Three complete novels, three romantic fantasies for those lazy, hazy, crazy days of summer.

Pull up a hammock and let a master entertainer take you away.

DALLAS SCHULZE

Summer DREAMS

D0189236

Dallas Schulze sold her first book when she was twenty-four and is eternally grateful to the publishing world for saving her from having to find a "real" job. The bestselling author of over forty books, she's won many awards, including the Lifetime Achievement Award and Storyteller of the Year from *Romantic Times,* plus two bestselling book awards from Waldenbooks, and her titles appear regularly on the *USA Today* bestseller list. Dallas describes herself as a sucker for a happy ending and hopes that her readers have as much fun with her books as she does. She lives in California with her husband, a couple of thousand books, lots of rosebushes and enough quilting fabric to cover half the earth's surface!

DALLAS SCHULZE

Summer DREAMS

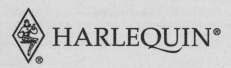

TORONTO • NEW YORK • LONDON
AMSTERDAM • PARIS • SYDNEY • HAMBURG
STOCKHOLM • ATHENS • TOKYO • MILAN • MADRID
PRAGUE • WARSAW • BUDAPEST • AUCKLAND

HARLEQUIN BOOKS

by Request—SUMMER DREAMS

Copyright © 1999 by Harlequin Books S.A.

ISBN 0-373-20164-8

The publisher acknowledges the copyright holder
of the individual works as follows:
OF DREAMS AND MAGIC
Copyright © 1989 by Dallas Schulze
THE MORNING AFTER
Copyright © 1989 by Dallas Schulze
A SUMMER TO COME HOME
Copyright © 1990 by Dallas Schulze

This edition published by arrangement with Harlequin Books S.A.

Visit us at www.romance.net

Printed in U.S.A.

CONTENTS

OF DREAMS AND MAGIC   9

THE MORNING AFTER   235

A SUMMER TO COME HOME   455

How was Jack going to explain Sheri
to his family and friends?
He couldn't even explain her to himself....

Of Dreams and Magic

Prologue

The flowers were a vibrant contrast to the mound of dirt on which they lay. White daisies and bright California poppies, the pale shades of columbines—a mixture at once wild and soft. The hand that arranged the delicate blossoms was slim and graceful, the fingers gentle.

"I would have brought roses, but you always said they looked better on the bush than cut."

The girl's voice was soft, with a lilting intonation and an accent impossible to place. As she knelt beside the grave, hair of a color somewhere between gold and silver spilled over her shoulder, down her back, and stopped just short of touching the ground.

Around her, the Sierra foothills spread out in endless vistas of beauty. The sky was a bright clear blue and the air was so clean it almost hurt to breathe it. A chickadee settled in a huge oak tree just above the girl's head. He cocked his head as if listening.

"I miss you." She moved a columbine a few inches before reaching out to touch the solid tombstone that marked the head of the grave. "In town they say he should be here soon." Her breath caught a moment and her teeth worried her lower lip. She continued in a rush, her fingers trembling as they traced the name on the marker. "I know you said that everything would be all right. You said he needed me more than you ever had. But does he *know* he needs me?"

There was no answer to the urgent question and she sighed.

"Can you really know him so well? I wish you'd told me more about him. If he doesn't want me..." Her voice trailed off and she stared out at the hills, seeing something else. "Do you know what that means, my friend? Did you truly understand?"

A quiet breeze brushed over the small graveyard. It tangled in the girl's pale hair, lifting it in a soft caress. She looked at the gravestone, her smile quivering around the edges.

"I know you did your best for me. I will be all right. Whatever happens, I will be all right. Perhaps you should have told him about me. It's not for everyone to accept such things. You could have explained." She sighed again. "But perhaps some things can't be explained."

She stood up, dusting her hands against the legs of her jeans. "I will always remember your kindness to me."

The breeze stirred the leaves above her and she smiled, her eyes lighting with a bright spark of blue that rivaled the sky. She lifted her head, looking at the chickadee. "Such a cheerful fellow you are."

Her hands came up, palm out, a crust of bread offered. The chickadee tilted its head first this way, then that before opening its wings and sailing across the short distance to light on her fingers and peck daintily at the offered crust. Her smile grew into a soft laugh of pleasure, stirring the deep quiet.

"Perhaps everything will be all right, after all."

Chapter One

"I simply don't understand why you have to make this trip, Jack. Can't you send someone else? Or hire someone from the area to take a look at the house and decide what to do with it?"

Jack set his suitcase down next to the front door and turned to look at his fiancée. Did Eleanor's mouth always have that pinched look?

"I told you why I'm going to see to the cabin myself." He struggled to keep the impatience out of his voice. It wasn't Eleanor's fault she didn't understand his reasons for going. He didn't fully understand them himself.

"You can't do anything for your uncle, Jack."

"I'm not trying to do anything for him." He heard the snap in his tone and stopped, drawing a deep breath before continuing. "I'm doing this for myself."

"I fail to see just what this is going to do for you. A long drive to some tumbledown little house in the back of beyond. That's hardly restful. And once you get there, the place probably won't be habitable."

"Uncle Jack lived there."

"I hardly think that qualifies as a recommendation. Your mother has told me about him."

Eleanor didn't do anything so inelegant as sniff. She didn't have to. The faint tilt of one patrician brow said it all.

"Don't believe everything Mother tells you about Uncle Jack," he said dryly. "He was the black sheep of the family and he was a bit eccentric, but I'm sure he lived in relatively civilized surroundings. He always appreciated the creature comforts. Besides, in the letter his lawyer forwarded he asked me to see to the place myself."

"Well, I think that's very inconsiderate of him."

"Eleanor, the man is dead. I hadn't seen him in almost two years." Guilt made his voice sharper than he'd intended. In the two weeks since he'd received word of his uncle Jack's death, guilt had become a familiar companion. How was it that he'd lost touch with someone who'd been so important to him? Uncle Jack, who'd encouraged his dreams, listened to his fantasies.

He swallowed the anger that was mostly self-directed. How could he blame Eleanor for not understanding how important Jack Ryan had been to his namesake? She'd certainly not seen any evidence of it before this.

His voice was calm when he continued. "It seems a small enough thing for him to ask. He left the property to me."

"Fine. I can see your mind is made up, but do you have to go now?"

From another woman the tone might have been coaxing, but coaxing was not Eleanor's style. The question came out more as a demand, and Jack swallowed his annoyance. Eleanor hadn't changed. He was the one who was suddenly chafing under her tone.

"Yes, I have to go now. I *want* to go now. I need a few days away."

She smoothed the collar of her tailored shirt, her wide brow puckered with annoyance. It wasn't that she was annoyed because her fiancé had announced he needed some time away from her. No, she was annoyed because he was being unreasonable.

It was at moments like this that Jack considered he was planning to spend the rest of his life with this woman. The prospect didn't bring him the satisfaction it once had. In fact, he was having a hard time remembering just why he and Eleanor had decided to marry. He rubbed at the ache gathering at his temple and tried to focus on what she was saying.

"You know the Smith-Byrneses' party is the day after tomorrow. I accepted for both of us almost a month ago. Will you be back in time for it?"

"No, I won't." He should have softened the flat refusal. The way Eleanor's mouth tightened told him she felt the same, but he didn't add anything more. He was sick of being polite, sick of going to dinner parties given by people he didn't know and wouldn't like even if he did know. He rubbed his forehead again. It seemed as if lately it was unusual *not* to have a headache.

"They're going to think it very odd if you don't show up."

"I'm sure they'll understand when you tell them there was a death in the family. Even in the best of families these things can't always be planned."

"I just don't understand you, Jack. You're being very flip about this whole matter. We have several important dinner engagements in the next week. Do you plan to simply miss all of them?"

"Yes, I do," he said bluntly.

"Good for you Jackson. Stick to your guns."

The new voice came from the doorway. Jack turned, grateful for the interruption.

"Roger! When did you get back from the Bahamas?" Jack strode across the room toward the other man.

Roger Bendon straightened from his slouched position against the doorjamb and took his best friend's hand. "Just this morning. You should have come with me, Jack. The weather was fantastic. The beaches were gorgeous and so were the women. Oops. Sorry, Eleanor." He nodded in her direction, his dark eyes holding a wicked glint that said he wasn't in the least sorry.

"Hello, Roger. I saw your mother yesterday." Her tone was accusing."

"Really? How is she these days?"

"She's well. She was surprised to hear you were out of the country."

"That's probably because I didn't tell her I was going," he admitted cheerfully.

Eleanor's mouth tightened, and her gaze took on an iciness. "Don't you think you should have let her know? After all, she *is* your mother."

"I can't be blamed for that." His tone was baiting and he watched her for the expected reaction, but Jack stepped in before she could reply.

"Stop it, you two. Why is it you can't be in the same room for more than twenty seconds without one or the other of you picking a fight?"

Roger shrugged, grinning innocently. "I didn't say a thing."

Eleanor stood up, smoothing one slim hand over her silk skirt, carefully ignoring Roger. "I think I'll be going now, Jack. I'll make your excuses where necessary. Call me when you return."

Jack bent to kiss the cheek she proffered. Her skin was smooth and soft, smelling vaguely of lavender. The scent reminded him of his great-aunt Alice, who'd died when he was ten. It occurred to him that his fiancée probably shouldn't remind him of his great-aunt Alice, but he pushed the thought away and forced a smile.

"I'll call you as soon as I know when I'll be back. I hope my absence doesn't cause you too many problems."

"I'm sure I'll be able to manage anything that comes up," she told him briskly.

She walked past Roger, according him a nod in farewell. He responded with a low bow, mocking her formality. Her stride was just a little tight as she crossed the wide hallway and pulled open the huge door.

"I'd frown if I was engaged to her, too."

Jack hadn't been aware of his expression until Roger's flippant comment. He rubbed his fingers over his forehead as if to erase the creases. "Lay off, Roger. I'm engaged to Eleanor. The least you can do is be polite."

"You're absolutely right. And I am polite. It's not my fault she doesn't like me." Roger perched on the arm of a Chippendale chair, his worn jeans a vivid contrast to the chair's ornate style.

The look Jack threw him made it clear his innocent pose wasn't fooling anybody. He had the grace to appear ashamed. "Sorry. I'll try harder."

"I'd appreciate that. Otherwise the wedding is likely to end up a war zone."

"Don't even mention the wedding. I can't believe you're actually going to marry—" He caught the warning in Jack's eyes and threw up his hands. "Okay, okay. Not another word. You know what I think of this engagement."

"Yes, I do."

The conversation lagged until Roger broke the awkward silence.

"So, tell me, where are you going? It's about time you took a vacation. You've been working like a dog at that bank for too long. Tahiti is nice this time of year."

Jack sat down opposite Roger. He'd planned to be on the road half an hour ago, but there was no set time he had to leave—a novel experience for him. In the ten years since he'd left college, he could barely remember an instance when he didn't need to be somewhere at a specific time. He wasn't entirely comfortable with this new freedom.

"I'm not going to Tahiti."

"How about Europe? I'll go with you. We could paint Paris red. I know this great little bistro. The food is out of this world and the waitresses—" Roger kissed his fingertips, his expression ecstatic.

Jack laughed, feeling some of his tension fade. Roger never failed to make people smile. It was one of his best qualities.

"Sorry. Paris is out. I'm on my way north."

"North? Alaska? No, really, Jack. I know things look bleak, but I'm sure they're not that bad."

"Northern California, you fool."

"Northern California? Land of latent Communists and ecologically minded citizens? No wonder Eleanor was so concerned."

"That's the place. I don't think Eleanor is concerned with *where* I'm going. It's the timing that bothers her."

"Ah, yes. How could you go in the middle of the season? Inconsiderate scoundrel."

The look Jack threw him was enough to make him raise his hands in apology.

"Sorry. Couldn't resist," he continued. "So, what's in the northern portion of our fair state? A local bank that Smith, Smith and Ryan Fiduciary, Inc. plans to swallow whole?"

"No. This has nothing to do with business."

Roger arched one dark brow, his face expressing amazement. "Nothing to do with business? I didn't think you knew how to do anything else anymore."

"Thanks," Jack told him dryly. Roger's comment had too much truth in it for him to be truly annoyed.

"You're welcome. So if it's not business, what's prying you away from your charming fiancée and your beloved desk?"

"My uncle Jack died and I'm going up to take a look at the place he left me."

"I'm sorry to hear that. I remember the summer he came to visit. We were what? Fifteen, sixteen? He smuggled us into that strip joint. I thought your mother was going to have a coronary when she found out."

Jack grinned. "I was grounded for a month. And Uncle Jack was forbidden to come near me for almost a year. I don't think Mother ever entirely forgave him for that."

"He was a great guy. What happened?"

Jack shrugged, his smile fading. It hurt to remember those good times. "Heart attack."

"Well, at least it was quick."

"Yeah. He wouldn't have wanted a lingering illness. Anyway, I'm going to drive up and take a look at the house and decide what to do with it. I shouldn't be gone more than a few days." He glanced at his watch. "I ought to get along."

Roger followed him out to the car, watching as he loaded his overnight case into the trunk of the gray Jaguar.

"You know, one of the best things about traveling is that it gives you a chance to think," Roger said casually.

Jack glanced at him. There was nothing in his friend's expression that hinted at deeper meaning, but he'd known Roger a long time. If anyone could understand the way he'd been feeling lately—the sensation of falling deeper into some dark hole—it would be Roger.

"Rog, I—" He stopped.

"What is it?"

Jack shook his head. "Nothing. Just a stray thought I had, but it's not important."

Roger wanted to press the issue, but didn't. "Have a good trip" was all he said. "I hope you find what you're looking for."

Jack was still pondering Roger's last remark a few minutes later as he drove onto the Ventura Freeway and joined the stream of cars heading west.

Find what he was looking for? Just what was he looking for? He had to admit there was something. There was a gap in his life. Something missing, an incompleteness he couldn't quite put his finger on. He shoved a hand through his hair, trying to shake the odd mood that had been with him ever since he'd gotten the letter telling him his uncle had died.

Though, if he were honest, the mood had been with him longer than that. It was just that Uncle Jack's death had sharpened the vague discontent, making it more real, more vivid. Just pointing the Jag's nose away from Pasadena, Los Angeles and Southern California as a whole made him feel he'd left a ball and chain behind.

But there was nothing in his life that justified that feeling. He wasn't being held prisoner or forced to do anything he didn't want to. Perhaps when his father had died his last year in college, he hadn't had much choice about jumping into the banking business. There'd been no one else to hold things together. But he'd stayed in the business because he enjoyed it. Didn't he?

He reached out and snapped on the radio, looking for something to fill the echoing silence left by that question. The soothing strains of Brahms filled the car, reminding him of concerts with Eleanor at his side, perfectly coiffed and immaculately dressed.

He punched a button and the rhythmic blast of the Beach Boys harmonizing "Little Deuce Coupe" effectively banished any concert-hall atmosphere. Tina must have set the station last time she'd borrowed the Jag. His little sister was not known for her sophisticated tastes in music.

He reached out to change the station again, then stopped. God, he hadn't heard the Beach Boys in years. They hardly suited his corporate image, but the song brought back memories of other times. He and Roger taking surfboards down into the Pacific, girls in bikinis, beach parties that lasted all summer. Life had been so much simpler then.

He left the station on, acknowledging a foolish feeling of defiance. Maybe Roger was right. Maybe he had forgotten how to play. It had been much too long since he'd taken time off just to relax.

Uncle Jack had wanted him to have a look at the property before deciding what to do with it and he was going to take his time, make sure that whatever he decided was what his uncle would have wanted. It wouldn't surprise him if that was exactly what the old scoundrel had had in mind when he'd made that will. He'd been pretty outspoken about his namesake's life. Maybe this was his final effort to get his nephew to break out of the corporate life-style he believed was just about the lowest way of living.

Jack grinned and reached out to turn the radio up another notch.

He made the long drive without stopping, except to get gas and have a late lunch—a thick hamburger and a mound of French fries, which he ate at a tiny café in a town so small he hadn't even noticed if it had a name. The napkins were paper, the booths were cracked vinyl and he could feel his arteries growing harder with every bite he took. Still, he couldn't remember the last time food had tasted quite so good.

As the sun began to set, he debated the wisdom of finding a place to stay the night, then continuing in the morning. From the instructions he'd been given, he suspected his uncle's home was easier to miss than find. But he didn't feel like stopping before he reached the end of the journey, so he went on, switching the high beams when he turned onto a winding country road.

It was almost midnight when he found the narrow dirt lane that led to the house. The road was just as he'd expected—unkempt, unmarked, barely usable. He found it more by instinct than sight, though he'd slowed to a crawl the last five miles, peering into the darkness for the shallow indentation in the overgrowth that was all the marker Uncle Jack had felt necessary.

The Jag grumbled in protest as it inched its way onto the rutted surface. Jack had the fanciful thought that it was complaining because the accommodations were hardly what it was accustomed to.

Now that he was nearly there, he felt a stirring excitement. He'd been right to make this trip himself. Not only did he owe his uncle this much, but he needed the time away himself. Time with no one making demands, no one expecting anything from him.

He stopped in front of the house and stared at the dark bulk of it. Funny, he thought he'd glimpsed lights when the lane curved and the house had been visible for a moment. But there were no lights now. He shrugged. It must have been an illusion. Maybe moonlight catching in the windows.

He opened the car door and stepped onto the coarse gravel that functioned as a parking area. Around him the night was still. No traffic noises, no distant wail of a siren. Just the rhythmic creak of a cricket and, in the distance, the mournful hoot of an owl. He took a deep breath, wondering if his lungs were up to handling air without smog.

This was exactly what he'd been craving. Total peace and quiet. He could spend a week up here and get a little perspective on his life. The only real problem was that he'd been too pressured lately. A small vacation was just the thing to shake everything back into its proper place.

He drew in another deep breath. This was exactly what he needed. No problems, no worries.

Chapter Two

The inside of the house did not live up to his expectations, considering the rather ramshackle look of the exterior. Or did he mean it didn't live *down* to his expectations? Whatever, it didn't match the outside, which even in the moonlight, showed signs of neglect and age. The sagging porch was sturdy enough, but in desperate need of a few coats of paint. In contrast, the hallway he stepped into was immaculately clean and had to have been painted within the past year or so.

So, the place was not the hut Eleanor had imagined and it wasn't exactly the shabby little building he'd been expecting. Uncle Jack had obviously kept it in good shape.

The hardwood floors were old and worn, but they were clean. In fact, they were much cleaner than he would have expected, considering the house had been empty for a month. He moved into the kitchen, and found it equally spotless. An ancient refrigerator hummed in one corner and Jack tugged open the door. He was only slightly surprised to find the shelves full of food.

He reached in and pulled out a bottle of beer, his mouth relaxing in a smile. Coors. Well, that told him Eleanor hadn't arranged this. She thought his taste in beer appalling. If he had to drink such a disgusting brew, at the very least couldn't he drink something imported? He twisted the cap off and took a long pull directly from the bottle, another action that would have made Eleanor's patrician nose wrinkle.

He left the kitchen, wandering toward the stairs that led upward from the front hall. The upstairs was as clean as the rest of the house. There were only three rooms on the second floor. A small but immaculately clean bathroom, a bedroom not much bigger than the bathroom, which his uncle had apparently used for storage, and another bedroom.

The larger bedroom was clean, which he had come to expect. The surfaces of the ancient oak furniture had that subtle glow that comes from generations of elbow grease. The bedspread— hand-crocheted, if he didn't miss his guess—was spotlessly white. When he flipped back the corner, he found the bed neatly made with linen sheets and a thick wool blanket.

He went back down the stairs and out to his car. The night was clear, the sky full of stars whose light never reached the city. The quiet *pop* of the trunk opening sounded loud in the thick stillness. He lifted his suitcase out and shut the trunk, wincing as the heavy *thunk* seemed to echo much too sharply.

When he stepped inside again, he had an odd sense of welcome, as if the old house were glad to see him. Jack smiled at the whimsical thought. Must be all this country air. It was bringing out a side of him he'd lost touch with so long ago he hadn't even remembered it existed. Shutting the front door behind him, he felt as if he'd come home. Not the way he felt about the huge house in Pasadena where he'd been born. That was home, but this was something more. This was— Just what was it?

He shook his head and carried his suitcase upstairs, setting it down in the old-fashioned bedroom. The stairs creaked as he walked back down. Maybe it was just that he was overtired from the long drive or the stresses of the past few months, but he couldn't shake the feeling that the house welcomed him. That it *liked* him.

He picked up his beer and carried it into the living room. There was firewood neatly laid in the fireplace and Jack hesitated only a moment before setting a match to it. The flames licked upward, burning through the crumpled newspaper before catching at the neatly stacked twigs, then licking up around the pile of small logs.

He hadn't even been sure his message to Mr. Jenkins had gotten through. The letter from the lawyer had said that Jenkins would be taking care of his uncle's property until Jack arrived or forwarded instructions. Jack had sent word he was coming up, but he hadn't asked Jenkins to get the place ready for him. He hadn't even known exactly when he'd be arriving. But apparently Jenkins had received the letter and had gone out of his way to get everything ready for his arrival.

The house had been cleaned, the kitchen stocked, even a fire laid. Maybe there really was something to the stories about country hospitality. Jack was going to have to make it a point to thank the man. He could go into the little town tomorrow and see about locating him. In a place this small, someone was bound to know where he lived.

The grandfather clock in the hall creaked like an old man going up a steep flight of stairs, then began to bong—a deep, dignified sound. Jack leaned his head against the back of the chair, counting the notes. It was late. If he had any sense at all, he'd go straight to bed, instead of lighting a fire he couldn't possibly stay awake to watch burn out. But he was tired of being sensible. Tired of doing the reasonable thing.

He'd been doing the reasonable thing since college. In this one small thing he was going to be unreasonable, unsensible. Unsensible? He smiled, taking another drink of beer. Even his command of the language was going to pot. It felt surprisingly good.

He stood up and adjusted the screen in front of the crackling flames, then turned to study the rest of the room. He'd barely glanced in here earlier, but his first impression had been accurate. Like the bedroom upstairs, this room had a vaguely Victorian flavor. The furniture was on the heavy side and

Of Dreams and Magic

looked as if it had remained in exactly the same place for decades.

But the room didn't feel like a museum. Jack settled back
into the chair and took another sip. Oddly enough, the room
looked just as he might have expected Uncle Jack's place to
look. It suited him. It was not quite of this time, and that was
exactly what Uncle Jack had been. A man in the wrong time.
He should have been born a century ago, when he could have
gone adventuring.

Jack's mouth twisted in a wry grin, and he lifted his bottle
in salute. "To you, Uncle Jack. I hope that wherever you are
now, it offers more excitement than this world had to give."

He took a long drink, angling his head back as the bottle
emptied. As he lowered the bottle, a golden gleam in one corner caught his eye. He tilted his head, but all he could make
out was something fairly large sitting on a low table in one
corner of the room.

He got up and moved to investigate. The light appeared to
shift as he approached, illuminating the corner. Then the firelight caught on gleaming brass. Settled on a low mahogany
table was an enormous samovar. The slightly squat urn shape
seemed to hunker in the corner as if trying to avoid being
noticed.

"What on earth were you doing with something like this,
Uncle Jack?" Jack asked the question out loud as he lowered
himself to his heels to get a better view of the object.

It was exquisite. Nearly three feet high, with curving lines
that flowed in an almost sensuous pattern. The brass glowed
as if lit from within. Every flicker of firelight caught on the
shining sides and Jack wondered how it was possible he hadn't
noticed the samovar the minute he walked into the room.

He reached out to stroke the shining surface. It felt warm to
the touch, warmer than he might have expected, given the temperature of the room. It must be a sensory illusion. The golden
brass *looked* warm, therefore it *felt* warm. Still, the illusion was

so strong he had the odd thought that the exquisite samovar was alive.

Jack drew his hand away, still staring at the urn. It was made in a pattern of overlapping leaves, each one intricately carved to match its mates so that the pattern appeared continuous. It was so bright. Not a spot of tarnish marred the perfect surface. No dust settled on the gleaming sides.

Jack reached out to touch it again, wanting to feel that warmth, but he drew back before his fingers contacted its surface. *If he touched it, he'd be lost.*

He shook his head as the bizarre thought flitted across his mind. Lost? Lost to what? In what? He shook his head, standing up and moving away from the low table. Maybe Eleanor was right. Maybe he should stay away from Coors. Would one bottle of a more respectable imported brew have had this effect?

He picked up the empty beer bottle and left the living room, refusing to acknowledge the uneasy itch between his shoulder blades when he turned his back on the samovar. Once he was in the kitchen the uneasiness slipped away, and he laughed at his strange fancies.

It must be the lateness of the hour and all this clean, healthy air. They were having a deleterious effect on his imagination. And speaking of healthy air, he was suddenly starving.

He rummaged through the refrigerator, finding a thick package of sliced ham and the rest of what he needed to construct a sandwich of truly mammoth proportions. He devoured his concoction hungrily, unable to remember the last time his appetite had been so sharp.

Once the snack was finished, tiredness rolled over him in a wave. He set his dishes in the sink and switched off the lights as he left the kitchen. He glanced into the living room to make sure the screen was in place around the fire. The samovar shone from its corner. Now that he knew it was there, it was impossible to ignore. In fact, he had the odd fancy it was watching him. He shook his head, turning away from it to climb the stairs.

He was tired and his imagination was working overtime. He'd been working too hard lately and he needed a rest. A long rest.

The mattress yielded beneath his tired body and Jack let out a long sigh. The bed felt like heaven. He could sleep as late as he wanted and tomorrow this place would look like an ordinary, slightly tumbledown house. He'd realize that this strange feeling of welcome, of homecoming, had been the result of too many hours on the road. And too many months of twelve-hour days before that.

He'd spend a few days here, get some rest, then go back to the real world. He drifted off to sleep on the thought, aware that the real world seemed very far away indeed.

Moonlight shone in through the open curtains, gilding the room in cool silvery light, catching the gilt of the watch lying on the dresser, the heavy brass latches of his suitcase, which he hadn't bothered to unpack. Outside, the owl hooted, the sound closer now. It hunted and some small creature would soon provide it with dinner, part of the cycle of nature.

Jack slept deeply, his breathing slow and shallow, his long body totally relaxed. He slept more soundly than he had in years. So soundly he was unaware of no longer being alone.

He didn't stir when a slim figure crept out of the shadows to stand beside the bed. Moonlight tangled in hair as pale as a moonbeam, shadowing more than revealing the delicate oval of a face and the slender hands clasped anxiously together.

She studied his face, all planes and angles. There was no softness there, but still...something drew her. A deep response she didn't fight. It wasn't in her to fight what her instincts told her was right.

He was handsome. And strong. She could read strength in the set of his jaw. She reached out, her fingers hovering over the lock of thick black hair that drifted across his forehead. She drew back without touching him, wondering at the odd tingling she felt. It was as if the air itself were alive.

He was her future, if a future she was to have. How would he react? She pressed her hand to her chest, feeling the slight acceleration of her heartbeat. She was nervous, but there was something more. Something she'd never felt before and couldn't quite define.

She watched Jack a few moments longer, tracing the strong lines of his face in the moonlight, wondering about a future she could only guess at. The future could never be predicted. Whatever was meant to be would be.

She slid back into the shadows, disappearing as silently as she'd come, like a wraith of smoke dispersed on a summer breeze.

Jack sighed and frowned slightly in his sleep, but he didn't awaken.

RIVERBEND, CALIFORNIA, was hardly a booming metropolis. It was, in fact, little more than a wide spot in the road—a narrow road at that. It had a gas station, a tiny post office, a café, two bars and a general store that carried everything from aspirin to videotapes. The two bars gave Jack a fair idea of what the residents of Riverbend probably did on a Saturday night.

Jack pulled the Jaguar into the narrow dirt parking area next to the general store. Overhead the sky was blue, a blue so bright it almost hurt to look at it. There was no traffic noise, there being no traffic to speak of in Riverbend. The mountains rose up on all sides, vivid reminders of the fact that so far man was only a visitor to this particular part of nature. Jack rather hoped it stayed that way. It was nice to know there were places where concrete and steel didn't reign supreme.

Entering the general store was like taking a step back in time. The aisles were packed with an assortment of items in no visible order. He assumed that the people who shopped there must simply memorize the position of any item they were likely to want. There was a single counter in front. Behind that was a display of rifles and shotguns and, in jarring contrast, a huge display of the latest movies on videotape.

Jack wandered up and down the aisles, picking up a Swiss army knife with enough gadgets to satisfy even the most avid of campers. He had no intention of going camping, but he remembered having wanted one when he was a boy. He bought a few groceries, thinking he should have given a more thorough check to the contents of the kitchen, since he wasn't sure if he was duplicating what was already there.

When he moved up to the counter, the man behind it gave him a measured look, as if trying to decide what he was doing in this sleepy little town.

"Find what you needed?"

"Yes, thanks." Jack nodded to the store behind him. "It would be pretty hard not to find what you needed. You've got a bit of everything, haven't you?"

The man's lean face softened into what could have been a smile.

"We try to keep most things on hand. It's a far drive to the next town and farther than that to a big city. Folks like to be able to get most things local."

"Well, you've certainly done a good job of choosing your stock."

"Thanks. You stayin' around here?"

The question was casual, but the look that accompanied it was sharp.

"I'm Jack Ryan." He held out his hand and the other man took it, his eyes sparked with interest.

"You must be old Jack's nephew. Knew you were supposed to come up and take a look at the place. I'm Burt Jenkins. When did you get here?"

"Late last night. I guess I have you to thank for taking care of the place. I appreciate the work you've done."

Jenkins shrugged. "Not much to do. We don't have any real crime up here, so I just looked in on the place once a week or so to make sure no animals had broken in. If I'd known exactly when you were going to get here, I'd have taken some lamps over. How'd you manage in the dark?''

Jack's smile took on a puzzled edge. ''Lamps? The electricity was on.''

It was Jenkins's turn to look puzzled. ''Electricity on? You must have gone to the wrong place. Jack had the electric cut off years ago. Said they charged too damn much, and besides, he preferred oil lamps. Bought all his oil here. You'll be wanting to get a supply for yourself, I reckon.''

''Yeah. Yeah, I guess I'd better. Are you sure about the electricity?''

''Sure as can be.'' Jenkins set two bottles of lamp oil on the counter.

''But I had lights last night. The refrigerator was working.''

Jenkins shrugged. ''Maybe the electric company heard the place was getting a new owner and figured he wouldn't be as stubborn as old Jack was. Maybe they turned it back on.''

He started ringing up Jack's purchases, obviously losing interest in the puzzle.

''Yeah. Maybe.'' Jack paid for his groceries.

''You going to be here long?''

Jack shrugged. ''I don't really know yet. A few days at least. There are a lot of decisions to make.''

''Well, if you need anything, let me know. I'm here most of the time.''

''Thanks. I'll keep that in mind. And thanks again for keeping an eye on the place.''

Jack loaded the sacks into the passenger seat of the car and started back toward his uncle's house. He drove automatically, a heavy frown drawing his dark brows together. He didn't know a whole lot about utility companies, but one thing he was willing to bet on was that they didn't just reconnect electricity in the hopes that a new owner was going to pay for it.

There *had* been electricity last night. He hadn't imagined it. But Jenkins had been so sure and having the electricity disconnected sounded exactly like something Uncle Jack would have done.

Jack pulled up in front of the house and studied it for a moment. This was definitely his uncle's house. The key he'd been sent fit the lock. He went inside and flicked lights on and off. They all worked, just as they had the night before. He went back outside, loosening the top few buttons of his shirt in response to the heat. It wasn't hard to find what he was looking for. The electric meter was on the side of the house, firmly nailed to the wood siding. The glass door hung drunkenly on one hinge. The meter inside was badly rusted and obviously hadn't worked in years. Squinting upward, Jack could see where the connecting line had once been hooked up to the house, but the line was long gone.

Curiouser and curiouser. He had electricity, but there was no way for it to be getting to the house. A quick check assured him there was no generator on the place. So where was the power to run the lights and the refrigerator coming from?

He stood in front of the house, his hands on his hips, and stared at the old building. A huge old rosebush rambled over the front of the porch. Big fat blooms the color of palest apricot covered the canes, filling the air with scent. It was a scene of domestic peace. Jack frowned. Roses were a passion of his mother's. Wasn't this awfully early in the year for them to be in bloom, especially at this altitude?

Now that he thought about it, there were other things about the place that were odd. The dishes he'd left in the sink the night before had been put away this morning. And the ones he'd used at breakfast were gone just now when he'd checked the power in the kitchen. He'd noticed it peripherally, but it hadn't registered that there was anything unusual about that. At home the housekeeper dealt with things like dishes. But this wasn't L.A. and there was no housekeeper.

And his car. Damn! Why hadn't he realized it before? The Jag had been in the garage this morning. Nothing odd about that, except that he'd left it in the driveway last night. And he'd had the keys with him. So someone or something had moved it into the garage. It was a measure of just how much he needed this time off that he was just now noticing things that should have hit him right away.

Despite the heat of the day Jack felt a shiver run up his spine. The sun didn't seem quite so bright. This whole thing was beginning to feel like something out of the *Twilight Zone*. He dismissed the thought as soon as it appeared. There was a perfectly logical explanation for all of this. At the moment he couldn't imagine what it was, but there was one.

He shivered again, and reached up to rub the back of his neck. It was stupid, but he suddenly felt as if he were being watched. Ridiculous. Yet the feeling persisted. Scanning the scruffy area around the house, he could see no signs of anyone, but the feeling grew stronger. He could feel eyes on him, watching, waiting. Waiting for what?

Every eerie story he'd ever heard flitted through his mind. According to childhood lore, there could be anything from a ghost to a banshee lurking in the underbrush.

"Right, Jack. In broad daylight." The sound of his own voice seemed too loud. A scrub jay started from the roof of the porch, his raucus cry making Jack jump.

"Don't be an idiot," he muttered to himself, but the feeling of unseen eyes persisted, until he had to believe someone was out there. Watching him.

He took a deep breath, squelching the urge to get in the car and drive away from this place. *If* there was someone out there, doing his dishes and moving his car and pulling electricity out of thin air, they'd already proved they weren't malevolent. There was a logical explanation for this, and whoever was out here could provide it.

"I think I'll go for a walk." He tried to sound casual, as if just talking to himself. Feeling like a total fool, he began to walk toward the thin forest of oaks that blanketed one side of the mountain.

The sky was still a brilliant blue. Another scrub jay called loudly, the harsh sound shattering the quiet air, leaving a thick silence behind. The dry grass crackled under his shoes. Ahead of him, a white butterfly flitted from one weed to another, pausing an instant before skipping to the next.

Jack noticed everything with senses that seemed more acute than they had just a few short hours ago. He walked into the woods until he judged that he was out of sight of the house, then turned and crept back, not sure if he really wanted to catch whoever—or whatever—had been watching him.

More than anything, he wanted to believe that the feeling had been nothing more than his imagination. That might leave him without an explanation for the odd occurrences, but it was better than what he was afraid he might find.

"Don't be an idiot," he mumbled. "*If* there's someone out there, it's probably just some local kid who's curious about a stranger in the area."

Sure. A local kid who just happened to know how to generate electricity from nothing. Who stocks refrigerators that shouldn't be working, does dishes without a sound and can move a ton and a half of car without a key. Sure. Just your average country bumpkin.

The mental argument continued, drawing Jack's nerves thinner and tighter. He moved carefully from tree to tree until he was within a few yards of the house, then waited. Around him, nature went about her business, oblivious of the little drama being played out. As he waited, Jack felt like more of a fool with each passing second.

He'd almost managed to convince himself that the only mystery was why he wasn't in a straitjacket, when he caught a glimpse of movement. Adrenaline surged through him. Someone was stepping out of the house onto the sagging porch. The sun was in his eyes, making it impossible to see more than just that it was a human shape. Jack felt a ridiculous flood of relief and he chided himself.

"What are you expecting, you idiot? A three-headed Martian?" The muttered comment made him feel a little better. Al-he had to do was talk to whoever this was and he'd have all the logical explanations he'd need. Then he'd see just how completely ridiculous this whole thing was.

He stepped out from behind the tree and started toward the house. "Excuse me."

Startled, the figure stiffened, then rushed off the porch and started to run. Jack saw all his logical explanations disappearing. Reacting instinctively, he gave chase. He hadn't spent four years on the UCLA track team for nothing. The distance between the figure and him shortened rapidly. He judged the space and threw himself forward in a flying tackle that caught his quarry behind the knees. The two hit the ground with a thud. Jack consolidated his grasp, his hands catching a pair of surprisingly slim shoulders and pinning them to the dirt as he straddled the stranger. He had a brief glimpse of masses of pale blond hair, so light it was almost white, and a pair of frightened blue eyes.

In the space between one second and the next, she was gone and he was suddenly flat on his face on the ground. He spit dirt out of his mouth as he pushed himself upright. She must have punched him when he wasn't looking. Though how such a fragile-looking creature could pack such a wallop he couldn't imagine.

"Are you all right? You aren't hurt, are you?"

The voice was soft, with the lilt of some accent he couldn't quite place. He turned his head to look at the speaker. He'd expected her to run, but she was still there, hovering a few feet away, her expression uncertain.

"Who are you?" He'd meant the words to come out as a demand, with a hint of righteous indignation, but the sheer beauty of her softened his tone. Never in his life had he seen a woman so exquisite. From the thick mass of pale hair to the tips of slender feet, she was like a painting of a fantasy.

"I'm Sheri." She reached up to coil a strand of hair around her fingers.

"I'm Jack." He stared at her, searching for some flaw but finding none.

"I know. Your uncle told me you'd be coming."

"You knew Uncle Jack?"

A smile flickered on the perfect oval of her face.

"He was my friend."

Jack moved closer, drawn toward her beauty, not believing the reality of it. Sheri shifted uneasily, watching him with a sort of nervous anticipation that Jack didn't understand.

"Are you the one who put the food in the house and cleaned the place up?"

"Yes. Was everything all right?" She twisted a lock of hair around her finger before releasing it to fall against the shoulder of her blue cotton shirt.

"Everything was fine," Jack replied, forgetting about all his questions, about the strange occurrences that had seemed so important a few minutes ago.

"Good. I wasn't sure what you'd like."

Jack was standing next to her now, and she tilted her head back to meet his eyes. My God, when had he ever seen eyes that color? Blue, yes, but more than blue. There was a touch of green in their depths. It was like looking into the heart of a pure sapphire and seeing a hint of emerald beneath.

She wasn't tall—not an inch over five feet—and she was slender. She looked as if a puff of wind would blow her over. But something told him she might be stronger than she appeared.

"Would you like to come in and have a cup of coffee or some iced tea or something? I guess iced tea would probably be better on a day like this. We could talk."

Unconsciously he'd lowered his voice, gentled the tone. She seemed so skittish, as if she might disappear in a wisp of smoke if he startled her. Maybe she hadn't seen many strangers.

She hesitated a moment, and he found himself wanting to know what she was thinking behind that wide blue gaze.

She nodded. "That would be nice."

As Jack led the way into the house, he had the feeling that nothing in his life was ever going to be quite the same again.

Chapter Three

"Shall I get the tea?"

Jack waved Sheri to a seat, shaking his head. "I'm the host. I'll get it. You just sit down and relax. It will have to be instant, I'm afraid."

"Oh, I think there's a pitcher of brewed in the refrigerator."

Jack glanced at her. "I don't remember seeing it."

"I think I put one in there. Your uncle was very fond of tea." She opened the refrigerator and reached in to pull out a tall white pitcher. "See? I was sure I'd left some in there."

Jack stared at the pitcher. It hadn't been in there last night. Had it? It was certainly possible he'd overlooked it. He'd been looking for sandwich makings, not tea. Still, he didn't remember seeing that pitcher.

Sheri poured tea into two glasses and set them on the table before looking up at him. Jack was still standing next to the cupboard, staring at the pitcher. Her eyes followed his and she seemed uneasy, but perhaps it was his imagination. Her voice was normal enough.

"It was way in the back. That's probably why you didn't notice it."

"Probably." He shook off the fruitless questions assailing him and sat down across the table from her. It took a conscious effort to keep from staring at her.

"Did you know my uncle long?"

"A few years. He was a very nice man."

"Yes, he was. A bit rasty but nice."

"'Rasty'?" Her forehead wrinkled as she tried out what was obviously a new word to her. "What's that?"

"Rasty. Ornery. Rough around the edges. Hard to get along with."

"Oh. Yes, he could be that, but underneath he was a very sweet man. A little lonely, you know."

Jack felt a surge of guilt. "I should have come up to see him years ago. Why is it that it always seems like there's plenty of time to do something, so you put it off, and suddenly there's no time left."

"That's the way things always are. But your uncle understood. He didn't mind. I think he was glad. He wasn't well the last few months, you know, and I don't think he would have wanted you to remember him that way."

"I didn't know he'd been ill." Guilt washed over him in a fresh wave. Why hadn't he made it up to see the old man?

Sheri's hand covered his on the table, her touch cool and soothing.

"Truly, he didn't want you to know. I suggested you should be called, but he said there would be time enough for you to visit when he was gone."

"Time enough for what?"

Her eyes shifted, flickering away from his, and she withdrew her hand. Jack found himself missing the light touch.

"I don't know. He didn't always tell me things."

"It sounds as if you spent quite a bit of time with him."

"I did. He was a good man."

Jack's eyes sharpened as a thought occurred to him. "Did you take care of him the last few months?"

She seemed to consider the question as if debating an answer, then she nodded slowly. "I did. He'd helped me when I needed help."

"My God. I had no idea." He shook his head, staring down at the scarred oak table, wondering how it was possible to lose touch so completely with someone so important to him. "You must have been very fond of him."

"I was," she answered simply.

"What about your family? Didn't they mind?"

"I...have no family."

He looked at her, another thought forming in the back of his mind. "Did you stay here with my uncle?"

She looked uncomfortable but answered quietly. "Yes, I did. He was quite ill and I preferred that he not be alone."

"Oh, God. I feel like a total scum. He didn't even feel as if he could come to me. I would have helped him."

Again she reached out to touch his hand. "He knew that. Please. He did not want you to feel this way. He wanted it this way. He said, 'I don't want the boy comin' up here and seein' me lookin' like a horned toad scared out of half a year's growth by a hoot owl.'"

Her soft voice had dropped into an uncanny imitation of Uncle Jack's gruff tone, and Jack had to chuckle. Yes, he could see the old buzzard saying that. "Uncle Jack always did go his own way," he murmured, remembering.

They were quiet for a while as they sipped the chilled tea.

Jack shook himself out of his memories and looked at her. "If you were living here with Uncle Jack, where did you stay last night?"

She reached up to twist her hair, a gesture he was already beginning to associate with her being nervous.

"There are a lot of places around here to stay."

He didn't press for a more precise answer, sensing she didn't want to say anything more, but he suspected he knew where she'd slept. He'd noticed that the old barn had a fairly good supply of straw. It wasn't hard to imagine her having spent the night there.

Maybe she didn't have the money to stay elsewhere. She'd said she had no family. She was so slim. Had she been living alone up here since Jack died? Maybe not eating enough? But she'd stocked the house with food. She must have had some money to do that. Still, she looked so waiflike.

"Are you hungry?"

"Not really."

But Jack didn't believe her. He could see that she had a fair share of pride. She wouldn't want him to know she was hungry. It was silly, really. If she'd taken care of his uncle in his last few months, a meal was the least Jack owed her.

"Well, I'm hungry. You'll stay for dinner, won't you?" Outside, the sun was beginning to lower. One of the disadvantages of having slept until almost noon was that the day was gone very quickly.

"I— Yes, that would be nice. May I cook for you?"

"I can manage."

"I'm sure you can, but I like to cook."

She gave him that shy smile he found so enchanting.

"Uncle Jack liked my cooking."

"'Uncle Jack'?" He raised one dark brow in teasing question. "Is that what you called him?"

"Yes. You don't mind, do you?"

"I don't mind. But I'm certain I don't have any cousins as beautiful as you."

Sheri flushed, dropping her eyes away from his, and Jack realized the remark had been unmistakably flirtatious. Not his usual style at all. He was an engaged man. Even without Eleanor to consider, flirting had never been his style. But, then, he wasn't feeling much like himself these days, anyway.

Sheri was so insistent about cooking the meal that Jack gave in, letting her shoo him out of the kitchen. He retreated to the living room and turned on a couple of lamps, dispelling the encroaching gloom. There was a fresh laid fire in the fireplace. Sheri's doing, no doubt. Her presence explained a lot of things, but it didn't explain the power that couldn't be on but was. Maybe she knew something about that.

He looked at the samovar. The last of the dying sunlight splashed across the table, casting golden rays onto the brass. It looked just as out of place now as it had the night before. Amid the worn, dated furnishings, the gleaming brass urn stood out, blatantly unsuited to its surroundings.

Jack moved closer. In better light the workmanship was even more remarkable. It really was a stunning piece of work. What on earth had Uncle Jack been doing with what looked like a museum piece? As far as he knew, the old man hadn't been a collector of anything except tall tales.

He reached out to lift the lid and his fingers had just settled on it, when Sheri spoke behind him.

"Dinner is ready."

Jack turned, startled, his hand dropping away from the samovar. She was standing in the doorway, her blue eyes on him, their expression wary. Wary? Now what made him think that? He shook his head slightly and smiled at her. He was getting paranoid in his old age.

"So soon? You must be a very fast cook."

Her smiled flickered. "It's nothing fancy."

Her eyes shifted to the samovar for an instant and Jack wondered if it was his imagination that her expression seemed distressed. He glanced over his shoulder at the gleaming urn. "It's beautiful, isn't it?"

"Yes."

"Do you have any idea where Uncle Jack got it? It doesn't seem like the kind of thing he'd have just had lying around the attic."

This time there could be no mistaking her expression. She looked almost frightened, and Jack's curiosity sharpened. Yet her tone was level, making him wonder if he was imagining the whole thing.

"I believe he said he found it in a shop in Hollywood. It amused him."

"Hollywood, huh? Land of dreams and magic." Jack looked at the samovar again, wondering what it was about it that drew him so. "Well, it seems a suitable place to find something like that. Odd that Uncle Jack would have bought it and hauled it all the way up here, though. Did he ever have it appraised that you know of?''

"He said it wasn't terribly valuable. Just something that amused him. Dinner will be getting cold.''

She appeared anxious to change the subject, and Jack didn't object. He could find out more about the intriguing pot later. Maybe he'd take it home with him and have it appraised himself. He'd love to know where it came from, how old it was.

Dinner was perfectly cooked fried chicken, with mashed potatoes, gravy and fresh corn on the cob. Jack was halfway through the meal before it occurred to him that he didn't remember seeing chicken or corn in the refrigerator, but when he mentioned it to Sheri, she just looked at him with wide blue eyes and said he must have missed them.

He pushed his chair back from the table with an exaggerated groan of contentment.

"Did you get enough to eat?''

Sheri's anxious question brought another groan.

"If I ate one more bite I'd probably explode. It was wonderful. I haven't had a meal like that in years.''

She flushed, her eyes sparkling with pleasure, and Jack found it was all he could do to keep from staring. She seemed completely unaware of her beauty, though that was hardly possible. In all his life he'd never met a woman so absolutely exquisite. She had to know how beautiful she was. But if she did, it didn't show in her mannerisms. She seemed eager to be liked, uncertain of being accepted.

"Would you like some coffee? It's fresh ground.''

"Sounds good.'' He watched her pour a cup of the fragrant brew. "Fresh ground, huh? I thought Uncle Jack was more of a tea drinker.''

Her hand froze over the cup for a moment. "He was. I drink coffee myself and your uncle insisted on buying a small grinder for me.''

She poured herself a cup and carried both cups to the table.

then sat down across from him. Jack sipped the coffee. It was perfectly brewed, smooth and rich.

"I hope it's as you like it."

"It's perfect. Don't you think so?"

Sheri lifted the cup and took a tiny swallow before smiling at him. "Perfect."

Now why did he have the feeling she didn't like coffee at all?

"You know, there's one thing that's been driving me crazy."

She started nervously, slopping coffee onto the table. "What?"

"The electricity."

"Electricity?"

"The lights, the refrigerator. I can't figure out where the power is coming from." He motioned at the lights.

Sheri's eyes followed his gesture. "The power?" she repeated uncertainly.

"The meter box is rusted out. There are no wires coming into the house, no generator. Jenkins down at the general store says that Uncle Jack used oil lamps for years. But all the lights work. So where is the power coming from?"

There was a long silence while Sheri stared at him wide-eyed. She finally shrugged, dropping her eyes to the table.

"I do not know. Your uncle never mentioned it to me."

Jack nodded and took another swallow of his coffee. He hadn't really expected her to say anything else. There had to be a logical explanation for everything else that had seemed so peculiar.

Except for the car being in the garage, when he'd left it outside. He frowned into his cup. Maybe he'd been mistaken. Maybe he really had put the car in the garage and he just didn't remember it.

"Is something wrong?"

Sheri's question broke into his thoughts. Jack shook his head. "I was just thinking about something."

"Something that disturbs you? May I help?"

"No. It's just something a little odd. No big deal." He finished his coffee and waved away her offer of more. "Tell me
about yourself?"

"Myself?"

She seemed startled by the request, and her hand rose automatically to grasp a lock of silvery hair. Jack found himself
wondering if it could possibly feel as soft as it looked. He
dragged his eyes away, hoping she couldn't read his mind.
"Yes. Yourself."

"What would you like to know?"

"I don't know. Anything. We've talked about me quite a
bit. It's only fair that we spend a little time on you."

"There is very little to tell."

"Where were you born?" Jack felt like an interviewer with
a nervous job candidate. "I can tell from your accent that
you're not from around here."

"No, I'm not from around here."

The idea seemed to amuse her.

"So where are you from?"

"Europe. I was born in Europe. My parents traveled a great
deal, so I'm afraid my accent is a mixture of many things."

"Well, it's very pretty."

"Thank you."

She flushed and changed the subject, obviously uncomfortable talking about herself.

Jack lost track of time as they sat around the old table, talking. He'd never met anyone quite so easy to talk to. They
talked about Uncle Jack. Sheri seemed interested in his memories of the old man and she laughed aloud at some of old
Jack's more risqué exploits. Jack found himself searching his
memory for stories that might amuse her just for the pleasure
of watching her laugh.

She was so natural, yet there was a fey quality about her
that made him want to shelter her, keep her safe. She appeared
fragile, a delicate porcelain figurine in need of protection.

He smiled at the thought. He sounded like some knight in shining armor looking for a damsel in distress. Like something out of a fairy tale. If there was one thing he'd learned, it was that fairy tales didn't exist. Damsels in distress were as rare as leprechauns and fairies.

The thought brought a twinge of regret. The world had seemed a much nicer place when he was young enough to believe in fantasies. Maybe that was the problem with life these days. There wasn't time for fairy tales. He shook his head, drawing in a deep breath, aware that the conversation had lagged and Sheri was watching him, her head tilted in question.

Jack shook his head, laughing at his own foolish thoughts. "I was just thinking about fairy tales and fantasies and how it's a shame we don't have more of them."

Something sparked in Sheri's eyes, but it was gone too quickly for him to identify. She looked down at the table, her lashes dark against her cheeks.

"Perhaps there are more fantasies and fairy tales alive than most people realize," she said softly.

"It's certainly a nice thought." Jack stifled a yawn. "Sorry. I guess this fresh air is taking its toll on me. I think my body misses the smog."

"It is late. Perhaps you would like to go to bed."

Jack's eyes sharpened. Was she aware that her words could be taken as an invitation? But her eyes were clear of anything more than concern. He shook his head. God, his imagination was working overtime lately.

"I am tired."

Sheri stood up and set their coffee cups in the sink. "I will just tidy up here and then I will leave."

"Why don't you stay here tonight?" She looked at him over her shoulder and Jack raised his hands. "I'm not making a pass. Look, you said you were living here when Uncle Jack was alive. I assume you've been staying here since he died. I suspect you slept in the barn last night rather than tell me you were here. I can't bear to have that on my conscience again tonight.''

"I was not uncomfortable last night." She ran water in the sink.

"Well, I'll be uncomfortable tonight if you don't agree to stay here. That couch in there is big enough for a football team. I can sleep there and you can have the bedroom upstairs. There's even a lock on the door, if it will make you feel better.''

"I do not need a lock. I know you would not hurt me.''

Such total faith took Jack a moment to absorb. He wasn't sure if he should be insulted that she didn't see him as a threat or complimented that she believed in his integrity.

"Then stay here tonight.''

She nodded slowly. "Yes. But I will sleep on the couch and you will keep your bed.''

Jack didn't argue, afraid that she might change her mind if he pushed the issue. Why it should be so important to him, he couldn't have said.

Within a few minutes, the lights were off—lights that shouldn't have been on in the first place—and the front door was locked, though Jack doubted the necessity of that. The two of them stood in the living room doorway a little awkwardly, not quite looking at each other.

"Well, good night," Jack said.

"Good night.''

"I've enjoyed this evening.''

"So have I." She looked up at him, her eyes shy. "I am glad to meet you. Your uncle told me much about you.''

"I wish he'd told me about you. I would have made it up here sooner.'' Was it possible to fall into someone's eyes. Hers were so blue, so clear. It was like drowning in a sea of sapphires, warm and cool at the same time. Sheri blushed, ducking her head. Jack tried to shake off the spell threatening to take hold of him, making him forget duty, family, fiancée and common sense. He cleared his throat.

"I'll see you in the morning."

"Yes, in the morning."

But Jack lingered, reluctant to give up the feeling of peace that seemed to surround her. He'd never felt anything quite like it. There was a gentle calm, as if the cares of the everyday world didn't affect her.

It took a conscious exercise of willpower for Jack to turn and climb the stairs. He had to force himself not to turn and look back down at her. He had the feeling he wouldn't be able to stop with just looking.

He shut the bedroom door behind him and leaned back against it for a moment, trying to remember that he was a man known for his cool logical mind.

When he crawled into the big bed a little while later, he found himself wondering how Sheri was settling in, found himself looking for an excuse to check on her.

Willpower kept him from going downstairs. Willpower and the memory of those trusting blue eyes. It it hadn't been for her trust in him, nothing could have kept him up there alone. Not duty, family, fiancée or common sense.

DOWNSTAIRS, Sheri stared into space. It had gone well. Not the way she'd hoped they'd meet, but perhaps best, after all. There'd been only a few awkward moments, fewer than she'd feared. Perhaps the old man had been right when he'd said his nephew needed her. She sensed a deep loneliness inside him, a yearning. And something inside her responded to that yearning, that need.

She frowned. He hadn't asked too many questions tonight, but he would. He wasn't like his uncle, who'd accepted so easily. No, the younger Jack was not the kind of human who accepted without question. Already he was questioning things. Probing, wanting answers she couldn't provide.

Still, if this was meant to be—and she believed with all her heart that it was—it would work out in the end. It had to work out. For as sure as she sensed his need, her own was just as strong, just as real.

THE SUN WAS JUST SLIPPING over the horizon, spilling warmth over the mountainside when Jack awoke. He slipped on jeans and a pale blue T-shirt, not bothering with shoes. He couldn't remember the last time he'd been quite so eager to start a day. He refused to speculate, even to himself, just how much his unexpected houseguest had to do with his anticipation.

The house was quiet as he opened the door and stepped into the hall, and he made a conscious effort to avoid the squeaky board at the top of the stairs. If Sheri was still sleeping, there was no reason to wake her. Maybe he'd make a cup of coffee and take it out onto the porch to enjoy the new morning, a bucolic pleasure he never had time for at home.

When he reached the hallway, he couldn't quite resist the urge to glance into the living room. Just to make sure she was all right, he told himself. He'd only intended a quick glance at the sofa to see if she was still asleep.

What caught his attention was the samovar. The squat urn stood stolidly on its table near the fireplace. The room was on the west side of the house, so it had yet to catch the rays of the sun. Yet the samovar seemed to glow as if lit with its own light. The brass didn't shine—it gleamed, it glittered, it drew his eye like a brilliant jewel.

Jack took a step closer. He was only peripherally aware that there was no sleeping form on the sofa. All his attention was on the samovar. The shining urn was mesmerizing, a warm golden pool of light. Gathering above the samovar was a vague misty cloud, gossamer thin at first, then slowly thickening.

Jack stared, aware of each separate beat of his heart, each shallow breath he took. He blinked and then blinked again, unable to drag his eyes from the gleaming samovar.

The smoke swirled lazily, growing thicker until it was impossible to see the wall behind it. It twisted as if guided by some intelligent hand, swirling and turning, coalescing into a solid, impossible shape.

Jack swallowed hard, feeling his pulse pounding in his ears, his heart threatening to push its way past his breastbone with the force of its beating.

The smoke wasn't smoke anymore. It had a shape, a form.

A woman's body, her back to him, her slender frame draped in a gossamer robe that revealed yet concealed, made of some glittering fabric that seemed to have no substance at all. A fall of pale, pale hair spilled down her back to the waist. It lifted as if with a will of its own, shifting in some unfelt breeze, seeming to beckon him closer. Slim hips and long slender legs ended in delicate ankles and bare feet.

She stretched, raising her arms over her head, her spine arching in a graceful gesture that was pure femininity. Jack felt beads of sweat rise on his forehead.

It wasn't the fact that she was stretching that bothered him.

It was the fact that she was floating in midair. Those slender little feet were at least two feet off the ground.

He'd obviously gone completely mad. He was probably not really here at all but locked in a padded cell in Camarillo State Hospital.

She drifted slowly to the floor, a leisurely descent that showed she was in complete control. He must have made some sound—possibly a murmur of disbelief—or maybe she'd heard the screaming denial in his mind. She turned suddenly, aware that she was longer alone, and her eyes met his.

Jack stared at Sheri, his tongue glued to the roof of his mouth. There was a logical explanation for this. He seemed to have been telling himself that ever since he arrived here. Their eyes held, hers frightened, his dazed.

"You were just floating." His tone said that he'd really appreciate a denial. He was amazed that he had a voice at all.

She didn't say anything, only stared at him with those wide frightened eyes. Jack waited, his mind working frantically, seeking the logical answer that just had to be there somewhere. But nothing came to mind.

"Who— What are you?" The question emerged on a whisper.

Sheri hesitated, lifting her hand to twist her fingers in that incredible mass of hair. A smile flickered uncertainly, then was gone.

"I am what I told you. A friend of your uncle's."

"Sure, and I'm Elvis Presley." The puzzled look in her eyes told him she hadn't the faintest idea whom he was talking about. That one silly thing was the final straw. The fact that the name meant nothing to her put the last touch of unreality on the moment.

"What are you?"

"I was your uncle's friend," she insisted.

"But that's not all, is it?"

"No." She dropped her eyes, her fingers twisted tightly in her hair.

"What else?" Jack felt almost calm as he waited for her answer. He was either dreaming or he was insane. Either way he didn't have anything to worry about. If he was dreaming, he'd soon wake up, and if he was insane, they'd probably come in to feed him anytime now.

"What else are you?"

Her voice was low, but not so low that he couldn't hear her. Every word came through clearly. Much more clearly than he would have liked.

"I am a genie."

Chapter Four

"I beg your pardon?" Jack groped behind him for a place to sit, beyond being surprised to find a chair where there shouldn't have been anything but floor.

"Are you all right?"

"No, actually. I'm not. I'm obviously insane," Jack said conversationally. "Or I'm dreaming. That's it. I'm not having this conversation at all. I didn't just see you form in a puff of smoke. You didn't just say that you were a genie. In fact, none of this is happening. I'm still lying upstairs asleep, and any minute now, I'm going to wake up and you won't be there."

Jack waited, but he didn't show any signs of waking. Sheri was still standing in front of him, her brow puckered in a frown. He closed his eyes, willing himself to wake up, willing himself to be somewhere else. When he opened his eyes, he was still sitting in the chair that shouldn't be where it was, looking at someone who shouldn't exist.

"Oh, God. You're still here."

"Yes. You would like me to go away?"

"Yes—no. Don't move. And don't do anything." He rubbed the bridge of his nose, aware of Sheri's anxious eyes on him. Did she have to look so eager to please? Didn't she know that her very existence was an impossibility, that what she claimed to be didn't—couldn't exist?

And yet it explained so much. The food, the car, the electricity. So many things that had defied logic were suddenly explained. Only the explanation was more impossible than the original puzzles.

"Good God! What am I doing?" He shot to his feet so suddenly that Sheri took a nervous step back. "I'm actually considering this."

"It is the truth."

"No. No, it's not." Jack put the chair between them, staring at her. "I don't know what the truth is, but you are not a genie. Genies don't exist."

"But I am here."

The simple statement left him momentarily speechless. It was undeniably true. She was there. No matter how much he wished she wasn't, she was right there in front of him. And he'd seen her materialize. Only he couldn't have seen it, because it was impossible. Wasn't it?

He laughed abruptly, a sound that held little humor. "I can't believe this. I must be more stressed out than I thought. I'm actually considering the idea that you really could be a genie. Since that's obviously not possible, there must be some reasonable explanation for what I think I've seen."

Sheri's puzzled expression mirrored his own. "I've given you an explanation."

Jack laughed again, a little more uneasily. She sounded so sincere. "Look, I don't know who put you up to this. Was it Roger? It sounds like exactly the kind of demented joke he'd love to play. I don't know how you did the tricks, but—"

"Tricks?"

She tilted her head looking confused. She was really an incredible actress. At least, he hoped that's what she was.

He waved his hand in the direction of the samovar, avoiding actually looking at it. "Tricks. You know, the puff-of-smoke routine."

"It is not a routine." She put the accent on the wrong syllable, giving the word a peculiar sound.

Jack stared at her, feeling desperation creeping around the

edges of his control. Looking into those wide blue eyes, it was difficult to believe she was part of some elaborate trick. On the other hand, it was impossible to believe what she was telling him.

"You can't be a genie," he told her firmly.

"Why not?"

The simple question left him without words for the space of several slow heartbeats.

"Why not? Why not?" He heard the barely restrained bellow of his own voice and stopped to take a deep breath. When he continued, his voice was painfully calm. "Why not? I'll tell you why not. Because there is no such thing. Genies are like elves and fairies and hobbits. They're all imaginary. Pretend. Things to tell little kids. They aren't real. They're fantasies. Dreams." He threw his arms out, emphasizing his point.

"And you don't think dreams are real?"

"No. Not that kind of dream," Jack told her firmly.

She nodded. "I think I understand."

While he watched, her figure seemed to blur around the edges, like a photograph just out of focus. The diaphanous robe that had hinted at so much more than it revealed vanished without a whisper. Sheri stood in front of him clad in jeans and a soft blue shirt just the color of her eyes. It all looked so normal. She might have been any one of a million young women walking down any street in America.

Only she wasn't walking down any street. She was standing right in front of him, wearing clothes that had been nowhere in sight a moment before. And she was claiming to be something that didn't exist.

"There are no such things as genies." He said it firmly, daring her to contradict him.

Sheri settled onto the sofa, drawing her feet up under her, one finger twisting idly in the thick fall of golden hair that fell over her shoulder.

"I can understand that it must be hard for you," she told him. "You've never known one of us before."

"I don't know one of you now, either. There's got to be a logical explanation for everything." But his denial was growing weaker. He could hear it in his voice. He sat back down, needing to feel something solid.

Sheri didn't try to argue with him. She nodded slowly. "I know it is not easy to accept. Your uncle was very unusual."

"Uncle Jack knew about you?" Jack demanded. "I mean, he knew what you claimed to be?"

"He knew what I was," she corrected gently.

"And he didn't mind?" Jack chose to sidestep the question of whether she was what she claimed.

"Your uncle was a man with vast dreams. Such people believe more than others."

"Believe? You honestly expect me to believe that you're a genie? Fine. Prove it. Wiggle your nose or blink or something and do something genie-ish."

"What would you like?"

The question threw Jack off balance—a position that was beginning to feel normal. She sounded so confident, so sure of herself.

"Let's start simple. How about a cup of coffee?"

He sat back, wishing he felt more smug. For the sake of his own sanity, he needed to believe that nothing was going to happen. He needed to know that this whole charade was going to end right here and now.

Sheri held out her hand, palm up. Jack stared at it, feeling less sure than he would have liked. He was almost unsurprised when the air over her palm began to shimmer as if she held a glowing light. There was an instant of disorientation and then her palm was no longer empty.

Jack reached out and wrapped his fingers around the mug of steaming coffee. It felt solid and real. The rich scent that wafted to his nostrils was real. He stared down into the dark liquid. The entire pattern of the world had just shifted, settling into a new design. Things he believed impossible beyond a shadow of a doubt were suddenly real and undeniable. And all he could do was stare at the coffee and wonder that she'd even added a touch of cream to it.

"Are you all right?"

Sheri's anxious question brought his eyes to her face. She looked so concerned. She looked so normal. Beautiful but normal. This wasn't real. *She* wasn't real. But here he was, with a cup of coffee in his hand.

"So, how did you get into this line of work?" The flip question was the best he could come up with. Maybe if he pretended this was all some kind of cosmic joke, it would go away.

"What do you mean, 'this line of work?'"

Sheri looked so genuinely puzzled that Jack laughed. It struck him as the final touch of absurdity that *she* should be confused by *him*.

He leaned back in his chair, feeling an odd sense of freedom. It was as if, in accepting the truth of Sheri's existence, he'd lost the heavy burden of reality. In a world where genies could exist, almost anything was possible.

Sheri watched him, toying with her hair, her expression puzzled but hopeful. He could have told her that the laughter was just the final evidence of his insanity, but it didn't seem important at the moment. The laughter faded, but the feeling of having shed a heavy weight lingered.

"Where did Uncle Jack find you?" He took a swallow of the coffee that shouldn't have been there and waited for her answer. Really, this wasn't that much different from interviewing someone for a job. It was just that he'd never interviewed a figment of his imagination before.

"Hollywood."

"Oh, yes, the samovar." He looked at the squat brass urn, wondering why it hadn't occurred to him immediately that it was the perfect place to hide a genie. The thought struck him as hilarious and he grinned. "It's better than an RV."

"An RV?"

"Recreational vehicle. It's a sort of home on wheels."

She tilted her head, puzzled a moment longer, and then made the connection.

"You mean because my samovar moves?"

Her laughter came softly, like warm breezes and blue skies. Her eyes were bright with humor.

"The thought did occur to me." Jack rested his ankle on his knee, relaxing. Whatever was happening here, he might as well sit back and enjoy it. Maybe there was something in the water in northern California that fed illusions and fantasies. When he left here, this whole thing would seem like a dream. "So how did Uncle Jack come to buy the samovar?"

"He told me that he was drawn to it. That happens sometimes, you know."

"No, I didn't know. I'm afraid I'm not really conversant with the circumstances that usually surround the acquisition of a genie."

"Well, it doesn't always happen like that, but sometimes a person is drawn. Usually because they can believe."

"And Uncle Jack believed?"

"Your uncle was a man of infinite dreams. To him all things were possible."

Her words brought back memories of his childhood. When his father had been so sure Jack would follow him into the family business, Uncle Jack had been the one to encourage him to dream of being an astronaut or a carnival barker.

For his fourteen birthday, when his father had given him a small portfolio of stock to manage, Uncle Jack had given him a pair of swords, souvenirs of World War II. They'd spent hours speculating on whom they might have belonged to and what might have happened to the officers who'd worn them.

Yes, Jack had certainly been a man of infinite dreams. It wasn't hard to imagine him being attracted to the samovar. It was just the kind of exotic oddity that would catch his eye. And when Sheri popped out in a cloud of smoke and announced she was a genie, Uncle Jack had probably accepted it with hardly a blink.

He'd always envied his uncle's ability to set reality aside in favor of a more pleasant fantasy. But reality had always been an overbearing presence in his own life and he'd long ago stopped trying to fight it.

"Why didn't Uncle Jack tell me about you? If not while he was alive, then in the letter I got after he died? All he said was that he wanted me to come take a look at the house. Not a word about any exotic surprises I might find."

"I told him he should have warned you about me, but he wouldn't do it. He could be very stubborn." Sheri shook her head, remembering.

"He must have had a reason for not telling me."

"He said that you wouldn't let yourself believe. That you'd have to see to believe."

"Well, I suppose he was right about that. I guess it's not the kind of thing you tell someone in a letter. 'It's been a long time since I've seen you. Hope you're well. By the way, I've got a genie in the house these days.'" Jack laughed, swallowing the last of the coffee and setting the cup down.

"Would you like some more coffee?" Sheri leaned forward, eager to help, but Jack shook his head.

"No, thanks. One cup of magic coffee is my limit. It's probably worse than caffeine."

"The coffee isn't magic," she assured him.

"Close enough." She seemed disappointed and he almost changed his mind. But he'd had enough demonstrations of the impossible. Enough to last him a lifetime. "How long were you with Uncle Jack?"

"Almost three years."

Sheri smiled, and the expression warmed her eyes in a way that would have taken his breath away if circumstances hadn't already left him with little to spare.

"He was very good to me. He taught me so much."

"I'm sure you must have taught him a thing or two," Jack said dryly, but the subtlety escaped Sheri. She took his words at face value.

"I don't know if I taught him anything, but I think he enjoyed my company. He was a lonely man. Did you know he had once almost married a woman he loved very much? She died, and I don't think he ever quite got over the loneliness of being without her."

"He never told me that." He wasn't sure why he should feel surprised. There were apparently a great many things the old man hadn't told him. "I wish I'd made it up to see him."

Sheri reached out to touch his hand. Comfort flowed from the light touch just as it had the day before. Of course, the day before he hadn't known she wasn't just an ordinary woman who happened to be particularly sympathetic. He shifted his hand, suddenly uneasy beneath hers. Not that he really believed she was what she claimed. But still...

He glanced at Sheri, catching the look of hurt that darkened her eyes before her lashes fell, concealing the expression. He felt as if he'd swatted a spaniel puppy unjustly. Whoever—or whatever—she was, she had been kind to him. More important, she'd been good to his uncle.

"I'm sorry."

"It's all right. I understand. I should have realized you would find it difficult to accept what I am."

Her words had been spoken evenly, without inflection, as if his reaction held little importance. But Jack had seen the look in her eyes and he knew he'd hurt her feelings by his withdrawal.

"Look, I didn't mean to be rude. You've been very good to me and I really appreciate all you did for Uncle Jack. It's just that...well, you're...I mean—" He broke off, at a loss. How did he explain what he was feeling when he didn't even *know* what he was feeling. He ran his fingers through his hair and stared at her.

"I understand. You don't like me," she said.

"No. No, it isn't that I don't like you," he protested. "I *do* like you."

"You do?"

Her eyes lifted to his and he found himself lost in the shining depths.

"I—yes, I do like you." Actually, he wasn't sure that was an accurate description at all. "Like" was such an anemic word. When he was with her, he felt a number of emotions, all of them confusing. There was a sweetness about her that made it impossible *not* to like her. Last night… What he'd been feeling last night was certainly something considerably more complex than simple liking.

He'd been drawn to her in a way an engaged man had no business being drawn. He'd felt the softness of her hand in his and he'd wanted to know if the rest of her could possibly be as soft. His dreams last night had held images of deep blue eyes and pale hair.

And then he'd come downstairs to find— No, he didn't want to think about what he'd seen. Better to try to block that memory if he wanted to retain any pretense of sanity. She'd tumbled his world upside down within the blink of an eye and now she wanted to know if he *liked* her.

Looking into those eyes, he found that reassuring her was more important than pinning down a precise description of his feelings at the moment. He didn't want to say anything to bring back that look of hurt.

"Of course I like you. It's just that you're the first genie I've ever met and I guess I'm having a hard time adjusting," he finished weakly.

Sheri's smile was dazzling. "You will get used to me. I'm really not all that different. You'll see."

Jack doubted he'd see any such thing. Whether she was a genie or a figment of his imagination, it was a sure bet he'd never met anyone like her.

"Would you like some breakfast?"

Breakfast was not high on Jack's list of priorities, but it seemed a safe enough thing to do. Maybe with some food in his stomach, he'd be able to make some sense of what was going on.

"Sure. Breakfast would be great."

"What would you like?"

"Whatever's out there." He caught Sheri's eye and realized that to her "whatever was out there" wasn't as limited as it might seem. "Bacon and eggs would be great."

He distinctly remembered seeing bacon and eggs in the refrigerator. However she chose to cook them, at least he wouldn't have to imagine them popping out of thin air.

"It will only take a moment."

Sheri slipped off the sofa, looking so normal, so average that Jack felt much as Alice must have felt when she toppled into the rabbit hole. At this point, if a white rabbit in a waistcoat popped out of the chimney, murmuring he was late, Jack wasn't sure he would feel any real shock at all.

Sheri left the room with a light, gliding step that seemed almost not to touch the floor. Jack pushed the thought away. God knows, she was probably quite capable of floating along. He reached for his coffee cup, taking a deep swallow before he remembered that there wasn't supposed to be any coffee left. Yet the cup was full. With a muttered oath, he set it down.

Somehow all his plans had gone awry. He'd thought he'd come up here and say a last farewell to his uncle. And he'd needed the time away, a chance to take a deep breath, figure out why his life wasn't as satisfying as it should be. A few days in the country with nothing to do but think. A simple enough concept.

Only it hadn't worked out that way. Electricity that shouldn't be on, dishes that shouldn't be clean and one delicate, exquisite person who claimed to be something that *couldn't* exist. Not only claimed it, but could prove it. No, this wasn't what he'd planned.

As he rubbed the back of his neck, his gaze settled on the samovar. The sun was creeping in through a south window and a beam of light splashed across the top of the brass urn. Jack glowered at it. It symbolized all the confusion that had entered his life. He would have loved to get up and pitch it out the window, as if he could throw the craziness with it.

"Breakfast is ready."

Sheri's voice made him jump. "Don't sneak up on me like that!" His tone held more of a bark than he'd intended, and her smile faded.

"I'm sorry."

"Oh, hell." Jack stood up, running his fingers through his hair and forcing a smile. "I'm the one who should be sorry. I didn't mean to snap at you. I guess I'm just having a bit of a hard time adjusting to this situation."

"That's all right."

Her ready forgiveness only made him feel guiltier. Did she have to be so damned nice?

The bacon was perfectly cooked, the eggs just as he preferred. He ate, refusing to think about the unconventional methods that had produced the meal. Jack leaned back in his chair, cradling a cup of coffee between his palms. Outside, the sun was shining with a brilliance that dazzled the eyes. The worn old kitchen looked so real, so normal, that it might have been a set in a movie. Which was exactly where Jack felt as though he was, smack in the middle of a Hollywood extravaganza. Any minute now the director would yell "Cut!" and life would go back to the way it had always been.

"The breakfast was delicious. Thank you."

Sheri beamed with pleasure and reached for the plates, but he stopped her.

"No, just leave them." He didn't want to see how she dealt with dirty dishes. It would spoil the fragile sanity he felt he'd achieved. "We should talk."

"All right."

She settled back in her chair, her hands clasped in her lap, her eyes on his face. She looked like a painting of an angel he'd seen when he was a child. There was the same gentle wonder in her eyes, the same fall of liquid gold hair. Only looking at the angel hadn't made him feel the way looking at Sheri made him feel.

"So, what do you plan to do now?" The question came out too loud, breaking the silence abruptly.

"Do?" Sheri was puzzled by the question. She tilted her head, a faint frown drawing her brows together. "What do you mean?"

"What do you plan to do? You know, now that Uncle Jack is gone. Where do you plan on going?"

"Wherever you go."

Her tone said that the answer was obvious.

"Wherever I go? What have I got to do with it?" Jack set his coffee down with a thud.

"Well, I'll go wherever you go."

She'd said it so calmly, as if her words weren't enough to shake the very foundations of his life.

"You'll what?" The thin-voiced question was all he could manage.

"I'll go wherever you go. Won't I?" A thread of uncertainty had crept into her voice.

"No." Jack got the word out quickly before the look in her eyes could change his mind. "Look, I'm sorry, but that's just not possible. You see, I'm a banker, and bankers don't have genies. We have Jaguars and houses in the best part of town, but we do not have genies."

"Your uncle felt that you needed me."

"Uncle Jack probably had a lot of odd thoughts. But I do *not* need a genie. It's nothing personal, you understand. It's just that my life is all set. I've got a career and I'm engaged to Eleanor. Eleanor! My God, I don't even want to think about what she'd say if I brought home a genie." Jack shuddered, imagining Eleanor's expression when he tried to explain about Sheri popping out of a samovar and pulling electricity out of thin air.

"But your uncle wanted me to stay with you," Sheri protested.

"Look, I'll tell you what. Why don't you just give me three wishes and we'll call it quits. You'll have done your duty by Uncle Jack."

"It's not about doing my duty. It's about fulfilling your uncle's wishes."

Jack pushed his chair back, standing up to pace to the back door. It looked so normal outside. The sun was shining. He could hear a jay squawking somewhere near the old barn. What was he doing in this worn old house, arguing with a woman who claimed she lived in a bottle?

He should have followed Eleanor's suggestion and sent a lawyer up here to take a look at the place. He could have sold it and never even known Sheri existed. Damn Uncle Jack! It was just like the old man to get his favorite nephew into a mess like this. The old goat was probably laughing his butt off somewhere. He'd finally managed to throw a huge monkey wrench into Jack's life. But he was damned if he was going to let Uncle Jack screw up all his careful plans.

It was one thing to admit that he'd had a few doubts himself. It was something else altogether for someone else to start pulling the strings. Especially from beyond the grave.

He turned abruptly, pinning Sheri with a look that had been known to make junior executives shudder. Sheri didn't even flinch. She just stared back at him with that wide-eyed gaze that seemed much too trusting, too vulnerable.

"Look, you owe me three wishes, right?"

"If that's what you want."

"Well, that's the way the stories all go. Is that the way it works or not?"

"Sometimes that's all that's required to fulfill the debt. But it doesn't have to work that way."

Jack moved back to the table, gripping the back of his chair and leaning toward her. "Suppose my first wish was for you to go away somewhere and stay out of my life. Would you do that?"

Sheri stared at him for a long moment, her face withou
expression. Then her eyes slowly lowered from his.

"Yes, I would do that."

Jack had to lean closer to hear her whispered assent.

He smiled, feeling as if he'd just concluded a particularl
difficult bargaining session. He could end this entire incider
right here and now. No one would ever have to know any c
this. Sheri could take her samovar and steal away into the nigh
and he could sell this place and pretend none of this had eve
happened. It was perfect. He opened his mouth to tell her h
wished exactly that: that she'd go away and never darken hi
door again. Nothing came out.

He stared at her downcast head, remembering the quiet sym
pathy she'd offered him; the way she'd tried so hard to mak
him comfortable; most of all, the way she'd cared for his uncl
If it hadn't been for her, Uncle Jack would have died alon
Genie or not, like it or not, he owed her.

"If I were to wish for you to go away, where would yo
go?"

She shrugged without looking at him. She'd drawn her hai
forward so that it formed a pale cape over her shoulders.

"Nowhere."

"Nowhere?" Jack questioned. "Come on. There must b
somewhere you'd like to go. God knows, airline tickets aren
going to be a problem. You can just twitch up a magic carp
or something, can't you?"

"There is nowhere."

She seemed to have withdrawn from him in some way h
couldn't quite put his finger on.

"How about Egypt?" he pressed. "If ever there was a coun
try built for a genie, Egypt has got to be it. Or Ireland. The
understand things like this. They've already got leprechaun
and pixies and things like that. I'm sure they wouldn't mind
genie. You could sort of expand their repertoire."

"No."

"No?" The simple refusal infuriated him. Here he was try

ng to be nice, trying to make sure she'd have a nice time when he left him. So maybe he wasn't doing the greatest job in the world, but he'd never wanted to be a travel agent for a genie.

"Why not? If you don't want to go to Egypt and you don't want to go to Ireland, where *do* you want to go?" he demanded. "There must be someplace."

"You don't understand. If I don't go with you, I shan't go anywhere. A genie who has no ties to a human is not truly alive."

Jack stared at her, appalled. "You mean you'll die?"

"Not death as you're thinking. It's more a state of nonexistence. Until someone appears who can believe." She glanced up at him with a sad smile. "There are fewer people in the world today who can believe in us."

"*I* don't believe in you!"

"Yes, you do. You don't want to believe, but you do."

Jack wanted to deny her words, but he couldn't. Against every grain of common sense he possessed, he did believe. He spun away from the table, throwing his hands out from his sides as if in plea to an unseen force.

"I don't need a genie. I've got my life nicely in order. I don't *want* a genie. Damn you, Uncle Jack. Damn you." He knew it had to be his imagination that put the sound of far-off laughter in his ears.

He turned back to Sheri, wishing he could say the words that would send her out of his life, wishing his damned conscience would keep its opinions to itself. But as his father had so often said, if wishes were horses, beggars would ride.

"I hope you're going to like Los Angeles."

Chapter Five

Jack pulled the Jag into the driveway of the big house an
stared at the lights blazing from the windows. The way his luc
had been going lately, he shouldn't have been surprised to fin
that everyone was home. It simply wasn't in the cards tha
something could go right. He'd hoped to find the house nic
and empty so he could get Sheri acclimated. Maybe get
chance to try to prepare his mother for her new housegues
How did a man go about preparing his mother for the presenc
of a genie in the house?

He glanced at the genie in question as he turned off th
engine. She was staring wide-eyed at the huge Spanish-sty
building he'd called home for the past thirty-odd years.

"It's so beautiful. How lucky you are to live here."

Lucky? Jack looked at the house again, trying to see
through her eyes. Yes, he supposed it was rather beautifu
Funny, he'd never really paid much attention to it. It was ju
the place his family lived.

"Well, I hope you like it. It looks like my mother and sist
are both home, so you'll get to meet them right away." H
voice must have reflected his uneasiness at that thought becau:
Sheri turned to look at him. Odd, how even in the gatherin
darkness, her expression was easy to read. It was as if she we
lit from within.

"You are worried about my meeting with your family."

It was more statement than question, but he answered her anyway. "It's not everyday that I bring home a houseguest who just happens to be something I don't even believe in."

"I know it will be difficult for you. If you'd like, I could—" She gestured at the back seat, where the samovar rested in stately solitude.

"No! No, thank you." One of the first things they'd established on the drive down the coast was that there was to be no more popping in and out of pots. Jack had always considered himself almost nerveless, but the idea of Sheri appearing and disappearing in a cloud of smoke was more than his nerves could stand. "That's all right. Mom and Tina are going to have to meet you sooner or later. It might as well be now."

Sheri shrugged and turned her eyes back to the house. "I will try not to cause you any problems, Jack. I know my arrival in your life is not welcome."

Jack's conscience gave a painful pinch. She sounded so forlorn. He reached out to touch her hand where it lay in her lap. It was the first time he'd voluntarily touched her since she'd set his world on end.

She looked at his hand and then her eyes lifted to his face. He forgot what he'd planned to say. His fingers tightened over hers. Awareness flowed into him. He should have known she was something more than human just by looking into her eyes. So blue so clear, so deep could never belong to a mortal.

She turned her hand so that their palms lay together, and the awareness intensified. Without thinking about it, Jack closed his fingers over hers. Her hand felt so small. Into him came the urge to protect her, to shield her from the blows life could so carelessly deal.

With his other hand he brushed back a lock of fine hair, feeling it twine around his fingers, another gentle link. There was such a sense of peace about her. And in him was a deep hunger for peace, a need he'd never acknowledged.

He leaned toward her, seeking... Seeking what? He couldn't

have said. He only knew that she could give him what h
sought. Surely it was possible to become lost in those eyes.

Behind him, the neighbor's dog barked sharply as a stray ca
leaped across the lawn. Jack jerked back, blinking to clear h
vision. What was he doing? He pulled his hands away fron
her, the silky lock of hair clinging as if to draw him back.

Sheri continued to watch him, but he avoided her eyes. H
must be feverish. What had he been saying? Oh, yes. H
cleared his throat, wishing he could clear his mind as easil
"I don't mean to make you feel unwelcome, Sheri."

"I know."

"It's just that—" He stopped. "Look, I—" How did he fin
the words to explain without hurting her that he needed th
complication is his life the way he needed a hole in his head

"Jack, you don't have to explain to me. I know that I'v
created a problem for you, but truly, everything will be a
right. You'll see. I will not cause problems in your life. I'r
going to learn how to be human. Soon I won't be different :
all."

She was so sincere, so earnest. Looking at her, he couldn
imagine how anyone could see her and not realize immediate
that she was not of this earth.

"That's good" was all he could manage. He reached for th
door handle, then hesitated. "Now remember, my mother an
Tina are *not*, under any circumstances, to be given any reaso
to think you're a— Well, that you're different."

"You mean I'm not to pop in and out of a cloud of smok
or wave up a dinner or twitch a new dress while they're watcl
ing."

She slanted him a mischievous look, and Jack couldn't hel
but smile. Did she have to be so damn cute? "Exactly. I wa
them to think you're completely normal."

"But I am completely normal." She gave him a wide-eye
look, her mouth tucked into a solemn line.

Jack was surprised by a sudden urge to kiss that look fro

er face, to see if her lips could possibly be as soft as they
ppeared.

"Completely normal for a genie, I suppose," he said dryly,
ushing stray and inappropriate thoughts away.

"Soon you won't be able to tell me from your sister."

"Oh, I don't think that's too likely." The thoughts he had
hen he looked at Sheri bore no resemblance to the way he
elt about Tina. Jack sighed, thinking wistfully of the joys to
e found in a Tibetan monastery. Did they allow genies in
nonasteries? "Come on, if we don't go in soon, Mother is
oing to think I've died out here."

He got out, but Sheri hesitated a moment before opening her
oor. Now that she was here, she was surprised by how uneasy
ne felt. With Jack, she felt a certain sense of rightness. They
elonged, even if he didn't realize it yet. But now, meeting his
amily, she was suddenly full of doubts. What if they didn't
ke her?

"Is something wrong?"

Cool air filled the car as Jack pulled open the door. He
ooked so handsome, his hair falling over his forehead in a
nick dark wave. She almost reached up to push it back, but
new he wouldn't welcome the gesture. With an effort she
orced a smile and shook her head.

"No. I am a little nervous." Jack's face softened into a smile
at Sheri thought more magical than anything she herself
ould produce.

"Don't worry about it. Tina is going to love you and
Mother... Well, Mother likes just about everyone." He reached
ut and took her hand, drawing her out of the car. "Just don't
o anything...odd and everything will be fine."

Sheri heard the doubt in his voice and knew Jack wasn't as
ure as he'd like her to believe. Well, it was up to her to make
ure that everything *was* fine.

Up close the house was even more exquisite. The smooth
aster walls gleamed pale in the twilight, reminding her of
ctures she'd seen of the Spanish missions, the red tile roof a

dark counterpoint. Arched windows spilled a warm glow ⟨
light onto the expanse of lawn.

The double front doors were heavily carved. A stylized su⟨
spread across the two doors, its deeply etched face offering
greeting. Sheri reached out, feeling the warmth of the carvin⟨
under her fingertips.

Jack turned his key in the lock and she felt the deep brea⟨
he drew before he opened the door and ushered her inside. T⟨
entryway was laid with thick red paving tiles, both warm an⟨
solid. To the right was an arched doorway, and she caught ⟨
glimpse of book-lined walls.

On the left, up two tiled steps, was the living room. T⟨
ceiling soared twenty-five feet above the floor. Small windov⟨
set high in the south wall broke the plastered expanse. A hu⟨
fireplace with a tiled hearth dominated the opposite wall. S⟨
could imagine that in the winter, a crackling fire would soft⟨
the almost overwhelming dimensions of the room.

She had only a moment to get an impression. Jack was lea⟨
ing the way up the steps. An older woman rose from a cha⟨
setting aside the needlework she'd been doing.

"Jack! We weren't expecting you, darling." She reached o⟨
to take his hands and lifted a cheek for him to kiss.

"Mother. I decided to come home rather suddenly. The⟨
wasn't as much to do at Uncle Jack's as I'd thought the⟨
would be."

"Well, it's certainly nice to see you. You know, Elean⟨
was not at all pleased with you—" Her eyes went past hi⟨
Sheri, hovering in the background. "You didn't tell me you⟨
brought someone with you, Jack."

"Mother, this is Sheri. She took care of Uncle Jack the p⟨
few years of his life. She's also taken care of the house sin⟨
he died. I thought it was the least we could do to offer her⟨
place to stay for a while."

Sheri wondered if his mother could hear the tension in Jack⟨
voice as clearly as she did. "Mrs. Ryan, I am very happy⟨
meet you."

"Ms....er...Jack, you didn't give me our guest's last name."

Sheri caught the panicked look Jack threw her.

"Jones. Sheri Jones," he answered.

"Ms. Jones, how nice to meet you." Glynis Ryan held out her hand and smiled graciously. "Of course you're welcome to stay with us as long as you'd like."

"Thank you, Mrs. Ryan. I'll try not to be any trouble." Was it her imagination, or did Jack look as if he doubted that were possible?

"Won't you sit down, Ms. Jones." Glynis gestured to the sofa, upholstered in deep red silk.

Sheri eased onto the sofa. When Jack sat next to her, tension in every line of his body, she wanted to reach out and take his hand, assure him there was no need to worry.

"Does your family live in northern California?" Glynis asked, settling back in her chair and picking up her needle and the rolled canvas she'd been embroidering.

Glynis Ryan's question was friendly, but Sheri sensed the concern under it. She was wondering just who her son had brought home.

Jack, even more than Sheri, was aware of the direction his mother's probing was likely to take. "Sheri is an orphan, Mother," he hastily explained.

"Oh, dear, how sad for you." Glynis's caution was overwhelmed by sympathy. "Were you very young?"

"She was just a child."

"Jack, really, let Ms. Jones answer for herself," Glynis said, giving her son a stern look.

"Jack's right, Mrs. Ryan. I was hardly more than an infant. I was raised by my godparents. Unfortunately they passed away a few years ago. They were acquaintances of Mr. Ryan, which is how I came to know him."

"So you're all alone in the world."

"Oh, no. At least not as long as people like you and Jack are so kind."

Glynis all but melted beneath Sheri's smile.

"Well, naturally, you must stay with us as long as you like."

"Thank you. I am grateful for your hospitality. Is that crewelwork you're doing? My godmother did crewelwork." Sheri leaned forward to view the embroidery Glynis held up. "Oh that's lovely. I've never seen anything quite like that. It must be your own design."

Glynis preened a bit, her pride evident. "You know, m dear, you really have to do your own designing these days you want anything truly unique. The needlework companie seem to be fatally infatuated with dancing teddy bears and kit tens playing the piano. Do you embroider yourself?"

"I dabble a bit, but I'm afraid my work isn't this fine."

Jack relaxed, knowing his mother was not going to be problem. Anyone who showed such a sincere admiration of he work would have to have a fault considerably graver tha merely being something out of a fairy tale. Whether she knew it or not, Sheri was in like Flynn.

There was a clatter of footsteps in the hall and a small dar whirlwind blew into the living room. At least, that was Sheri' first impression.

"Mom have you seen my red skirt? I wanted to wear tomorrow and I can't find it. Jack, what are you doing home Boy, Eleanor was sure ticked off when you hightailed north."

Jack stood up, catching his little sister's arm in a grip tha expressed his exasperation. He drew her forward as Sheri als stood.

"Yes, thank you, I'm glad to be home."

"Sorry."

The grin Tina gave him was unapologetic. "I didn't kno you'd brought a guest. Are you dumping Eleanor?"

Tina didn't seem in the least regretful. Jack gave her arm not-so-gentle shake. "You have the manners of a wartho Sheri, this is my obnoxious sister, Tina, the bane of the famil Tina, this is Sheri Jones. She took care of Uncle Jack and no she's going to be staying with us."

"Hi." Tina held out her hand, not in the least disturbed by her brother's uncomplimentary introduction.

"Hello." Sheri took the younger woman's hand, feeling the vibrancy of Tina's personality in the touch of her fingers. "I can see the resemblance between you and your brother."

"Horrors." Tina threw Jack an impish look, her eyes dancing with mischief.

Sheri had meant there was a similar feeling of intensity in both of them, but she could hardly say as much. And the physical resemblance *was* marked. Tina's eyes held more blue than Jack's pure gray and her hair wasn't as dark, but there was no mistaking their relationship.

"Tina, your manners grow more appalling every day. Is this the kind of behavior you're learning in college?"

Glynis's tone lacked any real bite. Her eyes held pride and affection as she looked at her children.

"Sure." Tina settled herself on the arm of her mother's chair, one jeans-clad leg swinging back and forth. "I'm taking Appalling Manners 101 and I'm getting straight A's."

"I can believe it," Jack said dryly, sitting back down. "Believe it or not, Sheri, underneath this ruffian is a mathematical genius. One of these days she's going to prove that the theory of relativity is all a bunch of hokum."

"Really?" Sheri searched her mind for some knowledge of the theory of relativity, but it hadn't been among the things old Jack Ryan had considered important for her education. She had a vague idea that it had something to do with an elderly gentleman with a shock of white hair. "I'm afraid I don't know much about math," she told Tina apologetically.

"That's okay. I only know enough to fake out my professors."

"Tina, why don't you show Sheri to the blue guest room," Glynis suggested, adding to Sheri, "I'm sure you'd like a chance to get cleaned up before dinner."

"I'll take Sheri up, Mother," Jack offered. He was a little uneasy about Sheri spending time alone with his boisterous

sister, at least until he was sure that disaster didn't lurk aroun
the corner.

"Let Tina take Sheri up to her room while you bring in h
luggage."

"She doesn't—" Jack broke off, coughing. He could hardl
tell his mother that not only did Sheri not have any luggag
she didn't *need* any.

"I would like to change before dinner."

At Sheri's words Jack met her look and he knew he'd fin
more than his own luggage in the Jag. He smiled weakly.

"You don't have to be so protective, Jack," Tina admon
ished. "I promise not to throw Sheri down the stairs."

"Thanks." Jack hesitated a moment longer, but there wa
really no graceful way to insist that Sheri stay in his sight. H
could hardly suggest she help him carry in the luggage. H
exited, feeling as if he were leaving a disaster in the makin
behind him.

"Gee, Jack must really like you," Tina commented, givir
Sheri a speculative look.

"I think he's just concerned." Sheri stood up, smoothing th
soft linen of her skirt. She was suddenly anxious to have a fe
minutes alone. There were so many conflicting emotions in th
room, too much to try to deal with all at once.

"Well, I think there's more to it than that," Tina persiste
"He's never worried about Eleanor."

"Tina, show our guest to her room." Glynis's voice too
on a firm edge. "And don't chatter her ear off."

Glynis watched the two women leave the room, Tina's cha
acteristic bouncy stride a contrast to Sheri's gliding step, s
light she almost seemed to float. She usually enjoyed this qui
time before dinner, immersing herself in her needlework, co
tent to know that her family was nearby. But tonight the del
cate embroidery lay forgotten in her lap.

The front door opened and Jack went through the hall, ca
rying a pair of ivory suitcases—pigskin, if she wasn't mistake
In fact, they looked identical to the set she'd bought Jack whe

he took his first trip to Europe alone, only the color was different. So Sheri must have a comfortable amount of money. Vuitton luggage was not inexpensive. If she was comfortably off, why had Jack brought her to stay here as if she'd had nowhere else to go?

Glynis stared at the fine wools in her lap without seeing the brilliant colors. Sheri Jones seemed like a perfectly nice young woman, but her instincts told her there was more to the politely spoken young woman than met the eye. Though she herself might have wished for more subtlety, Tina had expressed Glynis's own feelings quite well: Jack seemed quite protective of their guest. Too protective?

She set aside her needlework and stood up, crossing to the phone. She tried never to interfere in her children's lives. Still, this wasn't really interference: it was more in the nature of a reminder, she decided as she dialed a familiar number. The phone rang twice before being picked up.

''Eleanor, my dear, I have a wonderful surprise. I hope you don't have plans for this evening.''

SHERI RAN HER FINGERS over the top of the mahogany dressing table, avoiding her reflection in the mirror. She knew what she'd see there. Confusion. It wasn't an emotion with which she'd had a lot of experience, but since meeting Jack, it was becoming very familiar.

The room she'd been given was as exquisite as the rest of the house. Decorated in royal blue and a gray the color of palest smoke, it radiated serenity. She closed her eyes, taking a slow breath, trying to draw some of that serenity inside herself.

It was no use. Her eyes came open and she sighed. There was so much to think about, so many new things to understand. Life with Uncle Jack had never presented so many potential pitfalls. He'd lived alone and he'd been accepting of who and what she was. It had been much simpler.

This business of being human appeared to be somewhat complex. There were many aspects she did not yet understand.

She would have to learn quickly so that Jack wouldn't worry so much.

She frowned, staring at her reflection. Jack. In many ways he presented the greatest difficulty of all. She didn't understand her feelings for him. She felt warm when he was near. And alive. More alive than she'd ever felt before. It was not an entirely comfortable feeling.

With a sigh she turned away from the mirror. It had been so much simpler before. She wandered to the window, pulling aside the heavy drapes to look out into the darkness. Simple was not always best. She was needed here. Jack needed her. More than he realized.

She smiled softly, thinking of him. He didn't like the fact that she'd disturbed his orderly life. He didn't like it at all. But he'd still been kind to her.

Sheri allowed the curtain to fall and turned back into the room. Jack didn't know it yet, but she could help him. She would consider her own feelings later. Uncle Jack had been right. His nephew needed her help. All she had to do was prove it to him.

"MOTHER, don't you think it's a bit much to have invited Eleanor and Roger here on Sheri's first night with us?" Jack made an effort to keep his voice at a modulated level. His mother's news was the last thing he wanted to hear.

"Is there something you're not telling me about Sheri, Jack?" Glynis asked.

Jack twitched, spilling scotch onto the walnut bar top. "What do you mean?" Was that his voice? He sounded so casual. Not at all like a man on the ragged edge of insanity. He turned, leaning against the bar, the old-fashioned glass clutched a little too tightly in his fingers. "What could there be to tell about Sheri besides the fact that she took care of Uncle Jack and I think we owe her a place to stay?"

"I don't know." Glynis frowned down at the linen she held one finger stroking the swath of royal blue stitches. "You've been acting a little…strange this evening. And you seem worried about her.''

''Nonsense.'' Jack managed a light smile. ''I just think she's been through a lot of changes lately and I don't want her to feel overwhelmed. That's all. I hardly know her really.''

Glynis looked up at him, her eyes full of doubt. ''Perhaps I worry too much—''

''Of course you do.''

''But I don't want to see you make a mistake. You've done so well with the bank. Your father would be very proud of you. And Eleanor is a lovely girl. She'll be able to do a great deal for you once you're married. I'd hate to see you throw all that over on a whim. Your father and I always dreamed of seeing your life like this.''

And what about what he'd dreamed? The question popped up uninvited, and Jack tightened his fingers over the heavy glass. Where had the thought come from? He was doing what he'd dreamed, wasn't he? Not those silly adolescent dreams he'd had of living in the country some- where and raising horses. But the real, adult dreams of success.

''Don't worry, Mother. I'm not about to forget my responsibilities. You didn't have to invite Eleanor to remind me that I'm engaged. But if you're trying to remind me of the joys of being a responsible adult, Roger is an odd choice of guest. God knows, he's more likely to encourage me to run off and be a hermit in the South Pacific.''

''I thought Roger might be good company for Sheri. He may be a trifle irresponsible, but he really is a charming boy. As long as she's going to be staying with us, we might as well do what we can to make sure Sheri has a good time.''

''Matchmaking?'' Jack's tone was light and indulgent, a masterful piece of acting. Of course Roger and Sheri would be perfect together. If ever there was a man who knew how to dream, it was Roger. Wasn't that what Sheri had said—that it took someone who could dream? It would certainly solve his problems if Sheri and Roger hit it off. So why didn't the idea have more appeal?

Before he could answer that question, Sheri and his sister came downstairs. He'd forgotten to warn Sheri that they dressed for dinner, but Tina had apparently told her. Or she'd discovered it by methods he preferred not to know about. She was wearing a soft silk dress in a color that hovered somewhere between blue and green. She'd pinned her hair up into a pale gold coronet. She wore no jewelry and no makeup, but none was needed. Jack knew he'd never seen a woman look softer, more feminine, more exquisite. Next to her, every other woman he'd known seemed hard and overdressed.

He took a step toward her, but the doorbell rang before he could say anything. It was just as well. He wasn't sure what he'd planned to say, but it was a sure bet it was better left unsaid.

Later he was able to see that the evening had gone remarkably well. At the time he was convinced that his hair would be solid gray before the evening ended. It wasn't that Sheri said or did anything that extraordinary. It was just so obvious to him that she was something more than human, something different. At any moment he expected someone to leap to his feet, point a finger at her and announce that he knew her secret.

That never happened, but he couldn't quite get the scene out of his mind. In fact, he seemed to be the only one who was at all uneasy. Sheri met Roger and Eleanor with the same easy grace with which she did everything. Her shy smile had Roger eating out of her hand before the introductions were through. Eleanor was more reserved, but, then, that was just Eleanor.

He'd almost managed to relax by the time they sat down to dinner. After all, dinner table conversation should be safe enough. But the first words out of Eleanor's mouth shattered that hope.

"You have an interesting accent, Ms. Jones. I can't quite place it." Eleanor shook out her snowy linen napkin.

Jack wanted to shake her out. "Sheri has done a lot of traveling. I understand that tends to affect a person's speech patterns. Would you like a roll, Eleanor?''

"No, thank you, Jack." Eleanor gave him a polite smile and returned her attention to Sheri, who was sitting across the table from her. "Where are you from originally?"

"Didn't you say you were born in Europe, Sheri? Have some of this salad, Eleanor. It's really quite delicious." Jack thrust the bowl at her.

"Really, Jack, you'd think Sheri couldn't speak for herself."

That was Roger, ever-helpful Roger. Jack glared at him and received a bewildered look in return.

"Yes, Jack, do let Ms. Jones speak for herself," Eleanor said.

Jack sat back, trying to resign himself to the end of life as he knew it. Sooner or later Eleanor was going to ask Sheri something she couldn't answer. Something she *should* be able to answer. Something like "What do you think of Elvis Presley?" The fact that Eleanor despised Elvis Presley and probably knew no more about him than Sheri did was irrelevant at this point. Jack reached for his wineglass, wondering if he should casually spill it on his fiancée.

"Please call me 'Sheri,' Ms. Fitzsimmons."

"And you must call me 'Eleanor,' of course." Eleanor bared her teeth in a polite smile.

"Thank you. As a matter of fact, I have spent a great deal of time in Europe. I'm afraid my accent is impossible to trace. It's a little bit of everything, I guess."

"Well, I think it's lovely," Roger said, his eyes fixed on her face.

He looked like a lovesick calf, Jack decided uncharitably, downing most of his wine.

"Thank you."

Sheri's soft smile appeared to leave the never-without-a-reply Roger speechless.

"I myself have always thought it a pity that more people don't speak English correctly," Eleanor announced as she reached for her wineglass. "It's the reason Americans have such a terrible reputation, not only with other languages but with our own."

The edge in her voice made it clear she didn't share Roger's opinion of Sheri's accent. It was so clear that for a moment no one knew quite what to say. Roger's brows rose; Jack resisted the urge to kick Eleanor under the table; Glynis looked down at her plate. Only Tina opened her mouth, her eyes flashing indignantly.

But Sheri spoke first. "You are absolutely right. I have always been ashamed that my speech is so often incorrect. But it is quite difficult to hear one's own mistakes. Perhaps while I'm staying with Jack's family you would be willing to help me, Eleanor."

"Help you?" Eleanor reiterated in a scratchy voice.

"Teach me, perhaps."

"Teach you?" She was incapable of doing more than repeating Sheri's words.

"Oh, I did not mean that you should spend any of your time on something so unimportant, but maybe you could tell me when I have said something incorrect. So that I may learn, you understand."

The silence that settled over the table was nearly visible. There could be no doubting the absolute sincerity of Sheri's request. It was written in her eyes. She wasn't trying to make Eleanor look bad. There was no ulterior motive. Her request had come straight from the heart. She hadn't seen anything nasty in Eleanor's comment. Her very innocence made Eleanor look small, and everyone at the table knew it.

From the corner of his eye, Jack could see the color rising in Eleanor's smooth cheeks. Her fingers were rigid around her fork. The silence stretched to awkward lengths. Jack cleared his throat but couldn't think of anything to say.

"Have I said something wrong?" Sheri looked to Jack, sensing the atmosphere but uncertain of the reason for it.

"Of course not." Roger reached over and took her hand,

squeezing it gently. "You just caught us by surprise, that's all."

"I shouldn't have asked Eleanor to help me?"

Sheri turned those eyes on Roger and Jack was amused to see that Roger didn't handle that look any better than he did.

"Well, no. It's not exactly that. Really. It's just that—"

"What Roger is trying to say is that I hardly have a reputation as a teacher," Eleanor answered in a tight voice, but her tone was polite. "Besides, you don't need anyone to tutor you. You speak beautifully."

It was a gracious apology and Jack's respect for his fiancée inched up a notch. She'd made a mistake and she was acknowledging it.

"Well, I like Sheri's accent," Tina announced with a touch of belligerence. "I think it makes her sound very interesting and exotic."

If only you knew how exotic, Jack thought. However, the crisis was past. Conversation picked up slowly, but it did pick up. All in all, he supposed he should be grateful that that was the worst that happened. There were odd gaps in Sheri's education, but it was remarkable how much could be explained by a European upbringing.

By the end of the evening Tina was clearly a devoted fan, Roger was blatantly smitten, his mother liked her with reservations and Eleanor might not be crazy about his guest, but she'd pulled in her claws.

Jack couldn't even begin to describe his own feelings about Sheri. The last thing he'd wanted was a major complication in his life. He had enough on his plate now, what with the bank and his upcoming wedding—a wedding he couldn't seem to get up any real excitement about.

Still, there was something about Sheri, a sweetness. He couldn't put his finger on what it was exactly, but he couldn't bring himself to wish her away. God knows, he'd felt more alive in the past few days than he had in the past few years. That was something, wasn't it?

Chapter Six

"So, Jack, what's wrong?" Roger signaled for the waitress to bring a round of beer, then returned his attention to his friend.

"Why should something be wrong?" Jack leaned back as the waitress set the bottle in front of him. Harry's Pub wasn't known for its elegant presentation or even its smooth service. Nevertheless the place was always packed. The sign over the battered bar boasted the best chili size east of the Pacific. The clientele agreed.

"Something's got to be wrong."

Roger's voice drew Jack's attention away from the odd mix of hard-hat and business-suit types who made up the lunch crowd. He reached for his beer, taking a pull directly from the bottle. "Why does something have to be wrong?"

"Because this is the first time in the past five years that you've called me up and suggested lunch."

"Maybe I decided I'd been neglecting an old friendship," Jack offered.

"No, I don't think so. Something's bugging you, Jackson, and you want to tell your old pal all about it."

"How's the ranching operation going?"

Roger blinked at the abrupt question. He reached for his beer. "It's going okay. I don't get up that way very often and I leave the managing to the manager, but the reports look good.

We're turning out some good quarter horses. Another year or two and we may be in the black. Why do you want to know?''

Jack shrugged, his eyes on the scarred table. ''Do you ever think about the plans we made when we were in high school?''

''Which one? The one where we were going to become astronauts, or the one where we were going to become race-car drivers? Or just the general plan to become irresistible to women, means unspecified?''

''The one where we were going to move to Wyoming and raise the greatest horses in the world.''

''Oh, that one. Yeah, I think about it once in a while.''

''What happened to it?'' Jack asked moodily.

''Life, my friend. Life happened to both of us. I suppose my little operation north of Santa Barbara isn't quite the same as what we'd planned, is it?''

''No.'' Jack rubbed the back of his neck, wondering what he was doing here. He should never have called Roger and suggested lunch.

''What's bothering you, Jack? If you didn't want to talk about it, you wouldn't have called me.''

Jack leaned back as the waitress smacked plates heaped with chili down in front of them. Roger was both right and wrong. Something was certainly bothering him, but he didn't want to talk about it. It wasn't the kind of thing you could talk about, even with an old friend.

''I told you. I just decided I'd been neglecting an old friendship. Maybe I'll make a trip up to see what you're doing with this place. Just for old time's sake. I haven't been on a horse in nearly five years. Might be interesting to see if I can still stay on one.''

''It's Sheri, isn't it?'' Roger asked, cutting into what was threatening to become a monologue.

Jack lost hold of his fork, and chili splashed over the side of the plate and onto his pale yellow silk tie. ''Dammit!'' He dabbed at the spot and succeeded in spreading it into a large blotch.

"You should have dressed for the place," Roger told him without sympathy.

"Some of us work for a living." Jack glared at his friend's polo shirt.

Roger lifted his hands. "Don't blame me for that. I've offered several times to introduce you to the joys of hedonism, but you're always too busy doing something worthwhile. I've explained time and again that it's not as easy as it looks. There's a certain style that takes time and practice to achieve." He dunked a French fry in a mound of chili and bit into it, chewing reflectively.

Jack glared a moment longer, and then his sense of humor won out. "We all have to make the best of our skills, Roger. You have a talent for being useless. I don't."

Roger nodded thoughtfully. "Sad but true."

Jack laughed, feeling tension slip away. "Doesn't anything ever get to you?"

"Sure. Lots of things. Just the other day, I saw someone driving a maroon car with green upholstery." He shuddered. "It was enough to ruin my lunch."

"You are utterly worthless."

"Thank you. Now do you want to tell me what the story is on Ms. Sheri Jones—an alias if I ever heard one, by the way."

Jack started to shake his head, then stopped. If he didn't tell someone, he would surely go completely mad. On the other hand, Roger was likely to think he'd already gone over the edge if he tried to explain what was going on. He wasn't even too sure about his own sanity at the moment.

"Would you say I'm a relatively sane person?"

Roger raised a brow at the abrupt question. "Sure. Much too sane, if you ask me."

"That's what I've always thought. I mean, it isn't like I've been prone to flights of fantasy. I'm a practical, down-to-earth kind of guy. Dependable. Maybe even a little dull."

"Jack, you're beginning to babble, which is not a sign of mental health." Roger dunked another fry and fixed his friend with a demanding eye. "Spit it out. What's with the gorgeous houseguest? Are you considering eloping with her? Because I've got to tell you, if I had to choose between the lovely Sheri and the fair Eleanor, it wouldn't take me long to make a choice."

It was a measure of Jack's mental disturbance that he didn't even notice the slur to his fiancée.

"I'm not considering eloping. Not unless we go on a magic carpet."

"Excuse me?" Roger's brows rose in question. "Did you say 'magic carpet'?"

Jack looked up suddenly, his eyes showing the strain of the past few days. "Look, Roger, if I don't tell someone about this, I'm going to go completely crazy. Or maybe I'm crazy already. But one way or another, I've got to talk to someone."

"Sure. Sure, Jack. You know I'm always here for you." Roger put down his fork and gave Jack his undivided attention. "What's wrong?"

"It's Sheri."

"I'd gathered as much. What about her?"

"She's...not what she seems."

"Okay. She seems like a nice young woman who's staying with your family. What is she really?"

"Well, she's not a nice young woman—at least, that's not all she is. And she's not staying with my family for the reasons they think she is."

Roger frowned, trying to follow the convoluted sentences. His frown deepened as a thought occurred to him. "Jack, she's not— I mean, you and she didn't— She isn't—" He gestured, unable to finish the question.

Jack stared at him, trying to figure out what he was talking about. Light dawned slowly and he gave a short laugh. "Pregnant? God, no. I wish that's all it was."

"All it was?" Roger's voice rose. "My God, Jack, what the hell is it with this girl?"

"She's different. I mean, she's not like you and me."

"I noticed that."

Jack seized on his words eagerly. "Did you really? Because sometimes I think it's obvious, and then I'm not sure."

Roger reached for his beer, taking several long swallows before setting it down with a thump. His eyes were beginning to take on a slightly wild look.

"Jack, I was referring to the fact that she's female and we're not. It was a little joke. Very little, obviously. Now if you don't just spit out what the problem is, I swear I'm going to forget that we're friends and I'm going to climb over this table and do my best to drown you in Harry's chili. *What is wrong with Sheri?*"

"She's a genie." The words seemed to fall into a pool of sudden quiet, so that Jack had the feeling everyone in the bar must have heard them. He glanced around, but no one appeared to be paying any attention to their table.

"What?"

He looked at Roger, who was looking at him as if wondering whether or not to call for the men in the white coats.

"I know." Jack nodded. "It's hard to believe, isn't it? I didn't believe it at first, but then I didn't really have any choice. There was the electricity and the food and my car. And then I saw her in the smoke and the coffee. And that doesn't even take into account the luggage that wasn't there and then it was. And yesterday. Yesterday there were Mother's rosebushes."

"Jack. Jack. You've been working hard." Roger pitched his voice to a soothing tone. "It's been years since you've taken any kind of a vacation. And then there's been the engagement and your uncle's death. It's no wonder you're feeling a little strained."

"You think I'm crazy."

"No, of course not. You're a lot saner than I'll ever be. It's just that—" Roger paused, trying to choose his words carefully. "Even you have a cracking point, and maybe you just need a little rest."

"I'm not crazy, Roger. Sheri really is a genie."

"Jack, that's ridiculous. Next you're going to tell me that she lives in a lamp."

"A samovar," Jack told him gloomily.

"A samovar?" Roger reached for his beer and found it empty. He signaled the waitress frantically. "You're serious, aren't you?"

"I can't believe I'm saying this, but yes, I'm serious. I'm not crazy. At least, I'm reasonably certain I'm not crazy, and I am sitting here telling you that the girl you met last week is an honest to God puff-of-smoke genie."

The waitress brought another round of beer and Roger reached for his, taking a deep swallow before setting it down. He pushed his plate away and leaned his arms on the table.

"This I've got to hear. Start at the beginning, Jackson, and tell me everything that happened. Between the two of us, we'll get at the real truth."

"I thought the same thing, that there was going to be a logical explanation for it. Only there wasn't. I should have noticed that something was wrong when there was food in the refrigerator."

"At home."

"No, at Uncle Jack's. And the place was clean." He proceeded to tell Roger every detail of his relationship with Sheri, from realizing there shouldn't be any electricity, to seeing her form in a cloud of smoke, to his decision to bring her back to Los Angeles.

Around them the lunch crowd finished their meals and went back to work, but neither man noticed the place emptying out. The waitress cleared away their barely touched plates and kept them supplied with beer.

Roger didn't say a word until Jack had stopped speaking. There was a long silence while he digested his friend's incredible story.

Jack leaned back in his chair, feeling a tremendous relief now that he wasn't the only one who knew the truth. Even if Roger promptly called the nut patrol to haul him off, he couldn't manage much concern. It was wonderful to have actually told the entire story, to know that somebody else knew what had happened.

"A genie. It's impossible." Roger shook his head, his eyes on the wet circles created by the bottom of his beer bottle. "But there was something kind of...otherworldy about her. And the way she handled Eleanor's cattiness. Only a very clever woman or a total innocent could have managed that."

"I don't think she even knew Eleanor was being catty," Jack said lazily. Now that the secret was out, he felt almost light-headed.

"I can believe that, but a genie?" Roger shook his head again. "You're asking a lot, Jackson. We've been friends for a long time, but this is a hell of a lot to ask."

"She doesn't carry a purse," Jack offered, as if it were final proof.

"What?"

"She doesn't carry a purse. Not even a wallet. Nothing. Nada. Zip. Now I ask you, have you ever known a woman who didn't carry some kind of purse?"

It might have been the beer, but this seemed to strike both men as weighty evidence that Sheri was something other than an ordinary human.

Roger nodded solemnly. "It's true. Most women carry half a house in their purses."

"Well, Sheri doesn't even own one. Of course, I suppose she could snap one up in a minute, but she doesn't even bother." Jack leaned forward, his eyes meeting Roger's. "What would a genie need with a purse? Why carry all that stuff around if you can just pop it out of the air?"

Roger nodded, but he was still hesitant. He signaled for another beer, waiting for the waitress to bring it before speaking again. "You said something about your mother's roses. What was that about?"

Jack moaned, burying his fingers in his hair. "I thought everything was going fine. I mean, she's been here a week and nobody suspects a thing. Tina thinks she's 'rad' and Mother is teaching her to needlepoint. I was just beginning to relax a little, to believe that maybe having a genie in the house wasn't such a bad thing.''

"I can think of a few things a genie might come in handy for.''

Jack ignored Roger's innuendo. "Day before yesterday, Mother and Sheri were talking about the rose garden, and Mother commented, in all innocence, that it was such a pity that even in L.A. roses don't bloom year-round.''

"They don't?'' Roger interrupted. "The florist always has them.''

"Maybe they import them from Australia or something,'' Jack suggested impatiently. "Anyway, the point is that Mother said that *her* roses probably wouldn't bloom for another month and wasn't it a pity. She wished they'd bloom right away.'' He stopped, looking at Roger intently.

Roger looked back, aware that he'd somehow missed an important point.

"Don't you see?'' Jack asked.

"See what? Your mother loves roses. So what?''

"She said she *wished* they'd bloom right away. She *wished*.''

"She wished they'd bloom— Oh, I get it.'' Roger signaled for two more beers to celebrate this understanding. "So what happened? Did they burst into bloom right before her eyes?''

"No. It wasn't quite that bad.'' Jack leaned back to allow the waitress to set the fresh round on the table. "But yesterday morning she woke the whole household to come out and look at what had happened. The whole damned rose garden was in bloom. It looked like the middle of June.''

"And what did your mother say to this?''

"Well, at first she said it was a miracle. Then Sheri managed to convince her it must have been the Zoo Doo she'd used last fall. She claimed she'd seen it happen once in a garden in France.''

" 'Zoo Doo'?"

"You know, manure from the zoo. They gather it up and package it and sell it."

Roger stared at Jack, his mouth beginning to twitch. "You mean to tell me that your mother believes this miraculous occurrence was caused by elephant—" He broke off and leaned back in his chair, his shoulders shaking with laughter.

Jack's mouth curved in a barely suppressed grin, and then he began to chuckle. It did seem ludicrous, but no more absurd than the real truth of the matter. His eyes met Roger's and the chuckle became a laugh. It had been too long since he'd really laughed at something. Years too long.

Their laughter faded, leaving a lingering sense of ease. Jack took a swallow of beer, trying to remember the seriousness of the situation. But after several brews, it was difficult to feel the full weight of it.

"It's not funny, you know," he finally said into the silence. "What am I going to do with her?"

"Have her predict the stock market, become one of the richest men in the world, create a line of ever-blooming roses and corner the garden market?" Roger volunteered.

"Eleanor keeps suggesting I find her an apartment or a job or both."

"Ignore her."

"I can't ignore her. I'm going to marry her."

"All the more reason to ignore her now. You won't be able to after the wedding."

"What have you got against Eleanor? You've been sniping at her ever since I told you we were getting married."

"I don't have anything against her, Jackson. I just don't think the two of you are suited. She brings out the worst in you and you bring out the worst in her."

"Don't be ridiculous. She'll be a perfect banker's wife." Jack downed the last of his beer, wishing the thought of Eleanor as his mate gave him more pleasure.

"Exactly. But will she be the perfect wife for Jack Ryan?

That's the million-dollar question.'' Roger signaled for another round, ignoring Jack's vague protest that he ought to be getting back to the office. ''You can't go back to the office. You're drunk.''

This seemed so logical that Jack didn't even try to argue. ''Weren't you and Eleanor seeing each other for a while?''

Roger laughed, and if Jack's senses hadn't been more than a little dulled, he might have heard the note of bitterness there.

''That's ancient history. Ellie and I dated centuries ago, Jackson, my boy. Centuries ago. That was before I left this fair land for climes considerably less salubrious.''

Jack didn't have to ask what Roger was talking about. He remembered what Roger had been like when he'd gotten back from Vietnam. He'd never been inclined toward what he called ''earnest endeavors,'' but he'd come back seemingly determined to enjoy every moment he was given. As if he believed that at any moment his life might be snatched away.

''That was a rough time,'' Jack offered awkwardly, knowing the memories still haunted his friend.

''Yeah.'' The silence stretched until Roger broke it with a short laugh. ''But we're not here to discuss old times. We're here to decide what you should do with your inheritance. You know, it's just like old Jack to leave you a genie. None of my family ever does anything half as interesting.''

''Well, I could do with a little less interesting and a little easier to deal with. All I want is to get my life back to normal. How am I supposed to do that with Sheri in it?''

'' 'Normal'? Who's to say what's normal?'' Roger asked, waxing philosophical. ''In a more perfect world, we'd all have genies and *that* would be normal. Besides, you need something to liven your life up a little. Can you really tell me you wish you could go back to what it was before you met Sheri?''

JACK WAS STILL PONDERING the question several hours later as he made his way up the front walk. The bricks were showing a distressing tendency to shift beneath his feet and he had to concentrate on where he was stepping. He'd never before realized what a swell place to while away an afternoon Harry's Pub was.

In the back of his mind was the thought that he'd probably missed several meetings that afternoon, but it didn't really disturb him. He'd had important things to discuss with Roger. There'd been decisions to be decided, choices to be chosen. Off the top of his head, he wasn't sure whether he and Roger accomplished anything, but that didn't bother him, either.

He opened the front door and tiptoed into the hallway. At least, he tried to tiptoe, but someone had placed a palm in the middle of the entryway. Fighting his way free of the plant's vicious embrace, Jack glowered at it.

"Jack?" He turned at the sound of Sheri's soft voice, executing some rapid footwork to avoid tipping back into the killer plant.

She was standing on the stairs. Sun spilled in through the arched window on the landing, haloing her hair so that it seemed to be pure white gold. It came to him suddenly that he knew the answer to Roger's question. He did *not* want his life to go back to being just as it was before Sheri had floated into it.

He gave her a smile of singular sweetness. Sheri reached up, tugging on her hair, aware of the increased rate of her pulse.

"Hello."

"Hello." She came down a few more steps. "Are you all right, Jack? Your office called and said you hadn't come back from lunch."

"That's right."

He didn't seem interested in pursuing the topic, Sheri thought. He stared at her, an expression in his eyes she couldn't quite read.

"You don't look like a genie," Jack said abruptly.

"I don't?"

"No. You look exactly like an angel I saw in a picture book when I was a child."

Sheri felt a small shiver run up her spine as he continued to stare at her. There was something in his eyes—a look she'd never seen before—a need, a promise. Something that brought a feeling she didn't recognize, didn't quite understand. She cleared her throat and took another step toward him.

"We were worried."

The words broke the inexplicable tension. Jack blinked, looking around the hallway as if expecting to see someone lurking in the corners.

"'We'? We who?"

"Your mother and I. And Eleanor came by an hour or so ago."

"Ah, the fair Eleanor. Did you know that she hates being called 'Ellie'? Roger calls her 'Ellie.'"

Sheri crossed the last few feet between them and put her hand on Jack's arm. He looked at her, his eyes crossing slightly as he attempted to focus on her face.

"So what have you been doing with your day? Turning water into wine, feeding the fish on a loaf of bread? Or was that feeding the bread with a loaf of masses?"

"You're intoxicated!"

Jack grinned down into her wide eyes. "So I am. It's rather nice, don't you think?"

"I don't know. Perhaps you should go upstairs. I don't think your mother should see you like this."

"Quite right. Mother never has had any sense of humor about this sort of thing. She threatened to ground me for the rest of my life the first time I came home with a few too many under my belt."

Sheri pulled him toward the stairs. He was amenable enough to direction, though he showed a tendency to waver a bit.

"I told Roger all about you," he said solemnly. "He thought I was crazy, but then I told him you didn't carry a purse."

"A purse?" Sheri frowned, unable to make the connection that was obviously clear to Jack and Roger.

"That's right. Roger thinks it's great you're a genie." He frowned. "Don't go giving him tips on the races."

"I'll try to avoid that," she assured him, guiding him up the stairs.

"Do genies drink?" He turned to look at her, and caught his foot on a stair.

Sheri braced her arm across his back, exerting all her strength to keep him from tumbling backward.

The small crisis successfully resolved, Jack paused, devoting his full attention to her. "Well, do you?"

"Generally not." She tugged on his arm, getting him started up the stairs again. "Alcohol does not really agree with us."

They reached the top of the stairs, and she breathed a small sigh of relief. His room was just down the hall.

"That's too bad," he announced suddenly.

"What is too bad?"

"That you can't drink."

"I did not say I *could* not drink." She steered him toward his door. "I said that it's generally not a good idea. It can have a deleterious effect on my metabolism."

The door opened and Jack allowed her to push him gently through. "A del-e-te-ri-ous effect," he said, prounouncing each syllable separately, and then he grinned at her. "I like that. Next time someone asks me if drinking makes me sick as a dog, I'll tell them it has a dele—" His tongue stumbled over the word and he waved one hand expansively. "You know— that effect."

"Your mother will be home soon. I'm not sure you want her to see you in this condition."

Jack flopped down into a soft chair, tilting his head back to look at her. "Why don't you wave your wand and make me sober again? On second thought, I'm very dull when I'm sober. I'm much more interesting this way, don't you think?"

"I think you're always interesting." A lock of thick dark hair had fallen over his forehead and she had the urge to reach out and brush it back, to lay her palm against his brow and draw out the pain she could sense inside him.

"Always interesting, huh?" Jack leaned back in the chair and stared up at the ceiling. "Do they teach you that in genie school? That humans are to be told they're always interesting?"

He didn't wait for an answer. He reached up and caught her around the waist. Sheri gasped as he pulled her off balance and she tumbled onto his lap. Jack laughed, a low, masculine sound that sent a strange warm shiver through her. She shook her hair back out of her face, looking at him hesitantly.

His eyes were slightly glazed from alcohol, but there was something more there, a slumberous look she'd never seen before.

Jack reached up to stroke her hair. "Your hair is so soft," he murmured, almost to himself. "I've never touched anything so soft."

Sheri watched him uncertainly. She felt an odd tightness in her chest that made breathing an effort. His eyes swept up to meet hers, full of such pain that Sheri almost cried out.

"Did I ever tell you I wanted to raise horses?"

She shook her head.

"I did. Roger and I were going to have the biggest horse ranch in the country." Jack leaned his head back against the chair, his hand still tangled in her hair. "We were just kids with big dreams. Dreams. I used to be able to dream."

"You still can." Sheri brushed his hair back from his forehead.

"Can I?" He looked at her from under heavy lids. His mouth twisted suddenly in a wry smile. "I guess I must be able to. I dreamed you, didn't I?" His lashes drifted down.

"I am not a dream," she whispered.

But a deep breath was all the reply she received. The afternoon's drinking had caught up with him.

Sheri slid off his lap and settled him in a more comfortable position. Jack stirred as her fingers rested on his forehead, his brows puckering. She brushed the frown away, feeling him slip into a deeper sleep beneath her touch.

She backed away, her eyes on him. There was so much she didn't understand, so many things she hadn't been prepared for.

Jack needed her. She knew that, even if he didn't. And she should have been happy that it was so. To be truly needed was important. But there was something more. She wanted to be with Jack, wanted him to need her. But she wanted something more—something she couldn't define, didn't understand.

She reached out, almost touching him, then drew back, suddenly sure it would be a mistake. Shaking her head, she backed out of the room, easing the door shut behind her. The window at the end of the hallway beckoned and she drifted toward it.

It looked out on the rose garden, ablaze with bloom. She frowned. That had been a mistake. She should have realized it was the wrong thing to do. But she'd only been trying to make Glynis happy. She'd sounded so wistful when she'd spoken of her roses and it had seemed a small enough thing to do. Still, Sheri knew she'd have to be more careful.

Life had been so simple with old Jack. He'd asked nothing more of her than companionship, wanted nothing but a few small comforts and a smile. There'd been no need to worry about the truth of her origins coming out since he'd never had visitors. Her small magics had amused him.

But they didn't amuse Jack. He worried about them. He worried about her. She leaned against the cool glass, tracing her finger over its surface. Her expression grew dreamy. She liked the thought of Jack worrying about her, liked the idea that he cared enough to worry.

But it wouldn't do to like it too much. Jack was engaged to be married. She frowned, her finger tracing the same design over again. He and Eleanor did not seem well suited, but that was not for her to judge. She knew so little of his world. But she could learn.

She turned away from the view of the rose garden. Tina kept

a stack of magazines in the library. That would be as good a place as any to start.

Behind her on the windowpane, the tracing of a heart seemed to glow for a few minutes, as if catching the light of the fading sun.

Chapter Seven

Learning to be human was not a simple thing, as Sheri soon found out. The magazines were full of articles on how to improve oneself: how to lose weight, how to gain weight, how to find a husband, the joys of single life, planning a wedding, surviving a divorce. She'd hoped to find a clear-cut pathway to being normal, and instead found a bewildering array of choices.

Apparently a human woman was expected to be a high-powered career woman and a perfect mother whose children ate nutritionally complete meals at all times, attended only the best schools and participated in extracurricular activities. At the same time she should have the body of a twenty-year-old model, an unlined face, be a gourmet cook, a dietetic expert and have a home that was not only immaculate but exquisite—somehow combining both comfort and decor into one perfect whole.

Her relationship with a "significant other" was important, though not the sole focus of her life. A relationship was to be split right down the middle, fifty-fifty, and the magazines abounded with information on how to make sure your mate carried his fair share of the load.

Somewhere, in between jobs, classes, social engagements and self-improvement seminars, she should find time for herself.

Just reading about it all was enough to make Sheri's head spin. If this was what being human was all about, it was an exhausting affair altogether.

Still, in sorting it out, the one thing that seemed to be a constant thread was that a woman needed a job. Some article allowed, rather grudgingly, that if you had small children, perhaps raising them could be considered fulfilling. But if you were single, there was no question that you needed a job.

Since everyone had one, how difficult could a job be to find?

"Ms. JONES, I thought you said you had experience using a keyboard." Mr. Lewis ran his fingers through the few strands of hair remaining on his head, his eyes taking on a harried look.

"I...well, yes, I did. But it wasn't a keyboard of quite this type." Sheri stared at the rows of numbered and lettered buttons, wondering how she could explain to him that she'd been talking about a piano keyboard.

"Keyboards don't differ that much, Ms. Jones. Can you explain to me how you managed, in the space of less than two hours, to cause a total system crash?" Despite his best efforts, Mr. Lewis's voice was starting to rise.

"I—" Sheri stopped, raising her eyes to his, her expression helpless. "No."

The simple word seemed to leave him without words. When he'd hired her for the job, he'd been dazzled more by her fine-boned beauty than her qualifications. After all, she was only to answer the phone, type a few letters and act as a general receptionist to the small real estate office. The pleasure of watching her around the office—perhaps even more than just watching—would more than make up for any minor training he might have to provide.

She'd been honest about her lack of job experience. Looking into those big blue eyes, Gerald Lewis had seen the future in glorious Technicolor. He'd provide her with the necessary skills, she'd provide him with... Well, who could say just how grateful she might be.

Only now, staring at the lines of gibberish wending their way across the lit screen of the computer, he faced the possibility that the cost of hiring with his libido might be far higher than he'd ever dreamed.

"I am sorry, Mr. Lewis. I just pushed a few of the buttons. I did not mean to break it."

"Break it? Break it? I don't even know what it is you've done." He stared at the screen in despair.

"I suppose this means you do not want me to come back tomorrow morning?" Sheri questioned hesitantly.

The look he gave her spoke volumes.

Sheri was disappointed that her first venture into the working world had turned out badly, but not discouraged. According to the magazine articles, it was important to find a position requiring skills that meshed with your own. Apparently real estate was not her field.

She soon found that any job that required mastery of a computer was a mistake. Genies and computers simply didn't mix. She didn't understand them and they clearly disliked her. Her third attempt to master one ended with her prospective employer begging her not to return.

Wandering through the rose garden, she nipped a faded flower here and there and considered her options. If a job was necessary, then a job she had to have. She could ask Jack. He'd almost certainly find her a position. She scowled at a bee buzzing nearby, her jaw set stubbornly. She didn't want to ask Jack. This was something she wanted to do herself. She needed to prove—to Jack and herself—that she could live in his world, that she didn't have to be at best a helpless decoration, at worst a burden.

Still, it was difficult to know where to try next. With a sigh she set the problem aside. Given time, the Fates would provide. She just needed to have patience.

"YOU'RE GOING TO love this place, Sheri. They have the greatest seafood." Tina jerked the wheel, sending the little Mercedes skidding around a corner.

Sheri closed her eyes and tried to remember the names of all the presidents in order. Uncle Jack had sworn by it as a method of keeping calm. He'd obviously never ridden with his niece.

When Tina had suggested that she and Sheri go out shopping and have lunch, Sheri had jumped at the chance. Her job hunting had been discouraging, Jack had been spending long hours at the office and she was finding time lying a bit heavily on her hands.

Tina's offer of lunch was heaven-sent. Not only would but she get to see something beyond the walls of Jack's home, she could observe Tina and learn from the other woman's behavior. Besides, she liked Jack's little sister.

But she didn't need a lot of experience in this new life to know that one thing she did *not* want to learn from Tina was how to drive. The other woman was completely fearless and appeared to have a boundless faith in the ability of other drivers to anticipate her every move and compensate before disaster occurred. The fact that it had worked so far didn't reassure Sheri.

Tina spun the wheel again, and the car bounced over a shallow dip in the road as it hurtled into a parking structure. Sheri breathed a sigh of relief when they were safely parked between a gray Honda and a bright red Corvette. Tina threw herself out of the car with the enthusiasm she showed for everything she did. It was hard to reconcile her quick movements and impatience to get at each new experience with the kind of patience and discipline required by higher mathematics, but Tina seemed to balance the two.

Over the past few weeks, Sheri had learned that Tina was one person she could relax with. Tina never questioned any odd gaps in her knowledge, never probed for information she couldn't give. If Sheri didn't know something, Tina was more than happy to fill her in. She was quite capable of carrying ninety percent of the conversation by herself, and required little more than an occasional comment from her companion.

Now and then Sheri caught a shrewd look in Tina's eye that gave the lie to the scatterbrained image she projected. But she never questioned. Sheri was content with that.

The restaurant was in a slightly scruffy area of Pasadena. Tina referred to it rather sarcastically as a "revitalization target." Sheri followed her gaze out the window to across the street, where a bright neon sign advertised Chi Chi's vintage clothing. Next to it was a run-down storefront whose sign proclaimed adult movies for rent. She'd already learned that adult movies did not mean documentaries and educational specials.

"You don't approve of revitalization?"

"Oh, it's not that exactly." Tina picked up a breadstick and crunched into it, a frown puckering her forehead. "It's just that any time they revitalize an area, a lot of people are displaced. Sometimes it's people who've lived in the area for years. Look what's happening in Venice."

"Italy?" Sheri searched for anything she'd heard about the famous city, but the only thing that came to mind was that it was ever so slowly sinking.

"No. Venice, California. You know, on the beach."

"Sorry. I wasn't thinking." Sheri reached for a breadstick, hoping this lapse wasn't too severe. Tina seemed to take it in stride, however.

"A few years ago Venice was a pit. It was run-down and property values were really low. Only then property values in all the surrounding communities climbed so high that people started looking at Venice as an alternative to Santa Monica. A bunch of artists moved into the area. After all, what does an artist have that's worth stealing?"

Sheri considered pointing out that an artist might think his or her work was worth something, but she sensed it wasn't relevant.

"Anyway, before too long, Venice started to be seen as this

artsy community. Property values started to climb and all sort
of pseudo-artistic types began to move into the area. The street
were cleaned up and clever little shops opened up all along the
boulevard. Which brought the tourists in, which brought more
money, which made the property values go higher.''

Sheri frowned. ''Is that bad? It seems to me that it would
be a good thing that the streets were safer and nice shops were
opened.''

''That's just what it seems like on the surface. But that's no
all there is to it.'' Tina waved a breadstick for emphasis, her
face alight with emotion. ''There's another side to the story
As property prices increased, landlords suddenly realized they
could sell buildings they'd neglected for years and make hug
profits. If they kept the buildings, they raised the rent to out
rageous levels because all these artsy types were willing to pa
to live in Venice.''

''I still don't see what's so awful.''

''Well, what about the people who used to live in thos
buildings? The people who used to run businesses where thos
clever little shops are now? Some of those people were ther
for decades, renting their apartments or shops and going o
with their lives. Now suddenly they're forced out because Ven
ice is 'revitalized.' It's not right.''

Sheri crushed a tiny crumb with the tip of her finger, feelin
Tina's passion. ''And yet it's progress of a sort,'' she pointe
out. ''You said that this Venice was not a nice place to g
before the changes started. It's inevitable that something woul
change that. Cities are like people—they don't stay the sam
for long. If this hadn't happened, perhaps things would hav
gotten even worse.''

''Maybe.'' Tina stared moodily across the street. ''But
can't help but wonder how many people ended up homeles
because some nitwit wanted to try his hand at becoming th
next Picasso.''

''It's rare that a change doesn't displace someone or som
thing. Even good changes aren't good for everyone. All yo

can do is try to lessen the impact on those whose lives must change whether they wish it or not.''

''I suppose,'' Tina allowed, then eyed Sheri shrewdly. 'You're awfully philosophical for someone so young. You're not much older than I am, but you're so rational. Don't you ever get passionate about things?''

''Many things.'' Sheri glanced up, and smiled in relief when she saw the waiter approaching with their plates. ''Especially about food. It looks wonderful.''

The subject was safely dropped, but Sheri doubted it had been forgotten. Tina didn't forget much. The conversation moved in lighter channels over the meal, and by the time they left the restaurant, the tentative bonds of friendship had been drawn a little tighter.

''There's a shop across the street where they have the greatest Italian shoes.'' Tina caught Sheri's look and shrugged sheepishly. ''Well, if you can't beat 'em, you might as well enjoy 'em.''

The two women laughed and headed for the crosswalk. They were waiting for the light to change, when a gruff voice spoke from behind them.

''Excuse me. I'm sorry to bother you.''

They turned to see a man of about forty standing nearby. His clothes were ragged and dirty, but showed signs of having been cared for once. His hair was as neatly combed as fingers could manage. His face was lean and worn. But it was his eyes that caught Sheri. Never had she seen eyes so old, as if the man had seen centuries of hard living. There was almost pride there. Pride and strength. Beaten down and almost destroyed, but still struggling to survive.

''I'm sorry to bother you,'' he said again. ''But I was wondering if you could spare any change.''

Tina was already reaching for her purse, but Sheri took a step closer to the man, drawn by his need.

''Are you lost?''

He appeared surprised that she was addressing him, then he

laughed without humor. "Lost? In a manner of speaking, suppose. I haven't been able to find a job for over a year now.'

"How awful."

He drew himself up, pride in every line of his body. "I don' ask for your pity. We're managing all right. Most of the time.'

"Here. This is all I have." Tina held out a handful of bill and grasped Sheri's arm with her free hand, trying to draw he back.

The man looked at the money, and Sheri could see how much he hated needing it. She took the money from Tina' hand and thrust it into his.

"Please. She can afford it." Tina murmured a slightl alarmed protest, but Sheri ignored her. "You said 'we.' Ar you married? Do you have children?"

He shoved the bills into his pocket and half turned to wal away. But something in Sheri's eyes persuaded him to stay. ' have a wife and daughter."

"How old is your daughter?"

"Sarah is ten."

"Do you have a place to stay?"

"We've been living in the car for the past couple of month but it isn't going to last much longer."

"That's terrible! Don't you think that's terrible?" She turned to Tina for support.

Tina mumbled something, clearly at a loss about how to dea with the situation.

"You can't continue to live like that," Sheri said. She turne back to her new acquaintance, her expression determine "What's your name?"

"Melvin. Look, I didn't mean to start any trouble."

"You haven't started any trouble at all, Melvin. We ju can't allow this to continue. It's terrible to think that you an your family are living in your car. We'll have to do somethin about it, won't we, Tina?"

Tina stared at her helplessly. It wasn't that she didn't fee compassion for the man's situation. She felt tremendous con passion for him and his family. That's why she'd given him all the money she had with her. But never in a million years would it have occurred to her to engage him in conversation.

She had a sinking feeling that Sheri planned on a lot more than talking to him.

JACK STARED at the abstract print on the wall across from his desk. Squiggles of blue and red darted across a vaguely gray background. He wondered why he'd never noticed how much he disliked that print. He'd have to ask his secretary to find something that wasn't reminiscent of a depressed four-year-old's scribbling.

Of course, if he didn't manage to focus on the report in front of him, he would be telling his secretary she was going to have a new boss. He'd been working on the Carter deal for almost a year. Now that he had it virtually in the palm of his hand, it didn't seem all that important. It didn't even seem interesting. He rubbed a hand across his forehead, trying to remember what a coup this was. Where was his concentration these days?

He focused on the stack of papers again. Two lines into the report, his attention wandered once more, this time to the framed portrait of Eleanor that sat on one corner of his desk.

She really was a lovely woman. Not beautiful, and certainly nothing as frivolous as pretty. There was an elegance about her that he'd once found soothing. Why was it that lately it seemed more grating than anything else? When they went out together, he kept wondering what she'd look like with her hair mussed about her face, maybe her cheeks flushed.

He supposed that if he suggested it, she would have no objections to sleeping with him. But he had no desire to suggest it. He told himself that he was just observing a little propriety, something that was too seldom done these days. Yet he had a sneaking suspicion that it was lack of interest, not propriety, that kept him out of his fiancée's bed.

When he considered making love with a woman, it wasn't Eleanor's face he saw. It was Sheri's. No matter how firm he was in putting her from his mind, she always slipped under his guard, catching him at odd moments.

There was no reason for it. It wasn't as if he'd even kissed her. *But oh, how he wanted to.* He hadn't been so drunk that he hadn't noticed how right she'd felt on his lap. And he didn't have to concentrate to remember the soft scent of her—not quite a perfume, but a gentle scent that lingered in the memory.

With a muttered curse, he pushed his chair back from his desk and strode over to the window. Looking out over the Glendale financial district didn't do a thing to help him concentrate. Sometimes, if he tried really hard, he could almost believe his own story—that Sheri had been his uncle's nurse and nothing more. He could almost believe it.

It wasn't even the fact that she could twitch coffee cups out of the air and came with her own home away from home in the form of a samovar. Since the incident with his mother's roses, she'd been careful not to do anything out of the ordinary. She might have been just a normal houseguest, not too obtrusive and fairly easy to get along with.

In fact, he'd seen very little of her these past two weeks or more. Which was just the way he wanted it, he told himself. She was keeping out of trouble and that's all he asked.

So why couldn't he get her out of his mind?

The discreet buzz of the intercom interrupted his thoughts. He spun back to the desk and jabbed the button irritably. "What is it, Ms. Sanders?"

"It's your mother on line two, Mr. Ryan. She sounds very upset."

He jabbed line two and snatched up the phone.

"Mother?"

"Jack, you've got to come home immediately. It's just awful. I don't know what to do with these people. They're in the hall and they won't go away. They might go away, but she won't let them. She keeps insisting we've got to do something but it's not my responsibility, Jack. Really it's not."

"Calm down, Mother. She who? What people?"

"Sheri. And she brought them home. Eleanor is here and she agrees with me. Only, Tina and Roger are siding with Sheri, and I don't know what to do. It's not that I'm not a compassionate woman, Jack. You know I'm a compassionate woman."

"You're a very compassionate woman, Mother," Jack told her soothingly. "Now tell me what's going on."

"I told you. They're in the hall and she won't let them leave. It's not right, Jack. It's not proper. You've got to come home and do something."

"I'll be there in twenty minutes." Jack set down the phone in the midst of more protests from his mother that she really was compassionate. He didn't have the faintest idea what was going on at home, but it was obvious Sheri was right in the middle of it. That was enough to fill him with foreboding.

It was closer to fifteen minutes than twenty when he pulled the Jag into the driveway. The house looked much the same as it always had. From his mother's garbled explanation, he'd half expected to find people camped on the doorstep. Thrusting open the front door, he stepped into a scene he could guarantee the old house had never witnessed before.

The hallway was filled with people. On one side stood Sheri and Tina and Roger. Tina was arguing passionately that this kind of thing was everyone's responsibility. Sheri was silent, but her stance said she agreed with every word his sister uttered. Roger's eyes held more than a tinge of slightly malicious amusement, but his position bespoke his support.

On the other side of the hall stood Eleanor, looking a great deal like the paintings Jack had seen of Liberty on crusade. Her jaw was set, her dark eyes full of fury, and the flush on her cheeks made it clear the argument had been going on for some time. His mother stood next to her, her eyes full of confusion; she was clearly undecided about the proper stand.

In the middle was a ragtag trio of total strangers. Obviously a family: a man of about forty, a woman a few years younger, though hard living had etched premature lines in her face, and a little girl, who was holding her mother's hand so tightly her knuckles were turning white.

"Good grief!" The exclamation escaped his lips before he could think to back out the door, leaving this obviously volatile situation to resolve itself without him.

There was a moment of silence as everyone turned to look at him and then they all converged at once.

"Jack, thank heavens you're here. I don't know what to do with these people."

"Jack, you've got to tell Mother and Eleanor we can't turn our backs on these people. We have to do something."

"Jack, perhaps you can add a voice of reason to this whole mess. I've been trying to explain how impossible this situation is, but your sister and your 'guest' don't seem to understand."

"Jack, I'm sorry. I did not mean to cause trouble, but they haven't enough money for food and they have been living in their car and I just could not leave them there."

"Jackson, welcome to the circus. If you had any sense you'd have stayed at the office."

Jack realized that his back was pressed to the door, much like an animal at bay. He straightened up, raising his voice to be heard above the cacophony.

"Hold it! Hold it! I can't hear a thing when you're all talking at once." Silence descended and he drew a deep breath, trying to look as though he was in control of the situation. "Okay now somebody explain to me exactly what's going on."

"We were—"

"They brought—"

"I couldn't—"

"I can't believe—"

"QUIET!"

The bellowed command had the desired effect. They all stared at him, waiting. He thrust his fingers through his hair his gaze settling on the strangers, who looked as bewildered a he felt. He gave them a distracted smile before looking at th assembly in front of him.

"Roger, you seem to know what's going on. Do you think you could explain it to me?"

"Sure. It's really very simple."

Jack braced himself, recognizing the look in Roger's eyes. Roger was enjoying this entirely too much. Which meant that simple or not, things were not going to be easy.

"Tina and Sheri went out for lunch, and when they came out of the restaurant, this gentleman—" he gestured lazily to the strange man "—approached them and requested a small amount of money, apparently to buy food for his family." This time his gesture encompassed the woman and child. "Tina gave him some money, but Sheri engaged the man in conversation. When she discovered he'd been without work for over a year and he and his family were attempting to make their car into a home, she felt he needed more than money."

"And she brought them home?" Jack questioned weakly, beginning to understand his mother's hysteria over the phone.

"Yes, indeed. She brought them home. I personally think it was an act of great humanitarian spirit that puts the rest of us to shame," Roger answered, his eyes sparkling with amusement. It wasn't that he didn't sympathize with the man's plight, but he could see the humor in the current circumstances.

Jack was not really up to seeing the humor at the moment.

"Jack, Sheri's absolutely right. Melvin and Louise need more than just a handout. And there's Sarah to consider. Do you want to think of her growing up on the streets?"

"Tina, be quiet." He raised his hand when Eleanor started to speak. "Pardon me for being rude, but if you'd all just shut up for a minute, it would make it a lot easier to think."

He met the stranger's eyes again, and he saw pride beneath the confusion. Yes, he could just imagine Sheri taking one look at the man and deciding she had to help him.

"Sheri, could I talk to you for a moment? If you'll all excuse us?" He drew her into the library, shutting the door on the odd little gathering in the hallway.

"I'm sorry I have caused trouble, Jack. I know I promised

I would fit in. But I could not leave that man on the street. He was so full of hurt and pride. He hated asking us for money but his family had no food."

"Sheri, I know it's a terrible tragedy, but I'm not sure that bringing him into my mother's house is the right thing to do."

"I did not know what else to do, and I knew you would know how to help them. You can help them, can't you?"

When she looked up at him with those eyes, he was ready to promise her the world. He dragged his gaze away, trying to order his thoughts.

"Look, there are agencies who handle this sort of thing. It's too big a problem for individuals to deal with." He broke off as Sheri set her hand on his arm.

"They've been to the agencies, Jack. They would not be able to stay together. They're a family. All they want is a chance to stay together. That's not so much, is it?"

"No, of course not, but—" He stopped, running his hand through his hair again. How did he explain this to her? How did he make her understand that this wasn't the way things were done? She made it seem so reasonable, as though she'd done the obvious thing.

"Sheri, I—" He stopped again, caught by the shimmer of tears in her eyes.

"Jack, I am sorry I have caused trouble again, but I could not leave them there."

He reached up, catching a tear on the end of his finger. "No, of course you couldn't." And he knew it to be the truth. She could no more have left Melvin and family on the streets than she could have stopped breathing. "It's all right. Don't cry anymore. It's all right."

Somehow, she was in his arms, her head pressed against his chest, her tears dampening the front of his shirt. He bent his head over hers, inhaling the sweet fragrance of her hair.

Jack felt an ache in his chest, as if her pain were his. He wanted to comfort her, to take the hurt away. Her gentle soul could never understand the harsh realities of the world. Yet he realized he wouldn't want it any other way. He tightened his arms around her and pressed his cheek to the top of her head, his expression tender. "It's going to be all right."

"I don't see how you can say that, Jack."

He jerked his head up. Eleanor stood just inside the door, her eyes cool as she took in the sight of her fiancé with another woman in his arms. "This whole situation is ridiculous."

Jack dropped his arms from Sheri. She turned to look at Eleanor, apparently unaware of the possible implications of the scene the other woman had just witnessed. Eleanor stepped farther into the room, shutting the door behind her. The furious color faded from her cheeks, and she was as coolly in control as ever.

"Really, Jack. Maybe you should explain the realities to your little guest. This kind of thing may be acceptable in some places, but this is hardly the place. One just doesn't bring people of that sort into one's home. And especially not into the home of one's hostess. Glynis was practically in tears when I got here."

Sheri flushed. "I'm sorry if I upset Glynis, but I couldn't leave Melvin on the street."

"So you brought him here where he can do God knows what sort of damage? I hate to point out the obvious, but you know absolutely nothing about these people."

"I know they are good people," Sheri insisted stubbornly.

Eleanor gave a short laugh, expressing total incredulity. "On the basis of a five-minute conversation on a street corner, you're willing to risk not only your life, but the lives of Jack's entire family? The man could be a killer for all you know. My God, that's a bit arrogant, don't you think?"

Sheri paled, her fingers furiously twisting her hair.

"That's enough, Eleanor."

Jack's abrupt tone only fueled Eleanor's anger. "Enough? Jack, you can't possibly condone this. What about your family? Have you thought of what could have happened to Tina when this woman so blithely invited these people home?"

"Nothing happened to Tina," Jack said wearily. "And I don't think any good can come of overdramatizing the situation."

"Pardon me. I thought I was simply showing a normal concern for the welfare of the people I thought you cared about."

Eleanor's tone could have created instant icicles in the tropics. She turned and left the room before Jack could say anything more.

"I'm sorry, Jack. I did not mean to cause trouble."

Sheri's eyes, wide and troubled, settled on his face.

"Stop apologizing. You did what you thought was right, which is more than most of us manage these days." He rubbed the back of his neck, feeling the tension settle in a knot at the base of his skull.

"Still, I have made Eleanor very angry."

"She'll get over it." He was vaguely appalled to realize how little he cared whether she did.

He pushed the thought aside to concentrate on the problem at hand. "You must have had some idea of what to do with Melvin and Louise when you brought them here."

Sheri brightened somewhat. "Well, I did think that perhaps you could hire them."

"Hire them?" He tried to picture Melvin or Louise on the payroll at the bank. Did Sheri see them as the executive types?

"Your mother told me the cook is going back to Europe next week. Louise is a good cook. Sarah told me so."

Jack thought of pointing out that what a ten-year-old considered good cooking might not be quite what his mother had in mind. Goodbye *osso bucco*, hello macaroni and cheese.

"And what about Melvin?"

"Well, he likes plants. He told me so when I asked. And your mother told me how hard it is to find a good gardener— someone who really cares about their work."

She was looking at him so eagerly, as if she'd just solved a major problem for him. He pictured his mother's immaculately manicured two acres and then tried to picture her face if he suggested that she hire the scruffy individual he'd seen in the hallway.

He sighed. Roger had been right. He should have run the minute he heard his mother was on the phone. Saint Thomas was nice this time of year.

"Why don't you ask Melvin and Louise if they'd like to come in here, and I'll talk to them. Maybe they have some idea of how they'd like their future settled."

Sheri flashed a dazzling smile. "I knew you would understand. I knew you could help them."

The light in Sheri's eyes told Jack she believed he could do anything. "I haven't helped them yet," he said hastily. She caught his hand in hers and he felt the same jolt of awareness he did every time they touched. It was like coming into contact with something so intensely alive that there was an almost electric shock. He pulled his hand gently away. There was nothing he wanted more than to take her in his arms and try to absorb some of that vibrancy into himself. But the very intensity of his desire made him pull back.

"Ask them to come in here. And see if you can calm Mother down a bit. I think this has been a bit of a shock."

If finding Melvin and Louise in her foyer had been a shock to Glynis Ryan, it was nothing compared to having her only son suggest that the couple be hired.

"Jack, we don't know anything about them." She stared at her elder child as if trying to decide where she'd gone wrong with him.

"They're good people, Mother."

"They're living in a car."

"They wouldn't be living in a car if we hired them. The guest house hasn't been used in years."

"Really, Jack. This is ridiculous."

Eleanor's tone left no room for doubt about her opinion of her fiancé's suggestion.

"You can't possibly be serious about this. You're willing to risk your mother's safety and Tina's just because your little 'friend' brought home this riffraff? I can't believe you've thought this out clearly.''

"If you manage to speak a little louder, Ellie, maybe the poor souls will get an even clearer idea of what you think of them.''

Eleanor flushed at the lazy sarcasm in Roger's tone, but she didn't back down.

"I don't think they're terribly concerned about my opinion. Tina is probably encouraging them to help themselves to everything in the kitchen, including the silver.''

"The silver isn't in the kitchen," Sheri told her soothingly.

Eleanor turned on her, her eyes bright with rage. "Don't get smart-alecky with me! This situation is entirely your doing, and if I had anything to say about it, you'd be leaving along with your filthy friends.''

"But you don't have anything to say about it.''

Jack's quiet words reverberated in the silence that followed Eleanor's harsh words. His eyes met hers, flashing cool gray to furious brown. Two spots of color appeared high on her cheekbones. There could be no doubting that Jack was letting her know she'd overstepped her bounds.

"You're right, of course," she said tightly. The rigid set of her back left no doubt as to her feelings. "I apologize.''

She didn't look at Sheri and her tone was flat, but Sheri didn't seem to notice a lack of sincerity.

"It's all right." Sheri's smile held no enmity. "I know you are concerned. Truly, Melvin and Louise would never do any harm.''

Roger pried himself loose from the wall and moved over to Eleanor. "The truth is, Ellie, my pet, this really isn't any of our business. What say we go explore the rose garden?''

Eleanor hesitated only a moment before rising and shaking out the folds of her full silk skirt. She looked at Jack. "I hope you give some consideration to my feelings in this matter. After all, after the wedding it *will* be my concern.''

"Of course, Eleanor," Jack said, his tone saying he was

apologizing for his earlier harshness. He watched Roger and Eleanor leave the room before turning back to his mother.

"You know I wouldn't suggest this if I thought there was any possibility at all that they weren't completely trustworthy. Melvin has a letter of recommendation from his former employer." He didn't mention that Melvin's former employer had been a garbage company.

"I don't know, Jack." Glynis pleated the folds of her shawl uneasily. "This all seems so peculiar."

Sheri leaned forward, taking the older woman's hand between hers. "I am sure Melvin and Louise would be a wonderful addition to your home, Mrs. Ryan. You know how much you need a gardener, and Louise would be a fine cook. Hiring them would solve many of your concerns."

"Do you really think so?" Glynis clutched at Sheri's fingers.

"I'm sure of it."

"Well, it still seems very odd, but I suppose if you're both so sure, we could give them a try. Heaven knows, Tina will make my life a misery if I don't agree. But on a temporary basis only, mind you."

Sheri looked at Jack, her smile dazzling, her eyes sparkling with pleasure. Seeing only her face, aglow with gratitude, Jack promptly forgot all his doubts.

Chapter Eight

"So, are you going out to celebrate?"

Bob's question shook Jack out of the fog he'd been drifting into.

"Celebrate? Celebrate what?" He looked at the company's youngest vice president, wondering what the man was talking about.

"The Carter deal," Bob said, surprised. "You've been working on this long enough. I'd think you'd want to do a little celebrating now that you've tied the knot."

"Tied the knot," Jack repeated, the Carter contract forgotten. "You're married, aren't you?"

Bob blinked, wondering what he'd missed. "Yes," he admitted cautiously.

"I'm engaged, you know."

"I know."

Jack toyed with a pen, his eyes on the aimless movement. "How long have you worked here?"

"Five years."

"Five years. That's a long time. Do you like it here?"

"Yes." Bob tugged at his tie, wondering if he was about to get the ax.

"Did you ever want to do something else?"

"Something else?" Bob questioned cautiously. Was this some kind of a test?

"Some other career. You know, scuba diving or raising horses or something."

Bob relaxed. Either Jack was kidding, or he was just making idle conversation. No one would ask that question seriously.

"Sure. When I was a kid, I wanted to be an astronaut." He grinned, but Jack's responding smile didn't reflect much amusement.

"Why didn't you?"

Bob shifted uneasily in his seat. Maybe Jack had been working too hard. He shrugged. "Well, you know. That's kid stuff. Everybody has silly dreams when they're a kid. When you grow up, you want other things."

"I guess you do." Jack toyed with the pen a moment longer before dropping it and straightening in his chair. "Thanks, Bob. You've done a great job on this project."

Jack watched the other man leave, then leaned back, his eyes focused on nothing in particular. Bob now thought he was crazy and he couldn't blame the guy. He rubbed his fingers over the niggling ache that lurked between his eyes. He couldn't seem to get up any real enthusiasm for the business of Smith, Smith and Ryan these days. Sometimes he wondered if he'd *ever* had any enthusiasm.

In those first months after his father had died and he'd thrown himself into the business, he'd busted his butt to keep the bank going. He'd enjoyed the challenge. But sometime in the past ten years, the challenge had gone out of it—out of the business, out of his life.

Maybe Sheri was right. Maybe he didn't dream enough these days.

But there had to be something more to life than dreams, he argued with himself.

If you didn't have dreams, what was life really worth?

Plenty. He'd accomplished a lot in his life. He knew men twice his age who hadn't done half as much.

But was he any happier than they were?

He slammed a desk drawer shut and shot to his feet. The

only problem with him was that he'd been spending too much time in this damned office. The fact that he was having arguments with himself was a strong indication that he needed a break.

His secretary looked up, startled, as he strode through the outer office.

"I'll be out the rest of the afternoon, Ms. Sanders. I don't have any vital appointments, do I?"

Since he was already at the outer door, it was clear it would have to be a very vital appointment, indeed, for him to be interested.

"No, sir."

"Good. If anyone calls, tell them I've gone fishing. Better yet, why don't you wrap up whatever you're doing and go home yourself."

He shut the door on her surprised expression. Climbing into the Jag, he felt pleasantly truant, a sensation he hadn't experienced in a very long time. The late-spring weather was particularly mild, even for Southern California. The temperature hovered in the seventies, just warm enough for shirt sleeves. He rolled the window down as he pulled out of the underground parking lot and into the sunshine.

With no particular destination in mind, he turned toward home. That was the trouble with keeping one's nose to the grindstone. When you lifted it, you didn't quite know what to do with it.

By the time he marched into the wide hallway, Jack was feeling vaguely disgruntled. Now that he'd fled the burden of responsibility, he wanted something to do, someone to share it with. He stopped just inside the door, frowning. He shouldn't have come home. You didn't go home when you played hooky. It had been a long time since his grade school days, but he distinctly remembered that you did *not* go home when you ditched school.

Guilt niggled at the back of his mind. He really did have a lot to get done. It was all very well for Roger to talk about running away and Sheri to make obscure comments about the importance of dreaming, but neither one had people depending on them.

He wandered into the library, still arguing with himself. There was a small fire burning in the grate, an odd circumstance when the weather was so warm. He moved closer, stepping off the rich Oriental carpet onto the oak floor. At the first click of his heel on the floor, the fire winked out as if it had never been, leaving no embers or ash to mark the immaculate marble hearth.

"Sheri."

Two slender legs disappeared from where they draped over the arm of a wing chair and Sheri peered over the side, her anxious expression fading when she saw that he was alone.

"Hello, Jack."

"Hello. You know, you can't just go around popping fires in and out of existence. People notice things like that."

"I'm sorry. It looked so pretty, even though it's warm out. I could not resist."

"Don't worry about it." He waved away her apology as he sat on a thickly padded footstool, stretching his long legs out in front of him.

She was curled up in the big chair, her feet tucked under her. She was wearing a soft cotton skirt of a yellow so pale it was hardly a color at all and a plain shirt in a shade that hovered somewhere between blue and green.

"What do you do with yourself all day?" he asked abruptly, suddenly aware he'd never taken the time to wonder how she occupied herself when he wasn't with her.

"I've been reading a lot. You have so many wonderful books." She gestured at the floor-to-ceiling shelves that lined the room. "Have you read all of these?"

Jack glanced at the volumes that filled the shelves, leather-bound first editions packed next to the latest paperback best-sellers.

"No. You know, when I was twelve, I swore I was going

to read every one of these books, shelf by shelf.'' He reached out to take the book she held, staring at the spine without seeing it.

''Why didn't you?''

''I got bogged down in *Plutarch's Lives*.'' He laughed, handing the first edition of *Little Women* back to her. ''The most god-awful dull book you can possibly imagine. By the time I gave up on it, I'd sort of lost my taste for literary endeavors. So what else do you do besides read?''

Sheri tilted her head, studying him, sensing that he wanted to be distracted. ''Your mother is teaching me to needlepoint. I'm halfway through a pillow.'' She wrinkled her nose. ''I'm not very good at it, I'm afraid. I think your mother's fingers twitch with the urge to redo everything I've done. But she's very tactful about it. You know, she's really quite a good teacher. I think she should open a shop where she could use some of those skills.''

''Oh, I've been trying to get Mother to open a shop or take up teaching for years, but she won't do anything about it.''

He picked up a delicate Meissen figure of a woman, studying it absently. ''Where is Mother, anyway?''

''She's arguing with Melvin, I think.''

''What are they arguing about this time?''

In the weeks since Melvin and Louise had entered the Ryans' employ, Glynis's arguments with Melvin had become legendary. She was determined that he do things her way and he was equally determined that he do them his. Whether it was roses or plumbing, they were bound to have differing opinions.

''He doesn't believe it was the fertilizer that made the roses bloom earlier,'' Sheri said, watching Jack, trying to sense his mood.

''Oh, he doesn't, does he?'' Jack's eyes met hers, an amused glint in them. ''What is Melvin's theory for the miraculous occurrence?''

''He thinks it was a convergence of Mercury with Mars. Or

was it Venus with Saturn?'' She wrinkled her brow, secretly pleased when she drew a laugh from him.

"Mother is sticking by the Zoo Doo theory, I take it."

"Oh, yes. She showed him the bag of manure and Melvin said it would take more than zebra—'' she hesitated, seeking a more delicate word ''—droppings to make roses burst into bloom like that.''

"Good for Melvin. I'm glad to see he's sticking by his guns. Of course, if he gets her too frustrated, she may fire him.''

"I don't think so. I think she rather likes arguing with him. Besides, Louise is a wonderful cook, and if your mother fired Melvin, she'd have to fire Louise. And she's teaching little Sarah to needlepoint. She wouldn't want to give that up. Sarah is a much better pupil than I am.''

"I would think there wouldn't be much you couldn't do if you set your mind to it,'' Jack said.

Sheri shrugged. "I guess I haven't spent much time working with my hands.''

He laughed softly. "I suppose it's a lot easier to twitch things up when you need them.''

She laughed but shook her head. "You overestimate the amount of…twitching I do.''

"Do I?''

There was something in his eyes that put an odd little flutter in her breathing. She touched her fingers to the base of her throat, feeling the quickness of her pulse. It was odd the way her heart beat sped whenever Jack looked at her this way. There was a warmth in his eyes, a feeling she couldn't quite put a name to. Just as she couldn't quite put a name to her own feelings.

He looked away and the moment was gone, leaving her to wonder if she'd only imagined it. Silence lay between them, not uncomfortable but holding something best left unexplored.

Jack stood up abruptly, making Sheri jump. She tilted her head back to look up at him, sensing something in his mood she'd never seen before.

"Let's go somewhere." He reached down and caught hold of her hand, drawing her to her feet.

It was one of the rare occasions when he initiated physical contact between them. Sheri wondered if he felt the same tingling awareness that she did, that feeling of being connected to something vibrantly alive.

"Go where?"

"I don't know." He frowned down at her, thinking.

"We could go on a picnic," she suggested tentatively.

"A picnic." Jack considered the idea and then nodded slowly. "I haven't been on a picnic in years." He grinned, looking suddenly years younger. "I take it you can supply the food?"

Sheri grinned back, picking up his lighthearted mood. "I can only do my humble best."

"I'm sure that will be good enough." He tightened his fingers around hers. "Let's get out of here before someone catches us and suggests we do something worthwhile."

"SO, WHAT DO YOU THINK of L.A.?" Jack leaned on one elbow, feeling wonderfully content. The sun was beating down, warming him in a way central heating could never match. His suit jacket lay in the back of the Jag, his tie stuffed in one pocket. His collar was loosened; his sleeves were rolled halfway to his elbows.

The rest of the world was hard at work, and here he was, slothing the afternoon away on top of a grassy hilltop, surrounded by tall pines. But not a twinge of guilt accompanied the thought. At the moment, work, responsibility and the rest of the world seemed very far away. He was determined to keep it that way, at least for a little while.

He was pleasantly full of fried chicken and potato salad, not to mention the half-dozen other dishes that Sheri had felt appropriate for a picnic. On the blanket between them, the remains of the meal invited nibbling.

He had to admit there were definite advantages to not having to worry about spending hours in the kitchen to prepare a meal like the one they'd just eaten. It certainly made spur-of-the-moment alfresco dining a lot easier.

Sheri sat on the edge of the blanket, nibbling on a grape, her skirt spread out around her like the petals of a pale flower. Her hair was pulled back from her face, and it spilled over her shoulders, all shining pale gold in the warm sunlight.

Jack thought lazily that he'd never seen anyone quite so exquisite.

"It's a strange place," she said thoughtfully.

Jack had to drag his mind back to the conversation and make an effort to remember what he'd asked her. Oh, yes, her opinion of Los Angeles.

"I think that's an understatement," he commented dryly, reaching for a grape.

"There are so many people. And they all go about their business. They hardly ever seem to know there are other people around them."

"Most big cities are like that."

"It seems rather lonely."

"Lonely?" He nodded, staring across the grassy park to the small lake that nestled in the midst of some pines. "I suppose it is lonely in a way. But you can't be friends with everyone."

"No, of course not. But it seems as if people have so few friends."

Jack thought of himself. How many friends could he lay claim to? Roger, of course. And one or two people he worked with. But he rarely saw them outside of work. When it came right down to it, he could count his friends on the fingers of one hand and have a finger or two left over. It was not a cheering thought.

"Are you lonely, Sheri?"

She looked at him, surprised by the question. "Lonely? No. There are many things to think about, to do. I don't feel lonely."

"Just what do you do all day? You can't spend all your time

reading and needlepointing." Jack felt a twinge of shame when he realized how little thought he'd given to how she was occupying her time. "Do you get bored?"

"Bored?" Sheri laughed. "Never. You don't realize how interesting it is for me, being in your world. It's very different. I've never known anything like it."

"Before Uncle Jack, who were you with? I mean, did you have another—" He stopped, wondering if he was treading on delicate ground. "That is, if this world is so different, I just wondered— Never mind." He waved one hand as if he could erase the words. "It's none of my business."

"No, it's all right," Sheri told him quietly. She smoothed a hand over her skirt, her expression pensive. "You know that a genie who has no human connections is not truly alive. We exist, but we do not live. Before your uncle…" She trailed off, shaking her head, the sadness deepening. "It had been a very long time, longer than you can perhaps imagine. That, for us, is true loneliness. Such times drain the soul, leaving us weak, our powers thin.

"Before that…" She shrugged. "I remember little. Some compensation. It would be too cruel if we had to forever remember all that was lost."

It occurred to Jack that he'd accepted her existence by pretending she was an ordinary woman, at least as much as it was possible to pretend that. Only now was he acknowledging that there were many unanswered questions.

"Sheri, do you mind if I ask you something?"

"From you I have no secrets."

"Are you immortal?"

"Not truly immortal. Our life spans are… different from yours, but all things have an end." She squeezed a crust of bread in her hand, watching as the bread crumbled. "When I read your books, immortality seems an end devoutly to be wished. But everything has a price."

"And what's the price of immortality?" he asked.

"To see those around you grow old and die. To be always left alone."

She'd uttered the stark words quietly, but there was pain in her eyes.

"I'd never quite thought of it that way."

They fell silent and Jack felt as if a cloud had passed over the sun, dimming the pleasure of the day.

Sheri spoke first, her tone deliberately light. "It's not all bad. There are advantages." She made a quick gesture with her hand and the remains of the picnic vanished, leaving the thick grass empty.

After a startled moment, Jack laughed. "I suppose there are a few advantages." He leaned back, hands behind his head, and stared up at the sky. "So what else do you do with your days?"

Her answer was so long in coming that he turned his head to look at her, his curiosity aroused by the hesitancy in her expression. "You look guilty. What are you doing?"

"I am looking for a career." She made the announcement with a mixture of pride and defiance.

"You're what?"

"I am looking for a career," she repeated a little less certainly.

"As what?" Jack sat up, staring at her.

"I do not know." She frowned. "I thought it would be simple, but it has turned out to be much more difficult than expected."

"I— Have you been on any interviews?" Jack was having a difficult time picturing her on a job hunt.

"Oh, yes. I was even hired twice."

"Twice? How long have you been looking?"

"Two weeks."

"And you've been hired twice?" Jack thrust his fingers through his hair. "Why are you still looking?"

"Those careers did not work out."

"They didn't? What happened?" he questioned weakly.

"Computers and genies do not go together," she informed him succinctly.

Jack shuddered, trying to imagine the damage she could have done to a system. "Why?"

"Perhaps it's because computers have no soul."

"No, no. I mean, why are you looking for a job?"

Her eyes dropped. "I have been trying to become as human as possible so as not to cause you so much trouble."

"And you thought that having a career would make you more human?"

"It seemed to be something I should have. Unless one has children. If one has children, it is suitable to stay home and see to their care."

The innocent words had a stunning impact on Jack. He could see Sheri, her slender figure full with the weight of a child. He shook his head, forcing the image away.

"I have done something wrong?" Sheri's anxious question dragged his attention back to the moment.

"No, no. You haven't done anything wrong. If you want a job, you should certainly have one. I could find you something if you'd like." He closed his mind to the possibilities for disaster that lurked in the concept of Sheri working at the bank.

"Thank you, but this is something I wish to do myself. You will be surprised at how human I can become."

Jack bit back the urge to tell her he didn't want to see her change too much. He lay back, staring unseeingly at a thick white cloud overhead. He hadn't realized he'd come to cherish Sheri for her uniqueness.

A flutter of movement caught his attention and he turned his head, rising up on one elbow as a mourning dove settled on the ground near Sheri, cooing softly as if in inquiry. She laughed and held out her hand. The dove hesitated a moment, eyeing the inviting crust of bread. Jack wondered if it was his imagination that made it seem as if those beady little eyes looked at him suspiciously before the dove sauntered forward and took the crust from Sheri's fingers. She was soon joined by a second dove and then a third.

Watching Sheri feed the small creatures, Jack wondered how it was possible to see her and not know that there was something unique about her, something that set her apart from everyone else. It wasn't just the fact that the birds ate from her fingers with such trust. There was something in her eyes, in her smile, in the tilt of her chin. She was different—special.

"Sheri." The birds started, taking flight as he sat up. Sheri turned her head, meeting his eyes in a look so open, so honest, it brought an ache to his chest. What did it feel like to have nothing to conceal? No secrets—even from yourself.

"Jack?"

Her tone was questioning, but he didn't have a reply. Perhaps he'd just needed to reassure himself that she was real, that her beauty wasn't a figment of his imagination.

The rustle of footsteps nearby and the sound of a child's crying provided a distraction. Sheri scrambled to her feet. Jack followed more slowly, not sure whether to regret the interruption or welcome it. Whatever he might have said was probably better left unspoken.

Stepping around a sprawling oleander shrub, he found Sheri kneeling on the grass in front of a little boy who couldn't have been more than three or four. Tears had left tracks down his grubby cheeks and sobs still made the small frame quiver, but his attention was irresistibly caught by the woman in front of him. Jack knew just how he felt.

"Look at this. See the pretty leaf?" Sheri was saying to the youngster.

As Jack moved up to join her, she closed her hands over a wide sycamore leaf, crumpling it. The little boy was no more interested in the results than Jack. Sheri opened her fingers and a baby bunny sat trembling in her palm.

Jack glanced over his shoulder, hoping there was no one over the age of four close enough to witness what she was doing.

"See the bunny?"

The little boy reached out to touch the creature, his tear-stained face reflecting his awe.

"This is Larry and his parents are lost."

She didn't change her tone from the same soft cadence she'd used with the child, and it took Jack a moment to realize she was talking to him.

"Do you think you could find them for him?"

Jack pulled his gaze from the bunny that shouldn't have been there and nodded. "Sure. I'll see what I can do. Try not to conjure up a pony or anything that's too big to be explained. Okay?"

As he strode off, he heard Larry say "Pony?" in a hopeful tone. He winced, hoping Sheri would use some restraint in her efforts to distract the child.

Larry's parents were not difficult to locate. Nearing the lake, he heard them calling their missing offspring in frantic tones. Jack felt vaguely heroic at telling them their son was safe. Since Larry's mother was at least ten and half months pregnant, only Larry's father accompanied Jack back up the hill. As they approached, Jack muttered a prayer that they weren't going to find a camel or an elephant in addition to little Larry.

Perhaps Sheri had heard them coming, because there was nothing untoward lurking behind the oleander. The minute the boy spotted his father, he was reminded of his lost condition and a wail of anguish shattered the quiet. His father snatched him up, scolding him about wandering away. Since he was also clutching him so tight that the child was having a hard time getting enough breath to sob, Jack didn't think it likely that the reprimand was going to have much effect. With a heartfelt thanks, Larry and his dad disappeared down the hill.

Jack turned to look at Sheri, surprising a wistful expression in her eyes.

"He is a beautiful child, don't you think?"

Jack considered the dirt-smeared countenance, filthy jeans

torn T-shirt and shock of tangled hair. "He was certainly...healthy."

The answer seemed to satisfy her. "Do you ever think about having children, Jack?"

"Sometimes," he admitted slowly. "But I'm not sure I'd make the best of fathers."

"You would be a wonderful father." Her eyes met his, full of belief.

"Would I?" He reached out, hardly aware of his actions as he fingers caught a lock of her hair. It felt like the finest of silks in his hand—warm, alive, full of promise.

"I think any child would be lucky to have you for a father."

"Do you?" His finger slipped deeper into the fall of her hair, as if irresistibly drawn.

"Yes."

There was a breathless quality to the word that drew his eyes to hers. As always, he felt lost in the clear blue, sinking deeper to find the green that lurked beneath the surface.

The sunlit park faded away until only the two of them existed—alone, isolated, in a private world that couldn't be touched by reality.

His fingers slipped through the silk of her hair to cup the back of her neck. Sheri's palms touched his chest, light as thistledown, yet the touch went straight to his soul.

His eyes held hers as he lowered his head until their lips were barely a breath apart. He hesitated and her lashes fluttered downward, forming dark shadows on her pale skin.

If he kissed her, he'd surely be lost. Yet kissing her was as necessary as breathing.

His lips touched hers and a feeling of homecoming flowed through him. How had he lived without this? Without her?

He slid his hands around her back and drew her closer. Sheri rose up on her toes, her hands slipping upward to his shoulders. Her body fit against his as if made to be there. Her taste, the warm scent of her, the feel of her in his arms...it was all so right, so inevitable.

A breeze whispered by. Sheri's skirt drifted forward, wrapping itself around Jack's legs as if in silken embrace. Desire swept over him like a slow tide. His hands tightened around her back as need replaced wonder.

He heard Sheri make a soft sound as her lips parted for his tongue, fanning the deep hunger that gripped him. She tasted of everything and nothing. Femininity, passion, warmth, strength and softness—all lay in the sweetness of her kiss. It was like nothing he'd ever experienced before. It was magical.

Magical. The word stayed in his mind. *Magical.* His hands loosened slowly. *Magical.* Sheri's fingers drifted down to rest against his shirt front. *Magical.* He broke the kiss slowly, reluctance in every movement. *Magical.*

Their eyes met and Sheri saw the question in his, read the thought in his expression. Her fingers touched his mouth, feather light.

"No, Jack. What is between us is not of magic." A smile flickered over her mouth. "It's more of dreams. But not magic. Never magic."

Jack stared at her, his arms still around her, reluctant to give up the contact. More than anything, he wanted to keep her in his arms and shut out the world with a kiss.

But he had responsibilities, commitments. He was engaged, for God's sake. The world existed. But for just a little while longer, he could pretend it didn't.

He grinned suddenly. "Do you like movies?"

THE KNOCKING on the door was not gentle. Roger dragged his eyes from the television set. He wasn't sure if he'd been watching a sitcom or a soap opera. It was getting harder and harder to tell the difference. The knocking came again as he reached for the remote control and shut the set off.

"Hold your horses," he muttered as the knocking came a third time before he was more than halfway to the door. He jerked it open, his eyes widening when he saw who was on the other side.

"Is Jack here?"

Eleanor's tone was not one of friendly inquiry. In fact, she looked furious. And beautiful. Her dark hair was swept up in a simple chignon that set off the strength of her features. A simple black sheath of watered silk molded to her figure. But not even the most carefully applied makeup could conceal the rage in her eyes.

"Well, are you trying to think up a lie?" she demanded when Roger stared at her in silence.

"No."

"No, what? Oh, you're impossible."

She pushed him out of the way with one disdainful hand and stepped into his apartment. Roger's mouth twisted with amusement as he shut the door and turned to lean against it, watching as she swept the living room with her eyes.

"Jack isn't here, Ellie."

She spun around, her eyes flashing frustrated rage. "Don't call me 'Ellie.' And how do I know he isn't here? You'd probably lie for him."

"Undoubtedly," he agreed without apology. "But it's hardly Jack's style to hide in a closet when his fiancée comes looking for him." He pushed himself away from the door and crossed to the built-in bar. "Why don't you have a drink? You look like you need one."

"I don't want a drink," she snapped, too angry even to try for good manners. "If Jack isn't here, where is he?"

"Well, at a guess, I'd say he's not where he's supposed to be." Roger turned away from the bar and held out a glass. Eleanor took it absently, clenching the cool glass. "Did he stand you up, Ellie?"

"I waited for almost two hours at that damned restaurant."

Roger's brows rose. If she was cussing, she must be pretty far gone.

"How rude of him," he commented mildly. "Have a sip of scotch. It's good for the nerves."

"I told you I didn't want a drink."

But she took a swallow, anyway. It didn't seem to help her mood.

Roger poured himself a gin and tonic, then leaned one hip against the edge of the bar, watching as Eleanor paced restlessly across the room to stand at the window. He didn't think she was admiring the panoramic view of the Los Angeles basin.

"He's out with her. I know he is."

He didn't have to ask whom she was talking about. He took a swallow of his drink and wandered over to join her at the window.

"What makes you think Jack is out with Sheri?"

"I just know it. Nothing's been right since he brought her here. Nursing his uncle, indeed." She spit the words out, making them sound like a curse. "More likely she was hoping to bilk the old man out of his money."

Roger considered what he knew of Sheri. "I don't think so. She seems like a nice enough girl."

The remark was like throwing gasoline on a fire.

"Nice! She's not nice. She's manipulating Jack, using him. Look how she talked him into hiring those awful people."

"They seem to be doing quite well."

"Hah!" Eleanor tossed back the glass of scotch and thrust it out for a refill. "They're probably cohorts of hers. God knows what they're stealing."

Roger picked up the scotch bottle, weighing it in one hand, weighing obscure concepts like ethics and morality in the other. With a faint shrug for obscure concepts, he filled the glass with straight scotch.

"It's possible they're just what they seem, you know."

"None of this is what it seems." She took a swallow. "That woman isn't what she seems. I know she isn't."

Roger stared at his drink. She didn't know just how right she was, and he wasn't going to be the one to try to explain it to her.

"Jack seems to like her." He carefully tipped a little more fuel on the fire.

"Jack is like most men. You all think with your zippers. Just because a woman is pretty and looks helpless, you think she's an angel of goodness and light. Hah!" She tossed back another gulp. "That's the trouble with men. They don't have any sense. It's so easy to fool them just by batting your eyes at them. They're gullible."

"Do you think Jack's gullible?" he questioned idly.

"I thought he had more sense than the average man. He *did* have more sense until that woman wound her fingers around him. *She's* the one to blame for this."

"You don't appear to have a very high opinion of Jack's ability to think for himself."

"I—" She stopped, frowning down into her almost-empty glass. "Naturally, my opinion of Jack is high on every score."

"Except when it comes to thinking for himself. Do you think the same of me, Ellie?"

Her eyes came up to meet his and he saw the memories there—reluctantly recalled and fought against, but still there.

"The trouble with you is that you're determined to go your own way. You don't care what the rest of the world thinks, do you?"

"Not much," he admitted. He set his glass down and took a step closer to her. "I care what you think, Ellie."

"No, you don't." She backed away a step, but bumped into the window. She watched him, her eyes wide, showing a vulnerability few had seen.

"I do care, Ellie. I've always cared."

"No." She stopped and swallowed hard. "If you'd cared, you wouldn't have gone away."

"But I came back." He stopped inches away, so close he could see the way the pulse fluttered at the base of her throat.

"Roger, no…"

She tried to turn away, but his hand wound into her hair, holding her where she was. He stepped closer, pinning her to the cool glass. Her hands came up, pressing against his chest in silent protest. A protest he ignored.

"It's been a long time, Ellie. Do you still remember what we were like together?"

"No." But her eyes told him that she lied. "Let me go."

"We weren't much more than kids, but I've never forgotten it. I've compared every other woman with you."

"And there've been so many," she spat at him, her eyes burning. Roger's mouth curved in a smile of pure male satisfaction and Eleanor realized just how much she'd revealed. Color mounted her cheeks and she stood rigid in his hold. "Let me go."

"Jealous, Ellie?"

"Never!"

"I'm glad." He stroked the soft skin behind her ear with his thumb. "I like the idea of you being jealous."

"You always were a conceited ape." She twisted in his hold, but he only crowded her closer against the window.

"And you always were a stubborn little idiot."

"Coming from you, I'll take that as a compliment."

"We used to fight like this. Remember?"

"No." But the word was uttered breathlessly. Her eyes met his and she pushed frantically at the solid wall of his chest. "Roger, no. Please."

It wasn't a gentle kiss. His mouth plundered hers, expressing fifteen years of frustration. Years of broken dreams, shattered hopes. For a split second she fought him. And then she melted against him, her lips opening to his.

He dragged his mouth from hers, his breathing ragged. "You tell me if Jack has ever made you feel this way. Tell me if you've ever felt with him a tenth of what I make you feel." His voice was raspy, all the lazy humor gone.

She didn't answer him with words. Instead her arms came up to circle his neck, her eyes pleaded with him.

With a groan, Roger bent, his arms sweeping her feet out from under her as he lifted her against his chest. His mouth found hers again, and tried to slake a thirst that burned deep inside both of them. But the thirst wouldn't be quenched.

"BREAK THE ENGAGEMENT, Ellie." She jumped at the sound of Roger's voice. Her eyes flew toward the bed, where he lay propped against the pillows, the sheet draped across his waist.

"I can't."

The refusal was barely audible. Roger could see her fingers trembling as she reached for her dress. "You don't love him."

"I'm very fond of Jack." She tugged the dress into place, reaching behind her back to struggle with the zipper.

"You can be very fond of a puppy. It's not enough to base a marriage on."

"Jack and I understand each other."

"And you and I don't?"

"I thought Jack was your best friend." She snatched up her shoes, clutching them to her chest.

"He is my best friend. If it wasn't for Jack, I'd probably be in a psych ward somewhere. When I came back, he's a lot of what held me together. There wasn't anyone else."

Eleanor sucked in a breath, feeling the impact of Roger's words like a blow. Her eyes were wide and vulnerable on his, but he didn't soften his look. He wanted her to remember just how grim that time had been for all of them.

"Jack is like a brother to me. And this marriage would be as disastrous for him as it would be for you."

Her eyes dropped from his and she shook her head. Roger swung off the bed, catching her halfway to the door, his hands firm on her shoulders.

"Let me go, Roger." She didn't look at him.

"No. Ellie, don't be a fool. You can't go on with the marriage, not after tonight."

"All the arrangements have been made."

"Arrangements can be canceled. Ellie, look at me." He shook her gently until her eyes lifted to meet his. "Tell me that you melt in Jack's arms the way you melted in mine."

"Don't."

Her voice held a wealth of despair, but he didn't back down. "Tell me you cry his name the way you cried mine tonight."

"Please. Don't."

"Tell me he makes you feel what I feel. Tell me that, Ellie, and I'll let you go."

Tears filled her eyes, spilling down her cheeks. Her mouth quivered with pain. "Roger, please don't. I beg you."

"Tell me."

"Jack and I haven't...we don't sleep together." The admission was soft, broken.

"I knew it." Roger's eyes blazed with triumph and he tightened his hands on her shoulders, pulling her closer to his bare form.

"No." She turned her head away, her hands pressing against his chest. "I'm going to marry Jack." She backed out of reach

"You can't marry him," Roger protested incredulously.

"I can and I will. The arrangements are made. Jack will make a good husband. He's steady and dependable."

"So is my car, but I'm not walking it down the aisle."

"He's your best friend."

"He's not going to be any happier in this marriage than you are."

"The arrangements are made." She repeated the phrase like an incantation.

"Damn the arrangements! Ellie, we're talking about your life. Jack's life. My life," he added more softly.

"Stop it." She pressed her hand against her mouth, her eyes tortured. "Just stop it. You don't understand."

"Explain it to me."

"It's not just Jack and I. People have expectations. My family." She caught her breath as fury blazed in his eyes.

"Is that what this is about? Your damn family! You wouldn't fight them fifteen years ago and now you're letting them push you into a marriage that's going to make you miserable. When are you going to grow up and stop worrying about what your family thinks?"

"Please." The word broke on a sob. "Please, Roger. If you care about me at all, just let me go."

He stared at her, his hands clenched. The dimly lit bedroom was taut with emotion. For several long moments neither of them spoke. Eleanor watched him, her eyes swimming with tears. Slowly, moving like a very old man, Roger stepped out of her way, clearing a path to the door.

She moved to rush by him, but his hand caught her forearm, holding her still for one last moment. Eleanor was rigid in his clasp, her eyes fixed on the door as if salvation lay beyond it. He was so close his breath stirred the hair at her temple.

"I'd feel guilty about what happened here if I thought Jack gave a damn. But he doesn't love you any more than you love him. You think about that while you're walking down the aisle."

He released her and she bolted out the door as if all the hounds of Hell were on her heels. Roger didn't move as he listened to the sound of her stumbling progress across the living room, then the opening and closing of the front door.

Chapter Nine

The restaurant was small, dark and crowded. It made Jack think of opium dens and dungeons, neither one of which put him in a particularly good mood. It also happened to be one of Eleanor's favorite places to lunch.

Ordinarily he would have tried to talk her into eating somewhere that the lights held bulbs of more than two watts. But considering the fact that he'd completely forgotten their date the night before, it had seemed that the least he could do was graciously agree to her choice of restaurant.

Eleanor was already seated at a table in the most dimly lit corner in the place. As Jack approached, she looked up, her expression shadowed and impossible to read. Jack bent to kiss the cheek she presented and then seated himself across the table.

"I'm sorry I'm late. I had a hard time finding a parking place." He reached for the menu in the vain hope that they'd added something edible since the last time he'd been there.

"That's quite all right. After last night, I suppose I should just be grateful that you showed up at all."

Jack shut the menu with a snap, feeling guilty and annoyed. "I've already apologized for that, Eleanor."

There was a moment of tense silence and then she sighed, the stiffness going out of her shoulders. "You're right. I'm sorry, Jack. I guess I'm just a little snappish today."

The unexpected apology threw him off balance and added to the guilt he was already feeling. "I couldn't really blame you if you held it over my head." He gave her a half smile. "I really am sorry I forgot our date. Things have been difficult at the office."

"It's okay. I know you're not all that fond of the opera, anyway."

"Well, I have to admit it doesn't break my heart to have missed it, but I am sorry to have been so rude."

"It doesn't matter." She waved one hand, dismissing the incident.

The waiter appeared just then and the subject was dropped as the orders were given. When he was gone, silence settled between them.

Jack reached for a breadstick, one of the few things in the place he didn't consider undercooked and overpriced. Eleanor was studying her fork as if she'd never seen one before and Jack took the opportunity to study her.

She was a lovely woman. Her features were strong but not unfeminine. Her hair was thick and dark, the style softer today than the one she usually wore. There was none of Sheri's gentle sweetness—

The breadstick shattered between his fingers. He was *not* going to make comparisons between Sheri and Eleanor. Eleanor was his fiancée. He was going to marry her. And Sheri was— Just what the hell was Sheri?

"Jack."

He looked at Eleanor, grateful for the interruption. She didn't say anything for a moment, as if debating her words.

"I think you should ask Sheri to move out."

The words were flat, lacking any real emotion. Jack wondered if it was his imagination that put an underlying passion in them. He drew a deep breath. Maybe he should have expected this, but he hadn't.

"Why?" It wasn't quite the brilliant reply he'd have liked, but he was groping for time.

She looked away, uncharacteristically indecisive. ''I think she's had a detrimental effect on our relationship.'' She lifted a hand, stopping him when he would have spoken. ''Please let me finish, Jack.''

Jack sat back, wishing he were almost anywhere but in this dingy restaurant. How was he supposed to explain to Eleanor that no matter how reasonable her arguments, he couldn't ask Sheri to leave. He didn't even fully understand why himself.

''I am not a jealous woman, Jack. I think you'd agree with that. Even if I were inclined toward jealousy, our relationship is not one where it would be an appropriate emotion. After all, I realize that what we share is more in the nature of a strong friendship than a grand passion.

''When we decided to marry, we both knew it wasn't a love match in the generally accepted sense of the term. I want the stability you offer. You need a wife who understands your world and your business. I am not unhappy with that bargain. I don't think you are, either.'' She paused, as if waiting for him to confirm this.

Jack stared at her, trying to think of an appropriate reply. He was grateful for the interruption provided by the arrival of their waiter, bearing plates of artistically arranged, semiraw vegetation. He tried to look terribly excited by the prospect of the meal, hoping Eleanor would forget what they'd been discussing, but Eleanor's memory was considerably better than that.

''I think your friend Sheri is creating an undue strain on our relationship,'' she reiterated.

Jack set down his fork and looked across the table at the woman he planned to marry. The reasons for that marriage were becoming more blurred in his mind lately. But then, everything in his life had grown a little fuzzy around the edges since the advent of Sheri.

Sheri. There was the crux of the whole problem. The center, it seemed, of most of his problems these days. Certainly she was central to Eleanor's problem.

"Eleanor, Sheri nursed my uncle for almost three years before he died. She did that without any expectations of recompense. I can hardly throw her out now."

"I didn't expect you simply to throw her out." Eleanor stabbed a sliver of carrot with more force than was necessary. Her smile was strained. "But I'm sure it wouldn't be that difficult to find her a job and a place to live."

"I don't see any reason to rush her into making any decisions."

She set down her fork and clasped her hands in front of her, her expression intent. "This is important to me, Jack. Important to our future together. I'll help you find her a job. I'll help her find a place to live."

Jack looked away. The request wasn't unreasonable. God knows, most women would have made it long ago. If this had been an ordinary situation, if Sheri had been an ordinary houseguest, if anything about this whole damn thing had been ordinary— But it wasn't and she wasn't.

He ran his fingers through his hair, feeling a headache nagging between his eyes. Around them, the other diners seemed unaware of the tension at their table. He envied them their oblivion.

"I'm sorry, Eleanor," he said finally, his tone flat. "After what Sheri did for my uncle—for the family, really— I simply can't urge her to move."

"I see."

The silence stretched interminably, until Jack felt forced to break it, offering her reassurances he wasn't sure he had faith in himself.

"There's nothing to be concerned about. I consider her a friend, but nothing more than that—" He broke off, remembering that kiss yesterday. There'd been nothing of friendship in that kiss. "I just wouldn't feel right about asking her to leave," he finished weakly.

"Then of course you mustn't do so," she said without inflection. She glanced at her watch. "Heavens, look at the time. I really must be going."

Jack automatically rose as she stood. "Eleanor, perhaps we should discuss this further."

"Are you going to change your mind?" Their eyes met and Jack shook his head. "Then I really don't see any reason to discuss it further."

Her tone was quite pleasant, as if they'd just disagreed on whether or not to serve lobster at the wedding supper. She leaned down to him and Jack kissed her. It was a light kiss, perfectly suited to their surroundings. It was disturbing to realize that even if they'd been alone, he wouldn't have had any particular urge to turn the kiss into something more.

After Eleanor left, he sat down again, picking at the meal he hadn't wanted in the first place. There were too many things changing too damned fast to suit him. For years his life had gone along on an even keel. He'd had things planned, organized, settled.

In the space of a few weeks, all his planning, organizing and settling had begun to totter like a badly stacked tower of children's blocks. He rubbed at the ache in his forehead and stood up, throwing a handful of bills on the table.

He'd been spending too much time thinking lately, that's all it was. This constant analysis of the state of his life wasn't healthy. Maybe he'd call Roger and see if he could arrange a game of racquetball. Some nice cutthroat physical competition was just what he needed right now.

SHERI WAS CURLED UP on the sofa, laboriously threading Persian wool through the appropriate holes in the needlepoint canvas. It didn't seem to matter that she had put the stitches in the right place, which Glynis Ryan swore was all that was necessary. They might be in the right place, but they managed to look unhappy there. In fact, the peony she was supposed to be needlepointing didn't look happy at all.

When the doorbell rang, she put the canvas down, grateful

for an interruption. From the direction of the kitchen, she could hear Louise drilling Sarah on her multiplication tables. She smiled, thinking of how Sarah had blossomed in the weeks since her family had moved into the guest house.

Her smile widened when she opened the door to find Roger standing on the step. She liked Roger.

"Hi. Twitched up anything interesting lately?" He wandered into the hallway.

"I've been trying very hard to restrain myself from 'twitching.' It bothers Jack." Sheri shut the door and followed him into the living room, watching as he slouched down into a chair. She returned to her position on the sofa, but didn't reach for the abandoned needlepoint.

"Jack doesn't know how to have fun," Roger complained. "Now if I'd been lucky enough to have an uncle leave me someone as interesting as you, I'd know how to take advantage of it."

"What would you ask for?" It was a pleasant change to be able to talk naturally with someone without worrying about her words revealing what she was.

"Oh, I don't know. Stock market tips, maybe."

"Jack says you have absolutely no interest in the stock market."

"True, but it might be amusing to know where everyone else is going wrong."

"A lot of things seem to amuse you," she commented.

"Most things," Roger agreed easily. "If you just have the proper perspective, there isn't much in life that isn't amusing in one way or another."

"Is there anything you take seriously?"

"Sure, food and drink. Two very serious subjects."

Sheri laughed at the exaggerated solemn expression he conjured up.

"Speaking of which," he continued, "I don't suppose you'd like to get me a drink."

"Of course." She uncurled her legs and stood up, moving to the bar. "What would you like?"

"No, no, no. I didn't mean for you to get up." Roger stood and joined her at the bar. "Now you're making me feel guilty. I just thought you could pop it up for me."

"I thought we'd just discussed the fact that I've given up that sort of behavior." She watched as he poured himself a very short scotch with a lot of water.

"Jack spoils all my fun," he whined pathetically, drawing a laugh from Sheri. "So, what have you been up to lately?"

"I'm looking for a career." Roger's brows rose, Sheri noticed, but he didn't seem to find the idea as remarkable as Jack had.

"Really? How's it going?"

"Not well. I seem to have a great deal of difficulty with computers. I do not think they like me."

"Then they have no taste."

"Thank you, but perhaps they are right. I do not seem to be very good for them, either."

"What you need is a job where you work with people."

"I would like that."

"How about charity work? Have you thought of that?"

"Charity work?" She frowned. "Can that be a career?"

"I don't see why not. Look at what a good job you did with Melvin and Louise. There are a lot of people out there just like them. Maybe you could help them."

She considered that, a smile slowly brightening her face. "That would be very nice. How would I go about finding some of this work?"

Roger looked uneasy and stared down into his glass for a moment before meeting her eyes. "I could put you in touch with some people," he muttered.

"You could?"

"I...ah...do a little work for an organization. Nothing major, you understand. Just a little now and then...." He trailed off as if he'd just confessed a crime.

"I promise to keep your secret," Sheri told him.

Roger laughed at his own foolishness and held out his hand. Sheri took it and they shook, sealing the bargain.

To Jack, who was just entering the room, the scene appeared cozy and intimate. Sheri and Roger were standing in front of the bar, Sheri's face tilted up to his, laughter warming her expression. They seemed like old and close friends, and Jack discovered he didn't like the idea at all. He cleared his throat. They turned to look at him, displaying none of the guilt he half thought they should.

"Jack, you are home early. How nice." Sheri's smile held nothing but pleasure at seeing him.

"Jackson, your wish is my command. I await the pleasure of trouncing you on yon court of racquet, just as you requested." Roger waved his hand in a vaguely medieval salute.

"That wasn't exactly what I had in mind," Jack said dryly, coming farther into the room.

"But that's going to be the end result. You're out of practice."

"Maybe, but I can still run your butt off." Jack wondered if it was his imagination that put wariness in his friend's eyes. And if it wasn't his imagination, what was causing that look? "Have you been here long?"

. "Just long enough to fail at convincing Sheri to demonstrate her unusual talents for me."

"Since I presume Mother and Tina are home, not to mention Melvin and family, I'm glad she had the good sense to turn you down," Jack commented, pouring himself a drink of mineral water.

"Your mother is upstairs," Sheri said, "but I'm afraid she and Tina had an argument and Tina left. She said she'd be spending the night with a friend."

Jack sighed, rubbing the back of his neck. "I suppose they fought about Tina going for her master's?"

Sheri nodded. "Don't worry. I'm sure they will work it out." She reached out to smooth the collar of his shirt.

Roger's sharp eyes noted the casual intimacy of the gesture, but there was nothing more than mild curiosity in his tone when he said, "Your mother isn't a fan of higher education?"

Jack shook his head, a frown drawing his dark brows together. "It isn't that. She's just worried that Tina's education is going to get in the way of her personal life. She's got this idea that no man is going to want to marry a math professor."

"Ah, the ever elusive 'suitable marriage,' She should be satisfied that one of you has made such an excellent choice."

There was a note in Roger's voice that Jack couldn't quite define. "Eleanor, you mean?"

"Unless you're engaged to two women, I must mean Eleanor."

"After the way lunch went today, I don't even know if I'm engaged to one woman."

Roger tightened his fingers around his glass, a subtle shift in his expression revealing his interest, but it was left to Sheri to ask the obvious question.

"Did you and Eleanor quarrel?"

Jack shook his head, obviously regretting having said anything. "Not really. A minor disagreement. I'm going to go change. I'll be down in five, Roger. You might as well have another drink. Alcohol can be a cushion to the pain of defeat."

Roger lifted his glass in acknowledgment as Jack left the room. Sheri watched Roger for a moment, tilting her head as if to get a better angle.

"You don't like the fact that Jack and Eleanor are going to be married, do you?"

Roger's eyes met hers. His look was guarded, but not so guarded that she couldn't see the pain he felt.

"I don't think they're suited," he admitted cautiously. "Do you?"

"I don't know. There are many things I don't yet understand." She frowned, feeling her way carefully. "It does seem as though they don't make each other very happy. And I do think that if you're going to marry someone, they should make you happy—and you them.''

"Eleanor appeals to the stuffy side of Jack, the side that thinks duty is the most important thing in the world.''

"Isn't duty important?''

"Sure. But it's not a god. And it shouldn't be the be-all and end-all of your life. Ever since Jack's father died, he's been trying to do everything his father would have done. What about what Jack wants to do?''

"You don't think Eleanor will encourage him to follow his own dreams?''

"Ellie is worse than Jack when it comes to doing what's 'right.' '' His tone held an odd mixture of bitterness and affection. "No, she'll encourage Jack to keep on doing just what he's doing because it's safe and predictable. Ellie's big on predictablity.''

"And you aren't predictable?'' she questioned softly.

"Not at all.'' His eyes met hers, a wry acknowledgment in their depths. "You know, for someone who's spent her life in a samovar, you're pretty shrewd.''

"I watch people. They're so interesting.''

"This coming from a woman of your 'interesting' talents?'' Roger's brows rose in comical question.

Sheri grinned and reached for his empty glass. "What talents?'' The glass shimmered in her hand for an instant and then was gone.

Roger stared at her hand and then lifted his eyes to hers. For once there wasn't a trace of cynical amusement to be found in his expression. It was one thing to hear Jack's descriptions, to see the evidence of Sheri's uniqueness in an out-of-season rose; it was something else altogether to see the impossible happen right before his eyes.

"Good God.''

"That's almost exactly what Jack said,'' Sheri commented mildly, her eyes sparkling with mischievous amusement.

Roger shook his head, some of the bemusement fading, to

be replaced by a look of genuine humor. "'There are more things in heaven and earth, Horatio,'" he quoted softly.

"Hamlet. Act 1, Scene 5," Sheri said demurely.

Roger laughed out loud. "Jack is a fool if he can't see what's under his nose."

Sheri cocked her head, puzzled, but before she could ask him what he meant, Jack walked in. Faded jeans molded to his thighs in a way Levi Strauss had never envisioned. A blue chambray shirt with the sleeves rolled up and a pair of slightly scruffy running shoes completed his transformation from executive to sportsman.

Sheri smoothed her hair, her pulse oddly accelerated. She'd never seen Jack look quite so...so masculine. The shirt emphasized the width of his shoulders, the open throat exposing a hint of dark hair. Another quote came to mind: "Yon Cassius has a lean and hungry look."

There was something lean and hungry about Jack tonight, a restlessness she could feel as if it were a fourth presence in the room. Out of practice or not, she didn't think Roger should count on winning tonight.

"Sheri?"

Jack's voice penetrated her preoccupation and she jumped, realizing it wasn't the first time he'd called to her.

"What?"

"You looked like you were a million miles away," Jack commented, his eyes curious.

"I'm sorry. I was thinking." She hoped the soft lighting would serve to conceal the flush that had crept up her cheeks. She was aware of Roger watching her with an expression she didn't quite understand.

"I just asked if you would tell Mother not to expect me for dinner. We'll probably get something at the club."

"Alfalfa sandwiches and watercress juice," Roger grumbled under his breath.

"It'll be a nice change for your stomach," Jack told him

without sympathy. "After a steady diet of burgers and fries, I suspect it will welcome a change."

"A hasty change in the diet can be hazardous to one's health."

Jack ignored him, his eyes on Sheri. "I guess I'll see you later."

"Yes."

The silence stretched for several slow heartbeats while they continued to look at each other. Sheri could only guess at Jack's thoughts. Her own were hardly more clear. This breathless feeling was new to her, still unexpected. It was left to Roger to break the moment.

"Sometimes I'm amazed by the stupidity of the human race." The apparently irrelevant remark was addressed to no one in particular. He clapped Jack on the shoulder. "Come on, I've been waiting all afternoon for a chance to grind you to dust on the court."

"Fat chance," Jack mumbled, turning to follow him out the door.

Sheri curled up on the sofa and picked up her needlepoint as she listened to the sound of the car backing out the driveway. It wasn't the well-bred purr of the Jaguar, which meant they must have taken Roger's ancient M.G. She smiled, remembering Jack's bitter complaints about the car having been built for someone without legs.

Her smile faded as she tugged the yarn through the canvas. She and Jack had spent a wonderful day yesterday. She hoped he didn't regret it. She'd felt almost normal. As though she really belonged here.

There was nothing she wanted more than for Jack to see her as normal. To have him look at her without wondering what new disaster lurked around the corner. To have him forget that she wasn't human. To live in his world as if she belonged.

She smoothed her fingers over the slightly lumpy surface of the canvas. Jack had asked her if she was ever lonely. She'd lied, not knowing how to express the deep loneliness of being different from those around her, so different that she could at best find only a shaky meeting ground. Oh, she could pretend to fit in, but deep inside, she was always on the outside looking in.

There had been moments when she'd felt truly a part of his life. She didn't need to close her eyes to remember the way his arms had felt around her. They'd felt strong and warm and right. Just as the kiss had felt. In Jack's arms she'd felt as if she belonged.

She sighed. If there was one place she didn't—couldn't—belong, it was in Jack's arms. Jack was engaged to Eleanor. She might not yet understand everything that went on in Jack's world, but she knew that engaged men were not supposed to kiss other women.

Yet it had felt wonderfully right. And it was a memory she would hold to her always—that moment of belonging.

Chapter Ten

"Now *that* is a gorgeous dress."

Sheri turned from the mirror as Tina plopped down on the bed. "Do you really think so? It's very plain."

"It's perfect. It'll make all the other women look fussy and overdressed."

Sheri frowned, turning back to her reflection. The dress was a pale gold crêpe de chine. It was, as she'd said, very plain. A high, rolled collar, long straight sleeves and simple bodice topped a wide waistband over yards and yards of fabric gathered into an extravagantly full skirt that fell to midcalf. There was nothing flashy about the dress, but it managed to catch the eye, anyway.

"I don't want to make anyone else uncomfortable," she said uncertainly, touching her collar.

"You're much too nice, Sheri." Tina sighed when she saw that the words didn't reassure the other woman. "You look perfectly appropriate."

"Are you sure?"

"I'm positive. And if you happen to make the other women just a teeny-weeny bit jealous, where's the harm in that?"

Sheri laughed, turning away from the mirror to study Tina. "You look very nice yourself."

Tina tugged at the narrow skirt of her simple black dress and grimaced. "I want Mother to notice that I'm in mourning."

"In mourning?" Sheri sat on the bed next to Tina. "Who are you mourning?"

"Not who," Tina corrected. "What. I'm mourning my career aspirations."

"Is this what you quarreled about night before last?"

"It's what we always quarrel about. I don't know why she's so stubborn about it. It's not as though I don't have the money to go for my master's."

"Then why don't you do it?"

"Because Mother has control of the trust fund. I don't get control of it until I'm thirty." She scowled. "Thirty. My grandfather didn't think women could handle money, so he tied mine up until I turn thirty. He didn't do that to Jack."

"It doesn't seem very fair," Sheri agreed cautiously. "Why doesn't your mother want you get one of these master's?"

"She thinks I'm going to forget all about my personal life in my pursuit of a degree. She also thinks that most men are going to be threatened by a woman with a master's in math."

"You don't agree?"

"Of course not. No man worth having is going to let something like that stand in his way. Besides—" she hesitated, her eyes flickering to Sheri and then away "—I've already met a wonderful man who doesn't care what kind of a degree I have."

"Have you told your mother that?"

Tina studied her fingernails. "No. She wouldn't approve of him."

"Why not?"

"Well, he's older than I am—almost ten years—and he's not exactly the conventional type. He has a degree in marine biology and he's working with dolphins, trying to break their language down so that we can understand what they're saying."

Once she started talking, the words seemed to tumble from her. "He's tall and he has the most incredible blue eyes you've ever seen and blond hair and I don't think he's ever been in a tux in his life. It's not that he thinks there's anything wrong with money. It's just that it's not very important to him. He lives in this tiny little apartment right next to the water and he drives the oldest, most beat-up VW I've ever seen in my life. But he doesn't care, because that's not important to him, either.''

She stopped, drawing in a quick breath, as if surprised to realize how much she'd said. "And he wants me to get my degree if that will make me happy," she finished defiantly.

"He sounds very special. Why do you think your mother wouldn't approve of him?''

Tina frowned, flicking a bit of lint off her skirt. "Because he's not rich and he doesn't have any plans to get rich. And because he isn't part of 'society' and he doesn't have any interest in being part of it. Because he's different.''

Sheri shook her head. "I think you're doing your mother an injustice. All she really wants is to see you happy. Maybe she'd prefer it if you married someone who shared her world, but that's only because that's what she understands and it's what she believes would make you happiest. It seems to me that you should talk to her about this man, reassure her that you're not so buried in your education that you're letting your personal life fall by the wayside.''

Tina's frown deepened. "I don't know.''

"What do you have to lose? She's already said she won't fund your education. What more can she do?''

"I guess. I hadn't thought of it that way.'' Tina brightened a little, her natural optimism coming through. "Maybe you're right. Maybe if she met Mark, she'd see how wonderful he is.''

"From your description, I don't see how she could help it.'' Tina caught the gentle teasing in Sheri's tone and flushed, but she laughed, too.

"You know, I'm really glad Jack brought you home. I think you're good for all of us.''

Sheri returned her quick hug, keeping her doubts to herself.

She'd feel better if she could be sure that Jack shared his sister's opinion.

JACK STRAIGHTENED his tie for the tenth time, aware of a deep feeling of foreboding. This was not where he wanted to be. Ordinarily he enjoyed his mother's parties. Good food and good conversation were not to be sneered at. But tonight was different. Tonight Sheri was going to be there.

He thrust his fingers through his hair. He wondered what Sheri was going to think of her introduction to a larger swath of society. God alone knew what they were going to think of her.

"Don't be an idiot," he muttered under his breath. He moved over to the heavy mirror that dominated one corner of the living room. Meeting his own gaze, he realized that he looked as panicked as he felt. His hair was standing on end and his eyes held a slightly wild look reminiscent of a man facing a firing squad. He drew in a deep breath, smoothing his hair back into its usual neat style.

"There's nothing to worry about," he told his reflection. "There's no reason for anyone to suspect a thing. She's just a houseguest. It isn't as if she has 'genie' tattooed on her forehead. She's just a perfectly normal young woman."

"Begging your pardon, but if you're talking about Sheri, you're one hundred percent wrong."

Jack jumped at the sound of Melvin's voice and turned away from the mirror. He'd been so busy concentrating on his one-sided conversation he hadn't heard the other man come in. With the small portion of his mind that was still functioning in a normal fashion, Jack noted that Melvin had been pressed into a tux for the occasion. With his habitual lugubrious expression and his lanky frame draped in black and white, he looked like something out of an Alfred Hitchcock movie. The thought did nothing to calm Jack's nerves.

"Wrong about what?" he asked. Just how much had Melvin heard? And what exactly had he said?

"Wrong about Sheri being perfectly normal."

"I am?" His voice threatened to break into a squeak and he cleared his throat, repeating the question in a deeper tone. "I am?"

"Anyone can see that she's not normal at all."

"Really?" Was that his voice? He sounded so casual. Just what the hell did Melvin know and how was he going to deal with whatever it was?

"Yes, sir. You just have to look at her to see that she's different," Melvin said earnestly.

"Different?" That was a masterpiece of understatement if ever he'd heard one. "In what way?"

"She's sweet and kind and there's not an ounce of malice in her."

"And you think you can see all that just by looking at her?" Jack felt limp with relief. The way his life had been going lately, he'd fully expected Melvin to have guessed the worst.

"I do. It's all right there in her eyes. When she looks at you, you know there's nothing but goodness in her." He might have continued, but Sarah appeared in the doorway just then, her frantic signals indicating some domestic crisis in the works. Melvin bowed in Jack's direction, his long face completely solemn again as he exited the room.

Jack tugged at his tie again, wishing his mother had held off on this little gathering. Just until he'd gotten used to the idea of having a genie in the house—say, another ten or fifteen years.

He heard them coming down the stairs, Tina chattering away at a mile a minute, Sheri making an occasional reply in her soft voice. Turning toward the doorway, he realized he felt like a teenage boy about to go on his first date. He was long past his teenage years and this was definitely *not* a date, but he couldn't shake the nervous tension that gripped him.

The feeling didn't ease when he saw her. Her hair swirled over her shoulders, a pale golden cape that almost exactly matched the color of her dress. He couldn't have said just what

the dress looked like, but he knew it made her look like
princess in a fairy tale. Her eyes were wide pools of blue i
the delicacy of her face.

He stepped forward, hardly aware that Tina was standin
next to Sheri. There was something about Sheri—a look o
wisdom mixed with such innocence. The unawakened expres
sion in her eyes drew him so, made him wish he could be th
one to awaken her.

He stopped in front of her, never taking his eyes from her
losing himself in their clear blue depths. For a moment the
weren't standing in his mother's living room. They were some
where far away, alone, the world a distant presence.

"Sheri." Just her name seemed to say everything he wa
feeling, all the thoughts he couldn't express. He started to reac
out, needing to touch her to assure himself of her reality. B
then Tina cleared her throat and shattered the fragile fantasy.

Jack dropped his hand and shook himself, dragging his eye
from the melting depths of Sheri's gaze to meet the shrewdnes
of his little sister's.

"Gee, Jack, for a moment there, I wondered if I was invis
ible."

"Don't be silly." His laugh was a little strained, but it *wa*
a laugh. "You both look stunning." His eyes flickered ove
Sheri and then away again. "Can I get either of you somethin
to drink?"

The moment was gone, but not so easily forgotten. In th
one instant Jack knew he could have walked away from ev
erything just for the chance to be with Sheri, to hold her in h
arms. The question was, why?

But this wasn't the time to try to answer it, for within a fe
minutes the guests began to arrive. Jack allowed himself to b
drawn into his duties as host, grateful for the distraction.

Sheri did her best to fade into the background, retreating
a quiet corner and watching the colorful swirl of guests. H
eyes drifted to Jack more often than not. He looked so hand
some in the dark dinner jacket.

There'd been a moment when she and Tina had first come downstairs—just a moment—when it had seemed Jack was about to say something important. What would he have said if Tina hadn't been there?

There was a stir in the doorway, and she smiled when she saw Roger come in, wearing a slouchy silk jacket and jeans. Utterly inappropriate but so suitable for Roger that he fit right in. He saw her and waved a greeting. As he reached for a glass of wine, his eyes fell on Eleanor. For an instant Sheri could see pain wash over his face, but just as quickly the expression was gone, leaving his habitual cynical look.

She reached up to toy with her hair, her expression thoughtful. There was something between Roger and Eleanor, something a great deal deeper than the surface animosity they both displayed. Why did they pretend to dislike each other, when it was obvious they cared very deeply?

Her eyes shifted to Melvin, who was moving silently about the room, refreshing drinks and making sure the trays of canapés were always full. His eyes caught hers and he returned her smile with a slow wink, making her laugh softly. She might not entirely understand this world of Jack's, but she'd been right in thinking that Melvin and Louise belonged in it. Even Glynis admitted, somewhat reluctantly, that the couple had been an excellent addition to the household.

"Sheri, I have someone who wants to meet you."

She turned at the sound of Roger's voice, meeting the amusement in his eyes before her gaze shifted to his companion.

She'd seen the young man come in with an older couple she assumed were his parents. He was perhaps nineteen years old and at that awkward stage when he wasn't quite an adult but well past childhood.

"Sheri, this is Alan Brinkman. His parents are old friends of the family."

Seeing the look in Alan's eyes, Sheri knew the source of Roger's amusement. She didn't need to have spent a lot of time around young men to recognize an instant infatuation when she saw it.

"Hello, Alan." The look she threw Roger carried equal amounts pleading and threat.

Roger simply grinned and wandered off.

"I saw you the minute I came in," Alan told her fervently.

"Did you really?"

"Yes. You are the most beautiful woman in the room. I've been told I have an eye for beautiful women."

The attempt at sophistication would have been laughable if it hadn't been clear that he was painfully serious. With a sigh Sheri resigned herself to the inevitable.

JACK WAS DOING HIS BEST to play the part of the attentive host. It wasn't easy when at least half his attention was on Sheri. He wanted to talk to her, hear her impressions of the guests. He wanted to make sure she was having a good time. He wanted to feel the peace that was such a palpable part of her presence.

He saw Roger introducing young Alan Brinkman to her and relaxed slightly. She'd be safe enough with Alan. The boy wasn't likely to ask any questions she couldn't answer. From the awestruck, worshipful look on his face, it would be a miracle if he managed to get out a coherent word.

"Jack, Mr. Toffler was just telling me the most interesting story about his trip to Greece." Eleanor slipped her hand through his arm, drawing his attention away from Sheri. "Perhaps we should consider going there on our honeymoon."

Jack knew Eleanor had no intention of setting foot in Greece but Harold Toffler was an important client at the bank and never hurt to make important clients feel as if their opinion were of vital interest. It was exactly this kind of social skill that made Eleanor such an asset to his career. It was unfortunate that *he* couldn't seem to get up more interest in his career these days. Jack shoved the thought away, smiling at the older man and commenting that Greece was certainly a lovely country.

Twenty minutes later Jack knew far more than he'd ever wanted to learn about the country. Mr. Toffler was just launching into a column by column description of the Parthenon, when Jack's eye fell on Sheri.

There was something odd about the way she was standing. Something slightly off balance. He shook his head as Eleanor drew his attention back to the conversation. It was probably just his imagination. But five minutes later, his eyes drifted in her direction again.

Alan was still with her, talking earnestly in her ear, but Jack didn't think she was listening. Her attention seemed to have wandered. And there was definitely something wrong with the way she was standing. She looked taller somehow. Almost as if she wasn't touching the ground.

"Holy—" He covered the exclamation with a cough.

"I beg your pardon. What did you say, Jack?"

"I said that it sounds wholly interesting, Mr. Toffler. But I'm afraid I'll have to ask you to excuse me. I'm neglecting the rest of the guests."

As departures went, it could have been worse. Toffler seemed willing to buy it, but Jack was vividly aware of Eleanor's eyes following him. She wasn't going to be happy that he'd abandoned her and an important client to go to Sheri. But he couldn't worry about that now. Right now he had more important things to worry about. Much more important.

He skidded to a halt at Sheri's side, pinning a bright smile on his face. He set his hand on her shoulder, pushing downward until he felt her feet hit the floor.

"Alan, good to see you."

"Jack." Alan did not look at all happy to see his host.

"I noticed you and Sheri over here talking and I couldn't help but wonder what you were talking about so earnestly." He kept the jovial smile in place, along with the heavy hand on Sheri's shoulder.

"We were just talking," Alan said, a touch of sullenness revealing his youth.

"Alan was suggesting that I might like to leave the party with him," Sheri announced brightly. She looked at Jack, her eyes showing a slight tendency to wander.

"He was, was he?" Jack took the glass from her hand. "Did Alan get you a drink?"

"Yes, a juice. Wasn't that nice of him?"

"Very nice." Jack took a swallow, tasting the vodka under the sickly sweet fruit juice. Alan squirmed under the anger in Jack's eyes. But Jack didn't have to worry about punishment. Sheri delivered that all unknowingly.

"Alan says that in the locker room, his nickname is 'Stud.' Why do you suppose that is, Jack?" She looked at him, her eyes wide with puzzlement.

Out of the corner of his eye, Jack could see the color climb in Alan's face until the boy looked as though he were going to have a stroke. Despite his irritation, Jack had a moment of genuine pity. Still, maybe this would teach the puppy a lesson. With a garbled farewell Alan beat a hasty retreat. Sheri didn't seem to notice his departure.

"What's a locker room, Jack?" She reached up to straighten his tie.

"It's a room full of lockers," he told her absently. The door was on the opposite side of the room, making a casual exit difficult. Eleanor was shooting dagger-sharp looks in his direction, but he couldn't worry about that now.

"Why did they call Alan that, Jack?"

He looked into her unfocused, totally innocent eyes that searched for an explanation. "Because he has a laugh like a horse," he finally offered in desperation.

She frowned. "That doesn't seem like a nice thing to call him."

"I'm sure he doesn't mind at all. Sheri, just what exactly happens when you drink?"

"When I drink? I'm not thirsty anymore." This seemed to strike her as amusing and she giggled softly.

Jack tightened his hand on her shoulder. "Sheri, what happens when you drink alcohol?"

"Alcohol? I told you. It has a deleterious effect on my powers." She drew the words out slowly, savoring them.

"Yes, I know. But what exactly happens?"

"I don't know. I've never drunk anything. Drank? Drinked?"

She giggled again, but this time the giggle ended in a sneeze. Over her head, Jack watched as a delicate Limoges vase lifted off the mantel, hovered in midair for a second and then crashed to the hearth. The sound of shattered porcelain brought a few startled cries, then complete silence as everyone turned to look at the shards of glass.

"Boy, these tremors are getting worse all the time." Jack knew his voice was too loud, a little too hearty.

"Tremor? I didn't feel a thing," said one of the guests, her face reflecting bewilderment.

There was a murmur of agreement as everyone checked with his neighbor to see if he'd felt the quake. One or two people muttered that maybe they *had* felt something.

Jack's smiled widened to a maniacal width. "It wasn't very strong. And quick. It was very quick."

"I'm surprised it would knock a vase off like that," Mr. Toffler commented.

Jack considered immediately canceling the man's account.

"It does seem remarkable," Eleanor commented, her sharp eyes still on her fiancé.

"You know, I noticed earlier that that vase was sitting right on the edge of the mantel."

That was Roger, reminding Jack of all the reasons they'd been friends since grade school.

Roger moved forward to give Glynis an apologetic smile. "I'm sorry, Glynis. I should have said something. I feel as if this is my fault."

Glynis rushed to assure him it was nothing of the kind. Melvin appeared with a whisk broom and removed the debris. Los-

ing interest, the guests resumed their conversations. Catching
the panic-stricken look in Jack's eye, Roger made his way over.

"Hello, Sheri. Jack."

"Hello, Roger. Did you know that Alan's friends all call
him 'Stud' just because he laughs like a horse? I don't think
that's very nice of them, do you?"

Roger met Jack's eyes over Sheri's head. He bit his lip,
trying to maintain a sober expression. "I'm sure they don't
mean any harm by it, Sheri. What's going on, Jack? You look
like you expect a police raid."

"That would be easier to deal with," Jack muttered, keeping
a firm grip in Sheri. "That little twit slipped Sheri a glass that
was at least fifty percent vodka."

"Alan? I didn't think he had it in him." He caught Jack's
eye and erased the half-admiring smile. "I take it genies don't
drink?"

"It has a deleterious effect on our powers," Sheri informed
him solemnly, then sneezed again.

In the blink of an eye, an immaculate arrangement of glad-
iolus became a tousled basket of daffodils. Jack held his breath,
but no one appeared to have seen the transformation.

"Look, I've got to get her out of here," he told Roger.

"That seems like a wise move. Why are you leaning on
her?"

"Because she was floating a few minutes ago."

"I was not. I have my feet planted firmly on the ground.
But I could float if you wanted me to," Sheri offered in a
helpful spirit.

"No! No, that's all right. We're going to leave now. Can
you walk?"

"Of course I can walk. I can fly, too."

Roger snorted with muffled laughter, drawing a rather fierce
look from Jack, who wasn't up to seeing the humor of the
moment.

They'd taken only a few steps, when Sheri sneezed yet again.
Roger lunged to catch a cut-glass plate of crudités as it lifted

from the table and executed a figure eight in midair. Several people turned to look at him. He looked back, wondering how to explain the fact that he was clutching a plate of carrot sticks to his chest.

"I...ah... was just noticing that the tray was a little low. Thought I might take it out to the kitchen." The explanation was weak, but it was better than the truth.

Melvin appeared at Roger's side, giving him a sideways glance that questioned his sanity. "I'll take care of that, Mr. Bendon."

Roger handed him the plate and edged away from the table. Jack had Sheri almost halfway across the room, but they'd run into a snag in the form of an elderly neighbor. Roger was almost to them, when Sheri sneezed once more.

Over Roger's shoulder, Jack watched almost resignedly as a tray of smoked salmon began to move, arranging itself into the shape of a fish, complete with two olives for eyes. For several long moments he almost dared to hope no one would notice this phenomenon. That hope was dashed by a shrill cry as the fish rose on its tail and began to walk the length of the table.

Everyone turned to look. There was the sound of breaking glass as fingers, slackened with shock, lost their grip on wineglasses. The fish stepped over a fork and Jack closed his eyes, shuddering. His entire life flashed beneath his lids, but it was the future he saw that bothered him.

"That's amazing!"

"Incredible! How are they doing that?"

"Must be a puppet."

Several people stepped forward to investigate, but before they reached the table, Sheri sneezed again and the lights went out.

The repeated shocks to their nerves had left the guests without a reaction to this latest assault. Jack waited numbly. Anything from Attila the Hun and his hordes to a troupe of singing dogs was to be expected at this point.

"Look! On the ceiling."

Jack recognized his sister's voice. He looked up, wondering what new disaster lurked above them.

Pinpoints of colored light hung in midair. They swung back and forth, slowly at first, then more rapidly. With each swing they showered colored light over the room, like droplets of sparkling rain. Where the drops landed they clung, still glowing. There was a general exclamation of wonder as hair and clothes developed bright patterns of warm light.

In the illumination cast by the shining dots, Roger made his way to where Jack was easing Sheri from the room. He took her other arm as they edged through the awestruck guests.

They were almost to the door, when Sheri drew a quick breath, preparatory to another sneeze. Jack's hand came up and clamped her mouth as they swept her out the door, no longer concerned with the fact that her feet weren't touching the floor.

From across the room, Eleanor couldn't see Jack's hand over Sheri's mouth. All she saw was Jack and Roger leaving the room with Sheri, their attention focused completely on her. She turned away, oblivious of the exquisite dancing lights.

IT WAS NEARLY midnight. The last of the guests had left an hour earlier, still talking about the dancing fish and the spectacular light display. Jack had explained them away by the use of mirrors and a friend who worked for George Lucas. Lucky for him, no one had insisted on names and details.

He'd gotten through the rest of the party running on adrenaline, hardly conscious of what people said to him or what he said in response. He and Roger had tucked Sheri safely in her room, where her sneezing couldn't cause any new disasters. By the time they'd closed the door on her, she'd been sound asleep.

He'd made excuses to his family for Sheri's absence. Now the headache he'd claimed for her nagged at his temples. Still it could have been worse. Nothing had happened that couldn't be more or less explained away. At a safe distance he could even see the humor in the evening.

Jack grinned, shutting the door to his room behind him. The fish had really been a classic. All it had needed was a top hat and tails and he could picture it doing a little soft shoe in the dill sauce. He took a deep swallow of black coffee. The caffeine would probably keep him awake all night, but right now he needed its restorative effects more than he needed sleep. Many more evenings like this and he was going to grow old before his time.

He rubbed the back of his neck as he crossed to the window to pull the drapes. He paused, looking out into the moonlit garden. The roses were covered in blooms, the wonder of his mother's garden club. In the glow of the full moon, the blossoms of pale yellow and white caught the milky light.

A flutter of color near the far end of the garden caught his eye, and his hand tightened on the drapes. He shouldn't go out there. It was midnight, the witching hour. If Sheri was in the garden at midnight, she wasn't looking for company.

He took the stairs two at a time, turning toward the rear of the house when he reached the darkened entryway. He barely noticed the chill in the air as he stepped out the back door. Sheri fingered a rose washed white in the moonlight. Her golden gown glowed and her pale hair seemed the color of moonlight itself—neither silver nor gold but an amalgam of the two.

She turned at his approach, her face in shadow. "Hello." Her voice was subdued.

"A little late for a walk in the garden, don't you think?" Though there was no one to hear, he'd automatically lowered his voice in response to the stillness.

"I like the way it looks at night." She caressed a showy blossom. "All the color is washed away. It's so clear and simple."

As life should be and so rarely was, Jack thought.

"You looked very beautiful tonight."

She turned to face him, her eyes wide. "How can you say that? I caused so much trouble."

"Well, it could have been worse."

"I don't see how." She refused to be comforted.

"Well, nothing that awful really happened. The vase can be replaced. The fish had a certain air about him that I rather liked. Everyone thought the light show was spectacular. I've already had five people ask me for the name of the firm that did the special effects," he lied. When he saw some of the tension go out of her shoulders he laughed.

"You aren't furious with me?" She tilted her head questioningly and Jack had to suppress an urge to take her in his arms and kiss her thoroughly.

"For what? It wasn't your fault Alan spiked your drink."

"But I should have realized. I promised I wasn't going to cause any trouble. I wanted to make your life easier. Better. Not cause difficulties."

Jack caught her hands in his, drawing her forward so that the moonlight illuminated her face. "You didn't cause any real problems. You just livened things up a bit. Don't beat yourself over the head about this."

"But I—"

"No." He placed a finger across her lips. "Not another word about it. Do I have to make that an order?" he asked with mock sternness.

Her hands slowly relaxed in his and he saw a smile flicker over her face. "Your wish is my command."

"That's much better. For a minute there, I thought I was going to have to get tough with you."

"You have only to ask," she said softly.

He had to drag his eyes away from the softness of her. He released her hands, realizing how much he wanted to pull her closer, instead. If he had any sense at all, he'd go in. That would be the safe thing to do. The sane thing.

"So, do you always come out to the rose garden at midnight?"

"It's a nice place to think." Sheri half turned from him

looking out over the quiet garden. "If you listen carefully, you can almost hear the roses whispering to one another."

"What are they saying?" Jack watched her profile.

"Oh, silly things. They wonder why we're out here instead of safe in our beds where we belong. They discuss the weather. They gossip about their neighbors."

The moonlight made the curve of her cheek like porcelain, the drift of her lashes a silken shadow. Sheri seemed unaware of his regard. She cupped a rose in her palms, bending down to inhale the night-gentled scent.

"I love roses. They're so full of beauty and mystery."

"Like a beautiful woman," Jack murmured, his eyes never leaving her face.

"Don't you think all beauty has an element of mystery?" she asked, her fingertips caressing the full bloom. "We're never quite sure just why something is beautiful, what it is that takes it out of the ordinary."

"Sheri, do genies ever fall in love?" She was quiet for so long he had time to ponder the foolishness of his question.

"Sometimes," she said, her voice so low it was nearly a whisper. She tugged uneasily at a rose leaf. "But we have to be very careful. Love isn't the same for us as it is for humans."

"Why not?"

"Love is something we are, not just something we feel. Many of our powers are lost when we fall in love. We don't have as much to lose in these times. We had more power when the world had more dreams." She sighed, her expression troubled. "If something happens to that love…"

She trailed off and Jack could see the frown that creased her forehead. "What happens, Sheri?" He caught her hand, stilling its restless movement. "What happens?"

"We die."

The simple reply caught at his breath.

"A human dies of a broken heart only on the inside," she continued. "For us it's more than that."

Jack reached out to cup her cheek, feeling the softness of her skin against his palm, the warmth of her in his very soul. "You are so very beautiful."

She didn't move as he bent to her. Her lips were soft under his, parting to welcome him, her body pliant in his arms.

Moonlight spilled over them, the stillness of the garden surrounded them, and for one magical instant Jack was sure he, too, could hear the roses whispering secrets to one another.

Chapter Eleven

The party affected the Ryan household in unexpected ways. Tension seemed to creep through the house, catching everyone in its grip. Sheri could sense the change in atmosphere, but couldn't quite grasp the reason for it. It wasn't in anything anyone said. It was in the way they avoided one another.

Tina and her mother were still at odds over the future of Tina's education. The two women were polite, but the distance between them was obvious. Jack threw himself into his work with a new fervor, leaving early in the morning and coming home late at night.

Sheri was left to her own devices and she filled her time exploring the area around Jack's home, enjoying the warmth of spring.

On this particular day she was in a mood to like the whole world. Roger had kept his promise, introducing her to Marty and Lisa, a young couple who ran a shelter for the homeless. They'd been more than grateful for her offer of help, taking Roger's word for it that she would be an asset to their small endeavor. In fact, it was clear that anything Roger said was okay with them.

When Roger and Marty left the room, Lisa took the opportunity to pump Sheri for information, showing her disappointment when it became clear that Sheri and Roger were nothing more than friends.

"He's such a good man, you know." Lisa smoothed her hand over the bulge of her stomach.

"I do not think Roger would want you to spread that around," Sheri told her with a smile.

"No, he doesn't like people thinking he does good things," Lisa agreed. "He finances all of this, you know." Her wave encompassed the shelter. "Marty and I could never have managed this without Roger. It was a dream of ours to help the homeless, but Roger made it happen."

"He is very kind."

"Yes, but lonely, don't you think?" Lisa sighed, her hands resting on her stomach as if she took comfort from the life she carried.

"I think perhaps Roger has not yet found what he seeks. But he will."

"I certainly hope so."

"When is your baby due?" Lisa's pregnancy fascinated Sheri.

"Another two weeks." Lisa smiled, her thin features suddenly pretty. "It seems like centuries. Besides, he's been trying to kick his way out today."

"Could I— Would it be very rude of me—" She broke off, wondering if she was breaking a taboo she didn't know about. Her eyes met Lisa's, wide and uncertain.

Lisa's smiled softened. "Have you ever felt a baby move?" Sheri shook her head. "Here. Give me your hand." She took Sheri's palm, pressing it to her stomach.

Sheri closed her eyes, dizzy with the strength of the life force she felt beneath her fingers. "A boy," she murmured, only half-aware of speaking out loud.

"Yes. How did you know?"

Sheri opened her eyes to meet Lisa's puzzled gaze. "I'm...lucky with guesses." She drew her hand away. "He seems very strong."

"But he didn't kick just then."

"I...it is just a feeling I got," Sheri said weakly.

"I hope you're right. We lost a baby before this."

She stroked her stomach, her expression full of such protective yearning that Sheri looked away. What would it be like to carry another life inside you? Sheri wondered. *That* was surely true magic.

She was still thinking about Lisa and Marty and her new job, which she was to start in two weeks, later that afternoon. The shelter was small, but its purpose was to get people off the street for good, not to merely offer them a place to stay temporarily.

She liked the idea of working with people, helping them. This was something she could do and do well. Her smile widened as she thought about her attempt to thank Roger. He'd brushed the words away, as embarrassed as if he'd been caught doing something shameful. Such an odd man.

She shook her head, aware she'd been paying no attention to her surroundings. On a beautiful day like this, it was a crime to miss even a moment. This was a day to savor. Which is how she came to meet Mrs. O'Leary.

Mrs. O'Leary lived on the block behind Jack's. The houses were smaller there, the properties not as large. Mrs. O'Leary's home could best be described as midwestern farmhouse, with a wide front porch and neat blue shutters against the white paint.

Sheri had walked by it several times before she actually saw its owner. She liked the house. It seemed to smile at her. And the yard was a lavish tangle of plants. She liked that, too.

Today she slowed as she approached the house, just as she always did. She paused by the waist-high picket fence, admiring the tangle of hollyhocks, calendulas and pansies that filled one corner of the yard.

"Well, don't just stand there, my girl. Come here and give me a hand with this."

The voice came from behind a sprawling shrub rose. Peering

toward the sound, Sheri could just make out a tiny figure wearing what seemed to be chartreuse coveralls.

"Hurry up," the voice commanded.

Sheri let herself through the gate, hurrying up the old brick pathway until she came to the huge rose.

"Here, hold this while I get the saw. Darn thing keeps whacking me in the face. Watch the thorns. Trouble is, I didn't discipline it like I should have when it was small. Now it's got the idea that it can do what it wants. Plants are like children. They need a firm hand."

Sheri held the long cane out of the way while the old woman grasped a saw and proceeded to remove the cane at ground level.

"There now. That's better. Most of the time, he's well behaved, but this past year or so, he's been getting a mite above himself. Thinks because I'm getting old I'm getting soft. Do you like plants?"

Faded blue eyes, still fierce with life, glared up at Sheri from under the brim of a bright green baseball cap. The cap just matched the coveralls.

"Yes. I like plants very much."

"Thought so. I'm Cassie O'Leary. Mrs. O'Leary," she added firmly. "I've seen you walking by the yard. Had a feeling you liked plants."

"I am Sheri." Sheri reached out a hand to help the old woman to her feet, half expecting it to be brushed aside.

But Mrs. O'Leary took it in a strong grip, pulling herself up to her full height, which was several inches less than Sheri's.

"Sheri. Not a bad name. Here. Hold these while I help these sweet peas find the trellis. Stupid creatures. They just wave in the air as if the trellis wasn't right under their nose. Still, nothing smells quite like a sweet pea… I've seen you at all times of the day. Don't you work?"

"I do now. In two weeks I'll be working three days a week in a shelter for the homeless." Sheri set the pruning shears down and reached out, her slim fingers guiding the delicate green tendrils to their holds on the net trellis.

"The homeless, huh? I've seen articles about them. Tragedy, that's what it is." She knelt in front of the sweet peas, deftly nipping spent blossoms from the mat of pansies at the foot of the trellis. "The trouble is that we've lost sight of the family. Used to be that you took care of your own, but people don't think like that anymore. This place could use someone young about. Liven things up some. You may come here when you have time."

Sheri bit back a smile, wondering if it was a command or a request. "Thank you. I'd like that."

Mrs. O'Leary's eyes met hers. "I'm a pushy old woman, I should warn you."

"I would never have thought that," Sheri said demurely.

A surprised bark of laughter met the comment. "I like you. At my age, you've got to make up your mind quickly. You never know how much time you've got."

Sheri laughed and the old woman gave her an approving look. "You've got a sense of humor, too. We'll work well together."

And so they did. Sheri found Mrs. O'Leary's companionship as welcome as the old woman seemed to find hers. Jack was home so rarely. The big house was empty without him. She needed something to distract herself from the gap his absence left in her life. When she wasn't puttering in Mrs. O'Leary's tangled gardens, she walked.

This seemed a reasonably harmless way to spend time. And so it was, until a day when she didn't come home alone.

"BUT, SHERI, you don't know where he's been. And surely he belongs to someone."

Glynis eyed the "he" in question uneasily. "He" was a medium-size dog. He looked somewhat gray, though it was possible that beneath the layer of dirt he was another color entirely.

"I don't think so." Sheri reached down to stroke the animal, who sat quietly beside her. "He was very hungry. Louise fed him a few scraps of meat."

"Well, I certainly wouldn't want to see any animal go hungry, you know that. But he simply can't stay in the house. I'm allergic to dogs." Glynis confirmed this by sneezing violently.

Sheri turned to Roger, who was lounging nearby. He met her pleading look and lifted his hands in self-defense. "Sorry. My building has strict rules about pets. They aren't allowed even if they have a pedigree, and that thing certainly does not have a pedigree."

There the problem rested when Eleanor came into the room. She hesitated when she saw Roger, but it was too late to back out gracefully. With a vague smile in his direction, she approached Glynis's chair, bending to touch cheeks with the older woman.

"I thought I'd give you time to recover from the party before visiting. Good God, *what* is that?" She'd seen the dog, and her expression reflected her opinion of his presence in the immaculate living room.

"It's a dog, Ellie," Roger offered helpfully.

The look she shot him would have withered a lesser man where he stood. It had no visible effect on Roger.

"Sheri brought him home, but I've explained to her that he can't stay. Melvin and Louise were one thing. I mean, they're people after all. I'm not allergic to them. But I am allergic to dogs." Glynis sneezed again.

"I'm very sorry, Mrs. Ryan, but I couldn't leave him on the street." Sheri looked at her, distress in her eyes. "He was so frightened and hungry. I thought maybe I could find a home for him."

"Well, that's very kind of you, Sheri. But I'm afraid he simply can't stay in here. Please ask Louise to vacuum thoroughly after he's gone." Glynis retreated from the room, muffling a string of sneezes with a handkerchief.

"I can't imagine what kind of a home you'd find for a

scruffy-looking bundle of fur like that," Eleanor said disdainfully.

The dog had been watching her since she'd entered the room and he chose this inopportune moment to leave Sheri's side and approach Eleanor.

"Don't you come near me. You're probably crawling with fleas." At her harsh tone, he cowered on the floor, whimpering as if expecting a blow.

"He just wants to be friends," Sheri said reproachfully.

"I have no desire to be friends with a dog." But Eleanor's tone had softened considerably. "Do get up. I'm not going to hurt you." When the animal continued to cower at her feet, she bent and patted him gingerly. "There. Now go away."

But all he'd needed was that one touch to be convinced he'd found a friend for life. He rolled over onto his back, his entire body wiggling with delight. Despite herself, Eleanor smiled and scratched his stomach.

"Looks like you've made a conquest, Ellie," Roger commented lazily. "Maybe you'd like to take him home."

"Certainly not." But her fingers found a particularly sensitive spot just behind the dog's ear.

"You know, Eleanor, he really is a very nice dog. Well mannered, too. He'd make a wonderful companion."

"I don't need a companion." Eleanor was kneeling on the floor, rubbing the dog's back. He yelped suddenly and then cowered on the floor once more. She touched the sensitive spot again, gently brushing aside dusty fur to reveal a welt. She looked up, her eyes flashing. "Somebody has struck him."

"People aren't very friendly toward strays." Roger's voice was soft. "You've got room at your place. You could take care of him, just until you find him a home."

Eleanor stroked the scruffy dog, her fingers gentle. Her expression was soft and compassionate, a far cry from her usual haughty look.

"Well, I suppose I could let him stay with me for a little

while," she said hesitantly. The dog turned to lick her wrist, looking up at her with worshipful eyes.

"He loves you already," Sheri told her. "Animals can sense when someone has a kind heart."

"A kind heart," Eleanor repeated, standing up. "I suppose so." She reached for her purse. "I guess I'd better get him home. I'll have to get food and things." She looked at the dog doubtfully, as if she wasn't quite sure how he'd come to be her responsibility.

"Did you come over for something specific? I could take care of him for you if you want to talk to Mrs. Ryan," Sheri offered.

Eleanor paused, looking at her, an odd expression in her eyes. She shook her head. "No, that's all right. Actually, I came to talk to you, but it can wait. It was nothing important." She snapped her fingers at the dog, who leaped to his feet and ran to the door, clearly eager to be on his way. Eleanor smiled. "He seems to be a bit of an ingrate," she told Sheri, her tone friendly.

"That's all right."

"Well, I guess I'll be going, then. Tell Glynis goodbye for me, won't you?"

"Of course."

Eleanor's eyes flickered over Roger, her smile fading. She strode toward the door, only to gasp when her toe hit an invisible high spot in the rug. She stumbled and would have fallen if Roger hadn't lunged and caught her under the arms, pulling her against his chest.

For an instant they stood pressed together, their eyes locked. An instant only, then Eleanor pulled away, mumbling a thank-you before she rushed from the room. Roger watched her go, not turning back to Sheri until the front door had closed behind Eleanor and her new companion.

"It's a very dangerous thing to meddle in other people's lives," Roger remarked.

"Meddle?" Sheri widened her eyes innocently.

"The rug. She didn't trip without a little help."

Sheri shrugged. "Maybe it's the lingering effects of that drink I had at the party."

"That was a long time ago. I don't think it's still affecting your talents. Don't interfere in things you don't understand."

He seemed more weary than angry, and this gave Sheri the courage to pursue the subject.

"You and Eleanor care for each other, don't you?"

Roger was silent so long she thought he was going to ignore the question. When he spoke, his tone was flat. "Once, a long time ago, we cared a great deal. But that was a very long time ago. She's engaged to Jack now and I've learned to accept that."

"Have you? When you look at her, your eyes haven't accepted it."

Roger's face tightened. "Look, no matter what you think you see in my eyes, it doesn't matter. She and Jack are going to be married. That's the end of the story."

"There are so many things I don't understand."

"Join the club," Roger told her bitterly.

"You and Eleanor love each other, yet she's going to marry Jack. But they don't love each other." She frowned, puzzled.

"What makes you think they don't love each other?" Roger asked in a tone of mixed hope and pain.

"They aren't happy when they're together."

"Who told you love was supposed to make you happy? It's been my experience that love does a lot of things, but making you happy isn't one of them." He reached for his jacket.

"But it's obvious they aren't in love," Sheri protested. She'd caused Roger pain in some way she didn't quite understand.

Roger shrugged into his jacket before looking at her. "Is it obvious because of your own feelings for Jack? Don't let love fool you into seeing what you want to see. It's a painful experience."

Sheri watched him go, too stunned to speak. What he was implying wasn't possible. She cared for Jack. Of course she cared for him. She wanted to see him happy. That was the only reason she was concerned about his engagement. She just wanted him to be happy. But it wasn't because *she* loved him, at least not in the way Roger was suggesting. She wasn't *in* love with Jack.

Was she?

She reached up to smooth her hair, aware that her fingers were trembling. The luxurious room faded away and she was standing on a grassy hill, Jack's arms around her; then she was in a rose garden at midnight, Jack's hands gentle on her skin.

Shivering, she wrapped her arms around her waist, trying desperately to refute Roger's words. In love with Jack? It just wasn't possible. It would be foolish. But, then, when had love ever been wise?

But if she loved Jack, how could she be sure of her motives in trying to force Eleanor and Roger together? It seemed clear that they loved each other. It was in their eyes, in the tension between them. Was Roger right? Was it clear because that's what she wanted to see? Had her motives been selfish all along?

Sheri heard Glynis's footsteps in the hallway. Without a second's thought, the air around her shimmered and she was gone. She sought the sanctuary of the rose garden instinctively, slipping into reality in the shadow of an arbor that arched over one end of the pathway. The afternoon sun spilled over the garden, bringing out a wondrous richness of perfumes.

For once Sheri didn't notice the beauty around her. Her eyes were turned inward, trying to comprehend the impossible. She couldn't be in love with Jack. Yet how could she not love him? The question slipped in, and she closed her eyes against the truth it held.

How could she not love him? She should have asked that question weeks ago. When she thought of the kindness in his eyes, the way he could laugh at himself, the way his lightest touch seemed to go right to her soul, it seemed almost inevitable that she should fall in love with him.

She'd been such a fool. She closed her eyes, shutting out the bright sunshine around her. The price for loving him was high, but she'd have paid it in an instant if she thought there was any chance of him returning that feeling. But he didn't, couldn't. Even if he wasn't in love with Eleanor, he planned to marry her. And even without that barrier, there was still the reality of what she was.

Jack had accepted the disruptions she'd brought to his life, but only because he saw them as temporary. In the end he expected his life to continue along the path he'd set for it. That path didn't include her.

JACK SHRUGGED out of his suit jacket and threw it on the passenger seat as he slid into the Jag. Leaving work these days felt more and more like escaping from a prison. In the office above, he'd left half the company celebrating the successful conclusion of the Carter deal. He should be there. After all, it had been his project, his baby from the start. He should be at the celebration.

Only he didn't feel much like celebrating. Somewhere along the way, the Carter deal had become just another duty to be discharged. He'd lost the enthusiasm, the excitement.

He turned the key in the ignition, frowning at the windshield. There had been a time when he'd enjoyed his work. He was almost sure of that. At least he'd enjoyed the challenge it presented. But that seemed like a very long time ago now.

He flipped on the Jag's lights as he backed out of the parking place. The problem was, he'd been thinking too much lately. And what he kept thinking about was that long-ago dream of raising horses. Stupid. He'd grown out of that years ago. It was a kid's dream. But he kept thinking about it. About how much he'd like to ride again, how much he'd like to teach Sheri to ride.

Sheri and her talk about dreams. That was what had started

this line of thinking. Sheri. Everything in his life seemed to circle back to her in one way or another. No matter how hard he tried to put her out of his mind, she lingered there.

He turned on the radio as he hit the on ramp for the Ventura Freeway. The soothing strains of Mozart washed over him and he scowled, flipping the radio off. Mozart made him think of Eleanor. And Eleanor made him think of his upcoming marriage, which was beginning to loom on his horizon like an iceberg before the *Titanic*. He'd been so clear on his reasons for marrying Eleanor, so sure that it was the right thing to do that they could make each other happy.

"She died and he never quite got over the loneliness of being without her." Sheri's voice echoed in his mind, telling him about the woman his uncle had almost married. Jack scowled at a Toyota in the next lane. There was Sheri again, poking in where she didn't belong. But her words lingered. He tried to imagine how he'd feel if something happened to Eleanor. He'd miss her. Of course he'd miss her. But spend years of his life grieving for her? No, he couldn't honestly say he would.

"But every marriage can't be based on a grand passion," he muttered aloud. There was no answer except the abiding uncertainty in his mind.

By the time he got home, he was feeling restless and just little put upon. After all, he'd been quite content with the arrangement of his life until a few weeks ago. Maybe he was going through a midlife crisis. It was a decade or so early, but that didn't make it impossible.

The house was dark and quiet, and Jack assumed that everyone was in bed. But when he shut the front door, there was glow of light coming from the library. He stepped into the room, already sure of what he'd find. The room was dark except for the dancing glow of the fire on the hearth. Sheri was visible only as a pair of slender legs draped over the arm of heavy leather chair.

He cleared his throat and the legs disappeared to be replaced by a head of tousled hair and wide blue eyes. She smiled when she saw him, though he thought a touch of wariness lingered in her expression.

"No, don't put it out," Jack told her when the fire flickered on the verge of disappearing. "It's nice. Even if it is almost summer."

"You look tired." The lilting softness of her voice soothed his ragged nerves. He sank into a chair near hers, barely noticing when a footstool appeared in just the right place. Putting his feet up, he sighed. "I guess I am a little tired."

"I'll leave you alone." She stood, but Jack leaned forward, catching her arm.

"No." He realized how abrupt the word sounded and softened it with a smile. "If you're not too tired, I'd like the company."

She hesitated. Odd, Jack thought, how he could feel her uncertainty where his hand touched her arm. He wanted her to stay. She'd turned his life upside down, put a permanent crimp in his picture of the world as he'd always thought he knew it, but there was a certain peace in her company. And he wanted that right now, needed it.

"All right." She sank back into the chair, tucking her feet under her legs so that the swirl of her gray skirt covered her legs.

Silence settled over the room, a pleasant, undemanding quiet. Jack let it seep into him. Staring into the fireplace, he was reminded of those few short days at his uncle's house. That was the last time his life had seemed simple and under control.

"Do you ever think of Uncle Jack's?" he asked, his voice low.

"Sometimes. It was so peaceful there."

"I've thought about selling the place, but I can't bring myself to do it."

"It is a special place for me, too."

Jack turned his head to look at her. She was staring into the fire, her expression pensive.

"Are you ever sorry you came here?" He wasn't sure where

the question had come from, but the answer was suddenly im
portant.

She was silent for a moment. When she turned her head to
look at him, there was something in her eyes he couldn't define
a deep sadness.

"No. No, I could not be sorry that I came with you."

Jack had the feeling there was some meaning in her word
that he couldn't quite catch.

"You know, I wish we could be at the cabin right now. I
must be beautiful."

He'd spoken impulsively, out of desire to find a simpler tim
more than anything else. Scarcely had the words left him tha
he felt a tingling that started at his fingertips, then swept ove
his body. There was a moment of warm darkness, a darknes
so intense that it was impossible to imagine light ever piercin
it. A quick wrenching feeling, like stepping off a stair tha
wasn't there, and then he was sitting in a thick leather chai
that was not in his library.

He clutched at the arms of the chair, staring around him a
the living room of his uncle's home. Everything was just as h
remembered it, with the exception of the golden samova
which no longer sat in the corner. Sheri sat in the chair acros
from him, her feet curled under her, just as they'd been a mo
ment before. Only a moment ago she and Jack had been si
hundred miles away.

"Your wish is my command," she said.

"I guess I'm going to have to be careful of what I wis
for." Jack wasn't surprised to hear the shaky note in his voic
He had to make a conscious effort to unlock his fingers fro
their grip on the chair arms. He was aware of a tingling se
sation again, a feeling of being vibrantly alive unlike anythir
he'd ever felt before.

He grinned suddenly, leaning back. Maybe Roger was righ
Maybe he didn't appreciate the advantages of having a geni
He laughed.

"This gives new meaning to the words 'Beam me u

Scotty.'" He laughed once more, feeling totally carefree. His life, his fiancée and all his problems were hundreds of miles away.

"That is from *Star Trek*. I have been watching it in reruns." Sheri was pleased that she recognized the reference.

Jack laughed again. "I wouldn't think they could teach you much. Was that my first wish?"

"I have told you that it does not work that way."

"Are you sure?" He lifted his feet, watching without concern as a footstool shifted into position. "In all the fairy tales I read when I was a kid, you got three wishes."

"Those were stories. This is real life." She stared at him, puzzled, when he threw back his head and laughed deep and long.

"If I'm going to believe in you, I can hardly refuse to believe in fairy tales," he explained.

"I suppose not." Sheri laughed, too, seeing the humor in her words.

"Okay, for my second wish I'd like a cognac. The very best cognac, if you please." Jack waved his hand in a kingly gesture, but it was still a shock to see the snifter at his elbow. He lifted it, finding it warmed to the perfect temperature.

"Thank you." He lifted the snifter, inhaling the heady fragrance. "Do you suppose anyone will worry that we're not where we're supposed to be?"

"Your mother and Tina went to Santa Barbara to visit someone."

"Aunt Lydia, probably. Mother and Tina went together? I thought they were still at odds with each other."

"I believe Tina wanted to talk with your mother. She wants to try to reassure her that continuing her education does not mean she's not thinking about a personal life."

"Well, I wish her luck on that one. God knows, I've talked until I'm blue in the face. About the only thing that would reassure Mother is if Tina turned up married."

"I don't believe she is going quite that far, but she does

have a man she cares very much about. I think she's going t
tell your mother about him."

"Tina has a boyfriend?" Jack frowned into his cognac, nc
entirely sure he liked the idea of his little sister with a man.

"A man who works with dolphins," Sheri told him.

"Great. Now we'll be inviting Flipper to tea. Translation c
'works with dolphins'—he's a beach bum."

"That is one of the reasons Tina has not told you abo
him," Sheri informed him reprovingly. "She said you woul
not approve because he wasn't on the same social level. I tol
her you were not that narrow-minded."

There was a momentary silence.

"Ouch," Jack said. He looked at her, his eyes rueful. "Fc
such a nice little thing, you certainly do pack a wicked punc
But you're right." He lifted one hand, palm out. "I promis
to keep an open mind about Tina's friend. How's that?"

"Tina will appreciate it."

"You've been avoiding me," Jack said abruptly.

"Have I?' Sheri reached up and tugged on a soft curl.

"Yes, you have." He swirled the brandy in the bottom •
the snifter. "For the past two or three days. When I appea
you disappear. You're not mad at me, are you?"

"No, of course not."

Her eyes appeared haunted, Jack thought, the tilt of her smi
a little fragile.

"I guess I just thought that maybe you could use a litt
distance from me."

Jack leaned forward, catching the hand that twisted in h
hair, feeling her fingers quiver in his. Their eyes met and I
forgot what he'd planned to say. Where their fingers touche
electricity sparked. He drew a deep breath and released h
hand. "When I need distance, I'll let you know, okay?"

"Okay." Her smile was brighter, but there was still som
thing in her eyes—vulnerability. He took a sip of cognac a
stared at the fire.

Around them the old house was quiet. Outside, the night I

quieter still. Somewhere far off came the hoot of an owl. Los Angeles seemed a million miles away. Part of another world.

"Did I ever tell you that I wanted to raise horses?" The question came from out of nowhere. He hadn't planned to say anything at all, and certainly not that. But now that it was out he couldn't call it back.

"It sounds wonderful. I think you'd be very good at that."

"Oh, it was just silly kid stuff." Jack swirled the cognac, watching the patterns of light in the amber liquid. "Roger and I were going to move to Wyoming. Or was it Montana? And we were going to have the greatest horse ranch the West had ever seen. Stupid, really."

"Why is it stupid?" Sheri questioned.

Jack shrugged. "Oh, I don't know. We didn't really know that much about raising horses. You know, all kids go through a cowboy stage. I guess we were just a little older than most when the urge hit."

"What happened?"

"Life. I guess life happened. God, that sounds pompous and philosophical, doesn't it?" He pushed the footstool out of the way, setting his feet on the floor and leaning forward to stare into the fire. "Roger went to 'Nam. By the time he came back, I was halfway through college. We talked about it. Roger even bought a place up above Santa Barbara. Not the million acres we'd dreamed of, but a start. I was going to join him after I got out of school—it meant so much to my father that I have my degree."

He stopped, but Sheri didn't prompt him. After a long moment he went on, feeling the need to finish now that he'd started. "Then my father died. The bank was in trouble and I had a majority interest. There wasn't any one else, so I tackled it. I worked blind at first—I didn't know what the hell I was doing. But I made a few lucky choices. The job was only going to be temporary, but there never seemed to be a good time to step out. After a while I stopped thinking about leaving."

He shrugged again, suddenly uneasy. He had the feeling he'd said a great deal more than he'd intended.

"It's not too late, you know." Sheri's quiet words broke the stillness. "You could still have your dream."

"You mean the horses? I told you, that was just kid stuff." He finished off the last of the cognac without tasting it.

"Was it?"

"I don't know." He stared into the empty snifter broodingly. "If you'd asked me that three months ago, I could have said yes. But something's happened since I met you." His mouth twisted. "I guess I'd forgotten all about dreams and magic before I met you."

"Are you sorry?"

The question brought Jack's gaze to her. Her face was shadowed, her expression impossible to read.

"No. No, I'm not."

He reached out, catching her hand in his, drawing her toward him. She slipped from her chair with the grace of a drifting leaf and knelt in front of him. Jack cupped her cheek with his hand and let himself be lost in her eyes.

"I want only your happiness."

How was it possible for her to be utterly perfect? The firelight cast shadows in her hair, turning it into a cloud of red gold. Her eyes were soft pools of blue, danger and sanctuary in one glance. And her mouth— How could he possibly describe her mouth? His thumb brushed across the sweet bow feeling her lips soften beneath his touch.

"You've turned my life upside down. You've made me believe in the impossible. And you've almost made me believe in dreams again. Almost."

"Jack—"

He pressed his fingertips to her mouth, stopping her words. "Don't say anything. For now let's pretend that this is a dream. There's no one in the world but the two of us. This is all there is, only the here and now. A dream, Sheri. A sweet, sweet dream."

For a moment they stared at each other. He couldn't define what he saw in her eyes, he couldn't guess what she saw in his. But he knew that nothing had ever felt quite so right as this moment. He cupped her neck, tilting her head back, and saw her eyes widen, and knew she was half frightened, half eager.

"Jack, no." Her breathless protest didn't match the need in her eyes.

"Sheri, yes." The words ghosted against her lips an instant before his mouth touched hers. She opened to him like a flower drinking in rain. Her mouth was soft and inviting. His tongue slid between her lips, the taste of cognac mingling with a sweetness that could belong only to Sheri.

Jack felt all rational thought slip away and he let it go gladly. The past, the future—neither mattered.

He stood up, drawing her to her feet, his arms catching her close so that nothing could have slipped between them, not even a shadow. All that mattered was the here and now, the feel of her in his arms, the taste of her on his tongue and the desperate need that burned deep inside him. A need only she could satisfy.

He dragged his mouth from hers, but only to explore the length of her delicate throat. He heard her sigh, a soft sound of pleasure, another brand on the fire. He'd wanted her forever, needed her always. The pulse that beat at the base of her throat fluttered beneath his touch. Jack's mouth claimed it for his own.

She arched over his arm, trusting him with her helplessness, offering him whatever he chose to take. But in the taking there was giving.

His hand slid downward, cupping the gentle weight of her breast in his palm. His mouth closed over hers again, swallowing the quiet moan.

He lifted her in his arms, her weight as insignificant as a fairy's wing. Her lashes fluttered upward, her eyes meeting his in the golden firelight. Jack waited. She seemed to be searching

for something in his eyes. Whatever it was, she must have
found it, for she relaxed against him, her head coming to rest
on his shoulder; she gave herself into his keeping with a trust
so complete it made him ache.

The house was still as he carried Sheri up the stairs, the only
sound his footfall on the steps. He shouldered open the bedroom door, unsurprised when the lamp beside the bed came
on.

Stopping beside the bed, he let Sheri slide down his body
until her feet touched the floor. Her hands rested on his chest,
one palm over the rapid beat of his heart.

Her blouse opened at his touch, seeming to melt away. The
skirt dropped to the floor with a whisper of sound and she stood
before him, wrapped in nothing more than the silken fall of her
hair. Jack stared at her, her beauty leaving him without words.
She was all pale gold. He reached out, needing the sense of
touch to prove her reality.

She caught his hands, a half smile tilting her mouth as she
placed them at his side, a silent command. Jack obeyed with
an effort that became greater with each passing moment. His
shirt fell open beneath her touch and Jack's breath caught at
the feel of her fingers against his chest.

Sheri looked up at him, her eyes reflecting wonder as she
explored the muscles she'd bared. There was such innocent
sensuality in the look that Jack groaned. He buried his hand
in the rich length of her hair, letting it spill over his forearms.
Her mouth yielded to the hungry pressure of his, her body
pliant in his arms.

Jack released her only long enough to tug the rest of his
clothes off, impatient with anything that kept him from her. He
lifted her onto the bed, following her down, fitting the length
of his body to hers.

The bed cradled them, a gentle cocoon against the world
outside. There was no tomorrow, no yesterday. Nothing that
mattered beyond this place, this moment.

Jack's hands shook as he explored her slender body. He'

never wanted—needed—like this. There was a soul-deep need that only Sheri could fulfill. Her soft touch, her murmurs of pleasure fed that need, yet stoked it until it threatened to consume him.

He lifted himself above her, bracing his weight on his hands. Her legs came up to cradle him, but he hesitated a moment. Her hair was spread across the pillows, framing her delicate features, her deep, shining blue eyes. In that moment, he knew that he'd never been complete. Without her, he'd never know completion.

Her body opened to his, accepting him as if made for him only. The movements were older than time itself, but they'd never felt so new. And the fulfillment, when it came, was like nothing he'd ever known before. It wasn't only a fulfillment of body, it went deep into his soul, cleansing him, making him whole.

Chapter Twelve

Jack came awake slowly, aware that he'd slept deeply, dreamlessly. He shifted against the pillows, reluctant to open his eyes. He wanted to linger in the limbo between sleep and waking. As he breathed deeply his nostrils were teased by a delicate scent, a soft floral with overtones of sandalwood. He rolled over, his arm reaching out, seeking, but the bed was empty.

He opened his eyes and a sense of loss drifted over him. Sheri was gone. He didn't need to look for her. After last night he could sense her absence as easily as her presence. He was back in his own bedroom at home, the old house in the mountains once more hundreds of miles away. Her clothes were gone; his had been neatly folded and set on a chair. All that remained was the lingering scent of her on his skin, and even that was fading in the morning light.

Jack pulled himself up, propped his elbows on his bent knees and buried his head in his hands. What had happened last night? It had all seemed so clear-cut, so obvious. The feel of her in his arms, in his bed, had seemed inevitable, preordained.

He hadn't thought of anything but the need that had burned in his gut. He hadn't thought of duty or commitment or responsibility. Most of all, he hadn't thought of Eleanor.

"Dammit!" He jerked back the covers and stood up. Striding into the bathroom, he twisted the shower on with vicious orce, then stepped under the scalding water, as if the heat ould burn away the guilt he felt.

Eleanor. How could he have forgotten his engagement? He'd ever pretended to be madly in love with her, but at least she ad the right to expect fidelity. And he hadn't even managed hat.

And Sheri. He leaned against the cool tile, letting the hot ater pound on his back. What was Sheri thinking right now?)id she have regrets? She'd been so soft in his arms, yielding ut not passive. There'd been passion in her touch, a need as reat as his own.

He groaned as his body reacted to the memories. God, he as worse than a randy teenager. He wrenched the controls, asping when ice-cold water poured over his overheated skin. t this rate he was going to give himself a heart attack. At ast then he wouldn't have to worry about dealing with the onsequences of his actions.

Jack toweled dry and dressed for work without paying any ttention to what he was doing. His instincts told him he should nd Sheri, talk to her. But what would he say? He didn't know ow he felt, didn't know what she would want to hear. And ere was Eleanor to consider. Although, having already slept ith another woman, he supposed that simply talking to her as no great crime.

Still, shouldn't he talk to Eleanor first? And what was he oing to say to her? He groaned, his fingers fumbling with a avy silk tie. He was supposed to see Eleanor tonight...some inner party they were attending as a couple. How was he oing to face her? And what was Sheri going to think?

A headache nagged at his temples. What had happened to is neatly ordered life? Where had it gotten off track? Nothing as turning out as he'd planned. Nothing was going as he'd xpected.

He couldn't talk to Sheri until he had a chance to think ings through. Besides, she must feel the same, or she ouldn't have stolen out of his bed. Feeling like the lowest

worm on earth, Jack grabbed his briefcase and all but fled th
house.

SHERI STOOD BACK from the window, watching the Jag bac
out of the drive. Even from this distance she could sense Jack'
confusion. Or was it her own? The car sped out of sight an
she turned away from the window, her fingers twisting in he
hair, her expression troubled.

When she'd slipped from the bed this morning, she'd tol
herself it was for Jack's sake, to give him time. But she ha
to be honest with herself and admit that she was the one who'
needed time. Time to come to terms with the changes in he
self, time to wonder how Jack was going to feel about la
night.

She wandered outside, seeking the quiet peace of the ros
garden. She lifted a hand to Melvin, who was carefully nippin
faded blossoms, but she didn't seek out his company.

Had last night been wrong? Denial rose inside. Surely some
thing that felt so good, so right, couldn't be wrong. Her ex
pression softened, her eyes warm with memories. She felt a
if she'd been half-alive until now. All that had come befor
faded into insignificance.

And yet she'd lost something. She reached out to touch
rosebud, exerting all her willpower. The petals unfolde
slowly, reluctantly. Sheri's hand dropped to her side, her fi
gers trembling. She'd known the price she'd have to pay fc
loving. She was no longer part of either world. She'd sacrifice
most, if not all her powers for one night in Jack's arms.

And she'd do it again, she thought fiercely. For those fe
hours, she'd been complete in a way she'd never known befor
If that was all she ever had, it was surely worth any price. An
to have Jack's love— She hardly dared even dream of that.

How did he feel about her?

JACK COULDN'T HAVE answered that question to save his sou
The only thing he knew for sure was that he didn't know ho

he felt. He wasn't sure if that was a significant advance over knowing nothing at all, but at least it was something.

Work sat unattended on his desk while he stared out the window, his thoughts so tangled he couldn't even begin to sort them out.

On the one hand, there was Eleanor. Sophisticated, elegant, a product of his world, a world he understood. She'd make a wonderful hostess, a good companion, a helpmate in the true sense of the word. And he could give her the security and stability she wanted. She'd be an asset to his career, a good mother to their children and she wouldn't leave him in a perpetual state of confusion.

And then there was Sheri. His face softened. How could he possibly describe Sheri? Sweet, giving, full of light. She'd never understand his career, never give a socially important party. She'd bring home stray people and stray animals and expect him to help them. She'd turn his life upside down without even knowing it. He didn't even know if they could have children.

Good God! What was he thinking of? He turned away from the window he was looking out of and glared at a potted palm. He was acting as though it were a matter of choosing between the two of them. As though, if he didn't marry Eleanor, he and Sheri might—

"It's a ridiculous idea," he muttered to the palm. "She isn't even human." But she'd felt very human in his arms last night. "Besides, it's arrogant to think like that. I don't even know if she'd have me. And after last night, I can almost guarantee that Eleanor won't. And would it be fair to her even if she did?" His scowl deepened.

"I don't love her. Not that I love Sheri," he added hastily. "I care for her, but I can't be in love with her. I *won't* be in love with her." The words seemed to echo hollowly in the office and Jack was grateful when there was a quick knock on the door. A distraction was just what he needed right now.

"Come in."

But Tina was already in, poking her head around the door. "Your secretary said you might be busy, but I knew you wouldn't be too busy to see me."

"You knew that, did you?" Jack grinned affectionately. "What if I said I *was* too busy?"

"You'd be lying," Tina told him cheerfully, stepping into the office and shutting the door behind her. She was wearing jeans and a green top so bright Jack put a hand over his eyes.

"Is that thing legal? It's enough to cause traffic accidents."

"Of course it's legal. Besides, it reflects my mood."

Jack's brows rose. He perched on the edge of his desk, watching as his sister sat down in a chair, then bounced to her feet again. "Well, this is certainly a change. You've been drooping around the house for days now."

She turned to look at him, her face wreathed in smiles. "I have the best news."

"I thought you and Mother were going to be in Santa Barbara another day."

"We came home early," she told him, impatient with details.

"How was the trip?" he asked, just for the pleasure of watching her turn, full of impatience.

"Jack! Do you want to hear my news or not?"

"We-l-l." He dragged the word out, backing up when she took a threatening step toward him. He laughed. "Okay, what's the news?"

"Mother has agreed to let me go for my master's. She's going to give me the money from my trust fund." The words tumbled over themselves, so tangled they were almost incoherent.

"She did? You mean she ignored my advice?"

"Jack!" She threatened him with her purse and Jack ducked laughing.

"Okay, okay. I'm really happy for you, brat." He held out his arms and she threw herself into them, hugging him exuberantly.

"Can you believe it? I was just about to give up hope."

"So what changed her mind?" Jack's smile lingered as he watched her pace the office, too excited to sit still for even an instant.

"Well, I suppose it was Sheri, in a way."

"Sheri?" Jack's smile faded, his eyes growing watchful. "Sheri talked with Mother?"

"No. But she and I talked, and she told me I should tell Mother about Mark."

"Mark? The guy with the dolphins?"

"How did you know? Oh, Sheri must have told you. Oh, Jack, he really is wonderful, and I think you'll like him. Sheri was right. I was an idiot not to tell you and Mother about him months ago. She said I was underestimating you."

Jack remembered his initial reaction when Sheri had told him about the man in Tina's life. Luckily Tina was too absorbed in her story to notice the guilty flush that rose in his face.

"Yes, well, I suppose it's understandable," he muttered uncomfortably.

"Sheri said that all Mother cared about was seeing me happy. So I told her all about Mark. She was a little hesitant at first, but when I told her how wonderful he was, she said she didn't care if he had fins himself as long as he made me happy. How could I have been so wrong? Really, Jack, I don't think she'd have cared if I'd told her he was a practicing warlock and carried a magic wand."

Jack coughed uneasily.

"So, has she met this marvelous man?"

"No, but he's coming to dinner next week. You'll be there, won't you? And I want Sheri to be there, too. After all, if she hadn't been so sure that Mother would accept Mark, I might not have told her. And we'd still be fighting."

Jack listened to her rattle on. From her description, Mark seemed to be a cross between Jacques Cousteau and Robert

Redford. He was relieved that everything had turned out so well, but he couldn't help a mild feeling of pique.

He'd been talking himself blue in the face for almost six months, trying to convince his mother to release Tina's trust fund. He'd finally come to the conclusion he was going to have to give her the money himself, which would have caused considerable hostility on his mother's part.

In a matter of weeks, Sheri had managed to turn the whole situation around so that everyone was delighted. It would have been some consolation if she'd had to use magic to accomplish it, but she hadn't. Still, the important thing was that the problem had been resolved. He wasn't going to quibble over the means.

His good humor was stretched a little thin when his mother came to visit him midafternoon. It wasn't enough that he hadn't managed to get any work done. It wasn't enough that he felt like a total cad every time he thought of his fiancée. It wasn't enough that thinking of Sheri left him completely confused.

His own mother applied the coup de grace when she visited later in the day. He was delighted, of course, that she'd decided to open her own needlework shop, pleased that she felt it was time she put her skills to work. He'd been telling her that for years. And it certainly didn't bother him at all that she attributed her change of heart to Sheri's suggestion that it was almost a duty not to hide talent like hers away.

No, he didn't mind a bit. He smiled and told his mother he was sure the bank could arrange a business loan. He'd see to it personally that she got their very best business advisor to help her set up shop. The smile didn't last past seeing her out the door, however.

"Hell and damnation!" He shoved his hands into his pockets and stalked to the window, glaring out at the cloudless blue sky.

In the space of a few short weeks he'd lost control of his life. It was all sliding out from under him. Everything he'd worked for, planned for. So what if he'd begun to have doubts that he even wanted what he'd planned. It should have been his choice that it had all changed. Where had he lost control? Was it the first time he'd kissed Sheri? When he'd found out she was a genie? The moment he'd met her? Or did it go even farther back?

He'd leaped at the opportunity to check out his uncle's house, desperate for an excuse to leave L.A. Had things been slipping away from him even then? So he'd started to sense that some changes were necessary. But he hadn't wanted to make them all at once, with no control over their direction.

By the time he got home, the headache that had nagged at him all day was pounding in his temples. A last-minute emergency had kept him at the office late. Eleanor was due to arrive in half an hour. He didn't know what he was going to say to her—didn't even know what he *wanted* to say. And he needed to talk to Sheri, though he had no idea what he was going to say to her, either.

He pushed open the front door, rubbing the back of his neck. When had life gotten so complicated? He didn't have to look far for an answer. Sheri was in the living room, a slightly mangled needlepoint canvas in her lap. Jack doubted if she'd done much stitching, any more than he'd done much work.

She looked up and their eyes met for an instant before they both looked away. Seeing her brought memories flooding back. The way she'd melted against him, the sweet taste of her mouth, the delicate scent that lingered in his mind. His first instinct was to go to her. Everything had felt right with her in his arms. But Jack hadn't built his life on his instincts. He'd built it by thinking things out clearly, logically, making decisions based on facts. How did you apply logic to someone who couldn't even exist in a logical equation?

He thrust his fingers through his hair, feeling an irrational surge of annoyance. Everything had been so much easier before she'd popped into his life on a cloud of smoke. He cleared his throat.

"Sheri."

"Jack."

She watched him, her eyes reflecting the same uncertainty he felt. Just where did they go from here? Jack was damned if he knew.

He went to the bar and poured himself a stiff scotch before turning to face her again. Did she have to look so damn beautiful?

"How are you?" *Brilliant, Jack. Absolutely brilliant. Why don't you ask her if she'd like to do lunch next week?*

"I'm fine," she said softly. "How are you?"

"Fine. Just fine." *Sure, if you don't count budding insanity as a problem.*

Silence stretched again. Jack was vividly aware of Eleanor's impending arrival. He needed to say something about that. *Gee, I realize that we spent last night making passionate love to each other and that we need to talk. But my fiancée is going to be here any minute, so let me check my calendar to see when I can fit you in.*

Sheri reached up and twined her fingers in her hair. Jack remembered the feel of that hair in his hands, draped over his chest. He swallowed a groan and a large gulp of scotch. Maybe if he kept talking he wouldn't keep remembering.

"Tina came to see me today." His voice was a little too loud, he knew, the tone overly hearty.

"Did she?"

If Sheri was puzzled by the choice of topic, he couldn't tell it.

"That's nice."

"Wasn't it. Did you know that my mother has decided to release Tina's trust fund so she can stay in college?"

"No." She smiled, the first natural expression he'd seen. "That's wonderful. Tina must be very happy."

"Ecstatic," Jack agreed, staring into his drink. "Absolutely ecstatic." He looked up suddenly, pinning her with a cool gray stare. "She seems to feel she has you to thank."

"Me?" She shook her head. "I don't know why."

"She says you're the one who convinced her to talk to Mother."

"I suggested she do so, but I didn't do anything more than that."

"Well, it was apparently enough." Jack heard the edge in his voice and took a deep breath. He felt as if he were boiling inside. All the guilt and frustration was churning. "And this afternoon Mother came to see me."

"Did she?" Sheri tilted her head, sensing his volatile mood but uncertain of its origin.

"It seems she's decided to open up a shop specializing in needlepoint."

"That's good, isn't it?" she said hesitantly.

"It's great. I've been trying to talk her into something like that for years. But it seems that you just suggested she shouldn't waste her talents, and presto change-o, she decides it's the thing to do."

"Are you angry with me, Jack? Should I not have spoken to Tina or your mother?"

"Hell, no, talk away." He swallowed the last of his drink and set the glass down with a thump. "You've done a great job of fixing up their lives. I'm delighted."

"I didn't really do anything. I just helped them to see what they wanted. They had to make the decisions themselves."

"Don't apologize. I think it's great." He bit the words off, struggling against the irrational anger he felt. He wanted to quarrel. He needed to quarrel with her. She was so bloody perfect. Didn't she ever get angry?

"Since you're so good at this sort of thing, why haven't you helped me to see what I really want?"

"You are a man who needs to find his own way."

The quiet answer did nothing to soothe his mood. "Tell me what it is I want," he demanded. He leaned back against the bar, gripping its edge with his hands. "Tell me what's wrong with my life. What do I need to be happy?"

"Those are things only you can know."

"No, no. You did a great job with my family. Don't tell me you don't have some theories on where I'm going wrong." He waved one hand. "Tell me what you think."

"Jack, I—"

"Don't beat around the bush about it. What if I make it a wish? Don't you owe me another wish? You know we've never really discussed the details of this whole arrangement. What do I need to change in my life? Tell me."

Sheri's eyes dropped from his. "You know as well as I do."

"Tell me."

"You've chosen an easy path," she said softly. "You're doing what's expected of you, not what you want to do."

"And that's an easy path?" he asked incredulously.

"You're not taking any chances with your life." She looked up, catching him with that clear blue gaze. "You're doing what's safe. And yes, for you, that is easier."

Jack stared at her, feeling her words sink into him with the impact of blows. He wanted to deny what she was saying, but he couldn't. There was too much truth in it. In a few short sentences, she'd made him face things he'd been avoiding for years.

The rage that had been eating at him for months was suddenly white hot and uncontrollable.

"Keep your damned magic nose out of my business," he said hoarsely. "And keep it out of my family's business." He saw her eyes widen at his tone, but he was too angry to soften it.

"Jack, I did not mean—"

"I don't care what you meant. You pop into my life and you turn everything upside down. And then you start poking your nose into things that don't concern you. Well, you may be able to tidy up other people's lives, but leave mine alone. I've been managing just fine without you."

He started for the door, but stopped halfway there. "Eleanor is going to be here in a few minutes. We're going out to dinner." He said it quite deliberately, wanting to get a reaction from her. Anger, hatred, reproach, something that would justify his anger, something that would satisfy his need to quarrel with her.

Hurt flared in her eyes the instant before she lowered them. Jack's rage flared higher. "Well, aren't you going to say something?"

"What would you like me to say?"

The simple question had no answer.

"Aren't you going to tell me I'm a cad, say that I owe you better than this after last night?"

She looked up at him, her eyes clear and shining, hiding nothing. "You don't owe me anything because of last night. I don't expect anything from you."

"Dammit!"

She jumped as the curse exploded out of him.

He stalked over to her, his eyes fierce as he stopped in front of her. "Why the hell *don't* you expect something from me? Do you always have to be so bloody self-sacrificing?"

She stared at him, her eyes wide. He turned away from that look, his rage flaring higher still. Everything had been going just fine without her.

The clock in the hall struck eight, interrupting him. "Look, Eleanor is going to be here any minute. We need to talk, but not tonight."

Sheri nodded without looking up. Jack rubbed the back of his neck. He wanted to say something more, wanted to tell her he was sorry. But he couldn't get the words out. With a muttered curse, he left the room.

Sheri watched him go. There was an ache in her chest that made breathing difficult. She lowered her eyes to the canvas in her lap, only then noticing that it was twisted in her hands. Her fingers shook as she smoothed it out.

She'd never seen Jack so angry. But there'd been pain beneath the anger and that was what lingered in her mind. Was she the cause of his pain? That was the last thing she'd wanted. Was he angry because of last night? Did he feel they'd done something wrong? The thought deepened the ache in her chest. How could something that had been so right, so inevitable, possibly be wrong?

But Jack didn't necessarily share her feelings. Maybe it hadn't been as wonderful for him. Could humans share that kind of physical closeness without feeling the kind of soul-deep connection she'd felt last night? Was that what it had been to Jack? He couldn't have been so tender if she hadn't meant something to him. Yet it didn't have to be more than friendship.

Sheri pressed a hand to her chest, trying to soothe the pain lodged there. She'd let herself hope for so much, too much. Maybe she'd been dreaming of something Jack couldn't give her. Not because of his engagement, but because of what she was. Sometimes she almost forgot how far apart their worlds really were. Maybe Jack couldn't forget.

The doorbell rang, interrupting the endless circle of her thoughts. She got up, setting aside the hopelessly twisted canvas. It was a good thing Glynis was going to have a shop to occupy herself, because Sheri's lack of progress with a needle and yarn was enough to send the woman into the depths of despair.

"Hello, Eleanor." She stepped back to let the other woman enter, then shut the door and followed Eleanor into the living room, wondering if she should feel self-conscious. If she'd thought for even a moment that Eleanor loved Jack, then perhaps she'd feel guilty over last night.

Eleanor stopped near the fireplace, shrugging off the light cape that covered her slim gray dress. "Is Jack here?"

"He's upstairs changing. I'm sure he won't be long. If you'd like, I could make you a drink."

"No, thank you." Eleanor tugged off her gloves, her expression uneasy.

"How is the dog?" Sheri asked.

"He's fine." Eleanor's mouth softened in a faint smile. "He's getting a bit spoiled, I'm afraid. I rather think I may keep him."

There was a hint of defiance in the announcement but Sheri smiled, pleased. "That's wonderful. He really did seem to be a very nice dog."

"Yes, he is." The smile faded.

Sheri was at a loss. Since Eleanor remained standing, Sheri moved over to the bar, leaning against it as she'd so often seen Jack do. "I'm sure Jack won't be much longer," she offered, thinking that perhaps the other woman was getting annoyed with the delay.

"Actually, I'm rather glad we have a few moments alone."

"You are?" Sheri asked, surprised.

"Yes." Eleanor drew a deep breath, her fingers tightening on the soft kid gloves she held. "There's something I've been wanting to say to you."

"All right." Sheri gave her an encouraging smile.

Eleanor hesitated, wondering at her own motives. But she'd started now, and it really did need to be said. "I wouldn't mention this if it weren't for my concern for Jack. A concern I'm sure you share."

"Is there something wrong with Jack?"

"No. At least, nothing serious. That is, nothing that can't be dealt with." *Get to the point,* she told herself, annoyed with the way she was beating around the bush.

She drew in a deep breath and reminded herself that she wasn't doing this out of selfish motives. "You see, people are beginning to talk."

"About what?"

Sheri's bewilderment was obvious and Eleanor felt a stab of irritation at being forced to explain what should be obvious. Why wasn't anything as it should be with this woman?

"They're talking about you and Jack. The fact that the two of you are living in the same house has raised a few eyebrows. Naturally, *I* don't think there's anything going on, but there are those who do." She paused, but Sheri didn't say anything, only continued to watch her with those big blue eyes.

Eleanor jerked her gloves through her fingers. "I wouldn't

say anything it if weren't for the fact that, as a banker, Jack really can't afford to be gossiped about. His reputation is very important.''

''You mean people think that Jack and I are—'' she hesitated, searching for the words ''—more than friends, and because you and he are engaged, they think Jack is a bad person?''

''Well, not a bad person exactly,'' Eleanor said. Dammit, why couldn't the woman just understand these things the way everyone else did? Why did she have to look so worried and confused? ''I mean, it's not just the engagement, though that's part of it. Even if we weren't engaged, it wouldn't be a good idea for people to think that you and Jack were— Well, that you were having an affair. I'm sure you understand what I mean,'' she finished hastily, sorry she'd even brought the subject up.

''No, I don't. Please tell me what you mean. I want to understand.''

''Well, I—'' Eleanor felt as if she'd somehow gotten in over her head. She'd thought that a polite warning would be enough to protect her engagement. She'd make a few comments, Sheri would get the point and it would all be over, nice and civilized. She wished Jack would come down and put an end to this. But there was no sign of him, and Sheri was looking at her, waiting for her to continue.

''Well, I just mean that you're hardly the type of woman who gets involved with a banker. I don't mean to say there's anything wrong with that,'' she added quickly. ''I suppose that a banker's wife needs to be rather dull and conventional. Like I am.''

Sheri didn't smile at the mild humor and Eleanor cleared her throat, continuing uneasily. ''You're more the bohemian type. Bankers can't really afford to be bohemian.''

Sheri stared at her. ''You mean, my being here could cause Jack harm?''

''No, no. Not harm precisely.'' How had the conversation

gotten so completely out of control? ''I just think that some people—stuffy people—might be concerned about your relationship with Jack.'' She stopped, drawing a shallow breath. ''Don't you think it's awfully hot in here?''

Sheri didn't seem to hear her. She smoothed her hands over the skirt she was wearing, her expression sober. ''Thank you for telling me this, Eleanor. Please excuse me.'' She didn't wait to hear Eleanor's mumbled reply, but walked quickly across the room.

Eleanor watched her go, her hands knotted around her gloves. What had she done? She felt as if she'd just struck something totally defenseless. She started forward. ''Sheri, wait.''

But the only response was the quiet click of the front door. She sank into a chair, tossing the abused gloves on an end table. She'd only been doing what she had to to protect her engagement, to protect Jack. She hadn't said anything that wasn't true. It wasn't as if she'd set out to hurt the woman.

Why didn't the justification make her feel any better?

SHERI WALKED BLINDLY. Her direction didn't matter. She just had to keep moving. Everything had gone wrong. She should never have come here. Nothing but trouble had resulted from her presence. She'd made Jack unhappy, when all she'd wanted was for him to be happy. The idea that her presence could cause him trouble cut deep.

Eleanor's motives were a little tangled. Sheri was not such a fool that she didn't see that. But there had been a ring of truth to the woman's words. People might think less of Jack because of his association with her. She bit her lip to hold back a sob.

Her pace increased until she was almost running. Trying to outrun her own thoughts. But they were relentless. It was her fault. She'd been so sure that his uncle was right, that she could help Jack. How could she have been so arrogant? Jack didn't need her. He'd never needed her. He'd be better off without her, better if she'd never entered his life.

Jack had been so angry with her. He'd known that she was causing him trouble and he hadn't told her. That was why he'd been so angry. She was such a fool, a stupid little fool. And she'd lost everything. She belonged nowhere. She should have known she couldn't step out of her world into his. She dashed a trembling hand across her eyes, feeling the dampness of tears.

As if tears could return any of what she'd lost. She stepped blindly off the curb. She had nothing. No future. No life.

Nothing.

Chapter Thirteen

Jack turned away from the mirror, his hand going to his throat. He suddenly felt as if he were choking. He tugged at his tie, his chest aching. Something was wrong. Something was horribly wrong. He drew a shuddering breath, trying to steady his pulse. This was absurd. Nothing was wrong except that he'd made a total ass of himself.

He'd flown off the handle with Sheri. He tugged at his tie again. *Sheri. There's something wrong with Sheri.* He was halfway to the door before he caught himself, slowing his footsteps to a normal pace. This was ridiculous. There was nothing wrong with Sheri except that he'd hurt her. He'd go downstairs and apologize calmly, like an adult.

But he found himself hurrying downstairs, his heart beating too fast. He couldn't explain the urgency he felt. He had to talk to Sheri. Explain to her how wrong he'd been to take his frustrations out on her. He hadn't meant to hurt her. That was the last thing in the world he wanted. She meant too much to him. He had to assure her that it was all going to work out. He'd make it work out.

He took the last two stairs in one long stride, his heart pounding with anxiety. He had to talk to her before it was too late. Too late? He stopped in the hall, drawing in a deep breath. Why would it be too late? He pushed his fingers through his hair, trying to pinpoint the source of his urgency. He had to explain, to tell her— Tell her what?

He shook his head, once more trying to slow his pulse. He had to talk to Sheri, but there was no reason it had to be this instant. The feeling lingered, driving him into the living room.

"Sheri—" He stopped as Eleanor rose from a chair, her faultlessly made-up face arranged in a faultless smile of greeting. "Eleanor." The name came out on a flat note and he tried again, going forward to kiss her cheek. "Eleanor." There wasn't much more enthusiasm the second time and his eyes were already searching the room. "Where's Sheri?"

Pique flashed in Eleanor's eyes, and her mouth tightened.

"She went out."

"Out?" Jack looked at the dark windows, fear clutching at his throat. "Out where?"

"She didn't say. We really should be on our way, Jack. We're running a trifle late."

"Didn't she say anything? It's dark out."

"I'm sure she realized it was dark out. I don't know what you're worried about. She's a big girl."

Eleanor reached for her cape, but Jack was still staring at the darkness. "It's not like her to just wander off without saying something," he muttered. He turned suddenly, and his eyes caught Eleanor's. She was unable to prevent the flush that rose in her cheeks, and Jack's eyes darkened to storm gray.

"What did you say to her?"

"I don't know what you mean." She looked away.

"You said something to her. I want to know what it was."

"Really, Jack, you're making a ridiculous fuss over this. Jack!" she said on a startled note as he stepped forward and grabbed her arm with ungentle fingers, his eyes burning into hers.

"What did you say to her?" he demanded.

"I—I didn't say anything," she stammered, half-frightened by the look in his eyes.

"Tell me." He shook her arm slightly. The cool voice of

reason suggested he was overreacting. It was swallowed in the choking feeling of disaster that threatened to overwhelm him.

"I only said what needed to be said," she defended herself.

"Tell me, dammit."

"I told her that people were beginning to talk. Well, they are. And I told her that it wasn't going to be good for your reputation if she stayed here, that a banker had to be very circumspect."

Jack released her arm, turning away with a gesture of disgust. Eleanor rubbed her arm, staring at his back.

"How could you hurt her like that?" His voice was low, rough with anger. "She's never hurt anyone in her life."

"I didn't mean to hurt her," Eleanor told him, unaware of the pleading note that had entered her voice. "I didn't say anything that wasn't true, Jack. People *are* beginning to comment on your relationship."

He spun, pinning her with a fierce look. "I don't give a damn what people are saying. That's something you probably can't understand. All I care about is Sheri." He stopped, struck by his own words. "All I care about is Sheri," he repeated, letting the truth sink in.

"Don't you think that's a rather awkward thing to be telling me," she asked stiffly. "I *am* your fiancée."

"You don't love me." He looked at her as if seeing her clearly for the first time. "You never have."

"That's not true."

"And I've never loved you," he continued, overriding her feeble words. "We never pretended otherwise. We were safe for each other and convenient. I thought it was enough, but it's not."

"Jack—"

"No. It's the truth and you know it."

She stared at him, her face paper white. "What are you going to do?"

"I'm going to find Sheri. I have to talk to her." The wonder of finally realizing his true feelings was swept aside by a growing fear. He couldn't define the source, but he didn't doubt its validity. Something was wrong. Terribly wrong. "I've got to find her."

He was halfway to the door before he realized the futility of his action. She could be anywhere. Remembering their impromptu journey the night before, she could literally be anywhere in the world by now. He stopped and turned back into the living room. Eleanor stood near the fireplace, but Jack was oblivious of her.

Something had happened to Sheri. He knew it beyond a shadow of a doubt. She needed him and he didn't have the slightest idea of how to find her.

He tugged aside the curtains, staring out the window as if the answer might lie in the darkness outside.

"I'm sure she's all right."

"Shut up, Eleanor." The words were without heat. His anger hadn't really been for her, anyway. It had been for himself. For his own blind stupidity. Sheri hadn't run away because of anything Eleanor had said. She'd left because she thought he didn't want her. And for that, he had no one but himself to blame.

He turned away from the window with an abrupt movement that made Eleanor jump. "I'm going to look for her."

"I'll go with you."

"No."

The flat refusal didn't have an effect. She followed him out the door, swinging the cape over her shoulders.

"I'm going with you."

Jack whirled so quickly she almost walked into him. "*If* I find Sheri and *if* she's all right, I don't want you with me."

Eleanor swallowed hard at the blunt words, but she set her chin, meeting him eye to eye. "*When* you find her and nothing is wrong, I want to know it. After all, you seem to think it's my fault she left. I have a right to know that she's all right."

Jack spun away from her with a growl of impatience. He didn't have time to argue. Let Eleanor do as she liked. All he cared about now was finding Sheri, telling her what a fool he'd been.

As it happened, finding her was not hard. Turning right at the end of the block, Jack felt as if his heart had stopped. The eye-searing flash of red lights shattered the darkness. This was what he'd feared, what he'd expected.

Beside him, Eleanor was silent as he pulled the car to a halt at the curb and flung open the door. A small crowd had gathered at one corner, staring at the spot of activity in the normally quiet neighborhood. Jack hurried past, barely aware of their existence.

A policewoman moved to block his advance, but she wasn't quick enough. Jack stopped next to the small cluster of white-coated men who knelt in the street. Someone reached for something, shifting out of the way.

Jack knew he would never forget the picture he saw. Sheri's hair drifted across the pavement, a delicate cloud of white gold. The red lights flashed across her face, throwing a garish imitation of life into her waxen features. One hand lay across her chest, the fingers, lax, lifeless.

"Get back now."

The policewoman had to take hold of Jack's arm to get his attention. The paramedic shifted, blocking Jack's view of Sheri's still figure.

The officer tugged on Jack's arm again. "Please move back, sir."

"She's a friend of mine." He turned blindly toward her.

"You can't do her any good by getting in the way," she told him with professional sympathy. "Move back onto the sidewalk."

Jack backed away, recognizing the truth in her words. He wanted nothing more than to push them all out of the way and take Sheri in his arms, but that wasn't the way to help her. He stumbled up onto the curb, his eyes still on the tableau in the street.

"Are you Jack?" a thin voice asked at his elbow.

He turned reluctantly, and stared down at the old woman. He didn't recognize her, was sure he'd never met her, but she seemed to know who he was.

"I'm Jack Ryan."

"She was always talking about you. I'm Mrs. O'Leary." When Jack didn't appear to recognize the name, she clarified, "Sheri helps me with my garden two or three times a week. I'm sure she's mentioned it."

"I…yes, of course." Sheri hadn't mentioned it, but, then, he hadn't asked. Pain sliced through him. He should have spent more time with her and less time trying to deny his feelings. He'd been such a stupid, stupid fool. He hoped to God he'd have a chance to make it up to her.

"It's a tragedy. A lovely girl like her." Mrs. O'Leary shook her head.

"What happened? Do you know what happened?"

"Saw the whole thing. My eyes are just as good as they were when I was twenty," she told him proudly.

"What happened?"

"I was sitting on the porch, enjoying the night air. It's nice this time of year, you know. Saw her go tearing by like the hounds of Hell were right on her heels. Seemed real upset. I called her name, but she didn't hear me. Guess she didn't hear the car, either. She stepped right off the curb in front of it. He tried to brake but…" She shook her head.

Jack closed his eyes, seeing it all just as if he'd witnessed it himself. The car, the girl caught in the flare of headlights.

"Sir, they're taking your friend to the hospital."

He opened his eyes to see the policewoman standing in front of him. Behind her, they were loading a stretcher into the ambulance.

Mrs. O'Leary's reedy voice followed after him as he moved toward the Jag. "You be sure and let me know how she goes on."

Eleanor said nothing on the short ride to the hospital. She

huddled in her seat, the cape drawn around her as if she were chilled. Jack hardly remembered her presence.

They reached the hospital just moments after the ambulance, but Jack had only a glimpse of the stretcher as Sheri was rushed through the door. He strode into the emergency room, hating the cold clinical scent of it.

During the short drive from home, his mind had been filled with remembrances of Sheri: laughing in the sunlight; her eyes full of concern over the plight of Melvin and his family; the innocent sensuality with which she'd come to his bed. He could lose it all. And there was no one to blame but himself. His own blind stupidity could cause him to lose the most precious thing he'd ever known.

"There was a young woman just brought in." He hovered over the admitting desk.

The woman behind it looked up, her eyes full of professional compassion. "Her name?"

"Sheri. Sheri Jones."

"The young woman who was struck by the car."

"Yes," he managed hoarsely. "Is she all right? Where is she?"

"Are you a relative?"

"She doesn't have any relatives. I'm a close friend."

"She's with the doctor now. I'm afraid I don't have any information about her condition. If you'll take a seat, the doctor will speak with you as soon as he can." She gestured to a narrow waiting room and returned her attention to the paperwork in front of her.

Jack stood there, his mind a blank. Sheri was lying somewhere, behind one of those closed doors, alone and hurt. Eleanor took his arm and he followed her automatically as she led him to the waiting room.

"I'm going to see if I can find your mother. This is her bridge night, isn't it?"

Jack nodded. He didn't care whom she called. He didn't care about anything but Sheri. Was she badly hurt? He kept seeing her lying so still and pale on the street. What if she— He cut the thought off. She was going to be all right. She *had* to be.

He was staring out the window, when he heard the door open. He spun around, but it was only Eleanor. He didn't bother to hide his disappointment.

Eleanor didn't feel any offense, however. She handed him a coffee and he took it, though she wasn't sure he was aware of it in his hand.

The waiting room was empty but for the two of them. Eleanor sat on one of the padded benches, staring at a painting on the wall. The soft golden fields seemed inappropriate in this place so full of fear. Jack continued to stare out the window, his shoulders tense.

When the door opened, Eleanor looked up, relief flooding her features as Roger walked in. Jack turned, looking beyond his friend, hoping to see a white coat. Seeing that Roger was alone, he turned back to the window without a sound.

"Any word?" Roger asked Eleanor, since it was clear Jack wasn't going to be talking.

"No." She shook her head.

Roger glanced at Jack and then sat down in the chair next to her. "Have they told you what happened?" he asked quietly.

"It was a hit-and-run. I don't think Jack knows any more than that." She smoothed the folded length of her cape, her fingers trembling. "I don't think he even knows I'm here."

Roger reached out and caught her hand in his, his expression tender. "It's going to be all right." He gave her fingers a reassuring squeeze before getting up and moving over to Jack.

"What happened?"

Jack glanced at him. He had to make an obvious effort to focus his attention on Roger. "She stepped in front of a car. It was only a couple of blocks from home. She was upset, not paying attention."

There was a sharp sound and he looked down to see that he'd crushed the cup Eleanor had given him. Lukewarm coffee poured over his hand and dripped onto the floor. Roger took the remains of the cup from him and tossed it in a trash can before handing him a handkerchief.

"Anything else?"

"They called the paramedics. She didn't have any ID. She never carried a purse. She should have carried a purse, even if she didn't need it." That point bothered him. He rubbed his hand across his forehead, momentarily lost in thought.

"How did you find out?" Roger asked gently, leading Jack back to the present.

"I was looking for her. I knew something was wrong. I could feel it. There was an old woman there. Sheri had been going to see her a couple of times a week, helping her in the garden. She talked about me. I didn't even know she was doing something like that. I should have known. I should have asked."

"It's going to be all right, Jack. Sheri's stronger than she looks. Besides, she's probably got some pretty strong powers of recovery in that bag of tricks. It's going to take more than a car to get her down."

"Then why is it taking so long?" Jack asked fiercely. "Why haven't they come to tell us she's all right? Why hasn't she come out herself."

Roger couldn't answer. He put his hand on Jack's shoulder, offering support. The door opened again, this time yielding the white coat they'd all been longing to see.

"How is she?" Jack covered the distance between him and the doctor in two long strides. "Is she all right?"

The doctor was young, with a shock of thick black hair and blue eyes that looked as if they were accustomed to laughter. But there was no laughter in them now.

"Your friend is still unconscious."

"Is that bad?" Jack demanded.

"We don't really know yet. There isn't an obvious reason for her continued unconsciousness. We'll be running some tests."

"She has a head injury?" Roger asked, his expression as anxious as Jack's.

"Not that we've found," the doctor admitted. "Actually, we can't find any sign of injury. She doesn't even have a bruise. If it wasn't for the fact that we have witnesses to her being struck by a car, we wouldn't have any idea what was wrong with her."

"No sign of injury?" Eleanor questioned. "Isn't that rather odd?"

"Miraculous might be a better word."

"If she wasn't hurt, then why is she unconscious?" Jack asked.

"We don't know yet. We've done a blood workup and there's no sign of drugs or alcohol."

"I could have told you that." Jack was furious they'd ever had to check.

The doctor lifted one hand in a soothing gesture. "It's pretty routine these days, especially in a case like this. With no obvious injuries, we had to check."

"So what you're telling me is that you haven't the slightest idea why she's unconscious," Jack said.

"More or less. Her body has had quite a shock. There could be injuries we haven't found yet. As I told you, we're going to run some tests. We should know more when the results of those are in, which won't be before morning. I'd suggest you go home, but I don't think you'd pay any attention."

Jack didn't answer. He didn't have to. The set of his jaw made it clear that nothing short of a military escort would get him to leave. The doctor sighed. With a promise to let them know if there was any change, he left them alone.

It was left to Roger to break the silence. "Well, that doesn't sound too bad," he said, his tone too hearty. "Sheri will probably wake up in an hour or so with nothing but a nasty headache to show for this."

Jack's expression didn't change.

Eleanor put her hand on his arm. "I'm sure Roger is right, Jack. She's going to be fine."

Jack didn't even glance at her as he turned away, returning to his silent vigil by the window.

Roger and Eleanor looked at each other, uncertain in the face of the wall Jack was erecting between himself and the rest of the world.

"I'm sure she's going to be all right," Eleanor said uneasily.

"Sure she will," Roger agreed. "By tomorrow morning, we'll all be laughing with her about this."

BUT SHERI WASN'T LAUGHING with anyone the next morning. She was still unconscious and the doctors were beginning to worry. Roger took Eleanor home in the wee hours of the morning, returning just after dawn with a change of clothing for his friend. Jack took it with a word of thanks.

In the men's room, he shrugged out of his dinner jacket. It seemed as if centuries had gone by since he'd put it on. He changed into the jeans and cotton shirt Roger had brought, stuffing his dinner clothes into the satchel. Splashing water on his face, he tried to drive the grit from his eyes.

As he entered the waiting room, his eyes sought Roger. "Any news?"

Roger shook his head slowly, his expression somber. It didn't take a medical degree to know that the longer Sheri remained unconscious, the greater the reason for concern.

It was midmorning before a doctor came to talk to them. She didn't say much that her colleague of the night before hadn't said. They still didn't know why Sheri was unconscious. They had ordered more extensive tests, in hopes that they could find the source of the problem.

Jack listened to everything the woman said, absorbing the implications behind the actual words.

"Can I see her?"

"I don't see why not." Dr. Jeffries nodded, her eyes taking in the pallor of Jack's skin beneath the dark shadow of beard.

"But you have to promise me you'll get some rest afterward." She lifted her hand, stilling his protest. "I don't need another patient."

"I'm not leaving."

There was no arguing with that flat tone. The doctor didn't even try. "I'm sure we can find someplace for you to stretch out. Now if you'd like to see your friend, I'm going that way. I can show you to her room."

Roger caught Jack's arm when he moved to follow the doctor. "Tell her I'm here."

Jack nodded. "I will."

Stepping into Sheri's room, Jack was struck by the stillness. It was more than just the physical quiet. There was something more. It gradually sank in that what he was sensing was Sheri's absence. He'd never consciously realized how life filled a room when she was in it. But that feeling was missing here.

He let the door shut behind him and reluctantly approached the bed. Once he actually saw her lying there, it wouldn't be possible to pretend that this was a mistake of some sort, that Sheri was safe at home. It would be real then.

He stopped next to the bed and looked down at her. She was so pale and still. Not the woman he knew at all. Her hair was spread over the pillow, framing her face. Her lashes created dark shadows on her ashen cheeks.

"Sheri?" He picked up her hand. Her skin felt cool to the touch. Her fingers were lax in his. It was as if he were touching a shell—the mind that should have been occupying it was elsewhere.

"Sheri? Sweetheart, wake up." He patted her hand gently but there was no response. "You have to wake up. I have so much I need to tell you.

"Roger is here. He's worried about you, too. You know, the doctors don't know what's wrong with you, so I know you could wake up if you wanted to. But you've got to fight, Sheri. You've got to fight. Sheri?"

She didn't move, in fact, she seemed barely to breathe. H

night have been talking to himself. And he had a sudden, terrible premonition that it was always going to be this way, that he'd never hear her voice or see her laugh again.

"Please." The one word was all he could get out past the choking feeling in his throat. He gripped her hand as if he could will her to wake up with the force of his need.

He had no idea how long he'd been standing there, Sheri's unresponsive hand in his, when Dr. Jeffries entered the room.

"Are you still here?" She clucked her tongue in annoyance. "You're not going to do her any good if you collapse."

"I'm all right." Jack didn't look up as she stopped beside him.

Dr. Jeffries took Sheri's hand from Jack's, checking the pulse automatically. "Did she respond at all?"

Jack shook his head slowly. "Nothing. I can't lose her."

"Well, we're going to do our best to see that you don't," she told him briskly. "I want you to get some sleep now."

"I'm not leaving her."

"We're going to be taking her for some tests in a few minutes and you can't come along, so you might as well sleep." She took his arm, leading him out the door, ignoring his mumbled protest.

He stumbled into the bed she showed him, and was nearly asleep before his head hit the pillow. But his sleep was troubled, haunted by nightmare images of glaring headlights that bore down on him. He could hear the scream of brakes, smell the burning rubber and then, just when it was inevitable that the lights would strike him, the whole sequence would start over again.

Jack woke suddenly, sitting up in bed, panicked and breathless. Sweat beaded on his forehead and his chest heaved with the effort of breathing. Rubbing one hand over his face, he fought to swallow the panic that threatened to smother him.

If something had changed with Sheri, he knew someone would have woken him. He didn't draw a steady breath until he found a nurse who told him there had been no change.

The pattern repeated itself many times in the days that followed. Jack's life centered on the hospital, and all his concentration was on Sheri. He spoke to people when they came to visit, but five minutes after they were gone, he couldn't remember what he'd said. His mother and Tina visited every day. Eleanor came often, her eyes haunted.

It was almost a week before it occurred to Jack to wonder why Eleanor was so concerned. It wasn't hard to come up with an answer. She felt guilty. Her words had sent Sheri out into the darkness. Or so she thought.

"Eleanor." She jumped, looking up from the magazine she'd been staring at.

Jack sat down next to her. It was an effort to focus on anything but Sheri, but it wasn't fair to let Eleanor continue to suffer. Sheri wouldn't want that.

"Is there any change?" Her anxious fingers creased the magazine.

"No." The answer hurt every time he gave it. He rubbed his hand over his jaw, grimacing at the rasp of several days' beard. He knew from the brief glimpses he got of himself in the men's room mirror that there was little of the respectable banker about him these days. Unshaven, his clothes creased from sleeping in them more often than not, he was hardly the Jack Ryan he had been. What would Sheri think if she saw him now? Most likely she'd laugh and tell him he looked like a pirate.

Eleanor shifted beside him, her slim fingers folding and unfolding the magazine. Jack forced the image of Sheri, her eyes sparkling in a smile, from his mind.

"I'm sorry," he told Eleanor. "My concentration isn't all it should be right now."

"That's okay. You've got a lot on your mind."

"I think you do, too. More than you should have."

"I don't know what you mean." Her eyes flickered to his and then away.

"You think you're responsible for Sheri's accident."

She winced at the blunt statement, her hands trembling. "I should never have said those things to her," she said.

Her voice was so low, Jack had to strain to hear it. "No, you shouldn't have. But that's not what upset her so. At least that's not the bulk of it. It was my fault. We quarreled before you got there. Or maybe it would be more accurate to say that I quarreled. I don't think Sheri knows how to quarrel." He stopped, thrusting his fingers through his hair, his eyes dull with pain.

"She told me some things I didn't want to hear. I lost my temper and said some hurtful things to her. I was a fool," he admitted bitterly. "I hope I get a chance to tell her how much of a fool."

"You will. You have to keep believing that." Eleanor touched his hand tentatively.

Jack noticed that his ring no longer rested on her finger and he took her hand in his, running his thumb over the faint mark at the base of her third finger. "We'd never have made it work, you know." Eleanor's hand rested in his more comfortably now than it ever had.

"I know," she said.

Jack released her hand and stood up. The momentary distraction was slipping and his thoughts were returning to Sheri. Nothing else could hold his attention for long.

Eleanor clenched her hands as she watched him leave the waiting room. He'd looked so lost, shattered. His heart and soul were wrapped up in the still figure who lay down the hall. If she died— She bit her lip against the sob that welled up in her throat, but it was not to be denied.

Roger found her hunched in the chair, her face buried in her hands, shoulders shaking with sobs. He crossed the room in an instant, sitting next to her, his heart pounding with fear.

"Eleanor. My God, what's happened? Is it Sheri?"

"No, it's me." She looked up at him, her eyes red rimmed with tears. "I'm an awful person."

He reached out and took her in his arms. "You're not a awful person. What happened?"

"Jack." The one word broke on a sob.

Roger tightened his arms around her. "Jack is in a lot c pain right now. I wouldn't take anything he said too seriously."

"He told me it wasn't my fault. But it was. I shouldn't hav said those things."

"Shouldn't have said what things?"

It took several minutes to get the story out of her. She sobbe it into his shirtfront, her voice thick with tears. Roger listene his heart aching for her pain.

"I had no right to say those things to her. She'd never do anything to me. How could I be so cruel? And now she's goin to die and it's my fault."

"She's not going to die." He shook her lightly for emphasi his hands gentle on her shoulders. "And the accident wasn your fault."

"That's what Jack told me. I don't know how he can eve stand the sight of me," she wailed. "He's not even mad me." She looked up at him, heartbreak in her eyes. "I'm n a very good person, Roger."

Her hair was a mess. Her eyes were swollen from cryin Her nose was red, her skin blotched. Roger had never seen h look more beautiful in his life. His mouth quirked in a tend smile as he reached up to brush the hair from her forehead.

"I'm not too great myself. Maybe between the two of us v could work on it. Okay?"

Eleanor's breath caught and her eyes widened. There was gentle promise in his eyes. A promise she hardly dared to b lieve. But she wanted to believe it. She wanted it desperate! She clutched his shirt.

"Yes. Oh, yes."

"Sheri? Sheri, it's Roger." There was no response and Rog stepped closer to the bed, reaching down to take her han

hocked by the lifelessness he felt. It had been over a week
nd there'd been not a flicker of life.

Looking at her, it was almost impossible to believe that she
nerely slept, but there was a transparency to her features, a
ragility in the stillness of her form. Roger had the feeling that
f he glanced away, she might disappear, simply wink out of
xistence. He held her hand tighter.

"Sheri, you can't do this to Jack. He's not going to get
hrough this one. If you love him, you can't leave him like
his."

There was no response and Roger stared at her, feeling help-
essness slip over him like a dark tide. He'd never seen Jack
his way. He moved, he answered when spoken to, but he was
ne of the walking wounded, and there was a look in his eyes
hat was frightening to see.

"Sheri, you've just got to wake up." He tried a brisk tone.
You were right about Eleanor and me. She's not engaged to
ack anymore and I think we're going to work things out. If
ou'll just wake up, you can say 'I told you so' as much as
ou like. Sheri?" He leaned closer, seeking some sign of life,
owever subtle.

But there was nothing. If it hadn't been for the barely per-
eptible rise and fall of her chest, he would have believed that
he'd already gone beyond reach.

"Ah, Sheri, wake up, honey."

"Do you think she hears?"

Roger started at the sound of Jack's voice, turning to look
t him. He was a far cry from the man he'd known for almost
wenty years. His clothes were creased, his face unshaven, his
yes bloodshot from lack of rest. He hadn't left the hospital
nce Sheri had been brought in and his skin held the pallor of
omcone who'd been too long out of the sun.

"I don't know," Roger said at last, releasing Sheri's hand
s Jack stepped beside the bed.

"Sometimes I think she has to be able to hear me. And then

I think I'm crazy." He reached out, stroking a lock of hair from her forehead.

Roger glanced away from Jack's face, feeling as if the look in his eyes was something too intense, too private for another to see. "I guess it helps to think she can hear us," he offered.

"If she can hear me, why doesn't she respond?"

"I...Jack, you've got to face the fact that maybe she *can't* respond." Roger said the words as gently as he could, prepared for the wild denial that sprang into Jack's eyes.

"No!" Jack said. "No," he repeated more quietly, utter determination in his face. "I won't believe that. I *can't*." He looked at Sheri, then lifted his eyes to Roger's. "I don't know what I'll do if she—" He broke off, unable to complete the sentence.

Roger didn't know what to say. There was no comfort he could offer Jack. No comfort anyone could offer. He reached out and grasped his friend's shoulder, offering silent support.

THE MORE TIME that passed, the more the doctors shook their heads and expressed complete bafflement. There was no sign of injury, no reason Sheri shouldn't wake up, yet she continued to sleep, growing paler and more wraithlike with each passing hour until she seemed to be nothing but a thin husk lying in the hospital bed.

With every day, Jack's helpless rage grew, bubbling inside him. Sleep became a distant memory. Every moment was spent at Sheri's bedside. He was terrified to leave her for even a moment, afraid she might lose her frail grip on this world—his world. The world she'd wanted so desperately to be a part of.

He pressed his forehead against the metal rail that bordered her bed, remembering how she'd talked of learning to be human. Why hadn't he told her then that it was hardly something she should wish for? Why hadn't he told her that she was perfect as she was? He'd been so caught up in petty concerns that he hadn't offered her the reassurance she'd needed.

He didn't deserve her. He knew that now. And if she'd only open her eyes, he'd set her free, though it would be like tearing his heart out. He'd give anything, his very life, if only she'd smile at him one more time.

JACK PACED back and forth in the waiting room. His mother and Tina sat in one corner, their eyes on him, saying nothing, their hands linked for support. Roger leaned against the window, staring out into the parking lot. Eleanor sat quietly, her hands in her lap, staring at nothing in particular.

There was an unspoken sense that some crisis point was near. They'd all gathered here, waiting. Outside, the sun blazed down with a heat that hinted at what summer would bring. To those inside, it might as well have been pouring rain.

"You know, she really was learning to needlepoint." Glynis broke the silence. "I'm sure she could have been quite good if she'd just had a few more lessons."

"She was reading a book about Einstein," Tina offered, her usual vibrance muted by the circumstances and surroundings. "I don't think she understood any of the formulas, but she told me he seemed like a nice man."

"She's the one who gave me Lucky," Eleanor said to no one in particular. "She told me animals could sense someone with a kind heart." Her voice cracked on the last words and she bent her head, fumbling for a handkerchief.

"She really brought an extra sparkle to the house. And no one understood the garden quite like—"

"Stop it!" Jack barked the words, his voice hoarse.

Startled, they all looked at him.

"Just stop it! You're all talking about her like she's dead."

"Jack, they didn't mean—" Roger stepped away from the window, his voice soothing.

"I know you all think she's going to die," Jack said furiously. "But you're wrong. She's going to get well. I'm not going to let her die. She can't die. God, she can't." His voice broke on the words and he spun on one heel, stalking out of the room before anyone could say another word.

"I didn't mean to imply—" Glynis broke off, her eyes showing her distress.

"Jack knows that, Glynis," Roger told her. "He's just a little ragged. We're all a little ragged."

Just then the door of the waiting room opened again. But it wasn't Jack returning. It was Dr. Jeffries, her comfortably middle-aged face holding out little promise of good news. She looked around the small gathering.

"Is there a change?" Roger asked, voicing the question on all their minds.

She shook her head slowly. "Not the change we've all been hoping for. I saw Mr. Ryan leaving the hospital." She stopped, drawing in a deep breath. "It might be a good idea if he were here. She just seems to be fading away. It can't be much longer now. I'm sorry."

There was a long, still moment when no one spoke, no one looked at anyone else. It was what they'd all been expecting, and yet, now that the moment was at hand, they were totally unprepared.

"I'll go find Jack," Roger muttered, pushing past the doctor.

JACK STALKED OUT of the hospital, blind to his surroundings. It wasn't right. It wasn't right. The phrase repeated itself in his head, echoing over and over again. No matter how far or how fast he walked, he couldn't escape it.

A sharp tug on his shirt brought him to a halt. He jerked loose from the thorn that had snagged in the fabric. Blinking, he looked around, realizing that he was standing in the middle of a small rose garden. Around him, roses blazed in half a dozen different colors. Their perfume hung in the warm air, heavy and sweet.

He reached out to touch a delicate blossom the color of sweet butter. Sheri loved roses. His hand shook as he stroked the velvety surface of the petals. His mouth twisted in a half smile as he remembered his mother's garden ablaze with flowers weeks too soon.

It wasn't right. He blinked against the burning in his eyes. They should have had a chance to share many gardens together. There were so many things he wanted to do with her, so many things he wanted to say to her. He wanted a chance to tell her that he loved her. They should have had more time, all the time in the world.

"Jack." He didn't turn toward Roger's voice, but stared blindly at a rosebud the color of a gentle sunrise.

"Look, I know I snapped in there. I'll apologize when this is all over. I guess I'm running on a ragged edge, but when Sheri wakes up—" His voice broke and the rosebud seemed to blur. He drew a deep breath. "When she wakes up, things will get back to normal."

"Jack, Dr. Jeffries came in after you left."

Jack spun, his eyes pinning Roger with a look of desperate hope. "What is it? Is there a change? I knew I shouldn't have left her."

Roger caught his arm, stopping his headlong rush back to the hospital.

"Jack, Dr. Jeffries says that Sheri is fading away. She says...she says that it probably won't be long until...until..." He couldn't finish the sentence. He looked away from the dawning realization in his friend's eyes.

"No." Jack murmured the word. "No. I won't let it happen. I can't." He looked around the rose garden dazedly. "I don't know what I'd do without her."

"Jack, I... I'm sorry." The words seemed worthless, but it was all he could say.

"You know, she wanted to be human," Jack said to no one in particular. "She wanted to fit in my world. My world." He laughed roughly. "My world is what's destroyed her. My God, how could I be so blind?" He slapped at one of the rosebushes, oblivious of the thorn that caught his palm, tearing at the skin.

"It's my fault she's lying in there. It's all my fault."

"Jack, it's not your fault. There was an accident. It could have happened to anyone."

"To anyone, yes. But not to Sheri. She should have been able to avoid it. Didn't it ever occur to you to wonder why she didn't avoid it?"

"No one can avoid every accident. Not unless you're a wizard or—" Roger broke off, realizing what he was saying.

"Or a genie," Jack finished bitterly.

"I hadn't thought of that. What happened? Why didn't she just disappear when she saw the car?"

"Because of me."

"Don't be an idiot. Sheri might have been hurt, but she'd never let herself get hit by a car."

"She didn't *let* herself get hit. She couldn't prevent it. She told me once, only I didn't listen. I was too bloody selfish to think about what was happening."

"Told you what?"

"I asked her if genies ever fell in love," Jack said softly, remembering another rose garden, another time. "And she said that they did, but that it wasn't like a human falling in love. She said that they lost most of their powers." He snapped a rosebud off, staring blindly at the delicate shape. "They lose most of their powers," he repeated as much to himself as to Roger. "I should have thought... But I didn't. I only worried about what was happening to me. Not about what it could do to her."

"Jack, you're not making any sense."

"Don't you see? She didn't get out of the way of that car because she *couldn't*. She didn't have her powers anymore because she loved me. She loved me. And now she's going to die."

He watched understanding come into Roger's eyes, before looking away. Since the accident he'd lived with the knowledge that Sheri's love for him might be the cause of her death. It ate into him with the bite of acid—a burning pain he'd live with the rest of his life.

He looked at the rosebud he held, remembering how Sheri had loved roses. How was he going to go on without her? Pain emptied his mind of thought. Softly, as if drifting on the perfumed air, Sheri's voice slipped into his mind.

"Love is something we are, not just something we feel. A human dies of a broken heart only on the inside. For us it's more than that."

And Dr. Jeffries's voice. *"She just seems to be fading away."*

Something struggled to life in his mind, something so delicate he hardly dared label it hope. *Love.* Sheri had believed in that. *"It won't be long,"* Dr. Jeffries's voice reminded him. There was so little time. Was it possible?

He pushed past Roger, unaware of the other man's presence. It was a foolish hope, his desperation showing in the fact that he even dared consider it.

There was a nurse in Sheri's room, but Jack didn't see her. He ran to the bed and took Sheri's cold hand in his, the forgotten rosebud caught between his palm and hers. He could see the change in just the short time since he'd left her. She was so pale, her skin almost translucent.

"Sheri. Sheri, I love you. I didn't tell you before because I was a fool. You've got to come back, sweetheart. I love you."

He waited, hardly drawing a breath, but there was no response. Behind him, Roger stepped silently into the room. He didn't know what had sent Jack rushing back here, but he wanted to be present in case his friend needed him.

"Sheri." Jack made his voice more commanding, no longer pleading but demanding. "Sheri, you've got to come back."

"Mr. Ryan, please keep your voice down."

Jack didn't even turn to look at the nurse. All his attention was focused on Sheri, all his will.

"Sheri, you have to come back. I didn't get my third wish."

"Mr. Ryan, lower your voice."

The nurse's scandalized tone was no more than an annoying noise. Roger reached out, silencing her with a hand on her arm.

He thought he could guess what was going through Jack's mind, through his heart. He was unashamed of the tears that burned in his eyes as he watched his friend's last desperate efforts.

"Sheri, I want my third wish. You owe me that."

There was no response from the still figure on the bed, no life in the hand that lay slack in his.

"Sheri?" His voice cracked on the name. "Oh, God, please don't leave me alone. I can't make it without you. Please. You owe me that third wish. You can't go without giving me that much. I'll let you go after that, but I want that wish. It was part of the deal. Remember?"

His voice fluctuated between demand and pleading. Still no response, and Jack seemed to shrink in on himself, his shoulders hunching like those of a very old man.

"Please. Please don't leave me alone," he said brokenly.

Roger started forward, unable to bear the agony in his friend's voice. The nurse didn't move, understanding that this was an intensely private moment. Roger was halfway to the bed, when he stopped as if he'd run into a wall.

He heard Jack's breath catch and knew he hadn't imagined the flicker of movement.

Jack leaned forward, his eyes intent. Surely her lashes had moved. "Sheri." He kept the edge of demand in his voice.

Her lashes flickered again and Jack's fingers tightened over hers.

"I want that last wish. You promised me that."

Her lashes lifted slowly, as if carrying a heavy weight. She looked at him, her eyes a faded blue, so little of her left in them that Jack felt a terrible fear. What if it was too late?

"You promised," he told her firmly, gripping her hand as if he could hold her there with his strength alone.

She took a shallow breath and moistened her lips. "I have...nothing to give you."

The whisper was so low, he had to bend close to hear it. "I only have one wish," he persisted.

"Mr. Ryan!"

"I have nothing to give," she repeated, the dim awareness fading from her gaze.

Her eyes started to drift shut and Jack's hand tightened fiercely.

"You can give me this. You have to give me this."

She moistened her lips again, the effort clear. "What do you wish?"

"I want you to love me as much as I love you."

She stared at him for a moment and then her eyes fell shut.

"Sheri!" Jack's voice held raw panic. Had he been wrong? For seemingly endless moments there was no movement and he tasted the bitterness of loss.

But then her lashes moved again, lifting slowly. The faded blue seemed a little darker, a little brighter.

"I love you, Sheri. I love you more than life itself. You've got to come back to me. We'll raise horses or sail around the world or fly to the moon. It doesn't matter as long as we're together. I want you to love me. That's my last wish. The last command I'll give you."

Her fingers shifted in his, curling over the rosebud. Jack's hand closed over hers. He had to lean over to hear her words, but they settled into his heart.

"You don't have to wish for what you already have."

He took a deep breath, feeling the tightness ease in his chest. Roger drew a deep breath, aware that his cheeks were damp. It was going to be all right. Against all the odds, it was going to be all right.

"I love you." Jack bent to kiss her, knowing he could never say it too much. She'd taught him how to dream again and she'd taught him that magic was real. Together they'd learn about love.

And ever afterward, the nurse would tell the story of how the rosebud unfurled before her eyes until it was a magnificent golden bloom, the color of sunshine and promises.

Something was terribly wrong!
Lacey Newton woke up with a stranger.
Worse yet, she was *married* to him!

The Morning After

Chapter One

"An old maid. I've raised a daughter who's going to spend her life as an old maid." Mamie Newton's voice was filled with despair.

"Nobody uses that term anymore, Mother." Lacey smiled to take the edge off the words, wondering if Mamie would notice that her voice was a little too tight.

"What else can you call it?" Mamie looked at her daughter, her beautiful blue eyes reproachful. "Here you are. You're thirty years old and you aren't married. You don't even have a man in your life. Don't you want to get married, have children?"

Lacey took a swallow of tea, aware that her fingers were knotted around the fragile bone-china cup. It took a conscious effort to loosen them and smile.

"Of course I want that, Mother, but until it comes along, I'm leading a full, productive life. I have my shop and I have friends. I'm hardly living like a hermit."

Mamie didn't return her smile. She stared at Lacey as if trying to understand where she'd gone wrong in raising her only child. Lacey said nothing, keeping her expression calm, slightly amused. It wouldn't do to let Mamie know she'd struck a nerve. If she'd learned one thing in thirty years, it was that her delicate Southern belle of a mother had the tenacity of a bulldog. She never meant to be cruel, but if she had the least suspicion that Lacey was anything but content, she'd prod and push and poke until she had all the reasons laid out in front of her, and then she'd start looking for ways to fix whatever she thought the problem was.

The problem was that Lacey herself wasn't sure why her life didn't seem quite as full as it should have. Until she'd worked it out to her own satisfaction, she wasn't going to lay herself open to her mother's tender mercies.

"I just don't understand, Lacey. Sometimes I wonder if maybe your daddy dying when you were so young didn't affect you more than I thought. Maybe I should have remarried. A child should have a father in her life."

Mamie picked up a cucumber sandwich—thin white bread, the crusts removed, of course—and nibbled at it, her expression mournful.

Lacey watched her, torn between the urge to laugh and the urge to scream. Only the laughter would have had a hysterical edge and, if she started screaming, she might not stop.

"Mother, I'm thirty, not ninety. Lots of women wait to have families these days. It's no big deal."

Mamie sighed and swallowed the last of the tiny sandwich before wiping her fingertips on a snow-white linen napkin. If the world itself depended on it, Mamie would never speak with her mouth full.

"I don't mean to be a pushy mother, Lacey, but I worry about you. I never would have thought you'd get to your thirtieth birthday without at least being engaged a time or two. You don't even have a special man in your life."

"Having a man in your life doesn't guarantee happiness. Look at the divorce rate these days."

"You can't dwell on the negative, honey. It's just a matter of finding the right man, that's all." Thirty years in Southern California had not taken the Georgia from Mamie's voice. The tea table, the perfectly decorated room, her mother's soft lavender dress—all of it could have come out of a modern-day Tara. The rest of the world might have embraced "casual" as a way of life, but Mamie Newton believed that the finer things were what made life worth living.

Lacey stared at her beautiful refined mother and wondered how it was possible that she'd missed all the changes in the world around her. Lacey's father had died when she was barely four. What her life might have been like if he'd lived, Laccy would never know. Mamie had chosen to stay in Southern California, but she'd raised her daughter as if they were in the Deep South.

Lacey had worn dresses when other little girls wore jeans. She knew just how to crook her pinky while sipping tea. She was the only woman she knew who actually owned a pair of white gloves for church. To this day, she felt underdressed walking into a church without them. How did she go about explaining to her mother that life wasn't lived on the simple terms Mamie thought it should be?

"When I find the right man, I'll be more than happy to latch on to him."

"Well, you aren't going to find him by shutting yourself up in that stuffy little boutique of yours, getting ink all over your fingers from doing the books and all."

"You've been reading too much Dickens. I have a computer to help me with the books. And Lacey's Lovelies isn't stuffy. It's very chic, and my customers know they can get the best there. I notice you don't hesitate to buy from me."

Mamie waved her fingers, dismissing the shop. "I didn't mean to criticize what you've done, sugar. I'm real proud of you, and your daddy would have been, too. But you take my word for it. A store just doesn't make up for not having a man in your life. And I'm not talkin' about the bedroom, neither. It's important to have somebody there to lean on, someone to share thc good times and the bad."

Lacey reached for her tea, trying to ignore the twinge of pain her mother's words brought. "That sounds great, Mother, but wonderful men aren't hanging around like ripe peaches just waiting to be picked."

"Well, you aren't going to find one the way you're going at it. When was the last time you had a date?"

"As a matter of fact, I had lunch with a charming man last week."

She could almost see Mamie's ears perk up. "You did? What's his name?"

"Brad. He's nice, good-looking, and we had a wonderful time." She sipped her tea to hide a grin. She hadn't told a lie. Brad was all those things. He was also gay, but she didn't have to mention an irrelevant detail like that. She also wouldn't mention the fact that he had been trying to sell her an insurance package. For now, Mamie was distracted.

An hour later, she stifled a stab of guilt as she kissed her mother goodbye. Tucked into her purse was an exquisite pair of diamond earrings, Mamie's birthday gift to her only child.

The problem with her mother was that it was impossible to get too angry with her meddling. Mamie genuinely wanted nothing but Lacey's happiness. It was hard to get mad at someone who had your best interests at heart. Still, Mamie's constant concern about her daughter's single state did get on Lacey's nerves.

She settled behind the wheel of her car and started the engine, lifting her hand to wave to her mother before backing out of the driveway. She flicked the radio on, setting it to a station that was playing old rock and roll. The quick rhythms and silly lyrics rarely failed to raise her spirits. Today they failed abysmally. She shut the radio off as she turned onto Foothill Boulevard and headed toward Pasadena.

Thirty. She was thirty years old today. She'd never thought that she was going to be one of those people who was depressed by the big three-o. But here it was, and boy, was she depressed. Her thirties stretched in front of her, endless and empty. No, not empty! She made the correction angrily, her fine brows drawing together.

She'd accomplished a lot in thirty years. She had her own very successful shop and she loved the work. Lacey's Lovelies was proving to be a major success in one of Pasadena's terribly with-it neighborhoods. She'd bought before the prices climbed out of sight, and she was now in a remarkably secure position. She'd even been thinking about opening another shop.

There. Her life was hardly a barren wasteland. But the defiant thought didn't do much to lift her spirits. Neither did the bright California sunshine. In fact, she couldn't remember the last time she'd been so depressed.

Thirty. It sounded so...old. All the magazine articles described it as the prime of a woman's life—the time when she really came into her own. But right now Lacey didn't feel particularly prime. She felt slightly dusty and a little unwanted.

She flipped on a signal and turned into the parking garage beneath her apartment building. The elevator whisked her to the fourth floor and she stepped onto thick carpeting. Her apartment was sleek, charming, beautifully decorated. She was proud of it. So why was it that it looked so...empty? Maybe she should get a cat. Having someone to greet her when she came home would cheer the place up a bit.

Dropping her purse on the breakfast bar, she sank onto a stool and stared at nothing in particular. A cat. The classic symbol of the old maid.

"Next thing, I'll be wearing a doily on my head and talking to myself. All I need is a nice hot bath and some good company. Then I'll see how ridiculous this whole thirty thing is." She stopped suddenly. "Oh, my God, I am talking to myself!"

She laughed, hearing the sound disappear in the big room. Damn Mamie for making her feel like a dinosaur. There was nothing wrong with being unmarried at thirty. There were more things in a woman's life than husbands and children—not that those things wouldn't be nice, but they weren't the be-all and end-all.

She stood up, straightening her shoulders and forcing a smile. She was going to go out tonight, just as she'd planned. She and her friends were going to have a wonderful time celebrating her thirtieth birthday.

"Thirty. I'm thirty." There. She'd said it out loud, and she didn't feel anything awful happen to her. It was no big deal. It was just another birthday.

She walked briskly into the bathroom and turned the water on in the tub, adjusting it to just below scalding. While the tub was filling, she went into the bedroom and stripped off her skirt and blouse. After hanging them up, she caught a glimpse of herself in the mirror, and she paused to study her reflection.

Without giving herself time to think, she stripped off the pale peach camisole and tap pants and faced the mirror squarely. Her eyes were anxious as she studied herself. Her skin still looked firm and supple. She turned sideways, tightening her buttocks. Maybe they weren't quite as firm as they'd been when she was seventeen, but they weren't too bad.

She put her fingertips on the skin over her breasts and pulled upward. Her frown deepened. Were they sagging more than they had a year ago? Maybe she should get one of those things that you squeezed with your hands. They were supposed to build up the pectoral muscles, weren't they? Pectorals. Lord, it sounded like some prehistoric bird.

She leaned closer to the mirror and studied her face. It looked much the same to her. The same delicate bones, inherited from her mother. The same mouth, the lower lip just a bit too full. Her eyes were her best feature, wide set and a clear green. She smiled experimentally, counting the lines at the corners of her eyes. Was she aging too quickly? She'd given up the sun years ago, afraid of having her skin turn to saddle leather. But maybe those careless teenage days at the beach had done too much damage...

She frowned and then quickly erased the expression. Frowning gave you lines. How many times had Mamie told her that? But so did smiling and no one ever suggested that you stop smiling. Lacey stepped back and studied her reflection. No, the signs of deterioration weren't too obvious yet, but she had the gloomy feeling that they were lurking just below the surface, ready to leap out and cause her to wrinkle and sag overnight.

Maybe it wasn't on the birthday itself that all the hideous changes occurred. Maybe it was the day after the birthday. Maybe she was going to wake up tomorrow morning looking like the portrait of Dorian Grey.

The thought should have made her laugh, but she didn't even feel like smiling. Maybe she'd call Jimbo and tell him she really didn't feel like going out tonight. Somehow, turning thirty didn't seem like something to celebrate. She turned away from the mirror and walked into the bathroom. If she called to cancel, he'd want to know why and he'd think she was an idiot. She'd known Jimbo for almost five years now. Despite the considerable age difference, they'd hit it off immediately. But one thing he wasn't, was tactful. No, she'd just have to go tonight and pretend she didn't mind leaving her youth behind.

Sinking into the steaming water, she leaned her head back, staring at the tiled wall. Old maid. At the moment, the description sounded depressingly accurate.

CAMERON McCLEARY smoothed the fine sandpaper carefully across the wood. Willie Nelson rasped out a tune from the radio in the corner, the only sound in the garage-turned-workshop besides the smooth hiss of the sandpaper. Cam paused and studied the piece in front of him, his eyes critical.

One of his better pieces, if he did say so himself. The fine grain of the oak suited the sweeping lines of the cradle. He brushed a bit of sawdust off the top edge, running his thumb along the curve, testing its smoothness. The wood felt warm and strong under his hand. The Martins would be able to rock more than one baby in this cradle. He'd built it to last for generations.

He picked up a rag and began wiping the sawdust from the delicate carvings that marked the head and foot of the cradle. It wasn't hard to picture an infant asleep in the sturdy oak. The image brought a peculiar pang to his chest.

What would it be like to build a cradle for his own child? The rag stroked gently over the oak, picking up a fine coating of dust and leaving the wood satin smooth. The thought of his own child held safe and protected by the work of his hands was appealing. More than appealing. But while the infant was easy to picture, its mother was something else.

He hadn't gotten to thirty-six without knowing a fair number of women. Once or twice he'd even thought he might be in love but, somehow, the relationships had never quite developed into the kind of commitment that went with marriage and children.

His brows came together, overshadowing his summer-blue eyes. Over the past year, he'd begun to feel a strange restlessness, a sense of something missing in his life. He finally had all the work he could handle, his life was in order, and yet there was something missing. Something indefinable. There was a gap.

Stroking the rag over the cradle, he began to sense what the gap was. He wanted a family. His mouth tilted into a smile. He had to be crazy. After growing up in a family of seven, any sane person would be glad for a little peace and quiet. But he liked the chaos that went with a family—the noise, the arguments, the clutter…the love.

Still, you didn't just walk out and buy a family. It was something that grew out of a commitment to a woman and her commitment to you. Sighing, he tossed the rag aside. These days that commitment seemed to be a little hard to come by.

Cam stretched and reached for the cup of coffee that had grown cold while he worked. Grimacing at the bitter taste, he set the cup down, promising himself that he was going to buy a Thermos so he could manage hot coffee while he was in the shop.

"Hey, not bad." Cam turned, startled, as the voice boomed out from the doorway. He relaxed, giving a half smile when he saw who it was.

James Robinson—Jimbo as long as Cam had known him—matched his voice. Average height but barrel-chested, so that he seemed shorter than he was, Jimbo was the epitome of the hail-fellow-well-met type. His mouth seemed destined to snap out witty comments, and his eyes viewed the world with a combination of good humor and cynicism.

"Come right in." Jimbo grinned at Cam's halfhearted sarcasm.

"You didn't answer the doorbell and the gate was open. I figured you'd be in the shop."

"Maybe I didn't answer the door because I didn't want to be disturbed."

"Nah. I knew you wouldn't mind me dropping in. You didn't answer the door because you didn't hear it."

Jimbo walked into the converted garage, studying the nearly completed cradle. Cam watched him, knowing before the words were out just what Jimbo was going to say.

"The best thing I've seen you do."

"You said that about the last six things you saw."

Jimbo shrugged. "What can I say? You just keep getting better."

Cam grinned. "Flattery will get you nowhere. What do you want?"

"Me?" Jimbo's eyes were the very picture of injured friendship. "Why do you assume I want something?"

"Because you usually do." Cam leaned against the edge of the workbench, studying his friend with good-natured skepticism. "Three weeks ago, you wanted to borrow my car. A month before that, you wanted me to cover for you on a date you couldn't make. So, what is it this time?"

Jimbo gave him a hurt look. "You wound me, you really do. I come here with an invitation for you, and you practically throw it back in my face even before I can say anything."

Cam ignored the exaggerated expression of pain. "What kind of an invitation?"

"Dinner. Tonight. It's a friend's birthday. Lacey. You've heard me mention her."

"Sure. But I don't see why I'm invited. I've never met her."

"No. But this would be a great opportunity. Lacey is a great gal. You'd like her. Besides, we're going out for Mexican. Picture it—enchiladas swimming in sauce, burritos stuffed to the brim with shredded beef and cheese, margaritas.''

Cam held up his hand, groaning. "Stop with the bribery. It sounds great, but I really can't.''

"Why not? It looks like you've got this project about done. I know you well enough to know you're not going to start on another project right away.''

"No, but—''

"You're becoming a hermit, Cam. When was the last time you went out to dinner with a beautiful woman?''

"Last week.''

"Yeah, and I bet it was your mother or one of your sisters.''

Cam grinned, lifting his shoulders. "Guilty.''

"Come on. This is going to be a great evening. Frank and Lisa are going to be there and I'm taking Betts.''

"Look, this Lacey isn't going to want a stranger along on her birthday dinner. Maybe another time.''

"Lacey wouldn't mind a bit. In fact, she's been anxious to meet you.'' He caught the dubious look Cam threw him and amended the statement. "Well, I know she'd be interested. Besides, this way we'll have even numbers in case we go dancing. I don't want Lacey to feel like the odd man out at her own birthday.''

"I don't think it's such a hot idea.''

"I do. Come on, Cam. You owe me. Didn't I drive all thirty of your brothers and sisters to Disneyland?''

"There's only six of them and that was almost ten years ago.''

"Well, it seemed like thirty, and my nerves still haven't recovered. Come on, it will do you good to get out of the house. You work too hard.''

Cam looked at him, recognizing the gleam in his friend's eye. If he didn't agree, Jimbo was fully prepared to hound him until he gave up and said yes. Jimbo was nothing if not persistent. Besides, he *had* been feeling restless. Maybe Jimbo was right. Maybe he did need to get out of the house for a while.

"All right. But if it's a disaster, don't say I didn't warn you."

Jimbo grinned, rubbing his hands together. "It'll be fun. You'll see. This is going to be a night to remember."

Cam looked less enthused. "As long as it's not a night to regret."

Chapter Two

Lacey pulled into the parking lot of Los Arcos and slowed th
car to a near halt as she looked for a parking place. She edge
into a spot that looked more suited to a motorcycle than a ca
and then realized that she was going to be lucky if she coul
get her door open. The door did open—barely.

She hesitated, debating the wisdom of finding another plac
to park, but the lot looked pretty full. She'd been lucky to fin
the spot she had. It seemed par for the course that she had t
squeeze uncomfortably through an opening that would hav
challenged Houdini.

Considering the way her day had gone so far, it shouldn'
have surprised her that, when she slammed the car door an
tried to take a step, her skirt was caught. Jerked to an abrup
halt when her dress refused to move with her, Lacey looke
over her shoulder with more resignation than irritation.

She wasn't particularly disturbed. It was a reasonably simp
matter to open the door and release the swatch of pale gre
cotton. And if the dress was ruined, that was only to be e
pected. So far, her thirtieth birthday was turning out to be
day full of unpleasant surprises. A ruined dress barely rat
any concern. She started to turn and felt her resignation sli
The skirt was full enough to catch in the door but not fu
enough to allow her the room to turn so she could get the k

in the door. She turned left and then she turned right, but the door remained stubbornly out of reach.

She stopped and stood next to her car, smiling vaguely at a group of people going into the restaurant. They smiled back. One of them even went so far as to comment that it looked like it might rain. Lacey nodded, keeping her smile pinned in place until the door closed behind them. It faded the minute they were out of sight. It was easy for them to smile. She'd be willing to bet that not one of them was over twenty-five. What did they know about turning thirty? Just wait until they reached that day.

She twisted again, reaching for the door handle. Her fingertips just brushed it but there was no way she could get the key in the lock. She stood still, staring at the parking lot. The light was fading. Soon it would be dark and she'd still be standing here, like some bizarre form of modern art. *Woman and Car.*

Remembering the comment about rain, Lacey glanced up at the sky. A few gray clouds scudded overhead. Rain. Great. Just what she needed to top off a fun-filled birthday. She could stand in the rain and catch pneumonia just like that little girl in *Jane Eyre.*

She twisted quickly with some vague idea of surprising the door into letting her go. It didn't work. She nodded to an elderly couple and bent her head over her purse as if she were looking for something terribly important.

She could take off her dress. Then she'd be able to reach the door and release it. Of course, in the meantime, she'd probably draw quite a crowd. Admittedly, Southern Californians were notoriously blasé but she'd be willing to bet that a woman tripping to her skivvies in the parking lot of a Glendale restaurant was going to draw a crowd. It might not get much attention in Hollywood, but Glendale was a bit more conservative.

She could call for help. She abandoned that option almost as soon as she thought of it. If she called for help, she'd have to explain what had happened, and there *was* no explanation.

Turning thirty was not a valid excuse for losing all of one's
coordination and shutting part of one's person in a car door.

She stood between the two cars and considered the possibilities. None of them looked reasonable. No. She might as well
face the fact that she was doomed to grow old and die trapped
in the parking lot of a Mexican restaurant. Years from now,
they'd find her moldering form lying on the macadam and
they'd never know what happened, because by then her skirt
would have rotted loose, freeing her at last from the deadly
grip of the door.

The image was so absurd that she couldn't help but laugh.
It started as a smile and turned into a full-throated chuckle.

"Excuse me. Are you aware that your dress is caught in the
car door?"

The voice cut through Lacey's laughter and she turned her
head, looking over her shoulder to see its owner. The light had
faded to the point where it was difficult to make out much
beyond a pair of very broad, very masculine shoulders and the
faint gleam of a smile.

"No kidding." Her smile took any sarcasm from the words.
"I thought my dress was shrinking."

She felt his eyes sweep down to where her dress was caught
and then back up to her face. She sensed the smile in them.
"No, it's definitely caught. Can I help?"

"Well, that all depends. If you can reach the lock, you could
open the door so that I can move."

He seemed to consider the idea for a moment and then nodded. "I think I can manage that. Do you have the key?"

"Fat lot of good it's done me so far." She handed the key
back to him and heard the click as he slid it into the lock. A
moment later, he had the door open and her skirt was free.

"Thank you."

"No problem. Any damage?"

Lacey brushed at her skirt and then looked up, wishing she
could see more of his face. His voice was wonderfully deep
and mellow, making her want to know what he looked like.

"Nothing permanent. I can always have the dress cleaned. Before you came along I was beginning to wonder if I was destined to die there."

"I'm glad I could help."

"Not as glad as I am, I'll bet." They were walking toward the restaurant as they talked, and Lacey wasn't sure whether she was glad or sorry when he opened the door and they stepped into the brightly lit restaurant. She wanted to know what her rescuer looked like, but it was going to be extremely depressing if he turned out to be a twenty-two-year-old weight-lifter.

Her first reaction was relief that he wasn't young enough to be her grandchild. Her second reaction was that he was almost too handsome. His features were all-American perfect—strong chin, beautiful mouth, wide brow and eyes the color of the bluest skies. His hair was light brown, sun-streaked and casually combed. This was a man a woman would cheerfully kill for. He was also well on the far side of thirty. Thirty-five or six, at a guess. The knowledge didn't make her feel much better. A man this good-looking could have his pick of women, most of them younger and prettier than she was. Not that she was particularly interested in him, of course. Heaven knew, she'd grown past the stage of wanting to date a man just because he happened to be quite possibly the most attractive specimen of masculinity she'd ever seen.

She flushed when she realized that he was studying her with just as much interest as she was studying him. She resisted the urge to run her hand over her hair. Surely, as of today she had left behind some of the insecurities of her twenties.

"Well, thanks again."

"You're welcome." His eyes were intense, and Lacey had the impression that he wanted to say something else, though she wasn't sure she wanted to hear it.

"I think I'll visit the ladies' room before I meet my friends. See if I can repair some of the damage." She gestured to her skirt and smiled vaguely, moving away before he could sa anything more.

By the time she'd wiped away as much of the mark on he dress as she could, she was cursing herself. The man was go geous. And he seemed nice. Why hadn't she waited to see wha he wanted to say? He might have asked her for a date. Not tha she was given to picking up strange men in parking lots, b she could have made an exception just this once.

She studied her reflection in the washroom mirror. Go knows, she might as well make hay while she could. In th relentless fluorescent lighting, every line or hint of a lin showed up perfectly. She grimaced. Somebody ought to mak a law that said all mirrors had to be lit with candlelight.

With a sigh and one last thought of her rescuer, she left th bathroom. There was no sense in putting this off. Jimbo ha insisted on celebrating her birthday in style, and celebrate the would. After all, what was so bad about turning thirty? Th small pep talk did not have much effect on her spirits.

Los Arcos was packed on Friday nights, and this was n exception. Lacey stared at the crowd of people and felt he spirits sink. They all looked like they were having so muc fun. Couples, families—no one was here alone. And the looked young. Everyone in the place looked like they ought be eating pablum.

She considered turning and slinking out, but it was too lat Jimbo had seen her and with his usual subtlety was waving h arms to attract her attention. The movements were so attentio getting that Lacey wouldn't have been surprised to see a 74 land on top of him, mistaking his gestures for a signal to lan

She smiled and edged her way through the crowd to th table, feeling as if every eye in the place was on her and eve one of them knew it was her thirtieth birthday. They were pro ably trying to count the wrinkles.

"Lacey! Happy birthday! We were beginning to think y weren't going to show."

"I'm not *that* late." Lacey accepted his hug and smiled at Frank and Lisa. "Hi."

"Lacey, I want you to meet Betts. I did her taxes for her this year."

Lacey's heart sank. If Betts was with Jimbo that must mean that the other man at the table was unattached. And the only empty seat was right next to him. She'd kill Jimbo for this. She'd kill him and enjoy every minute of it.

"Nice to meet you, Betts. Jimbo's done a great job on my taxes."

Jimbo gave the two women a moment to exchange smiles before making the final introduction. "And this is Cameron McCleary. Cam, this is Lacey."

She really looked at the other man for the first time since arriving at the table, and she felt her color rise until her cheeks were on fire. The man who was slowly unfolding himself from the table was none other than her parking-lot rescuer.

"Hello again." He held out his hand, and Lacey put hers into it, oddly reluctant. His palm felt hard and warm, callused as if he worked with his hands. Her eyes met his and her flush deepened.

"Hi."

"You two know each other?" Jimbo's sharp eyes went from one to the other, missing nothing.

"Not exactly." It was Cam who answered, since Lacey couldn't seem to find her voice. "Lacey was having some trouble with her car and I helped a bit." He shrugged, dismissing the incident as too minor to discuss, and Lacey gave him a grateful smile. She was feeling a little too vulnerable tonight to want everyone to know what a stupid predicament he'd found her in.

"I hope you don't mind that I've sort of crashed your birthday celebration. Jimbo was pretty insistent." Cam's smile made her feel as if he saw only her in the entire room. Lacey warned herself against reading too much into it. Some men were just born knowing how to make a woman feel important.

Her smile was a masterpiece of casual as she said, "He wa
probably downright obnoxious."

Jimbo shrugged, not in the least disturbed. He returned t
his chair, leaving Lacey to settle herself next to Cam. She trie
not to notice how close his thigh was, how large he seemed.

Frank leaned forward, his sandy hair falling into a questio
mark over one eyebrow. "So, Lacey, how does thirty feel? Yo
going to survive?"

She shrugged, forcing a grin. "I haven't kicked the bucke
yet. It's about to kill my mother, though. She thinks I'r
doomed to be an old maid."

Everyone laughed, but Cam threw her a quick look, his eye
sharp, and Lacey wondered if he'd heard something in he
voice that shouldn't have been there. She leaned back as th
waiter set an enormous margarita in front of her, the salty rir
a pale contrast to the icy yellow contents of the glass.

"Okay. Time for a birthday toast." Jimbo reached for hi
glass and everyone followed suit. "To Lacey. May all you
birthdays be spent in such charming company." He grinne
and reached across the table to touch his glass to hers. Lace
couldn't help but smile at him. It was impossible to stay ma
at Jimbo, no matter how irritated she was that he had dragge
Cam along as a semi-date for her.

Everyone touched their glasses to hers, adding their goo
wishes. Cam was the last. As their glasses touched, Lacey me
his eyes. His expression seemed to say that he knew exactl
what she was feeling. She wanted to look away. He made he
uneasy, as if he was seeing too much. But she couldn't loo
away.

"To the prettiest old maid I've ever met." His quiet ton
soothed in some indefinable way, taking the sting out of he
mother's words.

"Thank you, I think." She took a sip of her margarita, tas
ing the salty-sweet tang of it, her eye still on Cam's, and som
how, the evening didn't seem so bad.

It was impossible to stay depressed when everyone else wa

such high spirits. The food was hot and spicy, the *salsa* brought tears to her eyes, but so did the laughter. She couldn't have said if it was the tequila in the margaritas or the company, but her depression lifted and suddenly turning thirty wasn't such a big deal.

She ate too much, drank more than she usually did and tried not to stare at Cam. The man was really much too handsome. The fact that he was also a nice guy made him almost too perfect a package.

Somewhere during the course of the evening, she forgot that she'd only just met him. There was something about him that made it impossible to stay uptight. He was warm and friendly and had a quiet sense of humor that blended surprisingly well with the more raucous humor of Jimbo. And it didn't hurt that he looked at her as if he found her as attractive as she found him. In the condition Lacey's ego was in, she needed the boost.

"We should go out and do something exciting." That was Lisa, her voice ever-so-slightly slurred. Her husband looked at her, his expression indulgent.

"Like what?"

"Well, I don't know." She crunched a tortilla chip. "Something different. We should do something fun. After all, a woman only turns thirty once."

"I don't know. I seem to recall you turned thirty three or four times." Frank ducked the playful swat she aimed at him. Everyone laughed, and Lacey tried to ignore the envy that crept over her as she watched them.

"We should go to Las Vegas." Betts's breathy voice cut through the laughter. Everyone turned to look at her.

"Las Vegas?" Lacey didn't know who spoke but the tone expressed her feelings precisely. Nobody went to Las Vegas on a whim.

"Sure. Why not? Las Vegas is really exciting. We could have loads of fun and really celebrate Lacey's birthday in style. I mean, a woman really ought to go all out on her thirtieth." She blinked her soft, slightly owlish blue eyes at the rest of

the table. "I think Las Vegas would be loads of fun. Don't
you, Lacey?"

All eyes turned to Lacey. She stared at her friends. Nobody
drove all that way for no reason but to celebrate a birthday.
You made plans for something like that. You spent the weekend. It was an absurd idea.

"I have an aunt in Las Vegas. She's a terrible gossip. I avoid
her at all costs."

Everyone considered the matter solemnly. "You don't have
to go see her." Frank offered the solution and everyone nodded.

Lacey considered. If she said no, they might all decide to go
home. And then she'd have to go home. And there'd be nobody
there but that awful mirror that made her look like a hag. And
Cam would go home and she might not see him again for
years—maybe not ever. The tequila made her thinking slightly
fuzzy, but she knew she didn't want to go home.

"Las Vegas sounds great."

It seemed as if her agreement was all they'd been waiting
for. Suddenly everyone thought Las Vegas was a great idea. If
she'd had more time, Lacey might have changed her mind, but
no one gave her a chance. Before she knew what was happening, she was wedged into the back seat of Jimbo's 1955 Cadillac convertible and they were on their way to Nevada.

Jimbo was behind the wheel, the only one of the group who
was stone-cold sober, since he never drank. Betts was snuggled
up next to him, leaving most of the front seat empty. It was
the back seat that was a trifle crowded, with four.

It had started out that Lisa was going to sit in front and Frank
was going to sit in the back. That was why Lacey had gotten
into the back seat next to Cam. At the last minute, Lisa changed
her mind, deciding that she wanted to sit next to her husband.
The end result was that Lacey had ended up practically in
Cam's lap—a surprisingly comfortable spot. It didn't occur to
any of them that Cam or Lacey could have moved to the front
seat.

Halfway across the desert, Jimbo started to sing, his scratchy baritone murdering "Happy Days Are Here Again." The rest of the drive was filled with Top 40 songs from the past forty years. No one was safe. Everyone from Gershwin to Huey Lewis was offered up to the clear desert sky.

Lacey found herself snuggling closer to Cam, perfectly content to have his arm around her shoulders, his thigh pressed against hers. Funny, she'd always kept a bit of a distance physically between herself and other people. She wasn't the backslapping, hugging type. She'd only met Cam a few hours ago, but it felt right to have his long body so close. In fact, it felt rather nice.

Somewhere in the back of her mind, a warning bell sounded, but she ignored it. Tonight she wasn't going to think about anything but having a good time.

YOU KNOW, my mother thinks there's something wrong with me." Lacey waved a limp French fry for emphasis.

Lisa heaved a sigh. "Don't all parents think there's something wrong with their kids? My mother refuses to speak to me until I have a baby. I'll fool her, though. If I do have a kid, I'm going to teach it to bite my mother."

Frank shook his head, his expression solemn. "Be easier to get a dog. That's the thing. We'll get a dog and teach it to bite your mother."

Lisa gave him a fuzzy glare. "You never have liked my mother."

"So? Neither do you." The discussion might have degenerated into a fight, but Betts provided a timely interruption.

"My mother never understood why I wanted to be an actress. She wanted me to be a doctor."

Lacey and Lisa looked at Betts. Even after one too many drinks, it was impossible to imagine Betts—of the platinumblond hair and breathy voice and big blue eyes—having a bedside manner. She was enough to give a male patient a coronary, and any female patient would simply die of despair.

"That's a shame." Frank's sympathy might have been mor
believable if his gaze hadn't been firmly fixed on her ampl
cleavage. Lisa's elbow in his ribs recalled his wandering gaze

"I tried to explain to her that it wasn't a big deal these day
to be unmarried at thirty." Lacey's attention hadn't wandere
from the original subject.

They were seated in a shiny red vinyl booth in the back
a restaurant that was connected—inevitable in Las Vegas—
one of the casinos. At three in the morning, the casino was sti
lively, full of people determined to go home winners despi
the odds against them.

Arriving in Las Vegas, they'd agreed that food was the fir
order of business before they decided on just how to finis
celebrating Lacey's birthday. The food was mediocre b
cheap. The management wanted to encourage people to sper
their money at the gaming tables rather than on the dinir
tables.

Lacey dunked another French fry in catsup and chewed
feeling a vague melancholy threatening to creep over her.

"Does your mother hassle you because you're not married?
she asked Cam. If she'd been more alert, she might have n
ticed the strange gentleness in his eyes. But alert was not som
thing she had great quantities of in the wee hours of the mor
ing after a few too many drinks.

"She prods a little once in a while," he admitted.

Lacey shook her head sadly. "Parents are all alike. The
think marriage leads to eternal happiness."

"You know, Lacey, you and Cam should get married. Th
would solve all your problems." It was Jimbo who made th
suggestion, his eyes bright and sharp.

There was a moment's silence, and then everyone at the tab
laughed, long and hard. Nobody could joke quite like Jimbo

"Come on. We came here to celebrate Lacey's birthday.
think we should go dancing." Frank's suggestion was greet
with unanimous agreement and the restaurant was abandon
for a livelier atmosphere.

Half an hour later Lacey discovered that Cam's arms felt very bit as strong as they looked. Crowded onto the tiny dance oor, he held her close and she didn't object. It felt wonderful) rest her cheek on the soft cotton of his shirt. She could feel ie beat of his heart just under her ear, and that felt wonderful,)o.

She tilted her head back, her eyes meeting his in the dim ght. "You're a good dancer."

"Thanks. You're pretty good yourself. I got a lot of practice ancing with my sisters."

"Sisters? How many?"

"Three sisters and three brothers."

Lacey's brow furrowed. "That's six." She was pleased with erself for coming up with the figure.

"Seven, counting me."

"There's only one of me." She frowned. "Maybe that's /hy my mother worries about me so much. Although I can't ally blame her. Do you know what the probabilities are of a /oman my age getting married?"

"Thirty doesn't seem that old."

She ignored his attempt to alleviate harsh reality. "I read iis article once that said that a woman has a better chance of eing struck by lightning *twice* than she does of getting married fter she's thirty." She looked at him solemnly.

Cam grinned, his eyes a bright and shining blue. "Twice, uh? Those are pretty slim odds."

Lacey nodded. The margaritas and the wine she'd had before iey danced combined to make her melancholy a distant and ot totally unpleasant experience. Somehow, held close to 'am's broad chest, she just couldn't be depressed.

"I'll probably die an old maid."

"I don't think so."

She stared up at him, blinking owlishly. "No? Why not?"

"Gut feeling. You just don't look destined for old maid-ood."

"Thank you."

The music was a slow romantic ballad that talked of lov
forever lost. Cam's hand moved slowly up her back. Lacey fe
a slow shiver work its way up her spine, an awareness she'
never felt before. His feet barely moved, keeping up a pretens
of dancing. Lacey couldn't drag her eyes from his. The room
the day, everything faded away, lost in the brilliant blue of hi
eyes.

As his head lowered, she noticed vaguely that there appeare
to be something wrong with her breathing. But it didn't seer
important. Her fingers tightened on his shoulders, her lips par
ing in soft anticipation.

When his mouth touched hers, it felt so right, so perfect.
was as if they'd kissed before, as if he'd held her before. He
arms slid upward to circle his neck as her mouth softened be
neath the pressure of his.

He tasted of wine. His mouth was warm and firm, coaxing
hungry, demanding, promising. Lacey's head spun with th
pleasure of it. Tomorrow she might blame her reaction on to
much wine, but tonight she had a sense of destiny. Fate. Th
moment, this kiss, had to happen.

Her lashes fluttered and her eyes opened slowly as Cam dre
away. On the dark dance floor no one seemed to have notice
what had just happened. No one else seemed to feel the groun
rocking under their feet. Lacey stared up at Cam, feeling as
she was falling into the bright, bright blue of his eyes. Fallin
further and further until she could never climb out.

But then, she couldn't imagine ever wanting to.

After that, the night grew hazier. When she tried to recall
afterward, her memories came in sporadic bits, like glimps
of a countryside seen through train windows.

They'd danced some more. Another stolen kiss or two ha
followed that first devastating assault on her senses. There'
been more wine and a great deal of laughter. Then a shar
clear memory of a bouquet of flowers—neon flowers. The
was a volley of cheers and applause, and she had a vague sens

hat she was the center of this approval, and then the noise and
ights were gone.

She and Cam were alone, somewhere dim and private. A
small bell had rung in the back of her mind, a warning Lacey
gnored. She was floating on a sea of pleasure. No cares, no
esponsibilities, just these wonderful liquid sensations that
illed her, sweeping everything else aside. She was drowning
n them, but she wasn't frightened. There was someone with
her. Someone strong and warm who held her, kept her safe.

She'd drifted to sleep, aware that everything had changed.
Not in the way her life usually changed, which was only after
careful thought on her part. No, this was a sudden, cataclysmic
change that swept away everything before it.

She might regret it later, but at the moment all she was aware
of was that she'd never felt quite so content.

Chapter Three

The noise sounded like a sonic rendition of hell. It boome
through her aching head with relentless force, dragging he
away from the oblivion of sleep and forcing her to move
Movement was not a good idea.

Lacey groped for the source of the hideous sound, som
distant part of her mind telling her that the noise could b
stopped—and she had the power to stop it. Her hand connecte
with something smooth and cool. She fumbled with it, her fin
gers curling around a handle and pulling. The bells stoppe
and she sighed with relief.

The phone. That was it. The phone had been making th
awful noise. But when you picked up a receiver, the person o
the other end expected you to say hello. She dragged the re
ceiver toward her.

"Hello?" Her voice sounded as thick and fuzzy as she fel

"Lacey? Honey, is that you? Darlin', this is your mothe
Are you there?" The words sounded muffled, and it took Lace
a moment to realize it was because there was a sheet betwee
her and the receiver.

"Just a minute, Mother." She clawed at the sheet, pullin
it away from her face, and dragged herself into a sitting pos
tion. The pain in her head intensified. It seemed to be centere
right behind her eyes, radiating outward from there to mak
her entire body ache.

"Hello?" She tried again, this time turning the receiver so that the mouthpiece was next to her mouth instead of her ear. It made a remarkable difference in the sound.

"Lacey? Darlin', is that you? I know I shouldn't have called, but I just couldn't wait to scold you." Mamie's tone did not sound like a scold. She sounded as if she was about to burst with pleasure. Lacey tuned out the ecstatic ramblings, uncertain of their cause. She studied her surroundings through slitted eyes.

A hotel room. This was definitely a hotel room. A luxurious hotel room. She shifted her legs and was rewarded with a rolling sensation that didn't feel anything like a nice solid mattress. She was in a water bed. What on earth would she be doing in a water bed in a hotel room? She hated water beds.

A niggling sense of disaster gnawed at the back of her mind. There was something she should remember. She looked down and was surprised to find that she was nude. That was odd. She never slept in the nude.

A muffled sound penetrated her absorption and she froze, feeling her heart nearly stop. Mamie's voice droned on in her ear, but Lacey was no longer listening. She had more important things on her mind. More important than anything her mother might be saying. More important than where she was or what she wasn't wearing. Someone had just groaned. Someone very nearby. Someone in the same bed.

Lacey turned her head stiffly, the phone still held to her ear. There was someone else in the bed, someone whose tanned back contrasted with the snowy white sheets. Tanned, muscular and very bare. Her wide eyes traveled the entire length of it before stopping at the sheet that was draped low on a pair of masculine hips.

A man. There was a man in bed with her.

She squeaked and grabbed for the sheet, drawing it up over her bare breasts. She couldn't drag her eyes away from the bed's other occupant. Bits and pieces of the previous evening and night flashed through her aching head. Her dress caught in the car door, the Mexican restaurant, drinks, the mad drive to Las Vegas, more drinks, and then things became blurrier. She remembered dancing with a man, a man whose eyes had been bluer than a summer sky.

And there were other memories, a little mistier, a little harder to recapture. But they were enough to drive the last tinges of color from her cheeks.

There was another groan, and the bed's other occupant turned over, exposing an endless expanse of bare chest. His lashes flickered and then lifted. His eyes were still blue, but now they were bloodshot. Lacey stared at him, speechless. She was in Las Vegas, in bed—naked—with a man she'd known less than twenty-four hours, and unless she was delirious, they'd done more than just sleep together. And, as the final insanity, her mother was on the phone sounding as if she'd just won the lottery.

Cam stared at Lacey for a long silent moment. He shut his eyes and then opened them again as if hoping she would turn out to be a figment of his imagination. He couldn't possibly wish it as fervently as Lacey did. But nothing had changed when he opened his eyes again. He looked at her and then shut his eyes, groaning as he buried his face in the pillow.

Lacey knew just how he felt.

"Lacey? Honey? Are you there?" Mamie's voice was taking on a worried edge and Lacey responded automatically.

"I'm here, Mother." The words brought another groan from her unwanted bedmate.

"Oh, sweetheart, I'm so happy for you I could just cry. Why didn't you tell me about him? Phoebe says he's just the handsomest thing. What's his name, sugar?"

"Name? His name?" The ache in her head intensified. What on earth was her mother talking about? What did her awful Aunt Phoebe have to do with any of this? She'd made it a point to avoid the woman for years. She had a vague memory of someone telling her that they wouldn't visit her aunt. And why did Mamie want to know his name?

"Cam...er...Cam..."

"Cameron McCleary, for what it's worth." The words were muffled by the pillow, but distinguishable.

"Cameron McCleary, for what—" She parroted the answer into the receiver, catching herself at the last minute.

"Oh, honey, that's a lovely name."

Lacey pulled the receiver away from her ear and stared at it. Why was Mamie so happy about her only daughter being in bed with a total stranger? It was a dream. No, make that a nightmare. That was the only possible explanation. This was all some awful, horrible nightmare. And she'd wake up in her own bed and find that none of this had happened.

"You'll bring him to meet me when you get home, won't you?"

"Ah...if you'd like."

"If I'd like? Don't be silly, sugar. I'm dyin' to meet him. We'll have a wonderful reception just as soon as you're settled."

"Of course." Lacey gave up trying to make any sense out of it. If this was all a dream, then none of it would make sense anyway. She'd stop fighting it and just pretend she knew what was going on. "I really have to go now, Mother."

"Of course. I know I shouldn't have called, but I just couldn't wait to congratulate you."

"Talk to you soon."

She fumbled behind her for the phone, finding it more by accident than design, and set the receiver down. Her eyes didn't leave Cam's large form. The room was amazingly still. Nobody moved, nobody spoke. Lacey was still hoping to wake up and find that none of this had happened.

She jumped when Cam suddenly rolled over and sat up. He groaned, burying his head in his hands. He was too large, too bare, too male. Lacey edged toward the side of the bed.

"I'm going to die." He made the announcement with calm certainty. For an instant she felt a twinge of sympathy. She knew just what he meant. Her own head still felt as if it might roll off her shoulders at any moment.

Cam turned his head, his eyes catching hers, and Lacey jumped like a startled doe. She stared at him, trying to think of something witty to say, something to make it clear that she wasn't in the least disturbed to find herself in this situation. Nothing came to mind.

He didn't say anything. He just looked at her for a long silent moment and then returned his head to his hands, his fingers burrowing into tousled brown hair, his shoulders hunched, his whole position indicative of great pain.

Clearly someone had to take charge of the situation. They couldn't sit here all day. Lacey didn't need to look at herself to know that she was not dressed for taking charge. A sheet clutched to her chest was certainly not in any dress-for-success handbook. Her eyes skittered around the room, looking for her clothes.

Her cheeks flushed as she took in their location—scattered across the carpet, intimately entwined with a pair of jeans, a shirt and some decidedly masculine underwear. It was not how she was accustomed to seeing her clothes. Besides, they were well out of reach.

She glanced at her companion and then looked away. This was going to require some cooperation.

"Don't open your eyes."

"If I open my eyes, they're going to fall out of my head." Cam's voice was muffled, but there was no doubting his sincerity.

Lacey swung her feet off the bed, trying to keep one eye on Cam and one on what she was doing. It wasn't easy. Her right foot came down on thick carpeting, but her left landed on something crackly. Tucking the sheet behind her to make sure that nothing vital was exposed, she leaned down and picked up a sheet of heavy parchment paper. With a quick glance at Cam to make sure he hadn't opened his eyes while she wasn't looking, she glanced at the paper.

Her muffled shriek echoed in Cam's pounding head. He clutched at his ears, squeezing his eyes tightly shut, trying to keep the pain at a manageable level. A thousand small children wearing tap shoes were dancing behind his eyes. There was a pause and then a muffled moan from Lacey's direction.

Aware of his promise to keep his eyes shut, he opened them warily. If she was being attacked by a burglar, she surely wouldn't expect him not to look. Of course, in his current condition, he wasn't sure what good he'd be in the event of an attack by anything much larger than a gerbil.

Lacey was sitting on the side of the bed, and despite his pain, Cam couldn't help running an appreciative eye over the smooth length of her back. He was even capable of a vague twinge of regret when he got to where the sheet cut off his view.

She moaned again and he brought his eyes back up, noting the slump to her shoulders. "What's wrong?"

She jumped as if she'd forgotten his presence. It was a measure of how upset she was that she didn't automatically reach behind her to check the position of the sheet. Circumstances had gone beyond worry over modesty.

Lacey turned slowly and handed him the sheet of paper. Cam took it, his eyes on her face. She was pale, her eyes wide green pools of shocked disbelief.

"Read it." She sounded like the voice of doom.

Cam lowered his eyes to the paper, convinced he didn't want to see what was written on it. He was right.

It was a printed form, black ink on thick ivory paper. At the top, in elaborate script were written the words: Little Chapel of Happiness in the Desert Dell. What the hell was Desert Dell, he thought. Then he squeezed his eyes shut and then opened them again, focusing on the rest of the form.

Under ordinary circumstances, it wouldn't have taken him more than a moment to read and assimilate the information on the form. But these were far from ordinary circumstances, and he didn't want to take a chance on misinterpreting anything.

Unfortunately, it was pretty hard to misinterpret what he was seeing. It was all quite straightforward.

He was holding a marriage certificate. A simple piece of paper that united two people in the bonds of holy matrimony. Even more unfortunate was the fact that the names were clear and easily read. Cameron David McCleary. Lacey Anne Newton. It took several seconds for the significance of those names to sink in.

When it did, he shut his eyes, absorbing the impact. A marriage certificate with those names on it could mean only one thing. He was married. Married to the woman who was sharing this bed—*reluctantly* sharing this bed.

He opened his eyes and looked at Lacey, seeing the same questions and answers in her eyes. He dropped the certificate, letting it float to the rumpled covers.

"Good morning, Mrs. McCleary." The joke was weak, but it didn't deserve the appalled expression that crept over her delicate features.

She looked at him, skimming over his bare chest to where the sheet rested at his waist. She didn't have to see any farther to know he didn't have a stitch on. His shorts were lying on the carpet in intimate proximity to her silk panties. She didn't have anything on. He didn't have anything on. The implications boggled the mind.

Cam's thoughts were following a similar path. Looking at the provocative pairing of their clothing, he had a sudden vivid memory of skin even softer than the silk that covered it. A sweet response that had seemed so right, so inevitable at the time. And something else. He closed his eyes, feeling the pain in his head intensify.

"Look, I—"

"Obviously, that's a fake of some sort." Lacey pointed to the form he held.

If she knew what he'd been about to say, it was clear she didn't want to talk about it right now. Cam allowed the change of subject, at least momentarily. He glanced down at the certificate and shrugged. "Looks pretty authentic to me."

"Well, it can't be authentic. I mean we wouldn't have—*I* wouldn't have just—" She waved her hand at the paper, unable to get the words out.

"Gotten married?" Cam finished helpfully and was rewarded with her glare.

"Right. People just don't do that, no matter how much they've had to drink."

"Oh, I don't know. People have done stranger things."

"Well, *I* haven't done stranger things. I don't do things like that or like this." She waved her hand, indicating herself, the bed and—most of all—him.

Cam grinned, beginning to enjoy himself despite the headache that gnawed at the back of his eyes. Maybe he was still feeling the effects of overindulgence. Whatever it was, he had a slightly light-headed feeling that things weren't as black as they looked. "You mean you don't wake up in strange hotel rooms with men you barely know?"

"No, I don't."

"That's good to know. I'd hate to think that I'd married a woman of loose moral character and easy virtue."

Lacey's eyes turned frosty. "We are not married. And my virtue is—was—unimpeachable." Each word was bitten off, separate and distinct from the others so that there could be no mistaking their meaning.

Cam sobered. God knows, the latter was the truth. It was the first item that was still in question.

"This says we're married." He nodded to the paper in his hand and wished he hadn't. The movement got the children tap-dancing again.

"Obviously that's a fake." She spoke firmly, as if that would be enough to make it true.

Cam shrugged, resisting the urge to argue further. Maybe he was still drunk, but somehow this situation didn't upset him as much as it should have. Whether the marriage certificate was real or fake, he couldn't seem to work up any real anxiety about it.

"If you'll close your eyes," she said, "I could get my clothes." She didn't look at him, and Cam felt a twinge of guilt. He could see she didn't share his sanguine attitude toward the situation. He was acting too insensitively.

"Sure. I won't look."

Lacey hesitated, throwing a quick glance at his face. His eyes were tightly shut, but that didn't mean he couldn't open them again.

"Go on. I won't look. I promise."

Surprisingly she believed him. Something about Cameron McCleary made her trust him—which probably said something about her sanity, considering the current situation.

She eased off the bed and hurried across the carpet to her clothes. The air-conditioning felt chilly on her bare body, but the goose bumps that rose on her skin were caused more by nerves than the temperature. She snatched up her clothes, trying to avoid touching any of Cam's garments.

Throwing one last glance over her shoulder, she scurried into the bathroom and shut the door behind her with a feeling of relief. The bathroom was as luxurious as the bedroom, all pale green tile and chrome. But decor was not a prime consideration to Lacey at the moment. All that mattered was that she be alone, with a door between her and the rest of the world. Although, right now, the only part of the world that concerned her was what lay just beyond the door she was leaning against.

She drew a deep breath and forced herself to walk to the sink and turn on the tap. If she still retained some hope that this was going to turn out to be a dream, it was shattered when splashing cold water on her face didn't wake her up.

Lacey raised her head reluctantly, meeting her eyes in the mirror. She was really here, in this hotel room, with a man she'd apparently spent the night with. A man whose name was next to hers on a marriage certificate. It didn't bear thinking about. No matter how she looked at it, she couldn't quite figure out how it had happened.

She closed her eyes, trying to piece together the memories of the night before. She'd caught her dress in the car door and he'd helped her free it. Then he'd been sitting at the table and Jimbo had introduced them. Everyone had been having a great time, and someone had suggested they go to Las Vegas.

She groaned and splashed more water on her face, scrubbing at her skin. She should have known she was drunk when Las Vegas didn't sound like such a bad idea. Right then and there, she should have called a cab to take her home. Thirtieth birthday or not, there was no excuse for this insanity. Las Vegas, for crying out loud!

The marriage certificate had to be a fake. That's all there was to it. It wasn't possible that she'd actually married a man she'd just met. On the heels of the thought came a dim memory of someone saying that she and Cam ought to get married, that it would solve all their problems. Everyone had laughed, but after a few glasses of wine, maybe the idea hadn't sounded so funny.

Lacey sank down on the edge of the tub, one arm resting on the sink, her fingers trailing in the cold water. She stared at the fluffy white rug at her feet. Other memories were creeping in. They'd played the slot machines for a while and then they'd gone dancing. She didn't remember much about the music, but she recalled looking into his eyes and thinking that she'd never seen anything quite such a deep, clear blue.

She closed her own eyes, resting her forehead on her arm. He'd kissed her. That was surprisingly vivid. She could remember the way he'd tasted, the scent of him. She could also remember the way her body had tingled and how right his arms had felt around her.

After that, things grew considerably more fuzzy until there was a sudden, sharp image of a neon bouquet of flowers hanging over a pale pink altar and a solemn-faced man looking at her, looking at *them*.

Lacey swallowed a sob. She'd really done it. She'd actually married Cameron McCleary—a man she'd met only hours ago, a man she knew nothing about. And as if marrying him wasn't enough, she'd slept with him. Made love with him. Her memories on that point were even more vague, but they were enough.

She leaned her forehead against the cold tile, squeezing her eyes shut to hold back the tears. Crying wasn't going to solve anything now. What was done was done. Drunk or not, how could she have done something so stupid, so irresponsible? You'd think that, after thirty years, a certain kind of behavior would be ingrained enough to survive even the assault of too many margaritas.

A solitary tear, which escaped to trail forlornly down her cheek, was impatiently dashed away. She stood up, drawing in a deep breath before facing her reflection again in the mirror.

She straightened the slump of her shoulders and took another deep breath. One thing she'd learned by the ripe old age of thirty: there was no erasing what had already been done. You just had to learn to live with it.

Obviously this situation had to be straightened out. Sitting in the bathroom moping about it wasn't going to get them anywhere. They'd had too much to drink, and they'd done something stupid. Those were the facts and there was no changing them. What was done was done. But it could be undone.

Lacey might have felt a little better if she'd been able to read Cam's thoughts on the situation. The moment she was safely out of sight, he swung his legs out of bed and reached for his underwear and jeans. His calm facade cracked in several places, helped along by a steady stream of muttered curses.

A man didn't get to the ripe old age of thirty-six without doing some stupid things, things he shouldn't have done, but this certainly took the cake as far as he was concerned. He jerked the jeans on, trying to figure out just how this situation had happened. There wasn't an answer, and he cursed some more as he reached for his shirt.

He strode to the window and stared out at the sprawl that was Las Vegas. In daylight, it lacked the glitter that made it seem almost magical at night. Now it was just a sprawling desert town with little to recommend it unless you wanted to gamble.

God knows, he'd done enough gambling while he was here, even if it wasn't the kind that emptied his pockets. He turned his back to the window and stared at the bathroom door. What was Lacey thinking? Lacey. The woman he'd made love to last night. His wife.

Lacey steeled herself and reached for the doorknob. She smoothed her hair again, wishing for a brush. The best she'd been able to do was finger-comb the tangles out. While she was in the wishing department, she might as well wish that she was home safe and sound in her own bed, she thought, and that none of this had happened.

The situation had gone beyond wishing. She opened the door and stepped into the bedroom, hoping she looked like a calm adult and not like the nervous wreck she really was.

Cam was standing by the window, and he swung around as she stepped onto the plush gray carpeting. Lacey forgot how to breathe. He'd pulled on his jeans, which were zipped but unbuttoned. His shirt hung open, exposing his chest. His feet were still bare, but he didn't seem to feel as if that put him at any disadvantage. Of course, when you were six foot two, maybe it took more than being barefoot.

"Hi."

"Hi." She had to clear her throat before she could get the word out. It was nerves. It had nothing to do with the pattern of golden brown curls that swirled over his chest.

"How's your head?"

"Okay. It's not hurting much. How's yours?"

"Better." His mouth twisted in a self-deprecating smile. "I haven't had a hangover in a long time. I'd forgotten how awful they are. I guess that will teach me not to drink too much."

"Me, too." Lacey edged her way into the room, trying not

to look at his bare chest, trying not to notice the way his jeans clung to his legs, trying to look as if she did this sort of thing every day.

Cam slanted her a shrewd glance, and she had the feeling that he saw through her casual facade to the trembling little girl inside.

Lacey looked around the room, seeking something to distract her from him. She flushed when she saw her panty hose neatly laid out on the foot of the bed, her shoes lying drunkenly beneath them. Cam followed her glance.

"They were under my jeans." The minute he said the words, he wished he'd kept his mouth shut. He'd been trying for a casual approach that would ease some of her obvious embarrassment, but it would have been better to say nothing. Lacey's flush deepened to a fiery red as she snatched up the offending hose and stuffed it into the pocket of her dress.

"Thanks." The word was hardly audible. She didn't look at him.

Cam studied her averted face and gave a quiet sigh. He wished there was something he could say that would reassure her, but the situation was what it was and there wasn't much he could do about it. The pounding behind his eyes had eased, but his brain still felt as if it was functioning at half power.

Just beyond Lacey, on the bed, he could see the corner of the marriage certificate—their marriage certificate. If it was genuine, of course. He didn't really doubt that it was. So, he was married. He felt detached, as if he were watching a play. But this wasn't a play, this was his life—his and Lacey's. And there were things they had to talk about.

"Lacey—"

"We need—"

They both started at the same moment and then stopped. Cam gestured with one hand.

"Ladies first."

She hesitated a moment, her eyes flickering over his chest.

he looked away, staring at a point just over his shoulder. ''I
as just going to say that I think we need to talk.''

''Funny, that's exactly what I was going to say.''

His tone invited her to relax, but the best she could manage
as a weak half smile. Cam studied her, wishing he could think
f something to say that would put her at ease.

A knock on the door made them both jump. Cam cocked his
yebrow at Lacey, but she shook her head.

''Who is it?''

''Room service.'' The voice that answered Cam's inquiry
as muffled but understandable.

Cam shrugged in answer to Lacey's questioning glance. *He*
adn't called room service. He walked to the door and pulled
open. Standing outside was a waiter in a crisp white jacket,
room-service trolley in front of him. He smiled at Cam, his
xpression bright and helpful.

''Your coffee and croissants, Mr. McCleary.'' He wheeled
e cart in as Cam backed away, but Cam wasn't paying any
tention to him. Behind the waiter was another visitor, his
road face wreathed in a cheerful smile, his stocky figure en-
ased in a crisp shirt and jeans, a newspaper tucked under one
m.

Jimbo grinned, his eyes full of sly amusement. ''So, how's
e happy couple?''

Chapter Four

"You!" Cam made the word sound like a curse.

He pounced—there was no other word for it. His long finger closed over Jimbo's heavy shoulder as if afraid that, withou physical restraint, the other might try to escape. Jimbo's gr didn't waver as Cam all but dragged him into the room.

"You low-life scum. You did this on purpose. I suppose yo think it's funny."

The waiter backed away from the table, his eyes uneasy, bu Jimbo wasn't fazed by Cam's fierce tone. His grin widened, possible. He took the bill from the waiter, who hadn't bee quite nervous enough to leave without it and a tip, and signe it with a flourish, then handed it back with a crisp greenbac He waited until the man was gone before answering Cam accusation.

"Funny? What should I think is funny? And by the wa it's customary to offer a greeting beyond 'low-life scum Something along the lines of 'Good morning' or 'How's trick might be appropriate. Good morning, Lacey."

"Good morning." She responded automatically. Courtes was as ingrained in her as brushing her teeth. From the tir Lacey was tiny, Mamie had drilled into her only child the beli that bad manners were one of the cardinal sins. The good Lo had just forgotten to add them to the list.

"There. You see, Cam? That's how it's done. You really should work on it."

"The only thing I feel like working on right now is beating you to a pulp."

Jimbo blinked, widening his eyes in an expression of exaggerated innocence. "Why are you upset with me? I didn't tell you to order those last two scotches. I didn't force them down you. It's hardly my fault if you've got a hangover. You should have some coffee. It'll improve your mood."

The casual comment broke the spell that had been holding Lacey speechless. All the panic she'd been trying to hold back swept over her in a wave.

"Improve his mood? Improve his mood?" Her voice rose to something perilously close to a shriek. "What about *my* mood? How do you think I feel? *We* feel?" She waved one hand, linking herself and Cam with the gesture. "I woke up this morning in bed with a man I'd just met. I had to talk to my mother before I'd figured out what was going on and then—then I step on this."

She snatched the marriage certificate off the bed and waved it in Jimbo's face. "Do you know what this is? *This* is a marriage certificate with my name on it. My name and his. I didn't even know what his last name was when my mother asked.

"And that's another thing. How could you call my mother and tell her about this…insanity? Do you realize she thinks all this is real? How am I supposed to explain this to her?"

"I didn't call your mother," Jimbo told her, calm in the face of her rage.

"Ha! If you didn't call her, how did she find out about it?"

"Well, my guess would be that maybe someone saw the picture and called her with the news."

"Picture? What picture?" It was Cam who asked the question. Lacey seemed to have lost her voice.

"The one in the newspaper. I brought you a copy. I knew you'd want one for your wedding album."

The look Cam gave him should have fried him to a cinder

on the spot. Lacey was beyond even a weak frown. She looke
down at the paper Jimbo held out. It was folded in half and i
the lower left-hand corner was a photograph. She thought long
ingly of the blurred newspaper pictures that were often such
vital part of her favorite mystery novels. Why wasn't this phot
one of those vague images of shadowy figures? Why did thi
one have to be so clear and sharp?

The flash had caught them in a moment of laughter. He
head was tilted back against Cam's shoulder, her eyes smilin
up into his. He was in profile as he looked down at her, th
perfect masculine contrast to her femininity.

The picture was charming, romantic, and made Lacey wan
to scream. The headline above the photo stated: Love Bloom
in the Desert. She moaned and closed her eyes.

"Why did they print this photo?" Cam's question was su
picious, but Jimbo shrugged, the picture of innocence.

"Newspapers call it human interest. It's a change from al
the bad news. Give me a break, Cam. I didn't bribe the pho
tographer to take the picture."

"This still doesn't explain how Lacey's mother found o
about this mess." Lacey glanced up at Cam, surprised an
rather pleased by the protective tone of his voice.

"How should I know?" Jimbo shrugged. "Didn't you sa
you had an aunt in town?"

Lacey shut her eyes. "God, yes. Aunt Phoebe. A hideo
woman, and Mother did mention her this morning. I was ju
too groggy to make the connection."

"I bet your aunt saw the picture and called your mother."

"It's just the kind of thing she'd do." Lacey sighed an
rubbed at her aching forehead. "I keep thinking this is all son
kind of a nightmare and I'm going to wake up any minute sa
in my own bed."

"This is hardly my idea of good fun, either," Cam told h
sharply.

"Do I smell trouble in paradise so soon?" Jimbo's arch to

brought two pairs of slightly bloodshot eyes to bear on him. They were neither amused nor friendly.

"If you want to live to see another day, James, I suggest you resist the urge to make any more smart remarks. I'm barely restraining my desire to tear you limb from limb as it is."

Lacey nodded, showing her approval of Cam's bloodthirsty feelings.

"Hey, why do I get the blame?"

"Because you were the only one who was sober last night. You should have put a stop to this whole absurd mess before it got to this point." Cam pinched the bridge of his nose, trying to ease the pain that throbbed behind his eyes.

"I tried. Believe me, I tried." Jimbo moved to the table and poured two cups of coffee, handing one to each of his companions.

"You didn't try hard enough," Cam told him sourly, his disposition not visibly improved by a sip of the steaming black liquid.

"What was I supposed to do? Knock you out? You were bound and determined that getting married was a great idea. The only thing I could do was offer my services as best man." He took a sip of his own coffee. "It was a lovely service."

Cam did not look impressed. "What about everybody else? Why didn't Frank do something, or Lisa, or your friend, what's-her-name?"

Jimbo shook his head. "They were all as drunk as you two. Betts cried a lot. Weddings do that to her. Frank and Lisa thought it was so romantic that they renewed their vows right here on the spot."

"Oh, God." Lacey's gasp brought both men's attention to her. Her gaze skittered from Jimbo to Cam and then away. She didn't want to look at Cam. Looking at him reminded her of waking up in bed with him this morning. It reminded her that he was married to this man. Married, for heaven's sake. She paced to the window and then back again, her fingers knotted around the thick porcelain coffee cup.

Cam watched her quietly, his expression unreadable. Jimbo watched them both, his eyes bright with interest. Lacey started to speak, met Cam's eyes and stopped. She continued to pace.

Cam's gaze wandered to the soft swishing motion of her skirt. There was something so essentially feminine in the gentle sway of her hips. He remembered the way she'd looked earlier the sheet clutched to her chest, her hair a golden tangle on her shoulders, her wide green eyes full of shock at finding him in the bed beside her. Not even a hangover could dim the delicate beauty of her.

He was glad to see that his taste was impeccable, even when drunk. He pushed the frivolous thought away. This was a serious matter. Marriage was a serious matter. He should be horrified and appalled that he'd jumped into something so important in a moment of drunken stupidity. Yet he didn't feel particularly horrified.

Maybe it was the lingering effects of the scotch. Maybe it was the children who still tap-danced behind his eyes with malicious delight. Whatever it was, the situation just didn't seem as appalling as it should have.

Lacey paced back toward the two men and stopped. Her fingers gripped the coffee cup so tightly that Cam half expected to see it crack beneath the pressure. Her eyes reflected all the distress he should be feeling and wasn't.

"What's done is done. We're married and that's all there is to it. There's no sense in trying to place the blame." Her eyes settled on Jimbo and he shrugged his innocence. She took a deep breath and continued, "Obviously, what we need to do now is to figure out how to undo this mess. It shouldn't be a problem. We'll just get an annulment. That's simple enough."

Her announcement was greeted with total silence. Cam stared at her, his eyes a cool reflective blue, giving no clue to his thoughts. She glanced at him and then away. Every time she looked at him, she remembered too much. Things she had no business remembering about a man who was a total stranger. The ripple of sleek muscle beneath her palms; the feel of crisply curling hair against her breasts. She brought her thoughts to a skidding halt. She'd deal with that aspect of the debacle later.

"Why?" Jimbo's question echoed in the quiet room.

"Why what?" Lacey asked. Cam said nothing.

"Why get an annulment?" Jimbo spoke slowly and precisely, as if to let the impact of each word be felt separately.

Lacey's mouth dropped open, her eyes wide with disbelief. "Why? Are you nuts? The reasons are obvious."

"To whom?" Jimbo sipped his coffee, his expression calm, his English ever correct.

"To whom? To whom? To anyone with half a brain!" Lacey gestured wildly, splashing lukewarm coffee onto her wrist. Cam reached out, taking the cup from her and handing her a napkin. "You explain it to him, Cam. It's obvious."

Jimbo forestalled Cam's reply. "I don't think it's obvious at all. Think about it. What's so awful about being married? Don't tell me you weren't attracted to each other last night. It was obvious, even to someone with half a brain." He lifted his cup in Lacey's direction. "It would get your mother off your back. You're married. She doesn't have to worry about you anymore."

"We hardly know each other. Has that occurred to you?" Lacey looked to Cam for help, but he was staring at Jimbo.

Jimbo shrugged. "So what? You get to know each other after the wedding. People used to get married all the time to people they didn't know."

"This isn't the eighteenth century." She turned to Cam, her eyes fierce. "Why don't you say something? Why am I the one doing all the arguing? Why don't you tell him how ridiculous this whole idea is?"

Cam's eyes, cool blue and enigmatic, met hers. His broad shoulders lifted in a shrug. "We might as well hear what he has to say."

"But this is crazy. You don't want to stay married to me,

do you?'' When he didn't respond immediately, she repeated the question, her voice rising. "Do you?''

"I don't know yet." The simple response silenced Lacey. She stared at him, unable to believe what she was hearing.

Jimbo grinned and reached out to pick up a croissant. "I'll leave you two to talk. But think about it. It might not be such a bad arrangement. Besides, I think you're perfect for each other."

The door shut behind him, leaving Cam and Lacey alone.

"You were kidding, right?" Lacey's tone pleaded with him to agree. "You can't possibly be serious about this. I mean, we don't know each other. We can't stay married."

"We can do anything we want. Have some more coffee. I don't know about you, but my head still feels like it belongs to somebody else."

Lacey took the cup from him automatically. He gestured to one of the chairs the waiter had pulled up near the table, and she sat down, feeling as if she could use the support. Cam settled himself in the other chair, stretching his long legs out in front of him.

Lacey stared at his feet. They were still bare. She tucked her own bare toes back under the chair, feeling an absurd sense of intimacy that they were sitting here in this hotel room with no shoes on. The rumpled bed was only a few feet away, Cam's shirt was still unbuttoned, but somehow, their bare toes seemed much too intimate.

"How are you feeling?" His tone was so gentle that Lacey felt tears sting her eyes.

"Stupid. Confused. Like a total fool. You may not believe this, but I'm not in the habit of waking up in bed with a complete stranger."

"I know that." His tone was so easy that Lacey dared to look at his face. He was watching her, his expression difficult to read. But there was certainly no judgment or criticism there.

She drew a breath, feeling calmer. Things could have been worse. He could have been a real jerk about the whole thing, instead of doing what he could to put her at ease. Still, they had to decide how to go about getting out of this crazy situation. Preferably as quickly as possible so that she could start picking up the pieces of her life.

"I know you were only kidding," Lacey said, "about us staying in this situation. Jimbo can be hard to deal with."

"True. But I wasn't kidding. I think we should talk about our options. *All* our options." He looked up, catching Lacey's openmouthed surprise, and his lips twitched in a smile. "Is it so awful to contemplate being married to me?"

"To you? No. I mean, I hardly know you." She stopped, trying to gather her wits, aware that she was blushing like a bride. No, that was the wrong simile. She wasn't a bride. Well, she was a bride, but not really. She shook her head sharply, clearing the tangle of her thoughts.

"It's nothing personal." She spoke slowly and carefully, trying to sound as reasonable as possible under the circumstances. "But we don't know each other. People who don't know each other don't get married."

"Usually, they don't. But we've already done it. Don't you think it might be fate? Kismet?"

"How about too much to drink?" Lacey's tone was all the firmer for the fact that, looking into those blue eyes, she found herself wanting to believe in kismet.

"Maybe. But now that it's done, we should think about it before we go off half-cocked again."

Lacey took a quick swallow of coffee. He was actually suggesting that they stay married. The idea was incredible. Ridiculous. It made absolutely no sense at all. And she was going to tell him that.

Just as soon as they got over the shock of discovering that it wasn't as appalling as it should be.

"Think about it, Lacey. Is it really such an awful idea? I don't know about you, but I haven't had a whole lot of luck finding someone I want to share my life with."

"Yes, but this isn't the way to do it." *Why was he beginning to sound so rational?*

"Why not? I'm thirty-six. You're thirty. We're both still alone."

"That's not so old."

"No. But we're not kids anymore, and nothing's come along so far. Now, here we are, already married. Why not explore the possibilities?"

Lacey pushed her hair back from her face, wishing for a hair band. Wishing for fresh clothes and a hot shower. Wishing that she was home safe and sound in her own bed.

Her lonely bed.

She stole a glance at Cam. He looked so relaxed sprawled in the chair. Could he really be so calm? Didn't this thing bother him at all? He looked as if nothing ever disturbed him.

You could really lean on a man like that.

She didn't need anyone to lean on. She was a strong woman, proud of her independence. She was running a successful business. Had a home of her own. The day was long past when a woman married a man because she couldn't make it on her own.

But wouldn't it be nice to have someone to come home to?

She scowled into her coffee cup. She was actually considering this madness. Was it possible that the coffee was drugged? She'd done something incredibly stupid last night, but that didn't mean she had to stick by it. No one could expect that.

She shook her head. "No. No, it would never work. It's an interesting idea, but it would never work."

"Why don't you think about it before you make up your mind?"

She shook her head again. "No. I don't need to think about it. The idea is nuts."

Cam drew in a deep breath, letting it out slowly. "I think we need to talk about something."

"We really don't need to," Lacey said quickly. She had the

feeling that, whatever it was he wanted to say, she didn't want to hear it. "Let's just get ourselves out of this situation as quickly as possible. An annulment shouldn't be hard to get."

"An annulment is only possible when a marriage hasn't been consummated."

Cam's quiet words struck her with the force of a blow. She didn't know if what he'd said was true, but she was too embarrassed to pursue it. It was the first reference either of them had made to the fact that they'd done more than just share a bed the night before. She'd been holding onto the vague hope that Cam's memory was even hazier than hers.

"Okay, a divorce then." She had the feeling she was hearing someone else's voice. It sounded so calm. "If we could get married on a moment's notice, we ought to be able to get divorced almost as fast."

"Lacey." Cam's voice was quiet, but something in it drew her eyes to his face. He looked concerned, regretful, but there was an iron set to his jaw that said that he wasn't going to just drop the subject.

"What?" She sounded sullen but there was nothing she could do about it. She'd never felt so humiliated in her life. What must he think of her? That she fell into bed with every man she met? She could hardly blame him if that's what he thought.

"Lacey, we really need to talk about this. I'm not in the habit of marrying a woman, making love to her and then divorcing her the next day. It's just not my style."

He paused, as if waiting for some response. There wasn't one and he sighed before continuing, his voice gentle. "Especially not when that woman happens to have been a virgin."

Lacey's eyes jerked up to his and then away. She felt her skin flush and then pale. She didn't want to deal with this. She didn't want to deal with anything. She just wanted to go home to her own safe, lonely bed and bury her head under the covers and stay there for the next five or ten years.

But she couldn't do that. At least not until she'd dealt with

the current situation. Cam was watching her, waiting for her t
say something.

"It's no big deal." As soon as the mumbled words were ou
she felt like a fool. No big deal? Couldn't she have come u
with something a little more adult?

"No big deal?" Cam questioned. "Lacey, the first time
person makes love is generally a fairly big deal. The fact tha
you've waited this long means it must have been important t
you."

"Waited this long?" She flared up defensively. "You mean
there must be something wrong with me because I was sti
a..." She stumbled over the words. "A...you know...at thirty
Well, there's nothing wrong with me."

Cam caught the hand she'd been waving for emphasis. '
don't think there's anything wrong with you. All I'm saying
that it must have meant something to you."

Lacey tugged on her hand but he ignored her, watching h
with those damned eyes that were so sympathetic. She stoppe
struggling, her anger leaving her abruptly. It wasn't his fau
that they were in this situation. That was the annoying part
it. It wasn't really anyone's fault.

How was she supposed to explain why she hadn't slept wi
a man in all of her thirty years? It wasn't that she hadn't bee
tempted a time or two. There'd been that boy in college, b
something had made her hold back, and she wasn't sorry s
had. Now she could barely remember his face.

She'd just never found someone who made her want to ma
that commitment. And as the years passed, it had begun
seem like more of a commitment than it had when she w
eighteen. When she slept with a man, she wanted to at lea
feel as if there was a possibility of a lasting relationship. A
she'd never felt that with any of the men she'd dated.

She became aware that Cam was still watching her, st
holding her hand. She shrugged, trying to look casual.

"I didn't avoid going to bed with a man out of some de

religious conviction, if that's what you meant by it meaning something to me."

"That's not what I had in mind, but I'm relieved to know you weren't considering entering a convent."

"I'm not." She tugged her hands loose, wanting to end the conversation. "Look, I don't see why we're talking about this. It's over and done with and it can't be changed."

"No, but maybe we could build on it."

"You don't build on a drunken marriage."

"Why not? Lacey, we must have felt something for each other, or drunk or not, we wouldn't have gotten married last night. Come on, tell me you didn't feel an attraction between us when we met."

"An attraction, yes, but that doesn't mean I wanted to marry you!" she cried.

"So, we didn't plan it very carefully. But we might have ended up here anyway."

"In a sleazy hotel room in the world's sleaziest city? I don't think so."

"I mean, we might have ended up married," he said quietly.

Lacey opened her mouth to deny the possibility and found herself without a thing to say. She *had* been attracted to Cam, more attracted than she liked to admit. Was it possible he was right? Might their relationship have headed in that direction? She shook her head.

"No. It's crazy. Besides, that's not a good excuse to stay together."

"Why not?" Cam persisted. "Why not give it a shot now that we've gone this far? We could get to know each other just as well after the marriage as we could have before."

"No." But she was weakening. She could hear it. So could Cam.

"Laccy, you slept with me last night. We made love. That's clearly not something you do casually."

"I was drunk!"

"So was I, but maybe that just means our defenses were

down. Maybe it made it possible for us to skip all the prelim-
inary garbage and get right to the heart of things."

"You sound like a cross between Sigmund Freud and a liquor salesman."

Cam grinned, hearing the softening in her tone. "Come on,
Lacey, take a chance. Let's give it a try."

Lacey shot to her feet. "I can't believe I'm even considering
this! This is the most ridiculous idea I've ever heard. We might
not even like each other once we get to know each other.

"And what about the practical problems? I don't know
where you live. You don't know where I live. Who's going to
move in with whom? What if you're a slob and leave your
dirty socks all over the place? What if you hate my mother?
Oh, God, my mother! How am I going to explain this to her?"

Cam stood up, taking her hands and holding them between
his palms. Lacey was aware of the warmth of his skin, the
calluses on his fingers, the strength that radiated from him. "
already like you," he said. "I don't think I'm going to change
my mind on closer acquaintance. As for the practical problems—I'm reasonably neat, no dirty socks. I have a house in
upper Glendale. There's plenty of room for you to move in.
must admit that my moving would be a bit of a problem since
my workshop is in the garage, but if you hate the place, we
can work something out.

"I'm sure I'll like your mother but if I don't, I can still
manage to be civil. Lots of people don't like their in-laws, and
it doesn't mean the marriage is doomed. And there's nothing
to explain to your mother. You can tell her that we just couldn't
resist the chance to get married when we found ourselves surrounded by the romance of the slot machines and blackjack
tables. Overcome with emotion, we decided that only marriage
would do, and we rushed to the nearest chapel to pledge our
troth beneath the light of a neon bouquet."

His description drew a reluctant chuckle. He made it all
sound so reasonable, as if this wasn't the craziest thing she'

ever done in her entire life. Besides, Mamie was just enough of a romantic sucker to fall for his corny story.

Her smile faded and she shook her head, staring at their linked hands.

"I don't know. It almost sounds reasonable when you say it, but I know it's crazy."

"It doesn't have to be crazy. We're sane adults. If we go about this right, it could work." His tone grew more serious. "Lacey, I wouldn't expect anything from you until you were ready for it. My house has a sparc bedroom and I wouldn't pressure you."

She blushed, keeping her eyes down. She appreciated his reassurance, but she was surprised to find that she hadn't needed it. She trusted him. Despite everything, she trusted him.

"It's nuts." She was weakening.

"But it's worth a try, isn't it?" he coaxed. "Nothing ventured, nothing gained. No pain, no gain."

"No pain, no gain?" she questioned. "I'm not sure that one is relevant here."

Cam shrugged. "I always get my clichés confused." His fingers tightened around hers. "Come on, Lacey. Let's give it a try."

She looked at him, trying to read something beneath his calm facade. *It had to be a facade.* No one could really be that calm at a time like this. But there was nothing visible beneath the still blue of his eyes. *Still waters run deep.* She had the feeling the phrase applied to Cameron McCleary.

"You really want this, don't you?"

"Yes, I do."

"Why?"

Something flickered in his eyes, gone too quickly for her to identify. His fingers tightened on hers and then dropped away as he sat back in his chair.

"My mother always told me that I have a bad habit of refusing to admit when I've made a mistake. Maybe that's why I want to give this a try."

Reaching for her coffee cup, Lacey stared at the film of liquid in the bottom as if the answer to all her problems could be found there.

It was a crazy idea, and yet... She was thirty and she hadn't even come close to getting married. Now here she was, married to a man who seemed like the answer to a dream. Not only was he attractive, he was nice, intelligent and considerate. He had a sense of humor.

She'd always planned her life so carefully, looking before she leapt, trying to see what lay ahead before she chose any one path. She had a successful business, friends, a nice apartment. Everything she'd planned to have. Careful planning had gotten her exactly what she wanted.

Hadn't it?

In the end, the answer wasn't in her coffee cup. It wasn't even in her head. It was in her heart. She wanted to jump without looking just once in her life. Maybe she'd known exactly what she was doing last night when she married a total stranger. A few drinks had smothered the practicality that had been threatening to choke the life out of her life.

Maybe it wasn't the smartest thing to do. She might live to regret it, but if she walked away without giving this insanity a chance, she knew she'd spend the rest of her life wondering if it might have worked.

Lacey took a deep breath and looked at Cam. He was watching her, something in the set of his shoulders telling her that her answer was important.

"Okay." She couldn't seem to get out anything beyond that one word. Okay. Such a silly word to use to change her entire life.

"Great." Cam gave her a slow smile that made her knees quiver. "We'll make it work, Lacey. I've got a feeling about this."

Her laughter was shaky. "So do I, but I doubt if it's the same one. I must be crazy to even consider this."

He held his hand out. Lacey stared at it for a long moment

before putting her hand in his. Cam's fingers closed around hers, warm and strong. Her eyes widened as the grip on her hand drew her forward until only inches separated them.

"The groom should always kiss the bride," he told her, his voice husky.

"Don't you think you did that last night?" She swallowed, keeping her eyes on his chest.

"That doesn't count. This is our real beginning." He slipped a hand beneath her chin, tilting her head back until her eyes met his. "Do you mind if I kiss you, Lacey?"

She swallowed hard and shook her head, unable to drag her eyes from his.

His mouth touched hers gently, asking more than demanding. Lacey's hands came up to rest against his chest, crisp whorls of hair tickling her palms. Cam's arms circled her back, pulling her closer. She felt surrounded but not trapped. Sheltered in his strength. It was a kiss of exploration, as if he understood that they needed time to get to know each other.

But there was passion underlying the gentleness. Lacey could feel it quivering in her bones like a sound that lay just beneath the level of hearing, more felt than heard. She heard a soft sigh of protest as Cam moved back and was only distantly aware it was her own.

Her lashes quivered a moment and then lifted, staring up into eyes the color of a summer day. His look was questioning, his eyes full of warm hunger. A hunger that reflected her own.

Her gaze dropped away from his. She hadn't expected that response. Hadn't planned on melting against him like that. She wasn't sure if it was lust or insanity that made her suddenly feel more hopeful about this crazy plan.

Chapter Five

"Are you sure we shouldn't try and find the others? At least Frank and Lisa. They'll worry about us."

Lacey's anxious question was addressed to Cam's broad back as he moved ahead of her. He glanced over his shoulder as he opened the door marked Stairs.

"They'll just assume we did exactly what we're doing and left without them. Believe me, this is the safest way. Do you want to face Jimbo and tell him we've decided to take his advice and give this a try?"

"No." She didn't have to think about her answer, but she was still frowning as she followed him into the cement stair well. "But do you really think sneaking down the stairs is necessary? We're on the eighth floor."

"It would be just like Jimbo to have arranged some kind of a welcoming party at the elevators. He's probably found some old shoes to drape around our necks and a pile of rice to throw at us."

"But how is he going to know we're on our way down?" Lacey was growing a little breathless as they descended what seemed like endless flights of stairs.

Cam paused on the landing next to a door marked with five. "I called down to check out, remember? He could have asked the desk to let him know when we checked out."

She swallowed a moan of protest as he started downward again. Aerobics three times a week were clearly not enough.

"Don't you think you're being a little paranoid? He's not the CIA."

Cam threw her a quick look over his shoulder without pausing. "You can't have known Jimbo as long as I have, or you'd know just how devious he can be. He wouldn't have to threaten the desk clerk. He could spin him a story about us having just been married and he wants to congratulate us."

Lacey scowled, but she didn't argue anymore. For one thing, she didn't have enough breath. And for another, she did know Jimbo quite well, and the scenario Cam had just painted would be typical of him. Besides, they only had two more flights to go.

Cam opened the door to the lobby and they tried to step out as inconspicuously as possible. The continual clanging of slot machines mingled with the usual hustle and bustle of a big hotel. Palm trees filled an atrium in the middle of the lobby.

Cam reached out to take her hand, and Lacey wondered if he felt the little spark of electricity when they touched. She was so distracted by the tingling sensation that it took her a moment to register what he was saying.

"I told you he'd be lurking in the underbrush."

She looked in the direction he indicated. Lurking in the underbrush wasn't entirely accurate, but there was no mistaking Jimbo's stocky frame hovering on the other side of the planters. He was facing the elevators, clearly waiting. Lacey's fingers tightened around Cam's in silent gratitude that she'd been spared whatever loud and probably embarrassing greeting their friend had in mind.

Cam grinned down at her, waggling his eyebrows in a way that made her want to giggle. "Act natural and we may escape detection."

He moved toward the front doors, shortening his stride to match hers. Act natural. Now why did he have to say that? She felt as if she was wearing a neon sign that begged for attention.

Everyone within a fifty-yard radius must surely be looking at them. She was vividly aware of her bare legs, her rumpled dress, the fact that the only makeup she had on was a pale lipstick she'd found in the bottom of her purse.

How many people had seen that stupid picture in the paper? Unconsciously, her hand tightened around Cam's, but she needn't have worried. People who came to Las Vegas had other things on their minds. They slipped out the front door without incident.

The hot dry air was a shock after the hotel's air-conditioning. A line of taxis waited to the left, and it took Lacey a moment to realize that Cam wasn't heading in that direction. His grip on her hand pulled her to the right.

"Cam, the taxis are over there." She tugged against his hold but he shook his head.

"We're not going to need a taxi. I've got a better idea."

To the right of the hotel was the parking lot. She'd seen it from the window of their room, but she didn't see how the parking lot was going to offer them a better idea than a taxi. At least she didn't see until she realized where Cam was headed.

There was no mistaking the lines of the big black car he was approaching. The Cadillac was Jimbo's pride and joy. He'd restored it from the ground up, and Lacey had learned far more about the art of restoration than she'd ever had any desire to know. It was all he'd talked about for months. Three years after it was complete, he still treated the car as if it were made of porcelain.

"What are you planning on doing?" Her voice was hushed though there was no one within listening distance.

"I'm going to steal us a ride to the airport." He said it so calmly, as if grand theft was an everyday part of his life.

"You're going to steal Jimbo's car?" Her voice rose to an incredulous squeak before disappearing altogether.

"Sure. Why not?" The top was still down, and Cam opened

the door, his movements so casual she might have believed it was his car. Only she knew it wasn't.

"Do you know what Jimbo is going to do when he finds it gone? He's going to report it to the police and they're going to be watching for it. It's not like it's an easy car to miss. And when they catch us, they'll throw us in jail, which will just put the perfect cap on my birthday celebration."

Cam had slid into the driver's seat and was fumbling under the dash, his expression intent. Lacey wasn't even sure he'd heard her dire predictions. The engine suddenly turned over, catching with a well-bred roar. Cam grinned in triumph.

"Some things you just don't forget. Get in. And you don't have to worry about the police. We're going to make sure Jimbo knows exactly what happened to his car."

Lacey hesitated a moment longer before walking around to the passenger side and climbing in. Maybe it was Cam's smile. Maybe it was the look in those incredible eyes. Or maybe turning thirty had brought on insanity.

She closed her eyes as he backed the big car out of the parking space. She half expected to hear the wail of a siren and see the long arm of the law coming at her. But nothing happened. The car responded to Cam's touch just as it always had to Jimbo's. Looking out over half a mile of hood, she didn't see any Bonnie-and-Clyde-style roadblocks. She dared to relax a little.

"How are you going to let Jimbo know that we've got his car so he doesn't sic the FBI on us?"

"Watch."

They circled the back of the hotel, coming up in front of the entryway. Cam pulled the car to a halt but left it idling. A gray-coated valet hurried forward, but Cam waved him back. He leaned on the horn and the unmistakable, three-note blare echoed against the building. Lacey realized what he was doing. If Jimbo was still lurking in the lobby, he couldn't help but hear the horn.

She turned toward the doors just as they slid open to reveal

Jimbo's stocky form. He took one look at the car and his face dropped.

"Hey!" He started down the steps at a pace that threatened to send him rolling down rather than walking.

"Hey, yourself," Cam called as he put the car in gear "Have a nice trip home."

"McCleary!" Jimbo's bellow was probably audible halfway to the coast, but Cam didn't ease his foot off the accelerator Lacey turned to look out the back as they pulled away from the hotel. Jimbo came to a screeching halt in the middle of the driveway. For a moment, she thought he might be contemplating his chance of catching them on foot, but he must have rated it about as low as she did. He stood there watching them his hands on his hips, frustration quivering in every line of his body.

The car turned onto the road and Jimbo disappeared from sight. Lacey turned to face the front.

"He looked really upset."

"I know." Cam's grin took on a positively wicked edge.

"You should have told him that we were leaving the car a the airport. What if he thinks we're driving it back to L.A.?"

"He should at least think of the airport. I'll park it in some nice obvious place and bribe a guard to keep an eye on it Besides, he deserves anything he gets. I may not remembe much by way of details of what went on last night, but gu feeling tells me that Jimbo had a lot more to do with thing than he's going to admit.

"Nothing would make me happier than for him to get bac to Los Angeles, only to find that his precious toy is still in La Vegas." He spoke with such good-natured malice that Lace laughed.

THE FLIGHT to Los Angeles was quiet. The closer they got t home, the more surreal the past twenty-four hours seemed. I was hard to believe that this wasn't all some strange drear from which she'd awaken at any moment.

Lacey stole a quick glance at Cam. He looked so calm. He seemed to be taking this whole situation in stride, as if he woke up married to a stranger every day.

She turned her head to look out the window. The sky beyond was a clear pale blue broken by an occasional puff of cloud. The drifting shadows created dark patches on the featureless expanse of tan desert.

Was she crazy to give this marriage a try? Her logical mind shouted yes. Marriage was tough enough when two people knew and loved each other. It took a certain amount of blind optimism even then. But to go into it with a man she didn't know, had only just met—that had to be the height of insanity.

If she had any sense at all, she'd tell him right now that she was going to apply for an annulment—she'd see about this consummation thing—as soon as she set foot in Los Angeles. He'd probably be relieved.

But she didn't turn her head, didn't say anything. Weighed next to every logical argument against this marriage was a gut-level feeling that she'd regret it the rest of her life if she backed out now. She didn't know why but this was something she had to do. And buried deep inside was a building excitement, an anticipation that she wasn't ready to acknowledge. There was a feeling that Cam McCleary might be just what she needed to turn her life upside down and give it a thorough shake.

Once they arrived in Los Angeles, it didn't take long to rent a car. Cam drove, for which Lacey was grateful. Her thoughts were still too scattered, jumping from one thing to another. She was grateful she didn't have to try to concentrate on negotiating the freeway traffic.

They'd spoken very little since boarding the plane in Las Vegas. She wondered if Cam was feeling the same doubts and uncertainties that plagued her. As he eased the car into the heavy traffic on the San Diego Freeway she found herself watching his hands. A quick flash of memory reminded her of just what those hands had felt like on her skin.

"You know, I don't even know what you do for a living."

She spoke abruptly, as much to interrupt her own train o
thought as anything else. "You said something about a shop
in your home?"

"I'm a carpenter, more or less. I make furniture, cabinets
that sort of thing."

"It sounds interesting." Her tone was a little overenthused
Privately, she wondered if it was possible to earn a living tha
way. Some of her doubt must have shown. Cam's mouth
quirked into a half smile.

"I make a decent living. Enough to support a wife."

"I don't need anyone to support me, thank you. I make
very good living on my own. Besides, we don't have that kin
of marriage."

"What kind is that?" he inquired politely.

"A real one and, even if we did, I would still keep m
shop."

"Why wouldn't you? I gather your shop does very well."

"Yes, it does." Lacey spoke without arrogance but with
definite note of pride in her voice.

"Maybe I should give up my work and let you support m
in the manner to which I'd like to become accustomed." H
grinned, inviting her to share his amusement. Lacey smile
reluctantly. There was something wrong with this picture. The
shouldn't be talking and laughing like old friends. Where wa
all the angst and uncertainty? Didn't he ever worry about any
thing?

"You know, you really didn't have to drive me home," sh
said, "I know Pasadena is out of your way."

Cam slanted her a look of amusement. "It's practically ne
door. Besides, my mother taught me that a gentleman alway
sees a lady home after a date."

"This has sure been one hell of a date. Oh, my God."

"What?" Cam lifted his foot off the gas pedal in respons
to Lacey's horror-struck tone. "What's wrong?"

"Your mother."

"My mother?" He glanced in the mirror and stepped on the gas again to avoid being swallowed whole by a semi.

"I'd forgotten all about her."

"I didn't know you were supposed to remember her."

"She's going to hate me."

The light dawned, and Cam smiled. "Mom is going to love you."

"How could she love me? She doesn't know me and everyone knows that mothers always hate the woman their son marries."

Cam grinned. "My mother isn't the possessive type."

"All mothers are possessive," she said gloomily. "I was worried about how you were going to deal with my mother, but at least I know she's going to love you. She'd love any man I married."

"Gee, thanks. You make me feel so special." He made the transition to the Ventura Freeway before glancing at her again. "Take my word for it. My mother will like you. Anyway, you don't have to worry about her for a while. She lives in Virginia."

"What about the rest of your family? Didn't you say there were ten or twelve of you?"

"Only seven. And most of them are scattered across the country. The only one you're likely to meet is Claire. She lives in the Simi Valley. We usually all manage to get together for Christmas, but that's quite a ways off, so I don't think you need to panic yet."

Somehow that knowledge did little to allay Lacey's concerns.

IT SEEMED TYPICAL of Cam that he found a parking place right outside her apartment building. They were usually as rare as hens' teeth. Her steps were slow as she led the way into the building. She'd started trying to imagine Cam's reaction to her home even before they'd pulled off the freeway. Somehow,

Cam's tall form and her intensely modern decorating refused to connect in her mind.

Not that it really mattered, of course. It was none of his business how she'd decorated her home. She certainly didn't care what he thought. The elevator came to a halt on her floor and they stepped out into the carpeted hall. Lacey's steps slowed still further, but she could delay the inevitable only so long. Once they stopped in front of her door, they could hardly stand there staring at it. She fished the key out of her purse and unlocked the door, throwing it back with an air of defiance that caused Cam to give her a puzzled look.

She'd spent months fixing this place, studying magazines, getting just the right feel, the proper air of chic. It had cost a small fortune, but it looked exactly like a picture in *House and Garden*. She looked at the rich scarlet and gold tones and then looked at Cam.

"You hate it, don't you?"

"No. No. I mean, it's very…nice. It looks nice."

Lacey looked at the sofa that had cost her a month's profits, the carpet that had been carefully dyed to match the wallpaper, the rather malevolent-looking metal sculpture that dominated one corner of the room.

"Nice?"

"Well, I mean interesting nice. Really interesting nice. My place isn't anything like this." Cam studied the metal sculpture, tilting his head to the side as if wondering if the piece was upside down. "Nothing like this at all."

Lacey looked at him and then looked at the room and her mouth quivered. He looked so out of place. No, the room looked out of place. Funny, she'd lived with this for almost three years and had never realized how superficial it was, how little she actually liked it. Cam glanced at her and misread her expression.

"It really is very nice, Lacey. It's obvious you've worked hard to make it look this way," he told her earnestly.

The quiver became a chuckle. He so obviously hated it and

he was trying so hard to be complimentary. Cam cocked one eyebrow.

"Is it something I said?"

"Sort of. You really hate this place, don't you?"

He looked around and then looked back at her, reading the amusement in her eyes. His shoulders lifted in a sheepish shrug. "It's really not my cup of tea, but it does look like you spent a lot of time on it. After seeing this, I'm not sure you're going to like my place. It's very different. Simpler."

"You mean it's not gaudy?"

"I didn't say that. This isn't gaudy. It's just very…bright." Lacey laughed out loud and he shrugged again. "Sorry. Like I said, it's not my cup of tea."

"I'm not all that sure it's mine. Would you like some coffee or something to eat?"

"No, thanks." Cam ran his fingers through his hair. "I guess I ought to be going. I could use a hot shower and you'd probably like some time alone."

"I…yes, I guess I would." She couldn't explain, even to herself, why the idea didn't hold more appeal. Heaven knew, after the last twenty-four hours, being alone must be exactly what she needed. But once she was alone, she'd have to think about what she'd done, what she'd agreed to.

"You won't change your mind, will you?"

Her eyes swept up to meet Cam's. She felt swallowed in their intense blue. Slowly she shook her head. "I won't change my mind."

And she knew she wouldn't. No matter how crazy this whole idea was, she was committed to it.

"Good. Listen, why don't I pick you up for lunch tomorrow and we can discuss the particulars of our living arrangements?"

"Okay." She was surprised by the strength of her desire to see him again. She gave him the address of the shop and then followed him to the door. Cam hesitated in the doorway, his eyes skimming over her tousled hair and lingering on her mouth. For a moment, Lacey thought he was going to kiss her.

She wasn't sure whether or not to be disappointed when he didn't. With a quick smile, he strode down the hallway toward the elevator. Lacey watched him until he turned the corner and then shut the door slowly and leaned against it.

She'd been longing for a hot shower and clean clothes, but she didn't move. Married. She was actually married. It didn't seem real. In fact, the last twenty-four hours didn't seem real. Had it really been only yesterday that she'd sat in Mamie's living room, listening to her lament her daughter's single state?

She shook her head, moving away from the door and heading toward the bedroom. How quickly things had changed. She glanced around the living room, thinking about all the time and money she'd spent decorating it. Funny, she didn't feel so much as a twinge of regret at the thought of leaving the place. Seeing it through Cam's eyes had made her realize how little she really liked it. It was striking, but it lacked warmth. It was about as far from the elegant clutter she'd grown up with as it was possible to get.

Maybe she'd been making some kind of statement. But she was a little old for defiant statements. She was thirty now, whether she liked it or not. And a married woman, whether she liked it or not. Wedded and bedded. The old phrase came to mind and she blushed.

She might be going crazy, but she felt a definite twinge of anticipation at the thought of being married to Mr. Cameron McCleary. Shaking her head, she pushed open the bedroom door and headed for the shower. It had certainly been one hell of a day.

"You realize, of course, that I could have had you arrested for grand theft."

Cam glanced up. Jimbo stood in the doorway, the late-afternoon sun silhouetting his stocky body. Cam returned his attention to the workbench. "You realize, of course, that I could shoot you and any judge would call it justifiable homicide," he suggested conversationally.

"Shoot me? Shoot me!" Jimbo stepped farther into the shop, his voice rising on an incredulous note. "I'm not the one who stole his best friend's car and left it parked in a dingy corner of a parking lot, just waiting to be stolen."

"It wasn't a dingy corner. I parked it right next to the guard shack. Besides, no one would steal that thing. No one but an accountant could afford the gas it guzzles."

"What about the mental anguish I suffered?" Jimbo reached out and picked up a handful of pretzels from a bowl on the bench, crunching into one to punctuate his complaint.

"Any mental anguish you suffered was well deserved," Cam told him.

"For what? What did I do?" Jimbo's round face was the very picture of cherubic innocence. Cam was not impressed. He set down the plane he'd been using to shave thin strips of oak from a board and leaned one hip against the bench, fixing his friend with an implacable gaze.

"You set us up. I haven't figured out quite how, and I'm not totally sure about the why, but I *know* you set us up."

"Us? You mean you and Lacey? I told you, there was nothing I could do. You were hell-bent on marriage. I tried to talk you out of it, but there was just no changing your minds."

"Sure. The day hasn't arrived when you couldn't talk someone out of something. Like I said, you set us up."

"Look, I'm not denying that I think the two of you would make a great couple. But the only setting up I did was in arranging for you to meet. I admit to that much, but anything beyond that was purely your own idea. What could I do?"

He lifted his hands and shrugged, but Cam didn't look impressed. He picked up the plane again and turned his attention to the wood. Some people might have taken it as a hint, but Jimbo had never been much inclined to take hints. He lingered, crunching another handful of pretzels.

"So, how'd it go?"

Cam hid a smile. He'd known that Jimbo's curiosity wouldn't be restrained for long.

"How did what go?" He carefully planed another fraction of an inch from the board.

"You and Lacey."

"What about me and Lacey?"

"How did it go? What did you decide?"

"About what?" Jimbo fairly danced with impatience, and Cam bit the inside of his lip, enjoying the moment.

"What did you decide about staying married? Are you going to give it a try or what?"

Cam looked up, widening his eyes in apparent surprise. "Are you kidding? Nobody in their right mind would try and make a go of marriage to a total stranger."

Jimbo's shoulders slumped. "I thought, when you two left like that, that maybe you'd decided to give it a try."

"We did." Cam spoke so calmly that it took several seconds for the meaning of his words to sink in. Jimbo stiffened, staring at him.

"You did?"

"Lacey is moving in here tomorrow."

Jimbo's grin threatened to split his face in two. "Why didn't you tell me? It's been almost a week. I knew you were perfect for each other. I knew it."

"Well, that remains to be seen," Cam pointed out with a dry smile.

"You're perfect for each other. I'm never wrong about these things."

"It must be nice to be right all the time."

"Yes, it is," Jimbo agreed modestly.

Cam laughed. It was impossible to remain even mildly annoyed with Jimbo.

"You wait and see. You and Lacey are going to be great together."

"I hope you're right."

In fact, he'd never hoped anything quite so much in his entire life. Jimbo lingered a little while longer, but Cam's heart wasn't really in the conversation and he was just as glad to see him go.

Lacey was moving in tomorrow. As of tomorrow, he was going to have to start learning how to be a husband. It was hard to believe that a life could change so completely in a week. Would he have let Jimbo talk him into joining Lacey's birthday celebration if he'd known where it was going to lead? It was impossible to say.

It wasn't that he was exactly happy to find himself married to a woman he barely knew. But he wasn't precisely unhappy, either. He'd been thinking that he needed something to shake up his life. Maybe Lacey Newton was just the ticket.

Chapter Six

Cam's home was, as he'd promised, nothing like Lacey's apartment. It was a large house set in the foothills above Glendale. White stucco and a red-tile roof made a gesture toward the area's Spanish heritage.

Lacey turned her car into the brick driveway, parking under the branches of the huge live oak that dominated the front yard. She turned off the engine but made no effort to get out of the car.

She was really here. Over the past week, she'd never quite believed she'd get to this point. Even while she was packing her clothes into boxes and loading them in the car, it hadn't felt real. Now that she was here, she was seized by a sudden attack of nerves. What was she doing here?

Before she had a chance to answer that question, she saw Cam walking toward her. Lacey watched him, her hands still gripping the steering wheel. It had only been a few days since she'd seen him, but she'd almost managed to convince herself that she'd imagined the effect he had on her breathing.

"Are you coming in, or are you going to stay there permanently?" He rested one hand on top of the car and leaned down to look through the window, one of his brows raised inquiringly.

Lacey pried her hands off the steering wheel and gave him

what she hoped was a casual smile. "I was just getting a feel for the place."

"It's not huge but it's quiet. Like I said, if you don't like it, we'll work something out." Cam opened the car door and Lacey stepped out of the car, feeling as if she were taking an irrevocable step—as if marrying the man hadn't been irrevocable enough.

"It's a pretty neighborhood. Have you lived here long?" Great. She sounded like a ten-year-old at a tea party.

"Eight years. My grandparents left it to me. I thought about selling, but the garage was already set up as a workshop and it was a good location, so I stayed."

"I'm sure I'll like it."

"I hope so." There was no mistaking the sincerity in his words, and she felt some of her tension fade. He'd reminded her that she wasn't in this alone.

"You can't have brought much with you." Cam eyed her small blue compact car as if trying to imagine how a human being could fit inside. Considering his size, he'd have to wear the car rather than sit in it. The image made Lacey smile as he bent to push the front seat forward and reach for her suitcase.

"Mostly just clothes. Since the shop isn't far from the apartment, I thought it would be easier to move a little bit at a time. I've still got three months to go on my lease, anyway."

And with her apartment still available, she'd have an escape if she needed it. If the thought occurred to Cam, he didn't say anything. He reached past her and lifted the suitcase out easily. For a moment, Lacey was caught between him and the open car door. How could she have forgotten how large he was?

He was wearing jeans and a blue chambray shirt. She stared at the wedge of skin exposed by his open collar. She had a sudden memory of waking up next to him, of warm muscles and tanned skin. Her eyes swept up to meet his, and she wondered if it was her imagination that put the same memories in

his gaze. She looked away. Cam stepped back and the momen
was gone. But not forgotten.

"I fixed up a room for you."

"Thanks." Lacey had to clear her throat to get the word out
She shut the car door and followed him up the brick walk t
the door. He tugged open the screen door and stepped back
waiting for her to enter.

She paused on the threshold, wondering if he was thinkin
the same thing she was. Under other circumstances, he woul
be carrying her into her new home. But that was hardly appro
priate now. Not that she was in the least disappointed. The las
thing she wanted was romantic folderol.

Taking a deep breath, she stepped into the small hallway an
looked at her new home. She took in the polished hardwoo
floors, white plaster walls and chunky leather furniture tha
filled the living room. A fireplace with a rustic wooden mante
dominated one wall, and windows filled two more. Maple cab
inets flanked the fireplace, hand-forged wrought-iron hardwar
setting off the warm wood.

"Think you can live with it?" Cam's question was light, b
she heard the underlying concern. He really cared what sh
thought.

She nodded slowly. "I like it a lot." And no one could hav
been more surprised than she was to find that it was the truth
A high ceiling with exposed beams kept the modest-sized roor
from being overwhelmed by the bulky furniture. The huge ex
panse of windows further lightened the room. It was plair
almost stark, but there was something very soothing in its sin
plicity.

"It's very…honest. Nothing fussy or overdone."

"I'm glad you like it." The words were simple, but glancin
over her shoulder, Lacey saw the pleasure in his eyes. Th
knowledge warmed her.

"I'll show you your room and then we can take the gran
tour, if you'd like." Before she could reply, there was a strang

scrabbling noise she couldn't identify. It grew rapidly closer and she threw Cam a questioning glance.

"Derwent." That was all he had time for before a furry bundle hurtled around a corner and rushed toward them. Lacey took an involuntary step backward. For a moment, she couldn't identify a head or a tail. Even the species was in doubt. All she could see was a tawny-colored mop. Derwent skidded to a halt, nails slipping on the smooth floors. A sharp high-pitched bark clarified that it was a dog. Cam set Lacey's suitcase down and bent to scoop up the animal in one hand.

"This is Derwent. He actually owns this house, or so he'd have you believe. I hope you like dogs."

"I don't know. I've never had much to do with them."

"Well, Derwent is spoiled rotten, but he's friendly."

Lacey studied Derwent doubtfully. Now that she saw him at closer range, she could see a pair of bright button eyes under the ratty beige bangs that spilled over his face. He was regarding her with the same curiosity she was displaying. A pink tongue lolled over sharp little teeth.

"What is he?"

"A Yorkshire Terrier. They're very smart."

She reached out and tentatively scratched behind one ear. Derwent's eyes closed and his tiny body quivered with pleasure in Cam's hold.

"He'll probably be your slave for life. Actually, he likes just about everybody. Except Jimbo. He terrorizes Jimbo."

"A dog with good taste," Lacey commented dryly. She still hadn't forgiven Jimbo for his part in this insane situation. She stepped back, looking at the picture Cam and Derwent made, and her mouth curved in an irrepressible smile. The tiny dog sprawled comfortably in one of Cam's hands, his short legs dangling contentedly. "You know, he's not exactly the kind of dog I'd have pictured you with. I'd have thought you'd have had something a little more...in proportion."

Cam's grin showed that he shared her humor. "I know. An Irish Setter maybe, or a Lab. But Derwent followed me home one day and simply refused to go away. I guess the proportions don't bother him." He bent to set the dog on the floor, and Derwent took off at a dead run down the hallway.

"Does he ever walk anywhere?" Lacey asked as the furry little body disappeared.

"Not often. I think when your legs are as short as his, you pretty well have to run to keep up with the rest of the world." Then he added, "By the way, Jimbo came by yesterday."

"Did he find his car?"

"Actually, he came by to threaten me with arrest."

Lacey ran her finger along the edge of a chunky missionary style bench. "Did you threaten him with murder?"

"Yup." Cam bent to pick up her suitcase again, and she followed him toward the rear of the house.

"Did you tell him we were going to give things a try?" she asked.

"I told him. He said he was sure we were made for each other." Cam pushed open a door and set her bag down in the room before turning to look at her. "He said he's always right about things like that."

"Maybe he should hang out a shingle. Matchmaker With Excellent Track Record. Heaven knows, Southern California has enough palm readers and channelers. We could probably use a good old-fashioned matchmaker."

Lacey slipped by him and into the bedroom. The room wasn't large, but it had the same restful feel that characterized the rest of the house, a feeling she was beginning to associate with Cameron McCleary.

"Do you suppose he'll ask us for a testimonial?" Cam leaned in the doorway, watching her.

Lacey looked at him, trying to ignore the way her pulse seemed to pick up speed when he was around.

"I don't know. I suppose he'll have to wait and see if he was right again."

"I suppose we all will." Cam grinned and stood away from

the door. "I'll give you a chance to settle in. I'm going to go start dinner."

"Do you need help?"

"I think I can manage tonight. But don't worry, I'll let you take your turn in the kitchen."

"Gee, thanks."

Cam grinned at her dry tone, but he didn't linger. He lifted a hand and disappeared back the way they'd come. Lacey looked around the room that was to be hers for who knew how long. Until she moved into the master bedroom? Until she moved back to her apartment?

With a sigh, she lifted her suitcase onto the bed and opened it. Just take one day at a time. That's what she'd promised herself she'd do. It was the only thing she *could* do.

"I HOPE YOU LIKE fried chicken." Cam turned from the stove as Lacey stepped into the kitchen.

"Are you kidding? My mother is from Georgia. Fried chicken is practically the national dish in the South."

"Then maybe I should rephrase the question. I hope you like *my* fried chicken."

"I'm sure I will. Is there anything I can do to help?"

"Just sit down and relax. Tonight is my treat." He turned back to the stove. "Is your room okay?"

"It's beautiful. Did you make the dresser that's in there?"

"One of my early efforts."

"It's lovely."

"Thanks." He scooped chicken pieces out of the sizzling oil and set them on a layer of towels to drain. Lacey watched him, realizing it was the first time she'd ever seen a man cook, except at a barbecue. He seemed to be perfectly at home as he drained oil from the pan and set about making a thick gravy.

Outside, a light rain was falling, making the little house a cozy shelter from the elements. The chicken was perfectly cooked, as were the accompaniments, and despite herself, Lacey began to relax. Maybe it was the food. It was difficult to

be on guard while you were licking your fingers. Or maybe i
was the company. Cam seemed to take the whole situation ir
stride. It made it hard to worry about what she'd gotten hersel:
into.

They talked while they ate, nothing heavy or full of meaning
just light dinner conversation. Cam wanted to know how she'c
come to start Lacey's Lovelies, and Lacey found herself tellin
him the joys and problems of running her own business. He
was a good listener. Halfway through the meal, she stoppec
and apologized self-consciously.

"I should have warned you about my tendency to rambl
on about the shop. I'm inclined to be a bit of a bore about it."

"I wasn't bored. You've obviously worked very hard. Yo
should be proud."

Lacey pushed a crumb around the edge of her plate with th
tip of one pale pink fingernail. "I am proud of it. I've worke
very hard to make it a success."

"Success usually doesn't come without a lot of work."

"My mother thinks I've worked too hard. She thinks I'v
put my personal life on hold."

"Have you?"

She glanced up, reading the question in his eyes. Questior
but no judgment. She shrugged.

"I don't know. I suppose I have. Not consciously, but it'
hard to have a personal life when you're getting a busines
started."

"And it's easier to deal with business problems than rela
tionships," Cam said quietly. Lacey's eyes jerked to his fac
but there was no criticism there. Or, if there was, it was sel-
directed. His eyes met hers and his mouth twisted in a hal
smile. "I've done the same thing myself. Business is a lot saf
than people."

Lacey's eyes dropped from his, but she nodded slowly. '
suppose it is."

They sat without speaking for a few moments. Outside, th
rain continued to drizzle gently, a soft counterpoint to the qui

inside. Derwent stirred restlessly in his bed near the door, his short legs twitching in some canine dream. The scene was one of cozy domesticity.

Cam moved first, breaking the spell. ''Here's to two cowards thrust into the middle of commitment by the divine hand of the Little Chapel in the Desert Dell.'' He grinned, lifting his glass. Lacey hesitated, and then lifted her glass to his. She'd never expected to toast her marriage with a glass of milk, but the lack of champagne didn't bother her.

Meeting Cam's eyes, she was seized by a sudden, foolish sense of optimism. Somehow the situation didn't seem quite as mad as it had. It seemed possible—almost—that this marriage might actually work.

CAM PAUSED in the kitchen doorway, giving himself time to savor the scene before him. Lacey had her back to him, her attention on something she was doing at the counter. Her hair was pulled into a ponytail, a spill of golden blond that brushed her shoulders as she moved. She was wearing faded jeans that molded the smooth lines of her hips in a way that invited a man's hand to test those same curves. A red-and-gray striped top completed the outfit. She looked casual, comfortable and deliciously attractive.

He was surprised by the strength of his pleasure in seeing her so at home in his kitchen. There was something so right about the picture, as if she was just what the house had been waiting for to make it complete.

When he'd picked up on Jimbo's suggestion that they remain married, he'd been acting more from guilt than anything else. Despite what he'd told Lacey, he was well aware that the odds against this marriage succeeding were high. But seducing innocent women and leaving them high and dry was not something he wanted to add to a life that had already had its share of misdeeds.

He felt a strong sense of responsibility for what had occurred between them. It had nothing to do with the few years' difference in their ages; thirty to thirty-six wasn't that big of a jump. But there was something about Lacey that spoke of a certain innocence, as if maybe some of life's harsher realities had passed her by. He didn't want to see that innocence disappear, at least not because of him.

Besides, there was no denying the strong attraction that lay between them. And he did believe in fate. It had played a strong enough part in his life. Maybe this odd marriage was a gesture from fate. Whether it was a gift or a gag remained to be seen.

He must have made some sound, or perhaps Lacey felt his eyes on her, because she turned suddenly and their eyes met. She had a smear of flour on one cheek, her hands were covered in the same substance, and the front of her top was dusted with it. Cam couldn't imagine how she could have looked more attractive.

"Good morning," he said, his voice still husky with sleep.

"Good morning." Her face was flushed. She brushed self-consciously at the flour on her cheek, only succeeding in adding to it. "I heard the shower and thought I'd make some breakfast. I hope you don't mind me making myself at home."

"This *is* your home. Besides, I'd have to be a fool to complain about you making breakfast. I usually make do with a slice of toast and some coffee. That looks like biscuits."

He crossed the room as he spoke, and Lacey had to control the urge to back away. He was so large and…male. It was almost too much for her nerves to take at this hour of the morning.

"Biscuits," she confirmed a bit breathlessly.

"I haven't had real biscuits in ages. Where did you get the recipe?"

Lacey turned back to the counter and finished rolling out the soft dough, using a water glass in place of the rolling pin she hadn't been able to find. "I don't need a recipe. Mother taught me to make biscuits before she taught me how to read. A Southern lady should always know how to cook." Uncosciously, her voice took on a soft drawl in imitation of Mamie's speech.

She turned the glass upside down and deftly cut biscuits, transferring them to a baking sheet. Cam watched her, wondering why he'd never realized how sexy making biscuits could be.

"You seem very California."

Lacey's laughter held a touch of sadness. "I am, but Mother did her best to drum the old South into me. I can play piano and cook and sew. I know precisely how to hold a teacup and I can make a cucumber sandwich. All accomplishments that a lady should acquire."

"Cucumber sandwich? Sounds peculiar."

"You'll probably get a chance to try one this afternoon. Mother is bound to have made them for us. Unless you've changed your mind about going to meet her. I love her dearly, but I have to admit that she can be a little hard to take sometimes. She's very good at pushing you around. Very politely, of course. She's always polite."

She looked sincerely worried that her mother might be more than he could handle. Cam grinned down at her, reaching out to brush the flour from her cheek.

"I think I can stand up to a little polite pushiness. I'm tougher than I look."

Lacey was not completely reassured. Cam had never seen her mother in action. Throughout her teenage years, she'd squirmed with embarrassment every time she brought a date home to meet her mother. Mamie would pump the unsuspecting boy for information, everything from his family background to his future plans. That her dates never realized what was going on hadn't made Lacey feel any better. The fact that her mother was subtle didn't make the interrogation any easier to take.

Lacey didn't have much to say during the drive to her mother's home in San Marino. She was aware of Cam glancing at her, his look questioning, but she was careful not to catch his eyes. How could she explain her feelings? He'd think she was worrying over nothing, especially once he met her mother. Men adored Mamie, and the feeling was mutual.

She wasn't worried about whether her mother and her new husband would like each other. That was practically a foregone conclusion. Mamie would adore Cam because he was male and presentable and he'd rescued her daughter from spinsterhood. Cam would adore Mamie because men always adored Mamie.

What bothered Lacey was the idea of watching her mother twist Cam around her little finger the way she had always done with anything male. It hadn't mattered much in the past, but somehow, with Cam, it did. She didn't want to see him falling hook, line and sinker for her mother's sweet Southern charm. She didn't want to watch Mamie extract information he didn't even know he was giving.

"Relax." She hadn't been aware that her fingers were knotted together in her lap until Cam's hand covered them. "It can't be that bad. I'm sure your mother and I are going to get along just fine."

Lacey sighed softly. "I'm sure you will."

Cam wanted to ask her why that prospect seemed to depress her. He opened his mouth and then closed it without saying anything. Maybe he was safer not knowing. Despite his reassurances to the contrary, he was growing a little uneasy about this meeting.

Was Mamie Newton a dragon lady? He was beginning to picture her as a cross between Bette Davis and Irene Dunne—genteel bitchiness mixed with a touch of the scatterbrained. Despite her warnings, he didn't doubt that Lacey loved her mother. But he was beginning to doubt that he would feel the same. What kind of a woman made her daughter so uneasy?

Of course, he wasn't really in a position to judge. His childhood had hardly been conducive to developing a deep understanding of parent/child relationships. By the time Mary and David Martin had taken him in, it had been more a case of taming a small animal than raising a child.

"This is it."

Lacey pointed to a brick driveway on the left, and Cam shook himself out of his thoughts as he turned the nose of the small truck into it.

Well, for better or worse, they'd arrived, and he was about to have his first meeting with his new mother-in-law. He could only hope that it wasn't going to turn out as badly as Lacey seemed to expect.

Chapter Seven

The rain the day before had left the air sparkling clean, a rare circumstance in Southern California. Two houses away an elderly man pushed an old-fashioned reel mower over the wide sweep of lawn. The gentle whir of the blades fit right into the neighborhood. The homes were large, and there was a quiet elegance to them that spoke of money.

As he walked up the brick path beside Lacey, Cam studied the house with interest. This was where Lacey had grown up. Flower beds flanked the front porch, filled with a bright profusion of tulips and ranunculuses. The flowers were backed by the creamy stucco of the house, and colonial-blue shutters were paired at each window.

The overall feeling was one of controlled gaiety, welcoming but just a little restrained. The house presented a bright front to the street, yet somehow managed to hint that the best it had to offer lay out of sight.

He was aware of Lacey's tension as they stepped onto the porch. She pushed the bell and stood staring at the front door. Cam's brow arched, thinking of the open-door policy at Mary and David's home. It would never have occurred to him to ring the doorbell there.

They had only a moment to wait before the door swung open. He'd half expected to see a giant of a woman with a rolling pin in one hand and a book of etiquette in the other

He hadn't envisioned the petite woman who was pushing open the screen door.

"Lacey! Honey, it's so good to see you." Mamie hugged her daughter and then turned bright blue eyes on Cam. "You must be Cameron. I can't tell you how pleasured I am to meet you." She held out her arms, and Cam stepped forward to embrace his mother-in-law.

"Now y'all come in. I've got a little bite prepared. Nothing fancy, mind you."

Amused, Cam followed the two women into the house, wondering if Mamie was aware that she hadn't allowed him to say a word.

"Cameron, you just settle yourself on the sofa. It should be comfortable enough for a man of your size. Lacey, you sit next to him. I want to look at the two of you together."

Cam's eyes danced as he sat on the sofa. He could see what Lacey meant. In the nicest possible way, Mamie reminded him of a general positioning his troops.

"Now, tell me all about how the two of you met. I've already told Lacey what I think of her keeping this from me. You knew nothin' would make me happier than to see you married, darlin'. And I can see Cameron is a fine man, so you had no cause for hidin' him."

"I'm afraid that's my fault, Mrs. Newton," Cameron said easily, realizing that if he didn't jump into the conversation now, Mamie would probably carry it all by herself. "I was a little uneasy about meeting Lacey's family. Now that I've met you, I'm sorry we didn't meet sooner. You're just as Lacey described you."

Lacey's arm twitched where it rested against his. She was probably remembering exactly what she'd said about her mother. But Mamie saw nothing wrong with his words. Her soft features colored at the subtle compliment.

"Well, I'm just glad we've had a chance to meet at last. Lacey was always such a secretive child. I suppose I shouldn't be surprised that she kept you to herself. But I must admit I

The

Morning After

was more than a little surprised when she got married withou even telling me.'' Her words held gentle reproach and Cam could feel the guilt practically oozing out from Lacey.

''Mother—''

''I'll have to take the blame for that, too, Mrs. Newton.' Cam didn't have any qualms at all about interrupting. When i came to her mother, it was clear that Lacey needed some help ''I'm the one who convinced Lacey that we should get marrie the way we did. There we were in Las Vegas, and the chanc just seemed too good to pass up. I bullied her shamefully.''

He slid his arm around Lacey's rigid shoulders, hugging he close. He didn't dare look at her face, fearing what he migh see there. They should have discussed what they were goin to tell her mother before they got here, but they hadn't, and s he was winging it.

''You must call me Mamie, Cameron. I hope the ceremon wasn't too stark. I'd always pictured Lacey in a white dres walkin' down the aisle at church.'' Her eyes were suspiciousl bright as she looked at her daughter.

''Well, it wasn't quite that romantic, but we'll always trea sure the memories, won't we, Lacey?''

Since neither of them had a clear memory of the event i question, Lacey was hard put to manage anything more than nod. She hoped her mother would take her flushed face as sign of her adoration for Cam and not of what it really wa: She'd been holding her breath so much during this conversatio that she was surprised she was still conscious.

Cam's judicious stretching of the truth seemed to be enoug to satisfy Mamie. Lacey was grateful when the conversatio moved away from the subject of their wedding. As the after noon wore on, she allowed herself to relax. Incredible thoug it seemed, it looked like Mamie had met her match.

Her genteel probing was met with polite response, but it wa clear that Cam was telling her only what he chose to tell he If she fished for more information than he was willing to giv he turned her questions away with as much subtlety as she asked them.

"When do the two of you plan on starting a family?" Mamie asked as she passed around a plate of delicate little sandwiches. Lacey's teacup hit the saucer with a loud clink. Cam took two sandwiches, apparently undisturbed by the question.

"Mother, we just got married." Lacey laughed, wondering if it sounded as false to the others as it did to her. "Give us a little time."

"You don't always have the time you think you're goin' to have, Lacey, honey. Look at your daddy and me. We'd planned to have a big ol' family, but he died before we had more'n you. I've always regretted that I didn't have another baby right away. That way you wouldn't have had to grow up all alone, the way you did. You listen to me, and don't put things off."

There could be no doubting Mamie's sincerity. Her eyes sparkled with tears and her voice shook. As usual when dealing with her mother, Lacey was torn between two opposing emotions: guilt and resentment. She was consumed with guilt and the need to reassure her mother she'd been perfectly happy as an only child, and she wanted to say that she and Cam were starting a family immediately, anything to take that look from Mamie's eyes. At the same time, she felt a tremendous resentment. Why couldn't her mother keep her nose out of things that were none of her business? For heaven's sake, she and Cam hardly even knew each other. How could Mamie be bringing up children?

"Mother—"

Cam's hand closed over hers, squeezing gently. "We've got plenty of time to decide what we want to do about children, Mamie. I think it's a mistake to rush into something like that. Besides, Lacey and I want some time to ourselves, don't we, honey?"

"Honey" nodded. She was incapable of anything more. Cam was looking at her in a way that made speech impossible.

She reminded herself that it was all for her mother's benefit but the look of tender affection in his eyes was so real.

"Well, I can see your point, Cameron. But don't you g waitin' too long. I'm anxious to hold a grandbaby."

"I think you're going to be a wonderful grandmother whe the time comes, Mamie, though you look much too young."

Mamie flushed with pleasure. The compliment could hav sounded glib, but Cam's tone made it impossible to doubt hi sincerity. Lacey stared at her teacup. How did he manage it For thirty years she'd been trying to find a way to distract he mother. In the space of an afternoon, he'd apparently manage to find the key to directing the conversation where *he* wante it to go instead of where Mamie chose to take it. And Mami was loving every minute of it.

She wasn't sure whether to be delighted or annoyed that h accomplished so easily what had always been impossible fo her. She scowled at the inoffensive china cup. Why wasn't sh happier that everything was going so well?

Beside her, Cam could feel her tension. He wondered at it source. True, he could see that Mamie needed a little managin if you didn't want her to manipulate you into answering ques tions better left unasked. But under the subtle manipulatio her affection for her only child was obvious.

He took a sip of coffee, listening with half an ear as Mami and Lacey discussed some new silk scarves that had recentl come in to Lacey's shop. He was fascinated by his surround ings. Having seen Lacey's apartment, he'd never have guesse that the home she'd grown up in would be so diametricall opposed in style.

Mamie's home was impeccably decorated in a style th could have seemed dated, yet somehow managed to look time less. Elegant mahogany furniture settled perfectly into the larg living room. Exquisite crocheted doilies created delicate pa terns on the dark wood. A baby grand piano sat in one corne framed by tall windows draped in ivory silk. His attention se tled on the neatly arranged photos that covered the piano.

Taking his cup with him, he left Lacey and her mother to their discussion and wandered over to the piano. Sunshine pooled on the gleaming wood, catching on the shiny silver frames. He wasn't surprised to see that most of the pictures were of Lacey. But it wasn't the Lacey he knew.

Picking up a photo, he felt the weight of the silver frame—no aluminum here. The girl in the picture was probably about twelve, but she didn't look like any twelve-year-old he'd ever known. She was seated on a straight-backed chair, her legs neatly crossed at the ankles, her hands clasped in her lap. Her hair—a paler shade of blond then—was drawn back from her face on top and allowed to cascade in neat curls onto her shoulders. A pale pink dress fell over her lap, almost meeting the tops of her white knee-length socks. Black Mary-Janes gleamed on her feet. And her hands were encased in short lace gloves.

Cam had a sudden memory of his foster sisters at that same age. As he recalled, jeans had been the general rule. He doubted if they would have sat still long enough to have their pictures taken in all this finery, and he knew for a fact that not one of them had ever owned a pair of white lace gloves.

He set the photo down, his eyes thoughtful. He was beginning to understand what Lacey had meant when she said that her mother raised her to be a Southern lady. Looking around this house, remembering the maid who'd wheeled in the tea cart—God, who had a tea cart in this day and age, let alone a maid?—he wondered if Lacey wasn't going to find life with him a little too primitive.

"That's one of my favorite pictures of Lacey. She was almost thirteen there." Mamie's voice interrupted his thoughts, and Cam turned to smile at her. Behind her, he could see that Lacey was gone, leaving the two of them alone.

"She was a very pretty little girl."

"Yes, she was." Mamie's expression was tender as she looked at the parade of portraits that marched across the piano top.

"It must have been difficult for you, raising a child on you
own."

"It wasn't easy." She reached out to touch a picture of a
Lacey barely out of diapers. "When her daddy died, I was so
frightened. I'd never really been on my own, you see. I lived
with my parents until I married, and then Doug took care of
me. There I was with hardly a lick of sense and a little girl
who had no one but me.

"I grew up real quick. It was lucky Doug left us well-off
because I sure didn't have a job skill to my name. I made Lacey
my job, and I did my best to bring her up in a manner befittin'."

She looked up at him, her eyes full of pride. "I couldn't be
any prouder of her. She's made a real success with her shop.
I worried that maybe she was puttin' off a personal life, but I
guess maybe she was just playin' it close to the vest. I hope
the two of you are goin' to be real happy."

"I hope so, too."

Lacey entered the room again, her eyes anxious when she
saw the two of them talking. Cam grinned at her and gave her
a thumbs-up sign behind Mamie's back. It seemed to reassure
her.

He felt as if he was beginning to understand a little more
about the woman he'd married. She'd been raised with one foot
in both worlds. The modern, ever-changing world of Southern
California and the gentler, more refined world her mother held
dear.

It must have created quite a conflict for the dainty little girl
in the picture. How did you walk a line between being the little
lady your mother wanted and the more laid-back, casual life
her friends had undoubtedly lived? It explained some of the
contradictions he'd seen.

The strong woman who had created a successful business by
the time she was thirty. And the woman who seemed slightly
uncertain when it came to dealing with other people. The
woman who was still a virgin at thirty.

He found himself liking her all the more for the way she'd tried to balance her two selves. A lot of people would have taken the easy road and turned their back on the world Mamie had presented.

He sat down next to Lacey on the sofa, listening with half an ear to Mamie's plans for the reception she insisted they had to have. Reaching out, he took Lacey's hand in his. She turned her head, startled by the casual gesture, but Cam didn't release her fingers. He smiled at her, feeling her hand relax in his.

He was beginning to think that, drunk, he'd had more sense than he might have laid claim to sober.

"I LIKED YOUR MOTHER," Cam said. The car slipped neatly into the stream of westbound traffic.

"You certainly know how to handle her." Lacey couldn't help the twinge of illogical resentment she felt, but she struggled to keep it out of her voice. The look he slanted in her direction told her that she hadn't been completely successful.

"Are you sorry we got along?"

"Of course not." She reached up to flip the visor down to shield her eyes from the late-afternoon sun. Her reflection greeted her in the mirror, and she met her own eyes, full of mixed emotions. She was behaving like a nitwit.

"No, of course I'm not sorry." She sighed. "I'm glad you liked her and I'm glad she liked you and I'm glad the visit went so well. Really I am."

"So what is it you're not glad about?" There was a hint of amusement in his tone but no sarcasm.

Lacey sighed again, feeling like an idiot. "It's really stupid, but in thirty years I've never been able to handle my mother as neatly as you did today. I guess I feel a little outclassed."

Cam grinned, but his glance held understanding, as well as amusement. "The fact that I didn't have any problem with your mother doesn't really have anything to do with how you deal with her. You've got a lot of emotional history with her. That makes it harder. Besides, I think your mother was determined to like me and get along with me. She wants to see you happy. She loves you.''

"I know." Lacey scowled. "I love her, too."

Cam laughed and reached over to squeeze her knee. "Cheer up. Now that I've saved you from spinsterhood, that's one bone of contention gone. She won't have to worry about you wasting away all by yourself. That should make her happy."

"Maybe. More than likely, she'll just turn her attention to something else. She's probably going to start worrying about us starting a family. She'll dig up all kinds of statistics about my biological time clock running out." Her mouth quirked in a rueful smile. "At least it will be a change of subject."

Cam smiled, but his eyes were thoughtful. "Do you want children, Lacey?"

The simple question seemed to catch at her throat, choking off her voice. She stared at the freeway ahead of them, oblivious to the traffic. Her answer, when it came, was straight from the heart.

"Yes. Yes, I do want children."

"So do I."

Cam didn't say anything more. He didn't have to. Those few simple words had given Lacey more than enough to think about. Children. Just thinking about them made this marriage seem real. Children meant forever; they meant commitment.

Lying alone in her bed that night, Lacey stared up at the ceiling, trying to picture herself as a mother. The image was a little fuzzy around the edges. She'd never really given children a lot of thought, always putting it off until some unspecified later date. Now it was hard to imagine herself with an infant.

Cam was another story. The picture of him as a father was sharp and clear. He'd be a good father. She didn't have any doubts about that. She might not have known him very long, but she was sure he'd be good with children.

And how did she feel about the idea of having Cam's child?

She closed her eyes as a wave of heat washed over her. One hand pressed against her stomach as she tried to imagine what it would feel like to hold another life inside her. The idea of carrying Cam's child was disturbing, all the more so because it held a definite appeal. Especially when she thought about creating that child.

Her memory of their wedding night was hazy, but when she tried to conjure it up, she was left with an impression of pleasure. Somehow she knew that drunk or not, Cam had been a considerate lover. She only wished she could remember the pleasurable details. Especially since it had been her first time. In her teens she'd often wondered what it would be like to be made love to. Whatever she'd thought then it would be, for sure it would be an experience she'd always remember. But...

She turned over, suddenly restless. Willing her mind to other, less dangerous thoughts, Lacey took deep, slow breaths, forcing herself to relax. Around her, the house was quiet. Cam had no doubt gone to sleep ages ago. Derwent would be snoring away in his bed in the kitchen. And they both showed a great deal more sense than she did.

The thing to do was to take this marriage one day at a time. It was foolish to think too far ahead. And children were a long, long way in the future. If they could make this marriage work—and that was a pretty big if—then they could talk about children.

LACEY GLANCED at the door as the shop bell rang, her face relaxing in a smile when she saw who it was.

"Lisa!" She wove her way around the tables of scarves and silken dainties to hug her friend. "Where have you been? I haven't seen you since—" She stopped, remembering just exactly when they'd last seen each other.

"Since Las Vegas." Lisa returned the hug and then stepped back, studying her friend carefully. "I've been in New York on business. I just got back yesterday and Frank told me what happened. Lacey, I just can't believe it."

"Frank told you what happened? Didn't you remember?"

Lisa shook her head, setting her pale brown page-boy swinging. "Not a thing. I swear to God, Lacey, I haven't been that drunk since the night you and I soaped the dean's windows. The last thing I remember about you and Cam is seeing the two of you dancing. Then Frank suggested we go somewhere a little more private, and I don't remember much of anything after that. We flew home the next day—God, what a miserable flight—and I left for New York that afternoon. I could just kill Frank for not telling me about this. Of course, our schedules never meshed well enough for us to talk directly, but he could have left a message with a secretary or something, don't you think?"

"Maybe he didn't want to distract you," Lacey offered as she led the way back to her tiny office. She signaled to Margaret, her assistant, that she was going to be unavailable. Not that she really needed to let her know. Margaret generally knew what was going on in the shop before Lacey did, anyway.

"Are you kidding? There's nothing Frank would love more than a chance to distract me." Lisa flung herself into the chair across from Lacey's desk while Lacey sat down behind the desk. "He hates my job. He's been bugging me for months to slow down."

"Well, you have been working really hard."

"I know that. But he just doesn't understand. I've got a really important deal in the works right now. Once this is settled, I'll be able to take a little time off."

Lisa had been saying that she was going to take "a little time off" ever since she left college. So far, she'd never found the right time, and Lacey didn't see any reason this time should be any different.

"Frank loves you. Maybe he wants to see a little more of you."

"Don't you start in on me, too." Lisa reached for her cigarettes, lighting one with fingers that seemed a little too tense. She drew in a lungful of smoke and let it out with a sigh, meeting Lacey's eyes across the desk. "I'm sorry, Lace. I didn't mean to snap at you. Frank and I have been going at i a bit too often lately. And what with this deal dragging on like this, I guess my nerves are a little ragged.''

"It's okay.''

"No, it's not okay.'' Lisa stubbed out the cigarette. "But I didn't come here to unload my problems on you. What's going on with you and Cam?''

Lacey shrugged. "Well, we got married in Las Vegas.''

"I know that much. What I don't know is what's going on now. Frank said you'd moved in with Cam?''

"That's right.''

"You mean, you're going to go through with this?'' Lisa sounded incredulous.

"What's wrong with that?'' Lacey asked defensively. In all the years she and Lisa had been friends, Lisa had never lost her ability to put her on the defensive.

Lisa shrugged. "Well, nothing, I suppose. I just never thought of you as that much of a gambler. You were always inclined to play it safe.''

"Well, maybe I got tired of playing it safe.''

"Good for you. I must say, Cam is one very attractive hunk of manhood. And nice, too. How goes the gamble so far?''

"Okay, I guess.'' Lacey picked up a pencil and began to doodle on the back of an invoice. "I only moved in about a week ago, so we're still doing a lot of adjusting.''

"That stage never really ends.'' Lisa tilted her head to one side, studying Lacey as if she was seeing her for the first time. "You know, I'd never have expected you to do something like this. You're the one who always plans your life so carefully. You don't even like to go out to dinner unless you've made reservations in advance. I just wouldn't have pictured you jumping into marriage like this.''

Lacey gave a short laugh. "Believe me, it's not the way I'd pictured starting my marriage.''

"No, I don't imagine it is,'' Lisa said thoughtfully. "So, having started out rather unconventionally, how's it going?''

"I told you. We're still making a lot of adjustments.''

Lisa waved one hand in a dismissing gesture. "Besides that. How are the two of you getting along? Are you madly in love with him yet? Or at least madly in lust?"

Lacey flushed, wishing Margaret would turn up with some small emergency that she just *had* to attend to herself. But the ever efficient Margaret didn't appear in the doorway, and Lisa didn't look as if she had any intention of disappearing in a puff of smoke.

"I haven't really had time to be madly in love with Cam."

"Okay. Then how about the lust part? Come on. With a man that gorgeous, you can't tell me you don't have a major case of the hots for him."

"I find Cam very attractive," Lacey said. She knew immediately that her tone was repressive, but it was too late to change it.

"Very attractive?" Lisa gave a hoot of laughter. "Lacey, the man is a hunk. A bona fide hunk. I think he deserves something a little stronger than very attractive."

"All right. He's a hunk. But there's more to marriage than that."

"Not as much as you might think." Lisa's tone held an edge of bitterness that surprised Lacey. Before she could question it, Lisa glanced at her watch and gave a quick exclamation. "Good grief. I've got a dinner appointment in less than an hour and I still have to go home and change."

She stood up. Lacey circled the desk and reached for the door, but Lisa's hand on her arm made her pause. "You know all I want is for you to be happy. I really do wish you and Cam the best. You know that, don't you?"

"I know." Lacey hugged her. There were times when Lisa drove her crazy, but twenty years of friendship lay behind them. There'd been an awful lot of good times in those twenty years.

She saw Lisa out the door and wandered back to her office. The store would be closing soon, and they weren't likely to be swamped by a sudden rush of customers. If they were, Margaret could call her.

She settled down behind her desk, thinking about Lisa's visit, the look in her eyes that said she wasn't happy with her life. It made Lacey look at her own life more closely, and she was surprised to find that she was happy. She hadn't realized how dull and predictable her life had gotten until Cameron McCleary appeared in it and threw it on its ear.

It wasn't even that everything had gone perfectly since she'd moved in. What she'd told Lisa was true. They were still trying to adjust to each other and there'd been a few snags along the way. But they'd been minor snags.

Like the night she'd fixed chicken curry for dinner. Cam had taken one whiff and turned a delicate shade of green. Curry was one thing he simply couldn't face. He'd once had a landlord who cooked curry twenty-four hours a day, and the smell had permanently destroyed Cam's interest in even trying the food. He'd been as tactful as it was possible to be while opening windows to try to air the house out.

And then there was Cam's taste in music. He adored Willie Nelson. In Lacey's opinion, Willie Nelson had no business calling himself a singer—a musician, maybe, but not a singer. To her ears his whiny tones were like nails on a blackboard. On the other hand, Cam referred to Bach as elevator music. So far, they'd found a shaky common ground with big-band music from the forties and rock and roll from the fifties and sixties.

She smiled suddenly, leaning back in her chair. She supposed that, when it came right down to it, much could be forgiven a man who was a bona fide hunk. Even Willie Nelson and a dislike of curry.

Chapter Eight

"Are you sure I shouldn't have worn something a little dress ier?" Lacey smoothed the jade-green skirt over her knees, he eyes going to Cam. He glanced away from the road long enough to inventory the simple cotton dress with the extrava gantly full skirt and soft fitted top, and the simple low-heeled pumps. She'd pulled her hair back in a chignon contrived t make her look both elegant and casual.

He faced the windshield again, his fingers tightening on th steering wheel. Did she have any idea how utterly desirabl she looked? It was all he could do to resist the urge to pull of the road and kiss her thoroughly.

"Cam?" She interpreted his silence as a negative. "It's n dressy enough, is it? Your sister is going to think I didn't car enough to dress up to meet her," she said with despair.

"You look fine."

If the answer was a little abrupt, it reflected the way he fel He'd never considered what a strain this arrangement was go ing to be. Living with an attractive, desirable woman who jus happened to be his wife and who he'd promised not to lay hand on was not his idea of a pleasant, relaxing way to spen his time.

The vague memories he'd retained of their wedding nigh didn't make things any easier. The fogginess that cloaked ther only made them seem more enticing. Was it a fantasy, or ha it really been one of the more incredible experiences of his life? Not knowing was enough to drive him crazy.

The only way to find out what was truth and what was fantasy was to try it again without an excess of margaritas. But of course that was going to have to wait until Lacey was ready. And she wasn't. He had only to look at the way she still watched him with that half-wary expression to know she wasn't ready. Not that he blamed her. When you got right down to it, they hadn't known each other all that long. It was an odd quirk on his part that made him feel as if he'd known her forever.

Lacey reached up to fuss with the neckline of the dress. "First impressions are important. I don't— What are you doing?"

With a mumbled curse, Cam switched on the right turn signal and began cutting across the lanes of traffic. He ignored her question, easing into the emergency lane and pulling to a stop.

"What's wrong?"

"You need something to think about besides your dress."

Cam unbuckled his seat belt and then leaned over to do the same to hers. He reached for her, but Lacey hung back against the door, reddening as her eyes met his and his meaning became clear.

"This is nuts. You can't do this."

"I've just done it." His hands closed over her shoulders, drawing her forward. There was a wicked gleam in his eyes that brought an unexpected flutter to her heart.

"Cam, there are laws."

"Against a man kissing his wife?" His breath feathered over her cheek.

"Against using the emergency lane for anything but an emergency," Lacey told him, wondering at the breathlessness that seemed to have stolen her voice.

"This is an emergency." Lacey couldn't have argued the point even if she'd been so inclined. His mouth took the last of her breath.

Her hands slid upward from their half-protesting position against his chest to cling to his shoulders. His fingers settled against the back of her head, mussing the careful chignon, but Lacey didn't care. Tilting her head to allow the kiss to deepen, she wasn't aware of anything but the warm pool of heat that seemed to spread outward from her mouth until her whole body was flushed.

It wasn't the first time he'd kissed her, nor the first time she'd felt this heat. But this time, the warmth seemed to spread a little farther, demand a little more. And Lacey was finding that demand increasingly exciting. She wanted more. She wanted Cam to want more. Each night when he said goodnight, it was harder to go off to her lonely bed, knowing he was so close.

His tongue edged along her mouth and she opened to him. His free hand slid upward from the curve of her waist until his palm rested against the side of her breast. She'd forgotten where they were, where they were going. All that really mattered was the feel of Cam's mouth on hers.

The raucous blast of a truck's horn broke the sweet spell. Cam's mouth lifted from hers slowly, as if relinquishing something precious. Lacey felt dazed as she looked up at him. Never in her life had any man made her tremble with just a kiss. Cam looked at her for a long moment, something in his eyes that she couldn't quite read, and then he turned away to put the car in gear.

"Fasten your seat belt."

Lacey's fingers fumbled with the mechanism. Fasten her seat belt? She felt as if she'd just taken a short roller-coaster ride without a seat belt. It seemed a little late to be fastening it now.

Cam pulled the car back onto the freeway, continuing their interrupted journey as if nothing unusual had happened. Lacey stole a quick look at him, but his attention was all on the surrounding traffic. At least so she thought until his eyes flicked toward her and he gave her a quick grin.

"Not worried about your dress anymore, are you?"

She shook her head, coloring slightly as she lifted her hands to her hair, repairing the damage his fingers had done. No, she certainly wasn't worried about her clothes anymore.

Claire's home was on a half acre of land in the Simi Valley. The hills around the property were covered with chaparral, a soft green at this time of year, though in summer they would change to a dull, fire-prone brown.

The car had barely come to a standstill in the gravel drive when the front door of the house burst open and what seemed to be at least a hundred children clattered down the steps, all shouting at the top of their lungs. Lacey blinked once or twice and the hundred children sorted themselves into four or five. It was impossible to get an accurate count because the mini-mob kept moving around.

The shouts of "Uncle Cam! Uncle Cam!" were near to deafening, but Cam didn't seem to mind. He was laughing as he scooped up the two smallest members of the group, settling one on each hip.

The screen door opened again, but closed more genteelly this time. The woman who approached them was lovely. Skin the color of pale coffee was stretched over sculpted cheekbones that made Lacey wish she'd spent more time with blusher and a contour brush. Though her dark eyes remained watchful, the woman smiled at Lacey.

Cam fought his way free of the children long enough to make the introductions. "Lacey, this is my sister Claire. Claire, this is Lacey, who was kind enough to marry me."

Lacey blinked, her eyes unconsciously widening a bit, but Mamie's years of teaching had not been in vain. Her smile was natural as she stretched out a hand to Claire. Claire's grip was as straightforward as her words.

"I take it Cam didn't tell you that we're all adopted."

"I— No, he didn't." Claire's face softened as she looked at her brother, who was kneeling to exclaim over the bandage that decorated his niece's dusty knee. "I think he forgets most of the time. We grew up in a mixed bag of a family. It's easy to forget that other people may be shocked.''

"I wasn't shocked." Lacey was quick to correct that impression. "It's just that— Well, you don't look much alike, do you?''

Claire laughed, her eyes lighting with amusement. "No, I guess we don't.''

Lacey watched as Claire waded into the group surrounding Cam and proceeded to detach them from their uncle with calm efficiency. Freed of his small entourage, Cam moved over to Lacey, taking her hand and drawing her toward the house.

The house was larger than it looked from the outside, the rooms big and airy. The decor had a simple elegance that reminded Lacey of her hostess. Taupe and black tones were lightened with an occasional shock of burnt orange or peacock blue. It might have looked contrived, but instead the effect was one of hominess. It wasn't hard to imagine children running through these rooms.

Lacey noticed the decor only peripherally. Her attention was on the two men who sat near the fireplace. The taller of the two was clearly Claire's husband. One of them stood up, approaching with a quick stride that she was to learn was characteristic of Claire's husband. Joe was a total contrast to his wife, quick and impatient where she was slower and calmer. He shook Lacey's hand, giving her a wide smile.

"So, you're the lady who finally caught Cam. His mother will be delighted he's no longer on the loose. She's been telling him he needed a wife for at least ten years now.''

"Twelve," Cam muttered with feeling. Joe laughed, taking Cam's hand and shaking it with the same fervor he'd shown Lacey.

She heard Claire and the children come in and shut the door, but her attention had shifted over Joe's shoulder to the man now standing up. His eyes met hers uneasily, and it was all Lacey could do to keep from laughing out loud.

"Hi, Lacey.''

"Jimbo." She kept her tone neutral. There was no reason to let him off the hook too soon. Though Cam had told her about Jimbo's visit, it was the first time she'd seen him since that eventful night in Las Vegas, and she was enjoying watching him squirm. Not that she blamed him for the fact that she and Cam had gotten married. But it wasn't often that she had a chance to see Jimbo humble.

"You look really nice."

Lacey's chin quivered. He was throwing himself on his knees, at least verbally. She ought to let him grovel, but Mamie'd taught her better. "Thank you."

Jimbo saw the humor in her eyes and he grinned, his relief obvious. "I knew you wouldn't be able to hold a grudge."

"I should." Lacey held out her hand, and Jimbo took it, pulling her into a hug.

The evening turned out to be a great deal more fun and a lot less stressful than Lacey had expected. Claire's entertaining style was relaxed. She allowed her guests to amuse themselves rather than try to force the evening into any set pattern.

The children were everywhere. Even though Lacey had sorted them into only four small bodies, two boys and two girls ranging from ten years old down to three, they still seemed to form a mini-horde. If there was ever a moment when she couldn't see a child, she had only to seek Cam out. Chances were that at least one of his nieces and nephews was somewhere nearby. They all seemed to think that Uncle Cam was one of the best entertainments life had to offer.

Lacey found herself watching him, marveling at his ability to handle the children. He seemed to know just how to talk to them, never condescending and never talking over their heads. She watched him pick up the littlest one, a girl whose precarious balance had been upset by the passage of her older brother. Cam's hands were gentle, smoothing the ruffles on her powder-blue dress and, at the same time, soothing the damage to her dignity. She leaned her head against his chest, sticking her thumb in her mouth as she watched the bustle from the safe haven of her uncle's arms.

As if sensing Lacey's gaze, Cam looked up, his eyes meeting hers. There was a moment when the rest of the room faded away and they might have been all alone. Just the two of them in some place where nothing mattered but each other. She didn't know if he could see the sudden vulnerability she felt, but she saw his eyes darken. He moved as if to come to her, but then Joe was asking Cam's opinion on an armoire he was thinking of buying. Cam stared at her an instant longer, something in his eyes she couldn't quite read, and then he turned to answer Joe and the moment was gone.

"He'll make a good father."

Jimbo's comment followed her own thoughts so closely that Lacey felt as if he must have read her thoughts. "Yes, he will." She reached for her glass of wine, hoping her expression was as calm as her tone.

Claire was in the kitchen, taking care of some last-minute details. Joe and Cam were absorbed in a discussion of the finer points of furniture making. For all intents and purposes, she and Jimbo were alone.

"You know, I've known Cam a lot longer than you have."

Lacey glanced at Jimbo, lifting one eyebrow. "Almost anybody could qualify for that statement."

"I mean, I've known him a lot longer than a lot of people."

"I know the two of you have been friends for a long time."

It was clear he had something he wanted to say. It was so unusual to see Jimbo at any kind of a loss for words that Lacey's attention sharpened. She turned so that she faced him more fully.

"Has Cam told you much about his past?" Jimbo asked.

"No. I didn't even know he was adopted until tonight."

"He doesn't talk about it much, but if it hadn't been for his foster parents, he'd probably be behind bars right now, or dead maybe."

Lacey choked on her wine. Her eyes jerked to where Cam

ınd Joe were talking and then came back to Jimbo. "Cam? You've got to be kidding. Mr. Calm-and-steady?"

But Jimbo didn't look like he was kidding. His square face was set in unusually serious lines. "I met Cam when I was working in a program to help gang members."

Gang members? Lacey was beyond a verbal protest. She stared at Jimbo, her eyes reflecting her disbelief.

"I know it's hard to believe. Cam would probably murder me if he knew I was telling you this, but he'll never say anything, and it might help you understand him a little."

Lacey knew that she should probably open her mouth and say that she didn't want him to tell her anything Cam didn't want her to know, but she couldn't have spoken to save her soul. Now that Jimbo had said this much, she had to know the rest.

"Cam was only thirteen or so, but he was one tough kid. He'd been on the streets for a couple of years and he'd figured out that a gang offered him a way to survive. The police picked him on a robbery charge, and I just happened to get the assignment to talk to him.

"I was only nine or ten years older than he was and he took one look at me and announced I wasn't old enough to be telling him how to live."

Jimbo smiled, his eyes seeing things Lacey could only imagine. "When I met him, he gave me a look that just dared me to try and help him, but there was something in his eyes that made me think maybe it wasn't too late for him. I knew about Mary and David Martin. They'd taken in three or four troubled kids by then. God, Cam was hostile.

"His father was dead and his mother just left him one day and never came back. He was convinced that adults were the enemy in his own private war. He had the most explosive temper I've ever seen in my life. Even though he was just a kid, he could be pretty frightening when he was in a temper.

"But Mary and David took him in as foster parents and convinced him that not every adult was a rat. It took a while

to track down his grandparents, since Cam wasn't sure of hi
mother's maiden name—his paternal grandparents were long
dead. By the time they were found, he'd settled in so well with
Mary and David that they left him where he was.''

"I'd never have guessed,'' Lacey murmured.

"He'd never tell you, but I know that calm of his can be
little hard to take sometimes. I thought it might help if you
understand where it came from.''

"It does. It really does.'' She looked at Cam, trying to see
that angry little boy in the man. He glanced up, caught her eye
and smiled. Lacey smiled back, but she was glad for the dis
traction Claire provided by returning to announce dinner. Jimbo
had given her a lot to consider.

She was still considering it as they drove home a few hour
later. Was it possible she'd imagined the whole conversation
There'd certainly been nothing in Jimbo's manner to indicate
that they'd spoken of anything more serious than the next day'
weather. He'd been his usual jovial, off-the-wall self, joking
with Cam, playing with the children.

She studied Cam surreptitiously. In the light from the dash
board, he looked the same as he always did. But she was seeing
him in a different way. She was seeing an angry little boy
who'd had no one but himself to depend on.

"Have I got dirt on my nose?'' Cam's quiet question made
Lacey jump. "You've been staring at me for the last twenty
minutes.''

"Sorry.'' She shifted her gaze to the empty freeway ahead
"I was thinking, I guess.''

"About what?''

"You. Us. I was thinking that we haven't known each other
very long at all.''

"True. Does that bother you?''

"I don't know. I guess maybe that's the whole purpose of
our living together like we are—to give us a chance to get to
know each other.''

"Do you feel like we're not making progress?" Lacey felt Cam glance at her, but she didn't return it.

"I don't know. Do you think we're getting to know each other?"

"You must have taken Psych 101 in college. Answering a question with a question. 'And what do you think of this, Mrs. Smith?' I always thought that was a way for the psychiatrist to stall while he was trying to figure out just what Mrs. Smith's dreams of talking pigs really meant.

"But to answer the questions—I think we're getting to know each other. At least, I feel as if I'm getting to know you."

"You don't talk about yourself very much."

Out the corner of her eye, she saw his hands tighten on the wheel and then relax. With the new insight she'd been given, she realized that Cam's control was not as effortless as she'd always assumed.

"I wondered why Jimbo was talking to you so earnestly. Telling you about my misspent youth, was he?"

Lacey shrugged, sorry she'd brought the subject up, even in such an oblique way.

"He told me a little."

Cam laughed, though the sound didn't hold much humor. "I should have known he wouldn't be able to resist."

"He was concerned about us. He said he thought it might help me to understand you."

"And does it?"

"I think so," Lacey said quietly. There was a new tension in the car that she didn't understand.

"It isn't that simple. That's another lesson Psych 101 teaches you: that you can get to know somebody by knowing their past. It doesn't work that way in real life, Lacey. In real life it takes a lot of time and effort to get to know a person. And you have to get to know them in the here and now. You see how the past shaped them by looking at what they've become. When you look at their past and then try to see how it affected them, you're going at it backward."

"Don't you think the two go hand in hand? That you can get to know someone by knowing both their past and their present?"

"No. I think that can just confuse things." She felt his glance though she didn't look at him. "Take this situation. Now that Jimbo has told you all about my pathetic past, you're looking at me in a different way."

"Of course I am. I've just learned something about you."

"No. You've learned something about who I *was*. I'm not that screwed-up little boy anymore. I haven't been for a very long time."

"I didn't say you were," Lacey protested. This conversation wasn't going at all the way she'd hoped. Instead of being able to express her sympathy for what he'd gone through, she'd apparently managed to offend him.

Cam drew in a quick hard breath. "I'm sorry. I didn't mean to jump all over you. I guess you touched on a bit of a sore spot."

"I just wanted you to know that I was sorry you'd had to go through that," she told him softly.

"I know." He reached out, taking her hand in his. "I don't talk about those days because I've gotten past them. I've moved on, and I don't want you looking at me and feeling sorry for what I was. I want you to see what I *am*."

"I do, but I can't help but admire the fact you've pulled yourself up the way you have." Lacey turned her hand in his, her fingers curling around his hard palm. "A lot of people never manage to get away from a start like that."

"I had a lot of help. Jimbo, for one, though I may murder him after this latest routine."

"I really think he was trying to help," Lacey offered.

"I think he was poking his nose where it doesn't belong."

Cam didn't sound too upset. The cold note that had been so unnerving was gone from his voice. He sounded the way he usually did, calm and in control. Still, Lacey had had a glimpse of what lay beneath that control.

They didn't talk much during the remainder of the drive. Cam drew her hand to his leg and pressed it there before returning his own hand to the wheel. She could have drawn away then, but she didn't. No matter what Cam thought, knowing his past did change the way she saw him. It made him more human.

She remembered that moment when their eyes had met and she'd felt so connected to him, as if she was seeing a part of herself that had been missing for a long time.

"Claire liked you."

"I liked her." Lacey shifted, drawing herself straighter in the seat. She would have moved her hand, but Cam's fingers closed over hers, a silent request, and so she left her hand where it was, resting on the hard muscles of his thigh.

"Abby told me she thought you were a very pretty lady."

Abby? It took Lacey a moment to remember that Abby was Claire's youngest, the toddler who'd clung so determinedly to Cam's leg.

She felt as if there were two conversations being carried on. The one on the surface that was safe and comfortable and another that lay underneath and was anything but.

By the time Cam pulled the car into the driveway, several miles of silence lay between them. Midnight hovered just around the corner, and the neighborhood was still, the houses dark.

Lacey was vividly aware of Cam following her up the walkway to the door. The lock snicked beneath the pressure of his key, and they stepped into the silent house. Derwent ran in from the kitchen, and Lacey bent to scratch one ear, glad of the small distraction.

She wasn't quite sure why a distraction was desirable. Nothing had happened. Nothing had been said. This was just a night like any of the other nights she'd spent in this house. But it didn't feel like any other night. There was something different in the air, something she couldn't put her finger on, and she didn't think it was her imagination.

Derwent swiped at her hand with a wet tongue and then turned and headed back toward his bed in the kitchen. Lacey stood up, drawing in a deep breath. She was being ridiculous. There was nothing different about tonight except that her imagination was working overtime. It was late, she was tired, she'd spent too much time worrying about meeting Cam's sister, and her nerves were still a little overstretched. That's all it was.

She cleared her throat. "Well, it's pretty late. I think I'll go to bed."

"Good idea," Cam said. Lacey glanced at him, wondering if his words had a hidden meaning. But there was nothing in his expression to indicate that he'd meant anything more than just what he'd said.

What's wrong with me tonight?

"Well, good night." She hesitated a moment and then took a step closer. Their good-night kiss was a well-established ritual. Why did tonight feel different?

Cam's hand came up, cupping her cheek as his head bent to hers. Lacey could feel the gentle rasp of his callused skin against hers. She could catch the merest whiff of some cologne she couldn't identify, a vague woodsy scent she associated with Cam.

Her gaze lifted as he lowered his head. That look was in his eyes again. The one she'd seen this evening. The one that set her pulse to beating at a faster rate. And she was no closer to defining that look than she had been. Or maybe she was afraid to define it. His thumb stroked her cheekbone, the faint roughness strangely inviting. Lacey's lashes lowered as if drawn by gentle weights.

His mouth was warm, molding to hers in a way that was both demand and appeal. And she had to answer both. She'd been right in sensing that tonight was different. It was as if there'd been something in the air they'd been breathing. Something that had caused a subtle shift, leaving them almost but not quite the same.

His hand slid from her cheek to cradle her throat, his thumb resting in the hollow at its base. Lacey wondered if he could feel the accelerated beat of her pulse. His other arm slipped around her back, drawing her closer as the kiss deepened. Lacey's fingers wove into the thickness of his hair. From somewhere deep inside, need swept over her, warm and hungry.

Her mouth opened to his, inviting—no, demanding his possession. His tongue slid inside, fencing with hers in an ancient duel that had no winner, no loser. His hand swept her closer still, until not even a shadow could have fit between them. Lacey rose on her toes, molding herself to him, as eager for the contact as he was.

This was what she'd been missing. All her life she'd been only half-complete and she hadn't realized it until now. Everything had been leading up to this moment, this place, this man.

Cam's fingers found the pins that held her hair, pulling them loose. They hit the floor with faint clicks that seemed unnaturally loud in the quiet of the house. Lacey's hair spilled over his hand, a cascade of honey-gold silk. The feel of it against his skin seemed to loosen his control another notch. He tilted her head, deepening the kiss still further as his other hand swept down her back, tracing the gentle hollows at the base of her spine before flattening over the swell of her buttocks and pressing her into the cradle of his hips.

Lacey could feel the pressure of his arousal through the layers of fabric that separated them. A warm, liquid weight seemed to settle in her stomach. She'd never wanted anything in her life more than she wanted Cam in that moment. Her very skin ached with the need for him.

But the strength of that need frightened her. It was as if, in giving in to that need, she might lose something of herself, something she'd never get back. She wasn't ready for this. The realization had to fight its way into her consciousness. She didn't want to acknowledge it, didn't want to give up the sweet sensations pouring through her. But it wouldn't be denied. With each passing moment, her desire grew, but so did her uneasiness. It was too soon. Too much, too soon.

Her hands moved to his shoulders, clinging for a moment in helpless response to the desire still rocketing through her. If this continued, she'd regret it. With an effort she dragged her mouth away from his, drawing in a deep lungful of air.

"No."

The word was hardly more than a whisper. For a moment, she wasn't sure if he'd heard her. His hands continued to hold her close. She could feel the hunger in him, and she knew that if he chose to insist, there'd be nothing she could do to stop him. Looking into his eyes, she saw the same awareness there.

He wouldn't have to use force. Her own need would work against her. He could surely feel it in the way she still pressed so close against him.

His hands tightened their hold on her, and her heart gave a quick leap. For an instant, only an instant, she knew he was tempted to ignore her protest. Time was suspended; even her breathing seemed to stop. And then his eyes closed, and she felt the quick hard breath he drew before his hands moved away.

She stepped back, feeling as if she'd left a piece of herself behind. Cam didn't say anything, and the silence in the little hall grew thick with things unspoken.

"I'm sorry." Lacey's voice was hushed, and she avoided looking at him.

"Don't be. I shouldn't have pushed." But there was a rasp in his voice that told her just how tightly he was holding on to his control.

"No, really. I shouldn't have—"

"Lacey." She'd never realized that the sound of her name could cut across a sentence so neatly. She stopped, staring up at him, her eyes wide. In the dim light she saw his chest rise and fall as he took a quick breath.

"Just go to bed, Lacey. And don't start feeling guilty. I'm a big boy. Cold showers are good for me." His mouth twisted in a half smile that didn't quite reach his eyes, but it was enough to tell her that he wasn't upset with her.

Maybe he was right. It had been a long eventful day. First the visit from Lisa, and then meeting Claire and her family. Jimbo's revelations about Cam's past and now this. She was tired and probably exaggerating the day's events.

"Good night."

"Good night, Lacey."

She turned slowly, fighting the urge to turn back and throw herself into his arms.

Chapter Nine

During the following week, Lacey learned the true meaning of
sexual tension. If she'd thought she was aware of Cam before,
it was nothing compared to the acute awareness she felt now.
It didn't seem possible that one kiss could have changed things
so much, but she couldn't deny the results.

If Cam walked into the room, she knew it. She didn't even
have to see him. She could *feel* his presence, like a feather
being drawn slowly up her spine, bringing all her nerve endings
to tingling life.

And it wasn't just the physical awareness that was suddenly
so vivid. She felt a new awareness of him as a person. Despite
what he'd said, the past did make a difference. Now when she
looked at him, she saw where he'd come from, as well as where
he was now. And she had to admit that she liked what she saw.
Past, present and, she hoped, future. She liked Cameron
McCleary. There were moments when she thought it might be
more than merely liking, but she wasn't quite ready to debate
that issue with herself. For now it was enough that she liked
the man she'd married. Love could come later, when she was
more prepared for it.

Cam obviously felt the change, too, intangible as it was. He
seemed to watch her more. But it wasn't just that. Kisses were
no longer limited to a semi-chaste good-night gesture. He
kissed her when they met in the morning. He kissed her when

he left for the shop. He kissed her when she got home. And
ometimes he kissed her for no reason at all.

At first Lacey was thrown off balance, questioning the reason
or each small contact, analyzing her own reactions, wondering
f a larger demand was to follow. But when he didn't push any
urther, she gradually relaxed, enjoying the small attentions.

Cam wondered if he was being totally ethical. He could see
Lacey's uneasiness gradually being replaced with trust, and he
wasn't sure he deserved that trust. He was deliberately setting
ut to convince her he was harmless. Which didn't reflect re-
lity at all. In fact, there were times when he felt downright
redatory. He'd once watched a cat stalk a sparrow, first acting
asual, as if the presence of the bird was of no interest at all,
nd then pouncing.

Pouncing was exactly what he felt like doing. He didn't think
acey had any idea of just how desirable she was. If she had,
naybe she wouldn't have trusted him so readily.

It wasn't as if he was planning anything that would hurt her
n any way, he argued with his conscience. Yes, he was delib-
rately seducing her, but it was his sincere belief that the end
esult would be as satisfying to her as it would be to him. They
vere married. If they really wanted this marriage to work, then
ooner or later they were going to have to sleep together. Was
t really so terrible of him to soothe her uneasiness? To make
e path just a little smoother?

Besides, it wasn't as if all he wanted from her was a quick
mble in the hay. He wanted a lot more than that. For the first
ne in a very long time, he wanted to build something im-
ortant with someone else.

He hadn't been entirely honest with her when he'd told her
at his past was the past. He knew, better than anyone else,
st how long the scars lingered. He'd learned early in life that
usting people was likely to get him hurt, and he hadn't trusted
any people since. Maybe that was why he'd never married,
ver even come close.

But now, here he was, married to a woman he not only

desired, but liked. He liked the way she looked in the mornin‹ with her eyes still heavy with sleep. He liked the drive an‹ determination that had made her successful in business. In fac‹ he liked just about everything about her.

So really, when you looked at it from that angle, there wasn‹ anything wrong with what he was planning. It was all for th‹ best. Right?

MAMIE'S HOUSE was brightly lit, throwing out a welcomin‹ glow into the dusk. Cam pulled the car into the drive and g‹ out, coming around to open Lacey's door for her. She took h‹ hand, though she didn't really need any help getting out of th‹ car. What she did need was a little moral support. Cam's stro‹ grip provided that.

"Are you sure you don't mind Mother throwing this party‹ I tried to talk her out of it."

Cam looked down at her, his expression difficult to read ‹ the near dark. "I don't mind a bit. After all, we missed t‹ reception and the usual round of showers, didn't we?"

"Mother just wants to show you off to everyone. I think s‹ wants to prove that I really did get married."

"Nothing wrong with that. You know, you worry too mu‹ about your mother's motivations. If you'd just accept her ‹ face value, I think you'd find her a lot easier to get alo‹ with."

"Maybe," she muttered. "But you haven't known her ‹ long as I have. She may look like a helpless flower, but s‹ has a knack for getting what she wants."

"Well, then look at it this way. She's already *got* what s‹ wants. We're married. So, what do you think she's after w‹ this party?"

It was a reasonable question. Lacey hesitated, staring at t‹ brightly lit house. "Maybe you're right. Maybe she just wa‹ to do a victory dance now that she's successfully married ‹ off."

Cam laughed. "Your mother can hardly take credit for that‹

"You don't know my mother." She reached up to smooth her hair, checking to make sure that none of the pins had come loose. Cam's hand caught hers, drawing it down to her side.

"You look terrific. Stop fussing." Somehow, the casual compliment reassured her in a way more flowery words couldn't have. She laughed as they went up the walkway.

"I guess I'm inclined to be a little paranoid about my mother."

"Just a little." But his tone was more amused than critical. They'd arrived on the front step and he reached out to ring the doorbell. Lacey drew a deep breath, but she didn't get a chance to let it out as Cam's head suddenly dipped and his mouth caught hers. Off balance, she clutched at his shoulders. Thus, her mother opened the door to find her son-in-law kissing her daughter quite thoroughly. Whether he'd planned it or not, Cam couldn't have come up with anything more likely to put Mamie in a good mood.

"Stop it, you two. A doorstop is no place to be kissin' your wife, Cameron." But there was a pleased note in her voice that made it clear she was delighted by this evidence of cordiality in her daughter's marriage.

Cam took his time releasing Lacey. He lifted his head, his eyes meeting hers. Despite the rushing in her ears, Lacey caught the wicked gleam that sparked his eyes to sapphire. He turned away to greet her mother, and she wondered if she'd imagined that look. Lifting a hand to her mouth, she didn't think so.

As she stepped into the living room, Lacey saw that she and Cam were just about the last arrivals. Such tardiness would ordinarily have earned her a scold, but she didn't think Mamie had any such thing in mind. She was too delighted to have Cam to introduce to those of her friends who'd begun to hint that Lacey might never marry.

Lifting a glass of champagne from a table, Lacey edged away, leaving Cam to her mother's tender mercies. She ignored the pleading look he threw her. Served him right for kissing

350   *The Morning After*

her like that. But there was a faint curve to her mouth as she went to inspect the food.

"You realize you're one of the few people in the world for whom I'd stuff myself into one of these things."

Lacey turned as Jimbo spoke from behind her. Her smile became a full grin. He did look remarkably uncomfortable in the tailored dinner jacket. With his stocky build, the resemblance to a penguin was marked.

"You look like a penguin I saw on a *National Geographic* special one time. Only he looked more comfortable." She reached for a stuffed mushroom and bit into it with obvious pleasure.

"Heartless wench." But reproach was absent from Jimbo's voice. His eyes had gone past her. Lacey turned to see what had caught his attention. Cam and Mamie were standing with a small group of guests. Cam was speaking, and though it was impossible to hear what he was saying, it was apparently amusing because his listeners began to laugh.

"Looks like Cam and Mother are getting along." Lacey turned back to the buffet table, wondering why the thought didn't please her more. Not that she wasn't glad he'd made a hit with Mamie. But she had to admit she might have been a bit gladder if Mamie hadn't made such a hit with Cam. It was great that he liked her mother, but did he have to like her quite so much? She sighed, recognizing the absurdity of her thinking.

"Why didn't you tell me that your mother was so beautiful?" Jimbo's attention was still on the other group. The question surprised her. Beautiful? Her mother?

She turned, trying to look at Mamie through a stranger's eyes. Yes, she supposed she could be called beautiful. She had the fine bone structure that she'd bestowed on her daughter and it carried age gracefully. Her skin was still smooth and lovely. The years had laid only the gentlest of hands on her. Her pale hair carried more than a few lengths of silver, but they threaded through the strands in a way that seemed to highlight the gold, rather than overpower it.

She answered Jimbo's question after a long pause. "You didn't ask." It seemed to take a conscious effort for him to drag his attention back to her.

"I guess I should have known she'd be beautiful. After all, look at her daughter."

Lacey raised one brow at his exaggeratedly unctuous tone. "Flattery isn't going to get you anything. I've already forgiven you for your part in the whole Vegas thing."

"I'm not sure there's anything to forgive." He reached for a cracker and spread it with a healthy layer of Brie. "It looks to me like you and Cam are doing just fine. If you weren't married to him, would you really be happier?" The look he gave her demanded honesty, as if her answer meant as much to him as it would to her.

Lacey stopped, a shrimp halfway to her mouth, an arrested look in her eyes. Trust Jimbo to ask the wrong question. Or was it the right one? Would she be happier now if she hadn't married Cam?

"Don't try to wiggle out of your responsibility," she told Jimbo absently. She bit into the shrimp, trying to throw off the uneasy feeling that something significant had just happened.

Jimbo's eyes went past her. Even before she turned she knew who was approaching. The back of her neck tingled with awareness.

"Cam. Mother."

"Honey, did I tell you how pretty you look?" Mamie slid her arm through Lacey's in an affectionate gesture, her eyes sparkling with pleasure.

"Since you bought me this dress, Mother, you're somewhat obligated to think it looks nice." She took a sip of champagne, trying not to notice the way Cam's shoulders filled out his jacket.

"Well, since you mention it, I do think I did a good job. That color is perfect for you. Don't the two of you think she looks nice?" Mamie's eyes moved from Cam to Jimbo, a teasing light in them. Lacey felt her cheeks warm, but she didn't say anything. Later, she'd throttle her mother, but for now she'd remember her manners.

"I've already told Lacey my opinion." Cam's voice held a deep note that stroked her like a physical caress. Lacey's eyes swept up to meet his. There was a warmth in his gaze that brought heat to her skin. She looked away, taking a quick swallow of champagne.

"It's easy to see where Lacey gets her looks, Mrs. Newton." Jimbo's tone drew Lacey's attention, and she looked at him sharply, wondering if she was imagining the way he was looking at her mother.

"Please, call me Mamie. And I believe your given name is James. May I?"

"I'd be honored, Mamie." The formal words should have sounded silly, especially coming from Jimbo. Only they didn't sound silly at all. Lacey looked at Cam, her uncertainty about him forgotten in the light of this new development. He raised his brows, his half smile expressing the same surprise she felt.

Jimbo was looking at her mother as if he'd just been granted a glimpse of heaven. He might have been looking at an angel, judging from the expression in his eyes. And her mother. That one was harder to assess. There was a hint of delicate color in Mamie's cheeks, and her eyes seemed to sparkle a bit brighter. But Lacey had seen that look before. There was nothing her mother loved quite so much as a little genteel flirtation. It was impossible to judge whether she saw Jimbo as anything more than a pleasant divertissement.

"Lacey tells me you're an accountant, James. Let me introduce you to Harry Lapin. He has a little business, and he was just sayin' he'd give his right arm to find a good accountant. Now, I don't think you want Harry's right arm, you havin' a perfectly good one of your own and all. But a little of Harry's business might be welcome."

The two of them moved off, Mamie's hand set gently on the aforementioned right arm, Jimbo's head bent over hers as if every word she spoke was a jewel beyond price.

"What do you think?" Cam asked, his gaze following the odd couple just as Lacey's had.

"I don't know. Jimbo certainly seems smitten. It's a little harder to tell about Mother. She always told me that Southern women are born knowing how to flirt. That may be all it is." She set down her empty glass and moved down the table to pick up a fresh one.

"Were you?"

She turned at Cam's question, raising one brow. "Was I what?"

"Born knowing how to flirt?" His eyes met hers over his own glass, and Lacey felt the familiar flush of heat.

"To Mother's everlasting regret, that's a gift apparently given only to those actually born on the sacred soil of the South. And Southern California doesn't count. I'm afraid flirting is not one of my better talents."

"You have talents all your own."

Now why did his statement seem to have a double meaning? Her eyes dropped from his to stare into her champagne. The bubbles clung lazily to the side, giving the pale liquid a frivolous look. She only wished her mood could match them. She took a deep swallow, trying not to notice how close Cam was standing.

"You really do look beautiful tonight, Lacey." His voice slid over her skin, leaving warmth in its wake. Despite telling herself that it was only a compliment, Lacey's hand was trembling slightly as she smoothed it over the fragile silk of her skirt. The fabric caught the light, revealing threads of gold and blue woven through the jade green. If you watched it long enough, it seemed to change colors, shifting with every change of light.

Not unlike the man who stood beside her. Sometimes he appeared as harmless as that silly dog of his. But then, some shift of light would show a new side, and she'd find her pulse beating a little too fast, her breathing too shallow. She was beginning to realize that Cameron McCleary was more com plex than he seemed.

"Do you always go mute when someone gives you a com pliment?" he asked teasingly.

Lacey's head jerked up. She hadn't realized how the silenc was stretching. "Sorry. I guess I forgot where I was. Than you. I'm glad you like the dress. Mother bought the fabric o a trip to Japan and had it made for me."

"It suits you. Your mother was right. The color's perfect fc you."

"Thank you." She looked up at him, forcing herself to me his eyes without blushing. "You know, Cam, if I didn't kno better, I might think you were flirting with me."

"And what if I am?"

"It seems a bit of a waste. Flirting with your wife, I mea I thought men were supposed to flirt with other women whe they go to a party."

"Why would I want to flirt with another woman? I can with the most beautiful woman here. Besides, we're not tho oughly married yet, are we?"

The look in his eyes brought a rush of color to her cheek despite her best efforts to look calm. She knew exactly wh he was talking about. They didn't sleep together. It wasn't ha to guess that he'd be more than willing to change that part their arrangement.

She tried to whip up some annoyance that he'd brought such a personal matter at a party. But the teasing look made impossible. He wasn't reproaching her or complaining.

Before she could think of a suitable reply, Mamie interrupt them.

"Now I know the two of you haven't been married all th long, but that's no excuse for ignorin' your guests. Lace honey, your Aunt Phoebe wants to talk to you. Now, do look like that." This was in answer to her daughter's grima of distaste. "I know she's gettin' a little old and maybe she mite crotchety, but she's your great-aunt, sugar, and you hould say hello at least.''

''Aunt Phoebe was born crotchety, Mother. You and I both now it. The woman makes Godzilla look like a pleasant dinner ompanion.''

Mamie ignored Cam's snort of laughter. ''That may be so, ut she's come all the way from Las Vegas to see you and neet Cameron, and I think you can make the effort to be polite o her.''

''Why? *She* never made the effort to be polite to anyone.'' But Lacey's comment was muttered into her champagne glass. Her mother had taught her too well. No matter how much she isliked her Aunt Phoebe, she knew that she'd have to find the ld bat and try to make polite conversation with her. Just the nought was enough to make her down the last of her champagne and reach for a fresh glass.

Mamie was leading Cam off. Lacey shrugged in answer to ne look he threw over his shoulder. There was nothing she ould do to rescue him from Mamie's clutches. Once her nother had her mind set on something, she usually got it. Cam ouldn't be set loose until Mamie was satisfied that he'd met veryone he was supposed to meet.

''Lacey?'' She turned, smiling.

''Lisa? I thought you were going to be in New York and ouldn't make this shindig.'' She reached out to catch the other oman's hand, her eyes searching. She hadn't forgotten Lisa's range mood the last time they'd spoken.

Lisa shrugged. ''A meeting was canceled and I decided that really ought to make my best friend's reception, even if it is little late.''

''You know Mother. I told her that you couldn't have a eception this long after the wedding, but she insisted that it ouldn't be a proper wedding without a reception. I think she st wanted an excuse to throw a party.''

''Well, when Mamie throws a party, she certainly does a

great job. This place looks wonderful. And the food is fabu
lous.''

Lisa set her champagne glass down and took another fron
a waiter. Lacey watched her uneasily. She had the feeling tha
Lisa had had more than her share already.

''Where's Frank?''

''Oh, he's around somewhere.'' Lisa didn't seem concerne
or even particularly interested. ''Last I saw, he was talking t
a redhead whose dress appeared to have been applied with ㆍ
brush.''

''Sounds like Sally. Don't worry, she's harmless. Believe
or not, she's a devoted wife and mother. She's probably borin
Frank to tears with stories about her kids.''

''Great. Just what I need.'' Lisa downed her champagne, he
mouth set in an unhappy twist. ''Frank is all hot and heavy t
have kids now. He's probably lapping up her descriptions ᴄ
the delightful little darlings.''

''Lisa.'' Lacey reached out to catch her friend's hand ju
as Lisa was about to pick up another glass of champagne. ''ㆍ
something wrong? With you and Frank, I mean? I alway
thought the two of you were so much in love.''

''In love?'' Lisa stared down at their linked hands, her ha
swinging forward to conceal her expression. ''I suppose v
were. Maybe we still are, but it's not easy to keep a marriag
strong these days. We seem to be going in different dire
tions.''

She lifted her head suddenly, her eyes intent on Lacey'
''You take advantage of every good time you and Cam hav
Because they don't last as long as you think they will. Don
put things off because you think you'll have time later.''

Before Lacey could question Lisa's meaning, Mamie r
turned to make sure that Lacey mingled properly. Lacey ha
only a moment to tell Lisa that they'd talk later, but when lat
came, she found that Frank and Lisa had already left.

The conversation lingered in the back of her mind. She
always thought that Lisa and Frank had a perfect marriag

They'd been so much in love when they'd gotten married. And they'd seemed to be perfectly suited to each other; similar interests, Frank's easygoing personality a perfect balance to Lisa's more frantic ways. If Frank and Lisa couldn't make their marriage work, how could she and Cam possibly hope to succeed?

Her eyes sought Cam's tall figure. He was talking to her awful aunt Phoebe, bent slightly to listen to whatever she was telling him. Just the sight of his broad shoulders was enough to soothe some of Lacey's doubts. He looked so solid. Next to him, every other man she'd known was vague and shadowy. He must have felt her gaze because he turned, his eyes sweeping over the room until he found her.

He didn't smile or wave. He simply looked at her, and she could feel her chest grow tight, leaving her breathless. Someone said something to her and she dragged her eyes from Cam's, reluctant to break the small contact. With an effort, she forced herself to concentrate on the conversation.

But the awareness built as the evening wore on. Lisa's warning to take advantage of every moment niggled at the back of her mind. She'd taken a big gamble by jumping into this marriage, a bigger one by deciding to stick with it. It was a little too late to chicken out now. She wanted Cam, not just because he was physically attractive, but because she'd grown to like him. Maybe even— She shied away from acknowledging anything more than that. For the moment, it was enough that she liked him.

They'd made love once. The fact that her memories of that night were vague didn't change the events. If she was honest, she wanted more than vague memories. But it was such a commitment. Yet the marriage itself was surely an even greater commitment. And if she wanted that to work, didn't she have to throw herself into it wholeheartedly?

And she did want it to work. She wanted to see if what she felt for Cam now would deepen. She wanted to know if the attraction she'd felt from the first moment she saw him had

had its roots in some deep recognition of their belonging together.

Her eyes caught Cam's again. He must have read something in her expression, because he excused himself from the conversation he was in and made his way across the room toward her. Now that he was approaching, Lacey was caught in a sudden attack of nerves. She barely knew this man, marriage or not.

"Have I mentioned that you look particularly beautiful tonight?" Cam took a glass of champagne from a waiter and pressed it into her hand.

"I think you mentioned it," she managed, her voice husky.

"I've been watching you all night."

"Have you?" From somewhere inside, she felt a sudden bubble of giddiness explode upward. She lowered her lashes, looking at Cam from beneath their fragile shelter. "You should be careful. My husband might catch you."

Cam's eyes widened and the slow smile that curved his mouth set off tingles all the way to her toes. "Is your husband the jealous type?"

"I don't know. You see, we have a marriage of convenience." She experimented with batting her lashes a little and was rewarded by the look in his eyes.

"Oh, really." He braced himself against the wall behind her, cutting her off from the rest of the party with the breadth of his shoulders. "It seems to me that any man married to you wouldn't be able to keep it a marriage of convenience for long. You're much too beautiful."

"Thank you." She batted her lashes again, allowing her mouth to curve in a small smile. This kind of flirtation was new to her, but perhaps her mother was right and it was something in the blood.

"I bet he lies awake at night thinking of you lying only a few feet away, your body all warm and soft under the covers. I bet he falls asleep imagining you in the bed next to him, your skin against his."

Lacey stared up at him, unable to drag her eyes from the heated blue of his. His words warmed her skin like a slow-burning fire, setting nerves quivering in places she hadn't even known she had nerves.

"Do you think so?" The words came out more breathless than she'd intended.

"I know so." Was it possible for a man to seduce with his voice alone? Lacey was beginning to think it was. Cam reached out, taking her hand in his, running his thumb over the sensitive skin at the base of her palm.

"Now, I know you're still newlyweds, but that doesn't mean you get to just ignore your guests." Mamie's voice was like a lash of cold water in the face. Lacey blinked, shaking her head and trying to drag herself out of the spell Cam had woven.

Before she could say anything, Cam turned his most charming smile on her mother. "You know, it's getting kind of late, and Lacey and I have to get up early tomorrow. I'm sure you'll understand if we leave a little bit early."

"Well, I..." Mamie didn't look as if she understood at all. It wasn't part of her game plan to have the guests of honor leave at ten o'clock. But Cam didn't give her a chance to protest. He had Lacey's wrap in hand and was ushering her out the door before Mamie could marshal her arguments.

Lacey giggled as he opened the car door and saw her seated. It was the first time in years that she'd seen someone so completely outmaneuver her mother. As Cam settled in the driver's seat, she laughed out loud, feeling suddenly wonderfully wicked and wild. He turned to look at her, arching one brow.

"You didn't let her get a word in edgewise," Lacey marveled. "You didn't even tell her why we were leaving."

"I didn't think it was good politics to tell her I wanted to take my wife home to seduce her."

Lacey's breath caught in the brief moment of silence before he turned the key in the ignition. The low roar of the engine filled the car, shutting out the world outside. She could only stare at him, incapable of protest or agreement—and uncertain which response reflected her feelings.

Cam's hand cupped the back of her neck, and Lacey's head tilted back as his mouth lowered on hers. It wasn't a long kiss but what it lacked in duration, it more than made up for in passion. When his mouth lifted, Lacey couldn't have uttered a protest even if she'd wanted to, which she didn't.

The drive home wasn't long, but each second seemed to increase the awareness that lay between them. By the time Cam pulled into the driveway, Lacey felt as if every inch of her skin was sensitized, attuned to him.

Neither of them spoke as they walked the short distance to the doorway. They'd left a lamp on in the living room, and light spilled into the hallway in dim patches. Cam shut the door behind them and slowly, deliberately, turned to her.

Lacey also turned slowly, feeling as if something hung in the balance. Cam's face was shadowy, impossible to read. But she could feel his eyes on her, as vivid as a physical caress.

He reached out to cup her cheek, and her lashes seemed suddenly much too heavy. His thumb stroked, the callused skin rasping gently. Warmth quivered to life somewhere deep inside her.

"You look so beautiful tonight."

His fingers shifted downward, brushing along the side of her neck. "I couldn't stand being there any longer, with all those people. I had to be alone with you. Tell me you wanted that too."

His palm settled on the top of her shoulder, sweeping outward, taking the wide strap of her dress with it. Lacey's breath caught in the back of her throat, but she didn't protest. The strap draped just above her elbow. She caught a glimpse of his eyes, blue fire in the shadows, and then his mouth touched the outermost edge of her shoulder. Her eyes fell shut.

He nibbled the soft skin, inhaling the gentle scents of perfume and woman. Lacey's hands came up, fumbling to find his shoulders, as if without them to balance her, she'd tumble help lessly backward. Cam's arms slipped around her, bracing her without drawing her any closer, and she gave herself up to that support.

"Lacey, tell me you want me as much as I want you."

The words were half demand, half plea and wholly irresistible. Her eyes opened slowly to stare up into his. His thumb had replaced his mouth, sliding restlessly over the top of her shoulder. She felt drunk, but she knew it wasn't the champagne.

"Lacey?" He made her name a question. She knew what he was asking.

She needed time to think. It wasn't a decision to be made lightly. She had to think. But how could she when he was standing so close? How could she when her body wanted only to lean into his? Without willing them, her fingers lifted to touch his face, the sensitive line of his mouth, the strength of his jaw. Cam stood still under her light exploration, but she could feel the tension in the hand that lay across her back, see it in the glitter of his eyes.

And the answer was simple after all.

"Yes." The one whispered word was all she could manage, but it was all he needed to hear.

His head lowered, his mouth capturing hers in a kiss that sent shock waves all the way to Lacey's toes. Her zipper slid downward beneath his fingers, and his hand flattened against the warm skin of her back. All the need, all the hunger they had been denying for so long, was suddenly freed of the restraints they'd been holding so tight.

Shirt buttons seemed to slip magically open, and her hands were pressed against the hard muscles of his chest. He eased her a fraction away and the silk dress fell to the floor with barely a whisper of sound. His mouth caught her soft moan of pleasure as the softness of her breasts met the hard warmth of his chest.

Bending, he caught her behind the knees and swept her into

his arms. For an instant, Lacey had the dizzying sensation that the world was spinning around her, and she clutched at him.

"I won't let you go." Cam's voice was husky. Lacey tilted her head back to meet his eyes, but she couldn't hold them for long. There was something so intense in his gaze that she had to look away. She buried her face against his chest as he carried her into the bedroom.

Cam set her on the bed, following her down so that she was pressed into the pillows. She was surrounded by him, his warmth, his scent, the sheer masculinity of him. She'd never felt more protected, yet more threatened, in her life. She wanted him, but the very intensity of her desire frightened her.

She slid her fingers into the silky hair at the back of his head, drawing him closer, wanting to lose herself in him. She'd think about the right and wrong of this tomorrow. For now she wanted to think only of how good it felt to be in his arms.

This was right. This was meant to be.

Chapter Ten

Lacey woke slowly, aware of feeling warm and content. She snuggled deeper into the pillow. There was something special about this morning. She couldn't remember what it was, but she knew it was special. It was the same feeling she'd had when she was a little girl waking up on her birthday.

Her mouth curved in a soft smile and she lay in sleepy contentment, not really trying to remember what made this day special. It was enough to savor the feeling.

There was a movement behind her, and a long, definitely masculine arm fell across the curve of her waist. Her eyes flew open. The contentment fled abruptly, replaced with awareness.

Cam. How could she have forgotten, even for a moment, just why today was different? They'd made love last night. More than once, as a matter of fact.

Lacey stared at the patterns of sunlight on the wooden floor. Memories of the night just past slipped uninvited into her mind. Cam's hands, so sure and knowing on her body. His mouth finding erogenous zones she hadn't known existed.

But he hadn't been the only one to take an active part in their lovemaking. Her cheeks warmed as she remembered that she'd made more than a few explorations of her own. Her fingers tingled with the memory of heated skin and firm muscles.

She'd learned more about her own potential for passion last night than she had in all the years that had gone before. Cam was a wonderful lover, strong and considerate, not afraid to take the lead, yet confident enough to lie back and allow her to direct their path. Lacey flushed deeper. She'd taken advantage of that confidence. She'd been shameless last night. And she'd enjoyed every minute of it.

But that had been last night. This morning, the sunlight seemed to cast a slightly different light on things. Their marriage was no longer just writing on a piece of paper. It was real by any standard she cared to name. And now that it was too late, she wasn't sure she was ready for that reality.

She eased the covers back and then lifted Cam's arm, so that she could slip out from beneath it. The floor was cool beneath her bare feet, but it was a pleasant contrast to the heat that seemed to cover her from head to toe. Her own clothes were no doubt still in the hall where they'd been left last night, but Cam's shirt was lying on the floor. She picked it up, wrapping it around her body, wishing that it came to her ankles instead of ending at mid-thigh. Still, it was better than nothing.

Cam rolled onto his stomach, and Lacey hesitated, poised for flight but unable to resist the urge to look at him. The sheet was draped at his waist, baring a width of muscled shoulder and a length of strong back. She didn't need to close her eyes to remember the feel of that back under her hands.

For a moment, the urge to crawl back into bed beside him was strong. She wavered. But she had a shop to open. Besides, she felt too vulnerable, too fragile right now. She needed little time to gather herself before she faced Cam again.

CAM ROLLED OVER as the door shut behind Lacey. Her scent lingered in the bed, and he almost got up to follow her to her room, which he hoped would become the guest room again. He wanted to take her in his arms and coax her back to bed, but instinct told him that wouldn't be a wise move.

He propped himself up on the pillows, staring at the blank panel of the door as if some message were written upon it. Lacey's stealthy departure from the bed had awakened him and he'd almost pulled her back down beside him. But it had been so obvious that she was trying to get out of the room before he woke. So he'd forced himself to lie still, allowing her to make her getaway.

He didn't want to press her too hard. Last night they'd taken an enormous step. If she needed a little breathing room after that, he could give it to her.

But not too much. He didn't want her to start thinking of reasons this couldn't possibly work. She would be on her way to the shop. But even the owner had to take a lunch break.

LACEY'S LOVELIES was a success because its owner had worked like a dog to make it so. Looking around the small shop, Lacey was justifiably proud of her efforts. She didn't have the room to carry a large stock, but she didn't need to. She only carried the very best, whether it was handmade leather bags from Italy or lingerie made of a silk so fine that it could literally be drawn through a wedding band. Elbow-length suede gloves in rich jade nestled beside an embroidered fuchsia silk camisole.

Her clientele appreciated the best, and they were willing to pay for it. She also provided them with a luxurious atmosphere, the pale gray-and-peach decor a quiet contrast to the season's current spill of bright colors. Coffee and tea were always available, the rich scent of Jamaican beans adding a last fillip of luxury.

Ordinarily Lacey had no trouble concentrating on business. Surrounded by the evidence of the success of her hard work, she felt inspired to keep going throughout the day.

Today was different. Today her thoughts showed an uncontrollable tendency to wander to the night before. Or to wonder what Cam had thought when he woke to find her gone. Or to wonder what Cam was doing right at that particular moment.

Luckily she wasn't handling the shop by herself today. If she had been, she would probably have managed to lose half the customers who came in. Her mind simply wasn't on the here and now. But Margaret had worked for her for nearly three years, and she was more than capable of running the place on her own. Sensibly Lacey let her do just that.

She retreated to her tiny office behind the fitting rooms and tried to concentrate on updating the accounts. She didn't get very far with that, either. Cam's face kept intruding between her and the columns of figures, making her fingers fumble on the keys of her calculator. She looked up gratefully when Margaret stuck her head in the doorway. She'd just added the same column twice, coming up with impossible sums both times. An interruption was more than welcome.

"Problem?" Lacey asked, almost hoping there was one. Anything to take her mind off Cam. But Margaret was shaking her head.

"You've got a visitor. I do believe it's your husband." She waggled her eyebrows, her comfortably middle-aged face settling into an exaggerated expression of appreciation. "If I had something like that at home, I certainly wouldn't be spending my days here."

"You've got Stanley." Lacey stood up, fussing with a stack of papers and keeping her head bent over the task, trying to conceal the color in her cheeks. Her husband. Odd, the word made it all seem so real. As if last night hadn't already made it real.

"I love Stanley dearly, but you're comparing French fries to potatoes Anna." Margaret's voice called Lacey back to the present. She smiled at the joke, her thoughts only half on the conversation. She smoothed a hand over her hair and then tugged at her skirt, making sure that the seam was precisely aligned down the front.

Cam wasn't hard to find. His height alone made him impossible to miss. He towered over the racks and low tables. But that wasn't the only thing that drew the eye. That he was male in a decidedly feminine setting was part of it. He was wearing a soft blue chambray shirt and a pair of crisp blue jeans. The contrast between his simple work clothes and the silks and laces of her stock was vivid.

Oddly enough, he didn't look uncomfortable. Lacey was beginning to wonder if the situation existed that could throw Cameron McCleary off his stride. He looked perfectly at home, standing next to a table of sensual lingerie.

Drawing in a deep breath, Lacey threaded her way through the racks of garments. He turned as she halted beside him, his face creasing in a smile that caused a quick bump in her chest.

"Hi."

"Hi." She had to clear her throat before she could return the simple greeting. Had he gotten even handsomer since this morning? Or had she simply forgotten just how attractive he was?

"I hope you don't mind my just dropping in."

"No, no. I don't mind." She cleared her throat again. "It's good to see you." *Great, nitwit. You sound like a sixteen-year-old on a blind date.*

"It's a beautiful store."

"Thank you."

"I particularly like some of your stock." His smile took on a wicked glint, and Lacey's gaze dropped to what he held. Draped across his palm was an ivory teddy made of a silk Charmeuse so fine it was almost transparent. Coffee-toned lace decorated the silk, emphasizing the high-cut legs and low-cut bodice. Lying across his callused hand, the garment looked wickedly sexy and frivolous.

The color that rose in Lacey's cheeks threatened to scorch her skin, but she struggled to maintain a calm facade.

"I've sold quite a few of those. They're imported from France."

Cam stroked the silk, his eyes on her face. "I always did say that the French really know how to live."

Lacey dragged her eyes from the hypnotic motion of his fingers on the silk only to meet the equally dangerous look in his eyes. Was it possible for blue eyes to look so warm? She reached out to take the garment from him, folding it with brisk motions that concealed the trembling of her fingers.

"Some of our best products come from France." She set the teddy back on the table and looked at him again, clasping her hands together in front of her. "Did you come in for something specific?"

The question came out a little more abrupt than she'd intended, but he'd thrown her so totally off balance, she hardly knew what she was saying.

"I thought you might like to join me for lunch."

Lunch? What a mundane thought. She wasn't sure what she'd been expecting, but she definitely hadn't expected that.

"I really should stay here. A lot of our customers do their shopping during the lunch hour."

"Oh, don't worry about that, Lacey." Margaret's smile was so wide that it threatened to split her face in two. She'd been casually straightening some stock that didn't need straightening, not far from where Cam and Lacey stood. Now she decided it was time to add her helpful two bits to the conversation.

"I can manage the shop just fine. I've done it before and there's no reason today should be any different. It's not like we're having a sale or anything." Her wide smile indicated that they would undoubtedly appreciate her help.

"What do you say, Lacey?" Cam was leaving the decision up to her. Lacey nodded slowly, not sure why she was so reluctant. Heaven knew, what they'd shared last night was considerably more intimate than lunch.

"Sure. That would be nice. There's a great café just down the street."

Cam waited while she made a last—unnecessary—check of the office and got her purse, and then he held the door for her to step out onto the sidewalk. Once outside he reached for her hand. The casual touch sent tingles up Lacey's arm, and she suppressed the urge to pull away.

"This place doesn't serve nouvelle cuisine, does it?" Cam

asked, following Lacey's lead through the light pedestrian traffic.

"Not really. It's more California cuisine."

"California cuisine? Does that mean all they serve are goat-cheese salads barely big enough to fill a thimble?"

"Well, they do have goat-cheese salads, but they also have other things, and the servings are a reasonable size."

They were a little early, avoiding the worst of the lunch crowd, and they were lucky enough to get a table by the window. The spring sunshine spilled across the patio outside, which was already getting some use despite the lingering coolness in the air.

They didn't talk beyond discussing the menu until the waiter had taken their orders. Once that was done, there were no obvious distractions. Tension was a knot in the pit of her stomach. She felt irritable, irrationally annoyed with Cam, though she couldn't have said why.

She avoided looking at him and stared at the table, her fingers twisting the small bread plate around and around on the checked cloth. Cam's hand came out, his fingers closing over hers, stilling the restless movement. Lacey looked up, meeting his eyes. His mouth was quirked in a half smile, but his eyes held understanding.

"I don't bite, you know."

"I know." She shrugged, pulling her fingers away from his, twisting them together in her lap. "I guess I'm just a little nervous."

"Because of last night?"

"I...yes."

Cam leaned back as the waiter set small salads, complete with goat cheese, down in front of them. Cam looked at Lacey, his eyebrows raised, and despite her nervousness, her mouth twitched in a smile.

"Well, at least this is only the first course," he said. "Why are you nervous about last night?" The question was so casually asked that it left her momentarily without words.

"Just being stupid, I suppose," she snapped on a wave of irritation. Dammit! Didn't anything throw him off balance?

Cam winced. "Sorry. I didn't mean to get too nosy."

"No, I'm the one who should be sorry." It wasn't his fault she was so uptight. It wasn't even his fault that he wasn't equally uptight. "I guess I just got up on the wrong side of the bed this morning."

"Or the wrong bed entirely?" Something in his tone made her look at him sharply. Maybe he wasn't quite as unaffected as he'd have her believe. The thought made her feel a little better.

"I'm not sorry," she told him.

"Are you sure?"

Why, he needed reassurance just as much as she did.

"I'm sure." Her color might be a little high, but her voice was steady. "What about you?" She hadn't meant to ask the question, but now that it was out, she held her breath, waiting for his answer.

"Regrets? Me?" He seemed surprised. "You've got to be kidding. How could I possibly regret one of the greatest nights of my life?"

She couldn't doubt his sincerity and something eased inside her. Perhaps, unconsciously, she'd been afraid that last night hadn't proved satisfying for him, that she'd failed to measure up in some way. She smiled at him, the first completely natural smile she'd given. There was a subtle relaxing of tension between them.

She took a bite of her salad, barely tasting the tart dressing on the romaine. Looking around the restaurant, she saw that couples occupied several of the tables. Some of them were obvious business acquaintances, absorbed in discussions of profit and loss. But two or three looked like their meeting might be more personal. How would someone else label her and Cam after just a casual glance at their table? Did they look like a married couple? Just what did a married couple look like, anyway?

"What are you thinking about, Lacey?"

"Nothing all that interesting." She set down her fork, pushing the salad bowl to the side. "I was just wondering how we look to other people."

"Other people?" Cam glanced around the small restaurant. "These other people?"

She nodded, feeling a little foolish now that she'd voiced her thoughts.

"It's a habit of mine," she told him. "Wondering what other people are doing in their lives, wondering how they see me."

"And how do you think they see us?"

"I don't know. Do you think we look married?"

"How does married look?" he asked.

"I'm not sure."

"Well, if there's a look to it, I'm sure we'll develop it, given enough time."

"Are we going to have enough time?" The question was barely audible, and her eyes avoided his.

"I think we're going to have all the time we need. Don't you?"

"I hope so." She looked up, meeting his calm gaze and wishing she felt as sure as he seemed. "I guess I just can't help wondering where we're going to go from here. I mean, we've been sort of living together without spending a lot of time together. How do we know we're going to be compatible over the long run?"

"We don't. But nobody does until they try. Why don't we make it a point to spend more time together? It takes time to get to know someone. But even if we'd been engaged for five years, we'd still have to spend time learning how to live together. We're just doing things in reverse order, that's all."

"I suppose." The waiter arrived with their main courses and the conversation was temporarily halted. Lacey picked at her boneless chicken breast for a moment. "But what if—"

"Lacey." Cam stopped her before she could finish the question. "Let's not borrow trouble. We'll take this one day at a time, just like everybody else does. Don't look too far ahead. Okay?''

She nodded slowly. He was right. No one could predict the future and there was no sense in trying. One day at time. It wasn't a bad philosophy.

THEIR MARRIAGE SHIFTED into a new phase. Lacey no longer slept alone in the guest room. Cam's bed was more than big enough for the two of them. No matter what the stresses of the day had been, they were put aside once the bedroom door shut behind them.

But it sometimes seemed as if that was the only place they'd made any progress. Their attempts to spend more time together met with mixed success. Lacey's visit to his workshop could hardly be deemed a big step forward in their relationship.

It might have worked out a little better if she hadn't happened to show up just after Cam had misjudged the pressure necessary to shape a thin piece of facing to a curved shelf. The facing snapped with a pop that paled in comparison to the curse that followed it.

''Hello?''

Cam spun around at the sound of Lacey's tentative greeting, the pieces of facing clenched in his fists. She was standing in the open door, her expression as uncertain as her voice.

''Is this a bad time?''

Cam took a deep breath, forcing himself to relax. ''No. It's not a bad time. Aren't you home early?'' He set the ruined facing down and crossed the cement floor to where she stood. Lacey lifted her face to his, and Cam felt some of the day's frustrations slide away as her mouth softened under his.

''It sounded like you were having some problems,'' she commented as they drew apart.

Cam remembered the rather vivid curse and shrugged. ''Sorry about that. It hasn't been the greatest day. What are you doing home? Nothing wrong at the shop, is there?''

"No. I've got some things I wanted to do around here, so I'm letting Margaret close tonight."

"Things? What kind of things?"

"Nothing major. Just some cleaning."

"I thought the place couldn't get much cleaner. Don't you think you're working a little too hard?"

"I enjoy it. Is this where you do all your work?"

Cam was willing to let the subject of housework drop for the moment. "It's not huge, but I don't really need a whole lot of room."

"It's a little cluttered, isn't it?" She looked around the shop, trying to sort out some recognizable pattern to the stacks of wood, boxes of tools and half-finished pieces of furniture.

"I know where everything is." Cam eyed her warily. She'd already reorganized the house, but his shop was in exactly the right state of chaotic order.

Lacey caught his eye and laughed. "Don't worry, I'm not going to try and straighten out your hammers and nails and whatever else you have in here."

"Good."

His relief was so obvious that she laughed again. "Coward."

Cam threw his arm around her shoulders, drawing her close. He never tired of the feel of her against him, the scent of her. It never failed to make his heart beat a little faster.

"So what do you do with all these tools?" Lacey's voice carried a hint of nervousness and his mouth curved in a smile. She was a passionate partner in the privacy of their bedroom, but outside the safety of those four walls, she was inclined to shy away.

Cam pulled her closer, turning her so that her hands were caught between them. "Do you really want to talk about carpentry right now?" He murmured the question against the soft skin behind her ear, feeling the shiver of response that ran through her.

But Lacey was nothing if not determined. "I think what you

do is very interesting, and I don't really know anything about it.''

With a sigh, Cam released her and she sidled away, picking up a chisel and studying it as if it was the most interesting thing she'd seen in weeks.

''Unless you're thinking of adding carpentry to your list of accomplishments, there's really not much to explain. The basics of building furniture are pretty straightforward. It's the details that change a few pieces of wood into a potential Chippendale.''

''It must have taken you a long time to learn how to create those details.''

Cam picked up a piece of wood, his long fingers caressing the subtle grain. ''My grandfather taught me most of what I know. I didn't meet him until I was almost fifteen. My mother had quarreled with her parents and left home to marry my father. My grandparents told me that they had a share in the decisions she'd made, keeping me from them. But I never really believed it.''

Lacey watched his face, seeing the old hurts, wondering if he was aware of the pain that drew lines between his brows when he spoke of his past.

''Do you remember much of your mother?'' She asked the question tentatively, uncertain of the ground she was treading.

''Sure.'' Cam laughed, a sound without humor. ''I remember a succession of strangers who took care of me a lot better though. She breezed in once in a while, either showering me with presents or sneaking me out without paying the bill, depending on which way her fortunes had gone. She was a shallow vain woman with a soul smaller than her heart.

''I don't remember my father at all, but I never really blamed him for leaving her. I'd have left her if I'd had a choice. Of course, in the end, she made the decision for both of us. Looking back, I'm surprised she kept me with her as long as she did.''

''Maybe she loved you in her own way,'' Lacey offered

hesitantly, uncertain of the best way to handle the kind of bitter memories her question had called up.

Cam laughed again. "No. She didn't love anybody but herself."

There was no arguing with his certainty, though Lacey found it hard to comprehend a woman not loving her own child.

"It must have been very hard for you." The platitude seemed woefully inadequate.

"It was hell," Cam said simply. He lifted another piece of wood, weighing it in one hand. "But it all worked out in the end. I was lucky that Jimbo saw something that made him think I might be worth trying to save. He wasn't much more than a kid himself. God knows what he saw in the obnoxious little punk I was then. And Mom and Dad took an even bigger risk. Hell, I half expected me to turn out to be an ax murderer, but they kept insisting there was something worth saving. They believed in me so strongly that I just had to try and prove them right.

"And then they found my grandparents, and I got a chance to see something of my roots. I'm glad I did. It made it easier to straighten out when I saw that they were good people. I could believe that I didn't have to turn out like my mother. I could try and be like my grandparents instead. That's the way my mind worked."

Lacey crossed the few feet that separated them and stood next to him, looking at the wood he was holding.

"Is that why you decided to go into carpentry, because that's what your grandfather did?"

"Not really." He stroked his fingers over the smooth grain. "The minute he handed me a piece of wood, I felt as if I'd found something I'd been missing for a long time. I never wanted to do anything else from that moment on."

There was a long moment when there didn't seem to be anything more to say. Cam broke the somber mood, dropping the small board with a crash that made Lacey jump.

"Enough of all this solemn talk. You're looking much too

beautiful to be spending your time in a shop. Let's go out to dinner.''

''But I had things I planned to do.'' Lacey struggled to adjust her thinking from Cam's past to the idea of a dinner out.

''The house will still be dirty when we get back.'' Cam dismissed her arguments with a wave of his hand, shepherding her out of the shop and shutting the door with a finality that made her wonder if he wasn't shutting the door to his memories.

Chapter Eleven

Cam stroked the plane across the surface of the wood, shaving off fragrant curls of cedar. Approaching summer meant the sunlight lingered till later in the day, and it spilled across the workbench now, painting vivid patterns of light and shadow across the pale wood.

If he looked out the garage door, he could see the light shining from the kitchen window. But he didn't raise his head. Lacey was probably in there preparing some meal guaranteed to set new standards of epicurean excellence. The thought should have delighted him. God knew, it would certainly be enough to delight most men. He hadn't eaten so well in years. He straightened, patting his stomach absently. He'd had to add another mile a day to his run just to keep from developing a bulge.

But that wasn't what bothered him. And it wasn't that he minded Lacey spending her time making fantastic meals. Not if that was what she really enjoyed doing. But he didn't think she was spending so much time in the kitchen out of a passionate love of cooking.

She seemed to be trying to prove something. But what and to whom, he couldn't figure out. He shook his head. He was probably looking for trouble where it didn't exist. Maybe Lacey secretly envied Julia Child. Maybe she was just going through a phase.

After glancing at his watch, he put away the tools, leaving everything ready for the morning. Cam stretched, enjoying the cool of the early-evening air. Spring in Southern California was too brief to be fully enjoyed. Summer's heat followed hard on its heels, making the pavement sizzle and leaving the air a visible presence in the L.A. basin. He enjoyed summer's heat, but it didn't have the innocence of spring.

He opened the back door and came to a dead stop. The rich scent of spices mixed with the pungent and unmistakable aroma of ammonia. In the middle of the floor, on her hands and knees, Lacey tilted her head back to look at him.

"Oh, dear. I should have told you I was going to be stripping the floor. Dinner isn't going to be done for about an hour, and it seemed like a good time to get it done. You'll have to go around to the front door."

Cam leaned his shoulder against the doorjamb, trying to rein in the inexplicable surge of anger that threatened to find voice. Her hair was caught back in a ponytail, the golden blond darkened by perspiration around her face. Her faded jeans and sleeveless top were not complemented by the elbow-length rubber gloves that protected her hands.

"Did you get home early?"

Lacey looked up at him, her expression distracted. "No. I got home about half an hour ago. Why?" She scrubbed another square of tile with the brush she held.

"Well, it seems to me that you must be pretty tired after working all day. And then to come home and start dinner and tackle stripping the kitchen floor is a bit of overkill, don't you think?"

She either didn't hear or chose to ignore the subtle tightness in his voice. "I'm not tired. And the floor really was getting to look grungy. Wax builds up on it so quickly, you know."

"Lacey." He waited until she stopped scrubbing and looked at him again. "It really isn't essential that I be able to literally eat off the floor. A little wax buildup is not fatal."

"I know, but Claire is coming to dinner next week, and I want the house to be really clean for them."

Cam knew when he was licked. He backed out of the doorway and circled around the house, coming in the front door. He went straight to the bedroom, stripping off his clothes on the way to the shower. It was stupid to get annoyed. If he had any common sense, he'd just sit back and enjoy the clean house, the meals, her presence in his bed.

He twisted the shower on. The problem was, he didn't want Suzy Homemaker. He wanted a companion. Someone to talk to, someone who wanted to spend an occasional evening reading the paper together, or watching a movie. And Lacey never seemed to have the time for any of that.

No, that wasn't entirely fair. They *had* been spending more time together. There'd been a trip to the zoo. They'd spent a day at the beach. Cam's mouth curved, remembering Lacey's sunburned nose.

No, he couldn't really say they hadn't been getting to know each other. The more time he spent with her the more things he discovered he liked. Sometimes he thought it was more than liking, but he wasn't quite ready to make that decision.

The warm water pounded down on his back, easing some of the tension from his muscles. He stretched out his arms and placed his hands against the tiled wall, closing his eyes and letting the water wash over him. Slowly a smile covered his mouth, and then he laughed softly.

This marriage business wasn't as easy as he'd thought it would be. He was acting like an idiot. Getting upset over something as ridiculous as the fact that Lacey had a passion for spotless floors and big meals. If she liked to clean house and cook, it was nothing to complain about.

So he complimented Lacey on the floor, ate twice as much as he wanted and refused to be annoyed when she waxed the floor after dinner. He bided his time until they went to bed. At least in bed, she could neither cook nor clean.

Cam lay in bed listening to the sound of the shower. Marriage might not have been as simple as he'd planned, but it definitely had its moments. Such as watching Lacey walk out of the bathroom, her skin lustrous with lingering moisture, her hair tumbling onto her shoulders in honey-colored waves. She was wearing a pair of gray silk pajamas that looked like something Marlene Dietrich might have worn. There was a playful element in their sexiness.

She sat down on the side of the bed to kick off her slippers, and Cam saw the tired slump of her shoulders. It was her own fault she was so exhausted. If she'd stop trying to be superwoman, life would be a lot easier for both of them. But he couldn't resist the vulnerability he saw in her. He sat up, his hands settling on her shoulders.

She tensed under his hands, but only for a moment. His thumbs found the tight muscles at the base of her neck and she went limp.

"You're working too hard," he told her, his voice soft in the dim room.

"I'm enjoying myself." She shifted under his hands so that he could get to a particularly tense spot. "Besides, I want everything to be perfect for the dinner party next week. You know, it will be the first time our families meet."

"That doesn't mean the house has to gleam. No one is going to look behind the stove."

"You never can tell. I just feel better knowing it's clean."

"I think you're taking on more than you should," he insisted, kneading the taut muscles of her shoulders. "You can't do everything."

"It's not that big a deal. Besides, I've watched my mother do this hundreds of times. She always managed without a problem."

"Well, it's no skin off my nose. Let me know what I can do to help."

His hands left her shoulders. Lacey reached up to turn off

the lamp as she slid under the covers. She relaxed back against the pillows with a sigh as tired muscles felt the support of the mattress.

"You know, a funny thing happened today." Her voice was quiet in the darkness.

Cam put his arm around her shoulders, drawing her against his chest. He draped his other arm over the curve of her waist.

"What happened today?" These quiet moments before they fell asleep were strangely rewarding. Cam felt more married in this little space of time than he did at any other. There was something so cozy and intimate about lying in bed in a darkened room, hushed voices talking about the little unimportant things that made up most days.

"Jimbo came to the shop."

"Oh, yeah? What did he want?"

"Well, that was what was strange. He never did say what he wanted, but he kept bringing the conversation around to my mother. I invited him to dinner next week, and when I told him she was going to be here, he looked like he'd just been invited to the White House. You don't suppose he's interested in her, do you?"

"I don't know. Why not?"

"Well, she's my mother and she's older than Jimbo, and Jimbo is— Well, Jimbo. They aren't a very likely couple."

"I've seen more unlikely combinations succeed."

"True. Look at us."

"Hey!" Lacey giggled as Cam's fingers found a ticklish spot on her side. It was a measure of how far they'd come that they felt safe enough to tease each other. They might have a long way yet to go, but at moments like this, it was easy to believe that they were going to make it.

"Lacey, the table looks fine. Will you stop fussing with it?" Despite his efforts to sound teasing, Cam was aware of the bite that had crept into his tone.

Lacey turned away from the table and gave him an apologetic smile. "Sorry. It's just that I want everything to be perfect."

"It looks great. You look great. In fact, you look positively edible." He slipped his arms around her waist. She returned his kiss, but it was obvious that her thoughts were elsewhere. With a resigned sigh, Cam released her. Until this damned dinner party was over with, he might as well resign himself to living with an android.

Well, at least this was the last night he had to worry about it. In a few minutes people would start arriving. Surely, once this was over, she'd relax a little. She'd been wound so tight this past week that he'd felt as if the slightest touch or the wrong word would be enough to send her flying apart in a million pieces.

"Do I look all right?" Lacey asked the question as if it was the first time it had been asked. Cam forced himself to forget the fact he'd already answered it at least three times in the past hour. He looked at her carefully, though he didn't really need to. The ivory silk dress was the essence of elegant simplicity. With a bright fuchsia scarf cinched around her waist and her hair caught back from her face with fuchsia silk bows she looked like she'd stepped off the pages of *Vogue*.

"You look fantastic. The dress is perfect." His reassurance appeared to soothe her anxieties, at least momentarily. Her expression relaxed into a smile.

"Thank you. You look very nice, yourself." Her eyes skimmed his tobacco-brown slacks and light blue shirt. The color of the shirt echoed his eyes, making them seem even bluer than usual.

"We strive to please." But Lacey's attention had already returned to a nervous examination of her table settings. Cam didn't bother to try to distract her again. Maybe when people began to arrive, she'd relax a little. She was so uptight now she was making him uneasy.

The evening started out just fine. Lacey's mother arrived first, followed almost immediately by Jimbo. So immediately that Cam half suspected he'd been lurking in the underbrush awaiting her arrival. Mamie settled into a chair, a ladylike finger of bourbon beside her, "Because you know, Cameron, that bourbon is the only truly civilized drink. Wine is hardly worth the effort."

Jimbo leaned against the mantel, which just happened to put him close enough to Mamie to catch a whiff of her perfume. From the way his old friend was looking at his new mother-in-law, Cam didn't think there was any real need to speculate on the direction that relationship was going to take, at least if Jimbo had anything to say about it.

Claire and Joe arrived a few minutes late, full of apologies and explanations of the difficulties of getting a houseful of youngsters and a baby-sitter in the same place at the same time.

Cam's hopes that Lacey would relax once the evening was under way were met, at least for a while. Mamie clearly liked Claire and Joe and the feeling was mutual. And Jimbo could always be counted on to keep the conversation going if things began to flag. Lacey was the perfect hostess, relaxed yet in control. Halfway through the hour before dinner she'd planned for everyone to chat, she glanced across the room and caught his eye. The smile she gave him was dazzling, and Cam found it easy to forget the minor stresses and strains of the past couple of weeks.

Twenty minutes before dinner was to be served, Lacey excused herself and disappeared into the kitchen. She'd spent the previous few days making schedules, ones that rivaled those that launched D day. She knew to the second how long each dish was to take and in exactly what order they were to be prepared.

As Cam watched her go he took a sip of his bourbon, glad the anticipated night had finally arrived and was off to a smashing start. A few more hours and this would all be behind them.

His complacency was shattered by a muffled shriek from the direction of the kitchen. Conversations broke off and all heads turned toward the sound. Cam was already on his feet, waving the others back.

"Don't worry about it. I'm sure it's no big deal."

Lacey's expression told him that, whatever was wrong, it was a very big deal indeed. She was standing in front of the counter staring at a roasting pan wherein rested two large chickens—capons, Cam corrected himself. He'd picked the birds up himself the day before, paying an exorbitant sum for what looked to him like a pair of hens with steroid problems.

"What's wrong?"

Lacey didn't even look at him. She simply pointed to the capons, her face set in lines of horrified disbelief. Cam moved closer, not sure what he was supposed to be looking for. The birds appeared to be just fine, their legs neatly tied, their skin pale and smooth. Pale? He looked from the birds to Lacey and then looked away, biting his cheek to keep from laughing.

"I forgot to put them in the oven." She said it as if she were announcing a capital crime.

"It could happen to anyone," he said, trying very hard to look sympathetic.

She turned her head slowly, as if it took a great effort, and looked at him. Her eyes were dark green and full of such tragedy that Cam's urge to laugh faded. "Everything else is done and everyone is out there waiting to be fed, and I forgot to put the damned birds in the oven. How could I be so stupid!"

"Lacey, it could happen to anyone."

"No, it couldn't. It could only happen to someone who's a complete and total idiot."

She looked heartbroken. Cam searched for some consolation and couldn't find one. The fact of the matter was that the dinner she'd planned for the past two weeks was sitting on the counter in front of her completely raw. Her guests were waiting to be fed and her meal was now several hours away from being done.

"I'll tell you what. Why don't we send out for some pizza? I could call Dominic's. We could order a couple of large pizzas. Nobody will mind."

He trailed off as Lacey's gaze changed from near shock to something that looked a great deal like pure loathing.

"Pizza? You want mc to throw a dinner party so our families can meet and then serve pizza? I'd sooner serve them live ants. I'd rather—" But he wasn't meant to hear what else she'd rather serve. She broke off, looking past him, her expression a mixture of dread and embarrassment. "Mother."

"Lacey, honey, is everythin' all right? When Cam didn't come back, I thought you might have hurt yourself."

"I'm fine, Mother." She paused and Cam could feel the effort she made to dredge up a smile. "I'm afraid we have a small problem with dinner, however." She gestured to the cartons. "I forgot to put dinner in the oven."

"Oh, dear." Mamie laughed. "Don't look so tragic, sugar. We can fix it in no time at all."

"Fix what?" Jimbo appeared behind Mamie, taking in the situation in a glance. "You've got to remember that you're supposed to serve *beef* rare, Lacey. Not chicken."

"Thanks." Irony lay thick in her tone. "Cam just suggested that we could send out for pizza." Despite her best efforts the word came out sounding obscene, giving Cam final evidence— if he'd needed it—of just what she thought of his suggestion. Still, as a good hostess, she was determined that her guests wouldn't starve, and if pizza was all she could offer them, he'd at least make the effort.

"Pizza!" That was Claire, who'd appeared next to Mamie. She gave her brother a disgusted look. "If that isn't just like you to think of pizza. I always knew you had no class."

Cam shrugged sheepishly. He didn't see what was so bad about pizza. He liked it. Besides, hadn't some study decided that pizza was a nutritionally complete food? Or at least not as bad as it looked. It wasn't as if he'd suggested they eat sawdust.

"You know, sugar, it seems to me that you've got the makin's for a good ol' Southern dinner right here." Mamie had approached the capons, and she now poked one with a perfectly manicured nail. "If we cut these chickens up, dredge them in a bit of flour and drop them in a pan of hot oil, I don't think anybody would starve."

"Fried chicken?" It was obvious that, as far as Lacey was concerned, it was only a notch above the despised pizza.

"I haven't had homemade fried chicken in ages." That was Claire. "I'm afraid we usually rely on the Colonel. And the children are all such little plebeians, they'd never notice the difference."

"I'm a mean hand with a butcher knife," Jimbo offered. Cam wouldn't have been surprised to find that he'd never cut up a chicken in his life. He was just looking for an excuse to stay close to Mamie.

No one seemed to miss the more elaborate dinner Lacey had planned, and the fried capon disappeared at a rate that indicated no one was going hungry.

But Lacey picked at her food, while keeping up her end of the conversations that flew across the table. Her heart wasn't really in it. Her exquisite capons reduced to something that could have been bought in a red-and-white bucket. Of course, she was lucky there'd been a way to salvage the meal. And it could have been worse. Pizza. She still simmered when she thought about that.

Aside from the near disaster, the evening went well. Everyone liked everyone else, conversation was lively, and she could honestly feel that her first dinner party was a success. Her first dinner party as Cam's wife. Standing next to him in the doorway, waving as their guests left, she realized how married she felt. It was not an unpleasant feeling.

Cam shut the door and the house was suddenly very quiet.

"I think it went pretty well, don't you?" Lacey wandered back into the living room and began stacking cups and saucers.

"Everyone had a great time." Cam followed her into the living room, flopping onto the sofa. "Why don't you leave those till morning?"

"It won't take that much time to throw them in the dishwasher, and then I won't have to worry about them tomorrow."

Cam stifled a yawn, watching her out of sleepy eyes. "Leave them till morning and I'll take care of them."

"That's not necessary."

"Who said anything about necessity?"

"Really, it won't take long. I can— Cam!" His name came out on a shriek as his arm hooked around her waist. She had only an instant to set down the stack of saucers she was holding before he pulled her off her feet to land in an untidy heap on top of him.

"I said leave them till morning." His mouth nuzzled the sensitive skin behind her ear, sending dangerous tingles up her spine.

"Cam, I don't think—"

"That's right. Don't think." He twisted, and her head spun as she found herself suddenly beneath him, pressed into the sofa cushions by the weight of his body. His eyes seemed dangerously blue, warm and slumbrous.

"Cam—" She wasn't sure what she'd planned to say, for he didn't give her a chance to get it out. His mouth settled over hers, scattering her thoughts in a hundred different directions. It wasn't a lengthy kiss, but it was a thorough one.

"You know what your problem is, Lacey McCleary?" Her lashes lifted slowly. She barely remembered her name.

"What?" She had to clear her throat to get the one word out.

"You think too much." His teeth nibbled at one earlobe, and Lacey felt her toes curl.

"Do I?" she asked breathlessly, hardly aware of what she was saying.

"You do." His tongue traced a heated pattern around the

curve of her ear and her fingers dug into his shoulders, seeking something solid to cling to.

"I'll have to try to do less of it."

Cam braced himself on his elbow, his hand seeking out the tiny gold buttons that ran down the front of her dress. His eye were intent on hers.

"Do less of what?"

"Thinking," she whispered, her breath catching as his hand slipped inside to find the softness of her breast.

"Too much thinking can be dangerous," he breathed, hi head lowering.

"Dangerous," she agreed.

But it wasn't thinking that was dangerous. It was feeling Feeling something so strongly that it threatened to wash awa everything else. You could get lost in feelings that strong.

His fingers whispered over her skin, the faint roughness c his work-roughened skin a contrast to the softness of her breas She closed her eyes, her skin flushing a delicate rose as h spread the dress open so that she lay nearly bare beneath him The lace and silk of her teddy could hardly be considered decent covering.

They'd been lovers for weeks now. Certainly he'd seen eve more of her than this. But that had always been in the saf darkness of their bedroom. There was something so decade about this. Lying on the sofa with all the lamps lit. Decaden and exciting.

Cam's mouth found the nipple of one breast through the pal silk. She arched upward, feeling the gentle tugging sensatio deep inside, a warm pool of need spreading outward from th pit of her stomach.

Forcing her hands between them, she struggled with the bu tons on his shirt. They resisted stubbornly, but at last gave wa beneath her increasingly frantic efforts to tug the shirt open, that she could bury her fingers in the crisp dark hair that co

red his chest. His head left her breast, but only to return to
er mouth.

Strong fingers slid into her hair, tilting her face upward as
is chest settled over hers. Lacey moaned against his mouth as
he firm muscles pressed against her. Passion was no longer
played out in a languorous progression from one step to the
next. It had become a demanding, urgent presence.

Cam's knee thrust between hers, pressing upward against the
heart of her need. Lacey's fingers flexed against his shoulder,
a response and a demand. She arched into his knee, wordlessly
pleading for more. Cam dragged his mouth away from hers,
taking in a great lungful of air.

He stared into her eyes for a moment before pulling himself
up and away. She started a protest that ended on a pleased
murmur when she saw that he was standing up only so he could
strip away the rest of his clothes. She watched him, her eyes
half-lidded, her expression vaguely feline. He jerked his shirt
off and reached for his belt buckle, his hands freezing as she
reached up to cup him through the fabric of his slacks.

Never in all her life had she done anything so blatantly sexual. But then, no one else had ever made her feel the way Cam
did. He made her feel like a warm, sensual woman, not the
rather reticent, business-oriented Lacey she'd always thought
she knew.

Cam groaned as her fingers moved, gently caressing him.

"Lacey, you're driving me crazy."

"You told me I thought too much, so I'm not thinking anymore. I'm feeling. Only feeling."

"I think I'm the one who's feeling." His voice held a
strained note that pleased her enormously. He stepped back and
Lacey's hand dropped away. Her mouth pursed in a moue, only
to soften into a pleased smile when Cam all but ripped off the
rest of his clothes.

She could hardly believe she was lying here, on the sofa,
with all the lamps lit. Looking at Cam's muscled body, she felt

a deep aching throb, a need stronger than any she could re
member. She lifted her arms to him in a wordless invitation a
old as time. And Cam didn't hesitate to respond. Her teddy
was disposed of with a quick tug that threatened the fragil
silk. Lacey wouldn't have cared if he'd taken it from her i
shreds. All that mattered was her need to feel him against her

She opened to him, cradling him between her knees, he
body arching to that first slow thrust. For a moment, the fir
was banked, the emptiness filled, but it was only for a momen

There was an urgency in her tonight that she didn't under
stand. A powerful need that was all consuming. When Cam
started to move, she responded hungrily. Each movement ser
ripples of pleasure through her until she was drowning in ser
sation. Her hands slid down the sweat-dampened length of hi
back, feeling the ripple of muscle and sinew.

Cam's mouth found hers, his tongue thrusting inside t
tangle with hers, swallowing her soft whispers. Lacey felt a
if she couldn't possibly get enough of him. She wanted thi
feeling to go on forever, and yet the pleasure was so intens
that it had to end soon or she'd shatter into a million pieces.

The pleasure built higher until she was aware of nothing b
Cam, the scent of him, his weight on hers, the intense ecstas
of their joining. And then the pleasure crested, washing ove
her, sending her tumbling into pure sensation. From somewhe
a long way away, she heard Cam's muffled groan of comple
tion.

It was a long time before either of them moved or spok
Cam shifted at last, lifting his weight from her. Lacey mu
mured a protest, reaching up to clutch at his shoulders.

"Sweetheart, this couch ain't big enough for the two of us.
She heard his words, but she could also feel them where h
chest still rested against hers. It took a great effort to lift h
lashes.

"I don't mind," she mumbled, lost in the blue of his eye

"Well, I do. I want you somewhere where I can hold yc

properly.'' He pushed himself upright and then bent to scoop her off the sofa.

Lacey looped her arms around his neck, leaning her head against his shoulder. ''I didn't get the dishes cleared up.''

Cam's soft chuckle vibrated through her. ''I thought I'd distracted you from that. Apparently I didn't do a very good job.''

''You did a wonderful job. I was just making an observation.'' Her prim tone didn't fit very well with the fact that neither of them had a stitch of clothing on. Cam laughed again, carrying her out of the living room and toward their bedroom.

He set her on the bed and followed her down, sweeping her against him, holding her close. ''I'm sure I could do an even better job of distracting you if I had a little more room and a little more time.''

''More time? Who said you didn't have all the time in the world?'' She placed soft kisses along the line of his collarbone.

''You did. How was I supposed to take my time and show you all my best techniques when you were driving me crazy?''

''Sorry.'' She didn't feel in the least sorry. In fact, she felt very pleased with herself. Even more pleased when she felt an unmistakable stirring against her thigh. ''Is that a gun in your pocket or are you just happy to see me?''

''I don't have any pockets.''

''Then I guess you must be happy to see me.''

Cam buried his hand in her hair, tilting her head back until their eyes met. Lacey's pulse sped at the look of glittering hunger in his gaze. She'd never felt so completely feminine, so totally desirable.

''Hussy.'' He made the word a caress. ''I'll show you just how happy I am to see you.'' His mouth came down on hers, stifling any reply she might have made.

But Lacey didn't protest. Tonight was not about words. Sometimes a touch could speak far louder than any words ever could. She had the feeling there was something to be learned in the way Cam touched her, held her. Some message that was important, if only she knew how to interpret it.

But the meaning stayed just out of her grasp.

Chapter Twelve

The television was not turned up particularly loud, but the sound of it grated on Lacey's nerves like fingernails on a blackboard. Cam was sprawled in front of the glowing box, his long legs stretched untidily across the floor. The floor she'd mopped just yesterday.

Not that he seemed to care if the floor had been mopped yesterday or three months ago. She stabbed the needle through the button and into her finger. Jerking her hand from under the fabric, she saw a bright drop of blood welling on the tip of her finger. It only added to her annoyance.

"Yeah!"

She jumped at Cam's loud exclamation. Slightly tinny-sounding cheers issued from the speaker. A home run or an out. She stifled the urge to ask what had happened. She'd enjoyed baseball a time or two herself, but she wasn't in the mood for it right now.

She jabbed the needle through the button again, securing it to the fabric. Her frown deepened as she stared at the inoffensive fabric. Only it wasn't inoffensive. At the moment, it offended her mightily. The faded chambray made her grind her teeth. It was a beautiful sunny Sunday afternoon and she was sitting here doing mending. Not even her own mending, at that. It seemed as if Cam lost buttons off his shirts every time he wore one.

And if she wasn't mending *his* shirts, she was cleaning *his* house or cooking *his* meals. All this while she was trying to run a profitable business. It wasn't that she minded cooking and cleaning and mending. After all, that was part of being married. But she did mind the fact that Cam didn't seem to appreciate all the work she put into making a home.

Oh, he'd comment on the fact that the house looked nice, or he'd tell her that he'd enjoyed a meal she'd just spent two hours cooking only to have it gone in twenty minutes. He'd even suggested on a few occasions that she was working too hard. But he didn't *really* appreciate the amount of work she was doing.

She jabbed at the button again. Maybe it was impossible for men to understand the amount of work that went into making a house a home. Maybe they weren't genetically programmed to understand. But he could at least make an effort.

It was Cam's mistake that he chose that particular moment to speak to her.

"Why don't you come over here and watch the game with me?"

"There's nowhere to sit." She didn't lift her head from the shirt, though she'd looped the thread through the button so many times that nothing short of a nuclear blast could have detached it.

"You could sit on my lap. Or we could move the television so we could both sit on the couch. Come on, Lacey. You haven't stopped working since you got up this morning. It's making me tired just watching you."

"Well, pardon me for trying to get something done," she snapped. Folding the shirt with jerky movements, she stood up, injury in every line of her body. "I'll just go somewhere else so that my working won't bother you."

"What on earth?" Cam's eyes widened as she turned to stalk out of the room. He stood up, taking a quick step forward to catch her arm. "What's wrong?"

Lacey stared at his chest, refusing to lift her eyes any higher. The fact that he could even ask that proved he was the insensitive clod she'd begun to suspect.

"Nothing's wrong."

"Lacey, something's obviously eating at you. Spit it out."

The inelegant command did nothing to soothe her anger. "I told you, there's nothing wrong."

"Does it bother you that I'm watching the baseball game? I asked if you wanted to go for a drive, but you said you had things to do around the house today. I didn't think a little television would bother you."

"Of course it doesn't bother me," she said woodenly, still without looking at him.

"Look, why don't we go for a drive? It's a beautiful day. We could head for the coast and drive up 101."

"I can't. I have too much to do here."

Cam's fingers tightened on her arm a moment before dropping away. He took a deep breath, and she had the feeling he was trying to take hold of his patience. Though what he had to be impatient about, she couldn't imagine.

"Forget about whatever you've got in mind. Let's get out of here. You work too hard."

It was as if he'd lit a match to a Roman candle. How dared he act as if she worked as hard as she did out of choice! Did he think she liked slaving?

"Well, if I don't do it, it's not going to get done, now is it? You obviously have more important things to do." She gestured contemptuously at the television. There was a moment of dead silence broken only by the electronic roar of the crowd, and then even that was silenced as Cam reached out to snap the set off.

"Don't let me interrupt you," she went on. "This is undoubtedly an important game. Heaven forbid you should miss it." *My God, I sound like a harpy.* But she couldn't seem to stop the flow of rage now that it had been turned loose.

Cam stepped back, folding his arms over his chest. "You want to tell me what the hell this is all about?"

"Nothing. Absolutely nothing." Lacey twisted the shirt between her hands, all the pent-up anger of weeks boiling inside her, seeking a way out.

"Bull," he said bluntly. "You've been acting like Joan of Arc on her way to the stake for days now. I thought it was a passing mood, but obviously it goes deeper than that. You want to tell me what's bugging you?"

"Joan of Arc?" She stared at him, her voice failing her. He returned the look impassively. "Are you implying that I've been acting like a martyr?"

"The thought had crossed my mind."

"Why you…you…male chauvinist pig!" The insult didn't nearly express her feelings, but it was the best she could come up with in the midst of her anger. He didn't seem in the least disturbed, which only made her angrier.

"Why don't you get it off your chest, Lacey? You'll feel a lot better."

"I'm not going to feel better until I can be reasonably sure I won't ever have to see you again. You are the most inconsiderate, oblivious man I've ever known in my life."

"What have I been inconsiderate and oblivious about?"

How could he remain so calm when she felt like she might explode at any minute? It wasn't fair and it only went to prove her point. He didn't have an ounce of sensitivity in his body.

"It doesn't matter what I do around here—you never notice I've developed housewife's knees and a permanent bend in my back. I've ruined my fingernails. I've cooked and I've cleaned and I've mended your damned clothes until I feel like a slave, and you sit in front of that damned television watching a stupid baseball game. And then you have the nerve to act like you can't imagine why I'm upset. You—"

"Who asked you to?" The calm question broke into the middle of her tirade. Lacey stopped, bewildered.

"Who asked me to what?"

"Who asked you to cook and clean and mend my damned
shirts?"

"I— You—" she stammered, her train of thought broken.

"Oh, no. Don't try to pin this on me. I haven't asked you
to do any of that stuff. *You're* the one who's been running
around here like the pope was going to come to visit any minute."

This conversation wasn't going at all the way she'd imagined
it would. He was supposed to be apologetic and appreciative.
He didn't look like either. In fact, he looked more angry than
anything else. "But I—"

"But nothing. Have I once said to you, 'Lacey, why don't
you wear the grain off the floors with a scrub brush?' Or 'Lacey, why don't you cook like Julia Child every night?' Or
'Lacey, why don't you mend my damned shirts?'"

She jumped as he jerked the shirt out of her hands, throwing
it into a corner of the room. The violence in the small act told
her that his emotions were every bit as riled as hers.

"You didn't ask maybe, but it was obvious that—"

"No, it wasn't," he interrupted flatly. "The only thing that's
been obvious is that you've got a Donna Reed complex. I never
asked, implied or hinted that I expected you to take on the sole
responsibility for running this place."

"Well, if I don't do it, who will?" There. She had him on
that one.

"Lacey, it may not have occurred to you before, but I lived
alone for quite a few years. I didn't starve to death, the house
didn't vanish in a mound of filth, and my shirts all had buttons.
I may not be an immaculate housekeeper, but I'm not Pigpen,
either. I'm perfectly capable of taking care of things myself.
At the very least, we could share the work."

"Well, then why haven't you? Why have you let me do
everything myself?"

"When have you given me a chance to do anything? Every

time I suggested doing something, you told me you'd rather do it yourself. When I tried to do laundry, you acted like I was incapable of pushing the right buttons. You pick my damned socks up almost before I get them off my feet. I've been afraid to set foot in the kitchen for fear a spill of flour would send you into a cleaning frenzy. Just what do you suggest I do? Fight you for the privilege of mopping the floor?''

She stared at him, grasping at the anger she was sure she still felt and finding nothing. Had she really been like that? Surely he was exaggerating. Yet, looking back, she could remember a number of instances where he'd offered to do something and she'd immediately denied the need for any help.

''I guess maybe I have been a little compulsive about it,'' she murmured, trying to absorb this new picture of her own behavior. ''It's just that I wanted everything to be perfect.''

''Lacey, this is real life. Who needs a perfectly clean house or gourmet meals every night, especially when it cuts into time that could be better spent on other things?''

''Why didn't you say something before?'' she asked.

''I've been telling you ever since before the dinner party, but you didn't seem to agree, and I didn't want to push it.'' He shrugged. ''I thought maybe you really liked all that cooking and cleaning. You were so determined to do it.''

''My mother always kept the house immaculate and we always had beautiful meals. And she never forgot to put the capon in the oven, let me tell you. That's the image I grew up with of a properly run home. I just wanted to do the same.''

''Lacey, honey, think about it. Your mother didn't work full time. She may have spent a lot of time doing volunteer work and managing your father's investments, but she didn't hold a full-time job, let alone run a business of her own. She had a lot more time to spend on the house. Besides, from what you've told me, Mamie has always had a maid. Did it ever occur to you that the maid had a lot to do with cleaning the house and putting those beautiful meals on the table?''

Lacey shook her head slowly. It was stupid, but she'd never thought of that. All these years, she'd looked at the way her mother ran her home and she'd felt inadequate, sure that she could never do half as well. And these past few weeks had seemed to confirm that. The cooking, the cleaning, the dinner party—all had left her exhausted, with none of the cool elegance that characterized her mother.

But it had never once occurred to her that Mamie hadn't taken on so many roles at one time. She'd never tried to do everything all at once. It was a revolutionary thought.

"I don't know. Maybe you're right."

"Of course I'm right." He reached out, taking her shoulders and drawing her close. "Haven't you figured out yet that I'm always right?"

Lacey managed a smile. "Hardly."

"Close enough." His hand circled the back of her neck, warm and strong. "Between the *two* of us, I don't see any reason why anyone should die of ptomaine poisoning or disappear into a cloud of dust. We may not be able to eat off the floors, but I think we can keep the place in reasonably good shape."

"I'm sorry I snapped at you about watching the game."

"No big deal. You can make it up to me by sitting down and watching the rest of it."

"I really should—" He cut off her protest with a quick, thorough kiss.

"You really should sit down and relax. Come on, admit it. There's nothing you have to do right this minute."

"No, I suppose not." She let him draw her forward to join him on the sofa. She'd halfway planned on making fresh bread. But that was part of the old Lacey. The one who'd been trying to do it all. And she wasn't going to do that anymore, right?

Right. Only it was easier said than done.

If anyone had told her that she'd find it difficult to do less, she wouldn't have believed them. But it was a fact that she felt

somewhat lost when she didn't have tasks to fill her ever
waking moment.

The first time Lacey came home to find that Cam had alread
fixed dinner, she could barely eat it. When he started sendin
things to the laundry, just as he'd done before they were ma
ried, she almost hoped that his shirts would come back i
shreds.

It was ridiculous. She'd never fancied herself as a candida
for Housewife of the Year. And heaven knew, she'd bee
working herself into the ground. But she felt a niggling re
sentment with each task that was shifted from her shoulder
Resentment and a vague feeling of failure.

It was one thing to acknowledge that her mother had alway
had a servant. It was another thing to really let that penetra
and dissolve long-held notions. All the years she'd been grov
ing up, she'd measured herself against her mother and fr
quently come up wanting. Maybe it was because she'd nev
known her father. She didn't have two parents to divide h
attention between, so her mother had gotten more than her fa
share.

Mamie might drive her crazy but she was still a role mode
an unattainable goal. And no matter what logic said, Lacey st
felt as if she'd failed to measure up in some way. There w
a feeling that her mother would have been able to mana
everything somehow. She would have run the shop and cleane
the house and cooked and mended and done it all so easily th
Cam would never have questioned the fairness of it.

And she couldn't even be mad at Cam. He was concern
about her. The knowledge should have made her feel good.
did make her feel good. But it also made her feel threatene

She was beginning to wonder if the reason she hadn't ma
ried before she was thirty was that she wasn't really suited
the institution. Not that there weren't pleasant aspects of it.
was nice to come home and talk to someone about what h
happened during her day. Cam was wonderful company.

In fact, Cam was wonderful about almost everything. And that was a large part of her problem.

The man didn't seem to have any faults.

Lacey's hands paused in their task of folding a pile of batiste camisoles, and she stared at the mirror that hung over the table without seeing anything it reflected. Usually, the image of the quiet elegance of the shop was enough to draw at least a smile. But not today.

Today, nothing seemed able to lift her spirits. She'd been feeling restless and moody for days now. One minute, the world seemed like a pretty terrific place to be, and the next she was wondering if it wasn't time to join a nice convent so that she'd never have to deal with the real world again.

She'd awakened in a gloomy mood this morning. It hadn't helped to find that Cam was already up and had prepared breakfast for her. As she'd poked moodily at her scrambled eggs and bacon, she'd wondered if there was anything the man couldn't do. What did he need a wife for, anyway?

And now, here she was wondering the same thing, when she should have been concentrating on the best way to display this stack of very expensive garments.

"Boy, you look about as cheerful as I feel."

Lacey started, dropping the camisole she held as she turned toward the voice. "Lisa! What are you doing here?"

Lisa shrugged. "I thought maybe you might like to go out for lunch."

"Lunch? You drove all the way from downtown L.A. to see if I wanted to have lunch with you?"

Her friend shrugged again. "It's been a while since we got together. Did I catch you at a bad time?"

"No, of course not." Lacey shook herself out of her gloom, noticing the way Lisa's eyes avoided hers, the dark circles under her eyes that no amount of makeup could completely disguise. "Margaret can take care of the shop for me."

If Margaret hadn't been there, she'd have done the unthinkable and closed Lacey's Lovelies. Lisa obviously needed to talk. But Margaret was there, and Lacey didn't have to worry about losing any business.

She and Lisa walked to a restaurant a couple of blocks away. Lacey deliberately steered clear of the café she and Cam had gone to the day after they'd first made love; right now, memories of Cam were not what she wanted.

They were lucky enough to get a table right away. Lacey waited until they were seated and their orders given before fixing Lisa with a look that demanded honesty.

"What's wrong?"

"It's that obvious, is it?"

Lisa's laugh showed a tendency to waver in the middle and Lacey felt her uneasiness grow stronger. This was something serious.

"It's obvious to me. But I've known you for a long time."

"Yeah. Since before I met Frank." Lisa moved her water glass in small circles, her eyes on the damp loops it left on the polished table.

"Since a long time before you met Frank," Lacey agreed, thinking it was an odd comment to make.

"Well, it looks like you're going to know me *after* I don't know Frank anymore." The flip words broke at the end.

Lacey drew a quick hard breath. "Are you and Frank having more problems?" The idea was inconceivable, despite the evidence she'd already seen. Frank and Lisa were the perfect couple. Everyone who knew them knew they were meant for each other.

"No. No more problems." Lisa shook her head, still not looking at her friend. "In fact, we have no problems at all. He moved out last week and we're filing for divorce."

Lacey felt the world spin around her for a moment before it settled into a new pattern. "Divorce," she whispered. "Lisa, you can't be getting a divorce. You and Frank love each other. Everybody knows that."

"Well, everybody forgot to tell Frank that." Lisa laughed, a bitter sound that carried pain.

Around them, the restaurant was full of people talking to their companions, the clink of silverware on plates. But their table might have been on another plane of reality.

"What happened?" Lacey asked at last.

Lisa shrugged. "Damned if I know. At least not for sure."

"Is it another woman?" Perhaps she shouldn't have asked the question. But this was Lisa. They'd known each other for too long for her to feel as if she was sticking her nose in where it wasn't wanted.

"No," Lisa said and then laughed again, still with that same bitter note. "If it was another woman, I might not feel like such a total failure."

"Don't be an idiot." Lacey reached across the table, catching Lisa's hand in hers and holding it until the other woman met her eyes. The pain in Lisa's was so deep, Lacey could feel it in her own soul. "Whatever happened, you're not a failure. Marriage is a two-way street, Lisa. You're not alone in its success or failure."

"Look who's talking," Lisa jeered. "Are you an expert on the subject now?"

Lacey withdrew her hand, her face tightening. "I'm sorry. You're right. I didn't mean to sound preachy."

"Oh, hell. I'm sorry, Lace. That was nasty and you don't deserve it. I want to shred Frank into little pieces and feed him to a pit bull, but I've got no right to take it out on you. Forgive me? Please?"

She reached out her hand, and Lacey's hesitation was only momentary before she extended her own.

"That's okay. I know you must be in a lot of pain. And I suppose I did sound a bit like a cheap marriage counselor." She squeezed Lisa's fingers before drawing away. The waiter appeared with their food, and the conversation halted until he'd left again.

"You want to tell me what happened?" Lacey's tone gave Lisa permission to say as much or as little as she wished.

"I'm not sure I know what happened." Lisa poked at her salad, her gaze on things Lacey couldn't see. "I guess maybe I haven't been as observant as I should have been. I've been so busy. Concentrating on my career." She laughed. "My career. Well, at least I'll have something to occupy my time."

"Lisa, what happened? What did Frank say? Did he just announce that he was moving out and that was that?"

"More or less."

"But he must have said something, given you some reason."

"He said we didn't seem to need each other very much anymore. He said I seemed to be doing just fine without him." Lisa put her fork down next to her untouched food and rubbed her fingers over her forehead as if soothing an ache. "Remember I told you that he asked me to cut down on my hours a few months ago? That he wanted to start a family?" At Lacey's nod she went on, "I promised him then that we'd talk about it again when I finished the project I was working on."

"And did you?" Lacey asked quietly.

"No. By the time that project was through, there was another in the works and I thought Frank had forgotten about it. And I didn't want to remind him, at least not right away."

"Can't you talk to him, explain that you didn't mean you wanted to wait forever?"

"Oh, Lacey, I don't think he wants to listen anymore." Lisa's voice broke on a sob. "You didn't see the way he looked at me. It wasn't like he was angry. He wasn't even cold. He looked at me like I was someone he'd known once a long time ago. I *tried* to talk to him. I practically begged him to talk. But he said it was too late. He said it was obvious we didn't need each other anymore and there was no sense in staying together.

"But I still need him, even if I haven't shown it lately. Knowing that Frank was there was what kept me going. I don't know how I'm going to manage without him. Don't ever fall in love, not even with Cam. It hurts too damned much when you lose them. Just too damned much.''

She stopped talking, her breathing rapid as she fought the threatening tears. Lacey stared at the table, trying to control the panic about to wash over her. This couldn't be true. Not Lisa and Frank. They were so perfect for each other. They'd been so much in love. If their marriage couldn't survive, how could anyone's? Especially one begun on shaky foundations.

Like her own.

Later, she had little memory of what she said to Lisa. She tried to offer comfort and she kept emphasizing that this couldn't be the end of it. Lisa and Frank would talk and they'd realize that they had built too much together to let it go like this. She couldn't be sure if she was trying to convince Lisa or herself.

By the time Lisa left her at the shop, Lisa seemed to have regained her control. Her eyes were red-rimmed, and they held a haunted look that made Lacey ache for her. There were one or two customers, but she left them to Margaret to handle and shut herself in her tiny office.

Seated behind the desk that took up most of the room, she didn't even pretend she was going to accomplish anything. Picking up a pen, she began to doodle aimlessly on the back of an invoice.

Frank and Lisa getting a divorce. What would Cam say when she told him? Would he see things as clearly as she did? It seemed as if this was almost an omen, pointing out how foolish they were to think they could make this marriage work.

We didn't seem to need each other very much anymore. Lisa's words echoed in her mind. Surely needing each other was an important ingredient in any marriage. An ingredient she and Cam didn't have. And they didn't seem likely to develop a sudden dependency on each other, either. After all, how could they? They'd both lived alone a long time. They'd proven they could make it without anyone else.

"Lacey?" Margaret's quiet knock preceded her person by only a moment. Lacey looked up, pulling a stack of papers toward her as if she had been interrupted in the midst of something important.

"Yes?"

"Maude Higgins is here. She says you told her we were going to be getting some new silk scarves, and she wants to see them."

"We didn't get them in yet."

"That's what I told her, but I don't think she believes me. She asked for you." Margaret rolled her eyes, expressing her opinion of Mrs. Higgins. Lacey privately agreed. The last thing she wanted to do right now was deal with a neurotic customer. But Maude Higgins was a very rich and loyal neurotic customer, she reminded herself. And no matter what was going on in her personal life, she had a responsibility to her clientele. Even the annoying ones.

By the time she'd convinced Maude that the scarves truly hadn't come in and promised, again, that she would personally call the moment they arrived, Lacey had managed to put thoughts of Lisa's marriage and her own on a back burner.

But they simmered there, threatening to boil over by the time she pulled into the driveway at home. Cam's home, she reminded herself, suddenly feeling as if it could never be hers. Cam's truck was gone, and she remembered that he was supposed to deliver a desk to someone in Santa Monica. That meant she was alone. She wasn't sure whether she was sorry or glad.

Certainly, with Cam gone, she'd have time to think. But that might not be all to the good. There was an almost inaudible voice in her head that suggested maybe she was overreacting to Lisa's news. Logic struggled to point out that her friend's failed marriage didn't necessarily spell doom for her own.

Part of her wanted Cam to come home and make her believe that everything was going to work out. It was his calm confidence that had taken their marriage this far. He'd made it seem so reasonable. Like it could actually work.

But it couldn't work.

She hurried through the house, giving Derwent an absent pat on her way down the hallway. She was aware of him watching her, his head cocked to one side as if puzzled. It had become a small ritual that she took time to play with him each evening when she came home. But she wasn't in the mood to play tonight.

Right now she had a mission. She suddenly knew what she had to do: end this travesty of a marriage before it was too late. That they hadn't fallen in love was all she was grateful for. If Lisa was right, love would have only brought more pain.

Her movements took on a frantic edge as she dragged her suitcase down from the top of the closet. Lacey's hands were shaking as she reached for her clothes. The sight of Cam's shirts hanging next to her dresses almost destroyed her resolve. But just because their clothes looked good together, didn't mean she and Cam belonged together. She drew out a handful of hangers, stripping the blouses from them and folding them roughly before dropping them into the open suitcase.

This was the right thing to do. She was sure of it. At least, she thought she was sure of it. And it wasn't talking to Lisa today that made her feel that way. That had just been the final little push.

She'd been having doubts for weeks now. Had there ever been a time when she didn't have doubts? She should have recognized her mood swings for what they were—a clear sign that it was time to end this whole foolish experiment.

She packed quickly, wanting nothing so much as to be out of the house before Cam got home. It was cowardly, but she didn't want to face him. She didn't want to listen to his arguments about their marriage being viable. She'd made her decision, and now she just wanted to act on it without anyone trying to talk her out of it.

But luck wasn't with her. She'd just finished putting the last of her toiletries in a small tote when the bedroom door swung open and Cam stopped in the doorway. Lacey froze, the very picture of guilt. Cam's eyes went from her pale face to the full suitcase.

"What's going on?"

Chapter Thirteen

Lacey stared at him, her vocal cords paralyzed. She couldn't look away from him and she couldn't find the voice to answer him, so she said nothing. Cam stared at the suitcase a long moment before his gaze moved back to her, a frown drawing his brows together.

"Lacey? Why are you packing a suitcase?"

She dragged her eyes away from his face, staring at a point somewhere to his left. Just a few more minutes and she'd have been out of here. She could have explained it all in a note. But that was no longer an option. She was going to have to explain it to him face-to-face. How did you go about telling a man you were leaving him?

"I'm leaving." In the end, the bare words were all she could find.

"Leaving?" He stared at her, apparently trying to absorb the meaning of her words. "For good?" He said it as if he couldn't believe her, as if he misunderstood her.

"For good." It sounded appallingly blunt, but she couldn't think of any way to soften it.

Cam thrust his fingers through his hair, ruffling it into pale brown waves. His expression seemed more bewildered than anything else.

"Why?" The simple question was the one she'd been dreading. She understood why her leaving was the right thing to do, but it wasn't something she could explain. Still, he'd asked and she had to try.

"I saw Lisa today."

"Great. What does Lisa have to do with this?" Cam waved one hand, indicating the suitcase.

"She and Frank have separated. They're talking about a divorce."

"I'm sorry to hear that. They seemed to be suited to each other. But I don't see what that has to do with you moving out."

"Don't you see what it means?"

"No." He obviously didn't see at all.

"Lisa and Frank *were* suited. They were so much in love. They fell in love at first sight, did you know that?"

"No. But I—"

"They married before Lisa was out of college and I've never seen a couple more in love. Really in love."

"Well, that's great but—"

"And now they're splitting up. Don't you see?"

Cam frowned, showing the first sign of irritation. "I'm beginning to think I may see what you're getting at, but why don't you explain it to me just to make sure."

"Cam, if Frank and Lisa can't make it when they started out with everything going for them, how can we expect to do any better when we started out with nothing going for us?"

She looked at him, pleading with him to understand. But it wasn't understanding that turned his eyes to a stormy blue.

"Do you mean to tell me you're leaving me because Frank and Lisa couldn't hold their marriage together?"

"Not because they couldn't hold it together, but because of what their breakup represents."

"It represents that they had problems they couldn't work out It has nothing—absolutely nothing—to do with us."

"Yes, it does. Cam, they loved each other, really loved each other."

"So what?" he burst out, exasperated.

"So, that wasn't enough. We don't even have that much. All we've got is a wedding neither of us remembers, a piece of paper we don't remember signing and a crazy idea that we could make something out of nothing. Well, we can't, and I'm leaving before we end up hurting each other."

She snapped the suitcase shut, but before she could pick it up, Cam's hand slammed down, pinning it to the bed. She jumped, looking up into eyes that burned with anger.

"That is the stupidest argument I've ever heard in my life." He bit each word off. "I could just as well argue that, since Lisa and Frank started out with love on their side, their separation makes it obvious that that's the wrong way to go about marriage."

Lacey closed her ears to the logic in his argument. This was how they'd gotten into this situation. He could make anything seem reasonable.

"Cam, if you're honest, you'll admit that this whole idea was crazy from the start. People don't get married to people they don't know."

"It seems to me that we've muddled along pretty well for the past couple of months. Lacey, don't do this."

"We've muddled along because we both worked at it, but it's not going to work in the end. Take my word for it."

"No! I damn well won't take your word for it." His palm hit the suitcase with a sharp explosion, and then he spun away from her, running his fingers through his hair again. He hunched his shoulders, stretching the fabric of his shirt across the hard muscles.

"Cam, I'm sorry. I didn't mean to hurt you."

"If I understood your reasoning, I might be able to understand why you think you have to do this. But I don't understand it. I'm not even sure you understand it." He turned to face her and Lacey winced away from his blazing eyes.

"I just don't want either of us to get hurt, and I believe that if we go on with this we're both going to regret it."

"Thanks loads for protecting me." He didn't bother to disguise his sarcasm.

Lacey set her chin. She'd made this decision and she wasn't going to change her mind.

"I'm doing what I think is best."

"You're doing what you think is safest. You're a coward, Lacey." Cam's blunt declaration hurt more than she liked to admit. "You're afraid you might be hurt, so you're running away. Let's call it like it is."

"You can think what you like."

"You want to know what I think? I think you're a quitter. When I first met you, I admired your spirit. I thought you faced life head-on and met its challenges, but you don't. You'd rather live in a safe little cocoon than take a chance.

"Oh, you'll take chances on your business, but that's safe enough. What are you going to lose? Money can be replaced. But you're not going to risk your emotions. You've been fighting them ever since Las Vegas.

"You're falling in love with me, but that scares the hell out of you. So you're going to run away. Well, you go ahead and quit, Lacey. Because I'm through fighting to get you to see what we could have. Run away. Lock yourself in that safe little world. I hope you'll be happy there. Alone."

He turned on his heel and strode out. A moment later Lacey heard the front door slam and then the roar of the truck's engine. She sat down on the edge of the bed, aware that her knees were not quite steady. She'd never seen Cam so angry. Angry and hurt.

Still, this was the right thing to do. She was sure of that. Wasn't she?

ONCE SHE'D LOADED her suitcase in her car, there didn't seem to be any question about where she was going. She still held the lease on her old apartment. It would be empty, but she considered that possibility for only a moment. Those cold, empty rooms weren't home. Maybe they'd never been home.

It was after dark when she pulled into the driveway of the house she'd grown up in. Light spilled from the windows, creating welcoming patterns on the neatly mowed lawn. Lacey rang the doorbell, shivering as she waited for her mother to answer. The air still held a portion of the day's warmth, yet she felt chilled.

She was going to ask if she could spend the night here. Tomorrow, she'd go and open up her apartment. But tonight she didn't feel like dealing with the inevitable dust and stuffiness. She'd very calmly tell Mamie that she'd left Cam and that she didn't want to talk about it. After all, she was an adult now. The day was long past when she felt the need to spill her private difficulties into her mother's ear.

There was the quick tap of heels on the tiled floor and then Mamie was opening the door. Light poured out to embrace Lacey like a warm blanket.

"Why, sugar, what are you doin' here? Is Cameron with you?"

"Mother." Lacey's voice quivered on the word, and her eyes stung with tears.

"Lacey, honey, what's wrong?" Mamie reached out, catching Lacey's hand and pulling her inside. The door shut behind them, shutting the world out and shutting Lacey back in the world that had been so safe when she was a child. A world in which there'd been nothing her mother couldn't fix.

"Can I stay here tonight?" Despite her struggle to sound calm, her voice broke abruptly. She lifted her hand, pressing the back of her fingers against her mouth to stifle the sob that threatened to break through.

"You know you can always stay here, honey. You're pale, sugar. Come on in the livin' room and I'll get you a dash of bourbon. Put a little color in those cheeks."

Lacey let Mamie seat her on the sofa, watching without really seeing as she poured a small dose of amber liquid into a crystal shot glass and brought it back. She took the glass automatically, her fingers numb as they curled around it.

"Now you drink that down. You'll feel better."

Lacey obeyed mechanically, her eyes stinging as the fiery liquid hit the back of her throat. It burned all the way down and she gasped for air as it hit bottom. Mamie patted her back her fine brows puckered in a concerned frown.

"There now. There's not much that a bit of bourbon can' help. You want to tell me what's wrong, sugar?"

She didn't want to tell her mother what was wrong. She didn't want to tell anyone. She wanted to go somewhere and find a dark corner to crawl into.

"I—I've left Cam."

"Oh, Lacey, honey, why?" Mamie's tone expressed he shocked concern.

"Because it wasn't a real marriage." The top of her head felt light, as if it might float off at any moment. She stared a the bottom of the shot glass, and it occurred to her that sh hadn't had anything to eat since breakfast. That would explai why the bourbon seemed to be affecting her so strongly.

"Not a real marriage? Lacey, what are you talkin' about?'

"It was a marriage of convenience. Or maybe inconvenienc would be a better description."

Mamie reached out to take the shot glass from her daughte studying it as if it might contain an explanation for her bizarr behavior.

"Sugar, you're not makin' much sense. You want to tell m what's happened between you and Cameron? You seemed s happy together. Did you quarrel with him?"

"No, we didn't quarrel." Lacey leaned back, suddenly ver tired. "At least not until I told him I was leaving. And I'm n falling in love with him." She stopped, closing her eyes for moment, as if she could shut out the past months. "Oh, Mama, I've been so stupid."

"You just tell me what's happened and we'll see what we can do about it. There's no problem that can't be fixed, Lacey. Tell me what's gone wrong."

There was something in her that responded to her mother's brisk tone. She might be long past the age of believing that her mother could solve all her problems, yet there was enough of the child left in her that she couldn't help but half believe that something could be salvaged out of the tangled mess she'd created.

"It started off all wrong. Maybe things would've been different if it hadn't started off so wrong." She told her mother the true story from beginning to end.

As she sat in the quiet elegance of the living room she'd grown up in, the story behind her marriage seemed even more bizarre. The trip to Las Vegas, waking up in bed with Cam— it was all like something out of a movie. A bad movie.

The hardest part was trying to explain just why they'd decided to give the marriage a try. It had seemed so crazy at the time and the fact that it had almost worked didn't make it any more reasonable.

Her calm control began to crack again when she got to her decision to leave. She'd been right to leave. She knew she was right. But she hadn't expected it to hurt so much. Her voice dissolved into tears as she told her mother about Cam's reaction, how he'd called her a coward and then stormed out.

Mamie reached for her daughter, wrapping one arm around Lacey's trembling shoulders and pulling her close. With a sob, Lacey turned, burying her face in her mother's shoulder just as she'd done when she was a little girl. The simple comfort still had the power to make the world seem a little less bleak.

She cried until she didn't have the breath to cry anymore. Mamie held her, murmuring softly, not saying anything in particular. She didn't speak until Lacey's sobs turned into deep shuddering breaths.

"We're not going to talk about this anymore tonight. You're tuckered out and you're goin' straight to bed."

"I can't sleep."

"Yes, you can," Mamie told her in a brisk tone that brooked no argument. "You're goin' to sleep till mornin' and then we'll talk about this."

"There's nothing to talk about. I've left Cam and that's all there is to it." She sounded sulky and she knew it.

"We'll see. Now, I want you to go take a nice warm shower while I get your room ready."

It was easier to do as she was told than to try to make any decisions of her own. Lacey stood under the shower, keeping her mind a careful blank. The water pounded down, washing over her. She wished it could somehow wash away all her hurt and confusion.

Fresh tears came to her eyes when she stepped into her old bedroom. The paint and wallpaper were different, but this was the room where she'd spent her childhood. She'd played with her dolls here, then played with makeup. She'd studied at the desk in the corner and worked out her first plans for the shop there. The room held a lot of memories. And at the moment it felt safe.

It was that feeling of safety that made it possible to climb into bed and fall asleep almost immediately. She slept deeply, waking the next morning to bright sunshine, which failed to reflect her mood. Despite the long sleep, she was tired. But maybe that was to be expected. A recovery was going to take more than a few hours' rest.

Mamie was in the kitchen when Lacey left her bedroom. The shop was open only half days on Thursdays, so she had a few hours before she had to go in. She was glad of the extra time. She needed it to pull herself together.

Mamie looked up as Lacey stepped into the kitchen. She w

seated at the table wearing a pale yellow blouse and a pair of tailored gray slacks. Lacey ran her hands over her own worn jeans and faded T-shirt. She probably looked like the wrath of God, but she couldn't get up the energy to care.

"There's some coffee on the counter. You look like you could use some."

Lacey started toward the pot and then changed her mind. The smell of the coffee made her stomach turn over. After yesterday's upset it was no wonder. She poured herself a glass of milk instead. Sitting down across from Mamie, she picked up a doughnut from the plate on the table and bit into it.

"How'd you sleep?" Mamie asked, her eyes going over her daughter with maternal concern.

"Good, actually. I was surprised I slept at all."

"A dab of bourbon will help every time." Mamie took a swallow of her coffee, her eyes never leaving Lacey. Lacey shifted uneasily.

"I'm sorry I made such a scene last night."

"Don't be silly, sugar. That's what I'm here for. I'm just glad you came to me. Are you ready to talk about things?"

Lacey felt a quick spurt of panic. She didn't want to talk about anything. She'd made her decision and acted on it, and that was the end of it. On the other hand, she knew that look in her mother's eye. Mamie had made up her mind that there were things to be said, and nothing short of a nuclear blast was likely to change her mind. Still, she tried.

"Actually, Mother, I really should get to the shop."

"You don't open till one o'clock. That gives you a couple of hours before you even need to get dressed."

"Well, we got this shipment in yesterday and I really should work on the books."

"Lacey, you and I have known each other a long time. Why don't you just sit down and let me speak my piece."

Lacey sank back down into the chair. It was true that in the long run it would be simpler to let Mamie get whatever she

wanted to say off her chest. She was going to do so sooner o
later, anyway.

"All right, Mother. What is it you want to say?"

"It's real simple. Cameron was absolutely right when he sai
you were actin' like a coward. You're actin' like a scared littl
rabbit, Lacey, and I think you know it."

"I don't know anything of the kind," Lacey said with dig
nity. "It seems to me that after I realized that there was n
future in our marriage, I would have been pretty dumb to hav
stayed in it."

"Who says there's no future?"

"Well, it's pretty obvious. I mean, we hardly know eac
other. The way our marriage started was ridiculous. How ca
we build anything on a beginning like that?"

"Those aren't real reasons," Mamie told her. "It doesn
matter how long you've known a man before you marry hir
You still get most of the knowin' after the weddin'. Do yo
think if you'd known Cameron for years, you wouldn't hav
had any doubts after you were married?

"And as for the way your marriage started out, I don't se
what the problem is. I think it's a lot more interestin' than
big church weddin' would have been. Think of what a story
would be to tell your children."

"Well, there aren't going to be any children because the
isn't going to be a marriage," Lacey declared. Her mother
words were so close to the things Cam had said that she almo
suspected a conspiracy between the two of them.

Mamie went on as if she hadn't spoken. "I think the re
problem is that you're afraid of gettin' hurt. You're afraid
lovin' someone. But, darlin', everyone is afraid of that."

Lacey stared at the table, trying not to hear the truth in h
mother's words. "It's different when it's someone you kno
Then you can have some confidence that they aren't going
hurt you."

"Honey, that's just not true. We all hurt the people we lov

's a part of livin'. We don't mean to hurt them, but it happens. o matter how long you've known someone or how much you ove them, it's no guarantee that they're not going to break our heart. Do you think your father and I didn't have our hare of problems?''

"No, of course not," Lacey said impatiently. "I'm not so aive that I think you can have a relationship without some onflicts, but it's different when you know you love that person nd you know he loves you."

"It's not that much different." Mamie shifted her coffee cup ack and forth between her hands, her eyes on the aimless ovement. "You know, maybe I made a mistake in not re- arryin'. You never had a chance to see a relationship close o, all the give and take that goes into makin' a marriage work. fter your father died, I just never found someone else I anted to share my life with."

"I know you loved him very much."

"I loved him. And he loved me, but that didn't mean things ere always smooth for us. We fought, sometimes over silly ings, sometimes over big things." Mamie looked up, fixing r clear blue eyes on Lacey. "I almost left him once. I never ld you that."

"No, you didn't." Lacey looked away, absorbing the shock her mother's statement. She'd always pictured her parents' arriage as idyllic. Perhaps because she had no memories of em together, she'd painted a picture in her mind of what the rfect marriage was and decided that was what they'd had.

"What happened?"

"I thought he was having an affair."

"Was he?" If she'd expected a quick denial, Lacey was sappointed. Mamie hesitated and then shook her head slowly. don't think so."

"You don't think so?" Lacey demanded incredulously.

"Well, I reckon I decided that he wasn't." Her smile held hint of self-deprecation. "I loved him."

"But if he was having an affair..." Lacey's entire conce[pt] of her father had shifted drastically in a matter of seconds. Sh[e] stared at her mother. "How could you forgive him?"

"Well, like I said, I wasn't even sure there was anything [to] forgive. And in the end I forgave him because I loved hi[m] enough to want to keep our marriage together.

"We'd been fightin' somethin' fierce, sugar. And there wa[s] this woman who worked for him. She was real pretty, and [I] guess maybe I'd been jealous of her for a long time. When [I] accused your father of cheatin' on me with her, he just look[ed] at me real still and he told me to believe what I wanted. [He] wasn't goin' to argue with me.

"I realized I could either pack my bags and go home [to] Georgia, or I could believe that he'd been faithful and sta[y.] And I loved him enough to stay."

"But didn't it spoil things between you?" Lacey was st[ill] groping to accept this altered portrait.

Mamie laughed softly. "I reckon it didn't spoil things t[oo] much. You were born just a year later. We still fought, bu[t I] think we'd both learned that we meant a lot to each other."

Lacey shook her head, staring at her empty milk glass a[nd] the half-eaten doughnut in front of her. "I don't see what t[his] has to do with Cam and me. After all, doesn't it just prove [my] point? You two loved each other when you got married a[nd] you still came close to losing each other."

LACEY'S EMOTIONS were so raw a few days later that she beg[an] to wonder if she wasn't coming down with one of the thr[oat] infections that had been the bane of her childhood. She hadn['t] had one in years, but the exhaustion she was feeling was [a] typical symptom. She made an appointment with her doct[or;] in the meantime she tried to stave it off with vitamins.

But the vitamins didn't do anything to lift her spirits, whi[ch] had sunk so low she sometimes wondered if they'd ever [lift] again.

She didn't hear a word from Cam, and she told herself that was exactly the way she wanted it. After all, there was no reason to flog a dead horse—obviously she'd convinced him that their marriage was just that. She was glad he'd accepted it. Very glad.

Which of course didn't explain why she lunged for the phone every time it rang. Why each ring of the brass bell on the shop door brought her head around. It wasn't that she was expecting anyone in particular. It was just that her nerves were strung a little tight these days. Nothing more.

By the time a week had gone by, she'd calmed down so that she no longer jumped when the phone rang or someone entered the shop. It was becoming clear that Cam wasn't going to try to contact her. Which was just the way she wanted it.

It was late morning when the shop bell announced the arrival of Mamie.

"Mother. You didn't tell me you were going to be in town." She glanced at her watch. "Did you want to go for lunch?"

To her surprise, Mamie flushed a delicate shade of pink.

"Well, actually, I already have plans for lunch. I just came in to see if you had a scarf that would look nice with this suit."

Lacey looked at the classic silk suit that fit her mother's trim figure as if it had been tailored especially for her, which it probably had. The delicate ivory was set off perfectly by a warm coral blouse.

"I think I've got something that might look good." She led the way to a table across the shop. "You don't really need anything with that, you know. It looks just about perfect as it is." She began shifting a stack of silk scarves, looking for one that was a blend of just the right shades.

"I don't want to look 'just about' perfect." Mamie fussed with the gold clasp on her purse and Lacey paused in her search, leaning against the table to fix her mother with a searching look. For the first time in a week, something took precedence over her own miseries.

"Just who is this lunch date?"

"Well, it's someone who's become rather important to me."

"Oh, really. Anyone I know?"

Mamie looked away, her skin taking on a tinge of pink. "Well, as a matter of fact—"

The shop bell rang again and Lacey looked up automatically. Jimbo stepped through the door, his stocky form encased in a neat blue suit, complete with tie. Lacey stared at him for a moment. Jimbo never wore a suit—unless he was meeting an important client. And if he was meeting an important client what was he doing here?

He turned and saw the two of them, and his eyes skimmed over Lacey to settle on Mamie. His face lit up as if he'd just been given a glimpse of the Holy Grail. Lacey looked from him to her mother, surprising a look she'd never seen, a mixture of shy pleasure and coquetry.

She looked at her mother incredulously. "Jimbo?" Her voice was hushed as he began to make his way toward them.

Mamie threw her daughter a quick look that held a touch of defiance. "He's a very nice man."

"Well, sure, but—" She didn't get a chance to finish her sentence. Jimbo stopped in front of them, reaching out to clasp the hand Mamie offered. Her hand looked so tiny, lost on his broad palm. Lacey had to admit there was something very sweet about the way the two of them were looking at each other. For a moment, she felt very old, as if she and Mamie had reversed positions and she was suddenly the mother.

"Mamie. You look exquisite as always."

"Why, thank you, James. You look very handsome in that suit."

To Lacey's amusement, Jimbo blushed, though she wasn't sure if it was pleasure or embarrassment that caused the reaction.

"Hello, Jimbo." She had the strong feeling that if she didn't remind them of her presence, they might forget she was there altogether. Jimbo dragged his eyes from Mamie with obvious effort to focus on Lacey, his expression cooling.

"Hello, Lacey. I hope you know you're an absolute fool."

"Well, I guess I know it now, even if I didn't before. It's nice to see you, too." She carefully didn't ask why he thought she was a fool. She didn't have to be psychic to know the reason involved Cam. Maybe Jimbo would take a hint and let it go at that. She should have known better. Subtlety had never been his strong suit. This time was no exception.

"You realize how dumb this whole thing is, of course. Cam's miserable. You're miserable. And there's no reason it has to be this way."

So Cam was miserable without her. Lacey's heart gave a hard bump, but she kept her expression calm, disinterested. "Did Cam tell you that?"

"Hell, no. Talking to him is like talking to the great stone face these past few days. All he said was that you'd left. He also told me to mind my own business."

"You don't seem inclined to take his advice," Lacey commented dryly.

"I don't see any sense in minding my own business when two of my best friends are miserable."

"Just stay out of it. Cam and I know what we're doing."

"Hah!" Jimbo's inelegant snort exploded out of him, making Lacey jump and drawing the attention of two customers. "You don't have a clue about what you're doing. If you did, you wouldn't be hiding yourself in this place and Cam wouldn't be burying himself in the shop."

"Jimbo—" Lacey's voice held a warning, and Mamie reached out, setting her hand on his sleeve.

"James, I'm not sure we should try and interfere in this. After all, Cameron and Lacey are adults."

"I'm sorry, Mamie, but I can't just stand here and watch them make the biggest mistake of their lives. Any idiot can see that they're head over heels in love with each other."

"Aren't you going to be late for lunch or something?" Lacey chose to ignore his words, knowing that any response she gave him would only encourage him to continue arguing. And this wasn't something she wanted to argue about.

Jimbo glowered at her a moment longer, but he must have realized he was up against a stone wall. He shrugged. "I give up. I suppose the Constitution guarantees you the right to act like an idiot."

"Thank you."

Lacey watched the two of them leave. There was still something incongruous about that pairing. Jimbo's bull-like body and boisterous personality didn't seem to fit with Mamie's delicacy and refinement. Still, she couldn't remember the last time she'd seen her mother look so happy.

She turned back to the table of scarves, and the room suddenly spun around her. Grabbing at the table for balance, she closed her eyes, waiting for the dizzy spell to pass. Damn Jimbo. He had to dredge up the past and call up memories of Cam she'd been trying to bury. See what they did to her? She knew she was right: this marriage was no good.

Chapter Fourteen

acey managed to put off thinking about Jimbo's words for
several hours. But now, seated in the doctor's waiting room,
she found herself thumbing through a magazine and seeing
nothing in it.

Head over heels in love with each other. The phrase super-
imposed itself over an article lamenting the drought in the Mid-
west. *Cam is miserable* appeared while she was looking at an
ad for underwear featuring an impossibly thin model.

In love with each other? Impossible. She'd know if she was
in love with Cam, even if she didn't know his feelings. Surely,
you couldn't be in love and not know it. No, she wasn't in
love with him. But she did miss him.

The knowledge slid into her mind, startling her. Okay, so
she missed him. The admission was sulky. There was nothing
wrong with missing him. He was a nice guy and she liked him.
Liking was a long way from loving. And there was nothing
strange in missing someone you liked. In fact, if she was totally
honest, she also missed his house and his ditzy dog.

With a muttered curse, she shut the magazine and stared at
the wall. Just missing someone wasn't a good enough reason
to be married to them. Not even when you missed them so
much it felt like a piece of yourself was gone.

She absently dog-eared the pages of the magazine, her eyes
focused elsewhere. Cam had said she was a coward, that she

was afraid of commitment, afraid of getting hurt, and he mother had agreed with him. *Was* she a coward?

A week ago, it had seemed so clear, so obvious. Now he reasoning seemed a little foggy and blurred around the edge What had been so obvious was now obscure. Why had sh panicked when Lisa told her that she and Frank were splittir up?

But before she could come up with an answer to that que tion, the nurse called her into the inner office.

"WELL, YOU WERE certainly right about your throat." Dr. Rit man studied her over the top of his glasses. "It's been quite while since you had one of these infections, hasn't it?"

"A few years," Lacey answered.

"Well, you've got a pretty good one now." He studied th folder he had balanced on his knee, frowning absently. "I se you recently got married. Congratoulations."

"Thank you," Lacey murmured, wondering what he'd sa if she told him she was likely to be divorced before too lon

He made some notes on the chart, the scrape of his founta pen audible in the small examining room.

"Well, a round of antibiotics should take care of that thro of yours. Is there any chance you're pregnant?"

"No, I—" She stopped, feeling a sudden tightness in h throat that had nothing to do with infected tonsils. The routi question had caught her off guard. He'd always asked it, dra ing blushes when she was sixteen. She didn't feel like blushi now. She felt more like fainting.

It wasn't possible. They'd been careful. Except that nig after the party, when they'd made love on the sofa... Only th one time. One careless moment couldn't possibly—

"No," she repeated, as much for herself as the doctor. "N I'm not pregnant."

Shrewd blue eyes regarded her over the glasses. "Are y

ure, Lacey? Because, if there's any doubt, any doubt at all,
e don't want to endanger the baby.''

"I..." She started to tell him that she was sure, but she
ouldn't get the words out. The fact was, she wasn't sure at
ll.

Her eyes filled with quick tears and she looked down, blink-
ng rapidly. "I don't think I'm pregnant." But the words didn't
arry any conviction.

"When was your last menstrual period?"

"I don't know." She tried to think. "I'm late, I guess. But
ve been under a lot of stress."

"Do you have any other symptoms? Nausea, dizziness, lack
f appetite, tiredness?"

"I— All of those."

Her voice was shaking, and Dr. Riteman reached out to put
is hands over hers, stilling the restless twisting of her fingers.
is eyes were kind. "I'll tell you what. Why don't we take a
ine sample and check. Just to make sure. How does that
und?"

She wanted to scream at him that it was an awful idea. It
as an unnecessary idea. She wasn't pregnant. She couldn't be
egnant.

Lacey nodded slowly. "Thank you, doctor. I'd appreciate
at."

"It's no problem. Better safe than sorry and, this way, you'll
now for sure."

It wasn't possible. It just wasn't possible.

UT TWO HOURS later she walked out of the office with a hand-
l of booklets that said that it was more than possible. It was
reality.

Just the early stages, but it was never too soon to start taking
re of herself, the doctor had told her in a tone that was much
o cheerful for Lacey's distraught mind.

When she got in her car, she didn't start it right away. She

just sat, staring out at the beautiful summer day, trying to ab
sorb this sudden drastic change in her life.

She was carrying a child. Cam's child. The thought brough
a confusing rush of emotions tumbling after it. She'd alway
planned to have children. In the back of her mind, there'd a
ways been the image of one or two small people who were
part of her. The father had been a vague figure, there, but n
very real.

Until Cam. Since the odd beginnings of their marriage, she'
unconsciously substituted him for the amorphous masculi
image in her mind. There'd even been a time or two whe
she'd specifically fantasized about the kind of father he'd mak
But she'd been thinking of some distant time, so far in th
future that it was safe to dream about.

Only now it wasn't a dream anymore. It was reality. Preg
nant. Her hands settled on her stomach. It was still flat, givi
no sign of the momentous changes taking place inside. A chi
was growing within. A son or a daughter who'd hold a litt
of herself and a little of Cam and blend those bits into a total
new and unique person.

Cam. Lacey drew in a quick breath as a wave of longi
swept over her, bringing tears to her eyes. She wanted nothi
as much in the world as to go to him and tell him her new
She wanted to feel his arms around her, hear him say that l
was happy, that everything was going to be all right.

But she couldn't do that. She'd shut that door; slammed
in fact. How could she go to Cam now and tell him that s
wanted to give their marriage a try after all? He'd take h
back when he found out about the child—she didn't doubt th
for a moment. He had a strong sense of responsibility. And s
knew he'd want to be a part of his child's life.

But she didn't want him to take her back because of t
baby. She wanted him to take her back because he loved h
because he didn't want to live without her, any more than s

wanted to live without him. The realization took her breath away.

She was in love with Cameron McCleary.

She'd been such a fool, an unforgivable fool. She'd let her own fears and doubts blind her to the incredible gift that had been dropped into her lap.

Mamie was in the living room when Lacey came in. She looked up from a handful of knitting the color of a summer sky, her smile welcoming.

"You're home a bit early, sugar. There's some tea, if you'd like. Janey fixed it before she left for the day. Those cookies are absolutely divine. That girl has the lightest touch with anything baked. I've been tryin' to talk her into startin' a bakery of her own. I'd finance it. I do believe it would be a good investment. I think I've almost got her talked into it."

Lacey sat down, pouring a cup of tea and reaching for a cookie. Her appetite had been almost nonexistent for the past couple of weeks, but she was suddenly ravenous. Maybe having a reason for the way she'd been feeling had restored her hunger. She bit into the cookie, feeling it nearly melt in her mouth.

"Aren't those just the best things?"

"How was your lunch with Jimbo?" Lacey reached for another cookie. She still hadn't decided whether she wanted to tell Mamie her own news.

"James and I had a lovely meal. The fish was divine."

"The two of you seem pretty close," Lacey said casually.

"He's a charmin' man and he knows how to treat a lady." Mamie's color was a little high and her tone held just a touch of defiance.

"Well, if you're happy, then I'm happy for you."

"Thank you, Lacey. That means a lot to me. Now, all we need to do is work on your bein' happy."

Lacey shrugged, doing her best to discourage her mother from continuing. It worked better with Mamie than it had with

Jimbo. Mamie's lips tightened and she shook her head, despairing of Lacey's common sense, but she didn't say anything more.

Lacey munched another cookie, her eyes on the swift movements of the knitting needles. It crept over her gradually that these past few days with her mother were some of the best they'd ever spent together. For the first time she was seeing her mother as a person apart from her role as a mother. Mamie was a woman with hopes and dreams just like everyone else.

Lacey wasn't sure just what had effected the change. Maybe it was turning thirty, or maybe it was getting married. Whatever, she knew she'd never look at her mother in quite the same way again.

"Mother?"

"Yes, sugar?"

"Have I told you lately that I love you?"

Mamie looked up, startled, and Lacey felt a twinge of shame that her words should come as a surprise.

"I guess I don't tell you often enough, do I?"

Mamie shook her head. "I know you love me, Lacey. You don't always have to say the words."

"Maybe they should be said once in a while."

"Maybe they should," Mamie agreed. "In that case, I should tell you that I love you, too. You're just about the best thing to come into my life."

"Do you ever regret that you raised me alone?"

"Well, I always regretted that you didn't get a chance to know your daddy and that he didn't get a chance to know you. But I never regretted having you, if that's what you're asking. If it hadn't been for you, I just can't imagine where my life would have gone."

"But didn't you ever resent having a kid around? I mean, you were very young. Didn't you ever think of the things you could have done?"

"No. There was nothing I wanted to do that I didn't do. You'll understand when you have children of your own."

Lacey took a sip of her tea then cleared her throat nervously. "How do you feel about being a grandmother?"

Mamie shrugged, without looking up from her knitting. "I won't mind when the time comes. It would be nice to have a little one around the place. A house without a child in it once in a while is a pretty dull place.

"Of course, at the rate you're going, it's likely to be quite some time before I have a grandchild," she added sternly.

Lacey smiled, aware that her lips showed a definite tendency to quiver.

"Mama? I'm going to have a baby."

The knitting needles came to a halt, but Mamie didn't look up. The silence stretched. Then she lifted her head, her eyes reflecting her shock.

"You're havin' a baby?" Lacey nodded, biting her lip nervously. "I'm going to be a grandma?"

"Do you mind?"

"Mind? Do I mind? Have you taken leave of your senses, child?" She leaned forward, and Lacey took the hands she held out. "A baby. Do you know how long I've waited to see you rockin' my grandchild? Oh, sugar, this is about the best news I've had in a month of Sundays!"

Lacey laughed, her eyes sparkling with bright tears. She hadn't realized how real telling someone about it was going to make her pregnancy seem.

Mamie's face sobered abruptly. "You are goin' to tell Cameron." It was a statement, but her tone made it half a question. Lacey's gaze dropped away from her mother's and she shrugged.

"I don't know yet."

Mamie's fingers tightened demandingly on her daughter's. "You listen to me, Lacey. Cameron has a right to know he's goin' to be a daddy. You got no right keepin' it from him."

"I know, I know." She tugged her hands away, twistin them together in her lap. "I'll have to tell him, but not righ now. I just found out about it myself, and I need a little tim to adjust to the idea. And I need to pick the right time to te him."

"If you hadn't done such a damn fool thing and left th man, you wouldn't need to pick the right time to tell him," Mamie told her with asperity.

"Mother, please. Don't make me sorry I told you."

Mamie glared at her a moment longer and then softene "All right. I won't scold you anymore tonight. We should d something to celebrate. I think there's some apple cider in th refrigerator. Why don't I get us a couple of glasses? We'll toa the newest member of the family."

So they toasted the baby with cider served in fluted cham pagne glasses. They laughed and talked, planning out th child's life right through college. In some ways, it was one the most wonderful evenings Lacey had ever spent.

But she cried herself to sleep that night. No matter how muc fun they'd had, Mamie was not Cam. Right now, no one in th world could reconcile her to the unhappy fact that he wasn here to share these first few hours of excitement. And it didn make it any easier that it was her own actions that had sh her away from him.

GOING INTO THE SHOP the next day, Lacey found her conce tration at an all-time low. If she wasn't thinking about the bab she was thinking about its father, wondering how she wou break the news to him, wondering what his reaction would b

Cam was so much on her mind that it was hardly a surpri when the bell pinged and she looked up to see his tall figu step through the door. She'd been kneeling on the floor, chec ing some stock in a low drawer, and he didn't see her at fir It was a small mercy but one Lacey appreciated. It gave her moment to grab hold of the composure that threatened to slip away.

She stood up slowly, feeling the impact of Cam's eyes when he saw her. She wanted to run to him, throw herself into his arms and tell him that she'd been a fool. But she didn't. If there was any way to salvage something of the mess she'd made of their relationship, it was going to take time and care. It wasn't something that could be fixed in a few brief moments.

"Hello, Lacey." Cam spoke as she came near, his voice soft, though they were alone in the shop.

"Hello, Cam." She started to hold out her hand and then stopped before the move had a chance to be completed. Shaking hands seemed a little absurd.

"You look beautiful." His eyes didn't miss anything, from the top of her neatly pinned chignon, over her pale green silk dress to the toes of her neat pumps. Lacey had to restrain the urge to put her hands over her stomach as if he could somehow see the new life that was hidden there. But of course he couldn't possibly notice anything.

"Thank you. You look very well." God, she sounded so stilted. She could have been taking a class in manners.

"Thank you."

The silence extended, threatening to grow to unmanageable proportions. Lacey could feel her nerves stretching thin. If only a customer would come in. Anything to break the tension.

"So, did you come in for something in particular?" The words came out too bald, too shrill, as if she felt his presence needed an explanation. Cam's face tightened.

"No. I guess I've caught you at a bad time." He half turned, reaching for the door. In a moment he'd be gone, thinking she didn't want to see him. Lacey's hand caught at his arm.

"Wait. I'm sorry. I didn't mean to sound so abrupt. I guess I'm a little nervous." She felt the muscles tighten in his arm as he slowly turned back to her. His eyes met hers and it wasn't hard to read his doubt.

"Are you sure? I know you've probably got a lot to do here."

Lacey laughed nervously, releasing his arm to wave an eloquent hand at the empty shop. "As you can see I am swamped with customers, but I think I can spare a few minutes."

Cam glanced around and then looked back at her, and she could feel his tension ease.

"Slow day?"

"Slow season. Come summer, all my customers depart for St. Moritz and St. Thomas. It's always the slowest time of year."

"Well, you seem to be busy enough the rest of the year to weather a couple of slow months."

"We are. To tell the truth, it's nice to be able to take a bit of a break."

"I'll bet."

Silence fell between them again, but this time, Lacey spoke before it had a chance to build into something awkward.

"How have you been? Are you keeping busy?"

"Busy enough. I finished the desk."

"The one with all the inlays? It looked gorgeous while you were working on it."

"I'm happy with it. And so were the Masdens. They've asked me to make a matching secretary."

"Are you going to do it?" she asked.

"I think so. I've already told them it would be quite a few months before I could start on it. I've got other things in line ahead of them. It depends on whether or not they want to wait."

"They obviously appreciate the best. They'll wait."

Cam smiled, the first truly relaxed expression she'd seen. "I should hire you to run a PR department for me."

"Well, it's true."

His smile faded, replaced by a searching expression. "How have you been?"

She shrugged. "Okay. How have you been?"

"Okay, I guess. Derwent misses you. He sulked for two full days. He even refused to eat."

"Poor baby." Had Cam missed her, too? *Tell me you missed me. Ask me to come home.*

But he didn't say anything for a moment, and when he did, it was on a different subject. "I hope you don't mind my dropping by like this."

"No, of course not." If only he knew how much she'd missed him, how hungry she'd been for the sight of him.

"I'd hate to think that we couldn't still be friends."

"I would too." Friends? She didn't want to be his friend. Not unless she could also be his wife, his lover, the center of his life.

He stuck his hands into his pockets and then pulled them out again, staring at them for a moment as if he wasn't quite sure what they were doing on the ends of his arms.

"Well, I guess I'd better get going. I need to pick up some things."

Tell him, you nitwit. Tell him how you feel. Tell him how much you miss him, how much you want to come back to him.

She bit her lip against the urge to beg him to take her home with him. How could she tell him she'd changed her mind? What if he still wanted her and then found out about the baby? He'd think that was the only reason she'd changed her mind. And if she told him about the baby first, she'd never be sure if that wasn't the only reason he'd wanted her back.

So she didn't say anything. She murmured a goodbye and watched him leave, the bell jingling merrily behind him. Her hands were clenched into fists at her sides, her nails biting into her palms.

Well, Lacey, you certainly managed to make a royal mess of things this time.

WELL, I CERTAINLY blew that one. Cam stalked along the side-walk, long angry strides eating up the distance to his truck.

He hadn't said anything he'd wanted to say. He'd probably looked like a total fool, standing there gawking at her.

"I hope we can still be friends." He mimicked his own words under his breath in a tone so savage that a little old lady who'd been about to walk by him quickly turned and went into a men's shoe store.

He'd given her some time. So okay, it was less than two weeks, but the house felt so damned empty without her. He'd come here, half thinking that he'd ask her to reconsider, give their marriage another try. Instead he'd stood there like a mentally deficient gorilla and exchanged a bit of casual conversation with her. Brilliant.

Why didn't you tell her how you felt?

He snarled at the small voice inside, causing a mother with two toddlers to decide that she'd really rather walk on the other side of the street.

How could he tell Lacey that his life was empty without her, that he was in love with her, when it was obvious that she didn't feel anything of the kind for him? It was one thing to take emotional chances. It was something else to throw himself at the mercy of someone who so clearly wasn't interested. Still, he couldn't quite believe it was going to end here. Maybe that was only because it hurt too much to think an end to their relationship was possible.

"No, dammit!" He shoved the key into the door of the truck with such force it threatened to bend. They felt too right to-gether, too perfect for it to be a figment of his imagination. Lacey would feel it, too. She *had* to feel it. Anything else was unthinkable. All he needed to do was give her some time.

Just a little time.

"JAMES IS COMING to dinner, sugar. I hope you don't mind." Even if Lacey had been inclined to object, she wouldn't have said anything to take the excitement from her mother's eyes.

"Of course not. Shall I make myself scarce?" she asked teasingly.

Mamie blushed, looking as young as her daughter. "Don't be silly. Besides, if we wanted to be alone, there're always motels." The look she threw Laccy was pure mischief.

"Mother! I'm shocked and horrified. You're talking like a hussy."

"I know," Mamie said complacently. "Ain't it fun?"

The dinner proved to be more pleasant than she might have expected, considering her last encounter with Jimbo. She didn't know if Mamie had said something to him, or if he'd simply decided that tact might work better than the frontal attack he'd tried before.

Cam's name didn't even come up until dessert was served.

"Have you seen Cam lately, Lacey?" her mother asked.

"As a matter of fact, he stopped by the shop yesterday."

"Lacey, you didn't tell me you'd seen Cameron. Did you tell him—" Mamie broke off abruptly.

"Tell him what?" Jimbo looked from one to the other as his fork sank into the apple pie Mamie had baked especially for him.

"Nothing," Lacey said, without any hope of being believed.

"It doesn't sound like nothing." He lifted a bite of pie to his mouth.

"It's certainly not nothing," Mamie said. She caught her daughter's eye and lifted her chin. "Well, you're not going to be able to keep it a secret forever."

"Mother, I really don't think that this is the time."

"Oh, come on," Jimbo said. "Now you've got to tell me what's going on. I'll die of curiosity." He picked up his coffee cup.

"Mother—"

"I think James should know. He's practically family, after all."

Lacey threw her hands up. There was simply no stopping her mother once she got her teeth into something. It was a wonder she hadn't already told Cam.

"So tell me. My imagination's running wild."

"Lacey's goin' to have a baby."

Jimbo inhaled a mouthful of hot coffee and then choked, gasping for air. He coughed, his eyes watering with the pain of his scalded throat.

"You're what?" He squeezed the words out.

"I'm pregnant."

"Oh, my God."

Lacey raised her brows. She wasn't sure what response she'd expected, but this certainly wasn't it. He looked as if she'd just told him that the world was coming to an end.

"Whatever happened to 'Congratulations, Lacey?'"

Jimbo ignored her mild sarcasm. "Have you told Cam?"

"I don't think that's any of your business."

"Then you haven't told him. Oh, God." He ran his fingers through his short hair, making it stand up on top of his head like a bizarre hat.

"James, what's the matter?"

He gave Mamie a distracted look. "Nothing's the matter. I was just surprised, that's all." He looked at his watch. "Good grief. Look how late it is. I'd forgotten I had an appointment."

"At nine o'clock?" Mamie asked incredulously.

"An eccentric client," he told her, giving her a quick smile. "Sorry I've got to eat and run. The meal was wonderful."

"Jimbo—"

But Lacey was speaking to thin air. He'd already vanished from the dining room, and a minute later the front door closed behind him. Raising her eyebrows questioningly she turned to look at her mother.

Mamie looked as confused as Lacey did. "I have no idea. He seemed upset, didn't he?"

"He seemed demented."

Chapter Fifteen

Summer had truly arrived. The temperatures were creeping into the eighties, and the sun was shining down out of a sky not yet marred by the smog that would descend a little later in the season. In fact, it was an extravagantly beautiful day.

Cam was not in the mood to notice it. He was sitting in front of his workbench, ostensibly working. Except his hands weren't moving. Derwent sat next to the open garage door, apparently on guard, though Cam couldn't have guessed what he thought he was guarding against. Still, at least the dog was acting productive. Cam hadn't managed that much in several days.

The first few days after Lacey left, sheer rage had sustained him. He'd been so angry at her leaving that he hadn't really noticed the hurt. But the anger had trickled away, leaving a void that was too quickly filled with loneliness.

He'd lived alone for years and never felt the least bit lonely. When he developed a craving for companionship, he could always call a friend. But this was a different kind of craving. He didn't want company. He wanted Lacey. There was an empty space inside him that only she could fill.

He should have told her that he loved her. He should have told her weeks ago. He'd accused her of being a coward, but he was certainly no better. He'd known weeks ago that this trial marriage had become very real, at least for him. He should have said something then. But he'd been afraid to lay himself open to the hurt he'd feel if Lacey didn't return his feelings.

And now she was gone. But not for good. He was going to figure out some way to convince her that, despite its crazy beginning, this marriage was the best thing that had ever happened to either one of them.

Derwent growled low in his throat, distracting Cam from his thoughts. He glanced up, not surprised to see Jimbo standing a few feet away from the small dog.

"Kill, Derwent," he ordered without much force. Derwent grumbled, but he didn't attack. Jimbo kept one eye on him as he sidled into the shop.

"I don't know why he doesn't like me," he complained.

"Well, they do say that an animal's instinct is often far superior to a human's. Maybe he knows something about you I don't. Have a seat." Cam turned and leaned back against the bench, watching as Jimbo found himself a stool and sat down.

Once settled, Jimbo didn't say anything. He sat staring at the concrete floor, his expression somewhere between guilt and depression. Cam dragged his attention away from his own problem and studied his friend with a sharper eye.

"You look like the Grinch just stole your Christmas. What's wrong?"

"I want to remind you, Cam, that we have many years of friendship behind us." Cam arched his brows at this apparent irrelevancy.

"That's true. Did you run into my car?"

"No." Jimbo stared at the floor again and then heaved a sigh. "I saw Lacey last night."

Cam sat up straight so suddenly that the stool rocked on its feet. "Is she all right?"

"She's fine. Really, she's just fine."

Cam relaxed slowly, aware that his pulse was faster. "Don't scare me like that."

"Sorry. I didn't mean to upset you prematurely."

"Prematurely?" Cam stiffened again. "Why don't you just spit it out, Jimbo? What's wrong with Lacey?"

"Well, it's not really anything wrong. I mean, it's not like she's sick or anything."

Cam stood up and Jimbo slid off his stool, facing the much larger man with a nervous expression. "Remember our friendship."

"If you don't tell me what the hell you're trying to get out, the only thing left of our friendship is going to consist of my being one of your pallbearers."

"Okay, okay." Jimbo made soothing motions with his hands as he backed slightly away. "I probably shouldn't be saying anything at all, but under the circumstances—which no one else knows at this point—I sort of thought I ought to tell you. Even though Lacey will probably never forgive me."

"Jimbo—" Cam's tone was ominous as was the step he took toward the other man.

"Lacey's pregnant." Jimbo blurted out the announcement and then waited.

Cam stared at him, feeling as if he'd just stepped off a stair onto a floor that wasn't there.

"What did you say?" The voice that asked the question wasn't his. He heard it from far away, much too hoarse and barely audible.

"Lacey's pregnant."

Cam stared at him, but he wasn't seeing Jimbo. He was remembering the night of the dinner party, Lacey's sweet demand matching his own. There'd been no thought of practicalities that night, no thought beyond the heat and scent of her.

"My God."

"Funny, that was my reaction," Jimbo said.

"Why hasn't she told me? Does she plan on keeping it from me? What the hell is going on in her head?" His tone grew more forceful with each question, but he wasn't looking for answers. Derwent, sensing Cam's mood, jumped to his feet and barked sharply, his button eyes focused on Jimbo, who seemed the most likely source of the disturbance.

"I don't know what she plans on doing," Jimbo said, keeping one eye on Cam and one eye on the dog.

"Well, I know what I damn well plan on doing. I'm going to find her and get her to listen to reason, even if I have to kidnap her to do it." Cam turned and strode out of the garage, punching the automatic opener as he went. Jimbo ducked under the closing door, barely escaping a bash on the head.

"Cam, I really think we should talk before you go any where." He had to increase his speed to a near trot to keep up with Cam's longer stride. Derwent hurried along beside them, his tongue lolling like a tiny pink warning flag.

"The only person I want to talk to right now is Lacey. Dam mit! Why didn't she tell me? How could she keep something like this from me? I'm her husband, for God's sake."

"Well, you see, that's what I think we should talk about."

But Cam wasn't listening. He strode into the house, his en tourage of two following close behind.

"We lived together for almost three months." He crossed the kitchen into the hall, grabbing his keys from the small tabl before reaching for the front door.

"Cam, I really think we need to talk," Jimbo managed little breathlessly.

"Later. Shut the door, would you?" Jimbo pulled the door shut but not before Derwent had managed to slip through, ap parently anxious to see the finale to all this unusual excitemen

"Cam." He hurried down the steps and trotted across th lawn.

Cam turned at the door of the car, but it wasn't because he' heard Jimbo. "You know, I would have thought that she' gotten to know me well enough to feel she could come to m with this. We may not have gotten off to a conventional star but I really thought we had established a relationship. Wh wouldn't she tell me she was pregnant? I'm her husban

You'd think I'd be the first person she'd tell, no matter what the circumstances.''

"No, you're not." Jimbo leaned one hand on the hood of the car, trying to catch his breath.

Cam looked at him, making a real effort to focus his attention on something besides his burning need to see Lacey. "I appreciate your telling me this. This may be just what we need to straighten things out between us. There's more than just the two of us to consider now. Maybe I can convince Lacey to give our marriage another try.''

"No, you can't.''

"What?" He finally had Cam's full attention. "What do you mean, I can't? I can't what?''

"You can't convince Lacey to give your marriage *another* try.''

"Why not?''

Jimbo pulled himself away from the car and straightened, his expression a mixture of remorse and defiance. Cam felt an uneasy stirring in the pit of his stomach.

"Why can't I convince Lacey to give our marriage another try, Jimbo?''

"Look, Cam, I did it for the best possible reasons. I really thought you two belonged together and I was just trying to see that you got a chance to get to know each other.''

Cam stepped away from the car door. "What did you do?''

"It seemed like a really good idea at the time." Jimbo took an uneasy step back, his eyes on Cam's suddenly looming figure.

"Jimbo—" Cam's tone held a warning. "*What* seemed like good idea at *what* time?''

"Well, this goes back a ways. It's really kind of funny when you think about it, like something out of an old movie.''

Cam didn't look in a laughing mood. Jimbo cleared his throat uneasily and went on. "Well, you remember the night of Lacey's birthday?''

"Yes." The one word had an ominous tone.

Jimbo cleared his throat again. "Well, you know, you and Lacey had quite a bit to drink."

"Jimbo, I don't need a postmortem on the night we got married. I just want to know what you did."

"Well, actually, it's not exactly what I did. It's more what you didn't do."

Cam stared at him, a terrible realization creeping over him. "Just what didn't I do?"

His voice had dropped to something between a whisper and a growl. Derwent, sensing the new element in the atmosphere, ranged himself beside his master, his sturdy little body bristling with dislike as he looked at Jimbo. The pairing of very large man and very small dog might have been comical, but Jimbo was not really in a laughing mood.

"Look, I want you to remember that we've been friends a long time, and I really did think it was a good idea at the time."

"Jimbo!" Cam barked the name out, his patience clearly at an end.

"You and Lacey aren't really married." He rushed the words out so quickly that they slurred together, but Cam clearly didn't have any trouble understanding him.

"You son of a—" Jimbo didn't even try to dodge the fist when he saw it coming. Cam's blow got him squarely on the chin, rocking him back off his feet. The lawn that looked so soft didn't feel nearly as plush when he hit it. For an instant he saw stars, and he had a vague hope that maybe he'd been knocked out, but he wasn't that lucky.

"Get up. Get up so I can kill you." Jimbo's vision cleared enough to reveal Cam standing over him, his hands clenched into fists, his stance murderous.

"No, I don't think I will. Not that I don't deserve to be killed, mind you, but I don't want you to have my death on your conscience."

"My conscience can take the pressure. How could you do

this to me? To Lacey? My God, when did you plan on telling us?''

Jimbo pushed himself up on one elbow, careful not to rise any higher for fear Cam wouldn't be able to contain his wrath. ''I hadn't really thought things out. There the two of you were. You were the ones who decided to get married. And I did try to talk you out of it. But you were both convinced it was a great idea. Well, I couldn't let you get married in that condition.''

''Gee, thanks.'' Cam's tone lacked any sincere element of gratitude.

''So I set up a fake ceremony, got a fake certificate. But then the two of you disappeared, and I didn't find you till the next morning. You seemed upset enough about the idea of being married. I figured that finding out you weren't really married might be even worse at that point. Besides, it was obvious you were perfect for each other. So I just let things lie for a while.''

''With friends like you, a guy sure as hell doesn't need enemies. Does Lacey know?''

''No. When I found out she was pregnant, I decided maybe it was time to let you know the whole story.''

Cam growled. There was no other word for it. His eyes blazed with a murderous blue light, and the sound that came out of his throat could only be called a growl.

''I wish you'd get up so I could beat you to a pulp.''

Jimbo shook his head, fingering the tender skin on his jaw. ''I'm not that stupid. Besides, you don't have time to beat me up. You've got to talk to Lacey.''

''Lacey. My God, how am I going to tell her this?'' Worrying about it distracted him momentarily, but then his gaze sharpened on the prone man again. ''You're right. I don't have time to kill you. But you'd better stay out of my sight for the next seventy or eighty years or I swear I'll tear you apart with my bare hands.''

Jimbo was careful not to move until the car had pulled out

of the driveway. Well, he'd done his best. Cam would forgive him eventually, and Lacey wasn't inclined to hold a grudge. He wasn't so sure about Mamie. She wasn't going to be very pleased when she found that he'd been partially responsible for her daughter's living in sin.

A low growl brought his attention to Derwent, who was still watching him, stiff-legged and bristling with hostility.

"Oh, shut up. Cam already decked me. There's no reason for you to add insult to injury. Besides, you're too little to take me on."

Derwent promptly proved him wrong by sinking a set of very sharp little teeth into his ankle.

LACEY WAS NOT HAVING a good day. She hadn't slept well. Dreams of Cam and his reaction to finding out about his imminent fatherhood had kept her tossing and turning most of the night. And then she'd awakened to discover the real meaning of morning sickness.

Mamie had nagged her to tell Cam about the baby, her car had coughed and sputtered all the way to the shop, threatening to die at any moment and leave her stranded on the freeway. She'd made it without having to resort to hitchhiking, but that one small blessing hadn't done much to restore her mood.

The shop was unusually busy for a Tuesday morning, which was good for the ledger but not so good when it came to her need to take some time off and put her feet up. It was nearly eleven before she got a chance to pour herself a cup of coffee, and then it sat and got cold while she helped a portly matron select a scarf to go with a particularly hideous dress. Lacey restrained the urge to suggest that a large silk tent would be the only thing that could improve the effect.

When the bell over the door rang and she looked up to see Cam walking in, it seemed like the perfect touch to a day that was going rapidly downhill. The last thing she wanted to deal with right now was Cam. Her emotions were too raw, too close to the surface. She knew she was going to have to tell him about the baby, but she wanted to choose her own time and place. This wasn't it.

Cam saw her and started toward her. There was something in the set of his shoulders that made her uneasy. He didn't look like he was here for a casual hello or an invitation to lunch.

"Lacey, I need to talk to you." He didn't bother with a greeting, and her uneasiness increased. He looked upset, and her mind flew immediately to the child she carried. But he couldn't know about that. Jimbo wouldn't have said anything, would he?

"Cam, this really isn't a very good time." She gestured to the half-dozen customers browsing behind him. "Maybe tomorrow."

"No." Cam barely glanced at the customers. "We've got to talk now."

"Cam, I really can't talk to you now." She started to move away, but his hand caught her wrist, holding her gently but implacably where she was.

"We've got to talk right now. Why don't we move into your office."

Lacey felt a wave of panic. He had to know about the baby. That was the only thing that could have brought him here like this. She wasn't ready to talk to him. She wouldn't talk to him.

"Later." She gave him a tight smile, aware that one or two of the customers were watching them, sensing drama.

"Lacey, we can talk here or we can talk in your office or we can talk on the sidewalk, but we are going to talk now. This can't wait."

"You're being obnoxious, Cam." She smiled at a woman with shockingly red hair. "Don't make a scene."

"I'm not going to make a scene. I don't think it's unreasonable to want to talk to the woman who's carrying my child."

His final words came during a lull in the piped-in music, and they seemed to echo around the room. If Lacey thought it was her imagination, she had only to look at the women in the shop to know that they'd heard every word.

She'd known that her pregnancy had to be what he'd come to talk about, but she still wasn't prepared for the impact of his words. The fact that Cam knew about the baby threw her completely off balance. Foolishly she still tried to avoid the inevitable.

"Let's talk about this later, Cam. Maybe over dinner tonight?" She affected a relaxed, proper tone so as not to draw further attention from the customers.

His fingers tightened over her wrist, not painfully but demandingly. "Lacey, this isn't something you talk about over steak tartare and a glass of cabernet. Why didn't you tell me?"

"I haven't known that long myself. I was just trying to adjust to the idea before discussing it with you."

"So you *did* plan on telling me."

"Of course I did." This time she gritted the words out, then smiled at the portly matron in the ghastly dress.

"We've got to talk about this."

"Later. Margaret won't be in until this afternoon, and I've got a business to run."

"Now. There are things we have to talk about now that are more important than business."

"Cam, just because you're my husband doesn't mean I have to jump when you say jump. Times have changed."

Cam moved closer, his expression intent. "Look, I don't mean to be pushy about this, but I talked to Jimbo this morning—"

"I gathered as much. That worm. I should have guessed he wouldn't be able to keep his mouth shut. I'd like to knock his teeth out."

"I already did, more or less."

"You punched Jimbo?" For the first time since he'd entered the shop, she looked at him with something approaching pleasure. "Good. I hope he has to spend months in a dentist's chair while they repair the damage."

Cam grinned at her bloodthirsty attitude, but the expression was quickly gone. "Look, we need to talk about what he told me."

"I really can't talk about it now."

"You don't understand. Jimbo told me something that we really have to—"

"Cam, please. Come back this afternoon." She was vividly aware that most of the customers had stopped even trying to pretend they weren't listening. "We can talk about this after—"

"Lacey, we're not married."

She stared at him. She was hearing things. Was that a symptom of pregnancy? She hadn't seen it mentioned in any of the books Dr. Riteman had given her, but that was the only possible explanation.

"What?" she got out.

"Jimbo told me that we're not really married. The certificate was a fake. We're not married."

There was no mistaking his words this time. And no doubting that he'd really said them. Not married. Cam wasn't her husband. She wasn't his wife. The realization washed over her. Her lower lip began to tremble. This whole crazy arrangement hadn't ever existed. They hadn't had a marriage of convenience or inconvenience or anything else. They hadn't had a marriage at all.

Cam watched her eyes fill with tears and felt his heart crack. His hand slid up her arm to her shoulder, and he pulled her closer, bending to brush a quick kiss over her shaking mouth.

"Don't cry, honey. It's not a tragedy. We'll get married. For real this time."

She stiffened and pulled away from him, her spine rigid with pride. "No. I don't want you to marry me just because I'm pregnant. I don't need that kind of charity."

"It's not charity." He drew a deep breath but found that the words were easy to say after all. "I love you. I've been in love with you for weeks."

"You're just saying that because of the baby." She wanted to believe him. She ached to believe him. She wanted it so much that she didn't dare believe him.

"No, I'm not. I love you, Lacey."

"If you love me, then why didn't you tell me before this? Why are you only saying it now that you know about the baby?"

"I was scared. I accused you of being a coward, but I was the one who was afraid."

Her eyes searched his, trying to find the truth. She'd had one marriage for the wrong reasons—or so she'd thought. She wasn't going to go into another one for anything less than love.

"I'd believe him, honey. He looks sincere to me."

The voice came from one of the customers, a buxom and bejeweled blonde who was leaning on a rack of thoroughly risqué camisoles, her eyes fixed firmly on them.

"I agree. He looks like a guy who'd tell the truth." That was the woman with the shockingly red hair.

"I don't know, you can't trust a man." This from the matron in the terrible dress. "They're sneaky by nature."

Lacey looked up at Cam, wanting with all her heart to believe him. "Are you sure?"

"I love you more than I can ever tell you. These past couple of weeks without you, I've been empty. I need you and I love you."

"You'll never hear a prettier speech, honey. A man who can talk like that is worth taking a chance on." The buxom blonde threw her opinion into the ring, but Lacey wasn't listening to her. She was listening to her own heart, which was telling her to believe, to take another chance.

"It's not just because of the baby?"

"With or without the baby, Lacey, I want you in my life. I love you."

She drew a deep breath and let it out in a rush. "I love you, too."

Cam's mouth captured the last word as it left her. Lacey threw her arms around his neck, feeling his arms enfold her, holding her close, holding her safe. She'd finally taken the biggest gamble of all, and it felt wonderful.

The sound of applause broke them apart. Cam's arms loosened just enough to allow her to turn and face their small but enthusiastic audience. He bowed slightly, grinning at the watching women. Lacey blushed but smiled. She felt as if she'd never stop smiling.

"If you'll excuse us, ladies, we have a wedding to arrange. Las Vegas?" He looked down at Lacey, cocking one brow in question.

"Where else? We'll do it right this time."

"We did it right the first time," he told her. Looking into the loving blue of his eyes, she had to agree.

Their marriage of inconvenience had turned out to be very right indeed.

Sweet Paige Cudahy taking up
with Jake Quincannon, the town rebel,
for a summer fling? Who ever would have thought
it? And who could have predicted that the summer
would end the way it did....

A Summer To Come Home

A Summer To Come Home

Chapter One

Chapter One

Jake Quincannon was back in town.

The news filtered through Riverbend with a speed military commanders would have envied.

Ethel Levine got the scoop on everyone else by virtue of the fact that Maisie's Café, where she worked, was located near the edge of town. Anyone entering or leaving Riverbend had to drive past Maisie's so Ethel was in a position to keep tabs on who was going where and with whom. Not that she was nosy. She would have been indignant if anyone ever suggested such a thing. She was just interested.

If it had been a busier time of day she might have missed seeing him, but at two o'clock on a Tuesday afternoon, Maisie's didn't do a booming business and she had time off from her job as Maisie's sole waitress to look out the big front window and watch the doings on Maine Avenue. Of course, as she explained to her five very closest friends at the Curl and Twirl Beauty Salon, the big Harley-Davidson was enough to catch a body's eye, even at a busy time of day. But this wasn't a busy time of day, so there was no need to worry about the possibility of missing anything.

Still, she might not have recognized the rider if it hadn't been for the light at the corner of Maine and Maple turning red at just the right moment. The big bike had coasted to a stop behind Fred Turley's Chevy pickup. It was rumored that

Fred's four-year-old son had gotten his start in the back of that very pickup. Ethel studied the rusted bed for a moment before turning her attention to the new—and more interesting—vehicle behind it.

Like the motorcycle the rider was big and his hair was black. Thick and a little too long, in her opinion, it brushed the collar of his leather jacket. Worn jeans covered a pair of long legs, which were braced on either side of the bike. He wore black boots, as worn as the jeans.

Ethel sniffed, and pursed her thin lips disapprovingly. A thug. That's what he looked like. Just like the hired muscle the villains always had on television. Heaven knows what kind of big city filth he had hidden in the canvas duffel bag he'd strapped across the back of the bike. A gun, certainly. Maybe drugs.

Her speculations might have carried her even further if the man in question hadn't turned his head just then and looked directly at her.

Ethel gasped, too shocked to back away from the window. She gaped at the black leather patch that covered the man's left eye, giving him a villainous look. But it wasn't the patch or the thick black mustache that made her heart jump with shock.

Nearly twenty years had passed since she'd seen him but she recognized him immediately. There was something in the way he looked at her, one dark eyebrow cocked in arrogant amusement, that left her with no doubts about his identity. An unkind person might have suggested that Ethel's identification was aided by the fact that Margaret Quincannon had mentioned there was a possibility her eldest son might be coming home. But Ethel was sure she would have recognized Jake Quincannon even if they'd met in Timbuktu. There was just no mistaking the man. The way he lifted one black-gloved hand to his forehead in a mock salute confirmed his identity.

That arrogant gesture was pure Jake Quincannon, full of insolence and defiance. The boy had been trouble from the word go and Ethel now had proof that nothing had changed. She stepped back from the window but the move was wasted on the man riding the Harley. The light had changed to green and he lifted his booted foot from the pavement, giving the big bike gas as Fred Turley's truck started across the intersection.

Ethel craned her neck to get a final look at the bike as it disappeared down the road. Heading toward his folk's place, no doubt. Well, Lawrence and Margaret might or might not be glad to see the return of their prodigal son, but Ethel knew, as sure as if she were one of them psychics, that Jake Quincannon's return wasn't likely to be good news for anyone else.

Long before the dinner hour, most of Riverbend was aware of Jake's return. Those who'd lived in the town long enough to remember the elder Quincannon boy, shook their heads, wondering what mischief he might get up to this time. One or two kinder people ventured to point out that all that mischief was nigh on to twenty years ago now. Even Jake was bound to have settled down some by now. But there wasn't much support for this theory. Once a troublemaker, always a troublemaker.

Besides, who knew what he'd been up to all these years? It was a fact that the Quincannons were pretty closemouthed about Jake's doings. Government work, they said and that could cover most anything. It didn't seem likely that Jake had been toting up accounts for the past twenty years. More likely he'd been looking up trouble.

The news spread through town faster than a chicken could jump a june bug. It reached Paige Cudahy an hour or so before she was due to close the doors of Riverbend's tiny library. She was stacking books on the library's only book cart, preparatory to putting them back on the shelves.

Her movements were unhurried. Paige rarely felt that hurrying accomplished much. It was simply not a part of her makeup, a fact that had caused her endless conflicts with her older sister.

Josie believed that anything worth doing was worth doing quickly. Whether it was reading a book or bandaging a child's skinned knee, there was no sense in taking any more time than necessary. Time, to Josie's way of thinking, was a precious commodity to be used carefully.

Paige had simply never seen life quite the same way. She agreed that time was precious, but it was something to be savored, like a particularly rich piece of chocolate. It wasn't to be spent like coins, with a careful accounting made of each minute.

It wasn't the only thing the two sisters disagreed on, not by a long shot. In fact, it would have been hard to find something they *did* agree on.

Paige picked up a worn volume of Emerson's essays, and couldn't resist opening it, thumbing through to find a few favorite passages. The library was quiet. The only patron was old Mr. Wellington and he was dozing in a corner near the window.

Standing between the stacks, surrounded by the faint musty scent of the books, Paige smiled. One of the things she liked best about running the library was the fact that there was no one telling her to pull her nose out of a book. All the years she was growing up, if it hadn't been her mother, it had been Josie, telling her that she was going to go cross-eyed from all that reading. Why couldn't she play with dolls, like other little girls?

"Paige Cudahy, get your nose out of that book. I've got the most fabulous news."

The piercing whisper made Paige jump and drop the book she was holding. It hit the wooden floor with a smack that echoed off the high ceilings, startling Mr. Wellington out of his nap. He snorted, his head jerking up, rheumy eyes peering out from under bushy white brows as he looked for the cause of the disturbance. Seeing nothing out of the ordinary, he set-tled back into the chair, his chin dipping toward his chest.

"Didn't anyone ever tell you that you shouldn't sneak up on a person?" Paige bent to pick up the book before turning to give Mary Davis a reproachful look.

"Wait till you hear what I've got to say." Mary grabbed Paige's arm, tugging her toward the front desk, her dark eyes flashing with excitement.

"If you're about to tell me that Mrs. Simms is a kleptoma-niac, I've known that for years."

"Everybody knows that. Mr. Simms has been buying the stuff she's stolen for so long, it's a wonder the poor man hasn't gone broke."

"Maybe he's a drug dealer." Paige sat on the edge of her tiny desk, stretching her long legs out in front of her.

"Do you think so?" Mary was momentarily distracted from telling her news, intrigued with the idea that plump, balding Mr. Simms might be a drug kingpin. Paige watched her friend. She could practically see the wheels turning and she wondered if Mr. Simms was going to turn up as a character in one of Mary's books. She had been writing suspense novels for the past five years, and even though they'd all been rejected so far, she was determined to crack the doors of the publishing world wide open.

"I was only kidding about Simms," Paige said when the silence had dragged on long enough.

"But it could be true, don't you think?"

"Not unless he's selling crack to Holsteins. There aren't enough people around here to support Mrs. Simms's light fin-gers. The truth is that Mrs. Simms inherited quite a tidy sum from her grandfather. Some say that's why Mr. Simms married her. I suppose, if it's true, he got his comeuppance."

"Maybe he's planning to murder her for her money."

Paige raised her dark brows until they almost met the fall of her pale blond bangs. "After thirty years? He's waited a bit long, don't you think?"

"Maybe he hasn't gotten his courage up." Mary was reluctant to let go of a possible murder suspect.

"After this much time, I should think it wouldn't be worth the bother."

"I suppose." Mary was disappointed but she had to admit that Mrs. Simms's demise did not seem imminent.

Paige scooted farther onto the desk, crossing one knee over the other. "So, what's your news?"

"News?" Mary was still pondering the dramatic possibilities of the Simms household. "News!" She threw out her hands in a sharp gesture of exasperation. "How could I forget? Guess who just drove down Maine?"

"Tom Selleck."

"Don't be an idiot. This is someone you know. Actually, it's someone you used to know."

"Who said I couldn't 'used to know' Tom Selleck?" Paige asked lazily. The finish was wearing off the pine floor behind the desk. She was going to have to talk to the library committee about having the floor refinished.

"Well, it wasn't Tom Selleck. Guess again."

"Well…" Paige dragged the word out, giving it several syllables. "I suppose it's a safe bet it wasn't Robert Redford. And I know it couldn't have been Errol Flynn."

"He's been dead for thirty years."

"I know." Paige grimaced. "Think how unpleasant he'd look these days."

"Do you want to know who's back in town or don't you?" Mary scowled at her, but her eyes were laughing.

"I thought you wanted me to guess, and I'm doing my best." She ducked the small fist her friend raised. "Okay, okay. I give up. Who did you see driving down Maine?"

"Well, Ethel Levine saw him first and she told Gussie Marstan, who told Prissy Taylor, who told—"

"You can skip all that. I know the pattern the gossip mill runs in this town. Remember, I was born here. Besides, after the news has passed through all those hands, it's hardly a reliable source. God knows, Yasser Arafat could become Wayne Newton by the time his name had passed down *that* route."

"Well, this happens to be true," Mary told her with a trace of huffiness.

"What happens to be true? So far, you haven't told me anything."

"Ethel was looking out the window of Maisie's and she saw this big black motorcycle and you'll never guess who was riding it."

Paige rolled her eyes in exaggerated impatience. There was nothing Mary loved more than dragging out the suspense. In fact, that was one of the problems with her books.

"Mary, you have precisely ten seconds to tell me who you're talking about and then I'm going to close up the library and lock you in here with Mr. Wellington. They say he was quite a ladies' man in his day."

Not visibly impressed by the threat, Mary cast a quick look at the somnolent old man.

"You're no fun, Paige."

"Mary—" Paige slid off the desk, her movement in Mary's direction underscoring her ominous tone.

"Jake Quincannon." Mary rushed the name out, stopping Paige's threatening approach instantly.

"Jake Quincannon? Are you sure?" Paige sank back onto the desk, her surprise all that Mary could have hoped for.

"Ethel saw him plain as daylight. He was riding a motorcycle and wearing a black leather jacket. And he had a patch over one eye." Mary clearly considered the last piece of information the cherry on the sundae.

"A patch? I wonder what happened?"

"I don't know. But Ethel said he looked meaner than a junkyard dog. Said he sent shivers right up her spine."

"Almost anything sends shivers up that woman's spine," Paige said with disgust. "Maybe she has a neurological problem."

Mary giggled. "I'd like to see you suggest that to her."

"Maybe one of these days I will." Paige leaned against the desk, her expression thoughtful. "Quincannon. Lord, it must be twenty years since he left Riverbend."

"Weren't he and Josie real tight?"

"They dated in high school. Everyone thought they were going to get married. Everyone thought it was a terrible idea. Josie was the prom queen and Jake—Well, Jake wasn't really the prom type. He rode a motorcycle then, too. His hair was too long, he was too tough. But Josie seemed crazy about him. I think my parents had just about resigned themselves to having Jake in the family."

She stopped, her gray eyes focused on things Mary couldn't see. Paige had been a child when Jake left town for the last time but he was vivid in her memory—a dark, brooding boy who'd always taken the time to talk to his girlfriend's bookish little sister.

"So what happened?" Mary prodded impatiently. "Why didn't Josie marry him?"

Paige shook the memories away and shrugged. "I don't know. Jake left to join the army. He was hardly out of sight before Josie was suddenly spending every waking moment with Frank Hudson. By the time Jake came home a couple of months later, Josie and Frank were married. There was a terrible fight. I was hiding in the hydrangea next to the porch and I could hear them arguing. Of course, there wasn't really much to say. After all, Josie and Frank *were* married. Then Jake took off and hasn't been back since."

"Wow. Didn't you ever ask Josie why she married Frank?"

Paige raised her brows. "*Me* ask Josie why she did something? I don't think so. Besides, I was only a kid when it happened. I didn't totally understand what happened until years later.''

"I wonder why he's come back," Mary asked rhetorically, her ever-fertile imagination at work on half a dozen possibilities, each one more outlandish than the last.

"His parents are still here."

"I think this Jake Quincannon sounds like exactly what Riverbend needs to liven things up. It looks like it may turn out to be an interesting summer, after all."

Paige watched Mary leave, her small figure always in a rush, eager for the next experience life might offer her. She stared at the door long after it had closed behind her friend.

Jake Quincannon. A name out of the past. She wondered if Josie had heard the news yet. And how she'd react to it. Mary was right. It should be a very interesting summer, indeed.

JAKE COASTED THE BIKE to a stop at the end of the gravel driveway. Bracing the bike with one foot, he nudged the kickstand into place. Once the Harley rested securely, he reached up to lift off his helmet, running his fingers through his thick black hair.

The house sat on the edge of town, the valley sweeping away behind it, the mountains rising in the background. Snow capped the highest peaks, but summer had come to the lower levels.

The house hadn't changed, not in the twenty years he'd been gone, not in the twenty before that. The small lawn was a rich green, edged with neat flower borders. Fronting the modest house was a screened porch, and pots of calendula flanked the steps. Every year his mother would carefully place seeds in egg cartons and set the cartons next to the kitchen window. While the Idaho winter still howled outside, the tiny green seedlings held a promise of springtime.

Jake swung his leg over the bike, setting the helmet on the seat. His boot heels crunched on the gravel. Stepping onto the brick walk, he hesitated, wondering if coming back had been such a good idea.

Twenty years was a long time. Maybe he'd been a fool to think coming home could answer any of his questions. He reached up to touch the black leather patch that covered his left eye. Although the house hadn't changed in twenty years, a lot had changed in him.

With a mental shrug, he continued up the walk. He was here now, he couldn't really turn around and leave, though that was exactly what he felt like doing. Maybe it was mid-life crisis that had driven him to go back to his roots. His mouth twisted in a cynical smile. If he'd had any roots here, they'd died from lack of care a long time ago.

He knocked on the door, another thing that had changed. Twenty years ago, he'd have walked right in. But he didn't live here anymore. He was a visitor, probably an unwelcome one.

Footsteps came toward the door and Jake tensed, his stomach tightening the way it always did when he knew he was walking into a dangerous situation. He shoved his hands into his rear pockets and held his shoulders back as he waited for the door to open.

The man who opened the door was like a blurred photograph of the one he remembered. The years had not been kind to Lawrence Quincannon. Twenty years of riding ditch and peering into the rising sun, had etched themselves into his face. Deep lines fanned out from eyes that had faded to a lighter shade of blue than his son's. His hair, once as black as the obsidian that veined the hills behind him, was now completely gray.

The two men faced each other through the screen, each measuring two decades of change. Jake knew the years hadn't been much kinder to him than they had been to his father. Gray was sprinkled through the black of his hair; his face was hard

It took a conscious effort for him to control the impulse to reach up and check his eye patch.

"Jake."

"Dad." The word felt strange on his tongue.

"When you wrote, you didn't say just when you'd be getting here."

"I didn't know. I wanted to see a bit of the country on my way."

His father's eyes went over his shoulder to the big bike in the driveway and, for just a moment, his eyes lit with old memories. "Still riding one of those two-wheeled things, I see."

"No better way to see the country." Jake half smiled, remembering how his mother had protested the purchase of his first motorcycle. And how his father had supported him. They'd been almost close then.

"Lawrence, who is it?" The voice broke the tentative rapport with a force out of all proportion to its light, sweet sound. Jake tensed again, the knot in his stomach tightening.

"It's Jake, Mother." Silence greeted his words. With a half sigh, Lawrence opened the screen door. "Come on in, Jake."

Jake stepped through the door, his heavy boots loud on the polished hardwood floor. He drew in a deep breath, tasting the mingled scents of floor wax, baking and the lavender potpourri his mother had always loved. It was a combination that swept him back to his childhood. He was five and he'd just lost a frog in the hallway. He was twelve and his mother was furious at the mud he'd tracked over her newly polished floors. He was eighteen and leaving for the army and she was watching him with those guarded eyes that never quite seemed to see him.

"Mother is in the parlor." His father's voice dragged him away from his memories and Jake nodded, following the slightly stooped figure down the short hallway. He stopped in the doorway, aware that he didn't feel any differently now than he had when he was sixteen and about to be called on the carpet for some perceived crime.

Margaret Quincannon was sitting in her favorite chair, the one that caught the pure northern light. Her hair had gone from pale blond to light gray but it was still pulled back in the same soft bun she'd always worn. Her pink floral housedress was identical to the ones she'd worn during his childhood. The pile of knitting in her lap could have been the same yarn she'd held twenty years ago.

Her face was older, more lined, but her eyes were the same watchful gray he remembered. She looked at him as if wondering what he was going to do next. It was that look that had so often driven him to his most outrageous pranks, as if by fulfilling her expectations, he could somehow make her love him.

"Jacob." Her voice held neither welcome nor rejection. She was simply acknowledging his presence, nothing more.

"Hello, Mother." Before he could stop the gesture, he reached up to adjust the patch. He lowered his hand, cursing the vulnerability she could still make him feel.

"Come in and sit down." That was his father, settling into the chair across from his wife's, reaching for his pipe.

Jake crossed the worn carpet and sat on the sofa. It was the same hideously uncomfortable affair he remembered from childhood. And it was also his mother's pride and joy. He was aware of her watching him carefully as he tried to adjust his long frame to the rigid back and narrow seat.

"It's been a long time," Lawrence said, breaking the silence before it could grow to uncomfortable proportions. "We got your postcards. Seems like you did a good bit of traveling."

"Quite a bit." Jake gave up trying to be comfortable and settled for the least uncomfortable position he could find.

"Sounds nice." Lawrence tamped tobacco into his pipe.

"I enjoyed it."

"What happened to your eye?" Margaret asked over the click of her knitting needles, her eyes on her work.

"I lost it." Jake jerked his hand down halfway to the patch, feeling the familiar helpless rage his mother had always brought out in him.

"In a fight, I suppose." Her light, sweet voice was laced with contempt. Lawrence continued to focus on tamping down the tobacco in his pipe.

"As a matter of fact, it was a fight," Jake said, a challenging edge to his voice. "I suppose I should consider myself lucky, though. He was trying for my neck. Of course, there are those who might consider it a shame he missed."

"No one said anything about wishing you dead, Jacob." Margaret's needles continued to click along rhythmically, never dropping a stitch.

"No. But no one said anything about being glad I'm alive, either."

"Naturally, your father and I are glad you're alive. You're our son."

Lawrence cleared his throat before Jake could respond. "How long do you think you'll be staying in Riverbend, Jake?" His eyes pleaded with his son. Jake swallowed the lump of anger that threatened to choke him.

"I'm not really sure. Possibly for the summer. Maybe not as long as that."

"I can't imagine what a man like you would find to do in Riverbend for the summer," Margaret commented.

"But then you don't really know what kind of man I am, do you, Mother?"

"Where are you planning on staying?" Lawrence asked, verbally stepping between his wife and son. "You could have your old room, if you'd like."

Margaret's knitting needles hesitated, her fingers tightening on the thin wands. For one moment, Jake was tempted to say he'd stay in his old room, just because he knew nothing would please his mother less. But he hadn't come back to renew old feuds or open old wounds.

"Thanks, but I think it would be best if I found a place in town."

"There aren't many places to stay in Riverbend," Margaret commented.

"I'm sure I'll find something." He stood up. He felt stifled in this room. "Well, I guess I'll be going."

"You'll have to come to dinner, Jake." Lawrence stood up, his eyes showing a touch of anxiety.

"I'd like that, Dad. I'll let you know where I'm staying."

"Welcome home, son." Lawrence held out his hand. Jake took it, feeling the softness of old age in a grip that had once been rock hard.

"Thanks. Goodbye, Mother." Margaret looked up at her son, her expression remote.

"Goodbye, Jacob."

Jake stepped off the porch, drawing in a deep breath of warm air. He reached for the gloves he'd tucked into his back pocket. This had been a stupid idea. What had made him think he was going to find what he was looking for in Riverbend? Especially when he didn't even know what it was he was looking for. He tugged his helmet on, swinging his leg over the wide seat. The Harley started with a roar, as out of place in this sleepy little town as he was.

If he had any sense, he'd just take the road right back out of town and mark this little visit up to stupidity. He'd been called a lot of things in his time but sensible wasn't one of them. Stubborn was. He'd come home for the summer and he decided he wasn't going to leave before he'd even spent a single night here.

Chapter Two

Like everything else in Riverbend, the old Cudahy house hadn't changed much. It looked as if it needed more repairs than most of the houses, as if it had been a while since anyone had seen to the upkeep.

Old Mr. Cudahy had taken great pride in the smooth expanse of lawn that stretched from the porch to the sidewalk, in the immaculately clipped hedges that bordered the porch. The lawn was still green, but mowing was obviously not high on the current occupant's list of priorities. The hedges were gone and in their place were flowers, not neat little beds but wild tangles of blooms and color. Hollyhocks reached nearly to the porch roof, a stately background to the miniature jungle at their feet. The roses that had once marched in neat precision along the south side of the house now sprawled in extravagant abandon, their canes heavy with flowers, the scent almost overpowering in the warm air.

Jake leaned against the porch railing. There were memories here, too. How many times had he waited on this porch for Josie to come out, aware of her mother peering through the lace curtains at him, feeling her disapproval.

He half smiled. The clerk at the little store on the edge of town had said that Paige Cudahy owned the house now and that she sometimes rented rooms. The clerk had stared at him as if he were an alien, but she'd been forthcoming enough about the slightly scruffy index card he'd pulled off the bulletin board near the door.

Yes, the room was available, she'd told him, her fascinated gaze drawn to the patch over his eye. The last time Paige had had a boarder was nearly a year ago. A writer had been looking for a quiet place to stay while he finished a book. Hadn't stayed long. Apparently Riverbend was quieter than he'd anticipated.

Jake had nodded his thanks, resisting the urge to shout "boo" just to see her scuttle for cover. Taking the card with him, he'd gone back out to the Harley, aware of her peering cautiously out the door after him.

Nothing ever changed in this town, it seemed. Gossip was still the major form of entertainment. When he was growing up here, it had been the bane of his life that you couldn't spit on the sidewalk without half the town knowing about it before the day was over.

He ran his fingers over the peeling paint on one of the pillars that supported the porch roof. He wondered how long Bill Cudahy had been dead. And Mrs. Cudahy? Was she still alive? The clerk had mentioned only Paige. That would be Josie's little sister.

He narrowed his eyes, staring absently at a fat bee making one last visit to an overblown rose before heading back to the hive. He vaguely remembered Paige. She'd been just a child when he left—maybe five or six, he thought. A plump little thing with long blond pigtails.

He couldn't remember Josie having much time for her, but then, time and distance had made him realize that Josie's attentions had usually been devoted to herself. Paige hadn't been of much use to her, so Josie had ignored her.

Paige would be—what? Twenty-four, twenty-five now. Idly, he wondered what she looked like. Was she still short and plump?

His gaze lit on a figure walking down the street. Pure male appreciation straightened his spine. This was a woman who'd turn heads anywhere she went. In Riverbend, she was enough to stop traffic. She was tall, about five eight, he judged. She was slim but with curves in all the right places. And her legs— her legs went on forever. The snug denim skirt she wore ended several inches above her knee, a length of which any man would heartily approve. She walked with a long lazy stride that made a man think of hot summer nights and cool sheets.

She reached up to flick a length of pale blond hair over her shoulder. When she turned her head to wave at a woman across the street, he could see that her hair fell thick and straight down her back, ending just above her waist. Straight bangs fringed over her forehead, almost touching her dark brows.

So absorbed was he in watching her that she'd taken several steps up the brick walkway before he realized that she was walking toward the house where he waited. He straightened away from the porch, disbelief edging out lust when he realized that *this* must be short, plump little Paige.

"Jake Quincannon." Her voice was low and husky, wrapping around his name in a way that evoked images of bedroom whispers. Her eyes were wide set and dark, pure green.

"Paige Cudahy?" The name was a question, though he didn't doubt her identity.

"The one and only," she said, moving past him up the steps and onto the porch. She glanced over her shoulder as Jake followed her.

"You've changed." It was the only comment that came to mind. It sparked a husky laugh as appealing as her voice. She turned, her hair swinging with the movement. Her eyes flicked over him.

"You've done a bit of changing yourself."

"You mean this?" Jake's hand moved before he could stop it, touching the black patch that covered his eye.

Her eyes swept up and down again. Her mouth quirked as her gaze met his. "That, but I was thinking more of the way you're dressed."

"The way I'm dressed?" Jake glanced down at himself.

"Really, Jake, you never used to be so obvious."

"Obvious?" He ground his teeth. He realized he was repeating everything she said, like a parrot. He'd had conversations with deposed kings and reigning terrorists and he'd always managed to sound reasonably intelligent. In the space of two minutes, Paige Cudahy—little Paige, for God's sake—had managed to throw him off balance.

"The clothes, Jake. Where did you get them? Central Casting for the returning rebel?" She flicked her fingers in his direction. "Boots, jeans, black T-shirt, even a leather jacket. It's good, I'll give you that." She tilted her head to one side, studying him with wide green eyes. "It suits you but it would have created more of an effect to try a three-piece suit. Ethel Levine might not even have recognized you. Or you could have tried linen slacks and one of those shirts with the little animals on them. In pink, maybe."

"Pink?" he asked, wondering if he'd missed a piece of this conversation somewhere.

"Okay, maybe not pink," she said easily.

She was teasing him. The idea was nearly as shocking as if she'd drawn a gun on him. A gun he'd have known how to handle. This light teasing tone wasn't so simple. He couldn't remember the last time someone had teased him.

"The problem is that you've done exactly what they expected you to do," she told him. "You should surprise people once in a while. It's good for them."

"Do you surprise people often?"

"Not too often. It takes too much energy. I believe in conserving energy, my personal contribution to the environment. I suppose you want to rent the room."

The abrupt change of subject seemed hardly worth noting. Jake nodded.

"You had a card on a bulletin board."

"Must have been yellow with age. Nobody's rented the place in nearly a year."

"So the girl at the counter told me."

"She probably told you that the last boarder was a writer. Said he wanted peace and quiet to finish his magnum opus. He sat up there two hours a day, pondering the fickleness of his muse and then he spent the other twenty-two hours drinking down at the Dew Drop Inn. He finally announced that the bucolic atmosphere was detrimental to his creative spirit and left. Is that your bike?"

"Yes." Jake was becoming accustomed to her erratic conversational style.

"It looks wonderful. I thought of getting one when I turned eighteen but my mother was convinced I'd end up with my lipstick smeared all over the highway and I gave up on the idea. Personally, I think it was your fault."

"Mine?"

"She never approved of you, you know. She thought you were going to encourage Josie to do things unbecoming to a prom queen. Actually, I think it would have done Josie a lot of good if someone had tarnished her crown a bit."

"What does that have to do with your mother not wanting you to get a bike?" She'd lost him again, just when he was sure he was following the conversation.

"A motorcycle reminded Mother of you, of course. Why don't you come in and you can take a look at the room."

She pushed open the door and Jake realized that it hadn't been locked, another thing that hadn't changed in the years he'd been gone. Half the people in town probably didn't even know where the key to their front door was.

Paige kicked off her shoes as soon as she stepped into the entryway. The house was warm after having been shut up all day and she made a mental note to leave a few windows open tomorrow. The oak floor was cool on her feet and she curled her toes against it. It was too bad she had to wear shoes to work. The weather simply cried out for bare feet.

But the library committee of Riverbend would never approve of the librarian going barefoot. They didn't entirely approve of her as it was, but the one time Mrs. Hallard had ventured to suggest that her clothing wasn't really restrained enough for a librarian, Paige had threatened to quit. Since they were lucky to get someone with even part of an English degree, Mrs. Hallard had beat a hasty retreat.

Paige turned as Jake stepped in, shutting the screen behind him but leaving the door open. Funny, how the entryway seemed suddenly smaller. It wasn't just his size. Her father had nearly matched Jake Quincannon's six feet three inches and his presence had never made a room shrink.

No, there was something about Jake—an aura, Mary would probably say. The man simply commanded attention. It wasn't just the black leather jacket or the ominous patch over his eye. It was something that emanated from him, probably without his even being aware of it.

"Is something wrong?"

The question made her realize that she'd been staring. She smiled and shrugged, unconcerned about having been caught.

"I was just thinking that the room seems smaller with you in it. I can't wait for Mary to meet you. She's going to say that you have a special aura. She'll probably put you in one of her books. The room is upstairs."

"Mary?" Jake questioned warily.

"A friend of mine," Paige explained as she led the way upstairs. "She's going to sell a book one of these days. Just as soon as she learns that anticipation may make the heart grow fonder but it exhausts a reader. She writes suspense stories. She's been rejected by some of the very best publishers."

"Is that good?"

"Well, I guess it's better than being rejected by the worst."

"Is this part of the theory that if you're going to get hit by a car, it doesn't hurt as much if it's a Rolls?"

Paige turned as they reached the landing. "Why, Jake, I do believe that was a joke. And you're almost smiling. I have a feeling you don't do nearly enough of that. You should try it more often. It's very good for you."

She also had a feeling that it had been a long time since anyone had teased Jake Quincannon. Which was a pity. Everyone needed someone to keep them from taking themselves and the world too seriously.

She pushed open the door to what she grandly referred to as her rental unit. "This used to be Josie's room. When she moved out, my parents kept it more or less as a shrine but I'm not as sentimental as they were."

"It can't bring in much money, if you only rent it once a year."

"No, hardly enough to be worth the bother, I suppose. I just like to break up the monotony. Besides, my occasional tenants give the town something to talk about."

"They always used to find enough to talk about without anyone having to work at it," he commented, glancing around the large, plainly furnished room.

"But that was when you were in town. Once you left, they lost one of their favorite topics."

"Didn't someone come along to take my place?"

"Not really." She ran a finger over the top of the bureau, studying the pattern it created in the dust. "I suppose I should dust but it just gets dusty again. You'd be responsible for your own room. I don't do sheets, or clothes, or windows. There's a dust mop in the hall closet and you're welcome to use the washer and dryer in the basement." She named a sum that seemed reasonable, less than he'd have paid to stay at the scruffy motel that was Riverbend's only facility for visitors.

"That sounds fair. Do you want a month in advance?"

"Whenever you get around to it. I'm in no hurry." She

looked around, wondering vaguely if there wasn't something else she should tell him.

"Where does that door lead to?"

"The bathroom. We share it. I promise not to leave my underwear drying on the towel rack, if you'll promise not to leave shaving cream in the sink."

"I think I can manage that."

"Then we should get along just fine."

"Are those your only prerequisites for getting along with someone?"

"The most important ones. Why don't you bring up your stuff. I'll treat for dinner tonight."

Jake watched her leave the room, his eyes lingering on those incredible legs. Who would have thought that chubby little Paige would grow up into such a long-legged beauty?

Paige wandered back downstairs, went into the big kitchen at the back of the house and pulled a bottle of soda out of the ancient refrigerator. She heard Jake go through the front door as she was twisting off the cap. He came back in while she was rummaging through the freezer for something to cook. And then she could hear his footsteps overhead. She pulled out frozen pizza and set it on the counter.

Funny, how she hadn't felt any real surprise when she'd seen him leaning against the porch. Unless he stayed at his parents' house, which hadn't seemed likely, this was about the only place in Riverbend to rent a decent room. But it wasn't logic that had made his presence seem natural.

How many times had she seen Jake standing in just that same place, waiting for Josie? He wasn't the tough boy he'd been twenty years ago and she wasn't the plump little girl who'd had such a terrible crush on her sister's boyfriend.

One thing that hadn't changed was the way her heart had given a funny little bump when she'd first seen him. For just a moment, she'd felt as breathless as she had twenty years ago. It had seemed almost inevitable to walk down the street and find him standing in front of the porch, waiting for her. As if all those vague childhood fantasies had finally come true.

The gossip mill must have gotten to Josie by now. In fact, she was probably one of the first people to hear about Jake's return. Twenty years may have passed but Riverbend hadn't forgotten that Josie and Jake had once been an "item."

As Jake came down the stairs, the smell of oregano and cheese wafted upward, announcing dinner. Pizza. He couldn't remember the last time he'd had pizza. Paige was setting out plates when he entered the kitchen. The radio was on, and he could make out Sam Cook through the scratchy reception.

Paige was humming along, singing a word here and there, her bare feet moving in rhythm to the mellow tune. There was a huge bouquet of flowers in the center of the big oak table. She hadn't bothered to arrange them in any particular order. It looked as if she'd simply wandered through the garden, picking whatever caught her eye, and stuffed them into a vase.

There were thick cloth napkins in a somewhat eye-searing pattern of purple and yellow and plates that didn't match. She hadn't bothered with any silverware, assuming that, like any civilized American, he understood that pizza was finger food.

She turned and saw him, ostensibly not in the least disturbed at being seen dancing while she was setting the table. She smiled, the expression starting in her eyes before moving to her mouth. It struck Jake that it had been a long time since he'd seen someone smile with their eyes.

"Decided to give up the retro-rebel look, huh?"

"For now. It isn't pink and there's no little animals on the pocket but it was the best I could do in a pinch."

She looked him up and down, taking in the jeans and the blue cotton shirt with the sleeves rolled halfway up his forearms. Sneakers had replaced the black leather boots. He'd combed his wavy hair into place but one rebellious wave had fallen onto his forehead.

"Nice," she announced, having given it serious consideration.

"Thanks," he said dryly. "I think the last woman to critique my wardrobe was my mother."

If Paige caught any sarcasm in his tone, she chose to ignore it. "The glasses are in the cupboard to the left of the fridge. I've got wine—aged at least a week in aluminum barrels. There's water, milk or soda."

"I think I'll stick with water, it sounds the safest of the bunch."

"Pour me a glass of milk, would you?" She was leaning over the oven as she spoke and Jake couldn't resist a lingering look at the rather extraordinary length of leg her skirt exposed.

He dragged his gaze away as she lifted the pizza out and straightened. Getting the glasses, that was what he was supposed to be doing. It wasn't until he was setting them on the table that he realized they were decorated with cartoon characters.

Paige scooped an enormous slice of pizza onto each plate and settled in the chair across from his. She lifted her wedge of pizza and took a bite. It wasn't until she had swallowed that she noticed Jake hadn't moved.

"Don't you like pizza?" She raised her brows, as if the thought was inconceivable.

"My glass has a picture of Tweety Bird."

"Don't you like him? I've got Sylvester and I don't think I've broken the Bugs Bunny yet."

He met her eyes and wondered if he looked as if he'd fallen into the Twilight Zone. What would the people he'd worked with over the past fifteen years think if they could see Jake Quincannon now? Sitting in a homey kitchen with a slice of pizza in front of him and drinking from a glass with a picture of Tweety Bird on it.

"He's fine," he said somewhat weakly. He reached for the

pizza, unable to shake the feeling that there was something wrong with this picture.

Paige didn't seem to feel the need to make conversation to fill up the silence, a trait Jake admired. He'd never understood why people seemed to think that silence was dangerous. In his experience, it could be an ally.

Glancing across the table at Paige, he was struck by the fact that she seemed completely relaxed. People didn't usually feel so comfortable in his presence. His own parents had watched him as if he were a dangerous animal who might turn on them. For some reason, her calm acceptance of his presence was disturbing.

"Are you always this comfortable with strangers?" he asked abruptly.

"You're not really a stranger."

"You haven't seen me in twenty years. For all you know, I could have become an ax murderer." Jake couldn't explain his irritation.

"Have you become an ax murderer?" She didn't seem concerned with his answer and Jake scowled as he reached for another slice of pizza.

"You're too trusting."

"You take yourself too seriously." There was no bite in the words but they stung nevertheless.

"You don't know anything about me," he snapped.

"If you *were* an ax murderer, you'd hardly come back here to commit your dastardly deeds. The whole town is just waiting for you to sneeze crossways to prove that you turned into the criminal they all predicted you'd become. If you murdered me in my sleep, they'd hang you from the nearest tree without benefit of trial."

Jake set the glass down with a thump. "Doesn't it worry you?"

Paige eyed him over a slice of pizza that dripped cheese, her eyes a cool green. "Do you want me to be afraid of you, Jake Would it feed your ego?"

"My ego? What does my ego have to do with it?"

"I get the feeling that you're used to people being afraid c you. If you've come home to prove that you've turned out jus as wicked as they all predicted you would, don't start wit me."

She stood up, took her plate over to the sink and rinsed before setting it on the counter. Jake was still sitting at th table when she left the room, staring at the cold pizza, awar that he'd just made a total fool of himself. Maybe it had bee too long since he'd had any dealings with real people. Mayb he didn't know how to behave like a normal person anymor

He'd come home to find out who he was. Instead, he wa finding out that he had the manners of a warthog. With a sigl he shoved his chair back. Reaching for his glass, he had fleeting wish that it held something more potent than wate When he set the glass down, Tweety seemed to be staring him, his beak pursed in disapproval.

"Okay, so I blew it," Jake muttered. "Maybe they wei right. Maybe you can't ever go back. She's probably going throw me out on my ear and I can't say I would blame her.

He stared at the painted yellow bird, so absorbed in thoug that it didn't even strike him that he was talking to a cartoc character. Reaching up to rub the back of his neck, he wa conscious of a deep weariness that had little to do with tl miles he'd travelled in the last few days.

He wasn't sure what he'd been expecting when he can home but Paige Cudahy hadn't been part of the picture. Ai neither had his reaction to her.

The only thing he was really sure of was that he didn't wa her to ask him to leave.

Chapter Three

The house was quiet when Jake came downstairs the next morning. He assumed Paige had already gone to work, though he hadn't thought to ask where she worked. There were probably a lot of things he should have asked, instead of haranguing her for trusting a virtual stranger and renting him a room.

He hadn't seen her again last night after she'd left the kitchen. When he went upstairs, the door to her room had been shut and it hadn't seemed like a good idea to disturb her. Apologies were better made in the calm light of morning.

He strode into the kitchen, wanting nothing more than a cup of strong coffee. But the kitchen was occupied. Paige leaned on the counter as she watched a particularly fat sparrow gorging himself at the bird feeder that hung outside the window.

She hadn't heard him approach and Jake was glad of it. It probably wouldn't be the smartest move to start off his apology by staring at the stunning length of leg bared by a pair of very short shorts. Starting at her bare feet and traveling up over lightly tanned calves and thighs, his gaze lingered on the way the denim shorts molded the curves of her buttocks. The shorts were topped by a loose T-shirt in a shade of green that made him think of maple leaves in the spring.

It wasn't possible that Josie's little sister had grown up into this desirable woman. It wasn't fair. He shifted his weight and the oak floor creaked, announcing his presence.

"Good morning, Jake." Paige turned slowly.

"Good morning." Her expression was impossible to read. occurred to him that, for all her seeming openness, there wa a great deal of Paige Cudahy that was kept hidden.

"If you're hungry, there's Fruit Loops and Cocoa Puffs i the cupboard." She dipped her hand into the box of Cap' Crunch she held, pulling out a handful. Jake controlled a shue der.

"Actually, all I really want is a cup of coffee."

"All I've got is instant." She pointed to the cupboard behir him. "It's pretty old. I only keep it for guests. All that caffei is bad for you."

Jake glanced pointedly at the sugar-coated cereal she wa munching.

"Sugar is an energy food," she said defensively, looking if energy was the last thing she had any interest in acquirin

"Caffeine is a sanity food," Jake said, finding a pan in th cupboard she pointed to with one bare foot. He filled the pa with water and set it on the stove, turning the flame as high possible. He was aware of Paige watching him as he dump coffee into a thick mug.

Neither of them spoke until Jake had poured the hot wat over the coffee crystals and had taken his first swallow of t nearly scalding liquid.

Feeling as if he just might live another day, Jake eyed Pai over the rim of the mug. She looked completely relaxed, h hips braced against the counter, her long legs crossed at t ankles. She'd pulled her hair back into a thick braid that f over one shoulder, leaving only the slightly ragged bangs frame her eyes. At first glance she looked about fourteen—l only at first glance. There was nothing girlish about the wa curves of her figure, nothing childlike in the sensuous shape her mouth.

Jake took another swallow of coffee, grimacing at the st

aste. She hadn't been kidding when she said it was old. He radled the warm mug between his palms.

"Look, I'm sorry about last night." At his abrupt apology, 'aige glanced up from the box of cereal. "I guess I haven't pent enough time in polite company these last few years." He hrugged, his mouth twisting. "And maybe you're right, maybe am used to people being afraid of me. Anyway, I had no usiness jumping down your throat."

"No, you didn't." But there was no anger in the words. 'Why *did* you come home, Jake?"

He couldn't even answer that question for himself. "I don't now exactly. Maybe I just wanted to see if it had changed."

"Riverbend never changes. It won't take you very long to nd that out."

"Well, I've got the summer. I decided to take the summer ▸ come home and find…" He shrugged, not knowing exactly 'hat he hoped to find. "…whatever."

"I hope you find your whatever, Jake. I don't think most ▹ople even know when they've lost it." She smiled as she ▸ade her statement, and Jake wondered if it was his imagi- ▸tion that saw a fleeting look of discontent in her eyes.

The screen door pushed open before he could pursue the ◂ought any further. The girl who breezed in was in her late ◂ens and pretty enough to turn heads. Her dark hair was cut ◂ort, framing a pair of deep blue, thickly lashed eyes.

"Hi, Aunt Paige." Though she spoke to Paige, her eyes were ▸ Jake. "You must be Jake Quincannon. I'm Beth. Everybody ▹ys you and Mom used to be a hot item. She never told me ◂u were so good-looking."

"Beth, you have the manners of a chimpanzee," Paige told ◂r dryly, rescuing Jake from the necessity of finding a reply. ◂ake, this is Josie and Frank's daughter, as you've probably ▸eady guessed. Someone once told her that honesty was the ◂st policy and so she abandoned all efforts at developing any ◂t or discretion."

"You're the one who said that people should always expres their thoughts, Aunt Paige." Beth threw her aunt a mischievou look. Paige responded by throwing a towel at her. Beth caugl the towel, grinning at her before turning to Jake.

"Should I apologize for having said that you're goo looking?" The offer was made so demurely that Jake foun himself unable to resist her youthful charm.

"I think I can bear up under the burden," he said, givin her a half smile.

"Don't encourage her, Jake," Paige told him lazily. "She the bane of the family as it is." She caught the wadded tow Beth tossed back at her. "What are you doing here, anywa I thought you were going to work at the bank this summer.'

"I am, but I don't start till next week. Billy and I are goir on a picnic and I asked him to pick me up here."

The last part of the sentence came out in a rush. Annoyan flickered in Paige's eyes.

"I thought your parents didn't want you seeing him."

"Mom and Dad are such sticks-in-the-mud. You know th are, Aunt Paige."

"Whether that's true or not, I don't want you using th house to meet Billy behind their backs."

This was a new side to Paige—the stern aunt. Jake took sip of coffee, watching the little drama unfold. Beth shift uneasily beneath Paige's severe look.

"They can't make me stop seeing Billy. And neither c you."

"I'm not going to try and make you do anything. But I do want you meeting him here again."

Beth hesitated, her face flushed with anger and embarra ment. But there was no arguing with that look and she kn it.

"All right."

A hiccuping roar in the street outside shattered the sligh tense silence. Beth brightened immediately, her eyes sparkli

"There's Billy now. I won't do it again, Aunt Paige. It was great to meet you, Jake." A flash of tanned legs and she was gone.

Paige sighed, moving over to the counter to heap instant coffee into a cup. She reached for the water Jake had left on the stove.

"I thought you didn't drink coffee," he commented.

"I said it wasn't good for you. I didn't say I didn't drink ." She poured water over the coffee and took a swallow, grimacing at the taste.

"Pretty girl," Jake said, not sure why he was lingering. Hadn't he decided last night that it might be a good idea to keep some distance between himself and his landlady?

"She's usually intelligent, too. But this Billy—" Paige broke off, shaking her head. "For once, I agree with Josie. He's no good for Beth."

"Sounds familiar. Everyone said the same thing about me and Josie." His smile was rueful. "And they were probably right."

"No one ever said you were a creep," Paige said firmly. "They might have said you were wild and destined to come to a bad end, but no one ever said you were a creep. Billy Wilson is a creep."

It was clear that to her the former was preferable to the latter. Jake didn't question her logic.

"She'll probably figure that out herself, sooner or later," he said easily, glad it wasn't his problem.

"I hope so." Paige fixed him with a speculative look, the coffee in her hand forgotten.

"Did you come back here because of Josie?"

"Josie?" The question surprised him. "Why would I come back because of Josie?"

"Well, you were madly in love with her."

"It was a long time ago. I was nineteen."

"You were furious when you came back to find she'd married Frank. I was hiding behind the hydrangea listening."

Jake frowned, trying to remember how he'd felt. "I think was more hurt that Frank would marry my girl than that Josi married Frank. He was my best friend. When you're a nineteen year-old boy, best friends aren't supposed to do that kind thing." He shrugged and finished the last of his coffee. "A I've already said, it was a long time ago. Whatever I felt the is long gone, including any puppy love I had for your sister.

HIS MIND was still on the conversation half an hour later as pushed open the door of Riverbend's only bank. He seemed be thinking about Paige Cudahy more than he had any busine doing. Shaking his head, he reached for the envelope that stuc carelessly out of the back pocket of his black jeans.

"Jake Quincannon." Startled, Jake stiffened at the gru sound of his name, his hand twitching instinctively toward t gun he no longer wore. He turned slowly, his wary expressic easing into a smile that would have surprised many who we convinced they knew him.

"Pop! You old dog, I thought they'd have put you out pasture years ago."

He reached out to grip the other man's hand. Pop Bellov had been one of the few people Jake could have called a frie twenty years ago. He'd seemed positively ancient then, thou he probably hadn't been much over fifty.

"Hell, they made me retire but they couldn't make me at home waiting to die." Pop's eyes had faded and his sk had the worn look of old leather but the hand Jake gripped w still firm and strong. "I took over as security guard here wh old Smitty had a heart attack."

All Jake had seen at first was that Pop was still wearing uniform, just as he had twenty years ago. Now he noticed tl the uniform wasn't the tan he'd worn as the town's sheri This was a crisp navy blue.

"Who's keeping law and order now that you've retired?"

"You remember Martin Smith? Well, he joined the Marines a year or two after you left. When he got out, he came back home and settled down. Turned into a pretty fine officer. Trained him myself."

"You probably scared him into doing a good job," Jake said. "Just like you scared me into staying out of trouble."

"Some folks learn without having to have the fear of God put into them." Pop gave him a pointed look. "Don't look like you remembered everything I taught you. What happened to your eye?"

Jake reached up to touch the leather patch. He didn't mind the question coming from Pop, knowing that there was more than idle curiosity behind it. "I zigged when I should have zagged."

"Well, I'd guess it doesn't do you any harm with the ladies," the old man said. "They're bound to think it makes you look like a pirate or some such nonsense. What are you doing home after all these years? What's it been? Fifteen, sixteen years?"

"Almost twenty, Pop."

"That long?" Pop shook his head. "The older I get the faster time goes. So what are you doing home, Jake?"

"I don't know. It seems like everybody's asked me that and I still don't know the answer. It seemed like as good a place as any to spend the summer, I guess."

"Well, I suppose Riverbend ain't a bad spot to light for a while. I'm not sure I ever expected to see you back here though. I figured once you shook the dust of this town off your feet, you weren't likely to come back."

"Maybe I came back for some more of that lethal lemon cake of yours."

Pop looked blank for a moment, then his eyes widened and he laughed. "I'd nearly forgotten that cake."

"I'm not likely to forget. Not when it damn near killed me.

I hope you've been staying away from the kitchen. Otherwise, the cemetery must be just about full of your victims.''

''Now, Jake, I was trying to do you a favor,'' Pop protested, still chuckling.

Jake's smile softened. Funny how he'd almost forgotten the reason Pop had baked that inedible cake. It had been to celebrate his graduating high school.

His parents had given him a small check and said they were proud of him but their words had seemed empty to him. He could still remember the way his mother had looked at him, as if she thought he'd threatened the principal into giving him his diploma. His father had patted him on the back, awkward as always when any outward display of affection was required.

In a rare weak moment, Jake had said something to Pop about never being able to please them. He'd thought that getting his diploma would be something that would finally make them proud of him. He'd finally done something right. But it still wasn't enough. He went on to tell Pop that Frank's parents had driven all the way to Boise to take him out to dinner, while his own mother hadn't even bothered to bake him a cake.

Pop had told him not to whine but the next time Jake had dropped by for his self-defense lessons, there'd been a three-layer cake sitting on the counter in Pop's rarely used kitchen. A three-layer cake that was about an inch and a half high. Jake had manfully attempted to eat a slice—he wouldn't have hurt Pop's feelings for the world—but the cake was just the consistency of not quite hardened cement.

They'd ended the evening by going to Maisie's for a slice of apple pie after burying the cake with great ceremony. Jake shook his head. It was funny how the good memories had lingered while the reason they'd happened had all but been forgotten.

Pop peered up at him, his faded eyes searching Jake's face for answers. ''You look like you've had some rough times, Jake. It's good to have you home, boy.''

Emotion caught in Jake's throat. Here was the welcome he hadn't gotten from his parents. This old man had been about the only person in the entire town who'd believed in him, who'd believed he could make something of himself. He'd made something of himself all right, but he doubted it was what Pop had had in mind.

"Thanks, Pop." Jake squeezed the old man's shoulder. "I'll be seeing you around."

"I'll be here."

Pop settled back into his chair by the door and Jake moved toward the teller window. The clerk's eyes widened when she saw the size of the check he wanted to cash, but after making a call to the bank it was drawn on, she cashed it without protest. He'd considered opening an account but an inner voice had suggested that it would make things more difficult if he should decide to leave suddenly. Considering Pop was the only one who seemed genuinely glad to see him, that was a strong possibility.

He was tucking his wallet back into his pocket when he felt someone watching him. When he looked up, his gaze collided with that of a tall, dark-haired woman who was standing a few feet away. It had been twenty years but he didn't have any trouble recognizing her. She watched his approach much as she might have watched a cougar about to jump on its prey.

"Josie."

"Jake." She nodded, her eyes a cold brown. "I heard you were back in town."

"Doesn't look like the grapevine has withered any in the last twenty years."

She didn't bother to acknowledge his mild sarcasm. "Why are you here?"

"I was cashing a check," he said, knowing that wasn't what she'd been asking.

She made an impatient gesture with one manicured hand. "I

don't mean that. I mean, why have you come back to River bend?''

"Is there any reason I shouldn't have come back?" He wa getting just a little tired of answering the same question and his irritation showed in his tone.

"There doesn't seem to be any reason you'd want to come back.''

"I don't recall being run out of town on a rail."

"Well, you've been gone nearly twenty years, Jake. Yo can't blame people for being a little surprised to see you."

"Maybe." He looked at her, searching for something of th girl he'd loved so passionately. There didn't seem to be an trace of her left in the rather cool woman standing in front c him. "How's Frank?"

"He's fine. Are you staying long?"

It didn't take a psychic to figure out that nothing would hav made her happier than to hear that he was on his way out c town.

"I don't know. With the heartwarming welcome everyon has offered, it's a little difficult to think about leaving just yet.

Color mantled her cheeks but he didn't think it was out c embarrassment. Anger was a better bet.

"I really can't imagine that there's anything here for yo Jake."

"Can't you?" He allowed the silence to stretch.

The skin over Josie's cheeks seemed to tighten, the carefull concealed lines beside her eyes deepening. "I have to go."

Jake watched her abrupt departure, wondering why Josi should be so anxious to see him leave town. He hadn't ex pected her to be delighted to see him, but neither had he ex pected veiled hostility. He followed more slowly, waving Pop on the way out.

He started toward the motorcycle, slowing when he saw th man looking at it. The tan sheriff's uniform identified him eve before he turned around.

Martin Smith had been two years behind Jake in high school, not as big a gap in a town the size of Riverbend as it might have been in a larger place. Martin turned as Jake stopped in front of the bike. The hair that had been carrot-red twenty years ago had darkened to a more subdued shade and the stockiness that had tended to fat in high school had become solid muscle.

"Jake Quincannon." Martin held out his hand, his smile easy, his eyes watchful. "Figured this had to be yours. I know every other bike in town. Heard you were back."

"Martin. Pop told me you'd taken over his job."

"You haven't been in town long."

"I'd guess you know the exact moment I crossed the city limits." There was no rancor in Jake's words.

Martin laughed. "Probably pretty close. You've sure had the grapevine humming."

"The place hasn't changed," Jake muttered.

"That's the way people want it. You go away, and when you come back, everything is just the way you left it."

"Is that why you came back? Pop told me you were in the service."

"Yeah. I did two tours in 'Nam. When I got home, I thought this place would drive me crazy. It was like they'd never gotten out of the fifties. But there's a certain peace in it, too."

Jake couldn't argue with that. God knows, peace was something he hadn't found. Maybe that's what he was looking for.

While he and Martin were talking, an armored car pulled up in front of the bank. The guard got out of the car, two sacks of money carried casually at his sides. The bank manager met him in the lobby and the two stood talking for a moment before making their way farther into the bank, and then out of sight. Inside the door, Jake could see Pop sitting in his chair, watching the exchange without much interest.

"Friday's payroll for half the businesses in town," Martin commented, seeing where Jake's attention was focused.

"Doesn't look like there's much security around," Jake commented.

"I've mentioned that to Mr. Nathan a few times but he's too cheap to hire extra guards for the delivery. So, I try to be around when the delivery is made." He shrugged. "I doubt there's much to worry about. They'd have to find the place before they could rob it."

Jake turned back to the sheriff. Security or the lack thereof wasn't his problem anymore. He didn't even have any money in the bank.

"You're staying at the old Cudahy place, I hear," Martin said.

Jake swung his leg over the big motorcycle, settling into the wide leather seat.

"Does everyone in town know what I had for dinner last night, too?" The edge of sarcasm was resoundingly clear.

Martin narrowed his eyes as if trying to remember something. "Pizza." He grinned at the startled look Jake threw him. "I know Paige. Gussied-up frozen pizza is her one culinary talent."

Jake shook his head, half grinning. He knocked the kickstand back before starting the engine. Martin lifted his hand as the Harley roared away from the curb. Jake returned the gesture aware that the tension he'd felt since yesterday had eased.

Pop had been glad to see him and Martin didn't seem to have any problem with his presence in town. He couldn't say that Paige hadn't been welcoming but there was something about her— He broke the thought off, his mouth tightening beneath the thick dark mustache. He'd come home to try and figure out where he wanted to go with his life, as if coming back to where it had started would clarify things. The last thing he wanted to do was get involved with his landlady. It shouldn't be hard to keep a little distance between them.

It was an easy decision to make but not quite so easy to keep. Pulling the bike to a halt in front of the house, Jake snapped the kickstand into place absently, his attention on the big oak tree that spread its branches over the front yard.

Perched on a branch halfway up the tree was a calico kitten, his piteous wails telling a heartrending tale of woe. Balanced uneasily on the lowest branch was the landlady Jake had just decided to avoid.

That Paige was uneasy in her current position was clear from the way she clung to the trunk of the oak as if it was a lifeline. As he watched, she inched her fingers toward a higher branch. She was talking to the kitten. Jake couldn't hear what she was saying but he could hear the reassuring cadence of her voice. Not at all reassured, the kitten continued to yowl pathetically.

Jake crossed the yard to stand under the tree. From this vantage point, he had an excellent view of those endless legs and the snug fit of her shorts.

"You're going to fall," he said conversationally.

Startled, she turned to look down at him, nearly fulfilling his prediction as the sudden movement upset her careful balance. Jake held his breath as she teetered. But she regained her balance almost immediately.

"Harry is stuck," she said, as if this disclosure was part of an ongoing conversation.

"It's not going to do Harry any good if you kill yourself trying to get him down."

"I can't just leave him there."

"I'd guess that Harry will come down when he's good and ready."

"He's so little." Paige turned to look up at the kitten.

"He got himself up there, he can get himself down," Jake said heartlessly. "Let me give you a hand."

She wavered, clearly torn between the common sense of his words and the plight of the kitten. As if sensing that rescue might not be as forthcoming as he'd hoped, Harry raised his thin voice in a terrified yowl, confirming the desperation of his position.

"Listen to the poor little thing." Paige looked back down
at Jake, her eyes full of concern. "I can't leave him up there
What if he falls?"

"I'll go up after him." Jake heard the words as if they came
from someone else. He knew as well as Harry did that a cat
up a tree can come down any time he wants to. Furthermore
he didn't even like cats. And he was long past the age for
climbing trees.

He repeated these arguments to himself as he balanced or
one branch and caught hold of another, pulling himself up into
the huge oak. Harry watched him suspiciously from a branch
that was just out of reach.

But it was another pair of green eyes that had gotten him
into this situation. Eyes that had sparkled with gratitude when
he said he'd undertake the rescue. Paige watched him from the
ground and he was more conscious of that than he had any
right to be.

"Come here, cat," he muttered, pulling himself up onto a
branch just thick enough to support his weight. Harry edged
back, letting out a piteous mew. The branch beneath him
creaked in protest and Jake had a sudden vision of himself
plummeting to his death on a front lawn in Idaho. For fifteen
years he'd lived with the possibility of death as a constant
companion. Wouldn't it be ironic if he died in his own home
town, trying to rescue a kitten who didn't need rescuing be
cause he was trying to impress a woman he didn't want to get
involved with?

"Come on, Harry," he coaxed in a soothing tone. What he
really wanted to do was get his hands around that furry little
neck. Harry edged just a little farther out on the branch, keep
ing up his pathetic cries, even as he tried to murder his would
be rescuer.

"Can you get him?" Paige called up. "He's a little shy
sometimes."

Jake eyed the kitten, who eyed him back. Harry didn't look shy to him. Harry looked stubborn.

"Come here, you little pest." The words were said from between Jake's clenched teeth, which may have accounted for the cat's reluctance to obey the command.

Exasperated, Jake lunged upward, scooping the startled kitten from its perch with one hand and clutching at the tree for balance with the other. Harry wailed in fright, struggling wildly. But now that Jake had him, he had no intention of letting him go. He made his way back down the tree, one hand full of spitting, scratching kitten.

"You got him."

Though he knew he was being a fool, Jake felt suffused with the warmth of Paige's smile. Harry, no more content now that he was safely on the ground, fastened small but very sharp teeth into Jake's finger.

"Ouch, damn!" Jake dropped the furious kitten, who disappeared in an orange and black streak across the lawn.

"Are you hurt?" Paige caught his hand before he could deny any serious injury. "Oh, look what he did to your hand."

"It's no big deal." He would have pulled his hand away but Paige held it firmly.

"Come on into the house. I'll put some disinfectant on those. Cat bites can be nasty, you know."

Still holding his hand, she led him across the yard and onto the porch. Jake told himself that he was going along with her only because he didn't want to make an issue of retrieving his hand. Besides, the bite was beginning to sting like the devil.

Paige sat him in a chair in the kitchen and turned to the drawer where she kept her somewhat haphazard first-aid kit. She was vividly aware of Jake watching her. Her fingers felt clumsy as she fumbled in the drawer.

"I'm sorry Harry wasn't more grateful," she said, turning back to him with a tube of antiseptic cream held like a shield in front of her.

"I've. never really thought of cats as being grateful crea
tures," Jake commented.

Paige crouched down in front of him, reaching for his hand
trying not to notice the warmth of his skin. "Harry was a stray
when Lisa took him in. I don't think he trusts humans ver
much."

"You mean it isn't even your cat?"

"No. Harry belongs to the little girl who lives across th
street."

"What was he doing in your tree?" Jake demanded, sound
ing vaguely indignant.

"Maybe he liked the looks of my tree better than the one a
home." She finished dabbing the injury with ointment an
glanced up. "You know, the trees are always greener on th
other side of the street."

Jake gave her a pained look but she thought she caught
twitch of amusement at the corner of his mouth. "Maybe Harr
just wanted to see if he could get me killed," he muttered.

"It was really nice of you to go up after him," she sai
distractedly. It was funny how with only one eye, his gaz
managed to be so penetrating. She'd forgotten she was holdin
his hand. She was suddenly aware of the intimacy of her po
sition, crouched on the floor between his knees.

"No problem. Climbing into trees after cats that don't nee
rescuing is my speciality." Jake's gaze was on her mouth a
he spoke. He lifted his free hand to take hold of the pale brai
that hung over her shoulder. "I didn't remember how light yo
hair was—the color of sunlight."

Paige moistened her lips, aware of a sudden catch in he
breath. She really should get up, she thought absently. But sh
didn't move. Jake's hand moved to the nape of her neck. Th
feel of his fingers resting on the sensitive skin there sent
tingling sensation up her spine.

She was hardly aware of releasing his hand as he pulled h
upward. But she was vividly aware of the feel of his che

beneath her palms. As his face filled her vision, she closed her eyes.

His mouth was firm and warm. The brush of his mustache against her upper lip was a sensuous tickle. She edged closer as his hands splayed against her upper back. The kiss was slow, almost lazy. His mouth explored hers without urgency.

Jake hadn't planned on kissing her. But her mouth had looked so soft, so inviting. A small kiss, he told himself. No big deal, nothing to even really think about. But he hadn't planned on the way the kiss seemed to take on a life of its own. He'd thought that, if he kissed her, he'd be able to stop wondering what her mouth would taste like. Instead, he found himself wanting to draw her closer, to see if her skin could possibly be as soft as it looked.

Paige had experienced more passionate kisses but she'd never experienced a kiss that seemed to plunge right into her soul. When Jake lifted his head, she could only stare at him. His look was searching, as if the simple kiss had been more than he'd expected, too.

If he released her, would she melt into a puddle, just like the Wicked Witch of the West? It seemed a distinct possibility. The thought was enough to force strength back into her spine.

"Well, I've heard of kissing it to make it better but I thought *I* was the one who was supposed to kiss your injury." Her voice was a little too husky but it was steady, the tone just light enough.

Jake's hands slid from her back and she scooted back before standing up.

"Consider it a thank-you for my rescuing Harry," Jake said, rising from the chair. He didn't seem in the least disturbed by the kiss, she noted, feeling an odd twinge of irritation.

"In that case, maybe you should have kissed Harry."

Halfway out the door, Jake turned, raking her with a look of pure masculine appreciation. "Harry isn't nearly as pretty."

Paige stood in the middle of the kitchen floor, listening to the thumping of his feet as he took the stairs two at a time. She had the feeling that Jake Quincannon was going to shake up a lot of things in Riverbend this summer. If her accelerated pulse was any indication, she didn't think her own life was going to be immune, either.

The thought was not without appeal.

Chapter Four

"Okay, give me all the juicy details."

Mary's piercing whisper very probably reached every corner of the library. Early weekday afternoons were generally slow, so there was no one in the library to frown at Mary for disturbing the silence.

Paige had been returning books to the shelves but she'd stopped to peruse a book of poetry. She shut the book as she turned to look at her friend.

"Juicy details about what?"

"About Jake Quincannon," Mary whispered, her dark eyes sparkling with anticipation.

"There's really not much to tell." Paige turned to slip the book back onto the shelf. It might as well have been a treatise on nuclear physics. She hadn't really registered much of what she'd been reading. In fact, she hadn't been able to concentrate on anything today. But it certainly didn't have anything to do with her boarder. And nothing at all to do with that brief kiss they'd shared.

"Paige Cudahy, don't you dare clam up on me. Martin won't tell me a thing. You'd think it was a state secret or something."

"Maybe Martin thinks Jake wouldn't appreciate being front-page news," Paige said.

"Then he shouldn't have come back to Riverbend," Mary responded with irrefutable logic.

"What did Martin say?" Paige picked up the small stack of books she was supposed to be reshelving.

"Don't think I don't know that you're trying to avoid answering the question, Paige." Mary trailed along after her friend, her quick movements making it seem as if she was taking two steps for every one of Paige's. "All Martin would say is that Jake seemed like a nice guy. A nice guy! What kind of description is that? I could have strangled him."

"Strangling him would probably have jeopardized your wedding plans." Paige slipped a volume onto the shelf.

"I suppose. Sometimes I don't know why I agreed to marry him."

"Because you're madly in love with him and he's madly in love with you."

"That's true." Mary held out her left hand, admiring the way the small diamond on her third finger caught the sunlight that poured in through the front windows.

"But that doesn't change the fact that he's the most exasperating man in the world," she said, hurrying to catch up with Paige, who'd moved down one of the stacks.

"All men are exasperating."

"You're not doing too badly yourself." Mary took Paige's arm in a determined grip. "I want to know all about Jake Quincannon."

"You've come to the wrong source. I hardly know him."

"Paige."

How someone so short could inject so much threat into one word was something Paige couldn't understand. But she knew that look. Mary wasn't going to budge until she'd pried every detail from her victim.

"If you're going to pump me for information, I might as well be comfortable while you're doing it."

Sighing in defeat, Paige made her way to the desk and collapsed back into the huge chair she'd convinced the library committee was absolutely essential to a librarian's comfort.

Mary perched on the edge of the desk, crossing her jeans-clad legs at the ankle.

"Okay, tell me everything. What does he look like?"

"Actually, I guess he looks pretty much like a returning rebel should look. Dark hair, with just a touch of gray at the temples. Black mustache, very ominous-looking. And blue eyes, at least the one you can see is blue. He wears a patch over the left eye."

"I told Sally Ann Hartford I didn't believe her when she told me he wore an eye patch." Mary sounded guilt stricken.

"I wouldn't worry about it. It's probably the first time Sally's told the truth in the last five years. It's not your fault you didn't believe her."

Mary dismissed the mendacious Sally with a wave of her hand. "She doesn't like me anyway." She leaned forward, her dark eyes bright. "What's he like, Paige? Is he lean and hungry, or sullen? Does he send shivers up your spine?"

Paige devoted her attention to picking an invisible piece of lint from her skirt, her eyes focused on the task. Shivers up her spine? She had to admit that he did, though not in the way Mary meant. But that was something she'd decided not to think about, at least not right now.

"He's definitely not sullen," she told her friend. "And he's too big to be lean and hungry. He seems nice."

"Nice?" Mary repeated the word disappointedly. She'd been hoping for something a little more provocative than "nice." "Is that all? Just 'nice'?"

"A little lonely maybe."

"Why did he come back to Riverbend? Miss Leigh, over at the post office, says that he's sent postcards from all over the world to his parents. If he's been all over the world, why would he want to come back here?"

"Maybe he just got tired of traveling," Paige suggested, remembering how he'd told her that he'd come back because he was looking for something. "Maybe he wanted to see his parents."

"I suppose." Mary sighed, looking as disconsolate as her sunny personality would allow. "I was really hoping he'd stir things up a bit. Nothing awful, just something to add a little spice to the summer. I thought maybe I'd get some ideas for my next book."

"What happened to the one about the knife thrower who's also a spy?"

"I just got it back in the mail. They said it didn't ring true," Mary said indignantly. "After all the research on circuses I did. And they said it was too long. I needed every one of those pages for plot development."

Paige offered commiserations, controlling the urge to comment that eight hundred pages of plot development was enough to exhaust anybody.

Mary turned to glance over her shoulder as the big wooden door that fronted Oakwood Street was thrust open. It banged back against the wall and Paige made a mental note to talk to the library committee about that. Of course, most of the patrons were familiar with the door's idiosyncrasies and avoided throwing it open. But then most of the patrons weren't Josie.

Josie never just walked through a door. There had been a time when Paige had despaired of ever being able to enter a room like her older sister, so that all eyes immediately turned her way. She'd long ago stopped trying to emulate Josie's entrances or anything else about her, but she still felt a twinge of admiration as she watched her sister sweep into the small library. Her heels clicked on the old wooden floor, sending out an almost military tattoo that demanded attention.

"Oh-oh. It's Morgana le Fey," Mary muttered as she slid off the desk and turned to face Josie, who had just swept up to the desk.

"Hello, Josie. I like that suit." Paige tried to defuse the

anger she could see simmering in Josie's eyes. The diversion worked only for a moment.

"It was a gift from Frank. Chanel, you know."

She spoke condescendingly, and Paige saw Mary's hand twitch with the urge to smack Josie. It was an urge Josie brought out in a number of people. Paige didn't know how to explain that Josie didn't mean to be insulting. She felt she was so clearly superior to nearly everyone in town that it never occurred to her that anyone would be insulted by anything she said or did.

Not that she'd have cared much if they were insulted, Paige admitted to herself.

"Chanel?" Paige spoke quickly, forestalling anything Mary might be about to say. "Frank must have sold a house."

Josie's husband was an attorney by profession, but because Riverbend wasn't big enough to require a full-time attorney, he also handled most of the real estate deals that came up.

"Yes, he did. Over in Banning. You know, if you weren't so stubborn, Paige, he could take that old white elephant off your hands. You could get a smaller place, something modern and efficient."

"Sorry." She wasn't really sorry but there was no sense in telling her sister that.

"Really. I don't know why Mom and Dad left the house to you in the first place. *I* grew up there, too, you know."

"And it obviously holds great sentimental value for you," Mary commented sweetly.

"Of course it does," Josie said, oblivious of her own insincerity. "But I understand property values in a way you obviously don't, Paige. The place has gone up considerably in value. If you sold now, you could make a nice profit."

"And Frank could buy you another mink," Mary said, without trying to hide the sarcasm.

"Actually, we've been discussing the fact that Beth needs a car." There was a faint air of maternal martyrdom in her tone.

Paige was well aware that Josie was hoping that the idea of being instrumental in getting her niece a car was supposed to weaken her refusal. She leaned back in the chair, careful to keep the amusement from her expression. Josie was so transparent sometimes.

"I'm not interested in selling, Josie. Frank knows that and he seems to understand."

"Frank's just not firm enough," Josie said irritably.

"I can think of a few places he might have applied a firmer hand," Mary said sweetly.

Josie blinked, apparently surprised to see that Mary was still there. She frowned for a moment, as if trying to decipher Mary's meaning and then, with a toss of her head, she dismissed it as being of no importance. She returned her attention to Paige—and to the subject that had brought her to the library in the first place.

"I suppose you've heard that Jake Quincannon is back in town."

"Yes." Paige made the admission cautiously. Josie obviously didn't know that Paige had rented Jake a room, though how the grapevine had missed spreading that juicy tidbit, she couldn't imagine.

"I saw him yesterday at the bank."

"Really." Monosyllables were generally the safest way of responding to Josie's questions. Why hadn't Jake mentioned that he'd seen Josie?

"Arrogant bastard." Paige was startled by the venom in Josie's tone. She hadn't expected her sister to be thrilled with Jake's return, but there didn't seem to be any real reason for such hostility.

"What did he do?"

"Nothing." Josie spit the word out as if it were a condemnation. "He just looked at me. He was wearing a hideous eye patch. It made my skin crawl just to look at it."

"The man can't help it if he lost an eye, Josie." Paige's voice held a sharp note that, as usual, Josie didn't hear.

"He probably doesn't even need it. It would be just like him to put a patch over his eye just for effect." Josie tugged petulantly at the bottom of her jacket.

"I don't remember Jake going out of his way to impress people," Paige said, wondering, not for the first time, if it was possible that she'd been adopted. Sometimes it seemed unlikely that she and Josie were related by blood.

"What would you know?" Josie snapped. "You were just a fat little girl who always had her nose in a book."

Mary drew in a sharp breath and Paige grabbed hold of the back of her shirt, giving it a warning tug. She didn't need Mary leaping to her defense.

"Why should you care whether or not Jake is back, Josie? He's probably here to see his parents."

"Well, they aren't going to be any happier to see him than anyone else is. They never did like him." There was a certain smug satisfaction in Josie's voice. Thinking of the lonely boy she remembered from twenty years ago, Paige felt a rare urge toward physical violence.

"Anyway, I don't care," Josie said. "I just think it's a shame he came back. I thought I ought to warn you that he was in town. If you take my advice, you'll avoid him. Not that he's likely to have any interest in you," she added with casual cruelty. "I doubt if he'd even remember you."

"Probably not," Paige said, keeping a firm grip on Mary's shirt.

"Well, I have to go. I've a committee meeting this afternoon." Josie glanced around the library, her mouth pursed in a moue of distaste. "I don't know how you can stand this place, Paige. It's so gloomy."

"Libraries are supposed to be gloomy, Josie. It's a tradition."

"I suppose. You know, it's too bad you didn't finish your

degree. If you'd stuck with it long enough to get a teaching certificate, you wouldn't have had to take a job like this.''

Paige tugged so fiercely on Mary's shirt that the collar cut off her breath, preventing the anger inside her from exploding.

''It is too bad.'' Paige left it to Josie to decide just what was too bad.

''Now, don't forget what I said about Jake, Paige. I know how you tend to feel sorry for everyone, but Jake Quincannon is not one of your interminable stream of stray dogs.''

Josie swept out on a wave of Giorgio, banging the door back against the wall as she left.

Paige relaxed her grip on Mary's shirt, well aware that an explosion was inevitable. Mary didn't disappoint her. She turned, her round face flushed, her eyes fairly snapping with anger.

''That...that...bitch!'' She stuttered with rage. ''I'm sorry, Paige. I know she's your sister but she's really the most selfish, insensitive, stupid cow I've ever had the misfortune to meet.''

''You can't really say Josie's a cow, Mary.'' Paige made the correction blandly. ''You can't be a size eight and a cow at the same time.''

''How do you stand her?'' Mary paced back and forth in front of the desk.

''I don't see all that much of her.''

''How dare she make nasty remarks about you not getting your degree. I suppose she doesn't remember that if you hadn't come home after your mother's stroke, there wouldn't have been anyone to take care of her. Josie certainly had no intention of doing it.''

''Josie already had a husband and child to take care of.'' It was a discussion they'd had before and Paige saw no reason to go over it again. She stood up and stretched, aware of the knot of tension that had settled in the back of her neck. It didn't seem to matter that she understood her sister backward and forward. It didn't even help that Josie's single-minded devotion to herself was so exaggerated that it was amusing. Spending any time at all in Josie's presence still made her feel tense.

She half listened as Mary enumerated Josie's faults. She wondered vaguely if she should say something in her sister's defense but she doubted if she could manage it with any sincerity. It was unfortunate, but true, that Josie really was one of the most unlikable people she'd ever known.

The rest of the afternoon passed in welcome quiet. The citizens of Riverbend were proud of their library, but they didn't make much use of it. She was able to lock the big front door a little after five, drawing in a deep breath of warm air. The sun was slipping behind the mountains to the west, but daylight would linger for another hour or so.

Paige waved to several people as she walked home, but she didn't stop to talk to anyone. She wasn't in the mood for idle chitchat this evening, especially when the topic was almost certain to be her new boarder.

JAKE TAPPED THE HAMMER against the nail, coaxing it into the wood. The thin slats didn't require much force. He sat back on his heels, looking at the old swing with a critical eye. Not bad really, he decided. No one was likely to call on him to build a house but the porch swing was certainly in better shape than it had been. He hadn't planned on fixing it, but the sagging seat had caught his eye.

He arched his shoulders back, aware of a not unpleasant ache. Weighing the hammer in his hand, he grinned to himself, pleased with the results of his afternoon's work.

"It won't do, you know."

He stood up and turned. Paige was looking at him from the bottom of the steps, her head tilted to one side. Her hair fell over her shoulder in that thick braid that made his fingers itch to undo it. She was wearing a slim skirt that revealed a tantalizing length of leg and a tailored blouse in a shade that hovered between blue and green.

"What won't do?" He was no longer surprised by the way she always started conversations in the middle.

"You." She gestured to the hammer as she walked up the steps. "You look far too domestic. Not at all the image everyone expects you to project."

"Since there was no one around, I didn't think I'd put too many dents in my reputation."

"That shows how much you've forgotten about this town." She nodded toward the big yellow house across the street. "Mrs. McCardle's curtain is twitching so hard, it's a wonder it hasn't come off the rod. And Mr. Dumphy hasn't taken a pair of shears to that hedge in ten years."

Jake turned to look at the old man two doors down who suddenly seemed terribly interested in his hedge. When his eyes shifted to the window across the street, the plain white curtain gave a convulsive heave and then was still.

"That was not protocol," Paige said, as she slipped off her shoes, kicking them in the general direction of the front door. "You're not supposed to notice them."

"But it's all right for them to keep an eye on me?"

He arched one brow as she sank onto the newly repaired swing.

"Of course. Everyone has his place in Riverbend. Some people are watchers and others are watchees."

"Watchees?" Jake's mouth twitched in a smile. "There is no such word."

"There is now. You are a *watchee*. You're supposed to go around giving the *watchers* something to watch. Repairing my porch swing isn't what they've got in mind. But I appreciate it anyway." She stretched her legs out, propping her feet on an empty wicker planter that had once been white but had long since faded to a dusty gray. She leaned her head back and closed her eyes, apparently ready for a nap.

"I hope you don't mind," he said, with just a touch of sarcasm. "I should have asked before taking a hammer to your house, but I had some time on my hands and the swing looked a little rickety.''

"You don't have to be polite, Jake," she said without opening her eyes. "The swing was falling to pieces. I should have had it taken down years ago. But I'm glad I didn't. I'd forgotten how comfortable it was. Why don't you try it out?''

She patted the seat beside her. Jake hesitated. He'd already decided that getting involved with Paige would be a big mistake. In fact, he'd made up his mind to do no such thing. But sitting with her wasn't really getting involved.

He stepped over her legs and settled gingerly onto the seat next to her. She didn't move or speak, and Jake gradually relaxed back against the curved wooden slats. Somewhere on the next block, he could hear the shouts of children at play.

A bee buzzed lazily around a fat rose blossom that nodded over the porch railing. Watching it, Jake realized that *this* was the reason he'd come back here. Lazy summer afternoons with twilight creeping in from the mountains. Nothing to think about except what to have for dinner.

Peace. More than anything in the world, he'd come home looking for peace. He let his eyes drift shut, unconsciously pushing one foot against the plank floor to set the swing into gentle motion.

He'd spent two decades traveling around the world, learning to live with danger the way another man might live with a nagging wife. Always, in the back of his mind, had been the thought that there was something missing in his life.

It wasn't the stability of a home life exactly. He wasn't looking for a white picket fence and a lawn to mow. He'd had that growing up and he'd learned that it wasn't a magic cure-all.

After losing his eye, he'd had time to think and he'd realized that what was missing was a certain inner peace, an acceptance of himself, of what he'd been and what he was now. That's what he'd come home to find.

He had no idea how long they'd been sitting there when Paige broke the silence.

"Jake?"

"Hmm?"

"Why did you fix the swing?"

He didn't move but there was a shrug in his voice. "It's been a long time since I did anything constructive with my hands. I guess I just wanted to see if I could. Besides, I used to love this swing."

"Because it reminds you of Josie?"

"Not particularly. When I'd come to pick her up for a date, she was never ready. Your mother would answer the door and tell me that Josie would be down in a minute. I always sat on this swing while I was waiting. I dreamed a lot of dreams on this swing."

"Did any of them come true?" There was a wistful note in the question and he turned his head, looking at her profile.

"Some of them," he said, after a moment, thinking of how he'd always wanted to see the world. He'd done that, though it hadn't been quite the way he'd dreamed.

"I'm glad," she said simply.

"What about you? Have you done what you've dreamed of?"

She opened her eyes, rolling her head toward him. "Does anyone dream of being a librarian in the town where she was born?"

There was a note in her voice he couldn't quite place. Not sarcasm or bitterness. More a rueful acknowledgment that life hadn't turned out quite the way she'd planned.

"Librarian? I pictured you running some chic little boutique."

"In Riverbend?" She laughed, a husky sound that seemed to slide down his spine. "I don't think this town is ready for chic boutiques just yet. Besides, being the town's one and only librarian carries a certain cachet that merely running a store couldn't possibly match. *I* am invited to the meetings of the Library Committee, the Committee to Improve Young Minds *and* the Mayor's Committee for the Betterment of the Community.''

Jake blinked. ''I'm impressed.''

''Don't be. I'm not.'' Her smile took any sarcasm out of the words. ''Actually, it's not a bad job. The library is only open a few hours a day and we're closed Sundays and Wednesdays. It doesn't do a booming business, so there aren't any real demands on my time. The library committee is grateful to have someone with half an English degree, and it gives me something to do. Besides, now I can read all I want and no one ever tells me to get my nose out of a book or that all that reading is going to do for me is make me cross-eyed.''

''Is that what people told you when you were little?''

''Constantly.'' She watched as the bee abandoned the rose, buzzing importantly off toward the hive. ''Not that I blame them. If I was awake, I was probably reading. Actually, it's a wonder I'm not cross-eyed.''

''Your eyes look fine to me,'' Jake said, responding to the almost imperceptible note of recollected hurt.

''Thank you.'' She shifted, tucking her feet up under her as she turned to look him squarely in the face. ''You know, you're really rather nice, despite that gruff exterior.''

Jake drew back, emotionally as well as physically. Her casual honesty was both appealing and threatening. One thing he was learning about Paige Cudahy was that she didn't seem to see the barriers the rest of the world found so apparent.

''Don't you like being called nice?'' she asked, sensing his withdrawal.

When she put it that way, feeling threatened by her compliment seemed ridiculous. It wasn't that he didn't *like* it. He just didn't know how to respond to it.

''I don't really mind,'' he said cautiously.

''I promise not to tell anyone else,'' she offered.

She was teasing him again. He could hear it in her voice and see it in the way her eyes seemed to be laughing at him. He stifled a sudden urge to pull her into his arms and kiss her until that hint of laughter darkened into passion.

"I'm not worried. No one would believe you anyway, so I don't think my reputation would be threatened."

"We can still keep it our little secret."

She made the offer so solemnly that Jake felt a smile tugging at his mouth again. He reached out and took hold of the thick braid that lay over her shoulder, giving it a quick tug.

"You know, I seem to recall that you were a bit of a brat when you pulled your nose out of that book you seemed to have with you all the time. You haven't changed."

"Thank you," she said demurely.

Jake laughed, the sound rusty from lack of use. Leaning back in a corner of the swing, he could feel years of tension flowing out of him.

Chapter Five

Jake eased the Harley to a stop. He took his time putting the kickstand into place, half wishing he could change his mind about this visit. But it was too late. His father had been watering the flower beds that lined the porch, but he turned at the sound of the Harley, watching as Jake swung his leg over the bike and started up the brick path.

"Hello, Jake." His weathered face eased into a cautious smile, his eyes watchful.

"Hi, Dad." Jake walked up the pathway until he stood beside his father. "The roses look great this year."

"I've got a few prizewinners in there." There was pride in his father's voice and Jake felt a sudden twinge of old pain. Twenty years ago, he'd have given his soul to hear that same note of pride turned toward him. But then, he hadn't really given his father much to be proud of, if the truth were told.

The silence stretched, threatening to become awkward. Staring at the fleeting rainbow patterns in the spray of water, Jake groped for something to say. Why was it so difficult? After all, this was his father, his family.

"I think you grew a bit after you left home, boy." It was obvious that his father was struggling as much as he was to keep the conversation going. Well, at least they had something in common, Jake thought with a touch of sardonic humor.

"You look the same," he lied.

"Well, the hair's a little grayer, I'd guess."

"Mine too," Jake said dryly.

His father looked at him in surprise, really looking at him for the first time, seeing the gray at his temples, the lines that experience had drawn beside his eyes.

"I guess I tend to forget that you're a grown man now, Jake. You weren't much more than a boy when you left home."

"A boy with a chip on his shoulder," Jake admitted, half smiling.

"Well, I reckon most of us have had a bit too much pride one time or another."

Jake returned his father's smile, feeling as if the wall that Time had put between them shrank just a little. They'd never been close but there'd been fleeting moments of understanding. If they could recapture even that much, this trip wouldn't have been wasted.

"Lawrence, you're going to drown those roses of yours." His mother's voice preceded her out of the dim front hallway. The disembodied sound shattered the moment like a hammer on glass. Jake's father turned away, twisting the nozzle to stop the flow of water. Jake's smile vanished.

Margaret had pushed open the screen door and stepped onto the shady porch before she saw her son. The lines around her eyes seemed to tighten and deepen. "Jacob. I didn't realize you were here."

"Hello, Mother." Jake reached up to check the black leather patch, as if the gesture might somehow make it less noticeable. "I hope this isn't a bad time."

"Of course not." There was no emotion in her voice. She could have been talking to the mailman, though Jake suspected there might have been more welcome in it. "You're family. You're welcome anytime."

The words might have sounded more sincere if they hadn't been uttered in such a flat tone. Jake shoved his hands into his back pockets, wondering how you started repairing a twenty-year-old breach. No, come to think of it, there'd never been a time when he and his mother hadn't been at odds with each other.

"Thank you, Mother."

"You don't have to thank me, Jake. It's only what's right."

"And you always do what's right, don't you?"

"I try." If she heard the bitterness in his voice, she chose to ignore it. "Trying to do what's right is a Christian's duty, Jacob. It's what the good Lord asks of us."

"It seems to me there's also something in the Bible about loving your children."

"And a commandment to honor thy father and mother, Jacob," she shot back, her gray eyes suddenly flaring with emotion.

"Touché, Mother." Jake acknowledged the hit with a mocking lift of his eyebrow.

"Lunch is almost ready, isn't it, Mother?" Lawrence stepped between the two of them, literally and figuratively. "Why don't you join us, Jake? Mother made one of her potpies. Best in the county."

Jake hesitated. His first urge was to turn and walk away. But his father's eyes held a look that could almost have been a plea. He'd spent the first twenty years of his life walking away from his problems with his mother; it hadn't solved anything then and it wouldn't solve anything now.

"I'd like that, Dad. If it wouldn't be an inconvenience..." He looked up at his mother where she still stood on the porch.

"I've already said you're welcome here, Jacob." There was not a flicker of expression in her eyes. "If you're staying to lunch, you'll want to wash your hands."

Ten minutes later, Jake seated himself at the sturdy oak table that had sat in the corner of his mother's kitchen for as long as he could remember. A blue and white checked cloth covered the table, a fitting backdrop for the plain white dishes. The room was cozy and homey. The rich scent of chicken potpie filled the big kitchen. The scene was right out of a magazine article on country living.

But Jake didn't feel particularly cozy and he didn't feel at home. He bowed his head while his father murmured a blessing, struggling against the feeling of having fallen into a time warp. He had to keep reminding himself that he wasn't sixteen anymore. He was an adult, able to meet his parents on equal ground. He'd made his own way in the world.

"Pass the salt, please, Jake."

Jake reached for the white porcelain saltshaker in answer to his father's request.

"Now you know the doctor told you to stay away from salt, Lawrence."

"Doc Burnett is an old fussbudget." Lawrence liberally dusted the steaming potpie.

"Well, it's your decision, of course," Margaret said disapprovingly. "But you'll have no one to blame but yourself if your blood pressure goes even higher than it already is."

"Do you have a problem with your blood pressure, Dad?"

"It's nothing serious, Jake." Lawrence brushed his concern away. "Like I said, Doc Burnett likes to fuss."

"And I suppose that's why he's got you taking those pills and that's why he has you in for a checkup every few months," Margaret said tartly.

"I wish I'd known, Dad," Jake said with concern.

"There's nothing to know," Lawrence said. "I'm as healthy as a horse."

"If you'd come home a little more often than once every twenty years, Jacob, you *would* have known."

Jake's fingers tightened on his fork. "It's not as if I had dropped off the face of the earth, Mother. I did write."

"Postcards two or three times a year." She sniffed her contempt.

"I don't think you did much better. Most years, all I got from you was a note in a Christmas card."

"Can't the two of you stop your fighting for just one meal?" Lawrence asked in exasperation. "I swear, you argued for twenty years and now you're picking up just where you left off."

His words put an end to any conversation for several minutes. Jake ate his meal doggedly, without tasting it. His mother had put a glass of milk out for him, he noticed. Just as if he were still ten years old. He wondered what she'd do if he asked for a beer instead, but there was no sense in baiting her.

The milk made him think of his first night home. Paige had offered him milk in a Tweety Bird glass. He wondered what she'd think of this tense, silent meal. She'd probably tell him that it was his fault. And she would probably be right, he admitted grudgingly. He had to take at least a portion of the blame for the fact that he and his mother had never gotten along.

He hadn't come home to renew old problems. If anything, he'd come back to resolve them. And he might as well start here and now. He drew in a breath, forcing his face into what he hoped was a pleasant expression.

"It doesn't look like the town has changed much," he said to no one in particular.

"No, that it hasn't," Lawrence said, relieved to have the silence broken. "That it hasn't."

"Some people don't see much reason for change just for the sake of change," Margaret said, without looking up from her meal. "Most of us like Riverbend just the way it is."

"No reason you shouldn't," Jake said, determined to ignore the challenge in her voice. "It's a nice little town."

"With all the places you've been, I'd think Riverbend might seem a little dull," she said, dabbing at her mouth with a snow-white cloth napkin. "I wouldn't think there'd be much for you to do here."

"You've said that before, Mother." His voice sounded

forced and he stopped, trying to relax. "I'm sure I'll fin
enough to do."

She put down the napkin, fixing him with a cool stare. Jak
remembered that look from his childhood. It usually meant sl
was about to tell him to comb his hair or wash his face, alway
in that coolly critical tone that made him feel as if he'd faile
some important test.

"Why *did* you come back here, Jacob?"

"Why does everyone keep asking me that?" He put his fo
down, setting his hands on the edge of the table. "Other peop
have left town and then come back. Everyone acts like I robbe
the bank and was sent off to prison."

"If it hadn't been for Joe Bellows thinking you could do r
wrong, that's exactly where you would have ended up," sl
said harshly.

"Now, Mother," Lawrence put his hand on his wife's arr
"That's not rightly true. Jake never did anything harmful."

"Except that I didn't die when Michael did."

Margaret drew in a shocked breath, the color draining fro
her face. For a moment, the silence was so intense, it seem
like a fourth party in the room. Jake's gaze was locked wi
his mother's. He could read the struggle there as anger foug
with her habitual control.

Her slim hand was clenched on the edge of the table and
knew she was controlling the urge to slap him. He almo
wished she would, that just once, she'd let go and give h
something real to combat.

"I think you should apologize to your mother, Jake
Lawrence's tone was stern. "She's never wished that you
died when your brother did. That was all a long time ago a
there's no sense in bringing it up now."

The words broke the tension. Margaret lowered her eyes, l
hand slowly relaxing on the edge of the table. Jake kn
there'd be no explosion and no discussion. He didn't offer
apology, but it wasn't really expected. The little incident w

)ver, filed away as unfinished business, just as all such inci-
lents had been during his childhood.

"You must admit, Jacob, that it's a little strange that you
hould come home after twenty years of gallivanting all over
he world." Margaret picked up the conversation, as if the brief
ligression had never occurred. She stood up, picked up her
»late and her husband's and carried them to the sink.

"Gallivanting can be tiring." Jake pushed his plate away.
"he few bites he'd eaten couldn't account for the knot in his
tomach. He was beginning to wonder, along with everyone
lse, just why he'd come home.

The knock on the back door was a welcome interruption.
"he door had been left open to allow the light breeze to drift
1rough the house. The visitor was visible only as a silhouette
1rough the screen door.

"Hi, thought I'd drop by to see if there was anything you
·eeded." The sentence was punctuated by the creak of the door
•eing pulled open, as the newcomer, clearly feeling very much
t home, didn't bother to wait for an invitation.

Jake shoved his chair back from the table and stood, feeling
· new surge of tension enter the room. Frank Hudson stopped
·ead when he saw Jake, his expression startled.

There had been a time when he and Jake had been as close
; brothers. They'd grown up together, shared their dreams and
mbitions. But that had been a long time ago. The last time
1ey'd met had been when Jake came home to find that Frank
1d married Josie. They'd fought bitterly. Jake had taken away
· split lip, a black eye and what he'd then believed was a
·oken heart. He'd left Frank with a broken nose, a few loose
·eth and the girl he'd thought was his.

They were both a lot older now, with any luck a lot wiser.
·ank hadn't changed much. His sandy-brown hair had thinned
·bit and he'd gotten a little soft around the middle. He'd never
·en handsome but there'd always been a warmth about him, ·
friendliness that drew people to him. When they were grow-

ing up, he'd had more friends than Jake could count. Jake had had only Frank. At the time, it had seemed enough.

"Frank." Jake nodded, his expression watchful. His fingers curled as he resisted the urge to make sure the patch was safely in place.

"Jake. I heard you were back in town."

"The grapevine has Western Union beat all to hell."

"It always did," Frank said, smiling. He stepped forward extending his hand. "How are you?"

"I'm okay. And you?" Jake shook his hand, feeling the tension in the room ease. Out the corner of his eye, he could see his father relax back into his chair. What had they expected? That he'd go for Frank's throat?

"I can't complain," Frank said. "Josie said she saw you yesterday."

Jake would have bet any amount of money that Josie had had considerably more to say than just that she'd seen him. But there was no reason to bring that up.

"We ran into each other at the bank," he said nonchalantly. "I met Beth the morning after I got home. She seems like great kid. You must be proud of her."

Was it his imagination or was the tension suddenly back with a vengeance?

"I am." If the atmosphere had changed, Frank didn't seem to have noticed it. "How long do you think you'll stay?"

Jake shrugged. "My plans are loose. Maybe for the summer maybe less. What are you doing these days?"

"I got my law degree and I do a fair business."

"Sounds good. Lawyers are always in demand."

"I make out. Thanks, Mrs. Quincannon." Frank turned take a cup of coffee from Jake's mother.

"Frank is real successful," she said, looking at Jake as expecting him to disagree. "He's head of the chamber of commerce. He'll probably be mayor in a few more years. People look up to him."

"Oh, I don't know about that." Frank shook his head, clearly embarrassed by her words.

"They do so, Frank Hudson, and you know it." There was a wealth of affection both in her tone and in the way she looked at him. Jake tried to remember if she'd ever looked at him that way. If she had, he couldn't recall it. Maybe he should have joined the chamber of commerce.

"I've got to be going," he said abruptly.

"Don't go on my account," Frank said, looking concerned. "I can't stay."

"Frank comes by to see us real often," Margaret told Jake pointedly. "He's been a real help to us."

Implicit was the fact that Jake had not been a help. Frank flushed, clearly uneasy.

"Thank you for the meal, Mother. It was delicious," Jake said, carefully avoiding the conflict she seemed to be looking for.

"You didn't eat enough to tell one way or another," she said, moving past him to pick up his plate. There was a plea in his father's eyes that made Jake swallow the words hovering on the tip of his tongue.

He managed to say his farewells without further incident, escaping the house with the feeling that he was escaping a prison. He settled into the leather seat of the Harley and started it up. The afternoon stretched ahead of him. It was funny. He'd come home after all these years and now, three days into his stay, there wasn't anywhere he wanted to go or anyone he wanted to see. No one who'd be particularly glad to see him. The thought came back to him; maybe you really couldn't go home again.

"How could you do this to me, Paige?" Josie leaned one hand on the oak desk, looming over it like a lawyer demanding an answer from a particularly difficult witness.

"I don't see that I've done anything to you, Josie," Paige said calmly. "All I've done is rent Jake a room."

"*All* you've done?" Josie's voice rose. Heads turned, not even bothering to hide their interest in the little drama unfolding at the front of the library.

It was odd how the fact that she'd rented a room to Jake Quincannon had suddenly made the library a popular place. People who hadn't been near the library in years had suddenly taken a new interest in reading. And while they were there, there was certainly no harm in asking the librarian about her new boarder.

Paige's answers had been disappointingly vague, and the curious had generally left with a book tucked under their arms and with no more information than they'd come in with. Josie was certainly providing a lucky few with plenty to watch.

"Keep your voice down, Josie," Mary told her angrily. She'd arrived at the library before noon and had stayed glued to Paige's side with a loyalty that was deeply appreciated by her friend.

"Don't talk to me in that tone," Josie said, turning the full weight of her fury on Mary. Mary was unimpressed.

"Don't talk to Paige like that. It's none of your business what she does."

"Stop it. Both of you." Paige stood up, more irritated than angry.

"I don't see how you could do this, Paige. Have you no sense of loyalty?" Josie's tragic voice was worthy of a Sarah Bernhardt but it failed to visibly impress her sister.

"I don't see what the problem is, Josie. If I hadn't rented Jake a room, he'd just have found somewhere else to stay."

"That's no excuse." Josie dismissed the irrefutable logic of Paige's argument with a wave of her hand.

"I don't need an excuse. He wanted to rent a room. I had a room to rent. Plain and simple."

"It's not plain and simple," Josie said, in a whisper that

could probably be heard in every corner of the room. "I don't want that man in my house."

"*Your* house?" Paige raised her eyebrows, her tone ominous.

"You know what I mean. It used to be my house. It should have been my house." She tugged petulantly at the narrow strap of her purse. "But that's not the point."

"Then why don't you get to the point, Josie? What *is* the problem with my renting a room to Jake Quincannon?"

"I don't see how you can ask that. Everyone in town knows what he is. He was a hood twenty years ago and you can tell just by looking at him that he's no better now. Just look at the way he dresses and that horrible eye patch. And that disgusting motorcycle."

She twisted her purse strap around her fingers, clearly agitated.

"God knows what he's been doing all these years, but you can bet it was something terrible. The man is obviously a menace. For all we know, he's escaped from some prison. He could be wanted by the law."

Paige half listened to Josie's babbling. She noticed that two of the town's most notorious gossips were studying a display of science books near the desk.

The front door opened and she glanced toward it, her eyes widening when she saw who was entering. Josie was oblivious of the sound of the door, oblivious of the ripple of shocked interest that swept through the library. She was only part way through her listing of Jake's faults.

"I don't know why he came back here in the first place. No one wants him here, everybody knows that. I think he came back just to see if he could cause trouble. And you have to go and help him by renting a room to him. Really, Paige, I don't see how you could be so stupid.

"It probably comes of having spent all that time reading. You don't understand the real world at all. But he's got to go.

I'm sure Frank would be willing to ask him to leave, if you're afraid to do it yourself. I wouldn't blame you if you were. I don't know how you can stand looking at him with that awful thing over his eye.''

Jake had come to a stop a little behind Josie, listening to the end of her speech without any expression on his face. Paige met his gaze. There was a certain bleak loneliness there that made her angry in a way all of Josie's foolish ramblings had failed to do.

''I don't need Frank to ask Jake anything, Josie,'' she said calmly. ''Jake is welcome to stay as long as he likes. I've told him as much.'' She paused to give her furious sister a gentle smile before looking over Josie's shoulder. ''Why, hello, Jake.''

Time seemed to stop. Josie gasped, her eyes bulging unattractively as she realized that Jake had to have heard at least part of her tirade. Around them, the library was dead quiet. The sound of a pin falling would have reverberated like thunder.

Josie glared at Paige, a look Paige returned with a smile. As far as she was concerned, if Jake chose to tear Josie limb from limb, she'd earned it. Moving stiffly, Josie turned to face the man she'd so thoroughly vilified.

''I hadn't realized my past was quite so colorful, Josie.'' He sounded almost amused and Paige could see the color rise in her sister's cheek.

''I didn't realize you were there, Jake,'' she said stiffly.

''I've heard worse.''

''I'm sure you have.'' It had taken Josie only a moment to regain her composure. Paige could see the gears turning. *After all, it wasn't as if she'd said anything that wasn't true. And she wouldn't have said anything at all if she hadn't been concerned about her baby sister.* Sometimes, Josie was so transparent, she was almost amusing.

''Obviously, I didn't intend for you to hear that, Jake, but perhaps it's just as well that you did.''

"Well, I suppose it's better to know who your enemies are," Jake said, still with a touch of amusement in his voice.

Josie's fingers tightened over her purse. She didn't like the feeling that he was laughing at her. *No one* laughed at Josie Hudson.

"I'm not your enemy, Jake, but I *am* Paige's sister. Since our parents died, I'm the only family she has and it's only right that I should do my best to look out for her. After all, I am nearly eight years older than she is."

"Actually, it's thirteen years, Josie," Paige added helpfully. The look Josie threw her held little in the way of gratitude.

"Thirteen years," she said between clenched teeth. "You've been gone a long time, Jake," she continued, determined to make her point. "You may have forgotten what small towns are like."

"I've had plenty of reminders in the last few days," he said dryly.

"What I'm trying to say is that it may not have occurred to you that Paige could be harmed by your presence in her house. People do gossip. I'm sure you wouldn't want to damage her reputation."

"For heaven's sake, Josie, you sound like a dowager aunt in a regency novel," Paige said, irritated.

"You can laugh if you want to, Paige, but I'm sure Jake understands the seriousness of the situation."

Jake raised one eyebrow. "Are you expecting *me* to do the right thing and move out to protect her reputation? From what I heard when I came in, you seem to think I haven't a shred of moral fiber. What makes you think I'd give a damn about something like that?"

Caught in a trap of her own making, Josie was speechless.

"He's right, Josie. You can't have it both ways," said Mary, her expression thoughtful. The look Josie threw her should have withered her on the spot.

Paige looked past her furious sister to Jake.

"Were you just looking for a little abuse or did you come in for something specific, Jake?"

"You mean aside from giving the town something to gossip about?" He glanced at the two matrons who'd gradually sidled closer to the scene of the action. Though there was nothing threatening in the look, they both flushed and set down the books they'd been holding. A moment later, the door closed behind them.

"Yes, aside from that," Paige said.

"Actually, I was heading out to Borden Hill. You'd said the library closed early today and I thought you might like to come along. But I hadn't realized that it might brand you a scarlet woman."

"The library doesn't close for another two hours," Josie told him.

"I can take over for Paige." Mary's helpful offer earned her another of Josie's angry looks.

"You're not approved by the library committee."

"She's approved by me," Paige said calmly. "I'm sure they'll be delighted to have someone with a degree. I'd love to go with you, Jake."

She opened the bottom drawer of the desk and took out her purse. "You know where the keys are, Mary."

"Don't worry about a thing." Mary rolled her eyes expressively in Jake's direction. "Have fun."

Paige knew Mary would grill her for every detail of the afternoon. Seeing Jake in the flesh had restored all of Mary's faith. Paige could call him "nice" if she wanted to, but Mary knew "dangerous" when she saw it. And she couldn't have been happier for her friend. In her opinion, a little danger was just what Paige needed in her life.

Chapter Six

Jake had begun to doubt the wisdom of asking Paige to go with him even before he got to the library. He'd only headed that way on an impulse, an impulse he'd half regretted even as he was pushing open the door. If it hadn't been for Josie, he might have made some vague excuse about wanting something to read and left it at that.

But as soon as he'd walked in on Josie's tirade, that option had disappeared. Thinking about the scene in the library, he acknowledged the foolishness of letting his anger get the best of him.

Paige's arms tightened around his waist as he leaned the bike into a curve. Hadn't he already decided that he'd keep his distance from Paige Cudahy? This was a fine way to keep that resolution.

He turned onto the dirt road that lead up the hill. Borden Hill had known various incarnations. There were caves on the north side, all but hidden by shrubbery, that were reputed to have provided hideouts for assorted bad guys in the 1880s.

Twenty-five years ago the hill had provided a place to park and neck. And the long road that wound up to the top had been the site of illicit drag races. Jake had participated in more than one of those until Pop Bellows, then Sheriff Bellows, had put a stop to the races by installing heavy iron gates at two critical points. The gates could be opened, of course, but there was only room for one car at a time to go through.

Jake bypassed the gates, steering the big bike around them, aware of Paige's arms tightening as they came near the edge of the road. In fact, he'd had a hard time concentrating on anything beyond the feel of her slim body pressed against his back.

This definitely was not in line with his policy of keeping distance between them.

Paige's hands slipped from his waist as he stopped the Harley and nudged the kickstand into place. He slipped off the bike, then offered Paige a hand. The skirt she was wearing today was neither as short nor as slim as the ones he'd seen her in before. He was grateful for that. As it was, that slender length of tanned leg was enough to put thoughts into his head that he didn't want to entertain.

"That was wonderful." She smiled up at him, running her fingers through her hair. It lay in wild tangles about her shoulders.

"I didn't think about your hair."

"Neither did I," she admitted. "I probably look like I'm wearing a haystack."

"There is a certain resemblance."

"Thanks. You're great for my ego." She threw him a reproachful look as she pulled a comb out of her purse.

Jake turned away as she began to work the tangles out. The view was just as he remembered it. The whole valley lay spread out before them. Riverbend lay in the distance, the river that had given the town its name curving protectively around its western edge. The air was warm and so still it was possible to hear the church bells in town ring the hour.

"It's beautiful up here," Paige said quietly. "I haven't been up here in years. I'd forgotten how pretty it was."

"This was one of my favorite places when I was a kid. From up here, anything seemed possible."

"Did you really plan on asking me up here or did you do it just to spite Josie?"

He glanced at her, wondering how he should answer the question. But she wasn't the kind of woman you lied to, not even if you'd been telling lies most of your life.

"A little of both," he admitted.

She chuckled, a deep rich sound that made him smile. "Josie never seems to understand that her attitude sometimes drives people to do the very thing she doesn't want them to do. It's one of the things that makes her tolerable. So, if Josie hadn't been carrying on, would you have asked me to go with you?"

She had the most disconcerting habit of asking irreverent questions. And the very fact that she asked them made it difficult to tell anything less than the truth.

"I don't know. I was planning on it and then it seemed like a foolish idea." He shrugged.

"I think it was a great idea. Actually, you more or less owed me this." He glanced at her, raising one eyebrow questioningly. "I've spent the whole day answering questions about you. The least you could do was offer me an escape."

"What did you tell them?"

"The truth, of course. I told them that you perform arcane rituals in the attic and that you're planning on resurrecting great bikers of the past to form The Motorcycle Gang From Hell to take over the town."

She said it with such relish that, for one startled moment, Jake wondered if she'd actually told people just that. His bewilderment must have shown in his face because she laughed.

"Only kidding. I was suitably vague. Really, from my description of you, everyone went away with the idea that you're the dullest thing in town. Let's sit over there. I like that tree."

She linked her arm through his unself-consciously, tugging him in the direction she wanted to go.

Paige settled herself on the scrubby grass beneath the tree, stretching her legs straight out in front of her as she leaned back on her elbows. Jake sat a little behind her, his back against the tree, one knee drawn up to serve as a prop for his elbow.

The silence that settled between them was nothing like the strained quiet that he felt when he was with his parents. It wasn't the same stillness he'd often felt when he was alone, preparing for a job. That had been a waiting kind of silence and there'd been a certain loneliness in it. But he'd grown so used to the loneliness that he rarely noticed it.

This was different. It wasn't a lonely silence and there was no strain in it, no feeling that she was waiting for him to say something or do something. Maybe this was what he'd been looking for when he'd thought of bringing her up here. There was a certain peace in her company, something he didn't find when he was alone.

"I'm sorry you heard Josie say the things she did." She spoke abruptly. From where he sat, Jake could see her in profile. She was frowning.

"Like I said, I've heard worse."

"She still shouldn't have said them. It's one thing to criticize the things you can do something about. I mean, if you really had no moral fiber, for example, then it wouldn't be so bad that she said so. Rude, of course, but honest. But she shouldn't have been so nasty about your eye."

Jake blinked, absorbing this novel way of looking at things. "So you're not sorry I heard her call me a hoodlum and say that I'd just come back to make trouble. But you *are* sorry I heard her make nasty remarks about the patch?"

"That's not exactly what I meant." She rolled over onto her stomach. Leaning on her elbows, she propped her chin in her hands as she looked at him. "Do you mind talking about it?"

"Talking about what?" He'd lost the thread again, just when he thought he'd figured out how to follow her thought processes.

"Your eye. Does it still hurt?"

"No." Funny, that was the first time anyone had asked him

if it hurt. He couldn't even remember the doctors asking him that. They'd been more inclined to tell him what he would and wouldn't feel.

"When did it happen?" There was curiosity in the question but there was also concern for him, for what he'd gone through.

"A little over a year ago. I hardly think about it anymore."

"What happened? Was it an accident?"

"Only on my part," he said dryly. "Although, I guess you could say it was an accident on the part of the guy who had the knife, too. He was aiming for my throat."

"He was trying to kill you?" Her eyes widened, shocked.

"That was the general idea."

"How awful." Her synopsis of the event startled a laugh from him.

"It wasn't a whole lot of fun."

"Was it part of your job?"

"My job?" He looked vague, sorting quickly through a number of well-rehearsed answers.

"Mary thinks you must have been a spy, because of all the foreign stamps on the postcards you've sent your parents."

"Are spies the only ones who send postcards with foreign stamps?"

"No, but they're the most interesting possibility. Mary would be terribly disappointed to find out that you were an accountant who happened to work for an international firm."

"I hate to disappoint her. I did some government work but I'd hardly call myself a spy. More of a…courier, I suppose."

"A courier." She thought that one over while she reached out to pluck a dandelion. "Mary will be satisfied with that," she decided finally. "Not quite as good as being an international agent but close. Why did you quit?"

"How do you know I wasn't fired?" Just when he'd neatly skirted one topic, she came up with another one he wasn't sure how to address.

"I think you quit. I think it's part of the reason you came home."

"That pretty well sums it up," he admitted, slightly shaken to find his motives were so transparent to her.

"I thought so." Satisfied with her analysis, she blew on the dandelion, smiling as puffy white seeds dispersed.

She plucked another dandelion and rolled onto her back, twisting the stem between her fingers.

"So tell me how you came to be the local bad boy. I'm too young to remember all the heinous crimes you committed."

"I'm not sure I really committed any heinous crimes," Jake protested, vaguely disturbed that she seemed to take the whole thing so lightly.

"Oh, come on, you must have committed one or two." She rolled over again, propping her chin on one hand, twirling the dandelion between the fingers of her other hand. She watched him with such bright-eyed interest that Jake felt a smile tug at the corner of his mouth, finally breaking out in a full-blown grin.

"Do you manage to manipulate everyone into telling you all the details of their private lives?"

She frowned, considering. "Most people. So what did you do to get such a reputation?"

"Not much really." Jake's smile faded. He plucked a stalk of grass, pleating it distractedly between his fingers. "I was more obnoxious than dangerous, really. I had a chip on my shoulder the size of Montana and I guess it made people nervous. Not that I didn't commit a few minor misdemeanors in my time. I was the local drag king until Pop Bellows put up those gates."

He grinned reminiscently. "I considered trying to tear them down but I figured he'd tear a strip off me if I did."

"Pop Bellows? The old guard at the bank?"

"He was sheriff then and maybe I would have been a lot

more serious about a career as a criminal if he hadn't been around.''

''Were you afraid of *him*?'' She sat up, curling her legs under her. He could see that she was having a hard time picturing the old man who dozed in his chair near the bank door as someone who might inspire fear in anyone.

''I had a healthy fear of the law. But that wasn't why I stayed out of real trouble. When I was fifteen, he caught me trying to steal a car. Since I fancied myself as pretty tough and had no intention of going to reform school, I came at him with a tire iron. He was smaller than I was and much older than I was—he must have been nearly fifty. I wasn't trying to kill him. I figured I'd just knock him out and then steal the car and make my getaway.''

''What happened then?'' Paige leaned forward, her attention focused on his story.

''I took one swing at him and next thing I knew I was flat on my back on the pavement and he was sitting on my chest. He had his leg across my throat, not putting any real pressure on, just lying there.

''I started to cuss and he leaned on the leg a little. He waited until I stopped seeing stars and then he began to talk. He informed me that I was the poorest excuse for a criminal he'd ever seen and that he wouldn't shame the jail by hauling me in. He explained every mistake I'd made in attempting to steal the car and then told me that I was a little too old to be so stupid.''

''What did you do?''

''There wasn't much I could do. Every time I started to speak, he'd put just a little pressure on that leg and cut my wind off.''

''You must have been scared.''

''Scared?'' Jake laughed, shaking his head. ''I was terrified. The longer he talked, explaining what I'd done wrong when I came at him with the tire iron, the more I began to think he was a lunatic. And you never know what a lunatic is going to do. Then he let me up and told me to come at him again.''

"Did you?''

"Sure. He was blocking the only way out of the alley. He threw me on the ground again. By about the third time he threw me, I was getting really angry. I tried everything I could think of but he tossed me on my butt every time.

"When I was finally too tired to try again, he hauled me onto my feet and started showing me how he was able to throw me so easily.''

Jake stared at the blade of grass he held, remembering the incident. The light from the streetlamps hadn't reached very far into the alley. Sheriff Bellows had stood there, lecturing him as calmly as if he were in a classroom. Jake had at least four inches and thirty pounds on the older man but it hadn't helped. If anything, it just meant the sheriff hit harder. He'd been battered and bruised and was nearly shaking with exhaustion when Bellows started showing him some of the self-defense techniques he'd used.

In the twenty-four years since then, Jake had learned half a dozen different forms of martial art. He could use them all with deadly accuracy. He could kill a man in more ways than he cared to name and hardly miss a breath. But none of the lessons he'd learned over the years had impressed him the way the one he'd learned from Joe Bellows had.

"So he didn't arrest you?''

Paige's prompting made him realize that he'd been sitting there staring into space for quite some time. He shook himself back into the present.

"No, he didn't arrest me. He informed me that I was to come into the office every day after school. I could take out the trash and do odd jobs. In return, he'd teach me what he could about self-defense.''

"I'd almost forgotten that he was a sheriff,'' Paige said, shaking her head. "Martin has held the job for quite a while.''

"Pop was damn good at his job. He knew how to tell the difference between a criminal and a kid who was just stupid enough to be looking for negative attention. If he'd arrested me, and he had every right to, I'd probably have ended up a career criminal.''

"Why didn't he arrest you? I mean, you didn't really know him or anything, did you?"

"I asked him the same thing once and he just said there was no sense in cluttering up the jails with people who were more stupid than they were dangerous.''

She was quiet for a moment and then she sighed. "That's an interesting story, Jake. It shows that you can see someone all your life and never really notice them that much. I'd never have pictured that old man doing something like that. You were lucky.''

"I think I was bright enough, even then, to figure that out.''

Paige shifted to sit beside him, settling her back against the tree trunk, stretching her legs out next to his. Her shoulder brushed against his. She was so close, he could catch the faint clean scent of her hair.

It seemed natural when his arm slipped around her shoulders, natural when she moved a little closer, settling comfortably into the curve of his arm. They sat in that position without speaking, looking out at the view.

It was as if the visit with his parents had happened a long time ago, and it seemed to have lost the importance it had at the time. Paige made no demands, offered no criticisms. She didn't watch him as if she expected him to explode at any moment. She didn't seem to think it incredible that he'd come home.

After she'd combed out her hair, she'd twisted it into a loose braid. The braid now fell against his chest, a pale streak across his black T-shirt. His hand came up and his fingers threaded through the braid, loosening it until her hair spilled over his hand like threads of sunlight.

"I'll have to braid it again," she murmured.

She tilted her head back to look at him and Jake's gaze shifted from her hair to meet her eyes. He could only guess what she saw in his face but he knew what he saw in hers. She looked curious and just a little bit wary. There was nothing concealed behind her eyes, no secrets lurking behind a plastic smile. In the shade cast by the tree's spreading branches, her eyes were dark green. Everything she felt, everything she thought was there for him to read.

Jake's hand cupped the back of her neck, his fingers slipping through her hair to cradle her head. Her eyes widened but she didn't protest as his head lowered toward hers.

Paige closed her eyes at the first touch of his mouth against hers. The soft brush of his mustache against her upper lip sent a shivery sensation down her spine. His lips were warm and firm. It was a slow, gentle kiss but there was a promise of heat behind it. She was drawn to that heat, at the same time knowing it could scorch as surely as it could warm.

Her hand came up to touch his cheek, feeling the faint scratchiness of a day's beard, the solid strength of his jaw. The kiss deepened, slowly, inevitably. It was as if all her life had been leading up to this one moment, here on a hilltop, with the rest of the world miles away.

Her lips parted beneath his but Jake didn't rush to accept the invitation she was extending. His tongue caressed her lower lip, trailed along the edge of her teeth before at last slipping inside to parry with hers.

Paige had been kissed before. She'd found it a pleasurable if slightly overrated experience. This kiss was nothing like any she'd ever known. She felt this kiss to the soles of her feet.

Need shot through her, catching her off guard, stripping away any defenses she may have had, leaving her open and vulnerable. Her fingers slid into the thick blackness of his hair as her breath left her on something perilously close to a sob.

Jake's hand tightened in her hair and then he shifted her,

laying her back in the long grass without lifting his mouth from hers. Paige's arms came up to circle his shoulders, holding him against her as his mouth twisted over hers.

Neither of them had been prepared for the sudden rush of passion that exploded with the kiss. They'd been skirting their awareness of each other from the beginning, toying at the edges of it without really acknowledging it. Jake had been determined to keep his distance. Paige had no such clear-cut plan but she'd had no intention of getting involved in a relationship that was doomed to die even as the seasons changed.

With one kiss, everything had suddenly changed.

Jake lay half over her, supporting his weight on one elbow. His mouth assailed hers, demanding and receiving a response Paige hadn't realized she could give. Her fingers burrowed into his hair, wanting to draw him still closer.

His hand slid upward from her waist, resting against the side of her breast for a moment before moving to cup the full weight of her through her clothing. Paige shuddered, wrenching her mouth from his as his thumb brushed over her nipple. She stared up at him, her eyes wide, her mouth swollen.

His hand was still. His gaze was steady, holding something she couldn't read. For a moment, it seemed as if neither of them so much as took a breath. He didn't speak, didn't try to persuade her. Why was it so hard to say what she knew to be true?

"I don't think this is a good idea," she said slowly, her voice sounding strange to her ears. "I'm not ready for this."

The song of a meadowlark somewhere in the distance was the only sound to break the stillness. His hand shifted to the ground beside her and Paige's fingers slipped from his hair as he levered himself up and away.

A surprising sense of loss swept over her, so strong that for a moment she couldn't move. She shut her eyes, reminding herself that she'd done the right thing.

So why didn't it feel better?

THEY RODE HOME without speaking. Jake stopped at the house just long enough to let Paige off. Then he mumbled something about seeing her later and roared off into the gathering dusk.

Paige walked slowly up the pathway, aware that, across the street, Mrs. McCardle's curtain was open just far enough to allow one sharp eye to peer out. By tomorrow morning, it would be all over town that she'd gone riding on Jake Quincannon's big black Harley.

Letting herself into the house, she resisted the urge to turn and wave to the old busybody. She grinned at the image of Mrs. McCardle's shocked reaction to such a breach of etiquette. She'd lived in this town all her life and she could chart the path gossip took as clearly as if it were mapped out. Mrs. McCardle would call Essie Williams, who'd call Dodie Smith. From there, it would soon be common knowledge.

She kicked off her shoes in the hallway and headed for the kitchen, wondering, without much concern, just how garbled Mrs. McCardle's account would have become by tomorrow. At the very least, everyone would know that she'd had a passionate tryst with Jake. At worst, she would be pregnant with his child. Which would be quite a feat considering he'd been here less than a week. Still, little details like that had never bothered the grapevine before.

She pulled a carrot out of the crisper and rinsed it off before biting into it. Wandering over to the window, she stared out into the backyard, crunching absently. It was almost dark. Where had Jake gone?

She didn't doubt that he'd been upset by what had happened—or had almost happened—between them. He didn't want to get involved with her. She didn't need to be a mind reader to figure that one out.

She wasn't sure she wanted to get involved with him, either. She had other plans for her life, plans that didn't include a man with so many scars. It wasn't the physical scars that bothered her. It was the emotional ones; those would be hardest to heal

If she had any sense at all, she'd ask him to move out. After all, he'd made it clear that he was only here for the summer. And involvement between them could last only as long as the lazy days of summer lasted. It was inevitable that she'd get hurt.

But for a little while, she'd be intensely alive.

She'd walked such a safe path all her life. What would it be like to throw caution completely to the wind? Jake was the most exciting thing to come into her life. But maybe the risk was too high. It was one thing to take a chance, it was something else again to commit emotional suicide.

Of course, there was always the question of whether *Jake* was interested in taking a chance.

IF THERE WAS ONE THING Jake knew, it was that he was not interested in taking chances. He'd spent his whole life doing that and he was tired of it. He'd left that life behind. He'd made his plans when he'd quit his job. He was going to do a little traveling, see all the places he'd only passed through. Then, in a year or two, he was going to buy a small piece of property, somewhere at a pleasant distance from the rest of the world, and he was going to sit and vegetate until moss grew on his north side.

Nowhere in those plans was there room for Paige Cudahy, not even as a summer affair. He'd come back here to bring completion to a part of his life that had been left unfinished. It hadn't been his intention to meet a long-legged woman with hair the color of sunshine. A woman without a self-conscious bone in her body. A woman nearly fifteen years younger than he was.

A woman who made him feel almost whole again.

He bent to pick up a stone, hurling it into the river with a violent movement that eloquently expressed his frustration. Paige had no place in his plans. It would be one thing if she were the kind of woman he could have a casual affair with, if he could then walk away without looking back. But Paige was the kind of woman who made a man want to look back.

Even if she were in his plans, he sure as hell wasn't in hers. He had too many scars, too many nightmares and too little to offer. He hardly knew who he was himself.

No, the best thing to do was to stick to the original plan and keep things between them casual. No more kisses like the one they'd shared today. That had been a mistake.

A mistake he certainly wouldn't repeat.

He threw another stone into the river, hearing the splash as it hit, though it was too dark to make out more than just the faint gleam of the moving water.

Hunching his shoulders against the chill that had entered the air as the sun went down, he wondered, yet again, if it hadn't been a mistake to come back here. He could pack his bags and be gone in an hour. No one would be surprised. No one would miss him.

Except, maybe, Paige.

Staring at the dark water beneath him, he knew he wouldn't be leaving, at least not tonight.

Chapter Seven

"Jake!"

Jake turned at the sound of his name, narrowing his eyes against the sun that beat down on the concrete sidewalk. A girl waved at him from across the street, giving a perfunctory look right and left before darting across. It wasn't until she'd almost reached him that he realized who she was. Josie's daughter, Beth.

When he'd met her in Paige's kitchen, she'd been more casually dressed. Today she was wearing a crisp blue linen dress that complemented her eyes and dark hair.

"Should I call you Mr. Quincannon?" she asked, slightly breathless from hurrying. Just like her aunt, she didn't seem to feel any need to go through the usual formalities of polite conversation.

"Jake is fine."

"Good. Mr. Quincannon sounds old and fuddy-duddy and you don't look either one. Susie Rightman says you look like a pirate but I think that's much too obvious a comparison. I think you look more like a thwarted swain."

"A thwarted swain?" Despite himself, Jake grinned.

"Or a highwayman," she said, tilting her head to one side to look at him.

"You know, Paige was right, you don't even try to be tactful, do you?"

"I haven't found that being tactful is terribly useful," she told him solemnly. "Besides, I might as well get away with as much as I can while I'm young enough for people to think I'm cute."

Jake laughed. Beth Hudson had probably had everything she'd ever wanted and she was, he'd guess, a trifle spoiled. But there was a natural charm about her that suggested she didn't take herself too seriously and didn't expect anyone else to, either.

"I work at the bank. If you're heading that way, we could walk together."

"I've no objection." Jake turned, slowing his pace to suit her shorter stride. "I wanted to say hello to Pop, anyway."

"Good." She glanced up at him, her blue eyes sparkling with mischief. "Susie will be green with jealousy when she finds out I was seen with you."

"I gather Susie isn't one of your favorite people."

"She's a nasty little cat," Beth said, though there was no rancor in her tone. He had the feeling Beth didn't waste much time on disliking people.

"Would it help if I swept you up in my arms and carried you to the bank?" he asked.

"Would you really?" She looked up at him, her eyes wide and startled for a moment before she caught sight of the tuck in his cheek.

She laughed. "I don't think it's necessary to go quite that far. But thanks for the offer."

"It's the least I could do. No one's ever said I looked like a thwarted swain before."

He reached over her head to push open the door of the bank. Beth grinned up at him. "Anytime." She lifted her hand in farewell and moved off toward the rear of the bank, her quick steps holding a hint of bounce.

"Nice girl." Jake turned at Pop's comment, still half smil

ing. The old man was looking after Beth, a faint frown drawing his gray eyebrows together.

"She seems like a good kid. I thought I'd drop by to see if you were free to go for a beer, maybe some lunch."

"Sorry, Jake. I just got back from my lunch hour and Nathan would have a stroke if I took extra time. I swear, that man remembers every parking ticket I ever gave him."

Pop stood up, straightening with an effort. Jake glanced away, pretending not to notice how difficult the simple movement was for the older man. It hurt to see how old Pop had become. Twenty years ago, it had seemed as if nothing could ever age him. Stupid really. Time was the one thing no one escaped.

"Why don't you quit?" Jake asked.

"And do what? Sit home and wait to die?" Pop shook his head. "The problem is, I spent too much time on the job, Jake. I never married, never had kids. It was okay when I was younger. But once you get too old for the job, you don't have much left."

Listening to him, Jake felt a shiver run up his spine. He could see himself in the same place thirty or forty years from now. No one to care about, nothing but a job he couldn't do anymore. It was part of the reason he'd quit, but he'd had it in the back of his mind that he could always go back.

"You've made a lot of friends over the years, Pop. A lot of people admire you." Even as he said the words, he knew they offered cold comfort.

"Sure they do," Pop said easily. He smiled at Jake, his eyes faded but shrewd. "But it ain't enough. Don't ever get old, Jake, not alone, anyway. And don't let anyone tell you about the 'golden years.' Ain't nothing golden about them. Your reflexes slow, your bones ache when it's cold and sometimes they ache when it ain't cold."

There was no bitterness in the words, more a rueful acceptance of what couldn't be changed. But Jake could hear the loneliness beneath the touch of humor.

He talked with Pop for a few more minutes until he noticed Henry Nathan hovering in the doorway of his office, a scowl on his overfed face. Not wanting to give the bank president a reason to harass Pop, Jake made his farewells and left the bank.

Standing on the sidewalk, he shoved his hands into the back pockets of his jeans. The sun was hot on his back. There was no place he had to be, no one was expecting him to go anywhere or do anything. He could go see his parents, but his last visit had been neither pleasant nor productive.

"You know, we have laws about loitering."

Jake turned to face Martin Smith, raising his eyebrows. "You going to arrest me, officer?"

"Not today. It's too hot for arresting people. In order to get you off the streets, though, I'll buy you a beer."

A few minutes later they were seated across from each other at Pat's Place, a combination beer bar and café. The cracked red vinyl booths were probably the same ones Jake remembered. He'd earned the money to buy his first bike cleaning the kitchen here.

"Pat Roberts still run this place?" he asked Martin after the waitress brought their order—beer for Jake and a soda for Martin, who was on duty.

"Pat died about eight years ago. His nephew moved up here from Texas and took the place over. He put in a new pool table, but other than that, nothing has really changed."

"Sounds like the whole town," he commented, reaching for the icy beer.

"Just like living in the fifties," Martin agreed. "Change comes slow here."

"Doesn't seem like change comes here at all."

"Sure it does. Old man Dearborn just sold the '62 Buick he bought new. Bought himself a brand-new pickup."

Catching the laughter in Martin's eyes, Jake shook his head, smiling. "Like I said, nothing changes in this town."

They talked easily. Martin might have made the choice to come back to Riverbend, but he hadn't lost sight of how the rest of the world had changed. Talking with him, Jake didn't feel as much like an alien invader as he did when talking to most of the townspeople.

Jake couldn't have said just how it was that the subject got around to Paige. He certainly hadn't planned on talking about her. In fact, he'd been doing his best to avoid her since that disturbing kiss they'd shared nearly two weeks ago. He hadn't even let his thoughts settle on her for more than a moment or two.

It was inevitable that, living in the same house, they'd run into each other from time to time, but he'd made a point of not doing more than to exchange a polite greeting and then make his exit. It wasn't that he was running away. But a wise man knew his limits and he had a feeling that Paige could push him past limits he didn't even know he had.

Yet, somehow, her name had come up.

"Sure, Paige left home." Martin drained the last of his soda, gave Jake's beer a longing glance and signaled the waitress to bring them another cold drink.

"I wasn't home then, but Mary filled me in on what happened. She and Paige are pretty close."

"Little brunette with bright eyes?" Jake remembered the woman who'd volunteered to cover for Paige at the library.

"That's Mary. We're planning on getting married next April."

He took a drink from the fresh glass of soda before going on. "Anyway, Paige went off to college, all the way to L.A. But she'd only been gone a couple of years when her father had a heart attack and died. Paige came home for the funeral, of course. Her mother was pretty shaken up and Josie wasn't a whole lot of help. So Paige stayed to help her mother get on her feet again. Only a couple of months after her father died, her mother had a stroke.

"Josie was all for putting her in a nursing home, but Paige said her mother wouldn't want that. She kept her at home and took care of her. Mrs. Cudahy lived three more years. She never got out of bed, never could talk."

"Paige could have gone back to school after her mother died," Jake said.

"She could have, but I think she'd lost the drive for it. By then, she'd taken the job at the library, though they had their doubts about hiring someone as young as she was. But there wasn't anyone else beating down the door for the job, so Paige got it. And then, her folks had left her the house. Josie was the apple of their eye but I think they knew she had no feelings for the place. She'd tear it down and put up a condo if she could."

An insistent noise interrupted him. Muttering a mild curse, Martin reached down to shut off his beeper.

"Duty calls. Someone probably lost the keys to the jail." He slid out of the booth. "I'll be seeing you around."

Jake lifted his hand in farewell, watching the sheriff leave before returning a brooding gaze to his nearly empty beer glass.

It was bad enough being attracted to Paige and trying to keep his distance. It only made it worse that the more he learned about her, the more he found himself liking her.

THE LIBRARY WAS CLOSED on Wednesdays, which was one of the reasons Jake had left the house early, before Paige was out of bed. But he found himself drifting back as the sun began to set over the western mountains. Having thought about little else all afternoon, he'd realized that avoiding Paige was an impractical solution to the problem.

They lived in the same house and there was a limit to the number of things he could find with which to occupy himself in a town the size of Riverbend. Besides, he'd come home to find a certain peace within himself and he couldn't do it if he was dodging his landlady like a five-year-old trying to avoid a bath.

Stepping through the front door, he drew in a deep, appreciative breath. The scent of garlic drifted from the kitchen, rich and inviting. Before he could decide whether or not to follow that invitation, Paige stuck her head out of the kitchen, looking at him with those wide green eyes that had haunted more of his dreams than he cared to admit.

"I thought I heard you come in. Are you going to be here for dinner?"

"Am I invited to have whatever you're cooking?"

"Of course. I only cook once or twice a year but I always cook enough for thirty or forty people."

"The way it smells I may be able to eat enough for thirty or forty people."

"Good. Why don't you go pick up Beth and a bottle of wine?"

Thirty minutes later, Jake pulled up in front of a big two-story house, more suited to the Deep South than Idaho. Massive white pillars marched across the front of the wide porch and he wouldn't have been surprised to see Scarlett O'Hara come sweeping down the steps onto the huge expanse of lawn.

Looking at it, he had no trouble attributing its wholly inappropriate design to Josie's pretensions. It was obviously designed to impress the peons in town, but Jake suspected it had elicited more laughter than anything else.

Swinging himself off the bike, he walked up the long brick path. His boots sounded loud on the wooden porch floor. The doorbell rang an elegant peal somewhere inside the big house. When the door swung open, he found himself face-to-face with Josie—the first time he'd seen her since the incident at the library.

She stared at him, her fair skin flushing and then paling.

"What are you doing here?"

"Paige asked me to pick up Beth."

"Beth?" Her voice rose on the name, her eyes flickering with some expression he couldn't read.

"Mom, is that Jake?" Beth's voice came down the stairs ahead of her. Josie's fingers tightened over the edge of the door, and for a moment, Jake had the feeling she was going to slam the door and tell her daughter it had been someone else there. If that was on her agenda, she must have thought better of it. Instead, she tried a different tack.

"Where do you think you're going? You have to work tomorrow."

Through the open door, Jake could see Beth coming down the stairs. She was wearing jeans and a loose shirt, her dark hair flying out behind her.

"I'm just going to Aunt Paige's for dinner. She's making scampi. She called to let me know Jake would be picking me up." She looked past her mother at Jake, who was still standing on the doorstep. "Did you bring your motorcycle?"

"I won't have you riding on that awful machine, Elizabeth."

"Mom, it's perfectly safe. Jake is very careful, aren't you, Jake?"

"I haven't had an accident yet," he said noncommittally.

"I don't see how you can possibly drive that thing, what with having one eye and all." Josie's gaze flicked over his face and then away, as if the sight of the patch disgusted her.

"Mother!" Beth was shocked by the blatant cruelty of her mother's remark. Josie flushed, but she set her chin stubbornly in a look Jake remembered thinking rather cute when they were dating.

"I'm sorry if I've hurt your feelings," she said, though making her apology sound to the contrary. "But Beth is my daughter and I have to look out for her safety."

"Mother, don't fuss so much. I'm nineteen, not nine. *I* trust Jake and that's what matters."

Jake stayed quiet. It wasn't his place to interfere even if Josie's objection had little or nothing to do with Beth's safety.

"What's the problem here?" Frank stepped out into the hall-way, taking in the confrontation between his daughter and his wife in a moment. From the way he immediately stepped forward, Jake had the feeling that the scene was not a new one.

"Hello, Jake." Frank stopped behind Josie, putting his hands on her shoulders and smiling at Jake over her head. "That must have been you I heard ring the bell a few minutes ago. What are you doing still standing on the doorstep?"

Jake let his gaze linger on Josie's face until she flushed, her eyes angry as she waited for him to say that he hadn't been invited inside. He waited for the space of several slow heart-beats before lifting his gaze to Frank's.

"I just stopped by to pick up Beth. Paige asked me to bring her to dinner."

"Is Paige doing her annual cooking spree?" Frank grinned and Jake saw that his front teeth were slightly crooked, just as they had been when they were both boys. He half smiled.

"I gather she doesn't do this very often."

"Once or twice a year. Well, Beth, you'd better hurry before the food gets cold."

"Frank, I already told Beth I didn't want her riding on that motorcycle."

"And I already told Mother I was old enough to make my own decisions."

"Don't speak to your mother in that tone, Beth," Frank told her gently, but with a note in his voice that made her flush and mumble an apology.

"I'm sure she'll be fine, Josie."

"But—"

His hands tightened on her shoulders and she broke off, her eyes dropping to the floor. "Jake will take care of her, won't you, Jake?"

"I haven't lost a passenger yet."

Beth slipped out the door before anyone could change their minds. Jake nodded to Frank, glanced at Josie's still lowered face and turned to follow Beth, who was already halfway down the path.

THE DINNER WAS A SUCCESS. Paige might not bother to cook very often but it was clear that it wasn't because she lacked culinary talent. The shrimp were juicy and moist, redolent of garlic and butter, the rice pilaf was delicately seasoned, the vegetables perfectly cooked. And to top off the meal, she'd made an enormous apple pie, laced with heavy cream poured in just before it finished baking.

She hadn't cooked enough for forty people but she'd cooked more than enough for the small gathering she'd invited. Aside from herself, Jake and Beth, Martin and Mary were the only other guests.

It had been a long time since Jake had been part of a dinner party of any sort. Small talk was a skill he'd lost a long time ago, and as soon as he'd accepted Paige's invitation, he'd doubted the wisdom of it. He needn't have been concerned. These were people who'd known each other a long time and they included him in their small circle as if he'd been there all along.

The talk ranged from the latest news from Europe to whether or not Ethel Levine's hair actually grew out pale blue or whether she had it dyed in the dead of night since no one had ever seen her enter a hair salon.

After the meal, they moved into the living room. Jake deliberately chose a seat that fell just beyond the circle of light cast by the lamps. It was a habit, always sticking to the shadows.

He watched as Beth ran and got Paige's guitar from her bedroom, pushing it into her aunt's hands. Laughing, Paige strummed a few chords and then broke into a chorus of ''Bottle of Wine.''

Everyone joined in, just as she'd intended them to. Watching the others, Jake wondered what it must be like to feel so completely comfortable in the company of other people, to be able to relax and not fear revealing something you didn't want them to know.

An hour later, the more boisterous songs had given way to soft folk ballads. Martin had his arm around Mary's waist, her head resting on his shoulder. Beth sat on the floor, leaning back against the sofa.

Paige's voice was not particularly beautiful, but there was something about the husky contralto that wrapped itself around the music. Accompanied by vaguely minor chords, she sang of loves lost and found, of destinies intertwined. Jake thought it might be possible to lose himself in that voice.

She'd just finished a song about a gypsy's lost love, the last chord still quivering in the air, when the mantel clock chimed the hour. Jake counted the bells, surprised when they reached eleven.

"You'd better get home, Beth, before your mother sends out a search party." Ignoring Beth's automatic protest, Paige set down the guitar.

"And I've got to go to work tomorrow," Martin said. He stood up, drawing Mary to her feet. "We can give you a ride, Beth. Saves Jake having to make a special trip."

Jake lingered in the living room as Paige saw her guests to the door. He was trying to convince himself of the wisdom of going upstairs, when Paige came back.

"There's most of a bottle of wine left," she said by way of greeting. "It seems a shame to let it go to waste."

Jake took the bottle from her and filled both their glasses.

"I'm glad you decided to stay," she said a few minutes later. She was sprawled in a big leather chair, her legs draped comfortably, if inelegantly, across the arm.

"So am I. You have nice friends."

"It's the only kind to have. Where did you find this wine? It's nothing like the stuff they carry at Burt's Market."

"The new liquor store on the edge of town has a pretty decent selection." Jake swirled the Chardonnay in the glass before taking a sip. "Nothing fancy, but some decent stuff."

"Are you implying that the wine at Burt's Market isn't first-rate? I'll have you know some of that stuff has been aged for more than a month in aluminum tanks. Some of them even had an oak log or two floating in them. But you have to watch out for the splinters with those."

"I'm sure Burt has a lovely selection of varietals," Jake said solemnly.

"You'd better watch what you say about Burt. I'm sure he'd never allow a varietal in the place." She raised her nose in the air, looking very haughty. "He does have his standards, you know."

Jake grinned. "I'm sure he does. I wouldn't dream of casting aspersions on Burt's standards."

"I think it's illegal to cast aspersions in Riverbend."

"Probably."

A comfortable silence fell between them, broken only by the ticking of the clock on the mantel. Somewhere in the distance, a dog barked a few times and then was quiet.

"What's it like to travel all over the world?"

Jake shifted his gaze from his glass to her. She'd shut off most of the lamps when the others left, leaving one to hold back the darkness. Jake could see only her profile and the pale length of her hair. She looked, he thought, rather wistful.

"It's not as exciting as it seems," he answered at last. "After a few years one place looks much like another."

"Have you been to Paris?"

"A couple of times."

"What's it like? Is it as romantic as they say?"

"It's pretty, I guess." Jake struggled to remember what Paris had been like—not the Paris he'd known, which had been dark alleys and information passed surreptitiously in the night. That wasn't the Paris she was talking about. She wanted to know about Paris in the springtime; lovers walking along the Champs-Elysées; rich coffee in quaint little cafés.

"And Rome? Have you ever been there? Or Athens? Is the Acropolis as beautiful as it looks in pictures?"

Jake tried to answer her questions about the places he'd been, groping for images of things only half seen. How could he tell her that he was more familiar with the back alleys of the world's great cities than with their museums? He could have instantly named half a dozen hidden corners of London where a rendezvous would go unnoticed, but Buckingham Palace was only a dim memory.

The clock rang once as Paige poured the last of the wine, dividing it evenly between her glass and Jake's.

"You've seen so much of the world," she said, setting the empty bottle on the hearth before sinking back into her chair.

"A good part of it, I guess." Jake wondered if she knew that those wispy little bangs gave her a pensive look.

"I went to L.A. once. I was going to get my degree and then find some job where I could travel. I was going to go all over the world." She gestured expansively, the wine sloshing dangerously close to the edge of her glass. "But then, my father died and my mother fell ill. So I came back here to look after her."

"You could have hired someone to take care of her."

"I suppose." She sighed, cradling the glass between her palms, staring at the pale liquid as if she were seeing pictures in it. "But Mom wouldn't have liked that, having a stranger take care of her. She was a very private person.

"We weren't close, you know." She turned her head to look at him, so much vulnerability in her eyes that Jake wanted to take her in his arms and hold her, keep her safe.

"But you took care of her, anyway."

"Yeah." She sighed again, leaning her head back against the chair, closing her eyes. "People in town thought that I was very noble and self-sacrificing but I really did it for selfish reasons.''

''You quit school and came home to nurse your mother for selfish reasons?''

She didn't open her eyes but she must have heard the disbelief in his tone. She half smiled. ''I really did.''

''How was it selfish?''

''We never seemed to connect when I was little. It wasn't that she and Dad didn't love me. I always knew they loved me. but they didn't quite know what to do with me. I was a surprise baby. After Josie, they never expected to have another child, so they gave everything they had to give to her. When I came along, it was hard for them to shift gears and include me in the family. And I was so bookish. I think they thought it was unnatural to always be reading.''

There was no rancor in her tone, no recollected hurt. But Jake knew the hurt was there. He knew what it was like to be an outcast in your own family, to never quite fit in no matter how hard you tried. Pretty soon you gave up trying, but you never got over wondering what you'd done wrong.

''Anyway, when Mom had her stroke, the doctor told us that it was unlikely she'd ever fully recover. She was going to have to have full-time care. So I decided to take care of her myself. I thought maybe, if we had the chance, we could find some common ground.''

''And did you?''

''I think so. She couldn't talk but we found ways to communicate. She could blink and she could move her fingers a little. It sounds funny but I think we really got to know each other in those last couple of years.''

She finished the last of her wine, settling deeper still into the big chair. ''It was worth giving up college for that. I always thought I'd leave after she died, but somehow, I just never got around to it.'' The words trailed off on a yawn.

Without meaning to, Paige had summed up exactly what he

was looking for—a common ground. Not just with his family but with the world in general.

He'd spent so many years living on the outside. At first by choice and then because he didn't know how else to live. The time he'd spent recovering from the fight that had cost him his eye had given him a chance to think about his life—where it had been, where it was going. In an odd way, it was as if losing his eye had made him really see.

He shook his head. Maybe he'd had too much wine. This unaccustomed bout of philosophizing was hardly his style. But then he'd been doing a lot of uncharacteristic things lately. Like spending time thinking about a woman he had no intention of getting involved with.

Glancing at Paige, he felt the illogical twinge of resentment fade. While he'd been pondering the meaning of his life—or the lack thereof—she'd fallen asleep. She looked so vulnerable. It wasn't just himself he was trying to protect. He didn't want to hurt her.

Jake set his glass down and got up. She sighed when he removed her empty wineglass and placed it on the hearth. He lifted a hand that had been dangling over the floor and laid it across her body, but she didn't awaken. She slept like a child, her lips slightly parted, her face as innocent as a babe's.

The only practical thing to do was to wake her up and send her off to bed. But she looked so peaceful, so completely relaxed.

She weighed next to nothing in his arms. She stirred as he lifted her, but only to settle closer, to press her cheek to his shoulder. Jake carried her upstairs and into her bedroom, angling her feet through the doorway.

It was the first time he'd been in her room. In the darkness he could make out little beyond the vague shapes of bed and dresser. She sighed as he laid her on the bed, turning her face into the pillow. His hands left her reluctantly as he straightened.

Without thinking, he reached out to brush a lock of hair from her cheek. It slipped through his fingers like fine silk. He wanted to sink his fingers in her hair. He wanted to feel her awaken under his touch, feel her melt under his mouth.

With an effort, he stepped away from the bed. Maybe he really *had* had a little too much wine. Or maybe his willpower just wasn't what it had been. He'd almost reached the door when her voice caught him.

"Good night, Jake. I'm glad you stayed tonight." Her voice was slurred with sleepiness, and glancing back over his shoulder, Jake saw that she'd turned on her side, her hands tucked under cheek, apparently more than half asleep.

She looked like his destruction.

She looked like heaven on earth.

It took all his diminishing willpower to continue walking out the door.

Chapter Eight

The annual Fourth of July picnic was one of the great events on Riverbend's calender. Cynics might have said it was the *only* great event. But even the cynics had to admit that the weekend was a genuine, smalltown extravaganza.

A traveling carnival rolled into town the week before the holiday, setting up a haunted house, a Ferris wheel, a merry-go-round and enough rides to please even the most demanding youngsters. There were also shooting galleries and various games that enabled young men to show off their dubious skills as they attempted to win neon-pink stuffed animals for their dates.

People poured into town from miles away and Riverbend took on an atmosphere of unaccustomed bustle. There were horse races and shooting contests where the locals vied for prizes ranging from gift certificates for Hank's Feed and Seed to a new calf.

It was, Paige thought, her favorite holiday of the year. Especially this year. Dipping her hand into the bag of caramel corn that was sure to ruin her appetite for dinner, she glanced sideways at Jake. As usual, his expression was difficult to read. He didn't seem to work consciously on keeping his thoughts hidden. He didn't have to. It was, she suspected, a habit ingrained over the years. It would be interesting to know just what he'd done for a living since getting out of the service.

She didn't, for a minute, believe that he'd been a courier—or at least not *only* a courier.

One thing he hadn't been was a ladies' man, she thought with a grin. The extreme, offhand way he'd asked her if she'd like to go to the fair with him was hardly the sort of thing to make a girl's heart go pitter-patter.

She grinned. From the expression he'd worn, she hadn't been able to tell whether he was glad or sorry that she'd accepted. He'd stopped avoiding her since the night he'd carried her up to bed. In fact, they'd eaten together more nights than not since then. She wasn't surprised by the fact that Jake was a more than passable cook. She had the feeling that he was probably pretty good at anything he set his mind to.

But even though he wasn't going out of his way to avoid her, there was a reserve in his attitude toward her. A reserve at odds with the way he sometimes looked at her. She hadn't quite made up her own mind about where this relationship was headed, or where she *hoped* it was headed. But wherever it was going, she was willing to go along with it. At least for now.

"What are you smiling about?"

She glanced up, meeting his gaze. "I was just remembering how shocked you looked to find yourself asking me for a date."

"I wasn't shocked. Besides, this isn't a date," he protested with an uneasiness that made her grin widen.

"Sure it is." She reached for another handful of caramel corn. "When a man asks a woman to go somewhere with him, it's a date," she informed him with precise logic.

"Dating is something teenagers do."

"You don't have to be sixteen to go on a date. If you didn't want to go out with me, you shouldn't have asked me."

"The trouble with you is that you didn't get enough spankings when you were little," he told her. "You have no respect for your elders."

"My elders?" She raised her eyebrows in a gesture of exaggerated disbelief. She stopped as if struck, turning to look at him. There was a deep tuck in his cheek that told her he was holding back a smile. It was an expression she'd become familiar with over the last month and she found the urge to coax that smile out of hiding more and more irresistible.

"You know, now that you mention it, I suppose you are just about over the hill. Maybe we should buy you a cane. And you forgot to ask for the senior citizen's discount at the gate."

"Brat." He reached out, taking hold of her thick braid and tugging on it. "Like I said, someone should have spanked you regularly."

She tilted her head to one side, her spirit not visibly dampened. "You should smile more often, Jake. Did you know you have a dimple right there?"

She reached up to touch his cheek, setting her finger in the shallow indentation there. The small contact sent a warm tingling sensation up her arm. Her gaze lifted to his and the tingle spread down her back. She felt his hand tighten on her braid, drawing her closer.

Was he going to kiss her right here in the middle of the fair, where half the town would be sure to know about it before sundown? Did she care if everybody knew that she and Jake Quincannon were on the verge of becoming something more than mere acquaintances?

Not particularly.

But as it happened, she didn't get a chance to prove it.

Just when a kiss seemed inevitable, Jake suddenly seemed to realize where they were. He drew back, releasing her braid, almost shaking himself as if trying to snap himself awake.

Paige drew in a breath, plunging her hand into the sack of caramel corn, trying to look as if nothing had happened. Which, of course, it hadn't.

"Jake! Hey, Jake!"

They both turned in answer to the summons. Jake's face broke into a grin. Pop waved to him from beneath a purple-

and-yellow striped awning. Paige followed him over to the booth.

She'd known Pop Bellows all her life. But remembering the story Jake had told her, she found herself seeing him with new eyes. Looking at the two of them together, it was hard to imagine a time when Pop had been able to physically best Jake. It was funny how Time had a way of reversing people's positions in life.

"Paige Cudahy, what are you doing with this good-for-nothing?" As he glanced at Jake, Pop's eyes sparked with an affection that belied his words.

"I thought he might need someone to take care of him."

Pop chuckled. "You be sure to keep him out of trouble."

"I can keep myself out of trouble, Pop."

"Maybe. Maybe not. But if I had a girl as pretty as that willing to look after me, you can bet I'd try to find a bit of trouble just for the pleasure of letting her keep me out of it."

"I'll keep that in mind," Jake said, slanting an inscrutable look in Paige's direction.

"Aunt Paige!" Paige turned to see Beth hurrying toward them, a somewhat sullen-looking Billy Wilson in tow. "Isn't this fun? Hi, Jake."

Youthful enthusiasm bubbled in her voice, her blue eyes sparkling with pleasure.

"Hi, Beth. Billy." It took an effort for Paige to nod pleasantly to the narrow-faced youth standing behind Beth. How a girl as pretty and intelligent as her niece had settled on a scuzzy little weasel like that, was a question Paige couldn't answer.

"Did you just get here? You've got to ride on the Ferris wheel. It's higher than the one they had here last year." Beth paused to draw a breath and glanced into the booth they were standing in front of. "Oh, look at that adorable little kitty cat," she exclaimed, looking at a fluffy white stuffed cat on the top shelf.

Sensing he had a customer, the man behind the counter

smiled at Beth, displaying a rather awe-inspiring number of teeth. "That's our highest prize, little lady. Why don't you give it a whirl? All you got to do is hit the little ducks with the rifle and you can take the stuffed animal home."

"Billy?" Beth turned to the youth, her voice coaxing.

"I already told you I ain't no good at these dumb games," he muttered, throwing a surly look at the man behind the counter. "I didn't want to come to this stupid carnival in the first place."

Paige's fingers itched with the urge to smack him. Beth's look of eagerness faded, squashed more by his boorishness than by the loss of the stuffed cat she probably wouldn't have ended up with anyway.

"If you really want the cat, I could give it a try." Jake's offer brought Paige's eyes to his face. From the glance he threw Billy, she guessed that he found the boy as unpleasant as she did.

"Would you really, Jake?" Beth's spirits rebounded, her face breaking into a wide smile. Then she glanced at Billy, obviously concerned about his reaction. "You wouldn't mind, would you?"

Billy looked as if he was about to say that he minded very much, but after a quick glance at Jake, he mumbled something about it being no skin off his nose. Paige bit her lip to hold back a smile. She'd caught only the edge of the look Jake had given the boy but she wasn't surprised Billy had changed his response.

"Now, we'll see some shooting," Pop said quietly as Jake picked up the rifle. Jake studied the duck silhouettes that paraded back and forth near the back of the tent and then lifted the toy gun to his shoulder. Six shots later, five of the metal silhouettes had disappeared.

"Oh, too bad. Nearly a perfect score." The man who ran the booth was eyeing Jake uneasily, disliking the easy way he

handled the gun. "I'll tell you what, I'll give the little lady
consolation prize."

"No." Jake pulled a handful of change out of his pocke
and set it on the counter. "She wants the stuffed cat." He
picked up the rifle again.

"When he was a kid, Jake was the best shot I ever saw,"
Pop told Paige quietly. "I'd wondered if losing his eye would
have affected that."

"It doesn't look like it has." Paige watched Jake lay out the
little metal ducks.

"He was a good boy," Pop said suddenly. Paige glanced a
the old man, surprised to see him looking at her so intently.

"Jake told me how you caught him trying to steal a car."

Pop smiled, his faded eyes alight with memories. "Wors
car thief you ever saw. But he was a good kid. A bit of a hell
raiser and he never knew when to back down. People got th
idea in their heads that he was trouble and he could never quit
get out from under that reputation. That's the worst thing abou
a small town. Once they poke you in a slot, you stay ther
forever."

Jake annihilated another half a dozen ducks. The man behin
the counter had given up looking uneasy. Now he just looked
resigned. Beth squealed as each new round was demolishe
Billy looked as if he'd just swallowed something with a nast
taste. As usual, there was little to be read in Jake's expressio

"He doesn't show much of himself, does he?" Paige aske

"That's the way a lot of folks deal with bein' hurt," Po
said. "His folks had a real problem with him. After his broth
died, it seemed as if Jake couldn't do anything right."

"His brother?" Paige's head jerked around, her eyes sta
tled. "I didn't know Jake had a brother."

"No reason you should. You weren't even born when h
died. Jake was only about six or seven. He don't talk about i
Neither do his folks. Fact of the matter is, I think most foll
around here have forgotten there was another boy. But Jal

hasn't forgotten. He talked with me about it once. Only time I ever heard him mention it. It was that time he came home after he left to join the service.''

When he'd come home to find Josie married to Frank.

"What happened to his brother, Pop?" Pop studied her for a long silent moment, as if trying to decide whether to tell her.

"Well, I don't know all the details. It was a long time ago. Jake, he'd been drinking real heavy or he wouldn't have told me at all, I reckon. The boy was two or three years younger than Jake, so I guess he'd have been about four when he died. Jake said he was the prettiest little thing you ever did see. He had blond hair and blue eyes, looked just like an angel. The apple of their mother's eye, too. I don't know exactly what happened to him. Leastaways, if Jake told me, I don't remember. Some sort of accident, I think."

Pop paused and ran a hand over his thinning hair. "I pieced a bit of this together myself, you understand. Near as I can figure, after his little brother died, there just wasn't nothin' Jake could do that his folks didn't find fault with. He seemed to think they blamed him for being alive when the little one was dead."

"That's awful. He was just a little boy himself."

"People do funny things when they're grieving. Maybe they didn't mean to push him away, maybe they were trying to protect themselves against loving him too much, lest something happen to him, too."

"That's no excuse. He was hardly more than a baby himself."

"I ain't making excuses for their behavior. I'm just offering ideas." Pop's eyes narrowed on her. "Maybe I shouldn't have told you any of this. It ain't really any of my business. But that boy's been hurt a good bit in his life. I don't know what all he's been up to since he left, but you can see in his face that it ain't been a bed of roses. I'd surely hate to see him get hurt again."

It wasn't hard to understand what he was saying. He though
she might hurt Jake. She had the feeling that if anyone was
going to get hurt, it wasn't going to be Jake. She bent and
brushed a kiss over the old man's cheek.

"Jake is very lucky to have a friend like you."

Beth's ecstatic squeal interrupted anything Pop might have
said in response. Paige turned to see the stuffed cat being
handed across the counter. Beth clutched it to her with one arm
and threw the other around Jake's neck.

"Thank you, thank you, thank you." She planted a kiss on
his cheek. For once, Paige had no difficulty reading his ex
pression. The mixture of uneasy pleasure and embarrassmen
was easy to see and rather endearing.

She moved over to the little group, noting with amusemen
that Billy looked even more sour than he usually did.

"Now that the great white hunter has bagged his game, do
you think we could go eat?" He threw her a grateful look. I
seemed perfectly natural to slip her arm through his as the
moved off down the wide dirt fairway.

"You really made Beth's day," she commented.

"It was no big deal."

"And you ruined Billy's," she said with relish.

"I can see why you don't like the guy. I hope I wasn't tha
sullen when I was his age."

"You were more the brooding type."

"Brooding? Makes me sound like a chicken."

"That's broody and it's something else entirely. Lool
there's a corn dog stand."

"You can't really be hungry," Jake protested, as she le
him across the fairway. "You just ate all that sweet stuff."

"And now I'm ready for some real food. Come on, don
they smell good?"

"Do you know what they put in a hot dog?"

"No and I don't want to know." She ordered two corn dog

hrusting one of them into Jake's hand. "It's not a real Fourth
f July unless you have a corn dog."

If the truth were known, Jake suspected he'd eat a stick if
he gave it to him with that persuasive smile. He'd never been
articularly crazy about the Fourth of July picnic when he was
kid. But seeing it through Paige's eyes, he was discovering
ew pleasures in it.

She had the ability to see things as a child would see them.
he didn't see the garishness of the painted rides or the cheap
ostumes or the fact that, in the end, the house always won at
ny of the foolish games of skill. She enjoyed the spectacle of
t, oohing and aahing over tricks that were as old as Methu-
elah, responding to them as if she hadn't seen them a hundred
mes before.

It was, he decided, not a bad way to look at life.

Halfway through the afternoon, they bumped into Martin and
Mary. The four of them wandered through the fair. Martin won
Mary a vaguely obscene-looking Kewpie doll at the ringtoss
nd Paige insisted on trying her hand at dunking the clown.
Her throws were so wild, there was more danger of her giving
im a concussion than of her hitting the target to dunk him.
ke couldn't remember the last time he'd laughed so much.

It was late afternoon when they found themselves at the edge
f the field that served as the fairgrounds. The rifle shooting
ontest was due to start in a few minutes and, from the size of
ne crowd, it was obvious that this was one of the major events
f the fair.

More by accident than anything else, they found themselves
ear the front of the crowd. Jake looked over the setup and the
ontestants with professional interest. They were a mixed
unch; farmers, ranchers, some old, some young. Some of these
en provided a good bit of the meat for their families by hunt-
g. Some of them looked deadly serious, and some of them
oked as if they were just having a good time.

"Are you going to enter, Jake?" He glanced around, startle⌐
by the suggestion. He hadn't noticed Beth's approach.

"I don't think so."

"Come on. You're really good. Tell him he should enter
Dad. I told you how he won my cat."

Jake's gaze went over her head to where Frank stood
"Hello, Jake. Beth tells me you're still pretty good with a ri⌐
fle." Frank was carrying his rifle tucked under his arm, barre⌐
down, a box of shells in his hand.

"I can hold my own," Jake said. How many times had the⌐
competed as boys? Taking potshots at cans and bottles, they'⌐
been evenly matched then.

"Are you going to enter, Jake?" Beth asked again.

"I don't think so." He shook his head. "I don't even hav⌐
a gun."

"I've got one in the car," Martin offered.

"Come on, Jake." That was Mary. He noticed that Paig⌐
hadn't said anything. She only watched, her expression ur
readable.

"I've taken the trophy the last five years," Frank sai⌐
"Might be interesting to have some new competition. It's bee⌐
a long time, Jake."

Meeting Frank's eyes, Jake was suddenly sixteen an⌐
determined to prove that there was nothing he couldn't do ⌐
well as or better than his best friend. The look in Frank's ey⌐
was challenging, telling him that he remembered old times, to⌐

"Why not," Jake said, feeling reckless.

Paige stood near the front of the crowd, watching as th⌐
contestants lined up and the rules were explained. The conte⌐
was to be played in rounds, with only the top scorers going ⌐
to the next round, until it got down to the last two shooter⌐
At that point, it would be the best two out of three rounds.

There were fifteen contestants to start with. Within tw⌐
rounds, the field was narrowed down to five. Paige had ey⌐
only for Jake. All of the contestants had grown up handli⌐

uns but there was something in the way Jake held the rifle…as
f it was an extension of his arm. He didn't take as much time
iming as the other men, yet each of his shots were dead center.

As the field narrowed to four and then three, an odd hush
ame over the crowd. And then there were only two contestants
eft. Paige's teeth worried at her lower lip as she watched Frank
oad his rifle and bring it up to his shoulder. He took the first
ound and Jake took the second.

She could hear a muttering in the crowd as those who knew
ne history between the two men filled in those who didn't.
lancing across the crowd, she saw Josie watching, her hands
lenched into fists at her sides, her mouth drawn tight. If Jake
as aware of the tension building in the crowd behind him, it
idn't show. His hands were steady as he loaded the rifle.

Paige was no longer the only one to notice the way he han-
led the gun, the calm way he fired off his shots. Suddenly,
ne had the disturbing thought that he'd be just as calm if it
ere a man standing out there and not just a paper target. She
ushed the thought away. Sliding a look sideways, she could
e Mary's eyes, wide and fascinated. There was a certain
imness in Martin's face. He could feel the tension in the
owd as well as she could.

Frank shot first, his shots neatly spaced and all in the black.
ke barely glanced at Frank's target. He lifted the rifle, set it
gainst his shoulder and fired, all in one motion. The shots
me so close together, they were one blast of sound.

There was dead silence as Jake set the rifle down. Paige
ondered if she was imagining that there was something de-
nsive in the set of his shoulders. No one moved or spoke as
e target was brought in. From where she stood, Paige could
e the center. There was one neat hole only slightly frayed
ound the edges. She felt a shiver run up her spine as she
alized that he'd put all the bullets in a space that could have
en covered by a quarter.

No one moved when the judges announced the winner. Jake

turned slowly, his face completely expressionless and ye
somehow communicating defiance as he let his gaze sweep th
crowd. Paige suddenly thought of the boy he'd been, deter
mined not to show anyone how much he was hurting.

Jake saw her start toward him, but Frank was there first, hi
expression rueful as he held out his hand.

"Damn fine shooting, Jake. Congratulations."

"Thanks." All Jake wanted to do was leave. Over Frank'
shoulder, he saw Josie, her face white with fury. But ther
everything about Jake seemed to infuriate her these days.

Paige slipped her hand through his arm and he turned, n
caring if she could see how grateful he was for the interruptio
She exchanged a few pleasantries with Frank that Jake barel
heard.

He wondered how he could have been so stupid?

Paige finished her conversation with Frank and tugged o
Jake's arm. The muscles under her hand were like iron. A
they stepped into the crowd, space opened around them as pe
ple moved out of the way. She felt Jake's arm twitch but sl
kept her expression pleasant as if she were unaware of the fa
that people were watching him much as they might ha
watched a lion who'd just been set loose in their midst.

It wasn't until they were back on the fairway that Jake spok
"I think—"

"I want some cotton candy," Paige interrupted, not in tl
least concerned about being rude. She knew what he though
He thought he should go home, but she had no intention
letting him. "Mary, do you want some cotton candy?"

Mary, bless her, responded immediately, though she ey
Jake a bit uneasily. Paige dragged Jake to the cotton can
stand, thrusting a cone of the spun sugar into his hand. I
looked at it as if he didn't know what to do with it but sl
didn't give him time to consider. Next came the merry-g
round. If he'd looked surprised to find himself eating cott
candy, he looked even more surprised to find himself sitti

stride a garishly painted pony while tinny music blared out of cracked speaker.

By the time the sun had gone down, Jake's expression was longer so bleak. Paige rather ruthlessly insisted that he have n. She hadn't allowed him time to brood. By pretending that thing untoward had happened, she made it impossible for m to dwell on the shooting contest.

Nibbling on her second batch of cotton candy, Paige watched ke and Martin, who were discussing the relative merits of e stock cars that would soon be racing around the makeshift ick. Mary was talking to another friend and Paige was mo-entarily alone, or at least as alone as she could be in a crowd hundreds.

Her eyes narrowed on Jake. She'd never known a man like m before. And she was willing to bet she'd never meet any-e like him again. Her life had always fallen along safe path-ys, as much through circumstance as choice.

But there was nothing safe about Jake.

He was the kind of man her mother had warned her about. :'d be gone with the summer sun. A wise woman would keep r distance. To get involved with him was to court heartache. But if she took the safe path this time, she'd never forgive rself.

As darkness fell, the fair became a magical place. Everything)k on added mystery as the lights came on, gilding the abby canvas awnings, turning the rides into sparkling jewels moving color.

It was nearing midnight when Paige pulled Jake toward the rris wheel. The narrow gondola seat put them thigh to thigh d it seemed only natural for Jake to put his arm around her the wheel turned, lifting them upward. When they were at : very top, the wheel came to a halt.

Paige leaned back, letting her head rest on his shoulder. Be-v them, the fair was all movement and color. To their right, town was a more subdued glitter.

"It's beautiful, isn't it?"

When he didn't answer, she tilted her head back until sh
could see his face. He wasn't looking at the view. His han
came up to cup her cheek and Paige let her eyes drift shut.
was a slow gentle kiss that seemed to ask for nothing yet dre
a response from deep within her soul.

They drew apart as the Ferris wheel jolted into motion agai
Paige let her head rest on his shoulder and wished they cou
stay just where they were forever.

Walking home in the warm summer night air, Jake foun
his footsteps slowing. For a little while, he'd almost manag
to pretend that the last twenty years hadn't gone by. He'd tast
what it felt like to be young and innocent, with his whole li
stretched out in front of him again. He was reluctant to let th
fleeting innocence go.

Paige had forgotten to turn the porch light on and the por
was full of deep shadows where even the moonlight couldn
penetrate. As if viewing his actions from a distance, Jake sa
his arms go around Paige's waist, turning her to face him.

Kissing her here, on the dark porch, was another piece
those long-ago summers. How many times he had kissed Jos
good-night, knowing her parents were waiting inside, counti
the seconds he lingered with their daughter.

But this wasn't Josie and he wasn't a boy. Paige was wa
and pliant in his arms, her mouth parting under his, as if
were made for him alone. The feelings she aroused were no
ing like what he'd felt twenty years ago.

His hand flattened on her back, pulling her closer as the k
deepened, his mouth slanting across hers. He wasn't sure h
they'd come to be inside, but the shadowy darkness of the h
enclosed them, wrapping them together even more intimate

He pulled her T-shirt loose from her jeans, his hand findi
the warm skin of her back. She tasted of cotton candy a
heaven. His palm cupped her buttocks, drawing her upward
that she was cradled against his thighs. She sucked in a qu

reath at the feel of him boldly pressed against her and then
e seemed to melt against him, her fingers sliding into his
air, her tongue tangling with his.

They were halfway up the stairs before a tiny voice of reason
uld make itself heard above the pounding of his heart. And
ey were in the warm darkness of her bedroom before he could
ag a coherent thought out of the desire that seemed to beat
his head.

"Paige." He dragged the name out, struggling to remember
the reasons he couldn't let this happen.

"Jake." She'd unbuttoned the first three buttons of his shirt
d she bent to put her mouth to his chest.

He caught her shoulders, holding her a little away when all
wanted to do was crush her to him.

"Paige, this isn't a good idea."

"Hmm." She leaned into his hands, forcing him to support
r full weight. Her fingers found another button and slipped
loose.

"I'm not a good man, Paige. I've done things you couldn't
en imagine."

"That's okay." Her palm stroked across his chest, her fin-
rs threading through the thick mat of hair there. Jake swal-
wed hard, trying to remember what he wanted to say.

"I'm leaving in the fall."

"I know." His shirt hung open and her fingers were busy
buckling his belt.

"This can't be anything more than a summer affair."

"I know." The rasp of his zipper sounded loud in the quiet
om.

"I don't want to hurt you." The words were hardly more
n a whisper.

At last, she lifted her eyes to his face. The moonlight that
lled in through the open curtains caught in her eyes, making
m deep pools of mystery.

"I'm not asking you for anything more than tonight, Jake."

She was asking for so much more than that, whether she knew it or not. Paige wasn't the sort of woman a man gave only one night.

She didn't move as he reached up to loosen her hair from its braid. It spilled over his fingers, pale as the moonlight, warm as her eyes. Her palms settled on his chest as he drew her closer.

With her, he felt whole again in a way he'd never known. In the end, he couldn't walk away, no matter how much he knew he should. He needed what she was offering to fill his emptiness.

With a groan that was half curse, he bent to catch her up in his arms. Her eyes were fixed on his as he carried her across the room. Bracing one knee on the mattress, he lowered her to the bed.

The moonlight filled the room with silvery brilliance, blurring the line between shadow and light. Their clothing seemed to melt away. Paige's skin was cool against the fever that burned inside Jake. But there was nothing cool in her response.

She burned for him, twisting against the sheets as he explored her slender body. When he finally rose above her, his skin was flushed and feverish, her eyes heavy with passion.

His mouth caught her gasp as his body claimed hers. She was surely made for him alone. Never had anything felt so right, so inevitable.

Somehow, in the taking, he was taken. Somehow, in the giving, she received.

And in the aftermath, they were both left trembling and fulfilled.

Chapter Nine

ownstairs, the clock chimed. Jake listened, counting the bells.
ur o'clock in the morning. It would be dawn in another hour
two. Paige stirred and his arms tightened around her.

They hadn't talked after they'd made love. Somehow, words
ould have been an intrusion. She'd fallen asleep as naturally
if they'd been sharing a bed for years, her head on his shoul-
r, the fine silk of her hair splayed across his chest, like a
licate chain, binding him to her.

Jake brushed his cheek against the top of her head, feeling
sense of peace he thought he had no right to feel. It was as
this was something that had been destined to happen.

Only two more months of summer left.

His eyebrows drew together as the thought intruded on his
nsciousness. He didn't want to think about that. He didn't
nt to think about anything but the woman who slept so
acefully in his arms.

The woman he'd be leaving behind.

But he hadn't lied to her about that. She'd known from the
rt that he'd be leaving.

Did that make him feel any less guilty?

Outside an owl hooted, a lost, lonely sound that found an
o in his heart. He had the rest of the summer. He wasn't
ing to look beyond that. He buried his face in her hair, letting
gentle scent of it precede him into sleep.

PAIGE AWOKE SLOWLY. She couldn't remember the last tim
she'd felt so completely relaxed. Forcing her eyes open, sh
squinted at the bright sunshine that poured in through the ope
windows. Funny, she usually closed the curtains before sh
went to bed.

She started to turn onto her back but the arm across her wai
tightened and there was a rumble of protest in her ear. A
traces of sleepiness vanished and she was instantly wide awak

Jake.

He was lying against her back, his legs drawn up benea
hers, his body cupping hers. It suddenly seemed very importa
that she get up before he awakened. Considering what they
shared the night before, it didn't seem possible that waking
with him could seem even more intimate, but it did.

She inched her legs toward the edge of the bed but wh
she tried to lift his arm, it tightened around her. She gasped
she suddenly found herself flat on her back, his wide shoulde
looming over her. She had only a glimpse of his face befc
his mouth covered hers in a slow, bone-melting kiss.

She gave in without a struggle, her arms coming up to e
circle his shoulders. The crisp hair on his chest teased her ni
ples into wakefulness just as his kiss was stirring all her ner
endings to life. He drew back slowly, examining her face w
a look of such profound male satisfaction that she flushed.

"Good morning." His voice held an early-morning rasp t
sent a shiver up her spine.

"Good morning." She wanted to slide toward the side
the bed but he had her neatly trapped between the bulk of
body on one side and his braced arm on the other.

"Are you all right?"

Her gaze flickered to his face and then away while she
bated the proper answer to his question.

Was she all right? It probably depended on whom y
asked. She'd just slept with a man she'd known for less th
a month, a man who was going to walk out of her life at

nd of the summer. There were those who would have said that
he was definitely something less than all right.

"I'm fine," she mumbled, staring at the hollow at the base
f his throat. She moved slowly toward the side of the bed
gain, grateful when he moved his arm, allowing her to sit up
nd swing her legs off the edge.

That left her with a new problem. Her clothes were on his
de of the bed. And her robe was hanging in the closet, where
 did her no good at all. She supposed that, were she more
ophisticated, she could just get up and casually saunter across
ne room.

She felt the bed shift as Jake got out on the other side.

"I think we should talk."

Paige glanced over her shoulder and then jerked her eyes
way again. He was standing there magnificently, unself-
onsciously nude.

She wanted to run her fingers over his chest.

She wanted to scuttle for the safety of the bathroom.

Most of all, she wanted to know how to handle this awkward
tuation.

"Here. Why don't you put this on." Jake must have sensed
er confusion. Gratefully, Paige took the garment he handed
er. It was the shirt he'd worn yesterday. The shirt she'd so
ethodically unbuttoned the night before. It smelled like Jake,
arm and woodsy. It was like being wrapped in his arms again.

With it safely buttoned, she slid off the bed, tugging the tail
wn to midthigh. She heard the rasp of his zipper as he put
 his jeans, so she was able to face him with reasonable com-
sure.

He looked, she thought, so much like a buccaneer that she
ouldn't have been surprised to see a cutlass in his hand. A
ght's growth of beard shadowed his jaw, complementing the
ack leather patch over his eye. His hair was tousled, as much
om her fingers as from the pillow. Since she was currently
tching his shirt rather desperately around herself, he re-

mained bare chested. His jeans were zipped but not buttone
and rode low on his hips. Her eyes followed the line of da
hair that shaded his abdomen and disappeared beneath h
waistband. She quickly diverted her gaze.

"Paige? We should talk."

"About what?" She stared over his shoulder.

"About last night." He sounded puzzled by her behavic
She couldn't blame him. She was hardly the picture of cal
sophistication he was probably accustomed to waking up b
side.

"Can't it wait?" She sidled around to the end of the be
The bathroom door was so close. She could lock herself
there until she came to terms with last night. Like maybe f
a year or two.

Jake caught her before she'd taken two steps. There w
gentle but implacable strength in the arm that swept around h
waist. Paige cast one despairing look at the sanctuary of t
bathroom before his chest blocked her view.

"Paige? Are you really all right?" There was such conce
in his voice that she felt tears burn her eyes. She was acti
like an idiot. She was a grown woman, for heaven's sake. S
drew a deep breath, forcing her eyes up to his face.

"I guess I'm not very good at this. I'm a little nervous."

"I'm not surprised you're not good at it." Jake's face so
ened in a smile, his teeth gleaming white beneath the thi
mustache. "Why didn't you tell me it was the first time
you?"

Her flush deepened until her cheeks felt as if they were
fire. "Does it matter?" she mumbled.

"Well, if I'd known, I might have taken more time, be
more careful." He broke off, shrugging.

She realized suddenly that he was almost as uneasy abc
this discussion as she was. The knowledge made her feel mu
better.

"You didn't need to take more time or be more careful. I... You were wonderful."

"Then why are you trying to sneak away this morning?" He slid one hand into her hair.

"I guess I'm not sure what the protocol is," she admitted, letting her hands settle on his chest.

"Well, I'm no expert, but I think a kiss would be in order."

The teasing tone was a new side of him and Paige found the last of her tension draining away.

"But we already kissed," she pointed out demurely.

"That was a long time ago and it wasn't nearly enough." He was staring at her mouth as he spoke, his gaze hungry.

"Then I suppose we'll just have to do it again, won't we?" Her hands slid upward, her fingers slipping into the thick dark hair at the nape of his neck.

"I guess we will."

The last word was smothered against her mouth. Paige melted beneath his kiss, feeling her knees weaken as his tongue slid between her lips to tangle with hers. His mustache brushed across her upper lip, prickly and soft at the same time. When she remembered the way it had felt against her breasts the night before, she felt even weaker in the knees.

She wasn't sure what Jake had intended when he kissed her—probably only to relax the tension. But the minute their lips met, one tension simply became another. He broke off the kiss, drawing his head back to look at her. Paige could only guess at what he saw—a woman whose mouth was swollen, whose eyes were slumberous.

If she'd ever thought that passion was a thing best experienced in the dark, Jake was proving that daylight could be just as potent. She rose up to meet his kiss, her breasts crushed against his chest, her mouth hungry.

Jake's hand slid under the loose tail of her shirt, his fingers splayed over her derriere as he lifted her up, until the rigid length of his desire was pressed against her.

Paige murmured approvingly, her hands sliding over the muscles of his back. She'd never have believed it possible, but she wanted him even more now than she had the night before. It was as if last night had only stoked the fires of the attraction between them.

Jake was lowering her to the bed, his hands seeking out the buttons that held her shirt together, when the front door opened and closed with a bang.

"Paige?"

"Josie." Paige breathed the name out, her wide eyes fixed on Jake's face.

"Maybe she'll go away."

"Paige? Are you still asleep?"

The sound of Josie's footsteps on the stairs was like a bucket of cold water, dousing their passion. Jake straightened abruptly. Paige jerked upright, scrambling off the bed, trying to find the jeans she'd discarded the previous night. But there was no time. She yanked at the tail of Jake's shirt, wishing it covered her to her ankles, instead of just her thighs.

"Paige?" Josie pushed open the door as Paige turned to face it. Jake turned his back and Paige felt wild color rise in her cheeks when she realized the reason. Not that it would have made any real difference. It was blatantly obvious that they'd just climbed out of bed, and just as obvious that they'd been about to climb back into it.

Josie took one step into the room before the scene before her registered. Paige didn't need a camera to know what her sister saw. She saw Jake, shirtless, his back half turned, his hair tousled from her fingers. Herself, wearing nothing but a man's shirt, her mouth swollen, her face flushed and her hair tossed in wanton disarray over her shoulders. And behind them was the rumpled bed.

The picture could have been titled "Caught in the Act."

For the space of several slow heartbeats, no one spoke. Throwing a wild look at Jake, Paige wondered just what Mis

Manners would suggest as an appropriate greeting for such a situation.

"Josie. Hello."

As greetings went, it could have been more original. It hardly mattered since she didn't think her sister heard it anyway.

Josie's eyes went from Jake to Paige, the color slowly draining from her face. She threw one look at the bed and then turned and fled as if the hounds of hell were at her heels.

Paige listened to the sound of her sister's shoes clattering down the stairs. Then she heard the front door slam shut. Out in the street, a car engine roared to life and then the car took off from the curb at a dangerous speed.

The silence left behind in the bedroom was absolute. Paige stared at the doorway, desperately searching her mind for something clever and witty to say.

"I don't think she was happy to see us," she said at last.

"There's no reason for her to object," Jake said.

"No, of course not." But she wondered. In the instant before Josie had rushed out of the room, she'd looked absolutely shattered, almost like a woman betrayed.

The mood had definitely been spoiled and Jake didn't try to stop her as she gathered up her robe and went into the bathroom with a mumbled excuse about getting ready for work.

When she came back out, he was gone. She was just as glad. She needed a little time before she saw him again, time to come to terms with the probable foolishness of what she'd done.

She dressed and walked to work, opening up the library automatically.

The carnival folk would be packing up their rides and tents, preparing to go on to the next town. She'd watched them move one year but it had spoiled all the magic to see the mechanical side of it all. Maybe it would have been better if she'd seen a little less magic and a little more reality last night, she thought, carefully shelving Thoreau with the cookbooks.

Did that mean she regretted last night?

Now there was the sixty-four thousand dollar question. She frowned at a book of plays by Euripides before shelving it next to a children's picture book.

No, she didn't regret last night. She was remarkably clear on that, considering how fuzzy the rest of her thinking was. She'd been too careful for too long. The time had come to take a few risks.

"So you started out with a big risk," she muttered to herself, shelving a car repair manual among the modern poetry.

Well, she'd never been inclined to wade the shallow end. She either stayed out of the water or jumped in up to her neck. And this had been quite a leap.

The question was: What did she do now?

It was a question she debated most of the day. Usually, she was just as glad that the library saw so little business. But today, she could have done with hordes of children demanding help with their term papers. Since school was out, this wasn't likely to occur. Today, there was too much time to think.

By the end of the day, she was no closer to knowing what her next move should be than she had been when she'd slipped out of the house that morning, grateful that she didn't have to face Jake again.

When she got home, she could tell Jake was in the kitchen. She could smell garlic and ginger, which told her that he was probably cooking something oriental. She slipped off her shoes in the hall, setting them with military precision at the foot of the stairs.

Jake's back was to her when she stepped into the kitchen. He was wearing a pair of worn black jeans that molded his thighs in a way that was positively sinful and a blue T-shirt the color of his eyes.

Looking at the way the T-shirt stretched across his back, Paige's fingers curled with the remembered feel of hard muscle and warm skin. She must have made some sound because he turned away from the counter, his gaze finding her instantly.

He didn't come toward her and she realized he was uncertain of her reaction. A lock of hair had fallen over his forehead, making him look touchingly vulnerable. He reached up to adjust the eye patch and Paige found all of her doubts melting away.

"Hi."

"Hi," he said quietly, still trying to determine her mood. "If you're hungry, there's plenty."

"I'm starving." She reached up and loosened the top button of her blouse. Jake's gaze dropped to her hand as the next button opened and then the next. He reached behind him and very carefully set down the knife he'd been using to slice mushrooms.

Paige's blouse was open to the waist now and she began to tug it loose from her skirt. Her stomach tightened in anticipation as he started across the kitchen toward her.

He would be leaving at the end of the summer but that was two months away. She'd never know another man like him. Even if it was only for a little while, she was going to enjoy every moment they had.

IT HAD BEEN a rather rocky start to her first affair but Paige wasn't complaining. Jake was a marvelous lover and she didn't need prior experience to know that. He mapped her body with his hands, finding just the way to touch her to reduce her to quivering need.

But it wasn't a one-way street. He neither wanted nor expected her to be passive. Tentatively, at first, Paige explored the planes and angles of him. He was all lean muscles and sinew. And scars.

"What happened here?" She traced her fingers over a thin white scar on his shoulder.

"A bar fight in Hong Kong."

"And this one?" She traced an indentation low on his side.

"Someone was target practicing in Beirut," he said absently, more interested in the way the early-morning sunlight caught in her hair.

"And you were the target?"

"Only because I happened to be in the way."

"You seem to have been in the way a lot," she said, frowning. "Do all couriers get so banged up?"

"Only the clumsy ones." He ran his hand down her bare back.

"What about this scar? What happened here?" She traced her finger over a long, puckered scar on his upper thigh.

"Now, that was a bad one," he said. He sounded so solemn that she looked up into his face, wondering if she'd touched off a bad memory.

"What happened?" Any number of grim scenarios were spinning through her imagination, each more graphic than the one before. Her eyes were wide and full of sympathy.

Jake pulled the corner of his mouth down and shook his head as if not sure whether to tell her the gory details.

"Barbed wire," he said. Paige bit her lower lip, images of capture and torture gleaned from late-night movies, floating through her head.

"Oh, Jake."

He shook his head again. "I was lucky really. He was coming after me with a shotgun."

"You could have been killed."

"Well, not really," he said, seeming to consider it. "I'm pretty sure he just had it loaded with buckshot. I got that scar climbing over old man Grimes's fence."

"Old man Grimes?" It took Paige a moment to transform the images of swarthy torturers to the withered old man who had a farm and orchard operation on the south end of town. "Old man Grimes?" she repeated, her voice climbing.

"Yeah. I was fifteen. He had the best apples but he wasn't really crazy about having them stolen. Frank and I climbed through the fence but we barely had a chance to grab more than a couple of apples before Grimes came charging out of the house with a shotgun.''

''You and Frank.''

''We took off running. It's amazing what the sight of a shotgun can do for your speed.''

''And you tore up your leg going over the fence?''

''Like I said, I was lucky. Frank wasn't quite as fast and he got a seat full of buckshot. Couldn't sit down for a week. Ouch!''

She'd found the tender skin along his side and had pinched him. ''It's a shame you didn't get your rear end peppered with a little buckshot. It would have served you right.''

''You're a hard woman,'' he complained, lifting her so that she lay on top of him.

She smiled down at him, shifting subtly, feeling his response. ''And you're a hard man, Jake Quincannon. Just the way I like you.''

His mouth smothered her smile and she forgot all about scars and old men with shotguns.

THERE WAS NO TALK of commitment, no promises made between them, no words of love spoken. Paige tried not to think about the end of the summer. She'd deal with it when it arrived. She knew he would be taking a piece of her with him when he left, but she wasn't going to think about that now.

As the days passed, it was hard for Paige to remember a time when Jake hadn't been a part of her life. Everything seemed so much sharper, so much more interesting now. It was as if she'd spent her whole life waiting for him to come along and shake her out of her cocoon.

And there was a change in Jake, too. She didn't think it was her imagination that some of the tension had drained from him. He smiled more often. And though he was careful not to let her see him without the eye patch, he didn't feel the need to constantly make sure it was in place, something she knew he did when he was feeling uneasy.

There was only one real cloud in the sky and that was Josie.

Despite the fact that they lived in a small town, where it was hard to turn around without bumping into someone you knew, Paige and Josie usually saw very little of each other. Josie was busy with various committees and with trying to find ways to advance Frank's career. She had her eye on politics, though Paige didn't think Frank's eye was turned in the same direction.

Suddenly, Josie was finding excuses to drop by the library almost daily. Paige watched this development somewhat warily. She knew her sister well enough to know that Josie never did anything without a reason.

The first time Josie dropped by was two days after she'd burst in on Jake and Paige. Paige assumed she'd come to harangue her for getting involved with Jake, but Josie made no mention of the incident. She chatted about happenings around town and what Beth was doing. It was right before she left that Jake's name came up.

"You know, I was furious when Jake won the shooting contest at the fair the other day."

"Were you?" Paige continued sorting file cards, her hands steady.

"Yes. It was silly of me, really. It's just that I hated to see Frank lose. It's so important to him, you know."

Paige didn't know any such thing but she mumbled something noncommittal. She had the feeling that Josie was finally getting around to the real reason for her visit, but she still couldn't tell what it was.

"As soon as Jake entered, I knew poor Frank didn't have a chance."

"It seems to me that Frank held his own."

"Oh, yes, he did all right." Josie smoothed one hand over her bone-colored purse, her expression pensive. "But it wa easy to see that, whatever Jake has been doing all these years, he's had a lot of experience with guns.''

''Was it?'' Paige questioned vaguely, snapping one file drawer shut and opening another. She pulled cards out at random.

''You know, when we were younger, Jake used to take me target shooting with him. You were hardly more than a baby then, you wouldn't remember.''

Josie didn't notice the way Paige's eyebrows rose at that. Generally, Josie preferred to reduce the number of years between them, not increase them.

''I wasn't crazy about it. All that noise, you know. But Jake would just beg me to go with him and I usually gave in. It was so important to him to have me there. Really, he could hardly stand having me out of his sight.''

''That's nice,'' Paige said, as if she hadn't heard a word Josie had said. Out of the corner of her eye, she saw Josie's mouth tighten with irritation. She stood abruptly.

''You seem to be very busy,'' Josie snapped.

Paige looked up as if half-surprised to see that Josie was still there. ''I'm sorry, Josie. I didn't mean to ignore you. All this paperwork, you know.'' She gestured apologetically in the direction of her nearly empty desk.

She watched Josie leave before leaning back in her chair. It wasn't hard to see what Josie's game was. Dog in the manger had always been one of her favorite diversions. She didn't want Jake but it galled her to think that someone else might have him. Particularly when that someone else was her little sister.

No, the game wasn't hard to recognize. But there *was* a grain of truth in what she'd said. Jake *had* been madly in love with her. Paige had been old enough to see that. But Jake's reasons for coming back had nothing to do with any old feelings for Josie. He'd told her that and she believed him.

Didn't she?

"THIS IS ABSURD. No one picnics in front of an empty fire-place." Jake looked at Paige across the blanket she'd spread on the living-room floor.

"You have to use your imagination. It's ten degrees outside and we've got a roaring fire in the fireplace."

"It's the middle of summer. You're wearing shorts. And just the thought of a roaring fire makes me sweat."

Despite his complaints, Jake made no move to get up. Paige grinned at him across the remains of a cold chicken dinner.

"I could think of more interesting ways to make you sweat," she suggested.

"Oh yeah?" He raised one eyebrow, a half smile tugging at the corners of his mouth.

"Yeah."

She'd only just begun her demonstration when the sound of quick footsteps on the porch interrupted them. Jake heard it first and lifted his mouth from hers. She murmured a protest, her hands tightening on his shoulders.

"There's someone on the porch," he muttered, levering himself upward.

"Whoever it is, tell them we're busy." Paige's eyes held an erotic slumberous promise.

"I will." He dropped a quick hard kiss on her mouth before pushing himself to his feet. He grabbed his shirt, shrugging into it on the way to the door, stopping to button his jeans. Whoever it was, he had every intention of getting rid of them quickly.

"If you don't leave me alone, I'm going to scream and wake up the whole neighborhood." He recognized Beth's voice, anger and a touch of fear making it louder than usual.

He jerked open the door in time to see her trying to push away the lank-haired youth she'd been with at the fair. At the sound of the door, the boy released her. He backed off a step when he saw Jake's figure looming in the doorway.

"Is there a problem here?" Jake asked, his eyes never leaving the boy's face.

"Nothing but the fact that Billy thinks I owe him...things just because he's taken me out." Beth's voice was shaky.

"Did he hurt you?"

Billy blanched at the cold menace in Jake's tone.

"I'm all right." Beth's voice steadied, Jake's presence giving her confidence.

"Shall I beat him to a pulp?"

Billy backed off another step, his pale eyes never leaving Jake's face.

"I didn't hurt her," he whined. "She thinks she's too good to put out."

Jake stepped onto the porch, threat in every line of his large frame. With a terrified squeak, Billy broke and ran, tripping down the steps and nearly falling flat on his face before gathering himself up and sprinting down the walk.

"You want me to go after him?"

"No, that's all right." Billy's rattletrap car peeled away from the curb as if it were the starting line of a race.

"Are you okay?" Jake asked as the taillights disappeared around the corner.

"I'm okay." She startled him by turning and putting her arms around his waist, pressing her face into his chest in a quick hug. "Thank you, Jake."

"You're welcome." He patted her back awkwardly.

"What's wrong?" He was grateful for Paige's interruption.

Paige led the way into the kitchen, making a pot of tea while Beth talked. She seemed more angry than hurt.

"You know what's so infuriating?" Beth looked across the table to where Jake and Paige were sitting, her eyes dark blue with emotion.

"What?" Paige asked. She lifted her teacup. Her other hand rested on Jake's thigh beneath the table in a gesture so casual he wasn't even sure she was aware of it.

"Mom was right when she said he was a creep." Beth sounded so gloomy that Jake had to restrain a smile. Paige glanced at him, her eyes laughing.

"It is depressing to find your parents can be right sometimes," she agreed solemnly.

"You can laugh if you want," Beth said, not in the least fooled. "But you know how Mom is when she's right about something like this. It doesn't happen often but she never lets you forget when it does. I'll be hearing about this for the rest of my life. She'll use this as an excuse to vet every boyfriend I have from now until doomsday."

"I wouldn't worry too much about it. You're leaving for college pretty soon. Not even Josie is going to fly to Berkeley to investigate your love life."

"Wanna bet?"

Beth lingered over her tea, telling them that if she went home early, she'd have to explain what had happened and she just didn't want to face that tonight.

Despite the somewhat inopportune timing of her interruption, Jake didn't mind Beth's presence. He hadn't had much experience with nineteen-year-old girls over the last twenty years but she seemed to have more common sense than he'd have expected from someone so young.

She was taking Billy's loss philosophically, without any breast-beating or wailing about a blighted life. He didn't doubt that she was hurt, but she seemed to have a firm grasp on the fact that this was hardly the end of the world.

Oddly pragmatic, considering her mother's character. But Frank had always been a sensible sort. She must take after her father, he decided.

It was approaching eleven o'clock when Beth decided it was late enough for her to go home without having to explain herself. Jake took her home on the Harley. Beth was young enough to enjoy the ride, despite the recent blow to her love life.

He brought the bike to a halt at the end of the driveway so

that no one would hear its distinctive roar, forcing explanations Beth didn't want to give just yet. Balancing the big bike, he reached back a hand to help her slide off.

Feeling her eyes on his, Jake turned his head. In the moonlight, she looked very young and very serious.

"I want to thank you for what you did tonight, Jake."

"It wasn't much. I don't think he'd have hurt you, even if I hadn't been there."

"Maybe not. But it was sure nice to have you there."

She hesitated and Jake had the feeling that she was debating whether or not to say something more. He waited, his feet braced on either side of the bike. The night air was slightly cool. Paige was waiting for him. There was a pleasant sense of anticipation in the knowledge of that.

"Are you in love with Paige?"

The question startled him. It startled him even more to realize that the answer wasn't as easy to give as he'd have liked.

"I don't think that's something I want to discuss with you," he said carefully.

"I know it's none of my business. But Paige is really special. I don't want to see her get hurt."

"I don't, either."

Beth hovered a moment longer, as if wanting to say something more. Perhaps she decided she'd pushed her luck as far as she dared. With a mumbled good-night, she ran up the driveway toward the big house.

Jake watched her go, his eyebrows hooked together in a frown. He'd told her the truth when he'd said he didn't want to see Paige get hurt.

The question was: Was it already too late to prevent it?

Chapter Ten

August slipped slowly, inexorably by. Paige avoided looking at calendars and refused to think about summer's end. It didn't seem possible that there'd been a time when Jake hadn't been a part of her life, and she wasn't going to think about a time when he wouldn't be again.

They talked of anything and everything. Anything but his leaving and everything but the future.

She told herself it was enough and almost managed to believe it.

She submerged herself in the present, aware in the back of her mind, that she was creating warm memories to hold against what might be a very cold winter.

The only thorn on the rose of her days was Josie's niggling little comments about how special she and Jake had been together, how much he'd loved her, how he'd sworn to always love her. For the most part, Paige could ignore her remarks, recognizing them for the barbs they were. But doubts lingered in the back of her mind.

If she and Jake had some spoken commitment, she might have asked him, might have let him reassure her. But that wasn't the case and she told herself she was being a fool to let any of Josie's mud stick at all.

She wasn't going to worry about anything beyond living life

to the fullest. After all, the here and now were all the guarantees anyone had.

Her here and now was Jake. The future could go hang.

"SORRY I'M LATE." Mary slipped into the booth, settling herself into a seat across from Paige. Her short dark hair was tumbled around her face and her cheeks were flushed from hurrying.

"That's okay. I was just enjoying the ambience while I waited."

"Ambience? In Maisie's? You must be delirious. Or in love." The last was said with what Mary believed to be a casual air.

"Maybe it's the heat," Paige suggested, pretending that she hadn't noticed the innuendo.

Ethel, Maisie's only waitress, appeared beside the table, her lavender hair immaculately coiffed in a style that hadn't changed in thirty years.

"You girls ready to order?"

They both ordered hamburgers, fondly labeled a "speciality" on the plastic-covered menu. In truth, it had been so long since anyone had ordered anything but a hamburger, it was possible the cook would have been thrown into confusion if something different had been requested.

Ethel lingered after writing down the order. "I hear Jake Quincannon's been staying at your place, Paige."

Paige saw Mary roll her eyes but she kept her tone pleasant.

"Yes, he has."

"Don't see much of him around town."

"I guess he hasn't had much reason to spend time in town."

"I saw him when he came in that first day, you know," Ethel said, fussing with the salt and pepper shaker, arranging them just so in the metal holder that was attached to the edge of the table.

"So I heard from several different people." Ethel gave Paige a sharp look, wondering if Paige was implying that she gossiped, which the good Lord knew she certainly didn't. But Paige's expression was blandly pleasant, not a hint of sarcasm to be read.

"I knew him right away," she continued importantly. "It's been twenty years but I knew him right off. Couldn't be anybody else with that wicked look about him. He looked just the same when he was a boy. Younger, of course, but that same look. Always looked like he was up to no good."

"That's funny. I don't remember Jake getting into much trouble when he lived here before." Paige's tone remained even but her eyes had taken on a chill.

"You're too young to remember much about him. He was trouble, all right. Clean through. I swear, I used to pity poor Margaret havin' a son like that."

"Really? Just what did Jake do that was so terrible?"

"It wasn't what he did so much," Ethel said. "It was the way he looked. Sort of arrogant and know-it-all."

"So because you didn't like the way he looked, you labeled him a troublemaker?"

"Well, it wasn't just that," Ethel said, not sure how she'd come to be on the defensive.

"Then he *did* do something specific?" Paige pressed ruthlessly.

"Well...I...Not that I recall right off the bat," Ethel stammered.

"I didn't think so." Paige's smile would have done justice to a shark. "Would you add a side order of fries to that order, please?"

Ethel nodded, grateful for a chance to retreat.

"You were a little hard on her, weren't you?" Mary asked.

"I'm tired of hearing how bad Jake was, when not one person can substantiate it."

"You know," Mary said carefully, "some people would say that where there's smoke there's fire."

"And it's probably just a smudge pot. Look, I'm not saying he was a saint, but the way the people in this town act, you'd think he was Dracula or something."

She leaned back as Ethel set two milk shakes in front of them, then scurried off without a word.

"I think you've scared her," Mary said, reaching for her chocolate shake.

"Good. She's the most notorious gossip in town."

"So, how is Jake?"

"He's fine." Paige stirred her milk shake with her straw.

"I haven't seen him around and Martin hasn't mentioned seeing much of him. Not since the fair."

"He's been doing a lot of work around the house. He seems to be enjoying himself and I'm not going to complain. The window in the kitchen hasn't worked since Dad died and he fixed the leak in the basement."

"Paige." Mary fixed her friend with a worried look that sat oddly on her round face. "You're not falling in love with him, are you?"

"I haven't decided yet," Paige said in a flip tone.

"I know it's none of my business but I don't want to see you get hurt. And if he's leaving at the end of the summer, it would be a big mistake to fall in love with him. I'm not saying he's not a great guy and all. Although I've got to be honest and say he makes me kind of nervous. But it's just not a good idea to go falling in love with someone you know is leaving in a month."

"Mary." Paige stretched her hand across the table, catching her friend's fingers, which were mutilating a straw wrapper. "I appreciate your concern."

"It's just that you're my best friend and I want to see you happy."

"That makes two of us," Paige said lightly. "I'm not even sure what I feel about Jake. But he's a good man and I—care—about him. And I'm not going to worry about the end of the summer till it gets here. Now, tell me how the new book is going.''

Mary was willing to let herself be distracted and the conversation turned to other things. Paige listened somewhat absently to the problems Mary was having with a recalcitrant character, who simply didn't want to do any of the things she thought he should do.

When they said goodbye in front of Maisie's, thick gray clouds were scudding across a steely sky. It looked as though the rain that had been threatening for two days was finally going to arrive.

Paige brushed her hair back over her shoulders. She slipped her hands into the pockets of her jeans, and considered her options. The library was only open half days during the month of August, so the afternoon stretched out in front of her. She could go to Harl's Department Store. Mary had said that they had received a new shipment of shoes. She could go to the little park behind the courthouse and feed the ducks.

Or she could go home and see what Jake was up to.

JAKE WIPED the back of his hand across his forehead, brushing away beads of sweat. Glancing out the garage door, he could see heavy clouds. They seemed to press down on the land, holding the heat to the ground like a thick blanket. It had clouded up like this the last two afternoons but it hadn't rained. There was a good chance the storm would break this afternoon.

With a last glance at the sky, he turned his attention once more to the maple table he'd spent the morning sanding. It had been sitting on the back porch, layers of grime and a scuffed finish hiding the beauty of the wood. When he'd mentioned it to Paige, she'd shrugged and told him it had been there ever since she could remember.

He wasn't sure just why he'd decided to refinish it. Woodworking had never been a hobby of his. But it had seemed a shame to leave the warm beauty of the wood hidden. And

aybe he liked the idea that, when he left, he'd leave some-
ing behind that was in better shape than it had been.

Running his hand over the smooth grain, he half smiled. It
ad been a long time since he'd spent time doing something
ke this, something simple and productive. There was no hid-
en subtext, no need to look for deeper meanings. The wood
sponded to his efforts in a gratifyingly straightforward way.

Shaking his head, he picked up the sanding block and re-
aced the worn sandpaper with a finer grade. He was really
sing it when he began seeing the meaning of life in a simple
finishing job.

He ran the sanding block over the table top, using long
raight strokes, smoothing the grain. The temperature hovered
the eighties and the humidity felt almost as high. He'd dis-
rded his shirt earlier and his torso gleamed with a fine sheen
sweat.

"I don't remember you wanting to be a carpenter."

Jake cursed as he came down too hard on the sanding block,
e corner digging a shallow groove into the wood. Absorbed
his task, he hadn't heard Josie's approach. He straightened,
s hand automatically checking the eye patch as he turned and
oked at her.

She was standing just inside the door, wearing a pair of
lored ivory linen slacks and a blue silk blouse that looked
mpletely out of place in the cluttered garage.

"Josie," he said flatly, letting her name serve as a greeting.
'aige isn't home."

"I know." She came farther in, running her fingers over a
sty bike frame. "This used to be my bike. Remember how
ride out to the lake to meet you?"

"I remember how you used to complain about the road being
rough."

Josie slanted him an unreadable glance, wandering around
e edge of the garage, touching things here and there, her
pression pensive. Jake watched her warily. As far as he

knew, Josie thought he was one short step above an ax mu
derer. She'd avoided him quite successfully all summer. In fac
he hadn't even seen her since the morning she'd walked in c
him and Paige. So if she knew Paige was gone, why was sh
here?

"We had some good times, didn't we, Jake?"

"I suppose so."

"Do you ever think about those times?"

"Not much."

Her mouth tightened for a moment before she seemed
make a conscious effort to relax it into a soft smile.

"I think about them." Her meanderings had brought h
around the table until she stood in front of him. Now sh
looked up at him, her expression wistful. "Those were son
of the best times of my life."

"Were they?" She was too close but there was no way I
could move away without making it obvious. She had hi
neatly trapped. He reached for his shirt, feeling suddenly nake

"We were so much in love. I don't think you ever get ov
your first love completely."

"It was a long time ago, Josie. We were kids." He shrugg
into his shirt.

"We were old enough to know we loved each other. O
enough to make love."

"It doesn't take any maturity to do that," he said dry
wishing she'd back off.

"Don't you sometimes wonder what it would have been li
if you hadn't gone away, if I hadn't married Frank?"

"Not really." He didn't care if he was less than tactful. I
didn't like the direction this conversation was taking.

"I do. We were so good together, Jake. You remember he
it was between us. You couldn't get enough of me."

"I was a nineteen-year-old boy, Josie. I hate to be blunt, I
nineteen-year-old boys don't require a great deal of emotio
commitment as a prerequisite for sex."

Something flashed in her eyes, something very close to ha-
ed but it was gone so quickly he thought he'd imagined it.

She moved closer. He'd already retreated until his back was
ressed against a pile of boxes. Unless he darted around her
ke a frightened rabbit, there was nowhere left to go.

"It was more than that, Jake. We were in love. We had
mething special."

"It was twenty years ago, Josie."

She set her hands against his chest, bare between the open
des of his shirt. Her eyes were full of soulful nostalgia as she
oked up at him.

"Something so intense doesn't just die. Isn't there still a
ark there?"

Looking at her, Jake found it hard to remember why he'd
ice thought himself so passionately in love with her. So in
ve that he'd wanted to kill his best friend over her. Had she
en this shallow even then?

She was Paige's sister, he reminded himself. They might not
close but Paige would probably prefer it if he used a little
ct, rather than just shoving the woman away.

"Josie, it was a very long time ago. We were different peo-
e then. Even if that weren't the case, Paige and I are...
volved."

It seemed such an anemic word to describe his relationship
th Paige. He might as well not have spoken for all the effect
had.

"I know you still want me, Jake." Before he could prevent
she threw her arms around his neck and pressed her mouth
his.

Jake jerked back as if she were an adder. His hands caught
r shoulders, none too gently, thrusting her away. Josie stared
him, reading the revulsion he couldn't hide. An ugly flush
ntled her cheeks. Her mouth tightened into a pinched line.

"You can't possibly prefer *her* to me," she said, spitting the
rds out.

The light dawned and Jake wondered how he could hav been so stupid that he hadn't seen it from the start. This wasn about him. It was about Paige. She didn't really want him all. She just couldn't stand the thought that he was sleepin with Paige, not out of any lingering feelings for him or becau: she was worried about her sister. She simply didn't want an one else to have something that she'd once considered hers.

He didn't even try to hide the contempt he felt. "Paige ten times the woman you ever hoped to be, Josie."

Outside, thunder rumbled. Fat drops of rain began to fall the storm broke at last. Josie stared at him, fully aware of h contempt. Her angry flush faded, leaving a pallor broken on by her carefully applied rouge, now ugly steaks of color on h ashen face.

Never in her life had she lost anything to Paige. *She'd* be the golden girl, the one their parents had loved first and be: *She'd* been prom queen. *She'd* married well. *She* had a positic in society. It wasn't possible that anyone could prefer Paige her. Paige, with her casual clothes and carelessly styled ha Paige, who'd rather read a book than attend a party.

Jake read the emotions flickering across her face. Disbeli shock, rage. She simply couldn't believe that he would reje her. She'd probably thought he'd be grateful that she'd co descend to offer herself to him.

"Paige will be home soon. I suggest you leave before s arrives."

He pushed past her without waiting for a response. Ra splattered his shoulders as he crossed the short distance to t house. The screen door banged shut behind him. Stripping his shirt on his way upstairs, he headed straight for the show He felt dirty in a way that had little to do with the sweat he worked up sanding the table.

Josie's perfume seemed to cling to his clothes, the feel her hands still lingered on his chest. He pulled off his jea and turned on the shower with a wrenching motion. All

anted was to wash away the smell and feel of Josie from his
kin.

AIGE PUSHED OPEN the front door, pausing to shake the rain
om her hair before stepping into the hall. Luckily, she'd been
most home before the rain really started to come down.

"Jake?"

She shut the door behind her, tilting her head as she listened
r a response. The garage door was open and the Harley
arked just inside, so she knew he was home. She was about
call again when she heard the pipes bang as the shower was
ut off too quickly.

Grinning, she started up the stairs. It would be fun to surprise
m. What better way to spend a rainy afternoon than in bed?
e took the last half of the stairway two steps at a time.

She already had her fingers on the buttons of her blouse as
e pushed open the bedroom door. She came to a dead stop,
eling as if she'd just been kicked in the gut.

Josie started up from the bed, naked to where the sheet
aped across her waist. Her clothing lay tossed over a chair.
er usually immaculate hair was tousled.

"Paige!" She looked the very picture of guilt as she sat there
the middle of the bed.

The bed where she and Jake had made love only that morn-
g, Paige thought dully.

"Oh, Paige, I'm so sorry. Jake and I...I mean, we just..."
sie stammered. "I didn't mean for you to find out this way.
did try to warn you," she said, ending on a vaguely self-
ghteous note.

Josie's breasts were starting to sag, Paige noted. Had Jake
ticed that? Of course, he'd probably had other things on his
nd. How many times had Josie hinted at the possibility that
and Jake would get back together? Had it been going on
along?

Uneasy at the protracted silence, Josie drew the sheet up to her shoulders. She should say something, do something, Paige thought. But she couldn't seem to move, couldn't seem to think.

Somewhere deep inside her, someone was screaming.

Before she could break the spell that held her rooted to the spot, the bathroom door opened and Jake stood framed in the opening. Paige turned her head to look at him, her neck stiff

He wore nothing but a towel draped low on his hips. Moisture beaded on his shoulders and caught in the mat of hair on his chest, making his skin gleam like damp copper. His hair was damp, falling into a heavy wave onto his forehead, touching the black leather patch over his left eye.

The other eye widened as he took in the scene before him—Josie in the midst of the tumbled sheets, Paige standing as frozen in the doorway.

If Paige had been looking at Josie, she might have seen the fear that flared in her eyes when she saw Jake. But Paige looked only at Jake, such hurt and betrayal in her eyes that Jake felt the look as if it were a knife in his chest.

''Paige.''

His voice was hoarse as he took a step forward, reaching out one hand.

The movement broke her frozen stance. Before he could stop her, she spun on her heel and ran from the room as if pursued by demons.

Jake whirled, snatching up his jeans from the bathroom floor and thrusting his legs into them.

''She'll never believe you,'' Josie said spitefully as he reached the bedroom door. The look of rage he shot her made her flinch.

''You'd better be gone when I get back.'' His quiet tone made the words more menacing than if he'd shouted threats.

He'd already dismissed Josie from his mind as he ran down the stairs. He'd heard the front door bang behind Paige seconds after she'd run from the room. He had to find her, had to explain that it wasn't what it had looked like.

Paige was halfway down the street when she heard the front door slam again. She was oblivious of the rain that was now coming down heavily, soaking her clothes and hair. She was blind to everything but the stabbing pain in her chest.

"Paige."

The sound of Jake's voice deepened the pain and she walked faster, trying to escape the hurt as much as the man who'd caused it. The concrete was cold beneath her bare feet. She'd kicked off her shoes when she'd gotten home, when she'd planned on creeping upstairs to surprise Jake. Wasn't it funny that she was the one who'd been surprised. A stone on the sidewalk bruised her heel but the pain only registered vaguely.

"Paige."

His hand came down on her shoulder, spinning her around to face him. She stared at his bare chest, refusing to lift her eyes any higher.

"It wasn't what you think."

She shrugged. "It doesn't matter," she said without emotion.

"Look at me." When she didn't move, Jake grabbed her by the shoulders, his fingers bruising with urgency. "Paige, look at me."

Hot tears slipped from the corners of her eyes to mingle with the cool rain. Jake gave her a quick shake, demanding her attention, demanding that she listen.

"Nothing happened, Paige."

"It's none of my business."

"Nothing happened," he repeated, trying to break through the wall of ice she was setting between them.

"There's no commitment between us."

"Dammit, Paige!" He shook her again, less gently this time. "I did not sleep with Josie."

"It's none of my business," she said again.

"Look at me, dammit." Frustrated, he grabbed her chin, forcing her face up until she had no choice but to meet his gaze.

"I did not sleep with Josie."

"It's none of my business."

"If you say that one more time, I'm going to shake you until your teeth rattle." Frustration deepened his voice to a rough growl. "I didn't sleep with your sister. It was a setup. Nothing happened between us except that she offered me her dubious charms and I turned her down. She was angry."

Paige blinked up at him, her lashes heavy with tears and rain. The tight pain in her chest eased enough to allow her to breathe. It sounded plausible. Josie *was* capable of almost anything when she was angry.

"Nothing happened?" she asked, her voice shaky.

His hand gentled her face, his thumb coming up to brush rain and tears from her cheeks.

"Nothing. Even if I wanted to sleep with another woman, do you really think I'd bring her to your home, to the bed we've shared?"

She bit her lip, wanting so desperately to believe him that she was afraid to let herself do so. With a sound that was perilously close to a sob, she stepped forward, wrapping her arms around his waist, her face pressed to his rain-drenched shoulder.

Jake held her that way for a moment before slipping his hand under her cheek, tilting her face up to his. His mouth was hard, almost frantic, and Paige responded with an urgency of her own. Her lips parted for him, welcoming the heavy thrust of his tongue, pressing her body close to his.

They stood there, locked in an embrace, oblivious of the pouring rain, indifferent to the fact that they were standing in the middle of the sidewalk, in full view of the neighbors, who were undoubtedly watching the scene with shocked interest.

Paige ran her hands up Jake's bare chest, slick with rain, he arms encircling his neck as he bent to sweep her up into his arms. Cradled against him, Paige had never felt more complete.

Jake kicked open the back gate, carrying her into the fenced backyard. Laying her beneath a huge old weeping willow, he followed her down, the weight of his body pressing her into the thick, soft grass. The grass was cool and damp beneath her back. Above her, Jake was all heat and fire.

Her hands slipped on his wet skin as his mouth twisted hungrily over hers. She shuddered as he unbuttoned her blouse, his palms cupping her breasts, his touch searing.

Hidden from prying eyes by the fence as well as the sheltering branches of the tree, they made love with explosive passion. They'd come so close to losing the fragile security they'd only just begun to find. Now they were reaffirming it with their bodies.

He might be hers only until the seasons changed, but until then, she knew he was hers alone.

Chapter Eleven

Never had summer flown by so quickly. The days slid one into another, rushing toward September. Paige refused to think beyond the next day. The future would come soon enough without her worrying about it. Jake was here for now and she'd never felt quite so alive. It was enough.

She was in love with him.

She'd never lied to herself before and she couldn't start now. She'd fallen deeply in love with a man who'd only come home for the summer. A man whose scars ran as deep as the emotions he tried so hard to hide. A man capable of both deep tenderness and unbridled passion.

When he left, he was going to take a vital piece of her with him.

But that was for the future. She'd deal with that time when she had to. For now, she was going to enjoy what they had without thinking about its ending.

BETH WAS a frequent visitor to the big old house. She came as much to see Jake as Paige. Since the night she'd broken up with Billy, she and Jake had developed an easy rapport. Jake had had little experience with girls Beth's age but he found she was good company.

When she had an afternoon off from the bank, she'd some

times drop by and perch herself somewhere in the vicinity of whatever he was working on. Jake finally began putting her to work handing him tools and holding things for him.

She was as easy and natural as her aunt. If Beth wanted to know something, she saw no reason not to ask. On the other hand, she took no offense when he bluntly told her she was nosy. She grinned at him and said that she was practicing her interrogation techniques. If she was going to be an investigative reporter, she had to start somewhere.

Jake was surprised to find that he really liked her, despite her endless, disconcertingly blunt questions. Like Paige, you always knew where you stood with Beth.

Josie had suddenly become all but invisible. Jake saw her once or twice at a distance, but from the way she disappeared, he assumed she was no more anxious to run into him than he was to run into her. It wasn't so much what she'd done—or tried to do—that made him angry. It was the fact that she'd hurt Paige. He'd discovered he had a protective streak that Paige brought to the fore.

There was nothing all that complex about it, he told himself. He had a basic dislike of cruelty. Maybe because he'd seen so much of it. Josie hadn't wanted to accomplish anything with her little act beyond hurting Paige and, indirectly, Jake himself.

As AUGUST WOUND DOWN, Jake felt a strange restlessness. Summer was almost over. The days were still long and hot but there was a feeling in the air that autumn was just around the corner. In a few short weeks children would be back in school.

He'd taken this summer to come home and find out who he was, to try and figure out where he wanted to go with the rest of his life, to make peace with his family.

His attempts to reconcile with his family had been less than successful. Each time he visited them, it seemed as if the tension only grew stronger. They didn't seem to have any common meeting ground, any way around the barriers that Time had set between them.

As for finding out who he was and what he wanted to do with his life, he couldn't say that he was much closer to resolution there, either.

All he'd really accomplished was that he'd added a new complication to his life in the form of a long-legged blonde who filled gaps in his life he hadn't even known were there.

He'd given little thought to what anyone else might think about his relationship with Paige. It had been a long time since he'd had any reason to wonder what other people thought. Despite the reminders he'd had, it hadn't occurred to him that he and Paige might be considered a hot topic for the gossip mill

It had been a slow summer in Riverbend, with little to talk about. Oh, there was the standard gossip. Young Louise Denby had gotten herself into trouble with the Peters boy. Her parents were planning a hasty wedding and Mr. Denby was said to have oiled his shotgun in case of any reluctance on the groom's part.

Old Mrs. Murchison had decided to write her children out of her will again. It looked as if this time she might really do it. She'd called on Frank Hudson to draw up a new will leaving everything to a distant cousin. But she'd come close before and had always changed her mind. After all, blood was thicker than water.

One of the Fletcher twins had fallen out of the Baldwin' hayloft and landed right next to their milk cow, scaring her so badly her milk had dried up.

But this was the standard stuff any small town gossip mill was used to. Paige Cudahy and Jake Quincannon living in the same house together was something else entirely. She might call him a boarder if she wanted but everyone knew he was more than that. Hadn't Mrs. McCardle seen them kissing in the middle of the day? Bold as brass, standing there in the rain and im with no shirt on. And hadn't he picked her up and carried er off just like Rhett carrying Scarlett up the stairs.

There were a few who sighed and said they thought it was omantic but they were outnumbered by those who thought it vas a crying shame that a sweet little thing like Paige was eing so foolish. Jake Quincannon was trouble, sure as the sun ame up every morning. Besides, everybody knew he was only ome for the summer.

Just where was she going to be come September when he ode off on that motorcycle of his, leaving her alone? And Lord nly knew if she'd been careful about protecting herself. What she found herself in the family way? She had no menfolk to emand that Jake do the right thing by her. Besides, he could e long gone before she even found out.

Paige had always seemed so sensible. A bit reserved maybe, ut not like that sister of hers, always thinking of herself. ometimes it was the sensible ones who broke out and did the raziest things.

Though Jake had given little thought to what the local grape-ine might be saying, he was brought nose to nose with it one fternoon late in August.

He and Pop and Martin had met for lunch, reminiscing about eople and places. The old man had gone back to work, leaving Martin and Jake to linger over their cups of coffee.

"He was hell on wheels in his heyday," Martin commented s the door shut behind Pop's slightly stooped shoulders.

"He put the fear of God into me." Jake smiled nostalgically. I don't know where I'd be if he hadn't taken it into his head whip me into shape."

"Yeah. He sure had a way about him. When I came back, drifted for a couple of years, in and out of one job and an-her. I kept a machine gun under the seat of my car, like I ought the VC were going to turn up in Idaho. Man, I was ore than a few bricks short of a full load."

"Most of us came out of it missing a few gears," Jake said his expression dark with memories.

"I guess. But at the time, I felt like I was the only one seein demons in every shadow. I think Pop got tired of seeing m hanging around. He collared me one day and told me I wa worrying my parents sick. He said if I was going to shoc myself, I ought to go ahead and get it over with. And if I wasn going to shoot myself, I ought to damn well get on with m life."

"That sounds like Pop. The velvet hand in the iron glove. He twisted the adage with a smile.

"That's Pop. He taught me most of what I know about th job and I've always had the feeling that he didn't teach m *half* of what *he* knows. It was a crying shame when they force him to retire. He lived for that job."

There were only a few other customers in the bar. Two me played a desultory game of pool at the table in the center the room. There were half a dozen customers lined up at th bar, drinking beer and talking.

The jukebox in the corner was playing a twangy tune th complained of cheating lovers and broken hearts. It was, pe haps, unfortunate that the song came to a close just when did. The tinny music had served to drown out any sound mo than a few feet away. As the song faded out, the conversatic of the pool players was suddenly audible.

"Can't say I blame the guy. For years I've wondered wh it would be like to have those legs wrapped around me. If I known she was open to suggestion, I might have done som thing about it."

The speaker was a big man, six foot three and well over tv hundred pounds. Years of drinking had put a paunch on hi but it was backed by solid muscle. Jake barely heard what said. It was barroom talk and of no interest to him. Until t man's friend spoke and he realized whom they were discussir

"Wait till Quincannon leaves town, George. Maybe she'll
e lonely then."

In a flash Jake was out of his seat and halfway across the
om, his approach as silent as it was lethal.

"You never can tell now," George said, chalking his cue,
olivious of the fact that he was teetering on the edge of di-
ster. "Once she's had a taste of it, she ain't likely to be nearly
• snooty." He set down the chalk. "I wouldn't want to cross
at Quincannon, though. He looks like a mean son of a bitch."

"He is," Jake said from less than two feet away.

George turned, his eyes widening when he saw who had
•oken. He hadn't seen Jake and Martin in the corner booth or
• would certainly have been more discreet in his choice of
pics. But Jake didn't give him a chance to retract his words.

His left first buried itself in George's paunchy belly. As he
ubled over, Jake's right fist caught him on the chin. He
vung from near ground level and his fist carried the power of
mule's kick. George rocked back on his heels, his eyes rolling
ck in his head as he wobbled for a moment before collapsing
to the floor like a poleaxed ox.

Jake took a step toward George's friend but Martin's hand
ught his arm, stopping him.

"That's enough, Jake. I'm sure Luke wants to apologize."

Luke wanted to apologize in the worst way for anything he'd
d, anything he might have thought of saying or anything he
ght say at any time in the future that could possibly offend
ke in any way.

Jake nodded shortly, fighting back the urge to knock Luke's
eth down his throat. Any man who could talk about Paige
e that didn't deserve to live. The fact that George lay un-
nscious on the floor at his feet only began to assuage the
ge he'd felt when he'd realized whom they were talking
out.

Martin continued to hold on to Jake's arm and could feel the tension in it. Jake let himself be herded outside. He knew if h stayed, there was likely to be bloodshed.

The sun was bright. Jake stood, his hands clenching a unclenching at his sides, surrounded by an almost visible au of danger.

"George is a bit of a loudmouth," Martin said, reaching ir his pocket for a pack of gum. Jake said nothing. Martin u wrapped a stick of gum with neat precision. "You know, y can't really expect to have an affair in a town this size with stimulating a bit of comment."

"We're not having an affair," Jake snarled, slanting t sheriff a look that held pent-up fury.

Martin folded the gum into his mouth, chewing it a fe times to soften it. "Next weekend is Labor Day. End of su mer." He glanced up at the sky as if he could see the inevitab change of seasons in the clear blue arc overhead. "You s leaving come fall?"

"I've no reason to change my plans," Jake said flatly, wo dering if the words sounded as hollow to Martin as they to him.

THE SMITH FAMILY had been having an annual end-of-sumr barbecue for as long as most of the town's residents co remember. It was as much a part of the changing of the seas as returning to school and digging out the woolens.

Jake hadn't planned on going. He remembered the barbe from his childhood. A good portion of the town could counted on to be in attendance, including his parents. Spend the afternoon under his mother's cool gaze was not exactly idea of fun.

There was so little time left. Already, the nights were coo the days a little shorter. The end of summer was all but h and he still hadn't made any plans to leave. He kept think that there was no harm in staying just a few more days, another week or two.

But there was harm. The longer he stayed, the more tangled p in Paige he became. It was already almost impossible to emember a time when he hadn't known her, a time when he adn't awakened with her beside him. If he'd been another kind f man, led another kind of life, maybe things could have been ifferent.

But he was what he was and the choices he'd made couldn't e changed. He should never have allowed himself to get involved with her. She was going to get hurt. He couldn't lie to imself about that, couldn't pretend that it was nothing more an a summer fling for her. She thought she was in love with m. She'd never said it but sometimes he could see it in her es.

She'd get over it, realize that he wasn't worth it. That was hat he wanted. And if he told himself that a hundred more nes, he just might begin to believe it.

His smile held an edge as he gave himself a last glance in e mirror. He stopped, caught by the image. He saw a man, ng past his youth, all illusions beaten out of him by life. His ir held a scattering of gray. There were fine lines slanting vay from his eyes and deeper lines bracketing his thick black ustache. He reached up, fingering the patch, the final touch his battle-scarred appearance.

He wondered suddenly what Paige saw when she looked at m.

IE BARBECUE was already in full swing when Jake stopped e motorcycle at the foot of the driveway. The Smith house s a sprawling ranch, half a dozen miles from town. The iveway was already lined with pickups and cars, with more rked on the road in front. Jake slid the Harley into a narrow ot between a battered pickup and an even more battered se- n, nudging the kickstand into place as Paige hopped off.

She was wearing a pair of pale pink shorts that exposed the ng, smooth length of her legs. When he'd first seen her in them, he'd had to suppress the urge to suggest that she put on something that was less revealing, like a nice full-length coat. Feeling possessive was something new to him and it wasn't a comfortable sensation.

"It looks like everybody got here before us," Paige said, linking her arm through his. Her other arm was wrapped around an enormous bowl of pasta salad, the same bowl that had jabbed him in the back all the way over. Jake thought it was a pity everyone hadn't already left before they got here.

But it wasn't as bad as he'd feared. True, when they'd first arrived, they were the cynosure of all eyes but it wasn't long before people's attention moved on to other things, like food and swimming in the in-ground pool Bob Smith had put in only this spring.

Even though Jake couldn't fade into the background, he could at least linger on the fringes of the gathering. He watched Paige talking to various friends and neighbors. She'd braided her hair again. The thick braid looked almost platinum in the sunlight. Jake wanted to wrap it around his hand and pull her to him.

He took a long draft from his beer, turning his gaze elsewhere. Josie was standing just across the patio from him, looking as out of place in her immaculately tailored slacks, silk blouse and high-heeled pumps as he felt. He noticed that she hadn't spoken to Paige and Paige had made no effort to seek Josie out. Josie's eyes met his for a moment. Jake lifted his beer in mocking salute, admitting to a rather immature pleasure when she looked away, her mouth pinched.

"Are you going swimming, Jake?"

Beth darted up to him, her nose slightly sunburned, her blue eyes sparkling. She was wearing a bright pink terry sunsuit and he guessed she had a bathing suit underneath it.

"I don't think so."

"Too old and feeble?" she teased.

"Someone really should have spanked you more often," he complained, reaching out to tug a lock of her hair.

"People always say that when you touch a nerve. Come watch me dive."

Without waiting for an answer, she linked her arm through his, tugging him toward the pool. Jake saw a few speculative glances cast their way and, glancing over his shoulder, he saw Josie staring after them, her eyes dark with some emotion he couldn't read. She was probably worried about him contaminating her daughter.

"You really should come in, Jake," Beth coaxed. She stopped on the edge of the pool, reaching up to unzip the front of the sunsuit. Shimmying out of the modest terry cloth, she revealed a bikini of truly minuscule proportions. She laughed as Jake's eyes widened.

"Do you like it?"

"There's not enough of it to like," he said dryly.

"Isn't it great?" She waved to a girl already in the pool. "You sure you won't come in, Jake?"

Jake glanced at the pool, which was full of teenagers whose average age was about sixteen. "I don't think so."

"If you'd just take your vitamins, you'd have more energy." She dodged the casual swat he aimed in her direction, laughing over her shoulder as she turned toward the pool. Jake half smiled, raising his beer to take a drink as he watched her.

The bikini was outrageous, of course, but she had the figure for it. A tiny strap cut across her back, the only covering until the scrap of fabric that barely stretched across her derriere.

The bottle stopped halfway to his lips, his gaze riveted to a spot just above the slinky black fabric of her bikini bottom. Just to the left of her spine was a heart-shaped birthmark about the size of a fifty cent piece. It was a familiar mark.

A description and photo of just such a mark had been a part of his file at the agency, a means of identifying him, alive or dead. A heart-shaped birthmark just to the left of his spine.

A birthmark exactly like the one Beth had.

She dived into the pool, her body arching over the cool blue water. Jake didn't see the dive. He didn't see anything but that tanned back and that small red mark. A rather insignificant mark really, the kind of thing you hardly noticed and quickly forgot.

He remembered his father telling him once that he had a birthmark just like the one Jake had and that his father had had the same mark. He'd been a little boy at the time and he'd thought it was exciting that he and his father shared something so personal, a visible link between them.

A sort of inheritance passed from father to son.

To daughter.

He was aware that his hand was shaking as he lowered the bottle. He reached out blindly, setting it on a table.

Beth was his daughter.

The simple idea was stunning in its impact. He had a child. Why hadn't he ever made the connection? No one had lied about Beth's age. Was it possible that no one knew?

Feeling eyes on him, he turned his head, his gaze colliding with Josie's. She'd moved down to the pool—to keep an eye on him and Beth?—and now stood a short distance away. Staring at her, he read the truth in her eyes.

She knew. She'd known all along that Frank wasn't Beth' father.

He saw the realization come up in her eyes that the secret she'd kept for twenty years was no longer a secret. Hard on its heels came fear. Jake held her gaze for several long, slow seconds, watching the fear build in her eyes.

He looked away at last, glancing toward the pool where Beth was laughing and splashing with her friends. Out of the corner of his eyes, he saw Josie take a quick step forward as if to thrust herself between him and her daughter. His daughter.

Jake spun on his heel, feeling as dazed as if he'd just received a sharp blow to the head. The lawn full of laughing people looked out of focus, like something seen in a funhouse mirror. A tangle of emotions roiled in him, making him almost sick. Rage. Anguish. Elation. Shock.

Moving quickly through the crowd, he found Paige. She was standing next to Ethel Levine, her expression making it clear that she was only half listening to what the woman was saying. Relief sparked in her eyes when she saw Jake approaching.

"Let's go." He was beyond caring that he was being rude. If Paige thought of protesting, he didn't give her a chance. His hand closed like a manacle around her wrist. He nodded to Ethel, whose eyes were snapping with excitement, her pale blue hair almost quivering with pleasure at this opportunity to witness the way Jake Quincannon treated the woman everyone knew he was having an affair with.

Paige glanced at Jake, startled. But any protest she might have made died when she saw the look on his face. He barely gave her time to say goodbye to Ethel. She knew that Ethel wasn't going to waste any time in telling her cronies that Jake had practically dragged her off, but that couldn't be helped. Obviously, something was very wrong.

Jake led her through the crowd at a pace that raised a few eyebrows. Paige kept a pleasant smile on her face as if nothing was wrong but she was glad her legs were long enough to allow her to keep up with him. She had the feeling that he only half remembered he had hold of her.

She waited until they were almost to the bike before speaking.

"Are you going to tell me what happened or are you just going to drag me all the way home?"

Jake stopped next to the bike, turning a look of such intensity on her that she felt her heart skip a beat.

"Beth went swimming."

"I think half the teenagers in town are in the pool."

"She was wearing this bikini, hardly more than a couple of scraps of fabric." He stopped, staring blindly at her.

"Jake, you didn't drag me out of there because Beth was wearing an indecent swimsuit."

"She has a birthmark on her lower back. It's shaped like a heart. I recognized it." He blinked, his gaze finally focusing on her. "I have one just like it."

Paige sucked in her breath as she realized what he was saying. "Jake..."

"She's mine, Paige. My daughter."

Chapter Twelve

Jake rang the doorbell, listening to the elegant chimes ringing somewhere inside the big house. The columns and wide porch looked even more pretentious than they had the first time he'd seen them. Or maybe it only seemed that way because of the mood he was in.

He'd waited to confront Josie until he was sure Beth would have left for the bank. Beth. His daughter. He still couldn't quite grasp the reality of it. Paige had been nearly as stunned as he was. They'd talked but there hadn't really been much to say.

Beth was his daughter and he'd been cheated out of the chance to know her.

The door opened slowly. Josie stared at him, her expression haunted.

"I think we'd better talk." Jake didn't particularly feel like bothering with the niceties this morning. What he really felt like doing was shaking her until her teeth rattled.

"We don't have anything to talk about." She tried to sound haughty but her voice shook, betraying her nervousness.

"We're going to talk, Josie," Jake said with icy calm. "We can talk here on the doorstep or we can talk inside. I don't really give a damn *where* we talk but we *are* going to talk."

"You really are offensive," she snapped. But she opened the door wider. Jake followed her across the marble-tiled foyer and into the library. Josie shut the double doors behind them, moving nervously into the center of the room.

"What do you want to talk about?"

"Cut the games, Josie." Jake felt almost weary. "Beth is my daughter, isn't she?"

"Don't be ridiculous." But her voice lacked conviction and the look she shot him held more fear than indignation.

"Why didn't you tell me?"

"When?" She set down the figurine she'd been toying with, straightening her shoulders as she turned to face him. "You left, remember?"

"I came back. I told you I was coming back. If you'd written, I could have gotten leave or something and come back even sooner. My God, didn't you think I had a right to know you were carrying my child?"

"You left," she repeated stubbornly. "I didn't know if you'd really come back. When I found out I was pregnant, I was scared."

"So you married Frank? Without even giving me a chance?"

"I married Frank. He was nice and he'd been in love with me all the time you and I were going out together. Besides, you didn't have any plans for the future beyond the service. Frank was on his way to college and then law school."

"So his prospects were better?"

"That's right. I didn't particularly fancy the idea of living in a trailer somewhere and growing old watching you ride your stupid motorcycles. With Frank, I had a chance at a good life. The kind of life I wanted."

"And what about the baby? Didn't you think I might have wanted to know that I was going to be a father? Didn't you think I'd care? My God, did you even tell Frank it wasn't his?"

"She told me." Frank pushed the door the rest of the way open, stepping into the room. Jake turned to look at him. Meet

ng the other man's eyes, he felt a shock of pain. He hadn't
vanted to believe that Frank had known.

It was funny, even after twenty years, he'd always thought
of Frank as his best friend, as if the bonds they'd forged when
hey were young could never be truly broken.

Last night, staring up at the darkened ceiling, listening to
Paige's quiet breathing beside him, he'd gone over the events
of twenty years ago in his head. He'd almost convinced himself
hat Frank couldn't have known the truth then, maybe still
didn't know the truth.

If he'd known then, he surely couldn't have kept it from
ake, not from his best friend. And if he'd found out later,
maybe he'd thought it would cause more trouble than anything
lse. But he couldn't have known then. Not when Jake had
ome home from boot camp to find his whole world shattered.

"I'm sorry, Jake."

"Sorry? Are you apologizing for what happened twenty
ears ago or are you sorry I found out at all? God, Frank!"
ake swung away from the man he'd called friend, only to turn
ack, his expression full of pain. "You were my best friend,
he one person I knew I could trust. I came home to find you'd
married my girl and now I find out you kept my daughter from
me for nineteen years. Why?"

"Because that's the way Josie wanted it." Frank crossed to
his wife, touching her lightly on the shoulder as if reassuring
er that everything was going to be all right. "I had to respect
osie's wishes, Jake."

"Even at the price of my never knowing I had a child?"
ake questioned, his voice pained.

"If you'd never known, there'd have been no harm done,"
rank pointed out.

"I bet you're a hell of a lawyer, Frank." Jake didn't try to
ide his contempt. "So you felt it was a victimless crime. Since
didn't know, I couldn't be hurt."

Frank flushed. He ran his hand over his thinning hair. "I

guess it does sound like a rather spurious argument, but at the time it seemed like the best thing.''

''At the time? What about later? Did it seem as good later?''

''Later it was too late to change anything. We'd already made the decision. You were gone. There didn't seem to be any reason to stir up trouble.''

''God forbid we should stir up trouble,'' Jake said nastily. He stuffed his hands into the pockets of his jeans, afraid that if he didn't, he was going to break something, preferably someone's neck.

''Does Beth know you're not her father?''

Frank winced at Jake's dismissal of his role in Beth's life, but he didn't protest. It was Josie who jumped in to answer the question.

''She doesn't know and you can't tell her, Jake. She adores Frank. It would break her heart if she found out.''

''Found out you'd lied to her all her life, you mean?''

''We didn't lie to her. Frank *is* her father in all the most important ways. He's provided for her far better than you ever could have.''

''That's enough, Josie.''

Jake's mouth twisted into a bitter smile. ''It's a little late to be trying to spare my feelings, Frank.''

''Recriminations aren't important now,'' Frank said quietly. ''It's Beth's happiness that's most important now. What do you plan to do, Jake?''

Jake stared at him, the question tumbling around in his head. *What did he plan to do?* Why had he even bothered to come here? Because he wanted to hear Josie confirm what he already knew? He didn't know what he planned to do. He could barely think of anything beyond the fact that he had a fully grown daughter.

''I don't know what I'm going to do,'' he said at last.

''You can't tell her, Jake,'' Josie said, her voice rising. ''You can't do that to her. She'll never forgive me.''

Jake's eyebrow rose. "Never forgive *you*? Do you really think I give a damn about whether or not she forgives you, Josie? You kept my child from me. I'm afraid your feelings aren't a high priority with me at the moment."

"Josie and I are concerned about Beth, Jake. I don't think any of us want to see her hurt."

Frank's reasonableness was harder to deal with than Josie's impending hysteria. Jake wanted to go find Beth and tell her that he was her father. He wanted to go buy a bottle of whiskey and drink himself into oblivion. He wanted to be able to go back twenty years and change everything.

Suddenly the pretentious room with its walls of walnut shelves was suffocating. Without another word, he turned and strode from the room, aware that Josie started after him, only to be stopped by Frank.

It wasn't until he was astride the Harley, the engine's roar in his ears, that he felt as if he could breathe again.

What was he going to do, they'd asked. He didn't have the slightest idea.

"ARE YOU all right?"

Paige set her hands on Jake's shoulders, feeling the knots of tension. He'd been sitting on the back porch, staring out at the mountains which were visible over the fence. He'd been sitting there when she'd come home two hours ago and she didn't think he'd moved since. There was a whiskey bottle and a shot glass beside him but the bottle was still full, the glass empty.

She'd left him alone. There didn't seem to be much she could say, any real comfort she could offer. She couldn't give him back all the years he'd missed with Beth. She couldn't tell him why Josie had chosen to marry Frank rather than tell Jake she was carrying his child.

But he couldn't sit staring at the mountains forever.

"Jake, are you all right?" She had to repeat her question. He stirred as if coming awake, wiping his hand over his face.

"I'm all right."

"Did you see Josie?" Her fingers kneaded his shoulders, trying to work some of the tension out.

"I saw her," he said flatly. "And Frank."

"Frank?" Paige's hands stilled for a moment. "Does he know?"

"He's known from the start. Said it was what Josie wanted." He sounded more weary than bitter and Paige's heart ached for him.

"I'm sorry."

The words were completely inadequate but she couldn't think of anything else to offer. They sat there in silence, watching the last of the light fade from the mountaintops.

"Do you want me to call your parents and tell them we can't make it tonight?"

Jake shifted under her hands and shook his head. "No. It's okay. I'll go clean up."

Paige watched him as he went back into the house and then her eyes turned to the whiskey bottle as if she might find some answers there.

She was no closer to finding those answers an hour later when the Harley stopped in front of the Quincannons' neat house. It had been Jake's mother who had suggested that he bring Paige to dinner, issuing the invitation at the barbecue yesterday, her cool gray eyes studying Paige as if wondering what she might see in Jake.

Paige didn't doubt that the invitation had been issued more out of a sense of duty than real affection. She'd seen the way Jake looked when he came back from one of his infrequent visits with his parents—lost and almost beaten—and she didn't think there was a lot of affection there.

She'd dressed carefully for the visit, sensing that Jake wanted this to go well. The slacks she wore were neatly tailored black linen and she'd topped them with an emerald-green blouse that emphasized the color of her eyes. She'd thrown a jacket on over the outfit, feeling a twinge at the necessity of having to do so.

Summer was officially over with the passing of Labor Day. The nights were cooling off. It wouldn't be that long before frost blackened the marigolds that had been so bright and colorful all summer long.

And Jake would be leaving soon.

She'd forced herself to face that. He hadn't said anything but she could sense a certain restlessness in him, as if he'd been here too long already. She didn't think finding out Beth's true parentage was going to change his mind.

No matter how much he might wish it were different, Frank had been Beth's father all her life. Even if Jake were to tell her the truth—and it would have to come from him if she were ever to know—nothing could change the fact that he hadn't been the one to stay up nights when she was cutting her first tooth. Or to hold her first bicycle while she found her balance and kiss her bruised knee when she lost it.

All those memories, all those years belonged to Frank.

If anything, finding out that Beth was his daughter seemed more likely to encourage Jake to leave rather than stay.

But sufficient unto the day is the evil thereof, she told herself, running a comb through her hair. Motorcycles were not kind to elaborate hairstyles, so she'd settled on letting it hang straight down her back.

Jake waited while she combed out the tangles, his hands stuffed into his pockets, his shoulders hunched as if carrying too great a weight. The porch light barely reached the end of the path. He was little more than a dark shadow in the dim light.

She dropped the comb into her purse and linked her arm through his. It took an effort to put a smile on her face but she managed it, determined to make the best of the evening.

''Is there anything I should particularly avoid doing besides the usual stuff like eating with my fingers and blowing my nose on the tablecloth?''

Jake blinked and looked down at her as if trying to remember where they were. As they began to walk toward the front door, she could feel the muscles under her hand tense, becoming hard as iron. She wasn't sure how much of the tension was caused by the discovery about Beth and how much by the upcoming meal with his parents.

''You're asking the wrong person,'' he said at last. ''I always seemed able to drive my mother crazy just by breathing.''

''I'm afraid that's one thing I can't bring myself to give up.''

''She probably won't mind it as much when you do it.'' He reached up to push the doorbell, his arm tightening, trapping her hand against his side.

His father opened the door.

''Jacob. Paige.'' He nodded as he pushed open the screen door. ''You're a mite late. Mother's fit to be tied.''

Mother might be fit to be tied but she was clearly making an effort to hide it. Jake's father led them directly into the dining room. From the way Jake raised his brows, Paige guessed that this was something of an honor. The room was filled to overflowing by a heavy walnut dining-room set. Table, chairs, sideboard, china cabinet and linen chest all crammed into a room that would have been hard-pressed to contain the table alone.

''What a lovely dining room set,'' Paige said with sincerity.

''It was a wedding gift from my parents. Actually, we rarely use this room.''

''I seem to recall being threatened with dismemberment if I so much as set foot in here,'' Jake commented.

Margaret glanced at her son, her eyes cool in the lamplight. They held none of the affection one would have expected a mother's eyes to show.

''You were a destructive child,'' she said, as if all children weren't destructive.

It wasn't the last uncomfortable moment of the evening. Paige hadn't been close to her parents but she'd certainly never experienced the thinly veiled hostility that existed in the Quincannon household, particularly between Jake and his mother. His father seemed to serve as a sort of referee and occasional conciliator.

Mother and son disagreed on every subject that came up, from the way to prune and hedge to the meaning of life, or so it seemed to Paige. Jake generally tried to sidestep the issue but Margaret followed like a small dog with a bone, not satisfied until the disagreement had been brought out in the open. As if the fact that he disagreed with her was another piece of proof that he was unworthy.

Paige's appetite deserted her early in the meal. Was this what he'd grown up with? This constant harping on every fault, those coolly critical eyes watching every move he made, ready to pounce on the smallest mistake?

By the time the pie was served, Paige had a knot in her stomach. The flaky crust encompassing a thick layer of apples looked about as appealing as a dead fish but she pinned a smile on her face.

"This looks like a wonderful crust, Mrs. Quincannon. Perhaps you'll give me the recipe?"

She caught the look Jake slanted her and knew that he was thinking about how seldom she cooked anything more complicated than a frozen dinner. She didn't care if she was being obvious. If they started arguing over the pie, she was going to scream.

"Of course, Paige. It was my mother's recipe."

"Mother makes the best pie in the county," Lawrence said heartily. Paige wondered if he was also trying to keep the conversation neutral. It didn't matter. Surely it was possible to have ten minutes of normal conversation. Unfortunately, her next words destroyed any hope of that.

"My niece, Beth, thinks apple pie is one of the four food groups."

She'd been so desperate to keep the innocuous conversation going that she was halfway through the sentence before she realized what she'd said. Bringing up Beth had not been the most intelligent thing to do. She glanced at Jake, worried that she'd reminded him of something he'd probably like to forget, at least for a little while.

But Jake wasn't looking at her. His gaze was on his mother and the intensity of that look was enough to burn holes through wood. Glancing at her hostess, Paige saw that she was looking at her plate. This in itself was nothing unusual except that the knuckles of her fingers were white from the force with which she gripped her fork.

"You knew," Jake said hoarsely.

Paige's heart bumped as she realized what he was saying. He thought his parents knew that Beth was his child, their grandchild. It wasn't possible. But the guilt in his father's eyes gave her the answer even as she asked the question.

"Look at me, Mother."

The eyes she lifted to his face were as cool and unemotional as ever. But Jake didn't seem to have any trouble reading the truth there.

"How long have you known she was my daughter?"

"Now, Jacob, there's no call to go getting in a fuss about it. It's all long over and done with." But the waters that had been whipped up across the snowy tablecloth were much too turbulent for Lawrence's rather feeble effort at calming them down.

"My God, how long have you known? Answer me, dammit!"

"There's no call for profanity, Jacob." Margaret set her fork beside her untouched plate, arranging it with neat precision. "Your father and I have known almost from the beginning that Beth was our grandchild."

The fact that he'd already guessed the truth didn't cushion the impact of her words. He'd known all his life that his mother didn't feel about him the way mothers usually felt about their children. When he was small, he'd tried desperately to gain her approval. Failing that, he'd settled for any reaction he could pull from her, usually anger.

But he'd never have believed she'd keep something like this from him. If not for his sake, then for hers. Hadn't she wanted a chance to get to know her grandchild? He didn't realize he'd asked the question out loud until she answered him.

"Frank always made it a point to bring Beth by occasionally. We were able to watch her grow up."

"Why didn't you ever tell me?"

"It seemed best not to," his mother said in her quiet way. His father stared at the tablecloth.

"Why? Why did it seem best to keep my child from me?" Jake's hand clenched into a fist on the table. Somewhere inside he could feel rage and pain boiling, threatening to spill over and destroy his control.

"We felt Frank could do more for our grandchild than you ever could. With all your traveling all over the world, doing God knows what. Killing and destroying, no doubt. What could you possibly have offered a sweet little girl?"

The words were all the more cruel for having been delivered in that cool, unemotional tone. Jake felt the color draining from his face. Staring at his mother, he felt true hatred for the first time in his life.

He hated her for all the years he'd spent trying to make her love him and never understanding why she didn't. He hated her for sitting there looking as if they were discussing whether to have tea or coffee. And he hated her for keeping Beth from him.

Josie and Frank had made their choices in a tangle of emotions. Maybe they'd really believed they were doing the right thing. But he knew, beyond a shadow of a doubt, that his mother had kept the secret for twenty years, not out of concern for Beth, but because she enjoyed the knowledge of how much it would hurt him if he ever found out.

"That was uncalled for, Margaret." His father's voice held a stern note he'd never heard directed toward his mother, but the words couldn't be taken back, even if she'd wanted to. And she didn't want to.

Without another word, Jake shoved back his chair, barely noticing when it slammed against the china cabinet. He strode from the room, knowing that he had to get fresh air. Knowing that, if he stayed, he couldn't guarantee he wasn't going to hit his own mother.

The silence he left behind was deafening. Paige broke it by pushing back her chair. She paused long enough to fix Margaret Quincannon with a look of contempt that brought a flush to the older woman's face.

"You don't deserve to have a son like Jake. Someday you're going to be a lonely old woman because people like you always end up like that. And I hope to God you remember what you've done and have to live with regret to your last bitter breath."

She tossed her napkin on the table and strode from the room without another word. Snatching her jacket off the coat rack, she hurried out the front door. Jake was already astride the Harley, gunning the big engine to life as Paige ran down the path. She skidded to a halt next to him.

"You're better off walking home," he said without looking at her, his voice carrying easily over the roar of the engine. "Or call Martin and ask him to give you a ride."

"Where are you going?"

"I don't know."

"I'm coming with you."

"I don't want company," he said bluntly.

"Tough."

He looked as if he might carry the argument further but she was already hopping onto the back of the motorcycle. She'd barely settled in place when the big bike took off, the rear wheel spitting gravel as it fought for purchase.

Paige grabbed for his waist, winding her arms around him, burying her face against his back as they roared into the night.

Forever after, she could remember only pieces of that wild ride. Paige clung to him, leaning her body with his when they took corners so fast the bike seemed to lie on the ground. Jake drove as if a demon was riding his shoulder. Which she supposed it was.

When he turned onto the road that led up Borden Hill, she could only close her eyes tighter and offer up an incoherent prayer. He skidded around the iron gates, skirting the edge so close that Paige felt her right foot hanging over empty space.

Taking the last curve too fast, the rear wheel skidded in the loose dirt. Paige gasped as Jake fought to regain control, finally steadying the big bike more by brute strength than anything else.

They came to a halt on the packed dirt of the parking lot. For several seconds, Paige didn't move, not even to lift her head from Jake's shoulder.

"Are you all right?" Jake's voice rumbled beneath her ear. She lifted her head slowly, taking a deep breath before answering him.

"I'm all right."

"I warned you not to come with me." He reached back one hand to help her slide off the bike, waiting until she was on the ground before nudging the kickstand into place and dismounting.

"So you did," Paige agreed, brushing futilely at her tangled hair. "But you should know by now that I rarely do what I should."

He shoved his hands into his pockets, half turning away from her. She could feel his pain as acutely as if it were her own.

"You know she's wrong, Jake. You have to know it."

"Do I?" He stared out over the dark valley.

"You would have been a good father."

"Maybe she's right." He didn't seem to hear her. "Maybe Beth was better off without me."

"That's not true." Since he wouldn't look at her, she moved to stand in front of him, taking hold of his arm, demanding that he listen. "You're a good man, Jake. No matter how hard you try to pretend you're not, you are. Beth would have been lucky to grow up with you as her father. Your parents were wrong not to tell you about her."

"I used to try so hard to make her love me," Jake said, speaking as much to himself as to her. "Mothers are supposed to love their children. I always knew that and I couldn't understand why she didn't love me. I had a brother, you know."

"I know." Paige stroked his arm.

"He was three years younger than I was. Michael. He died when I was eight. He was everything I wasn't. Blond and sweet. She always said that he had the prettiest blue eyes she'd ever seen. I used to stand in front of the mirror and wonder why my blue eyes weren't pretty, too. Sometimes, I'd think that she'd love me if Michael were gone."

He seemed caught in the grip of memories she couldn't share. Paige wanted to ask what had happened to his brother but she couldn't get the words out past the ache in her throat. He answered the question as if she'd spoken.

"He drowned. It was winter and the river was iced over. She'd told us not to go out on the ice. We were playing and I was supposed to be watching him. Michael went out on the ice and it broke under him. I crawled out after him and managed to grab hold of his hands but he was too heavy and I couldn't pull him up.

"I kept telling him it was going to be all right, that Mama would come help us. 'Mama will come,' I kept saying, over and over again, but by the time she came, it was too late."

Paige could hardly see him through the tears that blinded her. In her mind's eye, she could see the two frightened children, Jake trying to comfort his little brother, trying to push his own fears back.

"It was a tragedy, Jake, but it wasn't your fault."

"I know. I even think I knew it then. But I *had* wondered if she'd love me if he were gone. That was almost like wishing him dead. She never said it was my fault that he died. But sometimes when she'd look at me, I knew she was wishing *I'd* been the one to fall through the ice."

"No. I'm sure she never would have thought that." Her own uncertainty made her denial even more forceful. Perhaps Jake heard the doubt because his mouth twisted as he looked down at her, his expression shadowed in the moonlight.

"She didn't tell me about Beth because she thought I'd be bad for my own child. Maybe she was right."

"No, she wasn't." But he didn't seem to hear her fierce denial.

"I've killed people, Paige. She was right about that. I have spent most of my life killing and destroying. It's all I really know how to do."

The pain in his voice was so profound it left her momentarily speechless. She stared up at him, groping for something to say.

"I love you, Jake." She felt him jerk as if the words had the impact of a bullet. She tightened her hand on his arm. "I love you and since I've always had impeccable taste, you can't be nearly as bad as you think."

"Don't." The word felt thick on his tongue. He looked down at her. The moonlight bleached the color from her skin and hair, giving her the look of a pale wraith. But there was nothing wraithlike in the strength of her fingers on his arm. Nothing ethereal in the steady gaze of those wide green eyes.

She'd just laid her soul bare for him, offered it as a bandage for his pain. No one in his life had ever made themselves so completely vulnerable. That she'd done it to comfort him only made it more threatening.

"God, Paige." He felt something breaking apart inside him,

something tight and hard that had been lodged like a rock in his chest. ''God.''

He caught her to him with bruising strength, burying his face in the tangled length of her hair, holding her as if he couldn't bear to let her go.

Chapter Thirteen

Paige was gone when Jake awoke the next morning. He missed the feel of her in his arms but he was somewhat relieved. He wasn't sure he was ready to face her yet. Last night she'd soothed his pain, even though it meant opening herself up to hurt.

She'd said she loved him.

He rolled the idea over in his mind, feeling it flow over him like cool water over fevered skin.

He'd have to leave. He scowled at the ceiling. No matter what she said, he knew, better than she ever could, that he was no good for anything more than a summer affair. She didn't understand what he'd been, the scars he carried, the nightmares that sometimes woke him up screaming things he couldn't even remember as the sound died.

No, he was carrying too much emotional baggage. He couldn't burden her with it. She'd never believe him if he told her that now. But maybe someday she'd understand.

He'd leave today. Other than Paige there was no one to keep him in this town. No one who'd care if he left and more than a few who'd be relieved. Summer was over. It was time to move on.

But he made no move to start packing. Telling himself that he wanted to say goodbye to Pop, he dressed and drove the Harley into town, parking behind the bank.

There seemed to be more people in town than usual. Jake wondered if he was imagining the faint autumnal bustle in the air. The sun was shining brightly but it didn't feel as warm on his shoulders as it had a week ago, as if some of the strength had gone out of it.

"Jake!" Pop's creased features lit up in a pleased smile as Jake pushed open the bank door. The air conditioning that had seemed pleasantly cool a few days ago now seemed chilly.

"Catch any bank robbers yet?" Jake asked as Pop got to his feet.

"Not yet, but I'm ready." The old man patted the holstered gun at his side, his grin emphasizing the joke. "Saw you at the barbecue the other day. You took out of there pretty fast."

Jake's smile faded. "I suppose I did." He glanced toward the back of the bank. "Beth Hudson working today?"

"Yup. Went to lunch about twenty minutes ago. Cute little thing."

"Yeah, she is." It was probably just as well that she was gone, Jake told himself. The fact that they shared blood didn't change anything. And he'd always hated saying goodbye.

He lingered with Pop a few minutes longer, talking about nothing in particular. He was delaying the moment when he'd have to say that he was leaving. Once he said it, it would be real, irrevocable. He could just leave without saying anything but he owed Pop more than that.

"Pop, I—"

"Mr. Bellows, I don't see how you can properly guard my bank when you spend all your time talking to your friends." Henry Nathan, president of Riverbend's only bank, puffed across the floor, his hushed voice preceding him.

Pop frowned, rolling his eyes at Jake before turning to his employer. "Sorry, Mr. Nathan. Seeing as how there wasn't anyone in here but you and Lisa Mae at the window—no customers and all—I figured there wasn't a whole lot to worry about."

"I pay you to be on guard duty at all times, Mr. Bellows, not when you think it's convenient. The payroll is due in this afternoon and it might help if you at least pretended to show an interest in its safe delivery."

Jake wondered if Nathan would look any better with his nose broken in two or three places. But it wasn't his place to interfere in his friend's business. To do so would only be an embarrassment to Pop.

"I was just leaving." He pushed himself away from the pillar he'd been leaning against, deliberately looming over Nathan, who took a quick step back. Jake gave him a slow smile, enjoying the uneasy look that came into the man's eyes.

"I'll be seeing you later, Jake."

"Sure. I'll stop by later, Pop." He could stop by on his way out of town and say goodbye.

He stepped out into the street, narrowing his eyes against the sun. He still had to tell Paige he was going. God alone knew how he was going to do that.

PAIGE GLANCED UP as the library door opened, her expression chilling when she saw who had entered. Josie caught her sister's eyes and seemed to hesitate a moment before advancing boldly.

Paige was vaguely surprised by the strength of the rage she felt. She'd never particularly liked her sister but her feelings for her now ran close to hatred. She'd never imagined she was capable of such an emotion.

"Have you come to check out a book, Josie?"

Josie flushed at Paige's tone but she didn't stop until she stood just across the desk. Paige stood up slowly, her eyes meeting Josie's straight on.

"I want to talk to you," Josie said.

"Really? I can't imagine what about."

"Have you...talked to Jake?"

"If what you're asking is do I know that Beth is his daughter, the answer is yes."

"Quiet!" Josie's eyes darted around to see if anyone could have overheard Paige.

"There's only the two of us here, Josie."

"Well, you can never be too careful."

"You would know. You've built your life so carefully haven't you? Never giving a damn about who you use in the process. Mom and Dad, me, Jake, Frank. Is there anyone you really care about?"

"I can see you're going to take Jake's side in this," Josie said, her tone hurt. "I only did what I thought was best for my baby. Even all those years ago it was plain to see that Frank could give us more security than Jake could.

"And I was obviously right. Look at the way he's come back here with nothing to show for the last twenty years but that awful motorcycle.

"Besides, it's not as if keeping Beth's parentage a secret caused Jake any harm. He's a little upset now but he'll see that I did the best thing."

Paige clenched her hands into fists as she struggled against the urge to smack Josie until her ears rang. To hear her dismiss Jake's anguish as "a little upset" made her blood drum in her ears.

"What do you want, Josie?"

Josie looked a little surprised by the flat question but she seized her opportunity. "I know you want what's best for Beth, Paige. After all, she's completely innocent in this. No one wants to see her hurt."

"Cut to the chase. What do you want?"

"I want you to talk Jake out of telling her that…that…"

"That he's her father?" Paige finished, arching one eyebrow.

"Yes. The truth isn't going to do anything but hurt her now."

"So you want me to convince Jake to walk out of her life right after he's discovered that he's her father."

"Well, it isn't as if he *knows* her or anything. I mean, they're really hardly more than strangers. Besides, you owe me this much, Paige."

"I *owe* you?" Paige asked, astonished to discover that Josie could still surprise her.

"If it hadn't been for you, he would have left town weeks ago," Josie said with a touch of indignation. "No one would have ever had to know about this."

"And that would make all the lies okay?"

"Don't sound so self-righteous," Josie snapped, suddenly dropping the pretense of maternal concern. "You fell into bed with him like a cheap tramp. Or a starved spinster," she added spitefully.

"A starved spinster?" Paige stared at her for a moment and then laughed, a sound of such genuine amusement that Josie's face flushed an ugly shade of red.

Paige was still smiling when the big door banged open, slamming against the wall behind it in a way guaranteed to put gouges in the paneling. Mary tumbled through the door, breathless, as if she'd been running. Urgency seemed to spill into the room with her.

"What's wrong?" Paige asked, coming around the desk, her heart thumping with fear. What if something had happened to Jake?

"There's been a robbery at the bank," Mary got out between gulps of air. "They've taken hostages."

"My God. Beth." Josie pressed her hand to the base of her throat. Glancing at her sister's pale face, Paige was surprised to realize that Josie really did love her daughter. "I've got to get over there."

She brushed past Mary, her heels clicking on the wooden floor as she ran out. Paige would have followed her but she suddenly thought to tell Jake. She punched out the phone number, her fingers shaking so badly that she had to redial. The phone rang and rang but no one answered. She slammed the receiver down, turning to Mary.

"Have you seen Jake?"

"He was with Martin earlier. I saw them talking."

If he was still with Martin, then he would already know what had happened.

JAKE WAS INDEED with Martin. They'd been standing beside Martin's patrol car when the call came in. On the heels of the alarm had come the sound of shots fired from the bank. Jake had spun into a crouch, reaching for the gun he no longer carried, every sense instantly alert.

That had been nearly thirty minutes ago. Since then, there hadn't been a sound from the bank. Martin had moved quickly, blocking off the street in front of the bank, clearing people out of the area.

He'd set up a temporary headquarters in the building across the street from the bank, which just happened to be the post office. No one had said a word when Jake joined the small gathering. The office offered a clear view of the bank. Too clear, Jake thought bleakly.

Pop Bellows lay sprawled just inside the doors, the gun he'd patted laughingly a couple of hours ago only half drawn. That he was dead was something Jake didn't doubt. He'd seen enough bodies to recognize the sprawl of limbs, the look of death.

Somewhere deep inside, Jake felt a terrible grief but there was no time to give in to it now. The man had been more of a father to him than a friend. He'd believed in the young Jake when no one else did. Jake turned away, forcing his grief down. Pop was dead but he'd died in the way he would have wished to, trying to help someone.

But somewhere inside the bank was Beth, alive and unhurt, he hoped. Beth and the other teller. Nathan had escaped out the window of his office when he heard the alarm go off and he'd told Martin that he didn't think there were any customers in the bank. Just the two women.

Looking at his pasty, sweaty face, Jake told himself that it was unfair to blame Nathan for escaping. There was nothing he could have done against two gunmen who were clearly prepared to shoot to kill.

But he kept thinking of how frightened Beth must be.

"They were crazy, Sheriff Smith." Nathan wiped one fat-fingered hand over his sweaty forehead. "On drugs or something. I saw what happened through my office door. They shot Pop Bellows as quick as stepping on a cockroach and then laughed about it."

He clutched the glass of water someone had handed him, his hand shaking so badly the water threatened to slosh over the rim. "There wasn't anything I could do. Lisa Mae must have stepped on the alarm button. I saw the light go on and then I climbed out the window."

Though Jake thought his face was expressionless, Nathan flushed when he glanced at him. "There wasn't anything I could do," he repeated defensively, though Jake hadn't said a word.

"No one said there was, Mr. Nathan." Martin's voice was calm, in control. There was a commotion at the back door, one of the deputies arguing with someone, and then Josie rushed into the room. Frank was behind her and behind him was Paige.

Jake's gaze met hers across the room. It was like falling into a cool green stream. He read comfort and sympathy in her eyes. He didn't have to ask if she knew about Pop. He could see that she did and that she understood his grief. That she knew about Beth being inside the bank was obvious when Josie began to speak, demanding that Martin do something.

Frank set his hands on her shoulders, leaning down to murmur something in her ear. For a moment, it seemed as if she was going to ignore him and then she seemed to crumple, turning to him and burying her face against his shoulder.

Frank glanced at Jake over her head and then looked at Martin. "What's the situation, Sheriff? Is Beth all right?"

"We don't really know much at the moment, Frank, and that's the honest truth. As far as we know, Beth and Lisa Mae are fine. But I'm not going to lie to you. There's two men in there with guns and they've already killed Pop Bellows. We got them on the phone a little while ago but they said they'd call us when they wanted to talk and not to call back or they'd kill one of the girls."

Frank's face had grown more pale and stern as Martin talked. Josie began to sob, her fingers digging into the front of her husband's jacket. Looking at Paige, Jake saw her bite her lip, the fear apparent in her eyes.

He wanted to go to her, hold her and tell her that it was going to be all right. But he was too full of fear himself to offer reassurance to anyone else. He turned back to the window, staring at the bank, trying not to think about Pop's motionless body. Behind him, he could hear Martin's quiet voice.

Pop had done a good job with him, Jake thought. Martin was one hell of a lawman. He'd responded to the emergency as if he did this every day in some big city precinct. Pop would have been proud.

"What do you think?" Martin had moved up to stand next to Jake, his eyes reflecting his own grief when he looked across the street at Pop's body.

"I think we've got a nasty situation here." Neither man noticed the use of the plural. "If Nathan is right and these guys are on something…" Jake let his voice trail off, shrugging. "There's no telling what they might do."

"If we go in with guns blazing, one or both of the girls could end up hurt or dead," Martin said, thinking out loud. "I say we wait for them to call."

"That's what I'd suggest, too. They can't stay in there forever. Sooner or later, they're going to have to try and bargain their way out of this.''

When the phone rang fifteen minutes later, everyone jumped. Martin let the phone ring once, twice before picking it up. The silence in the crowded room could have been cut with a knife as everyone leaned forward, their attention focused on Martin.

He listened, speaking mostly in monosyllables at first. It wasn't hard to guess that the robbers were making their demands.

''You're asking for a lot,'' Martin said, his tone calm and reasonable. ''It's going to take some time to arrange all this. No, I'm not trying to stall. I'm just going to need some time, that's all.

''If I'm going to arrange this for you, I'd like a little something from you. I need some proof that the hostages are all right.''

His jaw tightened but his voice didn't change. ''No. I have to have proof that they're alive and unhurt.''

The sound of a gunshot echoed clearly from across the street. Jake jerked as if the sound had hit him with the impact of a bullet. Josie screamed and went limp in Frank's arm. Paige tumbled back against the wall behind her, her eyes enormous in her pale face.

''Dammit! There was no reason to do that.'' Martin's voice had lost some of its calm reason. Jake saw his jaw knotting with the effort of staving off panic. ''All right. You've made your point. One hour.''

He set the receiver down and spoke without looking up. ''He says they've wounded one of the hostages. He says next time he'll shoot to kill.''

''Maybe he just fired into the air,'' Paige said, her face so pale Jake wondered if she was going to faint, too. ''Just to frighten us.''

''What do they want?'' Jake asked quietly.

''A helicopter in front of the bank and a plane waiting for

them at the nearest airport. The one I spoke to says he's a pilo
He claims they'll let the girls go as soon as they get to Mex
ico.''

''You don't believe him?'' That was Paige, who'd come u
to stand next to Jake.

Martin shook his head slowly. ''The guy doesn't sound ra
tional, Paige. I'm sorry. As soon as they don't need them fo
protection…'' Martin didn't have to complete his though
Everyone in the tight, suddenly airless room knew his meanin

Paige nodded, her teeth worrying her lip. ''What are yo
going to do?''

Martin ran his hand through his ruddy hair. ''I'm going t
arrange for a helicopter. We can't do anything about them a
long as they're inside, and they won't come out until they se
a chopper.''

''But you already said that you think they'll kill the girls.
That was Frank. He'd laid Josie on a low sofa where she wa
just starting to stir.

''We've got to get them out of the bank before we can d
anything, Frank. Once they're out, I think we have to try ar
pick them off.''

''Pick them off? My God, you mean, shoot them?'' Fran
sounded horrified. ''They're sure to bring the girls with them.

''I know. But it will be our best chance. Two snipers wi
rifles would have a good line of fire from the roof of th
building. I think it's the best chance we have.''

Frank looked as though he might have wanted to say mo
but Josie called his name and he turned back to her. She w
weeping quietly, her makeup running down her pale cheek
Gone was the sophisticated, self-centered woman; in her pla
was a mother terrified for the safety of her child. Paige almo
forgave her for hurting Jake. Almost.

''It's going to take some careful shooting,'' Jake sai
''You're only going to have one chance and if you miss..
He finished the sentence with a slight shrug.

"I've got a man who could shoot a dime off a fence post at fifty feet and never touch wood. He'll hit anything he aims at."

"You're going to need two men." That was Frank.

"I know." Martin looked at Jake.

Paige bit back a protest. Not Jake. Martin couldn't ask Jake to do this. He already carried a heavy load of guilt for the killing he'd done in his past. And this was Beth. Martin didn't know what he was asking Jake to do. If something went wrong, Jake would never be able to live with it.

Jake's stomach knotted as he looked at Martin. All eyes had turned to him, a mixture of hope and fear in them. He'd known what was going to happen. They all knew he had the skill required to hit a gunman without harming a hostage. They all guessed he'd done similar jobs in the past.

He turned away from those hopeful eyes, staring out the window. He'd sworn to himself that he was through with all of that. No more dark alleys, no more walking in the shadows, no more guns. No more killing.

Was he really through with it? Maybe you couldn't ever walk away from something like that. Maybe it followed you forever, haunting you, a part of you whether you wanted it to be or not.

He couldn't do it.

But this was for Beth. For her life. The daughter he hadn't even known he had.

And if he missed? If he missed and one of them killed her? Or God forbid, what if his own bullet…?

No. He wouldn't think about that.

He didn't really have a choice. He stared down at his hands. He was the best chance Beth had. He had, unknowingly, given her life twenty years ago. He had to try and preserve that life now.

"All right." He turned back to Martin. "You've got your second sniper."

THERE WAS A TOUCH of bitter irony, he thought thirty minutes later, in the way everyone's attitude suddenly changed when his dangerous skills came in handy. There was nothing Martin could do about the crowd that had gathered behind the post office.

It hadn't taken long for the news of the robbery attempt to spread. Everyone knew there were hostages. Most of these people had known Beth and Lisa Mae all their lives. There was the usual amount of gawking that any dramatic event was bound to draw. But there was also a more personal concern. This was their town, the people involved were known to most of the crowd personally.

There was a murmur as Jake stepped out of the back door of the post office. Jake ignored them as he followed Martin out to the patrol car to select a rifle. The barriers Martin had set up kept the crowd at a distance but he could feel their avid interest as he checked the balance of each weapon, sighting along it, looking for some indefinable feel that made the weapon fit his hand.

The news that they were going to try to pick off the robbers as they came out of the bank spread through the crowd like wildfire. Everyone knew Slim Johnson and no one was surprised to see him there. But seeing Jake Quincannon there was a bit of a shock. Those who had seen his shooting at the fair whispered knowingly to those who hadn't been there. People who had eyed him uneasily the day before were suddenly looking at him with hope.

Jake blocked the crowd from his mind, concentrating on what Martin was saying. He'd already been introduced to Slim Johnson, a tall lanky man who looked barely out of his teens though Jake would have put his age at closer to twenty-five. The rifle Slim carried was well worn and he held it as if it were a part of his body. Jake didn't doubt the man could hit anything he aimed at. The question was, had he ever had to shoot another man before?

"The chopper should be here in ten or fifteen minutes," Martin was saying. "I've told the pilot to set it down slightly to the south of the bank. That should give you a clear field of fire. If you can't get a clear shot, don't try anything. I've alerted the airport in Seattle, where the plane is waiting for them. If we can't end this here, we'll let the Seattle police handle it."

"We'll handle it," Slim said calmly.

"I hope so. Good luck." Martin's handshake was firm, his eyes direct. He knew what he was asking. Jake knew if there'd been another way to do it, Martin would have taken it.

Neither he nor Slim spoke as they climbed to the rooftop. Jake dropped to his belly when they reached the roof. Pulling himself along on his elbows, he crept toward the low parapet on the front of the building. Over the edge he had a clear field of fire that encompassed the entire front of the bank.

"When they come out, I'll take whoever is on the left," Jake murmured as Slim crept up beside him.

"Fine by me."

And that was the only conversation they exchanged.

Jake wiped the sweat from his forehead. Was it only today that he'd been thinking that the sun seemed to have lost its summer strength? Lying up here, waiting, it certainly seemed powerful enough.

It reminded him of other times, other places. Saigon, where the heat and humidity had sometimes seemed borne straight from hell. Beirut, which surely had been hell.

He reached up to adjust the eye patch. He couldn't miss. This time, of all times, he couldn't afford to miss. If his whole life had been leading up to this one point, then he had to make sure he didn't fail. Beth's life depended on his success.

Don't think about that. Think about something else.

Like the way Paige's eyes always seemed to smile before her mouth did. Or the way her skin heated beneath his hands. The way she teased him when she thought he was taking himself too seriously.

The fact that he had to leave her.

No. Don't think about that, either.

Don't think about anything beyond the moment. Don't allow a second's doubt to creep in. It wasn't a man he'd be shooting at. It was a target, a silhouette on a shooting range. Not a human being.

He rested his forehead on his arm, staring at the rough surface of the roof. This was just another job. The last he'd ever do.

The most important he'd ever had.

IT SEEMED AS IF hours went by, though in reality it was only a few minutes before he heard the helicopter in the distance. Jake wiped his hands on his jeans, making sure they were perfectly dry before taking hold of the rifle stock and laying i along his cheek.

The wind from the chopper's rotors whipped through his hai as the machine hovered overhead for a moment before slowl setting down in the street. A good pilot, he noted with one par of his mind. He'd set the chopper just south of the bank, fa enough to allow a clear field of fire but not far enough to mak the men inside too anxious.

There was movement inside the bank and Jake curled hi finger around the trigger. The stock rested solidly against hi shoulder, the wood warm to the touch. The weapon was a extension of his body, just as it had always been. Lookin through the scope, he took a deep breath, deliberately slowin his pulse, aware of each separate beat of his heart.

There was a flurry of movement inside and then the door were shoved open and the robbers came out, each holding hostage, using her body as a shield. Jake focused only on th one to the left. The other one was Slim's problem.

Beth. A muscle ticked in his jaw. His target was the on holding Beth. Her blouse, which must have been crisp an white this morning was torn and soaked with blood down one sleeve and side. Her face was white, her eyes wide and terrified.

Through the scope, he could see the man holding her, all ratty black hair and wild eyes. He was holding an automatic beside Beth's head but not pointed at her. That was good. Less chance of a convulsive finger movement pulling the trigger.

Jake forced Beth's face, her expression of shocked fear from his mind. He only had to think of one thing now. Just one thing.

TO PAIGE, the minutes since Jake had gone up to the rooftop seemed to tick by in slow motion. Martin had insisted that everyone wait in back of the post office, protecting them as much from what might happen in front of the bank as he was from stray bullets.

Josie and Frank were sitting in the back of a patrol car. Josie wept loudly, making Paige want to smack her and tell her to shut up. Frank was pale and stern-looking. Paige sat in the front seat, her thoughts torn between fear for Beth and concern for Jake.

She knew, better than anyone, what this could do to him. He'd never told her the details of what his job had been but she didn't need to know the details. She could guess quite a bit.

Whatever Jake had been, she loved him. He'd walked away from that part of his life, put it behind him. Now he was going to have to kill again, this time to save Beth's life.

She supposed that a more charitable woman might have felt some twinge of regret at the thought of the men inside the bank losing their lives. But she wasn't feeling very charitable. They'd killed Pop Bellows. They'd wounded one of the hostages—maybe Beth. They'd made their choices.

She sucked in her breath when she heard the helicopter. Unable to sit still a moment longer, she thrust open the car door and stepped out, shielding her eyes as she watched the helicopter go by so low the pilot was clearly visible. It hovered over the building for a moment before disappearing, as the pilot lowered it into the street.

Paige waited, hardly breathing. She wasn't aware of Frank and Josie getting out of the patrol car to stand beside her. Nor was she aware of the crowd of neighbors and friends who watched from behind the rope barrier.

The shots were so close together they sounded as though they were one—a heavy boom followed by a stunning silence.

Josie screamed, her knuckles turning white where she clutched Frank's sleeve. Paige didn't move. She forgot to breathe. A thousand incoherent prayers tumbled together in her mind.

Martin had been inside the building, watching what was happening on the street. The moments oozed by so slowly they seemed caught in a trap that was sucking them backward. Paige counted. One, two... By the time she got to fifty, he'd bring Beth out, alive and unhurt. Fifty-two, Fifty-three... By the time she reached one hundred, they'd know that everything was all right.

Her head jerked upward as Jake swung over the roof, feeling for the first rung of the ladder. The rifle was slung over his back. There was a murmur as the crowd saw him. Paige started toward him, hesitating as the back door of the post office was thrust open.

"Beth!" That was Josie, her strength suddenly returning. She tore herself away from Frank and rushed to her daughter who was being half supported, half carried by Martin.

Paige felt tears start to her eyes. She'd noticed, as Josie hadn't yet, the blood on Beth's arm, but she was walking. She was safe.

Jake's feet had just touched ground when he felt Paige behind him. He knew it was her, even before he turned. For a moment, he stayed where he was, staring at the brick wall in front of him.

He'd just killed a man. Was he going to see horror in her eyes? A look that questioned how he could have done such a thing, even to save a life? He'd seen that look before. He didn't think he could bear to see it in Paige's eyes.

"Jake?" Her hand touched his sleeve and he turned, bracing himself for whatever he might see.

"Are you all right?"

The question took his breath away. He'd been forced to kill before and he'd answered all the questions he was thrown afterward by his superiors and the battery of psychiatrists ever ready to jump on any sign that he wasn't properly aware that he'd taken a human life. No one had ever thought to ask him the simple question Paige had just asked.

Was he all right?

God, no. He'd just killed a man. A man who'd murdered Pop and would have killed Beth without hesitation, but another human being nevertheless. He felt filthy, as if he'd just rolled in a sewer. He felt weary, burned-out, used up. No, he wasn't all right.

But looking into Paige's eyes, seeing the concern, the love she didn't try to hide, all those disturbing feelings started to fade.

"I'm okay," he said huskily.

"Thank God." The tears she'd refused to shed earlier began to fall but it didn't matter. She had her arms around Jake, her face pressed against his chest. He hesitated, hardly daring to believe in the reality of her love and then his arms came around her, crushing her closer still. He buried his face in her hair, letting the soft scent of her drive away the memories.

They stood that way for a few moments, oblivious of everything going on around them. Well-wishers crowded around Beth as if they needed to see her up close to believe that she was all right. The other teller was unharmed and sobbing in her husband's arms.

Jake and Paige stood off to the side. When he lifted his head,

he wasn't surprised to see the small pool of distance that surrounded them. It wasn't that people weren't glad that he'd been
here, that his skills had come in useful. But now that the crisis
was over, they were uneasy.

It would have been different if he'd been wearing a uniform.
That formalized things somehow, made the killing more respectable. That was just the reason he'd quit. It had begun to
seem all right to him, too. And he didn't need a psychiatrist to
tell him that when killing no longer left a hollow ache in the
pit of your stomach, it was time to get out of the business.

Looking over Paige's head, he saw Beth. Other than the
wound in her arm, which didn't look serious from what he
could see, she looked all right. It might take her a while to
come to terms with what she'd experienced but she was young
and she had a good share of common sense. She'd be fine.

Frank had his arms around her shoulders and she was leaning
against him like a tired child. The image burned into Jake's
mind, settling into a deep ache in his chest. Beth was his daughter by blood but she'd never be his in any real sense. Frank
was the father of her heart. Nothing would change that.

He'd lost her without ever really having had her.

Jake's eyes met Frank's for a long moment before he looked
away. He bent over Paige.

"Let's go home."

Chapter Fourteen

It was, Paige thought, incredible how quickly life got back to normal. It had been only a week since the attempted robbery, yet everything seemed to be going on as if nothing at all had happened.

She went to work every day. School would be starting in less than a week, which meant the library would be open longer hours. There would be a steady stream of youngsters studying the American Revolution, tree frogs and Watergate.

She usually enjoyed this time of year. Mixed with the regret for summer's passing was a certain excitement at the changing seasons. She loved to see the first ragged vee of geese flying overhead, going south for the winter. But this year, when she saw them, all she could think was that she wished she were going with them.

Pop Bellows was buried two days after the shooting, laid to rest in the cemetery that held graves dating back to the days when the stagecoach had come through once a month, bringing news and supplies to the valley. Paige had stood beside Jake, worried about the total lack of emotion in his face. But when she'd slipped her hand into his, his fingers had closed convulsively over hers.

He'd had a terrible nightmare that night, muttering in his sleep, his face tortured in the moonlight. He woke himself before Paige could. Instinct made her lie still with her eyes shut

as if she were still asleep. She'd felt him studying her before
he slipped from the bed. Through slitted eyes, she watched him
walk to the window, staring out into the darkness as if seeking
answers there. He'd stayed there for a long time before finally
coming back to bed.

Paige's teeth worried at her lower lip as she stared at the
library cards she was supposed to be updating. He was pulling
away from her. It was a subtle withdrawal but she knew she
wasn't imagining it.

She knew he'd be leaving soon. Summer was over. Whatever
he'd hoped to find here was either found or it didn't exist. He'd
leave and life would go on but it couldn't ever be the same.

She'd thought that she could say goodbye to him and go on
with her life. Oh, it would hurt but she'd known from the
beginning that this was only a summer romance. He'd never
lied to her about it and she'd accepted their relationship on
those terms.

She'd felt it would be enough to have him for a few short
months. Her life had needed shaking up. She'd allowed herself
to get stuck in a rut, a safe, cozy one but still a rut. Jake had
been just what she'd needed to blow her out of that rut.

She hadn't planned on falling in love with him. But even
when she realized she was in love with him, she'd told herself
that she could watch him walk away. It was going to hurt—
more than anything she'd ever known. But it was worth it.

But was her life worth much without him?

She flicked her finger against the stack of cards, fanning
them out on the desk. Jake wasn't just going to leave a hole,
he was going to leave a gaping tear.

She'd go with him in a minute if he'd ask her. But he'd
never ask. Not even if his heart was breaking as much as hers.
He was pulling away now but whom was he trying to protect?
Her? Or himself?

JAKE SLID THE LAST of his clothes into the shallow duffel and
zipped it shut. He was taking only what he'd brought with him

Though in truth he was leaving a great deal behind.

Beth, the daughter he'd barely gotten a chance to know. Paige had visited her in the hospital, where she'd stayed overnight to be treated for the flesh wound in her arm. She was going to be fine, Paige had said. A small scar that would make an interesting story to tell her children. His grandchildren.

He shook his head, his mouth twisting into a half smile beneath the dark mustache. Grandchildren. He still didn't quite believe he had a child. He wasn't ready for the possibility of grandchildren. Not that he'd know anything about it, he thought, the half smile fading.

When he left town this time, there was going to be no looking back. He'd made his peace with the past, though not in the way he'd hoped. He couldn't go back and change anything he'd done. He couldn't change what he'd been. He could only go forward from where he was now.

He'd even, in an odd way, made his peace with his parents. At nearly forty, he'd finally gotten it through his head that there was nothing he could do to change the way things had been. And nothing could change the way they were now.

He couldn't make his mother understand him or love him, any more than he could understand or love her. He'd spent twenty years trying and it hadn't worked. It had been foolish to think that it could all be changed in three months.

He'd done what he'd set out to do. Now all that was left was to say his goodbyes. And there were few enough of those to say. Pop was gone, the pain of his loss still raw. Martin had been a friend but he wouldn't be surprised to find Jake gone.

Beth. Yes, he wanted to say goodbye to Beth. He didn't think it was his imagination that she'd come to look on him as a friend. He owed her a chance to say farewell. Besides, he wanted to see her again.

That left only Paige. Paige. How was he supposed to say goodbye to her?

HE WAS NO CLOSER to an answer thirty minutes later as he rang the bell of the big white house. Frank answered the door, his eyes widening when he saw Jake.

"Hello, Frank. I'd like to see Beth."

"Jake." Frank stepped back to allow Jake to enter. But he didn't move to lead him upstairs, where he assumed Beth's room would be. "I didn't get a chance to thank you for what you did."

"If I hadn't been there, someone else would have been."

"But you were there and I want you to know I appreciate what you did. Beth... Well, she means the world to me."

He shoved his hands into the pockets of his trousers and Jake had the feeling it was to hide the fact that they weren't quite steady.

"Are you going to tell her?"

"No." Jake shook his head. "I don't think she'd welcome hearing that I'm her father. I'm leaving tomorrow morning and I just thought I'd say goodbye."

Frank's relief was almost palpable. "She's asked about you since the shooting."

"Frank? Who is it?" Josie's voice preceded her into the entryway. She came to a dead stop when she saw to whom her husband was talking. "What are you doing here?"

"He came to see Beth, Josie."

"Well, you can't see her." She moved forward, stopping next to Frank, her eyes dark with hatred.

"Josie." Frank's voice was stern.

"Well, he can't," she said petulantly, shrugging off his implied reprimand. "I don't want him anywhere near my daughter."

"Don't you mean *our* daughter, Josie?"

She paled at Jake's words.

"You can't tell her that! It would just about kill her to find out that Frank isn't her father. That her real father was a.. a...murderer."

"Josie, that's enough!"

But it had been a long time since anything Josie said had had the power to hurt him. Jake smiled coldly.

"I was just telling Frank that I'd decided not to tell Beth the truth." He waited to see the flicker of relief in her eyes. "But I could still change my mind."

"Why don't you wait for me in the library, Josie," Frank suggested. "I'm going to take Jake up to see Beth. No." He stifled her protest. "Not another word about it."

Josie looked as if she were going to say something more but perhaps it had finally occurred to her that she would do more harm than good if she did speak. With a final venomous leer at Jake, she went into the library.

Frank looked as if he felt he should say something but realized there really wasn't anything to say. He could hardly defend Josie. Neither could he criticize her.

"Beth's room is upstairs." He turned and Jake followed.

"How is she?" Jake followed him up the wide staircase.

"Remarkable." The paternal pride was so natural that Jake doubted Frank was even aware of it. "Her arm is healing just fine. And emotionally she's doing better every day. She's had a bit of trouble sleeping, though."

"That's not surprising," Jake said as they stopped outside Beth's door.

Frank looked at him, obviously struggling with something he wanted to say. "I want to thank you for not telling her, Jake. I should have told her years ago but it never seemed like the right time and then it seemed too late, somehow."

"You did what you thought was best."

"Yes. But I wouldn't blame you if you hated me."

"I don't hate you." Jake was surprised to realize that he didn't feel any bitterness about what he'd lost. Maybe it was a case of you can't lose what you've never had. "You probably did the best thing for her. I couldn't have given her the home, the stability that you have. She's a good kid, Frank. You did a good job.''

Frank stared at Jake's outstretched hand for a moment before reaching out to take it.

"Thank you, Jake," he said, his voice slightly choked. "You're always welcome to visit, as a friend of the family."

"I don't think so. There's not much reason for me to come back here. And I don't think Josie would agree with you." His half smile took any criticism from the words.

"You're always welcome, Jake," Frank repeated. "I can handle Josie."

Jake waited until Frank had disappeared down the stairs before tapping on Beth's door. When she called to come in, he pushed open the door, stepping into a pretty, feminine bedroom in blue and white.

Beth was sitting up in the middle of the bed, her hair caught back with a headband, her face freshly scrubbed. When she saw him, her face lit in a smile and Jake felt a surprising ache. Her eyes were bright blue and it occurred to him that she'd gotten her eyes from him.

"Jake! Come in. Why haven't you come before?"

"I thought I ought to give you a little time to recover." He took the hand she held out to him, letting her pull him down onto the side of the bed.

"I *am* recovered. It's just that no one will believe me." Her faint pout changed into a more serious expression. "Dad told me that it was you who did the shooting last week."

"I wasn't the only one," Jake said.

"I should feel sorry that they're dead, I suppose." She'd kept hold of his fingers and her thumb worried absently at the back of his hand. "They were awful, Jake," she said, her voice a near whisper. "They laughed when they killed Pop. Such a sweet old man and they *enjoyed* killing him."

She lifted her head and Jake thought his heart would break at the tears that brimmed in her eyes. Acting on instinct, he put his hand behind her head and drew it to his shoulder, offering her the comfort of his strength.

"Try not to think about it, Beth. If Pop could have chosen a way to go, it would have been while he was trying to help someone. He wouldn't want you to dwell on his death."

"I suppose." She snuggled closer and Jake felt a sweet pain in his chest. She smelled faintly of powder. She must have smelled just as fresh when she was a baby. "Anyway, I want to thank you for what you did."

"I just happened to be there."

"If you hadn't been there, Lisa Mae or I would probably be dead right now."

"Well, you're not, so don't think about it."

She sat back and he had to fight the urge to pull her into his arms again, hold her just a moment longer to make up for all the years he hadn't been able to hold her. Her eyes were very direct as she looked at him.

"I know you don't want me to make a big deal out of this, Jake, but you did save my life. And I don't want you to feel bad about having to kill that man. They would never have let us go. You did what you had to do."

"Thanks for the pep talk," Jake said, his voice scratchy. He reached out to smooth back a stray lock of her hair. "But I didn't come by so you could reassure me. I wanted to see how you were and I wanted to say goodbye."

He hadn't expected the word to hurt so much and it came out sounding forced. Beth's eyes widened.

"You're leaving?"

"Summer's over. It's time I move on."

"Where are you going?"

"I don't know. I thought I might drive around the country a bit more, maybe head farther south where the weather will be a bit warmer."

"Does Aunt Paige know?"

She was shrewd.

"I haven't told her yet," he said casually.

"I thought the two of you had something going."

"I never planned to stay more than the summer," he said, sidestepping her comment.

"Don't you love her?"

She'd asked him that once before and he was no more prepared to answer that question now than he had been then. Love Paige? He didn't have any right to love her.

"You're nosy and you still don't have any manners," he told her lightly. He stood up. "I'd better let you get some rest."

"Any more rest and I'm going to go comatose," she groused. She caught his hand. "I'm going to miss you."

He looked down at her, feeling emotion catch in his throat. He'd known her such a short time. Just a few weeks out of her life.

"I'll…" He had to stop and clear his throat. "I'll miss you. For a tactless brat, you're not bad."

"Gee, thanks." She grinned at him and then grew serious again. "Will you write?"

Jake looked down at her, seeing himself in her eyes, in the shape of her chin.

Would he write? Hear about her life from a distance? The boyfriends he'd never meet, the graduations he wouldn't be there to applaud, the wedding where he wouldn't be the one to walk her down the aisle, the grandchildren he'd never hold.

He swallowed, forcing a smile.

"Sure, I'll write," he lied.

Standing outside her door a few minutes later, he thought he'd rather lose both arms than have to say such a difficult goodbye again.

And he still hadn't told Paige he was leaving.

HE KEPT TELLING HIMSELF that he was waiting for the right moment to tell her but that moment didn't seem to come. It certainly wasn't the right time to tell her over the dinner he'd prepared.

And after dinner wasn't the right time either. She took his hand to draw him into the living room. She turned the radio on, finding a station that played slow, dreamy music. Jake hadn't danced in more years than he could remember, but swaying in front of the fireplace with Paige in his arms, he felt as graceful as Fred Astaire.

She fit against him so perfectly, her head just under his chin, her slender body a sweet pressure on his chest, on his thighs.

His arms tightened convulsively around her. How could he possibly leave her?

Did he love her, Beth had asked.

Only if loving someone meant that the sun only came out when you were with that person. That you were only truly whole in their presence. If that's what it meant, then he loved her. Loved her so much it was like tearing away a part of himself to think about leaving her.

She'd said she loved him. If he asked her, would she go with him?

Yes. He didn't doubt it. But he wouldn't ask. He didn't know where he was going or what he was going to do with his life. She'd find someone who could give her all the things he couldn't. Someone young, with a few illusions left in him.

She'd be better off without him. But tonight... Tonight, she was his, only his.

His hand slipped into the silken length of her hair, tilting her head back for his kiss. She responded just as he'd known she would, melting against him, her arms coming up to circle his neck and draw him closer.

He wasn't going to think about tomorrow or the goodbyes he couldn't bring himself to say. Tonight they had all the time in the world. The future stretched out before them, rich and full.

There was a particular intensity to their lovemaking. Jake

was saying with his body the words he couldn't bring himself to speak. He loved her. She was his soul, his only hope of happiness. Throughout the night he used his hands and mouth to tell her all these things.

It was nearly morning when Paige collapsed against his chest, her breathing ragged, her tears dampening his skin. Jake held her trembling body close, knowing he wouldn't sleep. He wanted to savor every moment he could. The warmth of her skin, the delicate scent of her hair. The memories were going to have to last him the rest of his life.

PAIGE FELT THE WAY his arms cradled her, holding her as if he would never let her go, and she knew he was leaving. Her tears fell silently, without fanfare. There'd been something different about him all night, a part of him she couldn't quite reach.

Somewhere in the intensity of their lovemaking, there'd been a note of finality. As if this was the last time they'd ever be together like this. He was trying to tell her goodbye. He hadn't been able to find the words but he didn't have to. She knew him so well. He'd become a part of her life, a part of her soul.

How was she supposed to go on without him?

IT WAS BROAD DAYLIGHT when Jake awoke, startled to find that he'd slept at all. His hand swept out searchingly. But the bed was empty. As empty as he felt.

A glance at the clock told him Paige should have opened the library nearly twenty minutes ago. She must have slipped out of bed and gone off to work.

He hadn't told her that he was leaving. He leaned back against the pillow, his forearm over his forehead. Perhaps it was just as well. He wasn't sure what would be worse: if she asked him to stay or if she didn't.

He could leave her a note, a coward's way out but perhaps easiest for both of them. God knows, he couldn't bring himself to face her again.

Jake dragged himself out of bed, his gaze lingering on the pillow that bore the imprint of Paige's head. He forced himself to turn away.

He dressed automatically, pulling on black jeans and a T-shirt before stomping his feet into the black leather boots he'd hardly worn since arriving at the beginning of the summer. Shrugging into his jacket, he took a last look around the old house.

The maple table he'd refinished sat proudly in the kitchen, restored to its former glory. He ran his fingers over the smooth finish. Would Paige think of him when she looked at it? Shaking his head, he hitched the duffel bag higher on his shoulder. More than likely, she'd take a hatchet to it, wishing it was his head.

He strode out the back door without looking back. The sun was warm but it lacked the strength of summer. Autumn had arrived. It was time he was moving on, time to decide what to do with the rest of his life. He had to give Paige a chance to get on with her life.

It was best this way.

He swung around the garage and came to a dead stop.

The Harley was parked just where he'd left it, facing into the street, ready for his departure. But leaning against it...

His gaze started at a pair of black leather boots and moved up an endless length of leg encased in skintight black denim. A snug black leather jacket fitted her waist, failing to hide the feminine curves. Her hair was braided and draped over one shoulder, white-blond against the black leather. Tucked under one arm was a black helmet with a tinted visor. There was even a pair of black leather gloves tucked into her jeans pocket.

"Where are we going?" She asked the question coolly, as if there were nothing else to discuss.

"*We're* not going anywhere," he said slowly, trying to regain his balance.

"Then why are we dressed like this?" She widened her eyes in surprise and Jake felt his mouth twitch.

"I was going to leave you a note."

"Well, now you won't have to," she said cheerfully. "I'm going with you."

"No, you're not."

"Don't you want me to go with you?"

"I—" He broke off, unable to utter the lie.

He scowled.

She was not impressed.

He tried harsh fact.

"I'm not good for you. I can't ever be what you need."

She was not visibly moved.

"Why don't you let me be the judge of what I need and what I don't need. I love you, Jake. I told you that before and I don't think you believed me. I guess I'm just going to have to tag along to convince you."

"Look, you don't really know who I am. You've got some romantic idea about me having traveled the globe, getting into romantic fights and killing people to save the world. That's not the way it was. I was little more than an assassin, a hired gun, a loaded cannon. I was a wind-up soldier for them to point at a target."

She didn't seem impressed. Jake ground his teeth.

"If they'd told me to shoot the President, I'd have done it without question."

"I don't believe you. And even if I did believe you, I don't think it's particularly important now. Are you planning on killing people as a hobby now that you've given it up as a profession?"

"No."

"Then we don't have a problem. I'm not interested in what you *were*, Jake. I'm only interested in what you are."

"And what do you think I am?"

"I think you're a man who's been hurt a lot. I think you've

done things you regret. But I think you spend too much time thinking about them, instead of thinking of the good things in your life. You have a deep capacity for love, even if you won't admit it. You're stubborn and lonely and you take yourself too seriously. You're also kind and you have no tolerance for cruelty. And I love you.''

Jake had never wanted anything in his life as much as he wanted to take her with him. He ached with the need to snatch her up and carry her off, to make her a part of his life forever. But he had no right to do that. He was still convinced she'd be better off without him.

Steeling himself, he forced the coldness into his voice.

"I don't want you. I'm sorry to have to be so blunt but I don't want you."

She didn't seem disturbed.

He watched her warily as she crossed the short distance between them. She laid one slim hand on his chest and Jake could feel that gentle pressure burning through his clothing until it seemed as if she were touching his heart.

"If you can look me right in the eye and tell me you don't love me, I'll let you go, Jake Quincannon. But you have to look me right in the eye and say it."

He stared into her eyes, bracing himself to say the words that would tear his world apart. His throat seemed to close. Her eyes were endless green pools, full of love and understanding and a faintly perceptible fear.

It was that tiny glimpse of fear that was his undoing. She'd bared herself to him, made herself completely vulnerable. He couldn't utter the lie that would crush that vulnerability. He'd told more lies in his life than he cared to remember, but this was one he couldn't tell.

He wanted her too much, needed her too desperately.

"Damn you," he said thickly.

He crushed her smile under his mouth, his arms holding her so tightly she could hardly breathe.

HALF OF RIVERBEND saw them leave town. Ethel Levine just happened to be in the window of Maisie's as the Harley roared up Maine Avenue. She described it afterward to half a dozen of her closest friends.

There was Jake Quincannon on that wicked-looking motorbike, wearing black leather and with that eye patch that made him look just like a pirate.

And perched behind him, looking happy as a cat with cream, was sweet little Paige Cudahy, her arms wrapped around his waist as if she didn't ever plan to let go.

Ethel shook her blue-haired head, her lips pursed.

Who would ever have thought that a good sensible girl like that would have her head turned by the likes of Jake Quincannon?

 **HARLEQUIN®**
Makes any time special ™

WIN A DREAM

In celebration of Harlequin®'s golden anniversary

Enter to win a *dream!* You could win:

- A luxurious trip for two to *The Renaissance Cottonwoods Resort* in Scottsdale, Arizona, or

- A bouquet of flowers once a week for a year from **FTD**, or

- A $500 shopping spree, or

- A fabulous bath & body gift basket, including **K-tel**'s *Candlelight and Romance* 5-CD set.

Look for **WIN A DREAM** flash on specially marked Harlequin® titles by Penny Jordan, Dallas Schulze, Anne Stuart and Kristine Rolofson in October 1999*.

FTD

RENAISSANCE. COTTONWOODS RESORT SCOTTSDALE, ARIZONA

K-TEL

"Fascinating—you'll want to take this home!"
—**Marie Ferrarella**

"Each page is filled with a brand-new surprise."
—**Suzanne Brockmann**

"Makes reading a new and joyous experience all over again."
—**Tara Taylor Quinn**

See what all your favorite authors are talking about.

Coming October 1999 to a retail store near you.

HARLEQUIN®
Makes any time special ™

Silhouette®

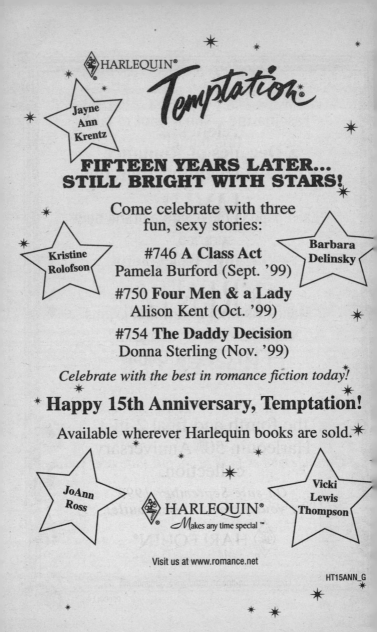